BEDSIDE BOOK OF
FAMOUS FRENCH STORIES

★★★★★★★★★★★★★★★★★★★★★★★★★★★★★★★★★★★★★★★

BEDSIDE BOOK OF

FAMOUS FRENCH

STORIES

★★★★★★★★★★★★★★★★★★★★★★★★★★★★★★★★★★★★★★★

Edited by

BELLE BECKER

and

ROBERT N. LINSCOTT

With an Introduction by

LEWIS GALANTIERE

★★★★★★★★★★★★★★★★★★★★★★★★★★★★★★★★★★★★★★★

RANDOM HOUSE   NEW YORK

Published simultaneously in Canada by
Random House of Canada Limited

MANUFACTURED IN THE UNITED STATES OF AMERICA

* Contents *

⋆ *Acknowledgments* ⋆

THIS collection is made possible by the generous permissions extended by the authors themselves, their publishers or the holders of copyright listed below. In several instances they allowed the editors to reprint stories that have never before appeared in an anthology.

The editors also gratefully acknowledge the valuable suggestions and assistance of Professor Henri M. Peyre, of Yale University, Madame Henri Focillon, of the French Embassy, Peter Rhodes, of OWI and Alice M. Schneider.

Every effort has been made to discover the owners of the copyright stories included in this volume. In case of any omission of acknowledgment, the editors offer their apologies and, if notified, will gladly rectify the omission in a subsequent edition.

Permissions:

J. M. DENT & SONS LIMITED: for *La Grande Bretêche* and *An Episode of the Terror* by Honoré de Balzac.

DODD, MEAD & COMPANY: for *The Procurator of Judaea* and *Crainquebille* by Anatole France.

WILLIAM HEINEMANN, LTD.: for *The Attack on the Mill* by Emile Zola and *The Sacrifice* by Georges Duhamel.

ALFRED A. KNOPF, INC.: for *The Escape* by Joseph Kessel.

LITTLE, BROWN & COMPANY: for *The Last Lesson* by Alphonse Daudet.

G. P. PUTNAM'S SONS: for *A Simple Heart* and *Herodias* by Gustave Flaubert; *The Venus of Ille* by Prosper Mérimée; *The Elixer of Father Gaucher* by Alphonse Daudet.

RANDOM HOUSE, INC.: for *Tank Trap* by André Malraux.

REYNAL & HITCHCOCK: for *Prisoner of the Sand* by Antoine de Saint Exupéry.

JEAN-PAUL SARTRE and *Chimera:* for *The Wall* by Jean-Paul Sartre.

EDITH THOMAS: for *The Professor and the Mussels* by Edith Thomas.

★ *Introduction* ★

HE great merit of any collection of short stories ought to be that its stories capture the reader's attention and hold his interest. A single story may be whatever it pleases: fantastic, comic, didactic, terrifying, heartbreaking, anything at all; but the collection as a whole should be something that can only be described as "entertaining."

It was for the reader's entertainment, and not for his edification, that this *Bedside Book* was compiled. Its editors have not been concerned to prove anything, either about France, or about literature, or about mankind. They might just as well have brought together a volume of American, or British, or Russian short stories. But as they happen to have read and enjoyed a good deal of French literature, it occurred to them that other people might find enjoyment where they found it.

There has never been a time, of course, when men have not entertained one another with story telling. Stories were spluttered out by the cave-dwellers, they were sung by Greek and Nordic bards, they were a customary accompaniment of coffee in Moslem bazaars (as we know from the existence of the so-called *Arabian Nights*), they were written down in the Middle Ages (whence we have, for example, the touching and delicate tale of "Aucassin and Nicolette"). But as a literary form, the short story is rare before the nineteenth century. It seems pretty clear that it came into its own, in Europe and America, with the spread of the popular newspaper and magazine. People who know about these things will tell you that the two most avid devourers of periodical publications are the American nation and the French nation. This may explain why, despite Gorky, Chekhov and Andreyev, despite Kipling, Conan Doyle and D. H. Lawrence, the short story has flourished most vigorously in France and in the United States, in the land of Maupassant and the land of Edgar Allen Poe.

The attitude to the short story displayed by first-rate modern writers is interesting: it is very like the attitude of modern painters to the portrait. True, Chekhov never wrote anything but short stories, nor did O. Henry or Katherine Mansfield. But with rare exceptions, every author who has written great short stories has wanted to be a great novelist, and not merely a story writer, whether it was Kipling or Maupassant, Sherwood Anderson or D. H. Lawrence, Liam O'Flaherty or Ernest Hemingway. And the rest have actually been great novelists: Hawthorne, Henry James, Joseph Conrad, Balzac, Dostoyevsky, Tolstoy, and so many others. Thus, on the whole, the bulk of short-story writing has been left to men and women who combine considerable skill with mediocre inspiration, men and women who read the newspapers and the popular-science journals to find their subjects, and look to the magazines for their market. In the same way contemporary portrait painters are most often conscientious and uninspired craftsmen who serve the whims of proud mothers, indulgent husbands, and aspiring boards of directors of clubs and corporations, for whom they do a job of work with such technical finish as they are able to command. As portrait painters rarely exhibit their work in galleries that anybody goes to, so short-story writers rarely publish books that anybody reads. And as, on average, portrait painters make the handsomest living among those whose trade is painting, so, on average, short-story writers have the highest income of those whose trade is writing. Whence it comes that in any collection of *great* short stories, the larger number will always be found to be the work of writers who have not "specialized" in the short story.

Whether or not a given novelist of world-wide reputation furnishes the full measure of his talent in the short story seems to be a matter of hit-and-miss. In this *Bedside Book* the results vary. Certain novelists—Flaubert, France, Duhamel, for example—come off here very well. Others—Balzac, Zola and Daudet—are bigger men than one would guess from the stories signed with their names in this collection.

Balzac was certainly at his greatest when he had something more than a story to tell, when he had a soul to depict in the grip of sin or a human heart to display in the exercise of Christian charity. He was not one of your tight, economical, analytical writers. To depict the soul or display the heart he needed space, he needed to pile up incident upon incident in order to show the inevitability of the disaster or the forgiveness which would come at the end of his prodigious demonstration. Meanwhile, he was a singularly naive man, greatly influenced in his youth by the so-called Gothic tales written in England by "Monk" Lewis and the once-popular Ann Radcliffe. It is out of that school that we get the romantic tale here reprinted, *La Grande Bretêche;* just as it is out of his deep fidelity to Church and Throne that we get the famous *Episode Under the Terror,* included in this volume.

As for Zola, whose *Attack on the Mill* remains a brilliant and absorbing story seventy-five years after it was written, he too required the largest possible canvas upon which to paint his view of the world. He was of the second or third generation of men and women writers who were appalled by the squalor and the misery which the industrial civilization had brought in its train. In our country, Harriet Beecher Stowe could presumably be put into this category; in England, Dickens, Carlyle, Read, Ruskin, and even Disraeli were among the early protestants against the exploitation of the poor; and in France, Victor Hugo, and the historian Michelet, were the forbears of Zola in this sense. At the same time, just as Balzac pinned his faith on Church and Crown, so Zola was a sincere and simple-minded believer in what might be called Science the Redeemer; and he had a notion that he could paint a picture of French life from which "scientific laws" or society could be deduced. All this meant that, the bigger the canvas, the more effective his work.

Alphonse Daudet is not wholly represented in his short stories for a different reason, and the reason is that there were in a sense two Daudets. One was the Southerner who wrote tall stories of the loquacious and idyllic country folk of Provence, the other was the Parisian who spent his time with men of politics and learning, wrote such Dickensian novels as *Jack* and *Little What's His Name,* and expressed his social consciousness, his sentimental sympathy with the worker, in lines like this one, for example, out of *Jack:* " 'Doctor,' exclaimed Labassindre, banging his fist on the table, 'the tool does not degrade the man, it ennobles him. Christ handled a plane when he was ten years old.' "

Had not a man named Denis Diderdot lived and written in Paris just before the Revolution of 1789, one might have said that Théophile Gautier was the first French professional man of letters, the first man prepared to write for you, on order, whatever you wished: a poem, a play, a story, a travel book, a dramatic criticism, a notice of a show of paintings—anything at all. He had been a younger contemporary of Victor Hugo and had participated in the noisy, defiant, and brilliant movement known as Romanticism whose beginnings are dated around 1830; but he was in his nature too cool, too clear-headed, too professional to be a true romantic. The single aspect of the romantics which remained with him throughout his life was their contempt for the money-grubbing middle-class. He, more than anybody else, made "bourgeois" a word of opprobrium; and though he did not originate the battle-cry, "Art for art's sake," he did more than anybody else to make it an article of faith with, say, the generation of Whistler and of Oscar Wilde. He was fascinated by ancient Egypt, he loved to play with outlandish words, and *One of Cleopatra's Nights* is certainly among the best fictions of the man who wrote *Mademoiselle de Maupin*.

Prosper Mérimée, whose *Venus of Ille* you will read in this collection, was acquainted with Gautier and his circle, but he inclined to hold himself aloof from the literary world. Mérimée was an *amateur* in the best sense of that useful word; he loved antiquity and was a respectable archaeologist, he loved the theater and wrote witty, sardonic comedies, he loved Spain and wrote *Carmen,* he loved France and when the Prussians defeated the French in the decisive battle of Sedan, on the 19th September 1870, he wrote to Madame de Beaulaincourt: "All my life I have sought to be free of prejudice, to be a citizen of the world before being a Frenchman, but the cloak of philosophy is of no avail. I bleed today from the wounds of these imbeciles of Frenchmen; I weep for their humiliation; and ungrateful and ridiculous though they be, I still love them." This side of Mérimée was little known to his contemporaries, who looked upon him as a cold fish; and in an age when color and sonority counted for more than form, his prose was dismissed (by Hugo, for example) as flat and insipid. Yet he was a tender and understanding admirer of Stendhal, and he sought with patience and affection to moderate the political imbecility of Eugénie, Napoleon III's meddling Empress, whom he had known as a child, in Spain. Though he possessed a more affirmative character, it would not be false to see in this erudite, skeptical and polished artist a precursor of Anatole France.

Among Gautier's contemporaries, the most gifted, the most successful, and the handsomest was the high-living and tuberculous poet and playwright, Alfred de Musset. His plays have the felicity of language and tenderness of sentiment of Shakespeare's comedies; his poems have the throbbing eloquence of the best of Tennyson. *Mimi Pinson* is one of his rare prose writings. The story, charming in itself, derives some importance from the fact that it created the idea of the Latin Quarter, brought forth Murger's (and Puccini's) *Vie de Bohème,* and, by inducing students to act as this literature said they acted, gave us another example of life imitating art.

But the writers of the nineteenth century did not stop at romanticism, the despising of the bourgeoisie, and the exaltation of long hair and velvet jackets. A Zola, or a Herbert Spencer might proclaim the infallibility of Science and the doctrine of perpetual progress; there were others, equally gifted, who spat upon Science and denied that there was anything valid in the modern world. These men were mainly poets, and they came to be known as the Symbolists. The strangest, most tenebrous, and most profound of them was Philippe Villiers de l'Isle-Adam. This extraordinary and solitary man claimed descent from a medieval Grand Master of the Knights of Malta, who bore the same name. Himself a kind of character out of Edgar Allen Poe, he wrote Poesque stories, savage satires of science, and plays, the most famous of which, *Axël,* furnished Edmund Wilson the title of that admirable volume of literary criticism, *Axël's Castle.*

When you read the greater works of Balzac you are entranced by them because of the vitality that is in them, and the quality of the story they tell. Afterwards, if you ask yourself what they are really about, you find that they are about the nature of a passion—the passion of avarice, of jealousy, of love, of ambition. In Zola you find an attempt to depict society, rather than an attempt to paint men and women. Flaubert, on the other hand, was infinitely less concerned with specific passions or with society as a whole than with the nature of the men and women he had chosen to write about. That tall, broad-shouldered, blond Norman, who lived in easy circumstances away from Paris, attended by a doting mother and sister, was sensitively, almost morbidly aware of all of his inner weaknesses and shortcomings. It was for this reason that he could say of Emma Bovary, his most perfectly portrayed heroine, that she was himself; and there can be no question but that Frederic, the hero of his *Sentimental Education,* is a piece of self-portraiture. Despite the fun he had recording the innocent stupidities of the half-educated city-dweller (in *Bouvard and Pecuchet*), Flaubert was a solemn fellow, something of a neurotic, and a slow, laborious writer. Whereas his friend Gautier loved words and handled them confidently and playfully, Flaubert respected words and was constantly afraid that he had not written down what he really meant to say. Whereas Gautier was a natural singer, Flaubert had first to "hear" the cadences of his sentences in his head, and then fret about finding the words to express the sense while retaining the rhythm. He had no use for "poetic" prose, but he sought to write prose with a poet's concern for diction and for economy of expression. The opening sentence of *A Simple Heart,* for example, looks as if it might have written itself, so simple is it, and so direct. Yet it gave Flaubert immense trouble, for he was determined to tell the reader, in that single brief sentence, the names of two characters in his story, the respective situations of the two characters, the place where they lived, and the length of time they had been under the same roof. No reader insisted in advance that he do this. Paid by the word, or the line, he would presumably earn less rather than more in return for his scruple. Yet he slaved over the blank page out of a pure, disinterested regard for his art. And it is Flaubert's triumph that with all his concern for the precise word, for the perfectly cadenced sentence, he never lost sight of the human heart and he portrayed it with a fidelity to truth as great as that of any artist who ever lived. The last of his great disciples was the author of *Dubliners.*

The first of his great disciples was, of course, Guy de Maupassant, who, although thirty years younger than his master, was admitted while still in his twenties into the society of Flaubert, Turgeniev, Zola and Daudet. Except that for seven years he served a severe apprenticeship under Flaubert, who confirmed rather than implanted in him a concern for "the humble truth" and the bare, simple, precise word, Maupassant had nothing in common with his elders. He saw in man and society nothing that was either pitiable or exalting, nothing susceptible of affection, admiration, or even amelioration. Whatever his subject, Maupassant so far disciplined himself that he refrained from even pessimistic moralizing about the characters he copied from life and the situations in which he found rather than set them. By his earliest critics, his writings were considered immoral; a later generation pronounced them repellent; and more recently the adjective most frequently applied to them has been "cruel." Nobody, however, has contested that he was the greatest master of the short story as a form of art that ever lived.

With Anatole France we enter a totally different world. His father was a well-known bookseller and he grew up a bookish young man, possessing some Latin, a bit of Greek, and a capacity for imitating the neo-classic verse of what was called the Parnassian School of which Leconte de Lisle was the leading light. *The Crime of Sylvester Bonnard,* a short novel on the professorial type he had observed as a boy in his father's circle, made his name. The post of literary critic on *Le Temps* deservedly enhanced his reputation. He was taken in hand, while still an awkward and not particularly attractive man of forty, by Madame Arman de Caillavet, who created a salon round this amateur of erudition who had so many droll stories to tell out of the minor Latin writers of the Middle Ages and the lives of the more obscure saints of both the Eastern and the Western Church. Ernest Renan, an historian thirty years his senior, had already given the French reading public a taste for impressionistic historiography and ironic commentary, written in limpid and fluent prose. Bookish, erudite, concealing a native timidity under the armor of irony; coddled by Madame Arman de Caillavet, but driven by her, also, to write more and talk less, France embarked in his middle years upon what was for him an ideal existence. He was surrounded by pretty women, revered by talented disciples (one of whom was Marcel Proust), honored in his own land no less than in other lands. With the new sense of security there came a new firmness into his work. The tales he wrote, that appeared on the surface to be innocent entertainment touched with merely literary irony, were in fact a long series of subtle and at times powerful commentaries upon the history of Western man. In this way he dealt with Hellenistic Greece, with declining Rome, with the Middle Ages, the Renaissance, the Revolution of 1789, and with his own age no less than the past. France was wont to proclaim himself a socialist. No man knew less about economic theory than he; his socialism was, as we see in *Crainquebille,* humanitarianism. For about a quarter of a century it has been the fashion in his own country to underestimate France's work. There is no question but that his name will come into its own again.

Georges Duhamel, from whose pen we have in this volume an admirable story of the war of 1914–1918, began his literary career as a member of a school who called themselves the Unanimists, and had Jules Romains for chief. They were not so much concerned with humanitarianism as with the notion that a city, a community, has a psychological life of its own, a life that is something more than the mere sum of the lives of its inhabitants. As a practising physician, Duhamel perceived this life among the people he treated. He saw it again as a medical officer in 1914–1918. But the longer he practised, and the more he saw of the war, the greater became his concern for the groups and even the individuals who composed the community. He expressed his hatred of what people call the "machine age" in an uninformed and ill-natured book about the United States, some twenty years ago. It would be absurd if a community as great as the American nation could not forgive that lapse of taste and intellectual probity in a writer of Duhamel's gifts.

Born in 1900, Antoine de Saint Exupéry (who should never be referred to as "Exupéry" any more than Admiral Mountbatten should be called "Batten") served in the French air force, and he vanished from this earth, nobody knows by what cause or exactly when, in June, 1944, at the controls of an observation plane somewhere between Algeria and the South of France. He has been called the Joseph Conrad of the air, and he was indeed a kind of Conrad in that his acknowledged professional skill as pilot was fused with an incomparable gift as writer and a profound concern with man's destiny. Saint Exupéry began by lending the form of fiction to his tales of the world he knew (*Southern Mail* and *Night Flight*), but with *Wind, Sand and Stars* and *Flight to Arras* he abandoned the pretense of fiction and dedicated his affection for mankind, his wonderfully precise eye and feeling for form to the intense narration of his own journey through the world. He was assuredly one of the best storytellers who ever lived, able to fascinate the reader by a description of a storm, a Patagonian town, a virtually eventless sojourn upon a plateau in the Sahara. For some years before his death, a mutation had been taking place in him: the pilot-poet had been giving way to the moralist, the inner world had been occupying a greater place than the outer world in his thoughts. In his reflective writing, he had not yet reached the point of dazzling clarity attained by that Pascal whom he so much revered. Nobody can say what he might have written, but what we already have assures his immortality.

The last four stories in this collection are stories of the world upheaval. Two—the stories by André Malraux and by Joseph Kessel—are stories of the war. A third—the story by Edith Thomas—relates an episode of the German Occupation. Jean-Paul Sartre's *The Wall* deals with the civil war in Spain. All of these make extremely good reading; but they have the advantage, also, of offering a remarkable account of what the French have been through in the past ten years. The Spanish civil war was a decisive event in the life of French youth: one was either intensely for the Loyalists or intensely for Franco. The fate of France seemed to many young Frenchmen to be foreshadowed by the struggle in the

Spanish arena. This was why Saint Exupéry had gone to Spain, it was why Jean-Paul Sartre, a young professor of philosophy, who had already begun to make his name as novelist and playwright, also went to Spain. Malraux, remembered among us as the author of *Man's Fate,* was in Spain as he had been in China in the 1920's and 1930's—and as he had been in the Maquis (in the hills), a colonel of the French Forces of the Interior, throughout the Occupation. And the same was true of Joseph Kessel, a captain of French aviation when the time came to fight in the open, but previously a man of the Resistance, a Jew who, when he was in Lisbon, safe from the Germans and bound for South America, suddenly said to his friends, 'No! My place is with the Jews who have not been able to escape"—and went back to German-occupied France. Edith Thomas' story, finally, was both written and published under the Occupation, by that most heroic of underground presses, the *Editions de Minuit,* the "Midnight Publishers" who brought out so much that was inspiring in the dreadful years from 1940 to 1944.

LEWIS GALANTIERE

New York, 1945

BEDSIDE BOOK OF
FAMOUS FRENCH STORIES

La Grande Bretêche

HONORÉ DE BALZAC

"AH! MADAME," replied the doctor, "I have some appalling stories in my collection. But each one has its proper hour in a conversation—you know the pretty jest recorded by Chamfort, and said to the Duc de Fronsac: 'Between your sally and the present moment lie ten bottles of champagne.'"

"But it is two in the morning, and the story of Rosina has prepared us," said the mistress of the house.

"Tell us, Monsieur Bianchon!" was the cry on every side.

The obliging doctor bowed, and silence reigned.

"At about a hundred paces from Vendôme, on the banks of the Loire," said he, "stands an old brown house, crowned with very high roofs, and so completely isolated that there is nothing near it, not even a fetid tannery or a squalid tavern, such as are commonly seen outside small towns. In front of this house is a garden down to the river, where the box shrubs, formerly clipped close to edge the walks, now straggle at their own will. A few willows, rooted in the stream, have grown up quickly like an enclosing fence, and half hide the house. The wild plants we call weeds have clothed the bank with their beautiful luxuriance. The fruit-trees, neglected for these ten years past, no longer bear a crop, and their suckers have formed a thicket. The espaliers are like a copse. The paths, once gravelled, are overgrown with purslane; but, to be accurate, there is no trace of a path.

"Looking down from the hill-top, to which cling the ruins of the old castle of the Dukes of Vendôme, the only spot whence the eye can see into this enclosure, we think that at a time, difficult now to determine, this spot of earth must have been the joy of some country gentleman devoted to roses and tulips, in a word, to horticulture, but above all a lover of choice fruit. An arbor is visible, or rather the wreck of an arbor, and under it a table still stands, not entirely destroyed by time. From the aspect of this garden that is no more, the negative joys of the peaceful life of the provinces may be divined as we divine the history of a worthy tradesman when we read the epitaph on his tomb. To complete the mournful and tender impressions which seize the soul, on one of the walls there is a sundial graced with this homely Christian motto, '*Ultimam cogita.*'

"The roof of this house is dreadfully dilapidated; the outside shutters are always closed; the balconies are hung with swallows' nests; the doors are for ever shut. Straggling grasses have outlined the flagstones of the steps with green; the ironwork is rusty. Moon and sun, winter, summer, and snow have eaten into the wood, warped the boards, peeled off the paint. The dreary silence is broken only by birds and cats, pole-cats, rats, and mice, free to scamper round, and fight, and eat each other. An invisible hand has written over it all: 'Mystery.'

"If, prompted by curiosity, you go to look at this house from the street, you will see a large gate, with a round-arched top; the children have made many holes in it. I learned later that this door had been blocked for ten years. Through these irregular breaches you will see that the side toward the courtyard is in perfect harmony with the side toward the garden. The same ruin prevails. Tufts of weeds outline the paving stones; the walls are scored by enormous cracks, and the blackened coping is laced with a thousand festoons of pellitory. The stone steps are disjointed; the bell-cord is rotten; the gutter-spouts broken. What fire from heaven can have fallen there? By what decree has salt been sown on this dwelling? Has God been mocked here? Or was France betrayed? These are the questions we ask ourselves. Reptiles crawl over it, but give no reply. This empty and deserted house is a vast enigma of which the answer is known to none.

"It was formerly a little domain, held in fief, and is known as la Grande Bretêche. During my stay at Vendôme, where Despleins had left me in charge of a rich patient, the sight of this strange dwelling became one of my keenest pleasures. Was it not far better than a ruin? Certain memories of indisputable authenticity attach themselves to a ruin; but this house, still standing, though being slowly destroyed by an avenging hand, contained a secret, an unrevealed thought. At the very least it testified to a caprice. More than once in the evening I attacked the hedge, run wild, which surrounded the enclosure. I braved scratches, I got into this ownerless garden, this plot which was no longer public or private; I lingered there for hours gazing at the disorder. I would not, as the price of the story to which this strange scene no doubt was due, have asked a single question of any gossiping native. On that spot I wove delightful romances, and abandoned myself to little debauches of melancholy which enchanted me. If I had known the reason—perhaps quite commonplace—of this neglect, I should have lost the unwritten poetry which intoxicated me. To me this refuge represented the most various phases of human life, shadowed by misfortune; sometimes the calm of a cloister without the monks; sometimes the peace of the graveyard without the dead, who speak in the language of epitaphs; one day I saw in it the home of lepers; another, the house of the Atridæ; but above all, I found there provincial life, with its contemplative ideas, its hour-glass existence. I often wept there, I never laughed.

"More than once I felt involuntary terrors as I heard overhead the dull hum of the wings of some hurrying wood-pigeon. The earth is dank; you must be on the watch for lizards, vipers, and frogs, wandering about with the wild freedom of nature; above all, you must have no fear of cold, for in a few minutes you feel an icy cloak settled on your shoulders, like the Commendatore's hand on Don Giovanni's neck.

"One evening I felt a shudder; the wind had turned an old rusty weathercock, and the creaking sounded like a cry from the house, at the very moment when I was finishing a gloomy drama to account for this monumental embodiment of woe. I returned to my inn, lost in gloomy thoughts. When I had supped, the hostess came into my room with an air of mystery, and said, 'Monsieur, here is Monsieur Regnault.'

" 'Who is Monsieur Regnault?'

" 'What, sir, don't you know Monsieur Regnault? Well, that's odd,' said she, leaving the room.

"Suddenly I saw a man appear, tall, slim, dressed in black, hat in hand, who came in like a ram ready to butt his opponent, showing a receding forehead, a small pointed head, and a colorless face of the hue of a glass of dirty water. You would have taken him for an usher. The stranger wore an old coat, much worn at the seams; but he had a diamond in his shirt frill, and gold rings in his ears.

" 'Monsieur,' said I, 'whom have I the honor of addressing?' He took a chair, placed himself in front of my fire, put his hat on my table, and answered while he rubbed his hands: 'Dear me, it is very cold. Monsieur, I am Monsieur Regnault.'

"I was encouraging myself by saying to myself, '*Il bondo cani!* Seek!'

" 'I am,' he went on, 'the notary at Vendôme.'

" 'I am delighted to hear it, Monsieur,' I exclaimed. 'But I am not in a position to make a will for reasons best known to myself.'

" 'One moment!' said he, holding up his hand as though to gain silence. 'Allow me, Monsieur, allow me! I am informed that you some-times go to walk in the garden of la Grande Bretêche.'

" 'Yes, Monsieur.'

" 'One moment!' said he, repeating his gesture. 'That constitutes a mis-demeanor. Monsieur, as executor under the will of the late Comtesse de Merret, I come in her name to beg you to discontinue the practice. One moment! I am not a Turk, and do not wish to make a crime of it. And besides, you are probably ignorant of the circumstances which compel me to leave the finest mansion in Vendôme to fall into ruin. Neverthe-less, Monsieur, you must be a man of education, and you should know that the laws forbid, under heavy penalties, any trespass on enclosed property. A hedge is the same as a wall. But, the state in which the place is left may be an excuse for your curiosity. For my part, I should be quite content to make you free to come and go in the house; but being bound to respect the will of the testatrix, I have the honor, Monsieur, to beg that you will go into the garden no more. I myself, Monsieur, since the will was read, have never set foot in the house, which, as I had the hon-or of informing you, is part of the estate of the late Madame de Merret. We have done nothing there but verify the number of doors and win-dows to assess the taxes I have to pay annually out of the funds left for that purpose by the late Madame de Merret. Ah! my dear sir, her will made a great commotion in the town.'

"The good man paused to blow his nose. I respected his volubility, perfectly understanding that the administration of Madame de Merret's estate had been the most important event of his life, his reputation, his glory, his Restoration. As I was forced to bid farewell to my beautiful reveries and romances, I now hoped to learn the truth on official authority.

" 'Monsieur,' said I, 'would it be indiscreet if I were to ask you the reasons for such eccentricity?'

"At these words an expression, which revealed all the pleasure which men feel who are accustomed to ride a hobby, overspread the lawyer's countenance. He pulled up the collar of his shirt with an air, took out his snuffbox, opened it, and offered me a pinch; on my refusing, he took a large one. He was happy! A man who has no hobby does not know all the good to be got out of life. A hobby is the happy medium between a passion and a monomania. At this moment I understood the whole bearing of Sterne's charming passion, and had a perfect idea of the de-light with which my Uncle Toby, encouraged by Trim, bestrode his hobby-horse.

" 'Monsieur,' said Monsieur Regnault, 'I was head clerk in Monsieur

Roguin's office in Paris. A first-rate house, which you may have heard mentioned? No! An unfortunate bankruptcy made it famous. Not having money enough to purchase a practice in Paris at the price to which they were run up in 1816, I came here and bought my predecessor's business. I had relations in Vendôme; among others, a wealthy aunt, who allowed me to marry her daughter. Monsieur,' he went on after a little pause, 'three months after being licensed by the Keeper of the Seals, one evening, as I was going to bed—it was before my marriage —I was sent for by Madame la Comtesse de Merret, to her Château of Merret. Her maid, a good girl, who is now a servant in this inn, was waiting at my door with the Countess's own carriage. Ah! one moment! I ought to tell you that Monsieur le Comte de Merret had gone to Paris to die two months before I came here. He came to a miserable end, flinging himself into every kind of dissipation. You understand?

" 'On the day he left, Madame la Comtesse had quitted la Grande Bretêche, having dismantled it. Some people even say that she had burnt all the furniture, the hangings—in short, all the chattels and furniture whatever used in furnishing the premises now let by the said M.—(Dear! what am I saying? I beg your pardon, I thought I was dictating a lease.) —in short, that she burnt everything in the meadow at Merret. Have you been to Merret, Monsieur? No,' said he, answering himself. 'Ah, it is a very fine place.'

" 'For about three months previously,' he went on, with a jerk of his head, 'the Count and Countess had lived in a very eccentric way; they admitted no visitors; Madame lived on the ground floor, and Monsieur on the first floor. When the Countess was left alone, she was never seen except at church. Subsequently, at home, at the château, she refused to see the friends, whether gentlemen or ladies, who went to call on her. She was already very much altered when she left la Grande Bretêche to go to Merret. That dear lady—I say dear lady, for it was she who gave me this diamond, but indeed I saw her but once—that kind lady was very ill; she had, no doubt, given up all hope, for she died without choosing to send for a doctor; indeed, many of our ladies fancied she was not quite right in her head. Well, sir, my curiosity was strangely excited by hearing that Madame de Merret had need of my services. Nor was I the only person who took an interest in the affair. That very night, though it was already late, all the town knew that I was going to Merret.

" 'The waiting-woman replied but vaguely to the questions I asked her on the way; nevertheless, she told me that her mistress had received the Sacrament in the course of the day at the hands of the Curé of Merret, and seemed unlikely to live through the night. It was about eleven when

I reached the château. I went up the great staircase. After crossing some large, lofty, dark rooms, diabolically cold and damp, I reached the state bedroom where the Countess lay. From the rumors that were current concerning this lady (Monsieur, I should never end if I were to repeat all the tales that were told about her), I had imagined her a coquette. Imagine, then, that I had great difficulty in seeing her in the great bed where she was lying. To be sure, to light this enormous room, with old-fashioned heavy cornices, and so thick with dust that merely to see it was enough to make you sneeze, she had only an old Argand lamp. Ah! but you have not been to Merret. Well, the bed is one of those old-world beds, with a high tester hung with flowered chintz. A small table stood by the bed, on which I saw an "Imitation of Christ," which, by the way, I bought for my wife, as well as the lamp. There were also a deep arm-chair for her confidential maid, and two small chairs. There was no fire. That was all the furniture; not enough to fill ten lines in an inventory.

" 'My dear sir, if you had seen, as I then saw, that vast room, papered and hung with brown, you would have felt yourself transported into a scene of romance. It was icy, nay more, funereal,' and he lifted his hand with a theatrical gesture and paused.

" 'By dint of seeking, as I approached the bed, at last I saw Madame de Merret, under the glimmer of the lamp, which fell on the pillows. Her face was as yellow as wax, and as narrow as two folded hands. The Countess wore a lace cap, showing abundant hair, but as white as linen thread. She was sitting up in bed, and seemed to keep upright with great difficulty. Her large black eyes, dimmed by fever, no doubt, and half-dead already, hardly moved under the bony arch of her eyebrows. There,' he added, pointing to his own brow. 'Her forehead was clammy; her fleshless hands were like bones covered with soft skin; the veins and muscles were perfectly visible. She must have been very handsome; but at this moment I was startled into an indescribable emotion at the sight. Never, said those who wrapped her in her shroud, had any living creature been so emaciated and lived. In short, it was awful to behold! Sickness had so consumed that woman, that she was no more than a phantom. Her lips, which were pale violet, seemed to me not to move when she spoke to me.

" 'Though my professon has familiarized me with such spectacles, by calling me not unfrequently to the bedside of the dying to record their last wishes, I confess that families in tears and the agonies I have seen were as nothing in comparison with this lonely and silent woman in her vast château. I heard not the least sound, I did not perceive the move-ment which the sufferer's breathing ought to have given to the sheets that covered her, and I stood motionless, absorbed in looking at her in a sort of stupor. In fancy I am there still. At last her large eyes moved; she tried to raise her right hand, but it fell back on the bed, and she uttered these words, which came like a breath, for her voice was no longer a voice: "I have waited for you with the greatest impatience." A bright flush rose to her cheeks. It was a great effort for her to speak.

" 'Madame,' I began. She signed to me to be silent. At that moment the old housekeeper rose and said in my ear, 'Do not speak; Madame la Comtesse is not in a state to bear the slightest noise, and what you would say might agitate her.'

"I sat down. A few instants after, Madame de Merret collected all her remaining strength to move her right hand, and slipped it, not without infinite difficulty, under the bolster; she then paused a moment. With a last effort she withdrew her hand; and when she brought out a sealed paper, drops of perspiration rolled from her brow. 'I place my will in your hands—Oh! God! Oh!' and that was all. She clutched a crucifix that lay on the bed, lifted it hastily to her lips, and died.

" 'The expression of her eyes still makes me shudder as I think of it. She must have suffered much! There was joy in her last glance, and it remained stamped on her dead eyes.

" 'I brought away the will, and when it was opened I found that Madame de Merret had appointed me her executor. She left the whole of her property to the hospital of Vendôme, excepting a few legacies. But these were her instructions as relating to la Grande Bretêche: she ordered me to leave the place, for fifty years counting from the day of her death, in the state in which it might be at the time of her decease, forbidding anyone, whoever he might be, to enter the apartments, prohibiting any repairs whatever, and even setting a salary to pay watchmen if it were needful to secure the absolute fulfilment of her intentions. At the expiration of that term, if the will of the testatrix has been duly carried out, the house is to become the property of my heirs, for, as you know, a notary cannot take a bequest. Otherwise la Grande Bretêche reverts to their heirs-at-law, but on condition of fulfilling certain conditions set forth in a codicil to the will, which is not to be opened till the expiration of the said term of fifty years. The will has not been disputed, so—' and without finishing his sentence, the lanky notary looked at me with an air of triumph; I made him quite happy by offering him my congratulations.

" 'Monsieur,' I said in conclusion, 'you have so vividly impressed me that I fancy I see the dying woman whiter than her sheets; her glittering eyes frighten me; I shall dream of her tonight. But you must have formed some ideas as to the instructions contained in that extraordinary will.'

" 'Monsieur,' said he, with comical reticence, 'I never allow myself to criticize the conduct of a person who honors me with the gift of a diamond.'

"However, I soon loosened the tongue of the discreet notary of Vendôme, who communicated to me, not without long digressions, the opinions of the deep politicians of both sexes whose judgments are law in Vendôme. But these opinions were so contradictory, so diffuse, that I was near falling asleep in spite of the interest I felt in this authentic history. The notary's ponderous voice and monotonous accent, accustomed no doubt to listen to himself and to make himself listened to by his clients or fellow-townsmen, were too much for my curiosity. Happily, he soon went away.

" 'Ah, ha, Monsieur,' said he on the stairs, 'a good many persons would be glad to live five-and-forty years longer; but—one moment!' and he laid the first finger of his right hand to his nostril with a cunning look, 'Mark my words! To last as long as that—as long as that, you must not be past sixty now.'

"I closed my door, having been roused from my apathy by this last speech, which the notary thought very funny; then I sat down in my armchair, with my feet on the fire-dogs. I had lost myself in a romance à la Radcliffe, constructed on the juridical base given me by Monsieur Regnault, when the door, opened by a woman's cautious hand, turned on the hinges. I saw my landlady come in, a buxom, florid dame, always good-humored, who had missed her calling in life. She was a Fleming, who ought to have seen the light in a picture by Teniers.

" 'Well, Monsieur,' said she, 'Monsieur Regnault has no doubt been giving you his history of la Grande Bretêche?'

" 'Yes, Madame Lepas.'

" 'And what did he tell you?'

"I repeated in a few words the creepy and sinister story of Madame de Merret. At each sentence my hostess put her head forward, looking at me with an innkeeper's keen scrutiny, a happy compromise between the instinct of a police constable, the astuteness of a spy, and the cunning of a dealer.

" 'My good Madame Lepas,' said I as I ended, 'you seem to know more about it. Heh? If not, why have you come up to me?'

" 'On my word, as an honest woman—'

" 'Do not swear; your eyes are big with a secret. You knew Monsieur de Merret; what sort of man was he?'

" 'Monsieur de Merret—well, you see he was a man you never could see the top of, he was so tall! A very good gentleman, from Picardy, and who had, as we say, his head close to his cap. He paid for everything down, so as never to have difficulties with anyone. He was hot-tempered, you see! All our ladies liked him very much.'

" 'Because he was hot-tempered?' I asked her.

" 'Well, maybe,' said she; 'and you may suppose, sir, that a man had to have something to show for a figure-head before he could marry Madame de Merret, who without any reflection on others, was the handsomest and richest heiress in our parts. She had about twenty thousand francs a year. All the town was at the wedding; the bride was pretty and sweet-looking, quite a gem of a woman. Oh, they were a handsome couple in their day!'

" 'And were they happy together?'

" 'H'm, hm! so-so—so far as can be guessed, for, as you may suppose, we of the common sort were not hail-fellow-well-met with them. Madame de Merret was a kind woman and very pleasant, who had no doubt sometimes to put up with her husband's tantrums. But though he was rather haughty, we were fond of him. After all, it was his place to behave so. When a man is a born nobleman, you see—'

" 'Still, there must have been some catastrophe for Monsieur and Madame de Merret to part so violently?'

" 'I did not say there was any catastrophe, sir. I know nothing about it.'

" 'Indeed. Well, now, I am sure you know everything.'

" 'Well, sir, I will tell you the whole story. When I saw Monsieur Regnault go up to see you, it struck me that he would speak to you about Madame de Merret as having to do with la Grande Bretêche. That put it into my head to ask your advice, sir, seeming to me that you are a man of good judgment and incapable of playing a poor woman like me false —for I never did anyone a wrong, and yet I am tormented by my conscience. Up to now I have never dared to say a word to the people of these parts; they are all chatterers, with tongues like knives. And never till now, sir, have I had any traveller here who stayed so long in the inn as you have, and to whom I could tell the history of the fifteen thousand francs—'

" 'My dear Madame Lepas, if there is anything in your story of a nature to compromise me,' I said, interrupting the flow of words, 'I would not hear it for all the world.'

" 'You need have no fears,' said she; 'you will see.'

"Her eagerness made me suspect that I was not the only person to

whom my worthy landlady had communicated the secret of which I
was to be a sole possessor, but I listened.

" 'Monsieur,' said she, 'when the Emperor sent the Spaniards here,
prisoners of war and others, I was required to lodge at the charge of the
Government a young Spaniard sent to Vendôme on parole. Notwithstanding his parole, he had to show himself every day to the sub-prefect.
He was a Spanish grandee—neither more nor less. He had a name in
os and dia, something like Bagos de Férédia. I wrote his name down in
my books, and you may see it if you like. Ah! he was a handsome young
fellow for a Spaniard, who are ugly, they say. He was not more than five
feet two or three in height, but so well made; and he had little
hands that he kept so beautifully! Ah! you should have seen them. He
had as many brushes for his hands as a woman has for her toilet. He had
thick, black hair, a flame in his eye, a somewhat coppery complexion,
but which I admired all the same. He wore the finest linen I have ever
seen, though I have had princesses to lodge here, and, among others,
General Bertrand, the Duc and Duchesse d'Abrantès, Monsieur Des-
cazes, and the King of Spain. He did not eat much, but he had such
polite and amiable ways that it was impossible to owe him a grudge for
that. Oh! I was very fond of him, though he did not say four words to
me in a day, and it was impossible to have the least bit of talk with him;
if he was spoken to, he did not answer; it is a way, a mania they all have,
it would seem.

" 'He read his breviary like a priest, and went to Mass and all the services quite regularly. And where did he post himself?—we found this
out later—within two yards of Madame de Merret's chapel. As he took
that place the very first time he entered the church, no one imagined
that there was any purpose in it. Besides, he never raised his nose above
his book, poor young man! And then, Monsieur, of an evening he went
for a walk on the hill among the ruins of the old castle. It was his only
amusement, poor man; it reminded him of his native land. They say
that Spain is all hills!

" 'One evening, a few days after he was sent here, he was out very
late. I was rather uneasy when he did not come in till just on the stroke
of midnight; but we all got used to his whims; he took the key of the
door, and we never sat up for him. He lived in a house belonging to us
in the Rue des Casernes. Well, then, one of our stable-boys told us one
evening that, going down to wash the horses in the river, he fancied he
had seen the Spanish grandee swimming some little way off, just like a
fish. When he came in, I told him to be careful of the weeds, and he
seemed put out at having been seen in the water.

" 'At last, Monsieur, one day, or rather one morning, we did not find him in his room; he had not come back. By hunting through his things, I found a written paper in the drawer of his table, with fifty pieces of Spanish gold of the kind they call doubloons, worth about five thousand francs; and in a little sealed box ten thousand francs' worth of diamonds. The paper said that in case he should not return, he left us this money and these diamonds in trust to found Masses to thank God for his escape and for his salvation.

" 'At that time I still had my husband, who ran off in search of him. And this is the queer part of the story: he brought back the Spaniard's clothes, which he had found under a big stone on a sort of breakwater along the river bank, nearly opposite la Grande Bretêche. My husband went so early that no one saw him. After reading the letter, he burnt the clothes, and, in obedience to Count Férédia's wish, we announced that he had escaped.

" 'The sub-prefect set all the constabulary at his heels; but, pshaw! he was never caught. Lepas believed that the Spaniard had drowned himself. I, sir, have never thought so; I believe, on the contrary, that he had something to do with the business about Madame de Merret, seeing that Rosalie told me that the crucifix her mistress was so fond of that she had it buried with her, was made of ebony and silver; now in the early days of his stay here, Monsieur Férédia had one of ebony and silver which I never saw later. And now, Monsieur, do not you say that I need have no remorse about the Spaniard's fifteen thousand francs? Are they not really and truly mine?'

" 'Certainly. But have you never tried to question Rosalie?' said I.

" 'Oh, to be sure I have, sir. But what is to be done? That girl is like a wall. She knows something, but it is impossible to make her talk.'

"After chatting with me for a few minutes, my hostess left me a prey to vague and sinister thoughts, to romantic curiosity, and a religious dread not unlike the deep emotion which comes upon us when we go into a dark church at night and discern a feeble light glimmering under a lofty vault—a dim figure glides across—the sweep of a gown or of a priest's cassock is audible—and we shiver! La Grande Bretêche, with its rank grasses, its shuttered windows, its rusty ironwork, its locked doors, its deserted rooms, suddenly rose before me in fantastic vividness. I tried to get into the mysterious dwelling to search out the heart of this solemn story, this drama which had killed three persons.

"Rosalie became in my eyes the most interesting being in Vendôme. As I studied her, I detected signs of an inmost thought, in spite of the blooming health that glowed in her dimpled face. There was in her soul some element of ruth or of hope; her manner suggested a secret, like the expression of devout souls who pray in excess, or of a girl who has killed her child and for ever hears its last cry. Nevertheless, she was simple and clumsy in her ways; her vacant smile had nothing criminal in it, and you would have pronounced her innocent only from seeing the large red-and-blue-checked kerchief that covered her stalwart bust, tucked into the tight-laced square bodice of a lilac- and white-striped gown. 'No,' said I to myself, 'I will not quit Vendôme without knowing the whole history of la Grande Bretêche. To achieve this end, I will make love to Rosalie if it proves necessary.'

" 'Rosalie!' said I one evening.

" 'Your servant, sir?'

" 'You are not married?' She started a little.

" 'Oh! there is no lack of men if ever I take a fancy to be miserable!' she replied, laughing. She got over her agitation at once; for every woman, from the highest lady to the inn-servant inclusive, has a native presence of mind.

" 'Yes; you are fresh and good-looking enough never to lack lovers! But tell me, Rosalie, why did you become an inn-servant on leaving Madame de Merret? Did she not leave you some little annuity?'

" 'Oh yes, sir. But my place here is the best in all the town of Vendôme.'

"This reply was such a one as judges and attorneys call evasive. Rosalie, as it seemed to me, held in this romantic affair the place of a middle square of the chess-board; she was at the very center of the interest and of the truth; she appeared to me to be tied into the knot of it. It was not a case for ordinary love-making; this girl contained the last chapter of a romance, and from that moment all my attentions were devoted to Rosalie. By dint of studying the girl, I observed in her, as in every woman whom we make our ruling thought, a variety of good qualities; she was clean and neat; she was handsome, I need not say; she soon was possessed of every charm that desire can lend to a woman in whatever rank of life. A fortnight after the notary's visit, one evening, or rather one morning, in the small hours, I said to Rosalie:

" 'Come, tell me all you know about Madame de Merret.'

" 'Oh!' she cried in terror, 'do not ask me that, Monsieur Horace!'

"Her handsome features clouded over, her bright coloring grew pale, and her eyes lost their artless, liquid brightness.

" 'Well,' she said, 'I will tell you, but keep the secret carefully.'

" 'All right, my child; I will keep all your secrets with a thief's honor, which is the most loyal known.'

" 'If it is all the same to you,' said she, 'I would rather it should be with your own.'

"Thereupon she set her head-kerchief straight, and settled herself to tell the tale; for there is no doubt a particular attitude of confidence and security is necessary to the telling of a narrative. The best tales are told at a certain hour—just as we are all here at table. No one ever told a story well standing up, or fasting.

"If I were to reproduce exactly Rosalie's diffuse eloquence, a whole volume would scarcely contain it. Now, as the event of which she gave me a confused account stands exactly midway between the notary's gossip and that of Madame Lepas, as precisely as the middle term of a rule-of-three sum stands between the first and third, I have only to relate it in as few words as may be. I shall therefore be brief.

"The room at la Grande Bretêche in which Madame de Merret slept was on the ground floor; a little cupboard in the wall, about four feet deep, served her to hang her dresses in. Three months before the evening of which I have to relate the events, Madame de Merret had been seriously ailing, so much so that her husband had left her to herself, and had his own bedroom on the first floor. By one of those accidents which it is impossible to forsee, he came in that evening two hours later than usual from the club, where he went to read the papers and talk politics with the residents in the neighborhood. His wife supposed him to have come in, to be in bed and asleep. But the invasion of France had been the subject of a very animated discussion; the game of billiards had waxed vehement; he had lost forty francs, an enormous sum at Vendôme, where everybody is thrifty, and where social habits are restrained within the bounds of a simplicity worthy of all praise, and the foundation perhaps of a form of true happiness which no Parisian would care for.

"For some time past Monsieur de Merret had been satisfied to ask Rosalie whether his wife was in bed; on the girl's replying always in the affirmative, he at once went to his own room, with the good faith that comes of habit and confidence. But this evening, on coming in, he took it into his head to go to see Madame de Merret, to tell her of his ill-luck, and perhaps to find consolation. During dinner he had observed that his wife was very becomingly dressed; he reflected as he came home from the club that his wife was certainly much better, that convalescence had improved her beauty, discovering it, as husbands discover everything, a little too late. Instead of calling Rosalie, who was in the kitchen at the moment watching the cook and the coachman playing a puzzling hand at cards, Monsieur de Merret made his way to his wife's room by the light of his lantern, which he set down on the lowest step of the stairs. His step, easy to recognize, rang under the vaulted passage.

"At the instant when the gentleman turned the key to enter his wife's room, he fancied he heard the door shut of the closet of which I have spoken; but when he went in, Madame de Merret was alone, standing in front of the fireplace. The unsuspecting husband fancied that Rosalie was in the cupboard; nevertheless, a doubt, ringing in his ears like a peal of bells, put him on his guard; he looked at his wife, and read in her eyes an indescribably anxious and haunted expression.

" 'You are very late,' said she. Her voice, usually so clear and sweet, struck him as being slightly husky.

"Monsieur de Merret made no reply, for at this moment Rosalie came in. This was like a thunderclap. He walked up and down the room, going from one window to another at a regular pace, his arms folded.

" 'Have you had bad news, or are you ill?' his wife asked him timidly, while Rosalie helped her to undress. He made no reply.

" 'You can go, Rosalie,' said Madame de Merret to her maid; 'I can put in my curl-papers myself.' She scented disaster at the mere aspect of her husband's face, and wished to be alone with him. As soon as Rosalie was gone, or supposed to be gone, for she lingered a few minutes in the passage, Monsieur de Merret came and stood facing his wife, and said coldly, 'Madame, there is someone in your cupboard!' She looked at her husband calmly, and replied quite simply, 'No, Monsieur.'

"This 'No' wrung Monsieur de Merret's heart; he did not believe it; and yet his wife had never appeared purer or more saintly than she seemed to be at this moment. He rose to go and open the closet door. Madame de Merret took his hand, stopped him, looked at him sadly, and said in a voice of strange emotion, 'Remember, if you should find no one there, everything must be at an end between you and me.'

"The extraordinary dignity of his wife's attitude filled him with deep esteem for her, and inspired him with one of those resolves which need only a grander stage to become immortal.

" 'No, Josephine,' he said, 'I will not open it. In either event we should be parted for ever. Listen; I know all the purity of your soul, I know you lead a saintly life, and would not commit a deadly sin to save your life.' At these words Madame de Merret looked at her husband with a haggard stare. 'See, here is your crucifix,' he went on. 'Swear to me before God that there is no one in there; I will believe you—I will never open that door.'

"Madame de Merret took up the crucifix and said, 'I swear it.'

" 'Louder,' said her husband; 'and repeat: "I swear before God that there is nobody in that closet." ' She repeated the words without flinching.

" 'That will do,' said Monsieur de Merret coldly. After a moment's silence: 'You have there a fine piece of work which I never saw before,' said he, examining the crucifix of ebony and silver, very artistically wrought.

" 'I found it at Duvivier's; last year when that troop of Spanish prisoners came through Vendôme, he bought it of a Spanish monk.'

" 'Indeed,' said Monsieur de Merret, hanging the crucifix on its nail; and he rang the bell.

"He had not to wait for Rosalie. Monsieur de Merret went forward quickly to meet her, led her into the bay of the window that looked on to the garden, and said to her in an undertone:

" 'I know that Gorenflot wants to marry you, that poverty alone prevents your setting up house, and that you told him you would not be his wife till he found means to become a master mason. Well, go and fetch him; tell him to come here with his trowel and tools. Contrive to wake no one in his house but himself. His reward will be beyond your wishes. Above all, go out without saying a word—or else!' and he frowned.

"Rosalie was going, and he called her back. 'Here, take my latch-key,' said he.

" 'Jean!' Monsieur de Merret called in a voice of thunder down the passage. Jean, who was both coachman and confidential servant, left his cards and came.

" 'Go to bed, all of you,' said his master, beckoning him to come close; and the gentleman added in a whisper, 'When they are all asleep—mind, *asleep*—you understand?—come down and tell me.'

Monsieur de Merret, who had never lost sight of his wife while giving his orders, quietly came back to her at the fireside, and began to tell her the details of the game of billiards and the discusson at the club. When Rosalie returned she found Monsieur and Madame de Merret conversing amiably.

"Not long before this Monsieur de Merret had had new ceilings made to all the reception-rooms on the ground floor. Plaster is very scarce at Vendôme; the price is enhanced by the cost of carriage; the gentleman had therefore had a considerable quantity delivered to him, knowing that he could always find purchasers for what might be left. It was this circumstance which suggested the plan he carried out.

" 'Gorenflot is here, sir,' said Rosalie in a whisper.

" 'Tell him to come in,' said her master aloud.

"Madame de Merret turned paler when she saw the mason.

" 'Gorenflot,' said her husband, 'go and fetch some bricks from the coachhouse; bring enough to wall up the door of this cupboard; you can use the plaster that is left for cement.' Then, dragging Rosalie and the workman close to him—'Listen, Gorenflot,' said he, in a low voice, 'you are to sleep here tonight; but tomorrow morning you shall have a passport to take you abroad to a place I will tell you of. I will give you six thousand francs for your journey. You must live in that town for ten years; if you find you do not like it, you may settle in another, but it must be in the same country. Go through Paris and wait there till I join you. I will there give you an agreement for six thousand francs more, to be paid to you on your return, provided you have carried out the conditions of the bargain. For that price you are to keep perfect silence as to what you have to do this night. To you, Rosalie, I will secure ten thousand francs, which will not be paid to you till your wedding day, and on condition of your marrying Gorenflot; but, to get married, you must hold your tongue. If not, no wedding gift!'

" 'Rosalie,' said Madame de Merret, 'come and brush my hair.'

"Her husband quietly walked up and down the room, keeping an eye on the door, on the mason, and on his wife, but without any insulting display of suspicion. Gorenflot could not help making some noise. Madame de Merret seized a moment when he was unloading some bricks, and when her husband was at the other end of the room, to say to Rosalie: 'My dear child, I will give you a thousand francs a year if only you will tell Gorenflot to leave a crack at the bottom.' Then she added aloud and coolly: 'You had better help him.'

"Monsieur and Madame de Merret were silent all the time while Gorenflot was walling up the door. This silence was intentional on the husband's part; he did not wish to give his wife the opportunity of saying anything with a double meaning. On Madame de Merret's side it was pride or prudence. When the wall was half built up, the cunning mason took advantage of his master's back being turned to break one of the two panes in the top of the door with a blow of the pick. By this Madame de Merret understood that Rosalie had spoken to Gorenflot. They all three then saw the face of a dark, gloomy-looking man, with black hair and flaming eyes.

"Before her husband turned round again the poor woman had nodded to the stranger, to whom the signal was meant to convey, 'Hope.'

"At four o'clock, as day was dawning, for it was the month of September, the work was done. The mason was placed in charge of Jean, and Monsieur de Merret slept in his wife's room.

"Next morning when he got up he said with apparent carelessness, 'Oh, by the way, I must go to the Mairie for the passport.' He put on his hat, took two or three steps towards the door, paused, and took the crucifix. His wife was trembling with joy.

" 'He will go to Duvivier's,' thought she.

"As soon as had left, Madame de Merret rang for Rosalie, and then in a terrible voice she cried: 'The pick! Bring the pick! and set to work. I saw how Gorenflot did it yesterday; we shall have time to make a gap and build it up again.'

"In an instant Rosalie had brought her mistress a sort of cleaver; she, with a vehemence of which no words can give an idea, set to work to demolish the wall. She had already got out a few bricks, when, turning to deal a stronger blow than before, she saw behind her Monsieur de Merret. She fainted away.

" 'Lay Madame on her bed,' said he coldly.

"Foreseeing what would certainly happen in his absence, he had laid this trap for his wife; he had merely written to the Mairie and sent for Duvivier. The jeweller arrived just as the disorder in the room had been repaired.

" 'Duvivier,' asked Monsieur de Merret, 'did not you buy some crucifixes of the Spaniards who passed through the town?'

" 'No, Monsieur.'

" 'Very good; thank you,' said he, flashing a tiger's glare at his wife. 'Jean,' he added, turning to his confidential valet, 'you can serve my meals here in Madame de Merret's room. She is ill, and I shall not leave her till she recovers.'

"The cruel man remained in his wife's room for twenty days. During the earlier time, when there was some little noise in the closet, and Josephine wanted to intercede for the dying man, he said, without allowing her to utter a word, 'You swore on the Cross that there was no one there.' "

After this story all the ladies rose from table, and thus the spell under which Bianchon had held them was broken. But there were some among them who had almost shivered at the last words.

2

An Episode of the Terror

HONORÉ DE BALZAC

ON THE 22nd of January, 1793, toward eight o'clock in the evening, an old lady came down the steep street that comes to an end opposite the Church of Saint Laurent in the Faubourg Saint Martin. It had snowed so heavily all day long that the lady's footsteps were scarcely audible; the streets were deserted, and a feeling of dread, not unnatural amid the silence, was further increased by the whole extent of the Terror beneath which France was groaning in those days; what was more, the old lady so far had met no one by the way. Her sight had long been failing, so that the few foot passengers dispersed like shadows in the distance over the wide thoroughfare through the faubourg were quite invisible to her by the light of the lanterns.

She passed the end of the Rue des Morts, when she fancied that she could hear the firm, heavy tread of a man walking behind her. Then it seemed to her that she had heard that sound before, and dismayed by the idea of being followed, she tried to walk faster toward a brightly lit shop window, in the hope of verifying the suspicions which had taken hold of her mind.

So soon as she stood in the shaft of light that streamed out across the road, she turned her head suddenly, and caught sight of a human figure looming through the fog. The dim vision was enough for her. For one moment she reeled beneath an overpowering weight of dread, for she could not doubt any longer that the man had followed her the whole way from her own door; then the desire to escape from the spy gave her strength. Unable to think clearly, she walked twice as fast as before, as if it were possible to escape from a man who of course could move much faster; and for some minutes she fled on, till, reaching a pastry-cook's shop, she entered and sank rather than sat down upon a chair by the counter.

A young woman busy with embroidery looked up from her work at the rattling of the door-latch, and looked out through the square window panes. She seemed to recognize the old-fashioned violet silk mantle, for she went at once to a drawer as if in search of something put aside for the newcomer. Not only did this movement and the expression of the woman's face show a very evident desire to be rid as soon as possible of an unwelcome visitor, but she even permitted herself an impatient exclamation when the drawer proved to be empty. Without looking at the lady, she hurried from her desk into the back shop and called to her husband, who appeared at once.

"Wherever have you put . . . ?" she began mysteriously, glancing at the customer by way of finishing her question.

The pastry-cook could only see the old lady's head-dress, a huge black-silk bonnet with knots of violet ribbon around it, but he looked at his wife as who should say, "Did you think I should leave such a thing as that lying about in your drawer?" and then vanished.

The old lady kept so still and silent that the shopkeeper's wife was surprised. She went back to her, and on a nearer view a sudden impulse of pity, blended perhaps with curiosity, got the better of her. The old lady's face was naturally pale; she looked as though she secretly practised austerities; but it was easy to see that she was paler than usual from recent agitation of some kind. Her head-dress was so arranged as almost to hide hair that was white, no doubt with age, for there was not a trace of powder on the collar of her dress. The extreme plainness of her dress lent an air of austerity to her face, and her features were proud and grave. The manners and habits of people of condition were so different from those of other classes in former times that a noble was easily known, and the shopkeeper's wife felt persuaded that her customer was a *ci-devant,* and that she had been about the Court.

"Madame?" she began with involuntary respect, forgetting that the title was proscribed.

But the old lady made no answer. She was staring fixedly at the shop window as though some dreadful thing had taken shape against the panes. The pastry-cook came back at that moment, and drew the lady from her musings, by holding out a little cardboard box wrapped in blue paper.

"What is the matter, *citoyenne?*" he asked.

"Nothing, nothing, my friends," she answered, in a gentle voice. She looked up at the man as she spoke, as if to thank him by a glance; but she saw the red cap on his head, and a cry broke from her. "Ah! *You* have betrayed me!"

The man and his young wife replied by an indignant gesture that brought the color to the old lady's face; perhaps she felt relief, she blushed for her suspicions.

"Forgive me!" she said, with a childlike sweetness in her tones. Then, drawing a gold louis from her pocket, she held it out to the pastry-cook. "That is the price agreed upon," she added.

There is a kind of want that is felt instinctively by those who know want. The man and his wife looked at one another, then at the elderly woman before them, and read the same thoughts in each other's eyes. That bit of gold was so plainly the last. Her hands shook a little as she held it out, looking at it sadly but ungrudgingly, as one who knows the full extent of the sacrifice. Hunger and penury had carved lines as easy to read in her face as the traces of asceticism and fear. There were vestiges of by-gone splendor in her clothes. She was dressed in threadbare silk, a neat but well-worn mantle, and daintily mended lace—in the rags of former grandeur, in short. The shopkeeper and his wife, drawn two ways by pity and self-interest, began by lulling their consciences with words.

"You seem very poorly, *citoyenne*. . . ."

"Perhaps Madame might like to take something," the wife broke in.

"We have some very nice broth," added the pastry-cook.

"And it is so cold," continued his wife. "Perhaps you have caught a chill, Madame, on your way here. But you can rest and warm yourself a bit."

"We are not so black as the devil!" cried the man.

The kindly intention in the words and tones of the charitable couple won the old lady's confidence. She said that a strange man had been following her, and she was afraid to go home alone.

"Is that all?" returned he of the red bonnet. "Wait for me, *citoyenne*."

He handed the gold coin to his wife, and then went out to put on his National Guard's uniform, impelled, thereto, by the idea of making some adequate return for the money; an idea that sometimes slips into a tradesman's head when he has been prodigiously overpaid for goods of no great value. He took up his cap, buckled on his sabre, and came out in full dress. But his wife had had time to reflect, and reflection, as not unfrequently happens, closed the hand that kindly intentions had opened. Feeling frightened and uneasy lest her husband might be drawn into something unpleasant, she tried to catch at the skirt of his coat, to hold him back, but he, good soul, obeying his charitable first thought, brought out his offer to see the lady home, before his wife could stop him.

"The man of whom the *citoyenne* is afraid is still prowling about the shop, it seems," she said sharply.

"I am afraid so," the lady said innocently.

"How if it is a spy? A plot? Don't go. And take the box away from her. . . ."

The words whispered in the pastry-cook's ear cooled his hot fit of courage down to zero.

"Oh! I will just go out and say a word or two. I will rid you of him soon enough," he exclaimed, as he bounced out of the shop.

The old lady meanwhile, passive as a child and almost dazed, sat down on her chair again. But the honest pastry-cook came back directly. A countenance red enough to begin with, and further flushed by the bake-house fire, was suddenly blanched; such terror perturbed him that he reeled as he walked, and stared about him like a drunken man.

"Miserable aristocrat! Do you want to have our heads cut off?" he shouted furiously. "You just take to your heels and never show yourself here again. Don't come to me for materials for your plots."

He tried, as he spoke, to take away the little box which she had slipped into one of her pockets. But at the touch of a profane hand on her clothes, the stranger recovered youth and activity for a moment, preferring to face the dangers of the street with no protector save God, to the loss of the thing that she had just paid for. She sprang to the door, flung it open, and disappeared, leaving the husband and wife dumfounded and quaking with fright.

Once outside in the street, she started away at a quick walk; but her strength soon failed her. She heard the sound of the snow crunching under a heavy step, and knew that the pitiless spy was on her track. She was obliged to stop. He stopped likewise. From sheer terror, or lack of intelligence, she did not dare to speak or to look at him. She went slowly on; the man slackened his pace and fell behind so that he could still keep her in sight. He might have been her very shadow.

Nine o'clock struck as the silent man and woman passed again by the Church of Saint Laurent. It is in the nature of things that calm must succeed to violent agitation, even in the weakest soul; for if feeling is infinite, our capacity to feel is limited. So, as the stranger lady met with no harm from her supposed persecutor, she tried to look upon him as an unknown friend anxious to protect her. She thought of all the circumstances in which the stranger had appeared, and put them together, as if to find some ground for this comforting theory, and felt inclined to credit him with good intentions rather than bad. Forgetting the fright that he had given the pastry-cook, she walked on with a firmer step through the upper end of the Faubourg Saint Martin; and another half hour's walk brought her to a house at the corner where the road to the Barrière de Pantin turns off from the main thoroughfare. Even at this day, the place is one of the least frequented parts of Paris. The north wind sweeps over the Buttes-Chaumont and Belleville, and whistles through the houses (the hovels rather) scattered over an almost uninhabited low-lying waste, where the fences are heaps of earth and bones. It was a desolate-looking place, a fitting refuge for despair and misery.

The sight of it appeared to make an impression upon the relentless pursuer of a poor creature so daring as to walk alone at night through the silent streets. He stood in thought, and seemed by his attitude to hesitate. She could see him dimly now, under the street lamp that sent a faint, flickering light through the fog. Fear gave her eyes. She saw, or thought she saw, something sinister about the stranger's features. Her old terrors awoke; she took advantage of a kind of hesitation on his part, slipped through the shadows to the door of the solitary house, pressed a spring, and vanished swiftly as a phantom.

For awhile the stranger stood motionless, gazing up at the house. It was in some sort a type of the wretched dwellings in the suburb; a tumble-down hovel, built of rough stones, daubed over with a coat of yellowish stucco, and so riven with great cracks that there seemed to be danger lest the slightest puff of wind might blow it down. The roof, covered with brown moss-grown tiles, had given way in several places, and looked as though it might break down altogether under the weight of the snow. The frames of the three windows on each story were rotten with damp and warped by the sun; evidently the cold must find its way inside. The house standing thus quite by itself looked like some old tower that Time had forgotten to destroy. A faint light shone from the attic windows pierced at irregular distances in the roof; otherwise the whole building was in total darkness.

Meanwhile the old lady climbed not without difficulty up the rough, clumsily built staircase, with a rope by way of a hand-rail. At the door of the lodging in the attic she stopped and tapped mysteriously; an old man brought forward a chair for her. She dropped into it at once.

"Hide! Hide!" she exclaimed, looking up at him. "Seldom as we leave the house, everything that we do is known, and every step is watched. . . ."

"What is it now?" asked another elderly woman, sitting by the fire.

"The man that has been prowling about the house yesterday and today, followed me tonight. . . ."

At those words all three dwellers in the wretched den looked in each other's faces and did not try to dissimulate the profound dread that they felt. The old priest was the least overcome, probably because he ran the greatest danger. If a brave man is weighed down by great calamities or the yoke of persecution, he begins, as it were, by making the sacrifice of himself; and thereafter every day of his life becomes one more victory snatched from fate. But from the way in which the women looked at him it was easy to see that their intense anxiety was on his account.

"Why should our faith in God fail us, my sisters?" he said, in low but fervent tones. "We sang His praises through the shrieks of murderers and their victims at the Carmelites. If it was His will that I should come alive out of that butchery, it was, no doubt, because I was reserved for some fate which I am bound to endure without murmuring. God will protect His own; He can do with them according to His will. It is for you, not for me that we must think."

"No," answered one of the women. "What is our life compared with a priest's life?"

"Once outside the Abbaye de Chelles, I look upon myself as dead," added the nun who had not left the house, while the Sister that had just returned held out the little box to the priest.

"Here are the wafers. . . . But I can hear some one coming up the stairs!"

At this, the three began to listen. The sound ceased.

"Do not be alarmed if somebody tries to come in," said the priest. "Somebody on whom we could depend was to make all necessary arrangements for crossing the frontier. He is to come for the letters that I have written to the Duc de Langeais and the Marquis de Beauséant, asking them to find some way of taking you out of this dreadful country, and away from the death or the misery that waits for you here."

"But are you not going to follow us?" the nuns cried under their breath, almost despairingly.

"My post is here where the sufferers are," the priest said simply, and the women said no more, but looked at their guest in reverent admiration. He turned to the nun with the wafers.

"Sister Marthe," he said, "the messenger will say *Fiat Voluntas* in answer to the word *Hosanna*."

"There is some on the stairs!" cried the other nun, opening a hiding-place contrived in the roof.

This time it was easy to hear, amid the deepest silence, a sound echoing up the staircase: it was a man's tread on the steps covered with dried lumps of mud. With some difficulty the priest slipped into a kind of cupboard, and the nun flung some clothes over him.

"You can shut the door, Sister Agathe," he said in a muffled voice.

He was scarcely hidden before three raps sounded on the door. The holy women looked into each other's eyes for counsel, and dared not say a single word.

They seemed to be about sixty years of age. They had lived out of the world for forty years, and had grown so accustomed to the life of the convent that they could scarcely imagine any other. To them, as to plants kept in a hot-house, a change of air meant death. And so, when the grating was broken down one morning, they knew with a shudder that they were free. The effect produced by the Revolution upon their simple souls is easy to imagine; it produced a temporary imbecility not natural to them. They could not bring the ideas learned in the convent into harmony with life and its difficulties; they could not even understand their own position. They were like children whom others have always cared for, deserted by their maternal providence. And as a child cries, they betook themselves to prayer. Now, in the presence of imminent danger, they were mute and passive, knowing no defense save Christian resignation.

The man at the door, taking silence for consent, presented himself, and the women shuddered. This was the prowler that had been making inquiries about them for some time past. But they looked at him with frightened curiosity, much as shy children stare silently at a stranger; and neither of them moved.

The newcomer was a tall, burly man. Nothing in his behavior, bearing or expression suggested malignity as, following the example set by the nuns, he stood motionless, while his eyes traveled around the room.

Two straw mats laid upon planks did duty as beds. On the one table, placed in the middle of the room, stood a brass candlestick, several plates, three knives and a round loaf. A small fire burned in the grate. A few bits of wood in a heap in a corner bore further witness to the poverty of the recluses. You had only to look at the coating of paint on the walls to discover the bad condition of the roof, and the ceiling was a perfect network of brown stains made by rain water. A relic, saved no doubt from the wreck of the Abbaye de Chelles, stood like an ornament on the chimney piece. Three chairs, two boxes, and a rickety chest of drawers completed the list of the furniture, but a door beside the fireplace suggested an inner room beyond.

The brief inventory was soon made by the personage introduced into their midst under such terrible auspices. It was with a compassionate expression that he turned to the two women; he looked benevolently at them, and seemed, at least, as much embarrassed as they. But the strange silence did not last long, for presently the stranger began to understand. He saw how inexperienced, how helpless (mentally speaking), the two poor creatures were, and he tried to speak gently.

"I am far from coming as an enemy, *citoyennes*. . . ." he began. Then he suddenly broke off and went on, "Sisters, if anything should happen to you, believe me, I shall have no share in it. I have come to ask a favor of you."

Still the women were silent.

"If I am annoying you—if—if I am intruding, speak freely, and I will go; but you must understand that I am entirely at your service; that if I can do anything for you, you need not fear to make use of me. I, and I only, perhaps, am above the law, since there is no King now."

There was such a ring of sincerity in the words that Sister Agathe hastily pointed to a chair as if to bid their guest be seated. Sister Agathe came of the house of Langeais; her manner seemed to indicate that once she had been familiar with brilliant scenes, and had breathed the air of courts. The stranger seemed half pleased, half distressed when he understood her invitation; he waited to sit down until the women were seated.

"You are giving shelter to a reverend father who refused to take the oath, and escaped the massacres at the Carmelites by a miracle. . . ."

"*Hosanna!*" Sister Agathe exclaimed eagerly, interrupting the stranger, while she watched him with curious eyes.

"That is not the name, I think," he said.

"But, Monsieur," Sister Marthe broke in quickly, "we have no priest here, and . . ."

"In that case you should be more careful and on your guard," he answered gently, stretching out his hand for a breviary that lay on the table. "I do not think that you know Latin, and . . ."

He stopped; for, at the sight of the great emotion in the faces of the two poor nuns, he was afraid that he had gone too far. They were trembling, and the tears stood in their eyes.

"Do not fear," he said frankly. "I know your names and the name of your guest. Three days ago I heard of your distress and devotion to the venerable Abbé de——"

"Hush!" Sister Agathe cried, in the simplicity of her heart, as she laid her finger on her lips.

"You see, Sisters, that if I had conceived the horrible idea of betraying you, I could have given you up already, more than once. . . ."

At the words the priest came out of his hiding-place and stood in their midst.

"I cannot believe, Monsieur, that you can be one of our persecutors," he said, addressing the stranger, "and I trust you. What do you want with me?"

The priest's holy confidence, the nobleness expressed in every line in his face, would have disarmed a murderer. For a moment the mysterious stranger, who had brought an element of excitement into lives of misery and resignation, gazed at the little group; then he turned to the priest and said, as if making a confidence, "Father, I came to beg you to celebrate a mass for the repose of—of—of an august personage whose body will never rest in consecrated earth. . . ."

Involuntarily the abbé shivered. As yet, neither of the Sisters understood of whom the stranger was speaking; they sat with their heads stretched out and faces turned toward the speaker, curiosity in their whole attitude. The priest, meanwhile, was scrutinizing the stranger; there was no mistaking the anxiety in the man's face, the ardent entreaty in his eyes.

"Very well," returned the abbé. "Come back at midnight. I shall be ready to celebrate the only funeral service that it is in our power to offer in expiation of the crime of which you speak."

A quiver ran through the stranger, but a sweet yet sober satisfaction seemed to prevail over a hidden anguish. He took his leave respectfully, and the three generous souls felt his unspoken gratitude.

Two hours later, he came back and tapped at the garret door. Mademoiselle de Beauséant showed the way into the second room in their humble lodging. Everything had been made ready. The Sisters had moved the old chest of drawers between the two chimneys, and covered its quaint outlines over with a splendid altar cloth of green watered silk.

The bare walls looked all the barer, because the one thing that hung there was the great ivory and ebony crucifix, which of necessity attracted the eyes. Four slender little altar candles, which the Sisters had contrived to fasten into their places with sealing-wax, gave a faint pale light, almost absorbed by the walls; the rest of the room lay well-nigh in the dark. But the dim brightness, concentrated upon the holy things, looked like a ray from Heaven shining down upon the unadorned shrine. The floor was reeking with damp. An icy wind swept in through the chinks here and there, in a roof that rose sharply on either side, after the fashion of attic roofs. Nothing could be less imposing; yet perhaps, too, nothing could be more solemn than this mournful ceremony. A silence so deep that they could have heard the faintest sound of a voice on the Route d'Allemagne, invested the night-piece with a kind of somber majesty; while the grandeur of the service—all the grander for the strong contrast with the poor surroundings—produced a feeling of reverent awe.

The Sisters kneeling on either side of the altar, regardless of the deadly chill from the wet brick floor, were engaged in prayer, while the priest, arrayed in pontifical vestments, brought out a golden chalice set with gems; doubtless one of the sacred vessels saved from the pillage of the Abbaye de Chelles. Beside a ciborium, the gift of royal munificence, the wine and water for the holy sacrifice of the mass, stood ready in two glasses such as could scarcely be found in the meanest tavern. For want of a missal, the priest had laid his breviary on the altar, and a common earthenware plate was set for the washing of hands that were pure and undefiled with blood. It was all so infinitely great, yet so little, poverty-stricken yet noble, a mingling of sacred and profane.

The stranger came forward reverently to kneel between the two nuns. But the priest had tied crape around the chalice of the crucifix, having no other way of marking the mass as a funeral service; it was as if God himself had been in mourning. The man suddenly noticed this, and the sight appeared to call up some overwhelming memory, for great drops of sweat stood out on his broad forehead.

Then the four silent actors in the scene looked mysteriously at one another; and their souls in emulation seemed to stir and communicate the thoughts within them until all were melted into one feeling of awe and pity. It seemed to them that the royal martyr whose remains had been consumed with quicklime, had been called up by their yearning and now stood, a shadow in their midst, in all the majesty of a king. They were celebrating an anniversary service for the dead whose body lay elsewhere. Under the disjointed laths and tiles, four Christians were holding a funeral service without a coffin, and putting up prayers to God for the soul of a King of France. No devotion could be purer than this. It was a wonderful act of faith achieved without an afterthought. Surely in the sight of God it was like the cup of cold water which counterbalances the loftiest virtues. The prayers put up by two feeble nuns and a priest represented the whole Monarchy, and possibly at the same time, the Revolution found expression in the stranger, for the remorse in his face was so great that it was impossible not to think that he was fulfilling the vows of a boundless repentance.

When the priest came to the Latin words, *Introibo ad altare Dei* a sudden divine inspiration flashed upon him; he looked at the three kneeling figures, the representatives of Christian France, and said instead, as though to blot out the poverty of the garret, "We are about to enter the Sanctuary of God!"

Those words, uttered with thrilling earnestness, struck reverent awe into the nuns and the stranger. Under the vaulted roof of St. Peter's in Rome, God would not have revealed Himself in greater majesty than here for the eyes of the Christians in that poor refuge; so true is it that all intermediaries between God and the soul of man are superfluous and all the grandeur of God proceeds from Himself alone.

The stranger's fervor was sincere. One emotion blended the prayers of the four servants of God and the King in a single supplication. The holy words rang like the music of heaven through the silence. At one moment, tears gathered in the stranger's eyes. This was during the *Pater Noster;* for the priest added a petition in Latin, and his audience doubtless understood him when he said: *"Et remitte scelus regicidis sicut Ludovicus eis remisit semetipse. . . ."* Forgive the regicides as Louis himself forgave them.

The Sisters saw two great tears trace a channel down the stranger's manly cheeks and fall to the floor. Then the office for the dead was recited; the *Domine salvum fac regem* chanted in an undertone that went to the hearts of the faithful Royalists, for they thought how the child-King for whom they were praying was even then a captive in the hands of his enemies; and a shudder ran through the stranger, as he thought that a new crime might be committed, and that he could not choose but take his part in it.

The service came to an end. The priest made a sign to the Sisters, and they withdrew. As soon as he was left alone with the stranger, he went toward him with a grave, gentle face, and said, in fatherly tones: "My son, if your hands are stained with the blood of the royal martyr, confide in me. There is no sin may not be blotted out in the sight of God by penitence as sincere and touching as yours appears to be."

At the first words, the man started with terror, in spite of himself. Then he recovered composure, and looked quietly at the astonished priest.

"Father," he said, and the other could not miss the tremor in his voice, "no one is more guiltless than I of the blood shed. . . ."

"I am bound to believe you," said the priest. He paused a moment, and again he scrutinized his penitent. But, persisting in the idea that the man before him was one of the members of the Convention, one of the timorous voters who betrayed an inviolable and anointed head to save their own, he began again gravely:

"Remember, my son, that it is not enough to have taken no active part in the great crime; that fact does not absolve you. The men who might have defended the King and left their swords in their scabbards will have a very heavy account to render to the King of Heaven. . . . Ah! yes," he added, with an eloquent shake of the head, "heavy indeed! For by doing nothing they became accomplices in the awful wickedness. . . ."

"But do you think that an indirect participation will be punished?" the stranger asked with a bewildered look. "There is the private soldier commanded to fall into line—is he actually responsible?"

The priest hesitated. The stranger was glad; he had put the Royalist precisian in a dilemma, between the dogma of passive obedience on the one hand (for the upholders of the Monarchy maintained that obedience was the first principle of military law), and the equally important dogma which turns respect for the person of a king into a matter of religion. In the priest's indecision he was eager to see a favorable solution of the doubts which seemed to torment him. To prevent too prolonged reflection on the part of the reverend Jansenist, he added:

"I should blush to offer remuneration of any kind for the funeral service which you have just performed for the repose of the King's soul and the relief of my conscience. The only possible return for something of inestimable value is an offering likewise beyond price. Will you deign, Monsieur, to take my gift of a holy relic? A day will perhaps come when you will understand its value."

As he spoke the stranger held out a box; it was very small and exceedingly light. The priest took it mechanically, as it were, so astonished was he by the man's solemn words, the tones of his voice, and the reverence with which he held out the gift.

The two men went back together into the first room. The Sisters were waiting for them.

"This house that you are living in belongs to Mucius Scaevola, the plasterer on the first floor," he said. "He is well known in the section for his patriotism, but in reality he is an adherent of the Bourbons. He used to be a huntsman in the service of His Highness, the Prince de Conti, and he owes everything to him. So long as you stay in the house, you are safer here than anywhere else in France. Do not go out. Pious souls will minister to your necessities, and you can wait in safety for better times. Next year, on the 21st of January"—he could not hide an involuntary shudder as he spoke—"next year, if you are still in this dreary refuge, I will come back again to celebrate the expiatory mass with you. . . ."

He broke off, bowed to the three, who answered not a word, gave a last look at the garret with its signs of poverty, and vanished.

Such an adventure possessed all the interest of a romance in the lives of the innocent nuns. So, as soon as the venerable abbé told them the story of the mysterious gift, it was placed upon the table, and by the feeble light of the tallow dip an indescribable curiosity appeared in the three anxious faces. Mademoiselle de Langeais opened the box, and found a very fine lawn handkerchief, soiled with sweat; darker stains appeared as they unfolded it.

"That is blood!" exclaimed the priest.

"It is marked with a royal crown!" cried Sister Agathe.

The women, aghast, allowed the precious relic to fall. For their simple souls the mystery that hung about the stranger grew inexplicable; as for the priest, from that day forth he did not even try to understand it.

Before very long the prisoners knew that, in spite of the Terror, some powerful hand was extended over them. It began when they received firewood and provisions; and next the Sisters knew that a woman had lent counsel to their protector, for linen was sent to them, and clothes in which they could leave the house without causing remark upon the aristocrat's dress that they had been forced to wear. After a while Mucius Scaveola gave them two civic cards; and often tidings necessary for the priest's safety came to them in roundabout ways. Warnings and advice reached them so opportunely that they could only have been sent by some person in the possession of state secrets. And, at a time when famine threatened Paris, invisible hands brought rations of white bread for the proscribed women in the wretched garret. Still they fancied that Citizen Mucius Scaevola was only the mysterious instrument of a kindness always ingenious, and no less intelligent.

The noble ladies in the garret could no longer doubt that their protector was the stranger of the expiatory mass on the night of the 22nd of January, 1793; and a kind of cult of him sprang up among them. Their one hope was in him; they lived through him. They added special petitions for him to their prayers; night and morning the pious souls prayed for his happiness, his prosperity, his safety; entreating God to remove all snares far from his path; to deliver him from his enemies, to grant him a long and peaceful life. And with this daily renewed gratitude, as it may be called, there blended a feeling of curiosity which grew more lively day by day. They talked over the circumstances of his first sudden appearance, their conjectures were endless; the stranger had conferred one more benefit upon them by diverting their minds. Again, and again, they said, when he next came to see them as he promised, to celebrate sad anniversary of the death of Louis XVI, he should not escape their friendship.

The night so impatiently awaited came at last. At midnight the old wooden staircase echoed with the stranger's heavy footsteps. They had made the best of their room for his coming; the altar was ready, and this time the door stood open, and the two Sisters were out at the stairhead, eager to light the way. Mademoiselle de Langeais even came down a few steps, to meet their benefactor the sooner.

"Come," she said, with a quaver in the affectionate tones. "Come in, we are expecting you."

He raised his face, gave her a dark look, and made no answer. The Sister felt as if an icy mantle had fallen over her, and said no more. At the sight of him, the glow of gratitude and curiosity died away in their hearts. Perhaps he was not so cold, not so taciturn, not so stern as he seemed to them, for in their highly wrought mood they were ready to pour out their feeling of friendship. But the three poor prisoners understood that he wished to be a stranger to them—and submitted. The priest fancied that he saw a smile on the man's lips as he saw their preparations for his visit, but it was at once repressed. He heard mass, said his prayer, and then disappeared, declining, with a few polite words, Mademoiselle de Langeais's invitation to partake of the little collation made ready for him.

After the 9th Thermidor, the Sisters and the Abbé de Marolles could go about Paris without the least danger. The first time that the abbé went out he walked to a perfumer's shop at the sign of the Queen of Roses, kept by the Citizen Ragon and his wife, court perfumers. The Ragons had been faithful adherents of the Royalist cause; it was through their means that the Vendéen leaders kept up a correspondence with the Princes and the Royalist Committee in Paris. The abbé, in the ordinary dress of the time, was standing on the threshold of the shop, which stood between Saint Roch and the Rue des Frondeurs, when he saw that the Rue Saint Honoré was filled with a crowd and he could not go out.

"What is the matter?" he asked Madame Ragon.

"Nothing," she said. "It is only the tumbril cart and the executioner going to the Place Louis XV. Ah! We used to see it often enough last year; but today, four days after the anniversary of the 21st of January, one does not feel sorry to see the ghastly procession."

"Why not?" asked the abbé. "That is not said like a Christian."

"Eh! But it is the execution of Robespierre's accomplices. They defended themselves as long as they could, but now it is their turn to go where they sent so many innocent people."

The crowd poured by like a flood. The abbé, yielding to an impulse of curiosity, looked up above the heads, and there in the tumbril stood the man who had heard mass in the garret three days ago.

"Who is it?" he asked. "Who is the man with . . .?"

"That is the headsman," answered M. Ragon, calling the executioner —the *exécuteur des hautes oeuvres*—by the name he had borne under the Monarchy.

"Oh! My dear, my dear! M. l'abbé is dying!" cried out old Madame Ragon. She caught up a flask of vinegar, and tried to restore the old priest to consciousness.

"He must have given me the handkerchief that the King used to wipe his brow on the way to his martyrdom," murmured he. "Poor man! There was a heart in the steel blade, when none was found in all France. . . ."

The perfumers thought that the poor abbé was raving.

3

The Venus of Ille

PROSPER MÉRIMÉE

'Ιλεὼς ἦν δ'ἐγὼ, ἔατω ὁ ἀνδρίας
Καὶ ἤπιος οὕτως ἀνδρεῖος ὤν
ΛΟΥΚΙΑΝΟΥ ΦΙΛΟΨΕΥΔΗΣ

I WAS descending the last slope of Canigou, and, although the sun had already set, I could distinguish in the plain below the houses of the little town of Ille, for which I was bound.

"You know," I said to the Catalan who had been acting as my guide since the preceding day, "you know, doubtless, where Monsieur de Peyrehorade lives?"

"Do I know!" he cried; "why, I know his house as well as I do my own; and if it wasn't so dark, I'd show it to you. It's the finest house in Ille. He has money, you know, has Monsieur de Peyrehorade; and his son is going to marry a girl that's richer than himself."

"Is the marriage to take place soon?" I asked.

"Soon! It may be that the fiddles are already ordered for the wedding. Tonight, perhaps, or tomorrow, or the day after, for all I know! It's to be at Puygarrig; for it's Mademoiselle de Puygarrig that the young gentleman is going to marry."

I had a letter of introduction to M. de Peyrehorade from my friend M. de P. He was, so my friend had told me, a very learned antiquarian, and good-natured and obliging to the last degree. He would take pleasure in showing me all the ruins within a radius of ten leagues. Now, I relied upon him to accompany me about the country near Ille, which I knew to be rich in monuments of ancient times and of the Middle Ages. This marriage, of which I now heard for the first time, might upset all my plans.

"I shall be an interloper," I said to myself.

But I was expected; as my arrival had been announced by M. de P., I must needs present myself.

"I'll bet you, Monsieur," said my guide, as we reached the foot of the mountain, "I'll bet you a cigar that I can guess what you are going to do at Monsieur de Peyrehorade's."

"Why, that is not very hard to guess," I replied, offering him a cigar. "At this time of day, when one has walked six leagues over Canigou, the most urgent business is supper."

"Yes, but tomorrow? Look you, I'll bet that you have come to Ille to see the idol! I guessed that when I saw you drawing pictures of the saints at Serrabona."

"The idol! What idol?" The word had aroused my curiosity.

"What! Didn't anyone at Perpignan tell you how Monsieur de Peyrehorade had found an idol in the ground?"

"You mean a terra-cotta, or clay statue, don't you?"

"No, indeed! I mean a copper one, and it's big enough to make a lot of big sous. It weighs as much as a church bell. It was way down in the ground, at the foot of an olive tree, that we found it."

"So you were present at the discovery, were you?"

"Yes, Monsieur. Monsieur de Peyrehorade told us a fortnight ago, Jean Coll and me, to dig up an old olive tree that got frozen last year— for it was a very hard winter, you know. So, while we were at work, Jean Coll, who was going at it with all his might, dug his pick into the dirt, and I heard a *bimm*—just as if he'd struck a bell. 'What's that?' says I. We kept on digging and digging, and first a black hand showed; it looked like a dead man's hand sticking out of the ground. For my part, I was scared. I goes to monsieur, and I says to him: 'Dead men under the olive tree, master. You'd better call the curé.'

" 'What dead men?' he says.

"He went with me, and he'd no sooner seen the hand than he sings out: 'An antique! an antique!' You'd have thought he had found a treasure. And to work he went with the pick and with his hands, and did as much as both of us together, you might say.'"

"Well, what did you find?"

"A tall black woman more than half naked, saving your presence, monsieur, of solid copper; and Monsieur de Peyrehorade told us that it was an idol of heathen times— of the time of Charlemagne!"

"I see what it is: a bronze Blessed Virgin from some dismantled convent."

"A Blessed Virgin! oh, yes! I should have recognized it if it had been a Blessed Virgin. It's an idol, I tell you; you can see that from its expression. It fastens its great white eyes on you; you'd think it was trying to stare you out of countenance. Why, you actually lower your eyes when you look at it."

"White eyes? They are incrusted on the bronze, no doubt. It may be some Roman statue."

"Roman! that's it. Monsieur de Peyrehorade says she's a Roman. Ah! I see that you're a scholar like him."

"Is it whole, well preserved?"

"Oh! it's all there, monsieur. It's even handsomer and finished better than the plaster of Paris bust of Louis Philippe at the mayor's office. But for all that, I can't get over the idol's face. It has a wicked look—and she is wicked too."

"Wicked! what harm has she done you?"

"None to me exactly; but I'll tell you. We had got down on all-fours to stand her up, and Monsieur de Peyrehorade, he was pulling on the rope too, although he hasn't any more strength than a chicken, the excellent man! With a good deal of trouble we got her on her feet. I was picking up a piece of stone to wedge her, when, *patatras!* down she went again, all in a heap. 'Stand from under!' says I. But I was too late, for Jean Coll didn't have time to pull out his leg."

"And he was hurt?"

"His poor leg broken off short like a stick! *Pécaïre!* when I saw that, I was furious. I wanted to smash the idol with my pickaxe, but Monsieur de Peyrehorade held me back. He gave Jean Coll some money, but he's been in bed all the same ever since it happened, a fortnight ago, and the doctor says he'll never walk with that leg like the other. It's a pity, for he was our best runner, and, next to monsieur's son, the best tennis-player. I tell you, it made Monsieur Alphonse de Peyrehorade feel bad, for Coll always played with him. It was fine to see how they'd send the balls back at each other. Paf! paf! They never touched the ground."

Chatting thus we entered Ille, and I soon found myself in M. de Peyrehorade's presence. He was a little old man, still hale and active, with powdered hair, a red nose, and a jovial, bantering air. Before opening M. de P.'s letter, he installed himself in front of a bountifully spread table, and introduced me to his wife and son as an illustrious archæologist, who was destined to rescue Roussillon from the oblivion in which the indifference of scholars had thus far left it.

While eating with a hearty appetite—for nothing is more conducive thereto than the keen mountain air—I examined my hosts. I have already said a word or two of M. de Peyrehorade; I must add that he was vivacity personified. He talked, ate, rose from his chair, ran to his library, brought books to me, showed me prints, filled my glass; he was never at rest for two minutes in succession. His wife, who was a trifle too stout, like all the Catalan women after they have passed forty, impressed me as a typical provincial, who had no interests outside of her household. Although the supper was ample for at least six persons, she ran to the kitchen, ordered pigeons killed, all sorts of things fried, and opened Heaven knows how many jars of preserves. In an instant the table was laden with dishes and bottles, and I should certainly have died of indigestion if I had even tasted everything that was offered me. And yet, with every new dish that I declined there were renewed apologies. She was afraid that I would find myself very badly off at Ille. One had so few resources in the provinces, and Parisians were so hard to please!

Amid all the goings and comings of his parents, M. Alphonse de Peyrehorade sat as motionless as the god Terminus. He was a tall young man of twenty-six, with a handsome and regular face, which, however, lacked expression. His figure and his athletic proportions fully justified the reputation of an indefatigable tennis player which he enjoyed throughout the province. On this evening he was dressed in the height of fashion, exactly in accordance with the engraving in the last number of the *Journal des Modes*. But he seemed ill at ease in his clothes; he was as stiff as a picket in his velvet stock, and moved his whole body when he turned. His rough, sunburned hands and short nails formed a striking contrast to his costume. They were the hands of a ploughman emerging from the sleeves of a dandy. Furthermore, although he scrutinized me with interest from head to foot, I being a Parisian, he spoke to me but once during the evening, and that was to ask me where I bought my watch-chain.

"Look you, my dear guest," said M. de Peyrehorade, as the supper drew to a close, "you belong to me, you are in my house; I shall not let you go until you have seen everything of interest that we have in our mountains. You must learn to know our Roussillon, and you must do her justice. You have no suspicion of all that we are going to show you: Phœnician, Celtic, Roman, Arabian, Byzantine monuments—you shall see them all, from the cedar to the hyssop. I will take you everywhere, and I will not let you off from a single brick."

A paroxysm of coughing compelled him to pause. I seized the opportunity to say that I should be distressed to incommode him at a season so fraught with interest to his family. If he would simply give me the benefit of his excellent advice as to the excursions it would be well for me to make, I could easily, without putting him to the trouble of accompanying me——

"Ah! you refer to this boy's marriage," he exclaimed, interrupting me. "That's a mere trifle—it will take place day after tomorrow. You must attend the wedding with us, *en famille,* as the bride is in mourning for an aunt whose property she inherits. So there are to be no festivities, no ball. It is too bad, for you might have seen our Catalan girls dance. They are very pretty, and perhaps you would have felt inclined to follow my Alphonse's example. One marriage, they say, leads to others. Saturday, when the young people are married, I shall be free, and we will take the field. I ask your pardon for subjecting you to the ennui of a provincial wedding. For a Parisian, sated with parties of all sorts—and a wedding without a ball, at that! However, you will see a bride—a bride—you must tell me what you think of her. But you are a serious man, and you don't look at women any more. I have something better than that to show you. I will show you something worth seeing! I have a famous surprise in store for you tomorrow."

"Mon Dieu!" said I, "it is difficult to keep a treasure in one's house without the public knowing all about it. I fancy that I can divine the surprise that you have in store for me. But if you refer to your statue, the description of it that my guide gave me has served simply to arouse my curiosity and to predispose me to admiration."

"Ah! so he spoke to you about the idol—for that is what they call my beautiful Venus Tur—but I will tell you nothing now. You shall see her tomorrow, by daylight, and tell me whether I am justified in considering her a *chef-d'œuvre,* Parbleu! you could not have arrived more opportunely! There are some inscriptions which I, poor ignoramus that I am, interpret after my manner. But a scholar from Paris! It may be that you will make fun of my interpretation—for I have written a memoir—I, who speak to you, an old provincial antiquary, have made a start; I propose to make the printing presses groan. If you would kindly read and correct me, I might hope. For example, I am very curious to know how you will translate this inscription on the pedestal: CAVE—but I won't ask you anything yet. Until tomorrow! until tomorrow! Not a word about the Venus today!"

"You are quite right, Peyrehorade," said his wife, "to let your old idol rest. You must see that you are keeping monsieur from eating. Bah! monsieur has seen much finer statues than yours in Paris. There are dozens of them at the Tuileries, and bronze ones too."

"There you have the ignorance, the blessed ignorance of the provinces!" interrupted M. de Peyrehorade. "Think of comparing an admirable antique to Coustou's insipid figures!

'With what irreverence
Doth my good wife speak of the gods!'

Would you believe that my wife wanted me to melt my statue and make it into a bell for our church! She would have been the donor, you see. A *chef-d'œuvre* of Myron, monsieur!"

"*Chef-d'œuvre! chef-d'œuvre!* A pretty *chef-d'œuvre* she made, to break a man's leg!"

"Look you, my wife," said M. de Peyrehorade in a determined tone, extending his right leg encased in a stocking of Chinese silk, in her direction, "if my Venus had broken this leg, I should not regret it."

"Gracious Heaven! how can you say that, Peyrehorade? Luckily the man is getting better. Still, I can't make up my mind to look at the statue that causes such accidents as that. Poor Jean Coll!"

"Wounded by Venus, monsieur," said M. de Peyrehorade, with a chuckle, "wounded by Venus, the clown complains:

'Veneris nec præmia noris.'

"Who has not been wounded by Venus?"

M. Alphonse who understood French better than Latin, winked with a knowing look, and glanced at me as if to ask:

"And you, Monsieur le Parisien, do you understand?"

The supper came to an end. I had eaten nothing for the last hour. I was tired and I could not succeed in dissembling the frequent yawns which escaped me. Madame de Peyrehorade was the first to notice my plight and observed that it was time to go to bed. Thereupon began a new series of apologies for the wretched accommodations I was to have. I should not be as comfortable as I was in Paris. One is so badly off in the provinces! I must be indulgent for the Roussillonnais. In vain did I protest that after a journey in the mountains a sheaf of straw would be a luxurious bed for me—she continued to beg me to excuse unfortunate country folk if they did not treat me as well as they would have liked to do. I went upstairs at last to the room allotted to me, escorted by M. de Peyrehorade. The staircase, the upper stairs of which were of wood, ended in the center of a corridor upon which several rooms opened.

"At the right," said my host, "is the apartment which I intend to give to Madame Alphonse that is to be. Your room is at the end of the opposite corridor. You know," he added, with an expression meant to be sly, "you know we must put a newly married couple all by themselves. You are at one end of the house and they at the other."

We entered a handsomely furnished room, in which the first object that caught my eye was a bed seven feet long, six feet wide, and so high that one had to use a stool to climb to the top. My host, having pointed out the location of the bell, having assured himself that the sugar-bowl was full, and that the bottles of Cologne had been duly placed on the dressing-table, and having asked me several times if I had everything that I wanted, wished me a good night and left me alone.

The windows were closed. Before undressing I opened one of them to breathe the fresh night air, always delicious after a long supper. In front of me was Canigou, beautiful to look at always, but that evening it seemed to me the most beautiful mountain in the world, lighted as it was by a brilliant moon. I stood for some minutes gazing at its wonderful silhouette, and was on the point of closing my window when, as I lowered my eyes, I saw the statue on a pedestal some forty yards from the house. It was placed at the corner of a quickset hedge which separated a small garden from a large square of perfectly smooth turf, which, as I learned later, was the tennis court of the town. This tract, which belonged to M. de Peyrehorade, had been ceded by him to the commune, at his son's urgent solicitation.

I was so far from the statue that I could not distinguish its attitude and could only guess at its height, which seemed to be about six feet. At that moment two young scamps from the town walked across the tennis court, quite near the hedge, whistling the pretty Roussillon air, *Montagnes Régalades*. They stopped to look at the statue, and one of them apostrophized it in a loud voice. He spoke Catalan; but I had been long enough in Roussillon to understand pretty nearly what he said.

"So there you are, hussy!" (The Catalan term was much more forcible.) "So there you are!" he said. "So it was you who broke Jean Coll's leg! If you belonged to me, I'd break your neck!"

"Bah! with what?" said the other. "She's made of copper, and it's so hard that Étienne broke his file, trying to file it. It's copper of the heathen times, and it's harder than I don't know what."

"If I had my cold chisel"—it seemed that he was a locksmith's apprentice—"I'd soon dig out her big white eyes, as easy as I'd take an almond out of its shell. They'd make more than a hundred sous in silver."

They walked away a few steps.

"I must bid the idol good night," said the taller of the two, suddenly stopping again.

He stooped, and, I suppose, picked up a stone. I saw him raise his arm and throw something, and instantly there was a ringing blow on the bronze. At the same moment the apprentice put his hand to his head, with a sharp cry of pain.

"She threw it back at me!" he exclaimed.

And my two rascals fled at the top of their speed. It was evident that the stone had rebounded from the metal, and had punished the fellow for his affront to the goddess.

I closed my window, laughing heartily.

"Still another vandal chastised by Venus!" I thought. "May all the destroyers of our ancient monuments have their heads broken thus!"

And with that charitable prayer I fell asleep.

It was broad daylight when I woke. Beside my bed were, on one side, M. de Peyrehorade in his *robe de chambre;* on the other a servant, sent by his wife, with a cup of chocolate in his hand.

"Come, up with you, Parisian! This is just like you sluggards from the capital!" said my host, while I hastily dressed myself. "It is eight o'clock, and you are still in bed! I have been up since six. This is the third time I have come upstairs; I came to your door on tiptoe; not a sound, not a sign of life. It will injure you to sleep too much at your age. And you haven't seen my Venus yet! Come, drink this cup of Barcelona chocolate quickly. Genuine contraband, such chocolate as you don't get in Paris. You must lay up some strength, for, when you once stand in front of my Venus, I shall not be able to tear you away from her."

In five minutes I was ready—that is to say, half shaved, my clothes half buttoned, and my throat scalded by the chocolate, which I had swallowed boiling hot. I went down into the garden and found myself before a really beautiful statue.

It was, in truth, a Venus, and wonderfully lovely. The upper part of the body was nude, as the ancients ordinarily represented the great divinities; the right hand, raised as high as the breast, was turned with the palm inward, the thumb and first two fingers extended, the other two slightly bent. The other hand was near the hip and held the drapery that covered the lower part of the body. The pose of the statue recalled that of the *Morra Player,* usually known, I know not why, by the name of Germanicus. Perhaps the sculptor intended to represent the goddess playing the game of morra.

However that may be, it is impossible to imagine anything more perfect than the body of that Venus; anything more harmonious, more voluptuous than her outlines, anything more graceful and more dignified than her drapery. I expected to see some work of the later Empire;

I saw a *chef-d'œuvre* of the best period of statuary. What especially struck me was the exquisite verisimilitude of the forms, which one might have believed to have been molded from nature, if nature ever produced such flawless models.

The hair, which was brushed back from the forehead, seemed to have been gilded formerly. The head, which was small, like those of almost all Greek statues, was bent slightly forward. As for the face, I shall never succeed in describing its peculiar character; it was of a type which in no wise resembled that of any antique statue that I can remember. It was not the tranquil, severe beauty of the Greek sculptors, who systematically imparted a majestic immobility to all the features. Here, on the contrary, I observed with surprise a clearly marked intention on the part of the artist to express mischievousness amounting almost to devilry. All the features were slightly contracted; the eyes were a little oblique, the corners of the mouth raised, the nostrils a little dilated. Disdain, irony, cruelty could be read upon that face, which none the less was inconceivably lovely. In truth, the more one looked at that marvelous statue the more distressed one felt at the thought that such wonderful beauty could be conjoined to utter absence of sensibility.

"If the model ever existed," I said to M. de Peyrehorade—"and I doubt whether Heaven ever produced such a woman—how I pity her lovers! She must have delighted in driving them to death from despair. There is something downright savage in her expression, and yet I never have seen anything so beautiful!"

" 'Tis Venus all intent upon her prey!" quoted M. de Peyrehorade, delighted with my enthusiasm.

That expression of infernal irony was heightened perhaps by the contrast between the very brilliant silver eyes and the coating of blackish-green with which time had overlaid the whole statue. Those gleaming eyes created a certain illusion which suggested reality, life. I remembered what my guide had said, that she made those who looked at her lower their eyes. That was almost true, and I could not help feeling angry with myself as I realized that I was perceptibly ill at ease before that bronze figure.

"Now that you have admired her in every detail, my dear colleague in antiquarian research," said my host, "let us open a scientific conference, if you please. What do you say to this inscription, which you have not noticed as yet?"

He pointed to the base of the statue, and I read there these words:

CAVE AMANTEM

"Quid dicis, doctissime?" ("What do you say, most learned of men?") he asked, rubbing his hands. "Let us see if we shall agree as to the meaning of this *cave amantem."*

"Why, there are two possible meanings," I said. "It may be translated: 'Beware of him who loves you—distrust lovers.' But I am not sure that *cave amantem* would be good Latin in that sense. In view of the lady's diabolical expression, I should be inclined to believe rather that the artist meant to put the spectator on his guard against that terrible beauty. So that I should translate: 'Look out for yourself if *she* loves you.'"

"Humph!" ejaculated M. de Peyrehorade; "yes, that is a possible translation; but, with all respect, I prefer the first, which I will develop a little, however. You know who Venus's lover was?"

"She had several."

"Yes, but the first one was Vulcan. Did not the artist mean to say: 'Despite all your beauty, and your scornful air, you shall have a blacksmith, a wretched cripple, for a lover'? A solemn lesson for coquettes, monsieur!"

I could not help smiling, the interpretation seemed to me so exceedingly far-fetched.

"The Latin is a terrible language, with its extraordinary conciseness," I observed, to avoid contradicting my antiquary directly; and I stepped back a few steps, to obtain a better view of the statue.

"One moment, colleague!" said M. de Peyrehorade, seizing my arm, "you have not seen all. There is still another inscription. Stand on the pedestal and look at the right arm."

As he spoke, he helped me to climb up.

I clung somewhat unceremoniously to the neck of the Venus, with whom I was beginning to feel on familiar terms. I even looked her in the eye for an instant, and I found her still more diabolical and still lovelier at close quarters. Then I saw that there were some letters, in what I took to be the antique cursive hand, engraved on the right arm. With the aid of a strong glass I spelled out what follows, M. de Peyrehorade repeating each word as I pronounced it, and expressing his approbation with voice and gesture. I read:

> VENERI TVRBVL—
> EVTYCHES MYRO
> IMPERIO FECIT

After the word *tvrbvl* in the first line several letters seemed to have become effaced, but *tvrbvl* was perfectly legible.

"Which means?" queried my host, with a beaming face, and winking maliciously, for he had a shrewd idea that I would not easily handle that *tvrbvl*.

"There is one word here which I do not understand as yet," I said; "all the rest is simple. 'Eutyches made this offering to Venus by her order.'"

"Excellent. But what do you make of *tvrbvl*? What is *tvrbvl*?"

"*Tvrbvl* puzzles me a good deal. I have tried in vain to think of some known epithet of Venus to assist me. What would you say to *Turbulenta*? Venus, who disturbs, who excites—as you see, I am still engrossed by her evil expression. *Turbulenta* is not a very inapt epithet for Venus," I added modestly, for I was not very well satisfied myself with my explanation.

"Turbulent Venus! Venus the roisterer! Ah! so you think that my Venus is a wine-shop Venus, do you? Not by any means, monsieur; she is a Venus in good society. But I will explain this *tvrbvl* to you. Of course you will promise not to divulge my discovery before my memoir is printed. You see, I am very proud of this find of mine. You must leave us poor devils in the provinces a few spears to glean. You are so rich, you Parisian scholars!"

From the top of the pedestal, whereon I was still perched, I solemnly promised him that I would never be guilty of the baseness of stealing his discovery.

"*Tvrbvl*—monsieur," he said, coming nearer to me and lowering his voice, for fear that some other than myself might hear—"read *tvrbvlneræ*."

"I don't understand any better."

"Listen. About a league from here, at the foot of the mountain, is a village called Boulternère. That name is a corruption of the Latin word *Turbulnera*. Nothing is more common than such inversions. Boulternère, monsieur, was a Roman city. I have always suspected as much, but I have never had a proof of it. Here is the proof. This Venus was the local divinity of the city of Boulternère; and this word Boulternère, whose antique origin I have just demonstrated, proves something even more interesting—namely, that Boulternère, before it became a Roman city, was a Phœnician city!"

He paused a moment to take breath and to enjoy my surprise. I succeeded in restraining a very strong inclination to laugh.

"It is a fact," he continued, "*Turbulnera* is pure Phœnician; *Tur*, pronounced *Tour—Tour* and *Sour* are the same word, are they not? *Sour* is the Phœnician name of *Tyre;* I do not need to remind you of its meaning. *Bul* is Baal; Bal, Bel, Bul—slight differences in pronunciation. As for *nera*—that gives me a little trouble. I am inclined to believe, failing to find a Phœnician word, that it comes from the Greek word νηρός, damp, swampy. In that case the word would be a hybrid. To justify my suggestion of νηρός, I will show you that at Boulternère the streams from the mountain form miasmatic pools. On the other hand, the termination *nera* may have been added much later, in honor of Nera Pivesuvia, wife of Tetricus, who may have had some property in the city of Turbul. But on account of the pools I prefer the etymology from νηρός."

And he took a pinch of snuff with a self-satisfied air.

"But let us leave the Phœnicians and return to the inscription. I translate then: 'To Venus of Boulternère, Myron, at her command, dedicates this statue, his work.'"

I had no idea of criticizing his etymology, but I did desire to exhibit some little penetration on my own part; so I said to him:

"Stop there a moment, monsieur. Myron dedicated something, but I see nothing to indicate that it was this statue."

"What!" he cried, "was not Myron a famous Greek sculptor? The talent probably was handed down in the family; it was one of his descendants who executed this statue. Nothing can be more certain."

"But," I rejoined, "I see a little hole in the arm. I believe that it was made to fasten something to—a bracelet, perhaps, which this Myron presented to Venus as an expiatory offering. Myron was an unsuccessful lover; Venus was irritated with him and he appeased her by consecrating a gold bracelet to her. Observe that *fecit* is very often used in the sense of *consecravit;* they are synonymous terms. I could show you more than one example of what I say if I had Gruter or Orellius at hand. It would be quite natural for a lover to see Venus in a dream and to fancy that she ordered him to give a gold bracelet to her statue. So Myron consecrated a bracelet to her; then the barbarians, or some sacrilegious thief——"

"Ah! it is easy to see that you have written novels!" cried my host, giving me his hand to help me descend. "No, monsieur, it is a work of the school of Myron. Look at the workmanship simply and you will agree."

Having made it a rule never to contradict outright an obstinate antiquarian, I hung my head with the air of one fully persuaded, saying:

"It's an admirable thing."

"Ah! mon Dieu!" cried M. de Peyrehorade; "still another piece of vandalism! Somebody must have thrown a stone at my statue!"

He had just discovered a white mark a little above Venus's breast. I observed a similar mark across the fingers of the right hand, which I then supposed had been grazed by the stone; or else that a fragment of the stone had been broken off by the blow and had bounded against the hand. I told my host about the insult that I had witnessed, and the speedy retribution that had followed. He laughed heartily, and, comparing the apprentice to Diomedes, expressed a hope that, like the Grecian hero, he might see all his companions transformed into birds.

The breakfast bell interrupted this classical conversation, and I was again obliged, as on the preceding day, to eat for four. Then M. de Peyrehorade's farmers appeared; and while he gave audience to them, his son took me to see a calèche which he had bought at Toulouse for his fiancée, and which I admired, it is needless to say. Then I went with him into the stable, where he kept me half an hour, boasting of his horses, giving me their genealogies, and telling me of the prizes they had won at various races in the province. At last he reached the subject of his future wife, by a natural transition from a gray mare he intended for her.

"We shall see her today," he said. "I do not know whether you will think her pretty; but everybody here and at Perpignan considers her charming. The best thing about her is that she's very rich. Her aunt at Prades left her all her property. Oh! I am going to be very happy."

I was intensely disgusted to see a young man more touched by the dowry than by the *beaux yeux* of his betrothed.

"You know something about jewels," continued M. Alphonse; "what do you think of this one? This is the ring that I am going to give her tomorrow."

As he spoke, he took from the first joint of his little finger a huge ring with many diamonds, made in the shape of two clasped hands; an allusion which seemed to me exceedingly poetical. The workmanship was very old, but I judged that it had been changed somewhat to allow the diamonds to be set. On the inside of the ring were these words in Gothic letters: *Sempr' ab ti;* that is to say, "Always with thee."

"It is a handsome ring," I said, "but these diamonds have taken away something of its character."

"Oh! it is much handsomer so," he replied, with a smile. "There are twelve hundred francs' worth of diamonds. My mother gave it to me. It was a very old family ring—of the times of chivalry. It belonged to my grandmother, who had it from hers. God knows when it was made."

"The custom in Paris," I said, "is to give a very simple ring, usually made of two different metals, as gold and platinum, for instance. See, that other ring, which you wear on this finger, would be most suitable. This one, with its diamonds and its hands in relief is so big that one could not wear a glove over it."

"Oh! Madame Alphonse may arrange that as she pleases. I fancy that she will be very glad to have it all the same. Twelve hundred francs on one's finger is very pleasant. This little ring," he added, glancing fatuously at the plain one which he wore, "was given me by a woman in Paris one Mardi Gras. Ah! how I did go it when I was in Paris two years ago! That's the place where one enjoys one's self!"

And he heaved a sigh of regret.

We were to dine that day at Puygarrig with the bride's parents; we drove in the calèche to the château, about a league and a half from Ille. I was presented and made welcome as a friend of the family. I will say nothing of the dinner or of the conversation which followed it, and in which I took little part. M. Alphonse, seated beside his fiancée, said a word in her ear every quarter of an hour. As for her, she hardly raised her eyes, and whenever her future husband addressed her she blushed modestly, but replied without embarrassment.

Mademoiselle de Puygarrig was eighteen years of age; her supple and delicate figure formed a striking contrast to the bony frame of her athletic fiancé. She was not only lovely, but fascinating. I admired the perfect naturalness of all her replies; and her good-humored air, which, however, was not exempt from a slight tinge of mischief, reminded me, in spite of myself, of my host's Venus. As I made this comparison mentally, I asked myself whether the superiority in the matter of beauty, which I could not choose but accord to the statue, did not consist in large measure in her tigress-like expression; for energy, even in evil passions, always arouses in us a certain surprise and a sort of involuntary admiration.

"What a pity," I said to myself as we left Puygarrig, "that such an attractive person should be rich, and that her dowry should cause her to be sought in marriage by a man who is unworthy of her!"

On the way back to Ille, finding some difficulty in talking with Madame de Peyrehorade, whom, however, I thought it only courteous to address now and then, I exclaimed:

"You are very strong-minded here in Roussillon! To think of having a wedding on a Friday, madame! We are more superstitious in Paris; no one would dare to take a wife on that day."

"Mon Dieu! don't mention it," said she; "if it had depended on me, they certainly would have chosen another day. But Peyrehorade would have it so, and I had to give way to him. It distresses me, however. Suppose anything should happen? There must surely be some reason for the superstition, for why else should everyone be afraid of Friday?"

"Friday!" cried her husband; "Friday is Venus's day! A splendid day for a wedding! You see, my dear colleague, I think of nothing but my Venus. On my honor, it was on her account that I chose a Friday. To-morrow, if you are willing, before the wedding, we will offer a little sacrifice to her; we will sacrifice two pigeons, if I can find any incense."

"For shame, Peyrehorade!" his wife interposed, scandalized to the last degree. "Burn incense to an idol! That would be an abomination! What would people in the neighborhood say about you?"

"At least," said M. de Peyrehorade, "you will allow me to place a wreath of roses and lilies on her head:

'*Manibus date lilia plenis.*'

The charter, you see, monsieur, is an empty word; we have no freedom of worship!"

The order of ceremonies for the following day was thus arranged: everybody was to be fully dressed and ready at precisely ten o'clock. After taking a cup of chocolate, we were to drive to Puygarrig. The civil ceremony would take place at the mayor's office of that village, and the religious ceremony in the chapel of the château. Then there would be a breakfast. After that, we were to pass the time as best we could until seven o'clock, when we were to return to Ille, to M. de Peyrehorade's, where the two families were to sup together. The rest followed as a matter of course. Being unable to dance, the plan was to eat as much as possible.

At eight o'clock I was already seated in front of the Venus, pencil in hand, beginning for the twentieth time to draw the head of the statue, whose expression I was still absolutely unable to catch. M. de Peyrehorade hovered about me, gave me advice, and repeated his Phœnician etymologies; then he arranged some Bengal roses on the pedestal of the statue, and in a tragi-comic tone addressed supplications to it for the welfare of the couple who were to live under his roof. About nine o'clock he returned to the house to dress, and at the same time M. Alphonse appeared, encased in a tightly fitting new coat, white gloves, patent-leather shoes, and carved buttons, with a rose in his buttonhole.

"Will you paint my wife's portrait?" he asked, leaning over my drawing; "she is pretty too."

At that moment a game of tennis began on the court I have mentioned, and it immediately attracted M. Alphonse's attention. And I myself, being rather tired, and hopeless of being able to reproduce that diabolical face, soon left my drawing to watch the players. Among them were several Spanish muleteers who had arrived in the town the night before. There were Aragonese and Navarrese, almost all wonderfully skilful at the game. So that the men of Ille, although encouraged by the presence and counsels of M. Alphonse, were speedily beaten by these new champions. The native spectators were appalled. M. Alphonse glanced at his watch. It was only half after nine. His mother's hair was not dressed. He no longer hesitated, but took off his coat, asked for a jacket, and challenged the Spaniards. I watched him, smiling at his eagerness, and a little surprised.

"I must uphold the honor of the province," he said to me.

At that moment I considered him really handsome. He was thoroughly in earnest. His costume, which engrossed him so completely a moment before, was of no consequence. A few minutes earlier he was afraid to turn his head for fear of disarranging his cravat. Now, he paid no heed to his carefully curled locks, or to his beautifully laundered ruff. And his fiancée? Faith, I believe that, if it had been necessary, he would have postponed the wedding. I saw him hastily put on a pair of sandals, turn back his sleeves, and with an air of confidence take his place at the head of the beaten side, like Cæsar rallying his legions at Dyrrhachium. I leaped over the hedge and found a convenient place in the shade of a plum tree, where I could see both camps.

Contrary to general expectation, M. Alphonse missed the first ball; to be sure, it skimmed along the ground, driven with astounding force by an Aragonese who seemed to be the leader of the Spaniards.

He was a man of some forty years, thin and wiry, about six feet tall; and his olive skin was almost as dark as the bronze of the Venus.

M. Alphonse dashed his racquet to the ground in a passion.

"It was this infernal ring," he cried; "it caught my finger and made me miss a sure ball!"

He removed the diamond ring, not without difficulty, and I stepped forward to take it; but he anticipated me, ran to the Venus, slipped the ring on her third finger, and resumed his position at the head of his townsmen.

He was pale, but calm and determined. Thereafter he did not make a single mistake, and the Spaniards were completely routed. The enthusiasm of the spectators was a fine spectacle; some shouted for joy again and again, and tossed their caps in the air; others shook his hands and called him an honor to the province. If he had repelled an invasion, I doubt whether he would have received more enthusiastic and more sincere congratulations. The chagrin of the defeated party added still more to the splendor of his victory.

"We will play again, my good fellow," he said to the Aragonese in a lofty tone; "but I will give you points."

I should have been glad if M. Alphonse had been more modest, and I was almost distressed by his rival's humiliation. The Spanish giant felt the insult keenly. I saw him turn pale under his tanned skin. He glanced with a sullen expression at his racquet, and ground his teeth; then he muttered in a voice choked with rage:

"Me lo pagarás!"

M. de Peyrehorade's appearance interrupted his son's triumph. My host, greatly surprised not to find him superintending the harnessing of the new calèche, was much more surprised when he saw him drenched with perspiration, and with his racquet in his hand. M. Alphonse ran to the house, washed his face and hands, resumed his new coat and his patent-leather boots, and five minutes later we were driving rapidly toward Puygarrig. All the tennis players of the town and a great number of spectators followed us with joyous shouts. The stout horses that drew us could hardly keep in advance of those dauntless Catalans.

We had reached Puygarrig, and the procession was about to start for the mayor's office, when M. Alphonse put his hand to his forehead and whispered to me:

"What a fool I am! I have forgotten the ring! It is on the Venus's finger, the devil take her! For Heaven's sake, don't tell my mother. Perhaps she will not notice anything."

"You might send someone to get it," I said.

"No, no! my servant stayed at Ille, and I don't trust these people here. Twelve hundred francs' worth of diamonds! That might be too much of a temptation for more than one of them. Besides, what would they all think of my absent-mindedness? They would make too much fun of me. They would call me the statue's husband. However, I trust that no one will steal it. Luckily, all my knaves are afraid of the idol. They don't dare go within arm's length of it. Bah! It's no matter; I have another ring."

The two ceremonies, civil and religious, were performed with suitable pomp, and Mademoiselle de Puygarrig received a ring that formerly belonged to a milliner's girl at Paris, with no suspicion that her husband was bestowing upon her a pledge of love. Then we betook ourselves to the table, where we ate and drank, yes, and sang, all at great length. I sympathized with the bride amid the vulgar merriment that burst forth all about her; however, she put a better face on it than I could have hoped, and her embarrassment was neither awkwardness nor affectation. It may be that courage comes of itself with difficult situations.

The breakfast came to an end when God willed; it was four o'clock; the men went out to walk in the park, which was magnificent, or watched the peasant girls of Puygarrig, dressed in their gala costumes, dance on the lawn in front of the château. In this way we passed several hours. Meanwhile the women were hovering eagerly about the bride, who showed them her wedding gifts. Then she changed her dress, and I observed that she had covered her lovely hair with a cap and a hat adorned with feathers; for there is nothing that wives are in such a hurry to do as to assume as soon as possible those articles of apparel which custom forbids them to wear when they are still unmarried.

It was nearly eight o'clock when we prepared to start for Ille. But before we started there was a pathetic scene. Mademoiselle de Puygarrig's aunt, who had taken the place of a mother to her, a woman of a very advanced age and very religious, was not to go to the town with us. At our departure, she delivered a touching sermon to her niece on her duties as a wife, the result of which was a torrent of tears, and embraces without end. M. de Peyrehorade compared this separation to the abduction of the Sabine women.

We started at last, however, and on the road we all exerted ourselves to the utmost to divert the bride and make her laugh; but it was all to no purpose.

At Ille supper awaited us, and such a supper! If the vulgar hilarity of the morning had disgusted me, I was fairly sickened by the equivocal remarks and jests which were aimed at the groom, and especially at the bride. M. Alphonse, who had disappeared a moment before taking his place at the table, was as pale as death and as solemn as an iceberg. He kept drinking old Collioure wine, almost as strong as brandy. I was by his side and felt in duty bound to warn him.

"Take care! They say that this wine——"

I have no idea what foolish remark I made, to put myself in unison with the other guests.

He pressed my knee with his and said in a very low tone:

"When we leave the table, let me have a word with you."

His solemn tone surprised me. I looked at him more closely and noticed the extraordinary change in his expression.

"Are you feeling ill?" I asked him.

"No."

And he returned to his drinking.

Meanwhile, amid shouts and clapping of hands, a child of eleven years, who had slipped under the table, exhibited to the guests a dainty white and rose-colored ribbon which he had taken from the bride's ankle. They called that her garter. It was immediately cut into pieces and distributed among the young men, who decorated their buttonholes with them, according to an ancient custom still observed in some partriarchal families. This episode caused the bride to blush to the whites of her eyes. But her confusion reached its height when M. de Peyrehorade, having called for silence, sang some Catalan verses, impromptu, so he said. Their meaning, so far as I understand it, was this:

"Pray, what is this, my friends? Does the wine I have drunk make me see double? There are two Venuses here——"

The bridegroom abruptly turned his head away with a terrified expression which made everybody laugh.

"Yes," continued M. de Peyrehorade, "there are two Venuses beneath my roof. One I found in the earth, like a truffle; the other, descended from the skies, has come to share her girdle with us."

He meant to say her garter.

"My son, choose whichever you prefer—the Roman or the Catalan Venus. The rascal chooses the Catalan, and his choice is wise. The Roman is black, the Catalan white. The Roman is cold, the Catalan inflames all who approach her."

This deliverance caused such an uproar, such noisy applause and such roars of laughter, that I thought that the ceiling would fall on our heads. There were only three sober faces at the table—those of the bride and groom, and my own. I had a terrible headache; and then, for some unknown reason, a wedding always depresses me. This one, in addition, disgusted me more or less.

The last couplets having been sung by the mayor's deputy—and they were very free, I must say—we went to the salon to make merry over the retirement of the bride, who was soon to be escorted to her chamber, for it was near midnight.

M. Alphonse led me into a window recess, and said to me, averting his eyes:

"You will laugh at me, but I don't know what the matter is with me; I am bewitched! the devil has got hold of me!"

The first idea that came to my mind was that he believed himself to be threatened by some misfortune of the sort of which Montaigne and Madame de Sévigné speak:

"The sway of love is always full of tragic episodes," etc.

"I supposed that accidents of that sort happened only to men of in-tellect," I said to myself. "You have drunk too much Collioure wine, my dear Monsieur Alphonse," I said aloud. "I warned you."

"Yes, that may be. But there is something much more terrible than that."

He spoke in a halting voice. I concluded that he was downright tipsy.

"You remember my ring?" he continued, after a pause.

"Well! Has it been stolen?"

"No."

"Then you have it?"

"No—I—I can't take it off that infernal Venus's finger!"

"Nonsense! you didn't pull hard enough."

"Yes, I did. But the Venus—she has bent her finger."

He looked me in the eye with a haggard expression, leaning against the window-frame to avoid falling.

"What a fable!" I said. "You pushed the ring on too far. Tomorrow you can recover it with a pair of pincers. But take care that you don't injure the statue."

"No, I tell you. The Venus's finger is drawn in, bent; she has closed her hand—do you understand? She is my wife, apparently, as I have given her my ring. She refuses to give it back."

I felt a sudden shiver, and for a moment I was all gooseflesh. Then, as he heaved a profound sigh, he sent a puff of alcoholic fumes into my face, and all my emotion vanished.

"The wretch is completely drunk," I thought.

"You are an antiquary, monsieur," continued the bridegroom in a piteous tone; "you know all about these statues; perhaps there is some spring, some devilish contrivance that I don't know about. Suppose you were to go out and look?"

"Willingly," I said. "Come with me."

"No, I prefer that you should go alone."

I left the salon.

The weather had changed while we were at supper, and the rain was beginning to fall violently. I was about to ask for an umbrella when a sudden reflection detained me. "I should be a great fool," I said to myself, "to take any trouble to verify what an intoxicated man tells me! Perhaps, too, he is trying to play some wretched joke on me, in order to give these worthy provincials something to laugh at; and the least that can happen to me is to be drenched to the skin and to catch a heavy cold."

I glanced from the door at the statue, which was dripping wet, and then went up to my room without returning to the salon. I went to bed, but sleep was a long while coming. All the scenes of the day passed through my mind. I thought of that lovely, pure maiden delivered to the tender mercies of a brutal sot. "What a hateful thing, a *mariage de convenance* is!" I said to myself. "A mayor dons a tri-colored scarf, a curé, a stole, and lo! the most virtuous girl imaginable is abandoned to the Minotaur! Two persons who do not love each other—what can they have to say at such a moment, which two true lovers would purchase at the cost of their lives? Can a woman ever love a man whom she has once seen make a beast of himself? First impressions are not easily effaced, and I am sure that this Monsieur Alphonse well deserves to be detested."

During my monologue, which I have abridged very materially, I had heard much coming and going about the house, doors opening and closing, carriages driving away; then I fancied that I heard in the hall the light footsteps of several women walking toward the farther end of the corridor opposite my room. It was probably the procession of the bride, who was being escorted to her bedroom. Then I heard the steps go downstairs again. Madame de Peyrehorade's door closed.

"How perturbed and ill at ease that poor child must be," I thought.

I turned and twisted in my bed, in an execrable humor. A bachelor plays an absurd rôle in a house where a marriage is being celebrated.

Silence had reigned for some time, when it was broken by heavy steps ascending the staircase. The wooden stairs creaked loudly.

"What a brute!" I cried. "I'll wager that he will fall on the stairs!"

Everything became quiet once more. I took up a book in order to change the current of my thoughts. It was a volume of departmental statistics, embellished by an article from the pen of M. de Peyrehorade on the druidical remains in the arrondissement of Prades. I dozed at the third page.

I slept badly and woke several times. It might have been five o'clock, and I had been awake more than twenty minutes, when a cock crew. Day was just breaking. Suddenly I heard the same heavy steps, the same creaking of the stairs that I had heard before I fell asleep. That struck me as peculiar. I tried, yawning sleepily, to divine why M. Alphonse should rise so early. I could imagine no probable cause. I was about to close my eyes again when my attention was once more attracted by a strange tramping, to which was soon added the jangling of bells and the noise of doors violently thrown open; then I distinguished confused outcries.

"My drunkard must have set fire to something!" I thought, as I leaped out of bed.

I dressed in hot haste and went out into the corridor. From the farther end came shrieks and lamentations, and one heartrending voice rose above all the rest: "My son! my son!" It was evident that something had happened to M. Alphonse. I ran to the bridal chamber; it was full of people. The first object that caught my eye was the young man, half dressed, lying across the bed, the framework of which was broken. He was livid and absolutely motionless. His mother was weeping and shrieking by his side. M. de Peyrehorade was bustling about, rubbing his temples with eau de Cologne, or holding salts to his nose. Alas! his son had been dead a long while.

On a couch, at the other end of the room, was the bride, in frightful convulsions. She was uttering incoherent cries, and two strong maid-servants had all the difficulty in the world in holding her.

"Great God!" I cried, "what has happened?"

I walked to the bed and raised the unfortunate young man's body; it was already cold and stiff. His clenched teeth and livid face expressed the most horrible anguish. It seemed perfectly evident that his death had been a violent one, and the death agony indescribably terrible. But there was no sign of blood on his clothes. I opened his shirt and found on his breast a purple mark which extended around the loins and across the back. One would have said that he had been squeezed by an iron ring. My foot came in contact with something hard on the carpet; I stooped and saw the diamond ring.

I dragged M. de Peyrehorade and his wife to their room; then I caused the bride to be taken thither.

"You still have a daughter," I said to them; "you owe to her your devoted care."

Then I left them alone.

It seemed to me to be beyond question that M. Alphonse had been the victim of a murder, the authors of which had found a way to introduce themselves into the bride's bedroom at night. The marks on the breast and their circular character puzzled me a good deal, however, for a club or an iron bar could not have produced them. Suddenly I remembered having heard that in Valencia the *bravi* used long leather bags filled with fine sand to murder people whom they were hired to kill. I instantly recalled the Aragonese muleteer and his threat; and yet I hardly dared think that he would have wreaked such a terrible vengeance for a trivial jest.

I walked about the house, looking everywhere for traces of a break, and finding nothing. I went down into the garden, to see whether the assassins might have forced their way in on that side of the house; but I found no definite indications. Indeed, the rain of the preceding night had so saturated the ground that it could not have retained any distinct impression. I observed, however, several very deep footprints; they pointed in two opposite directions, but in the same line, leading from the corner of the hedge next the tennis court to the gateway of the house. They might well be M. Alphonse's steps when he went out to take his ring from the finger of the statue. On the other hand, the hedge was less dense at that point than elsewhere, and the murderers might have passed through it there. As I went back and forth in front of the statue, I paused a moment to look at it. That time, I will confess, I was unable to contemplate without terror its expression of devilish irony; and, with my head full of the horrible scenes I had witnessed, I fancied that I had before me an infernal divinity, exulting over the disaster that had stricken that house.

I returned to my room and remained there till noon. Then I went out and inquired concerning my hosts. They were a little calmer. Mademoiselle de Puygarrig—I should say M. Alphonse's widow—had recovered her senses. She had even talked with the king's attorney from Perpignan, then on circuit at Ille, and that magistrate had taken her deposition. He desired mine also. I told him what I knew and made no secret of my suspicions of the Aragonese muleteer. He ordered that he should be arrested immediately.

"Did you learn anything from Madame Alphonse?" I asked the king's attorney, when my deposition was written out and signed.

"That unfortunate young woman has gone mad," he replied, with a sad smile. "Mad! absolutely mad! This is what she told me:

"She had been in bed, she said, a few minutes, with the curtains drawn, when her bedroom door opened and someone came in. At that time Madame Alphonse was on the inside of the bed, with her face toward the wall. Supposing, of course, that it was her husband, she did not move. A moment later, the bed creaked as if under an enormous weight. She was terribly frightened, but dared not turn her head. Five minutes, ten minutes perhaps—she can only guess at the time—passed in this way. Then she made an involuntary movement, or else the other person in the bed made one, and she felt the touch of something as cold as ice—that was her expression. She moved closer to the wall, trembling in every limb. Shortly after, the door opened a second time, and someone came in, who said: 'Good evening, my little wife.' Soon the curtains were drawn aside. She heard a stifled cry. The person who was in the bed by her side sat up and seemed to put out its arms. Thereupon she turned her head, and saw, so she declares, her husband on his knees beside the bed, with his head on a level with the pillow, clasped in the arms of a sort of greenish giant, who was squeezing him with a terrible force. She says—and she repeated it twenty times, poor woman!—she says that she recognized—can you guess whom?—the bronze Venus, M. de Peyrehorade's statue. Since she was unearthed, the whole neighborhood dreams of her. But I continue the story of that unhappy mad woman. At that sight she lost consciousness, and it is probable that she had lost her reason some moments before. She could give me no idea at all how long she remained in her swoon. Recovering her senses, she saw the phantom, or, as she still insists, the statue, motionless, with its legs and the lower part of the body in the bed, the bust and arms stretched out, and in its arms her husband, also motionless. A cock crew. Thereupon the statue got out of bed, dropped the dead body, and left the room. Madame Alphonse rushed for the bell-cord, and you know the rest."

The Spaniard was arrested; he was calm, and defended himself with much self-possession and presence of mind. He did not deny making the remark I had overheard; but he explained it by saying that he had meant simply this: that, on the following day, having rested meanwhile, he would beat his victorious rival at tennis. I remember that he added:

"An Aragonese, when he is insulted, doesn't wait until the next day for his revenge. If I had thought that Monsieur Alphonse intended to insult me, I would have driven my knife into his belly on the spot."

His shoes were compared with the footprints in the garden, and were found to be much larger.

Lastly, the innkeeper at whose house he was staying deposed that he had passed the whole night rubbing and doctoring one of his mules, which was sick. Furthermore, the Aragonese was a man of excellent reputation, well known in the province, where he came every year in the course of his business. So he was released with apologies.

I have forgotten the deposition of a servant, who was the last person to see M. Alphonse alive. It was just as he was going up to his wife; he called the man and asked him with evident anxiety if he knew where I was. The servant replied that he had not seen me. Thereupon M. Alphonse sighed and stood more than a minute without speaking; then he said:

"Well, the devil must have taken him away too!"

I asked him if M. Alphonse had his diamond ring on his finger when he spoke to him. The servant hesitated before he replied; at last he said that he did not think so, but that he had not noticed particularly.

"If he had had that ring on his finger," he added upon reflection, "I should certainly have noticed it, for I thought that he had given it to Madame Alphonse."

As I questioned this man, I was conscious of a touch of the superstitious terror with which Madame Alphonse's deposition had infected the whole household. The king's attorney glanced at me with a smile, and I did not persist.

Some hours after M. Alphonse's funeral, I prepared to leave Ille. M. de Peyrehorade's carriage was to take me to Perpignan. Despite his enfeebled condition, the poor old man insisted upon attending me to his garden gate. We passed through the garden in silence, he, hardly able to drag himself along, leaning on my arm. As we were about to part, I cast a last glance at the Venus. I foresaw that my host, although he did not share the terror and detestation which she inspired in a portion of his family, would be glad to be rid of an object which would constantly remind him of a shocking calamity. It was my purpose to urge him to place it in some museum. I hesitated about opening the subject, when M. de Peyrehorade mechanically turned his head in the direction in which he saw that I was gazing earnestly. His eye fell upon the statue, and he instantly burst into tears. I embraced him, and, afraid to say a single word, entered the carriage.

I never learned, subsequent to my departure, that any new light had been thrown upon that mysterious catastrophe.

M. de Peyrehorade died a few months after his son. By his will he bequeathed to me his manuscripts, which I shall publish some day, perhaps. I found among them no memoir relating to the inscriptions on the Venus.

P.S.—My friend M. de P. has recently written me from Perpignan that the statue no longer exists. After her husband's death, Madame de Peyrehorade's first care was to have it melted into a bell, and in that new shape it is now used in the church at Ille.

"But," M. de P. adds, "it would seem that an evil fate pursues all those who possess that bronze. Since that bell has rung at Ille the vines have frozen twice."

4

The Marquise

GEORGE SAND

THE Marquise de R—— never said brilliant things, although it is the fashion in French fiction to make every old woman sparkle with wit. Her ignorance was extreme in all matters which contact with the world had not taught her, and she had none of that nicety of expression, that exquisite penetration, that marvelous tact, which belong, it is said, to women who have seen all the different phases of life and society; she was blunt, heedless, and sometimes very cynical. She put to flight every idea I have formed concerning the noble ladies of the olden times, yet she was a genuine Marquise and had seen the Court of Louis XV. But as she was an exceptional character, do not seek in her history for a study of the manners of any epoch.

I found much pleasure in the society of the lady. She seemed to me remarkable for nothing much except her prodigious memory for the events of her youth and the masculine lucidity with which she expressed her reminiscences. For the rest, she was, like all aged persons, forgetful of recent events and indifferent to everything in which she had not any present personal concern.

Her beauty had not been of that piquant order, which, though lacking in splendor and regularity, still gives pleasure in itself; she was not one of those women taught to be witty, in order to make as favorable an impression as those who are so by nature. The Marquise undoubtedly had had the misfortune to be beautiful. I have seen her portrait, for, like all old women, she was vain enough to hang it up for inspection in her apartments. She was represented in the character of a huntress nymph, with a low satin waist painted to imitate tiger-skin, sleeves of antique lace, bow of sandal-wood, and a crescent of pearl lighting up her hair. It was an admirable painting, and, above all, an admirable woman—tall, slender, dark, with black eyes, austere and noble features, unsmiling, deep red lips, and hands which, it was said, had thrown the Princess de Lamballe into despair. Without lace, satin, or powder, she might indeed have seemed one of those beautiful, proud nymphs fabled to appear to mortals in the depth of the forest or upon the solitary mountainsides, only to drive them mad with passion and regret.

Yet the Marquise had made few acquaintances; according to her own account she had been thought dull and frivolous. The roues of that time cared less for the charms of beauty than for the allurements of coquetry; women infinitely less admired than she had robbed her of all her adorers, and, strange enough, she had seemed indifferent to her fate. The little she told me of her life made me believe that her heart had had no youth, and that a cold selfishness had paralyzed all its faculties. Still, her old age was adorned by several sincere friends, and she gave alms without ostentation.

One evening I found her even more communicative than usual; there was much of sadness in her voice. "My child," she said, "the Vicomte de Larrieux has just died of the gout. It is a great sorrow to me, for I have been his friend these sixty years."

"What was his age?" I asked.

"Eighty-four. I am eighty, but not so infirm as he was, and I can hope to live longer. *N'importe!* Several of my friends have gone this year, and although I tell myself that I am younger and stronger than any of them, I can not help being frightened when I see my contemporaries dropping off around me."

"And these," said I, "are the only regrets you feel for poor Larrieux, a man who worshipped you for sixty years, who never ceased to complain of your cruelty, yet never revolted from his allegiance? He was a model lover: there are no more such men."

"My dear child," answered the Marquise, "I see that you think me cold and heartless. Perhaps you are right; judge for yourself. I will tell you my whole history, and, whatever opinion you may have of me, I shall, at least, not die without having made myself known to some one.

"When I was sixteen I left St. Cyr, where I had been educated, to marry the Marquis de R——. He was fifty, but I dared not complain, for every one congratulated me on this splendid match, and all my portionless companions envied my lot.

"I was never very bright, and at that time I was positively stupid; the education of the cloister had completely benumbed my faculties. I left the convent with a romantic idea of life and of the world, stupidly considered a merit in young girls, but which often results in the misery of their whole lives. As a natural consequence, the experience brought me

by my brief married life was lodged in so narrow a mind that it was of
no use to me. I learned, not to understand life, but to doubt myself.

"I was a widow before I was seventeen, and as soon as I was out of
mourning I was surrounded by suitors. I was then in all the splendor of
my beauty, and it was generally admitted that there was neither face
nor figure that could compare with mine; but my husband, an old, worn-
out dissipated man, who had never shown me anything but irony and
disdain, and had married me only to secure an office promised with my
hand, had left me such an aversion to marriage that I could never be
brought to contract new ties. In my ignorance of life I fancied that all
men resembled him, and that in a second husband I should find M. de
R——'s hard heart, his pitiless irony, and that insulting coldness which
had so deeply humiliated me.

"This terrible entrance into life had dispelled for me all the illusions
of youth. My heart, which perhaps was not entirely cold, withdrew into
itself and grew suspicious. I was foolish enough to tell my real feelings
to several women of my acquaintance. They did not fail to tell what they
had learned, and without considering the doubts and anguish of my
heart, boldly declared that I despised all men. There is nothing men will
resent more readily than this; my lovers soon learned to despise me, and
continued their flatteries only in the hope of finding an opportunity to
hold me up to ridicule. I saw mockery and treachery written upon every
forehead, and my misanthropy increased every day. About this time
there came to Paris from the provinces a man who had neither talent,
strength, nor fascination, but who possessed a frankness and uprightness
of feeling very rare among the people with whom I lived. This was the
Vicomte de Larrieux. He was soon acknowledged to be my most favored love.

"He, poor fellow, loved me sincerely in his soul. His soul! Had he a
soul? He was one of those hard, prosaic men who have not even the elegance of vice or the glitter of falsehood. He was struck only by my
beauty; he took no pains to discover my heart. This was not disdain on
his part, it was incapacity. Had he found in me the power of loving, he
would not have known how to respond to it. I do not think there ever
lived a man more wedded to material things than poor Larrieux. He ate
with delight, and fell asleep in all the armchairs; the remainder of the
time he took snuff. He was always occupied in satisfying some appetite. I
do not think he had one idea a day. And yet, my dear friend, would you
believe it? I never had the energy to get rid of him; for sixty years he was
my torment. Constantly offended by my repulses, yet constantly drawn to
me by the very obstacles I placed in the way of his passion, he had for

me the most faithful, the most undying, the most wearisome love that ever man felt for woman."

"I am surprised," said I, "that in the course of your life you never met a man capable of understanding you, and worthy of converting you to real love. Must we conclude that the men of today are superior to those of other times?"

"That would be a great piece of vanity on your part," she answered, smiling. "I have little reason to speak well of the men of my own time; yet I doubt, too, whether you have made much progress; but I will not moralize. The cause of my misfortune was entirely within myself. I had no tact, no judgment. A woman as proud as I was should have possessed a superior character, and should have been able to distinguish at a glance many of the insipid, false, insignificant men who surrounded me. I was too ignorant, too narrow-minded for this. As I lived on I acquired more judgment and have learned that several of the objects of my hatred deserved far other feelings."

"And while you were young," I rejoined, "were you never tempted to make a second trial? Was this deep-rooted aversion never shaken off? It is strange."

The Marquise was silent, then hastily laying her gold snuff-box on the table—"I have begun my confession," said she, "and I will acknowledge everything. Listen. Once, and only once, I have loved, with a love as passionate and indomitable as it was imaginative and ideal. For you see, my child, you young men think you understand women, but you know nothing about them. If many old women of eighty were occasionally to tell you the history of their loves, you would perhaps find that the feminine soul contains sources of good and evil of which you have no idea. And now, guess what was the rank of the man for whom I entirely lost my head—I, a Marquise, and prouder and haughtier than any other."

"The King of France, or the Dauphin, Louis XIV."

"Oh, if you go on in that manner, it will be three hours before you come to my lover. I prefer to tell you at once—he was an actor."

"A king, notwithstanding, I imagine."

"The noblest, the most elegant that ever trod the boards. You are not amazed?"

"Not much. I have heard that such ill-sorted passions were not rare, even when the prejudices of caste in France were more powerful than they are today."

"Those ill-sorted passions were not tolerated by the world, I can assure you. The first time I saw him I expressed my admiration to the Comtesse de Ferrières, who happened to be beside me, and she answered: 'Do not speak so warmly to any one but me. You would be cruelly taunted were you suspected of forgetting that in the eyes of a woman of rank an actor can never be a man.'

"Madame Ferrières' words remained in my mind, I know not why. At the time this contemptuous tone of hers seemed to me absurd, and this fear of committing myself a piece of malicious hypocrisy.

"His name was Lelio; he was by birth an Italian, but spoke French admirably. He may have been thirty-five, although on the stage he often seemed less than twenty. He played Corneille; after this he played Racine, and in both he was admirable."

"I am surprised," said I, interrupting the Marquise, "that his name does not appear in the annals of dramatic talent."

"He was never famous," she answered, "and was appreciated neither by the court nor the town. I have heard that he was outrageously hissed when he first appeared. Afterward he was valued for his feeling, his fire, and his efforts at correct elocution. He was tolerated and sometimes applauded, but, on the whole, he was always considered an actor without taste.

"In those days tragedy was played 'properly'; it was necessary to die with taste, to fall gracefully, and to have an air of good breeding, even in the case of a blow. Dramatic art was modeled upon the usage of good society, and the diction and gestures of the actors were in harmony with the hoops and hair powder, which even then disfigured 'Phèdre.'* I have never appreciated the defects of this school of art. I bravely endured it twice in the week, for it was the fashion to like it; but I listened with so cold and constrained an air that it was generally said I was insensible to the charms of fine poetry.

"One evening, after a rather long absence from Paris, I went to the Comédie Française to see 'Le Cid.'† Lelio had been admitted to this theater during my stay in the country, and I saw him for the first time. He played Rodrique. I was deeply moved by the very first tone of his voice. It was penetrating rather than sonorous, but vibrating and strongly accentuated. His voice was much citicized. That of the Cid was supposed to be deep and powerful, just as all the heroes of antiquity were supposed to be tall and strong. A king who was but five feet six inches could not wear the diadem; it would have been contrary to the decrees of tastes. Lelio was small and slender. His beauty lay not in the features, but in the nobleness of his forehead, the irresistible grace of his attitude, the careless

* "Phèdre," by Racine.
† "Le Cid," by Corneille.

ease of his movements, the proud but melancholy expression of his face. The word charm should have been invented for him; it belonged to all his words, to all his glances, to all his motions. It was indeed a charm which he threw around me. This man, who stepped, spoke, moved without system or affectation, who sobbed with his heart as much as with his voice, who forgot himself to become identified with his passion; this man in whom the body seemed wasted and shattered by the soul, and a single one of whose glances contained all the life I failed to find in real life, exercised over me a really magnetic power. I alone could follow and understand him, and he was for five years my kind, my life, my love. To me he was much more than a man. His was an intellectual power which formed my soul at its will. Soon I was unable to conceal the impression he made on me. I gave up my box at the Comédie Française in order not to betray myself. I pretended I had become pious, and in the evening I went to pray in the churches; instead of that I dressed myself as a working woman and mingled with the common people that I might listen to him unconstrained. At last I bribed one of the employees of the theater to let me occupy a little corner where no one could see me and which I reached by a side corridor. As an additional precaution, I dressed myself as a schoolboy. When the hour for the theater sounded in the large clock in my drawing-room I was seized with violent palpitations. While my carriage was getting ready I tried to control myself; and if Larrieux happened to be with me I was rude to him, and threatened to send him away. I must have had great dissimulation and great tact to have hidden all this for five years from Larrieux, the most jealous of men, and from all the malicious people about me.

"I must tell you that instead of struggling against this passion I yielded to it with eagerness, with delight. It was so pure! Why should I have blushed for it? It gave me new life; it initiated me into all the feelings I had wished to experience; it almost made me a woman. I was proud to feel myself thrill and tremble. The first time my dormant heart beat aloud was to me a triumph. I learned to pout, to love, to be faithful and capricious. It was remarked I grew handsomer every day, that my dark eyes softened, that my smile was more expressive, that what I said was truer and had more meaning than could have been expected.

"I have just told you that when I heard the clock strike I trembled with joy and impatience. Even now I seem to feel the delicious oppression which used to overwhelm me at the sound of that clock. Since then, through the vicissitudes of fortune, I have come to find myself very happy in the possession of a few small rooms in the Marais. Well, of all my aristocratic *faubourg,* and my past splendor I regret only that which could have recalled to me those days of love and dreams. I have saved from the general ruin a few pieces of furniture which I look upon with as much emotion as if the hour for the theater were about to strike now, and my horses were pawing at the door. Oh! my child, never love as I loved; it is a storm which death alone can quell.

"Then I learned to take pleasure in being young, wealthy, and beautiful. Seated in my coach, my feet buried in furs, I could see myself reflected in the mirror in front of me. The dress of that time, which has since been so laughed at, was of extraordinary richness and splendor. When arranged with taste and modified in its exaggeration, it endowed a beautiful woman with dignity, with a softness, the grace of which the portraits of that time could give you no idea. A woman, clothed in its panoply of feathers, of silks, and flowers, was obliged to move slowly. I have seen very fair woman in white robes with long trains of watered silk, their hair powdered and dressed with white plumes, who might without exaggeration have been compared to swans. Despite all Rousseau has said, those enormous folds of satin, that profusion of muslin which enveloped a slender little body as down envelops a dove, made us resemble birds, rather than wasps. Long wings of lace fell from our arms, and our ribbons, purses, and jewels were variegated with the most brilliant colors. Balancing ourselves in our little high-heeled shoes, we seemed to fear to touch the earth and walked with the disdainful circumspection of a little bird on the edge of a brook.

"At the time of which I am speaking blonde powder began to be worn and gave the hair a light and soft color. This method of modifying the crude shades of the hair gave softness to the face, and an extraordinary brilliance to the eyes. The forehead was completely uncovered, its outline melted insensibly into the pale shades of the hair. It thus appeared higher and prouder, and gave all women a majestic air. It was the fashion, too, to dress the hair low, with large curls thrown back and falling on the neck. This was very becoming to me, and I was celebrated for the taste and magnificence of my dress. I sometimes wore red velvet with grebe-skin, sometimes white satin edged with tiger-skin, sometimes lilac damask shot with silver, with white feathers and pearls in my hair. Thus attired I would pay a few visits until the hour for the second piece at the theater, for Lelio never came on in the first. I created a sensation wherever I appeared, and, when I again found myself in my carriage, I contemplated with much pleasure the reflected image of the woman who loved Lelio, and might have been loved by him. Until then, the only pleasure I had found in being beautiful lay in the jealousy I excited. But from the moment that I loved I began to enjoy my beauty for its own sake. It was all I had to offer Lelio as a compensation for the triumphs which were denied him in Paris, and I loved to think of the pride and joy this poor actor, so misjudged, so laughed at, would feel were he told that the Marquise de R—— had dedicated her heart to him. These the dreams, however, were as brief as they were beautiful. As soon as my thoughts assumed some consistency, as soon as they took the form of any plan whatever, I had the fortitude to suppress them, and all the pride of rank reasserted its empire over my soul. You seem surprised at this. I will explain it by and by.

"About eight oclock my carriage stopped at the little Church of the Carmelites near the Luxembourg, and I sent it away, for I was supposed to be attending the religious lectures which were given there at that hour. But I only crossed the church and the garden and came out on the other street. I went to the garret of the young needlewoman named Florence, who was devoted to me. I locked myself up in her room, and joyfully laid aside all my adornments to don the black square-cut coat, the sword and wig of a young college professor. Tall, with my dark complexion and inoffensive glances, I really had the awkward hypocritical look of a little priestling who had stolen in to see the play. I took a hackney coach, and hastened to hide myself in my little box at the theater. Then my joy, my terror, my trembling ceased. A profound calm came upon me and I remained until the raising of the curtain as if absorbed in expectation of some great solemnity.

"As the vulture in his hypnotic circling surrounds the partridge and holds him panting and motionless, so did the soul of Lelio, that great soul of a poet and tragedian, envelop all my faculties, and plunge me into a torpor of admiration. I listened, my hands clasped upon my knees and my chin upon the front of the box, and my forehead bathed in perspiration; I hardly breathed; the crude light of the lamps tortured my eyes, which, tired and burning, were fastened on his every gesture, his every step. His feigned emotions, his simulated misfortune, impressed me as if they were real. I could hardly distinguish between truth and illusion. To me, Lelio was indeed Rodrique, Bajazet, Hippolyte. I hated his enemies. I trembled at his dangers; his sorrows drew from me floods of tears, and when he died I was compelled to stifle my emotions in my handkerchief.

"Between the acts I sat down at the back of my box; I was as one dead until the meager tone of the orchestra warned me that the curtain was about to rise again. Then I sprang up, full of strength and ardor, the power to feel, to weep. How much freshness, poetry, and youth there was in that man's talent! That whole generation must have been of ice not to have fallen at his feet.

"And yet, although he offended every conventional idea, although he could not adapt his taste to that silly public, although he scandalized the women by the carelessness of his dress and deportment, and displeased the men by his contempt for their foolish actions, there were moments when, by an irresistible fascination, by the power of his eye and his voice, he held the whole of this ungrateful public as if in the hollow of his hand, and compelled it to applaud and tremble. This happened but seldom, for the entire spirit of the age can not be suddenly changed; but when it did happen, the applause was frantic. It seemed as if the Parisians, subjugated by his genius, wished to atone for all their injustice. As for me, I believed that this man had at most a supernatural power, and that those who most bitterly despised him were compelled to swell his triumph in spite of themselves. In truth, at such times the Comédie Française seemed smitten with madness, and the spectators, on leaving the theater, were amazed to remember that they had applauded Lelio. As for me, I seized the opportunity to give full play to my emotion; I shouted, I wept, I passionately called his name. Happily for me, my weak voice was drowned in the storm which raged about me.

"At other times he was hissed when he seemed to me to be sublime, and then I left the theater, my heart full of rage. Those nights were the most dangerous for me. I was violently tempted to seek him out, to weep with him, to curse the age in which we lived, and to console him by offering him my enthusiasm and love.

"One evening as I left the theater by the side passage which led to my box, a small, slender man passed in front of me, and turned into the street. One of the stage-carpenters took off his hat and said: 'Good evening, Monsieur Lelio.' Eager to obtain a nearer view of this extraordinary man, I ran after him, crossed the street and, forgetting the danger to which I exposed myself, following him into a café. Fortunately, it was not one in which I was likely to meet any one of my own rank.

"When, by the light of the smoky lamp, I looked at Lelio, I thought I had been mistaken, and had followed another man. He was at least thirty-five, sallow, withered, and worn out. He was badly dressed, he looked vulgar, spoke in a hoarse, broken voice, shook hands with the meanest wretches, drank brandy, and swore horribly. It was not until I had heard his name repeated several times that I felt sure that this was the divinity of the theater, interpreter of the great Corneille. I could recognize none of those charms which had so fascinated me, not even his glance, so bright, so ardent, and so sad. His eyes were dull, dead, almost stupid; his strongly accentuated pronunciation seemed ignoble when he called to the waiter, or talked of gambling and taverns. He walked badly, he looked vulgar, and the paint was only half wiped from his cheeks. It was no longer Hippolyte—it was Lelio. The temple was empty; the oracle was dumb; the divinity had become a man, not even a man— an actor.

"He went out, and I sat stupefied without even presence of mind enough to drink the hot spiced wine I had called for. When I remembered where I was, and perceived the insulting glances which were heaped upon me, I became frightened. It was the first time I had ever found myself in such an equivocal position, and in such immediate contact with people of that class.

"I rose and tried to escape, but forget to pay my reckoning. The waiter ran after me; I was terribly ashamed; I was obliged to return, enter into explanations at the desk, and endure all the mocking and suspicious looks which were turned upon me. When I left I thought I was followed. In vain I looked for a hackney-coach; there were none remaining in front of the theater. I constantly heard heavy steps echoing my own. Trembling, I turned my head, and recognized a tall, ill-looking fellow whom I had noticed in one corner of the café, and who had very much the air of a spy or something worse. He spoke to me; I do not know what he said; I was too much frightened to hear, but I had still presence of mind enough to rid myself of him. I struck him in the face with my cane, and, leaving him stunned at my audacity, I shot away swift as an arrow, and did not stop till I reached Florence's little garret. When I awoke the next morning in my own bed with its wadded curtains and coronal of pink feathers, I almost thought I had dreamed, and felt greatly mortified when I recollected the disillusions of the previous night. I thought myself thoroughly cured of my love, and I tried to rejoice at it, but in vain. I was filled with a mortal regret, the weariness of life again entered my heart, the world had not a pleasure which could charm me.

"Evening came, but brought no more beneficial emotions. Society seemed to me stupid. I went to church and listened to the evening lecture with a determination of becoming pious; I caught cold, and came home quite ill. I remained in bed several days. The Comtesse de Ferrières came to see me, assured me that I had no fever, that lying still made me ill, that I must amuse myself, go out, go to the theater. She compelled me to go with her to see 'Cinna.'* 'You no longer go to the theater,' said she to me; 'your health is undermined by your piety, and the dullness of your

---

* "Cinna," a tragedy by Corneille.

life. You have not seen Lelio for some time; he has improved, and he is now sometimes applauded. I think he may some day become very tolerable.'

"I do not know why I allowed myself to be persuaded. However, as I was completely disenchanted with Lelio, I thought I no longer ran any risk in braving his fascinations in public. I dressed myself with excessive brilliance, and, in a court proscenium box, fronted a danger in which I no longer believed.

"But the danger was never more imminent. Lelio was sublime, and I had never been more in love with him. My recent adventure seemed but a dream. I could not believe that Lelio was other than he seemed upon the stage. In spite of myself, I yielded to the terrible agitations into which he had the power of throwing me. My face was bathed in tears, and I was compelled to cover it with my handkerchief. In the disorder of my mind I wiped off my rouge and my patches, and the Comtesse de Ferrières advised me to retire to the back of my box, for my emotion was creating a sensation in the house. I fortunately had had the skill to make every one believe it was the playing of Mlle. Hippolyte Clairon which affected me so deeply. She was, in my own opinion, a very cold and formal actress, too superior perhaps for her profession, as it was then understood; but her manner of saying 'Tout beau,' in 'Cinna,' had given her a great reputation. It must be said, however, that when she played with Lelio she outdid herself. Although she took pains to proclaim her share in the fashionable contempt for his method of acting, she assuredly felt the influence of his genius.

"That evening Lelio noticed me, either on account of my dress or my emotion; for I saw him, when he was not acting, bend over one of the spectators, who, at that epoch, sat upon the stage, and inquire my name. I guessed his question by the way both looked at me. My heart beat almost to suffocation, and I noticed during the play that Lelio's eyes turned several times toward me. What would I not have given to hear what the Chevalier de Bretillac, whom he had questioned, had said to him about me! Lelio's face did not indicate the nature of the information he had received, for he was obliged to retain the expression suited to his part. I knew this Bretillac very slightly, and I could not imagine whether he would speak well or ill of me.

"That night I understood for the first time the nature of the passion which enchained me to Lelio. It was a passion purely intellectual, purely ideal. It was not he I loved, but those heroes of ancient times whose sincerity, whose fidelity, whose tenderness he knew how to portray; with him and by him I was carried back to an epoch of forgotten virtues. I was bright enough to think that in those days I should not have been misjudged and hated, and that I should not have been reduced to loving a phantom of the footlights. Lelio was to me but the shadow of the Cid, the representative of that antique chivalric love now ridiculed in France. My Lelio was a fictitious being who had no existence outside the theater. The illusions of the stage, the glare of the footlights, were a part of the being whom I loved. Without them he was nothing to me, and faded like a story before the brightness of day. I had no desire to see him off the boards; and should have been in despair had I met him. It would have been like contemplating the ashes of a great man.

"One evening as I was going to the Carmelite church with the intention of leaving it by the passage door, I perceived that I was followed, and became convinced that henceforth it would be almost impossible to conceal the object of my nocturnal expeditions. I decided to go publicly to the theater. Lelio saw me and watched me; my beauty had struck him, my sensibility flattered him. His attention sometimes wandered so much as to displease the public. Soon I could no longer doubt. He was madly in love with me.

"My box had pleased the Princess de Vaudemont. I gave it up to her, and took for myself a smaller one, less in view of the house and better situated. I was almost upon the stage, I did not lose one of Lelio's glances; and he could look at me without it being seen by the public. But I no longer needed to catch his eye in order to understand all his feelings. The sound of his voice, his sighs, the expression which he gave to certain verses, certain words, told me that he was speaking to me. I was the happiest and proudest of women, for then it was the hero, not the actor, who loved me.

"I have since heard that Lelio often followed me in my walks and drives; so little did I desire to see him outside of the theater that I never perceived it. Of the eighty years I have passed in this world, those five are the only ones in which I really lived.

"One day I read in the *Mercure de France* the name of a new actor engaged at the Comédie Française to replace Lelio, who was about to leave France.

"This announcement was a mortal blow to me. I could not conceive how I should exist when deprived of these emotions, this life of passion and storm. This event gave an immense development to my love, and was well-nigh my ruin.

"I no longer struggled with myself; I no longer sought to stifle all thoughts contrary to the dignity of my rank. I regretted that he was not what he appeared on the stage; I wished him as young and handsome as he seemed each night before the footlights, that I might sacrifice to him all my pride, all my prejudices.

"While I was in this state of irresolution, I received a letter in an unknown hand. It is the only love letter I have ever kept. Though Larrieux has written me innumerable protestations, and I have received a thousand perfumed declarations from a hundred others, it is the only real love letter that was ever sent me."

The Marquise rose, opened with a steady hand an inlaid casket, and took from it a crumpled, worn-out letter, which I read with difficulty.

"Madame—I am certain you will feel nothing but contempt for this letter, you will not even deem it worthy of your anger. But, to a man falling into an abyss, what matters one more stone at the bottom? You will think me mad, and you will be right. You will perhaps pity me, for you will not doubt my sincerity. However humble your piety may have made you, you will understand the extent of my despair; you must already know *how much evil and how much good your eyes can do.*...

"You must know this already, madame; it is impossible that the violent emotions I have portrayed upon the stage, my cries of wrath and despair, have not twenty times revealed to you my passion. You can not have lighted all these flames without being conscious of what you did. Perhaps you played with me as a tiger with his prey; perhaps the spectacle of my folly and my tortures was your pastime. But no; to think so were to presume too much. No, madame, I do not believe it; you never thought of me. You felt the verses of the great Corneille, you identified these with the noble passions of tragedy; that was all. And I, madman that I was, I dared to think that my voice alone sometimes awoke your sympathies, that my heart echoed in yours, that between you and me there was something more than between me and the public. Oh, my madness was arrant, but it was sweet! Leave me my illusions, madame; what are they to you? Do you fear that I should boast of them? By what right should I do so, and who would believe me? I should only make myself a laughing-stock of sensible people. Leave me this conviction; it has given me more joy than the severity of the public has caused me sorrow. Let me bless you, let me thank you upon my knees, for the sensibility which I have discovered in your soul, and which no one else has ever shown me; for the tears which I have seen you shed for my fictitious sorrows, and which have often raised my inspiration almost to delirium; for the timid glances which sought, at least it seemed so, to console me for the coldness of my audience. Oh, why were you born to pomp and splendor! Why am I an obscure and nameless artist! Why have I not riches and the favor of the public, that I might exchange them for a name, for one of those titles which I have hitherto disdained, and which, perhaps, would permit me to aspire as high as you are placed! Once I deemed the distinctions conferred upon talent superior to all others. To what purpose, thought I, is a man a Chevalier or a Marquis but to be the sillier, the vainer, and the more insolent? I hated the pride of men of rank, and thought that I should be sufficiently avenged for their disdain if my genius raised me above them. Dreams and delusions all! My strength has not equalled my mad ambition. I have remained obscure; I have done worse—I have touched success, and allowed it to escape me. I thought myself great, and I was cast down to the dust; I imagined that I was almost sublime, and I was condemned to be ridiculous. Fate took me—me and my audacious dreams—and crushed me as if I had been a reed. I am a most wretched man! But I committed my greatest folly when I cast my eyes beyond that row of lights which marked between me and the rest of society an invisible line of separation. It is to me a circle of Popilius. I, an actor, I dared to raise my eyes and fasten them upon a beautiful woman—upon a woman, you, lovely, and of high rank; for you are all this, madame, and I know it. The world accuses you of coldness and of exaggerated piety. I alone understand you. Your first smile, your first tear, sufficiently disproved the absurd fable which Chevalier de Bretillac repeated against you.

"But then what a destiny is yours! What fatality weighs upon you as upon me, that in the midst of society so brilliant, which calls itself so enlightened, you should have found only the heart of a poor actor to do you justice. Nothing will deprive me of the sad and consoling thought that, had we been born in the same rank, you would have been mine in spite of my rivals, in spite of my inferiority. You would have been compelled to acknowledge that there is in me something greater than their wealth, and their titles—the power of loving you.

Lelio."

"This letter," continued the Marquise, "was of a character very unusual at the time it was written, and seemed to me, notwithstanding some passages of theatrical declamation at the beginning, so powerful, so true, so full of only bold passion, that I was overwhelmed by it. The pride which still struggled within me faded away. I would have given all the remaining days I had to live for one hour of such love.

"I answered in these words, as nearly as I can remember:

" 'I do not accuse you, Lelio; I accuse destiny. I do not pity you alone; I pity myself also. Neither pride nor prudence shall make me deny you the consolation of believing that I have felt a preference for you. Keep it, for it is the only one I can offer you. I can never consent to see you.'

"Next day I received a note which I hastily read and threw into the fire, to prevent Larrieux from seeing it, for he came suddenly upon me while I was reading it. It read thus:

" 'Madame—I must see you or I must die. Once—once only, but for a single hour, if such is your will. Why should you fear an interview since you trust my honor and my prudence? Madame, I know who you are; I am well aware of your piety and of the austerity of your life. I am not fool enough to hope for anything but a word of compassion, but it must fall from your own lips. My heart must receive it and bear it away, or my heart must break.   Lelio.'

"I believed implicity in the humility, in the sincerity of Lelio. Besides, I had ample reason to trust my own strength. I resolved to see him. I had completely forgotten his faded features, his low-bred manners, his vulgar aspect; I recollected only the fascination of his genius, his letters, and his love. I answered:

" 'I will see you. Find some secure place, but hope for nothing but for what you have asked. Should you seek to abuse my trust, you would be a villain, and I should not fear you.'

"Answer:

" 'Your trust would save you from the basest of villains. You will see, Madame, that Lelio is not unworthy of it. Duke —— has often been good enough to offer me the use of his house in the Rue de Valois. Deign to go thither after the play.'

"Some explanations and directions as to the locality of the house followed. I received this note at four o'clock. The whole negotiation had occupied but a day. I had spent it in wandering through the house like one distracted; I was in a fever. This rapid succession of events bore me along as in a dream.

"When I had made the final decision, when it was impossible to draw back, I sank down upon my ottoman, breathless and dizzy.

"I was really ill. A surgeon was sent for; I was bled. I told my servants not to mention my indisposition to any one; I dreaded the intrusion of officious advisers, and was determined not to be prevented from going out that night.

"I threw myself upon my bed to await the appointed hour, and gave orders that no visitors should be admitted. The blood-letting had relieved and weakened me; I sank into a great depression of spirits. All my illusions vanished with the excitement which had accompanied my fever.

Reason and memory returned; I remembered my disenchantment in the coffee-house, and Lelio's wretched appearance there; I prepared to blush for my folly, and to fall from the height of my deceitful visions to a bare and despicable reality. I no longer understood how it had been possible for me to consent to exchange my heroic and romantic tenderness for the revulsion of feeling which awaited me, and the sense of shame which would henceforth poison all my recollections. I bitterly regretted what I had done; I wept my illusions, my love, and that future of pure and secret joys which I was about to forfeit. Above all, I mourned for Lelio, whom in seeing I should forever lose, in whose love I had found five years of happiness, and for whom in a few hours I should feel nothing but indifference.

"In the paroxysm of my grief I violently wrung my arms; the vein reopened, and I had barely time to ring for my maid, who found me in a swoon in my bed. A deep and heavy sleep, against which I struggled in vain, seized me. I neither dreamed nor suffered; I was as one dead for several hours. When I again opened my eyes my room was almost dark, my house silent; my waiting-woman was asleep in a chair at the foot of my bed. I remained for some time in such a state of numbness and weakness that I recollected nothing. Suddenly my memory returned, and I asked myself whether the hour and the day of rendezvous were passed, whether I had slept an hour or a century; whether I had killed Lelio by breaking my word. Was there yet time? I tried to rise, but my strength failed me. I struggled for some moments as if in a nightmare. At last I summoned all the forces of my will. I sprang to the floor, opened the curtains, and saw the moon shining upon the trees of my garden. I ran to the clock; the hands marked ten. I seized my maid and waked her: 'Quinette, what day of the week is it?' She sprang from her chair, screaming, and tried to escape from me, for she thought me delirious; I reassured her and learned that I had only slept three hours. I thanked God. I asked for a hackney-coach. Quinette looked at me in amazement. At last she became convinced that I had the full use of my senses, transmitted my order, and began to dress me.

"I asked for my simplest dress; I put no ornaments in my hair, I refused to wear my rouge. I wished above all things for Lelio's esteem and respect, for they were far more precious to me than his love. Nevertheless, I was pleased when Quinette, who was much surprised at this new caprice, said, examining me from head to foot: 'Truly, madame, I know not how you manage it. You are dressed in a plain white robe, without either train or pannier; you are ill and as pale as death; you have not even put on a patch; yet I never saw you so beautiful as tonight. I pity the men who will look upon you!' 'Do you think me so very austere, my poor Quinette?' 'Alas, madame, every day I pray Heaven to make me like you; but up to this time—' 'Come, simpleton, give me my mantle and muff.'

"At midnight I was in the house of the Rue de Valois. I was carefully veiled, a sort of valet de chambre received me; he was the only human being to be seen in this mysterious dwelling. He led me through the windings of a dark garden to a pavilion buried in silence and shadow. Depositing his green silk lantern in the vestibule, he opened the door of a large dusky room, showed me by a respectful gesture and with a most impassive face a ray of light proceeding from the other extremity, and said, in a tone so low that it seemed as if he feared to awaken the sleeping echoes: 'Your ladyship is alone, no one else has yet come. Your ladyship will find in the summer parlor a bell which I will answer if you need anything.' He disappeared as if by enchantment, shutting the door upon me.

"I was terribly frightened; I thought I had fallen into some trap. I called him back. He instantly reappeared, and his air of stupid solemnity reassured me. I asked him what time it was, although I knew perfectly well, for I had sounded my watch twenty times in the carriage. 'It is midnight,' answered he, without raising his eyes. I now resolutely entered the summer parlor, and I realized how unfounded were my fears when I saw that the doors which opened upon the garden were only of painted silk. Nothing could be more charming than this boudoir; it was fitted up as a concert-room. The walls were of stucco as white as snow, and the mirrors were framed in unpolished silver. Musical instruments of unusually rich material were scattered about, upon seats of white velvet, trimmed with pearls. The light came from above through leaves of alabaster, which formed a dome. This soft, even light might have been mistaken for that of the moon. A single statue of white marble stood in the middle of the room; it was an antique and represented Isis veiled, with her finger upon her lips. The mirrors which reflected us, both pale and draped in white, produced such an illusion upon me that I was obliged to distinguish my finger from hers.

"Suddenly the silence was interrupted; the door was opened and closed, and light footsteps sounded upon the floor. I sank into a chair more dead than alive, for I was about to see Lelio shorn of the illusions of the stage. I closed my eyes, and inwardly bade them farewell before I reopened them.

"But how much was I surprised! Lelio was beautiful as an angel. He had not taken off his stage dress, and it was the most elegant I had ever seen him wear. His Spanish doublet was of white satin, his shoulder and garter knots of cherry ribbons, and a short cloak of the same color was thrown over his shoulder. He wore an immense ruff of English lace; his hair was short and unpowdered, partially covered by a cap with white feathers and a diamond rose. In this costume he had just played Don Juan in 'Festin de Pierre.' Never had I seen him so beautful, so young, so poetical, as at that moment. Velasquez would have worshipped such a model.

"He knelt before me. I could not help stretching out my hand to him, he seemed so submissive, so fearful of displeasing me. A man sufficiently in love to tremble before a woman was rare in those times, and this one was thirty-five and an actor.

"It seemed to me then, it seems to me still, that he was in the first bloom of youth. In his white dress he looked like a young page; his forehead had all the purity, his heart all the ardor of a first love. He took my hands and covered them with kisses. My senses seemed to desert me; I caressed his burning forehead, his stiff, black hair, and the brown neck which disappeared in the sofe whiteness of his collar. He wept like a woman; I was overwhelmed with surprise.

"I wept delicious tears. I compelled him to raise his head and look at me. How splendid, how tender were his eyes! How much fascination his warm, true soul communicated to the very defects of his face, and the scars left upon it by time and toil! When I saw the premature wrinkles upon his beautiful forehead, when I saw the pallor of his lips, the languor of his smile, my heart was melted. I felt that I must needs weep for his griefs, his disappointments, the labors of his life. I identified myself with him in all his sorrows, even that of his long, hopeless love for me, and I had but one wish—to compensate him for the ills he had suffered.

"My dear Lelio, my great Rodrique, my beautiful Don Juan! He spoke to me, he told me how from a dissipated actor I had made him a man full of life and ardor; how I had raised him in his own eyes, and restored to him the illusions of his youth; he spoke of his respect, his veneration for me, of his contempt for the species of love which was then in fashion. Never did a man with more penetrating eloquence speak to the heart of a woman; never did Racine make love utter itself with such conviction of its own truth, such poetry, such strength. Everything elevated and profound, everything sweet and fiery which passion can inspire, lay in his words, his face, his eyes, his caresses. Alas! did he deceive himself! Was he playing a part?"

"I certainly do not think so," I cried, looking at the Marquise. She seemed to grow young as she spoke; and, like the fairy Urgela, to cast

off her hundred years. I know not who has said that a woman's heart
has no wrinkles.

"Listen to the end," said she. "I threw my arms around his neck; I
shivered as I touched the satin of his coat, as I breathed the perfume of
his hair. My emotion was too violent and I fainted.

"He recalled me to myself by his prompt assistance. I found him still
kneeling at my feet. 'Pity me, kill me,' cried he. He was paler and far
more ill than I.

" 'Listen, Lelio,' said I. 'Here we separate forever, but let us carry from
this place a whole future of blissful thoughts and adored memories. I
swear, Lelio, to love you till my death. I swear it without fear, for I feel
that the snows of age will not have the power to extinguish this ardent
flame.' Lelio knelt before me; he did not implore me, he did not reproach me; he said that he had not hoped for so much happiness as I
had given him, and that he had no right to ask for more. Nevertheless,
as he bade me farewell, his despair, the emotion which trembled in his
face, terrified me. I asked him if he would not find happiness in thinking
of me, if the ecstasy of our meeting would not lend its charm to all the
days of his life, if his past and future sorrows would not be softened
each time he recalled it. He roused himself to promise, to swear all I
asked. He again fell at my feet and passionately kissed my dress. I made
a sign and he left me. The carriage I had sent for came.

"The automatic servant of the house knocked three times outside to
warn me. Lelio despairingly threw himself in front of the door; he looked
like a specter. I gently repulsed him and he yielded. I crossed the threshold, and as he attempted to follow me, I showed him a chair in the middle of the room, underneath the statue of Isis. He sat down in it. A
passionate smile wandered over his lips, his eyes sent out one more flash
of gratitude and love. He was still beautiful, still young, still a grandee
of Spain. After a few steps, when I was about to lose him forever, I
turned back and looked at him once more. Despair had crushed him. He
was old, altered, frightful. His body seemed paralyzed. His stiffened lips
attempted an unmeaning smile. His eyes were glassy and dim; he was
now only Lelio, the shadow of a lover and a prince."

The Marquise paused; then, while her aspect changed like that of a
ruin which totters and sinks, she added: "Since then I have not heard
him mentioned."

The Marquise made a second and a longer pause; then, with the
terrible fortitude which comes with length of years, which springs from
the persistent love of life or the near hope of death, she said with a
smile: "Well, do you not now believe in the ideality of the eighteenth
century?"

5

Mimi Pinson

ALFRED DE MUSSET

Among the students who attended the lectures, last year, at the School of Medicine, there was one called Eugène Aubert. He was a young man of good family, about nineteen years of age. His parents lived in the country and made him a small but sufficient allowance. He lived a quiet life and was considered to have a mild character. His friends loved him; always finding him kind and helpful, generous and open-hearted. The only fault with which he could be reproached was a singular liking for reverie and solitude, and he had such an excessive reserve in his conversation and his smallest actions that he was nicknamed the "Little Girl," a description, moreover, at which he laughed himself, and on which his friends did not place any construction that could offend him, believing him to be as courageous as anyone else when necessary; but it must be admitted that his conduct justified, in a small way, this appellation, particularly by the way it contrasted with the habits of his companions. As long as it was a question of work, he was the first; but if it was a suggestion of a pleasure party, a dinner at the *Moulin de Beurre,* or a dance at the *Chaumière,* the "Little Girl" shook his head and returned to his room. This was a monstrous state of affairs to the students; not only had Eugène no mistress, although his youth and his appearance would have helped him considerably, but he had never been seen flirting at a bar with a grisette, an immemorial custom in the Quartier Latin. The beauties who thronged the Montagne Sainte-Geneviève, and shared among themselves the love affairs of the schools, inspired him with such repugnance that it almost amounted to aversion. He regarded them as a species apart, dangerous, ungrateful, and depraved, born to disseminate illness and misfortune in exchange for a few pleasures. Avoid all the women there, he said to himself, they are bad lots.

And unfortunately he found too many examples to justify the horror with which they inpired him. The quarrels, the dissipations, sometimes even the ruin which followed these transient liaisons, with their outward aspect of happiness, were only too easy to name; last year like today, and probably the same as next year.

Naturally Eugène's friends laughed continually at his morals and scruples.

"What do you mean?" one of his friends called Marcel often asked him, who pretended to be a jovial fellow, "what does one fault prove, or one accidental happening?"

"That one should abstain," replied Eugène, "for fear of it happening a second time."

"Wrong reasoning," rejoined Marcel, "the argument of a *capucin de carte,* who falls if his neighbor stumbles. What are you worrying yourself about? Which of us has not lost at the game? Is that a reason for turning monk? One has no money and another only drinks water; is that a reason for Élise to lose her appetite? Whose fault is it if your neighbor pawns his watch so that he may go to Montmorency and cut a caper? No one is hurt by it. You make love to Rosalie and get a sword thrust through you; she turns her back on you, quite naturally: does she suffer by it? They are the little inconveniences of which life is full, and even so they are much less common than you suppose. Take a Sunday, when it is fine, and the many friendly couples in the cafés in the gardens, and the public-houses. Look at those great omnibuses, crowded with grisettes, going to Ranelagh or Belleville. Count those who go out, on a fête day, from the Quartier Saint-Jacques: the battalions of dressmakers, the armies of seamstresses, the crowds of tobacconists; they all amuse themselves, they all have their love affairs, they all go to lie down around Paris under the arbors of the countryside, like flocks of sparrows. If it rains they all go to the play, eat oranges and weep; for these people eat a lot, it is true, and weep readily; which goes to show a good disposition. But what harm do those poor women do, who have sewn, basted, hemmed, and mended all the week, in showing an example, on Sundays, of forgetting troubles and looking to the future? And what could an honest man do better, who on his part, having spent a week dissecting things unpleasant, clears his eyes by looking at a pretty face, a rounded leg, and life?"

"Whited sepulchres," said Eugène.

"I say and maintain," continued Marcel, "that one must and should sing the praises of the grisettes, and that friendship with them does no harm. First, they are virtuous, for they spend the day in making garments indispensable to modesty and decency; secondly, they are courteous, for there is no proprietress of a shop who does not see that her shop-girls speak politely to customers; thirdly, they are very careful and very clean, inasmuch as they constantly have in their hands lingerie which they must not soil, under penalty of being fined; fourthly, they are sincere, because they drink ratafia; in the fifth place, they are economical and frugal, for they have to work hard to make thirty sous, and if on occasions they show themselves greedy and extravagant, it is never with their own money; sixthly, they are very cheerful, because the work they do is in general deadly tedious, so they frisk like a fish in water as soon as their work is done. Another thing that one finds in them is that they are not at all exacting; for as they spend their life pinned to a chair from which they cannot move, they can't run after their lovers like ladies of good society. Besides, they are not loquacious, for they have to count their stitches. They do not spend much on their shoes, because they do not walk much, nor for their dress, for hardly anyone gives them credit. If they are accused of inconstancy, it is not from natural naughtiness; but from the temptation of the great number of different people who pass their shops. From another angle they prove convincingly that they are capable of genuine passion, by the great number of them who throw themselves daily into the Seine or out of the window, or asphyxiate themselves in their homes. It is true, they have the misfortune of being nearly always hungry and thirsty, precisely because of their temperance; for it is notorious that they can be satisfied with a glass of beer and a cigarette for a meal; a valuable quality that is rarely met with at home. In short, I maintain that they are good, lovable, faithful, and impartial, and it is regrettable when they finish in a hospital."

Whilst Marcel was talking like this, as they were seated at a café, he became rather heated, and filling his friend's glass, asked him to drink the health of Mademoiselle Pinson, who was their neighbor; but Eugène, while Marcel continued to harangue his comrades, took his hat and stole away quietly.

II

Mademoiselle Pinson could not exactly be described as a *jolie femme*. There is a great deal of difference between a *jolie femme* and a *jolie grisette*. If a *jolie femme,* recognized as such, in Parisian terms, bethinks herself of wearing a small bonnet, a dress of gingham, and a silk apron, she will be dressed, it is true, like a *jolie grisette*. But if a grisette puts on a hat, a velvet mantle and a silk dress, she does not become a *jolie femme;*

on the contrary, it is probable she would look like a portmanteau, and deceive no one. The difference arises from the conditions in which these two beings live, and principally in that cardboard wheel, covered with material and called a hat, which women consider correct to apply to all sides of the head, rather resembling a horse's blinkers. (It should be noted meanwhile that the blinkers prevent the horses from seeing one side or the other, and that the piece of cardboard does not stop anything!)

Whatever it is made of, a small bonnet demands a snub nose, which in its turn should be above a well-cut mouth, in which are good teeth, with a round face as frame. A round face should have sparkling eyes; it is better that they should be as black as possible, and the eyebrows well defined. The hair must be *ad libitum* and in keeping with the black eyes. Such an appearance is far from beauty as generally understood. One would rather describe it as a doll's face, the typical face of the grisette, who would perhaps be ugly under the wheel of cardboard, but whom the bonnet can somehow make charming, more pretty than beautiful. Such was the appearance of Mademoiselle Pinson.

Marcel resolved in his mind that Eugène should pay his addresses to this young lady. Why? Either I know nothing about it, or else because he himself was the admirer of Mademoiselle Zelia, the intimate friend of Mademoiselle Pinson, and it seemed to him natural and proper to arrange matters to suit himself, and to make love in couples. Such plans are not uncommon, and succeed fairly often, opportunity being, since the world existed, the greatest of all temptations. Who can say what events are brought about, happy or unhappy, of love, of quarrels, of joys or of sorrows, by communicating doors, a secret staircase, a corridor, or a broken-down wheel?

Nevertheless, there are certain characters who deny themselves these opportunities. They prefer to work for their enjoyments; not to win them by chance, and they are disposed to make love just because they find themselves next to a pretty woman in a carriage. Such was Eugène, and Marcel knew it; however, he had long ago formulated a fairly simple plan that he believed to be admirable, and above all infallible, to break down the resistance of his friend.

He made up his mind to give a supper, and could not think of any more appropriate day than his own birthday. He ordered two dozen bottles of beer to be sent to his rooms, a large piece of cold veal with a salad, an enormous *galette de plomb,* and a bottle of champagne.

First he invited two students of his acquaintance, then he told Mademoiselle Zelia that he was giving a party in his rooms, and that she was to bring Mademoiselle Pinson. They were on no account to fail to come.

Marcel had the reputation, quite justly, of being one of the "bloods" of the Quartier Latin, one of those people whom one does not refuse. Scarcely had the clock struck seven when the two grisettes knocked at the door of the student's room; Mademoiselle Zelia in a short dress, gray boots and a flower-trimmed bonnet, Mademoiselle Pinson, more modest, dressed in a black coat which she did not remove, and which gave her, so it was said, a slightly Spanish air, of which she was very proud. Both of them were ignorant, it is hoped, of their host's secret designs.

Marcel had not made the mistake of asking Eugène beforehand; he was too certain of a refusal in that case. It was only after the ladies had sat down to table, and after the first glass had been emptied, that he asked permission to absent himself for a few minutes to go and fetch a friend, and went to the house where Eugène lived. He found him, as usual, at his work, alone, surrounded by his books. After a few remarks, he started gently his usual expostulations; that he was overtiring himself, that he was wrong in not taking any kind of distraction, then he suggested a short walk. Eugène accepted; he was a little tired, in fact, as he had been working all day. The two young men went out together, and after strolling in the Luxembourg Gardens, it was not difficult for Marcel to persuade his friend to return with him to his rooms.

The two grisettes, left alone, and probably tired of waiting, had begun to make themselves at home; they had taken off their bonnets and shawls, and singing, danced a country dance, not without helping themselves to the refreshments, from time to time. With bright eyes and animated faces they ceased their dance, slightly out of breath, as Eugène bowed to them somewhat timidly, looking surprised. Because of his solitary habits, he was scarcely known to them; they had soon taken in his appearance, from head to feet, with that unabashed curiosity which is the privilege of their type; then going on with their singing and dancing, as if nothing had happened. The newcomer, somewhat disconcerted, took a few steps backward, when Marcel, having closed and locked the door, threw the key noisily on the table.

"No one else yet," he exclaimed. "What are my friends doing? But never mind, the wild man is ours. Ladies, allow me to present to you the most virtuous young man in France and Navarre, who has long wished to make your acquaintance, and is, particularly, a great admirer of Mademoiselle Pinson."

The country dance ceased once more; Mademoiselle Pinson bowed slightly and replaced her bonnet.

"Eugène," cried Marcel, "today is my birthday; these two ladies have very kindly come here to celebrate it with us. It is true I nearly brought you here by force; but I hope that, at our united request, you will stay here willingly. It is now nearly eight o'clock; we have time to smoke a pipe whilst waiting for our appetites."

Speaking thus, he threw a significant look at Mademoiselle Pinson, who, understanding it, bowed once more, smiling, and said gently to Eugène:

"Yes, Monsieur, we beg you to." At this moment the two students invited by Marcel knocked at the door. Eugène, realizing that he could not withdraw without being ungracious, resignedly took his seat with the others.

III

The supper was long and noisy. The men having commenced by filling the room with a fog of smoke, drank the more to refresh themselves. The ladies made most of the conversation, and amused the company with tales more or less scandalous, at the expense of their friends and acquaintances, and adventures more or less true, from the workroom. If the stories lacked probability, they did not lack spice. Two lawyers' clerks, if they were to be believed, had made a profit of twenty thousand francs by dealing in Spanish Funds, and had spent it in six weeks on two girls in a glove shop. The son of one of the richest bankers in Paris offered a well-known dressmaker a box at the opera and a house in the the country, which she had refused, preferring to look after her parents and remain faithful to a clerk at the Deux-Magots. A certain personage, who must not be named, and whose rank obliged him to keep the greatest secrecy, went incognito to visit an embroideress in the Passage Pont-Neuf; the latter had been suddenly carried away by the authorities in a post-chaise, at midnight, given a pocket-book full of bank-notes and shipped to the United States, etc.

"Enough," said Marcel, "we know that. Zelia invents, and as to Mademoiselle Mimi (as Mademoiselle Pinson was called familiarly), her information is not correct. Your lawyers' clerks only got swindled; your banker offered an orange, and your embroideress is so far from the United States that she is seen daily, from twelve to four, at the hospital of La Charité, where she has gone to live, owing to lack of food."

Eugène was seated near to Mademoiselle Pinson. He thought he saw her turn pale at this last word, spoken with such indifference. But, almost immediately she rose, lit a cigarette, and said easily:

"Silence in your turn. . . . I claim to speak. As Monsieur Marcel does not believe in fables, I will tell you a true story, *'et quorum pars magna fui.'* "

"Do you speak Latin?" said Eugène.

"As you see," Mademoiselle Pinson replied; "that sentence comes to me from an uncle, who served under the great Napoleon, and never failed to use it when telling the story of a battle. If you do not know the meaning of these words you may learn without payment. They mean, 'I give you my word of honor.' You know that I went last week, with one of my friends, to the Odéon. . . ."

"Wait a minute," said Marcel, "until I cut the cake."

"Cut, but listen," replied Mademoiselle Pinson. "I had gone with Blanchette and Rougette to the Odéon to see a tragedy. Rougette, as you know, has just lost her grandmother; she inherited four hundred francs. We took a box; three students were in the stalls; these young men noticed us, and, with the excuse of our being alone, invited us to supper."

"Outright—directly?" asked Marcel. "Really, it was kind. And I suppose you refused?"

"No, sir!" said Mademoiselle Pinson; "we accepted and, at the interval, without waiting for the end of the piece, we went to Viot.'"

"With your beaux?"

"With our beaux. The waiter, to be sure, began by telling us that there was nothing left; but such a state of affairs could not stop us. We insisted that they should send out and get what was wanting. Rougette ordered a regular wedding feast: prawns, a sweet omelette, mussels, fritters, eggs *à la neige,* everything there was to be had for a good dinner. To tell the truth, our young acquaintants looked rather sour. . . ."

"I should think so," said Marcel.

"We did not mind. The supper brought, we began to imitate fine ladies. We did not like anything, everything displeased us. As soon as one dish was tasted we sent it away and insisted on another being brought. 'Waiter, take that away . . . it won't do at all . . . where did you get such stuff from?' Our friends wanted to eat, but were not allowed to. In short, we supposed as Sancho dined, and anger made us even break some crockery."

"Good behavior! And what about paying?"

"Precisely the question the three unknowns were asking themselves. It seemed to us, from what we heard of a whispered conversation they had together, that one of them possessed six francs, another very much less, and the third only had a watch, which he generously drew from his pocket. In this condition the three unfortunates went to the cashier, with the object of getting some kind of credit. And what do you think the reply was?"

"I should think," said Marcel, "that they kept you as security, and sent them to the police station."

"You are wrong," said Mademoiselle Pinson. "Before going up to the supper-room, Rougette had taken their measure and paid for everything in advance. Imagine the sensation when Viot said to them: 'Gentlemen, the account is already settled!' Our unknown friends looked at us dumb-founded with woeful stupefaction mingled with pure gratitude. We, in the meantime, pretending not to notice anything, walked down and had a cab called.

" 'Dear Marquise,' said Rougette to me, 'we must take these gentle-men to their homes. . . .' 'Willingly, dear Comtesse,' I replied. Our poor lovers did not know what to say. Can you imagine how put out they were? They declined our offer, not wishing us to take them home, and would not give their addresses. . . . I really believe that they thought we were society ladies, and they lived in the rue du Chat-qui-pêche!"

The two student friends of Marcel, who, up to the present, had only smoked and drunk in silence, did not seem at all pleased with this story. They looked black; perhaps they knew as much as Mademoiselle Pinson did about this unlucky supper, for they looked at her uneasily as Marcel said to them, laughing:

"Give their names, Mademoiselle Mimi. As it was last week it will not hurt anyone."

"Never, Monsieur," replied the grisette. "One may laugh at any man, but damage his career, never. . . ."

"You are right," said Eugène, "and in this case you are perhaps acting more wisely than you think. Among all the young men who fill these schools, there is scarcely one who has not at some time or other made some mistake, or done some foolish thing, and yet the most respect-able and distinguished men in France come from them: doctors, magis-trates. . . ."

"Yes," responded Marcel, "that is true. There are peers of France who dine at Flicoteaux and do not always have the means to pay their bill. But," he added, winking, "have you never seen your friends again?"

"Who do you take us for?" replied Mademoiselle Pinson, in a serious and almost offended manner. "Do you know Blanchette and Rougette? And do you suppose that I . . .?"

"That's right," said Marcel, "don't be annoyed. But, listen, here is a nice trick. Three scatterbrains who have not perhaps sufficient to pay for their next day's dinner, and throw money away in order to mystify three poor devils as poor as themselves. . . ."

"Then why did they invite us to supper?" said Mademoiselle Pinson.

IV

With the cake appeared, in all its glory, the single bottle of champagne as dessert. With the wine the talk turned to singing. "I hear," said Marcel, "as Cervantes said, I hear Zelia coughing; that is a sign that she wants to sing. But, if these gentlemen agree, it is I who am being fêted, and give myself the pleasure of asking Mademoiselle Mimi, if telling her anecdote has not made her hoarse, to give us a song. Eugène," he added, "be agreeable and take a glass of wine with your neighbor, and beg her to sing a song for me."

Eugène blushed and obeyed. Just as Mademoiselle Pinson had not disdained to induce him to remain, he bowed and said to her: "Yes, Mademoiselle, we beg you to."

At the same time he raised his glass and touched that of the grisette. From this light contact arose a clear and silver note; Mademoiselle Pinson caught this note and sang it with a pure fresh voice.

"Yes, I will," she said, "for my glass has given me the 'la.' But what do you wish me to sing? I am not conceited, I would have you know, but I do not know any songs of the *corps de garde*. I do not fill my memory with such stuff. . . ."

"We know that," said Marcel, "you are above such stuff; go your own way, opinions are free."

"Well," resumed Mademoiselle Pinson, "I will sing you, to show there's no ill-feeling, some verses written about me."

"One minute. . . Who is the author?"

"My colleagues in the shop. It is what we compose while we are sewing, so you must not be too critical."

"Is there a chorus to your song?"

"Certainly; such a thing is always expected."

"In that case," said Marcel, "take your knives, and, when the chorus comes, beat on the table, but take care to do so in time. Zelia need not if she does not want to."

"Why not, rude boy?" demanded Zelia, angrily.

"For a very good reason," replied Marcel; "but if you wish to join in, take a cork, that will be less painful for our ears and your white hands."

Marcel had arranged all the glasses and plates in a circle and seated himself in the middle of the table, his knife in his hand. The two students, guests at Rougette's supper, a little more cheerful, removed the bowls of their pipes so as to beat with the wooden mouthpieces; Eugène dreamed, Zelia pouted. Mademoiselle Pinson took a plate and requested permission to break it, to which Marcel replied with a gesture of consent, so the singer, taking some pieces to use as castanets, began the song which her companions had composed, after having apologized for anything it contained flattering to herself. . . .

The knives and the pipes, even the chairs, had contributed their noise, of course, at the end of each verse. The glasses danced on the table and the bottles, half-full, rocked joyously, tapping each other's necks.

"And so your good friends," said Marcel, "composed that song for you? For my part I think it is too affected. Give me those good old songs in which they don't mind what they say . . ." And he tuned up in a loud voice:

"Nanette n'avait pas encore quinze ans . . ."

"Enough, enough," said Mademoiselle Pinson. "Let us dance, let us have a waltz. Can anyone here play?"

"I have what you want," said Marcel; "I have a guitar; but," he continued, while undoing the instrument, "my guitar is not all it should be; it lacks three of its strings."

"But here is a piano," said Zelia. "Marcel will play for our dance!"

Marcel glared at his mistress as if she had accused him of a crime. It was true he knew enough to play for a country-dance; but it was for him, as for many others, a species of torture to which he submitted very unwillingly.

Zelia, in betraying him, took her revenge for the cork.

"Are you mad?" said Marcel. "You know that that piano is only there for ornament and God knows you are the only one who can get anything out of it. Where did you get the idea that I could play dance music? I only know the *Marseillaise,* which I play with one finger. If you asked Eugène it would be much better; there is a boy who understands it, I am quite certain. You are the only one here sufficiently indiscreet to *do* such a thing without warning."

For the third time Eugène blushed and prepared, politely and tactfully, to do what he was asked. He sat down at the piano and a quadrille was arranged. This lasted nearly as long as the supper. After the quadrille came a waltz, after the waltz, the galop, for one still galops in the

Quartier Latin. The ladies especially were indefatigable, gambolling and shouting with laughter enough to wake the neighborhood. Soon Eugène, doubly tired by the noise and the late hour, fell into a sort of half-sleep, still playing mechanically, like the postilions who slumber whilst riding. The dancers moved to and fro in front of him like phantoms in a dream; and as there is nothing which makes a man melancholy so easily as listening to the laughter of others, melancholy, to which he was subject, took possession of him—Sorrowful joy, he thought, miserable pleasures . . . moments that one imagines snatched from sorrow. . . . And who knows which one of those five people dancing so gaily in front of me is certain of the wherewithal for tomorrow's dinner?

As he was thus reflecting, Mademoiselle Pinson passed near him; he thought he saw her, whilst dancing, take a piece of cake from the table and surreptitiously put it in her pocket.

V

It was nearly daybreak when the company separated. Eugène, before going home, walked about the streets for a short time to get some fresh air. Still possessed by his melancholy thoughts, he repeated quietly to himself the words of the grisette's song:

> *"Elle n'a qu'une robe au monde*
> *Et qu'un bonnet. . . ."*

"Is it possible?'" he said to himself. "Can misery get to such a pitch as to be freely shown and laughed at by one's own self? Can one laugh at one's lack of bread?"

The piece of cake that had been taken was a suspicious sign. Eugène could not help smiling and at the same time being moved with pity.

"Yet," he thought, "she took a piece of cake and not a piece of bread; perhaps this was greediness. Who knows? Perhaps it is a neighbor's child to whom she is taking a piece of cake, perhaps a talkative concierge, who would tell of her having passed a night out, a Cerberus to be appeased."

Not noticing where he was going, Eugène had wandered into that labyrinth of small streets behind the Carrefour Bucy, through which a carriage can scarcely pass. Just as he was retracing his steps, a woman came out of an old house, wrapped in an old dressing-gown, bare-headed, hair untidy, pale and wasted. She seemed so weak as to be scarcely able to walk; her knees bent; she leaned against the wall and seemed to want to go to a neighboring door where there was a letter-box, in which to post a letter that she held in her hand. Surprised and shocked, Eugène approached her and asked where was she going, what was she looking for, and could he help her. At the same time he put out his arm to support her, as she seemed about to fall to the ground. But without answering him, she drew back with a mixture of fear and pride. She placed her letter on a projection, pointed with her finger to the box, and seeming to summon all her strength, said: "There!" Then, still clinging to the wall, she returned to her house. Eugène vainly tried to make her take his arm and answer his questions. She returned slowly to the dark and narrow alley from which she had come.

Eugène had picked up the letter; he started to walk to the box to post it, but he hesitated. This strange encounter had troubled him greatly, and he felt overcome with a kind of horror mingled with a feeling of pity, so strong that, without thinking, he broke the seal almost involuntarily. It seemed to him hateful and impossible not to try, no matter how, to unravel such a mystery. Evidently that woman was dying; was it from illness or hunger? In all probability from misery. Eugène opened the letter: it was addressed: *À Monsieur le Baron de X.*, and contained the following:

Read this letter, Monsieur, and for pity's sake do not reject my appeal. You can save me, and you only. Believe me when I say to you, save me, and you will have done a good action, which will bring you happiness. I am suffering from a severe illness, which has deprived me of that small amount of strength and courage that I once had. In August last I returned to the shop; my belongings have been seized by my former landlady, and I am practically certain that before Saturday I shall find myself without shelter. I have such a horror of dying of starvation that I resolved this morning to drown myself, for I have had no food for nearly twenty-four hours. As soon as I thought of you, a ray of hope lit up in my heart. I pray that I have not deceived myself. Monsieur, on my knees I beseech you, however little you may do for me, let me live for a few more days; I am afraid of dying, for I am only twenty-three years old. . . . I shall perhaps, with a little help, succeed in surviving until the first of the next month. If I only knew with what words to arouse your pity, I would write them, but none come into my thoughts. I can only deplore my inability, for I am afraid you will treat my letter as is usually done when such are received: you will destroy it without thinking that a poor woman is there, watching the hours and the minutes go by in the hope that you would have thought it too cruel to leave her in such suspense.

It is not the idea of giving a louis, a small thing for you, that will restrain you, I am quite sure; it seems to me that nothing is simpler for you than to place your alms in an envelope and address it: "À Mademoiselle Bertin, 7, rue de l'Éperon." I have changed my name since going to work in a shop, as mine was my mother's. On leaving your house, give the letter to a commissionaire. I shall wait Thursday and Friday and pray fervently that something will soften your heart.

It occurs to me that you have no idea of such misery; but if you would see me you would be convinced.

Rougette.

If Eugène had at first been touched on reading these lines, one can well believe his astonishment when he saw the signature. So this was the same girl who had foolishly wasted her money on pleasure parties; and think of that ridiculous supper mentioned by Mademoiselle Pinson; it was she, reduced by misfortune to such suffering, and such an appeal. So much improvidence and folly appeared to Eugène as an unbelievable dream. But undoubtedly the signature was there; and Mademoiselle Pinson, in the course of the evening, had mentioned the *nom de guerre* of her friend Rougette, now become Mademoiselle Bertin. How was it that she found herself suddenly abandoned, without help, without bread, almost without shelter? What were her friends of yesterday doing, whilst she was perhaps dying in some attic of that house? And what kind of house was it in which one could exist in such a manner?

This was not the time for indulging in such surmises; it was most urgent to go and relieve the poor creature's starvation.

Eugène began by entering a provision shop, which had just been opened, and buying what he could find. That done, he proceeded, followed by a waiter, towards the lodging of Rougette; but he experienced a feeling of embarrassment at the thought of presenting himself so abruptly. The poor girl's pride, which he had discovered, made him fear, if not a refusal, at least a wound to her vanity; how to admit that he had read her letter? When he arrived at the door, he said to the waiter: "Do you know a young lady living in this house called Mademoiselle Bertin?"

"Oh yes, Monsieur," replied the waiter. "It is we who habitually serve her. But if Monsieur is going there, it is not the day. She is now in the country."

"Who told you that?" asked Eugène.

"Pardi, Monsieur . . . it was the concierge. Mademoiselle Rougette likes to dine well, but she does not like paying. She would as soon order roast chicken and lobsters as anything; but to get her money is a question of several visits. . . . We also know, in this neighborhood, when she is here and when she is away. . . ."

"She has returned," rejoined Eugène. "Go up to her room, deliver what you are carrying, and if she owes you anything, do not ask for it today. Should she wish to know who has sent her this, you will say it is the Baron de X."

With these words Eugène departed. On his way he readjusted, as well as he could, the seal of the letter and posted it. "After all," he thought, "Rougette will not refuse, and if she finds the answer to her letter somewhat prompt, she can get the explanation from her baron."

VI

But students, any more than grisettes, are not rich every day. Eugène understood full well that, to give an air of likelihood to the story that the waiter had to tell, he should have added the louis which Rougette had asked for to his gift; but there was the difficulty. Louis are not precisely common currency in the rue St. Jacques. On the other hand, Eugène had promised to pay the restaurant, but unfortunately at this moment his drawer was not better furnished than his pocket. That is why it was that, without any delay, he went on his way to the Place du Panthéon.

At this time there lived in this Place that famous barber who by going bankrupt ruined himself whilst ruining others. There, in the back shop, was carried on in secret large and small usury, where students poor and careless, perhaps in love, borrowed money at enormous interest, spending it gaily in the evening and paying dearly for it next morning. Grisettes entered there furtively, with lowered head and shamed look, borrowing in order to go to a country party, on a faded hat, a dyed shawl, a chemise bought at the pawnshop. There, young men of good family, having need of twenty-five louis, signed bills for two or three thousand francs. Minors spent their fortune before they had got it; the imprudent ruined their families and threw away their future. From the titled courtesan, longing for a bracelet, to the necessitous college servant coveting a hare or a plate of lentils, all went there as if to the springs of Pactolus, and the usurious barber, proud of his clients and his exploits to the point of boasting about them, kept the prison of Clichy in repair pending his own visit there.

This was the dismal resort to which Eugène went, though with much repugnance, to get the means to help Rougette, or to be in the position to do so; because it did not seem certain to him that the appeal addressed to the baron would produce the desired result. To run into debt for someone unknown was really an act of great charity on the part of the student; but as Eugène believed in God, every good action was a duty to Him.

The first face he saw on entering was that of his friend Marcel, seated in front of a mirror, a towel round his neck, pretending to be having his hair done. The poor fellow had probably come to procure the where-withal to pay for his supper of the previous evening; he seemed very pre-occupied and frowned with an air of dissatisfaction, whilst the barber, pretending on his part to curl his hair with a cold instrument, talked to him in a subdued Gascon accent. Facing another mirror in a small cabinet, a very restless stranger was seated, also wrapped in a towel, looking ceaselessly round about him, and one saw, through the partly opened door of the back shop, in an old cheval glass, the somewhat thin silhouette of a young woman who, aided by the wife of the barber, was trying on a dress of Scotch plaid.

"What are you doing here at this hour of the day?" cried Marcel, whose face regained its customary expression of good humor as soon as he recognized his friend.

Eugène sat himself by the mirror and explained in a few words the encounter he had had and the purpose that had brought him here.

"Ma foi!" said Marcel, "you are really sincere? As there is a baron why mix yourself up in it? You saw an interesting young lady apparently in need of food; you bought her a cold chicken, which was worthy of you; there is nothing more to be said. You do not ask any gratitude from her, you are pleased to remain incognito; this is heroic, to go a little further, it is chivalrous. To pledge one's watch or signature for a seamstress kept by a baron, and whom one has not the honor of visiting, has never been done in human memory, except in the Bibliothèque Bleue."

"Laugh at me if you like," said Eugène. "I know that there are many more unfortunates in the world than I can help. Those that I cannot help have my pity; but if I meet one I must help. Whatever I do, it is impossible for me to remain indifferent in the face of suffering. My charity does not go so far as to look for cases, I am not rich enough for that; but when I find a case I give."

"In that event," said Marcel, "you have much to do; you will find no lack of applicants in this country."

"What does it matter?" said Eugène, still moved by the incident of which he had just been a witness. "Is it better to let these people die and pass on one's way? That unfortunate girl is scatterbrained, flippant, anything you like to call her; she does not perhaps deserve the compassion which she evokes; but this compassion, I feel it sincerely. Is it better to act like her intimates, who hardly seem to worry about her any more than if she were dead, and who yesterday were only too pleased to lend a hand in her downfall?

"To whom could she turn to help? To a stranger who would light his cigar with her letter, or to Mademoiselle Pinson, I suppose, who is always dining out and going the pace, whilst her friend just—starves? I must say, my dear Marcel, that all that upsets me profoundly. That thoughtless little creature of yesterday evening, with her snatches of song and vulgar jokes, laughing and babbling at your party, at the time when the other, the heroine of her story, is dying in a loft. It makes my heart sick. To live in that way, as friends, almost as sisters, for days and weeks, going the round of theatres, dances, cafés, and not to know from one day to another whether one is dead or the other alive, it is worse than the indifference of the *égoïsts,* it is the indifference of an animal. Your Mademoiselle Pinson is a monster, and your grisettes that you boast about, their shameless manners, their butterfly friendships, I know nothing so contemptible!"

The barber, who, during this discourse had listened in silence, continuing to manipulate his cold tongs over Marcel's head, smiled maliciously as Eugène stopped talking.

In this way, chattering like a magpie, or rather like the barber that he was, when it was a question of something being said with an ulterior motive, taciturn and laconic, like a Spartan, as soon as things were moving, it was his habit always to let his clients speak first before joining in the conversation. The indignation which Eugène expressed in such violent terms nevertheless made him break his habitual silence.

"You are severe, M'sieur," said he, smiling rather boastfully. "I have the honour to *coiffer* Mademoiselle Mimi, and I believe she is a very kind-hearted creature."

"Yes," said Eugène, "excellent, as far as that goes, when it's a question of drinking or smoking!"

"Possibly," retorted the barber, "I do not deny it; these youngsters, they laugh, they sing, they smoke; but they are mostly very good-hearted."

"What are you trying to make out, *père* Cadedis?" asked Marcel. "Not so much tact; come to the point!"

"I'll prove it to you," replied the barber, pointing to the back shop, "that there is there, hanging on a hook, a little black silk dress that you gentlemen doubtless know, if you know the owner, for she does not possess a very extensive wardrobe. Mademoiselle Mimi sent me this dress early this morning; and I presume that, if she has not helped *la petite* Rougette, it is that she herself is not too well off."

"That's a strange thing," said Marcel, rising and going into the back shop, without consideration for the poor girl who was still trying on her tartan dress. "Mimi's song was hardly true to fact, as she had been forced to pawn her frock. But in the devil's name in what does she go visiting now? Isn't she calling on anybody now, then?"

Eugène had followed his friend.

The barber had not deceived them: in a dim corner, mixed up with all sorts and kinds of clothes, Mademoiselle Pinson's only dress was drooping humbly and sadly.

"That's actually it," said Marcel. "I recognize the frock, having seen it when it was quite new, eighteen months ago. It is the working dress, riding habit and afternoon frock of Mademoiselle Mimi. There should be on the left cuff a little stain about the size of a franc, caused by a drop of champagne. And how much have you lent on that, *père* Cadedis? For I suppose that that dress is not sold, and is only to be found in this boudoir as a pledge?"

"I have lent four francs," replied the barber, "and I assure you, M'sieur, that it was pure charity. To any other I would not have advanced more than forty sous; the dress is worn out, one can see through it, the whole thing's transparent. But I know that Mademoiselle Mimi will pay me; she is always good for four francs."

"Poor Mimi!" sighed Marcel. "I'll eat my hat if she's not borrowed this trifling sum to send to Rougette."

"Or to pay some pressing debt," said Eugène.

"No," said Marcel, "I know Mimi; I don't think she'd strip herself for a creditor."

"That may be true," said the barber. "I knew Mademoiselle Mimi in a better position than that in which she now finds herself; she had then a quantity of debts. One arrived daily to seize what she possessed, and one finished, as far as that goes, by taking all her furniture, except her bed, for you gentlemen will doubtless be aware that a debtor's bed cannot be seized. But Mademoiselle Mimi had at this time four very nice dresses. She put all four of them one on top of the other, and she went to bed on top of them so as to prevent their being seized; that is why I was surprised that, not having more than one dress now, she pledged it to pay somebody."

"Poor Mimi," repeated Marcel; "but how does she actually manage? Has she been gulling her friends? Has she got a dress we know nothing about? Has she made herself ill through eating too much sticky cake? As far as that goes, if she is in bed there's no necessity for her to dress. That's no matter, *père* Cadedis, the sight of that dress hurts me, with its dangling cuffs which seem to ask for help; here, take back four francs from the thirty-five livres that you were going to advance me, and wrap up the dress, and I will return it to the poor child. Well, Eugène," he continued, "what does your Christian charity say to that?"

"That you are right," responded Eugène, "to talk and act as you do, but perhaps for my part I am not wrong; I will have a bet on it if you like."

"Right," said Marcel, "let us have a cigar on it, like the members of the Jockey Club. You have nothing more to do here. I have thirty-one francs—we are rich! Let us go and see Mademoiselle Pinson; I am anxious to call on her."

He put the dress under his arm, and the two of them went out of the shop.

VII

"Mademoiselle has gone to Mass," the concierge informed the two students, when they arrived at the lodging of Mademoiselle Pinson.

"To Mass!" exclaimed Eugène in surprise.

"To Mass!" repeated Marcel. "It is impossible, she has not gone out; let us go in; we are old friends."

"I assure you, M'sieur," replied the concierge, "that she has actually gone out to Mass, about three-quarters of an hour ago."

"And which church has she gone to?"

"To St. Sulpice, as she always does; she never misses a day."

"Yes, yes, I know she plays to *le bon Dieu;* but it seems strange to me that she has gone out today."

"Here she is coming back, M'sieur; she is just coming down the street; you can see her for yourself."

In fact Mademoiselle Pinson, having left the church, was returning home.

Marcel had no sooner caught sight of her than he ran towards her, impatient to see her rig-out from close up. She had for a dress a skirt of dark Indian print, partially covered by a green serge curtain; out of which she had contrived a sort of shawl. Her graceful head, set off by a white bonnet, emerged from this singular garb, which owing to its somber color passed without comment, and her tiny feet were shod in dainty little boots.

She had draped herself in her curtain with such care and art that it really looked like a genuine old shawl, so that one scarcely saw the bound edge of it. In short, she had found the means of pleasing the eye in this contrivance, and of proving again to the world that a pretty woman is a pretty woman anyhow.

"How do you like me?" she said to the two young men, slightly parting her "curtain," and letting them have a glimpse of her finely-moulded figure, modelled by her corsets. "It is a morning deshabille that Palmir has just sent me."

"You are charming," said Marcel. *"Ma foi,* I would not have believed that anyone could look so effective in a window curtain!"

"Really," replied Mademoiselle Pinson, "in spite of the fact that I feel rather like a tied-up sachet."

"Sachet of roses," responded Marcel. "I almost regret now having brought you your dress."

"My dress? Where did you find it?"

"Where it was, apparently."

"Then you have liberated it from slavery?"

"Yes, indeed, I have ransomed it. Are you annoyed with me for my temerity?"

"Certainly not, if I may recoup you. I am very pleased indeed to see my dress again; for, to tell you the truth, the two of us have lived together for so long that I have become unconsciously very attached to it."

So speaking Mademoiselle Pinson tripped briskly up the five flights of stairs which led to her little room, which the two friends entered with her.

"I can only return you this dress on one condition," said Marcel.

"How shameful," ejaculated the grisette. "What nonsense! Conditions? I'll have nothing to do with them."

"I have made a bet," said Marcel; "you must tell us frankly why this dress was pawned."

"Let me first of all put it on," replied Mademoiselle Pinson; "I will then give you the reason. But I must warn you that if you will not use my wardrobe, or the gutter, as an antechamber you must cover your face like Agamemnon."

"We can't agree to that, we're better behaved than you think, and wouldn't even steal a glimpse."

"Wait," replied Mademoiselle Pinson. "I have every confidence in you, but experience tells us that two precautions are better than one."

Saying this she took off her curtain and put it gently over the heads of the two friends, and in such a way as to render them completely blind.

"Don't move," she said to them, "It's only for a second."

"Take care of yourself," said Marcel, "if there's a hole in the curtain I will answer for nothing. You will not be satisfied with our word, consequently it is withdrawn."

"Happily, so is my dress," said Mademoiselle Pinson; "and my figure as well," she added, laughing, and throwing the curtain on the floor. "Poor little dress! It seems to me quite new. It gives me great pleasure to snuggle in it again!"

"And your secret—you will tell it to us now? Listen! The truth! We're not given to gossiping. How and why a young person like you, knowing, experienced, virtuous and modest, could all at once put the whole of her wardrobe in pawn, at one fell swoop."

"Why, why?" replied Mademoiselle Pinson, seeming to hesitate. Then, taking the two young men, each by an arm, she said to them, pushing them towards the door: "Come with me and you shall see."

As Marcel expected, she took them to the rue de l'Éperon.

VIII

Marcel had won his bet. The four francs and Mademoiselle Pinson's piece of cake were on Rougette's table, with the remains of Eugène's chicken.

The poor invalid was a bit better, but still confined to her bed; and whatever her gratitude was towards her unknown benefactor, she made her friend tell these gentlemen that she asked to be excused, but she was not in a condition to receive them.

"How well I know that touch," said Marcel; "she would die on the straw in an attic, but she would still behave like a duchess in front of her water-jug."

The two friends, with much regret, were than obliged to return home as they had come, not without laughing together at the pride and discretion so strangely manifested in a garret.

After having been to the School of Medicine for their daily lecture they dined together, and the evening having set in they took a turn up and down the boulevard des Italiens. There, still smoking the cigar he had won in the morning:

"With all this," said Marcel, "are you not obliged to admit that I have at heart reason to love and also to esteem these poor creatures? Let us consider temperately these matters from a philosophic point of view. This little Mimi, whom you have abused so, has she not, in depriving herself of her dress, done an action more praiseworthy, more meritorious, I even venture to say more Christian, than the good King Robert in allowing a poor creature to cut a piece off his mantle? The good King Robert, on the one hand, had no doubt plenty of mantles; on the other hand, he was seated at table, said the historian, when a beggar approached him, dragging himself along on hands and knees, and with a pair of scissors cut the gold fringe from his sovereign. This the queen considered was taking a liberty, but the dignified monarch actually pardoned the thief; perhaps he had dined well! Reflect, what a difference between him and Mimi! Mimi, when she had learnt of Rougette's misfortune, was undoubtedly fasting, for you can rest assured that the piece of cake she took away from my supper was destined in advance to form her own breakfast. But what did she do? Instead of breakfasting, she goes to Mass, and in so doing she shows herself once more the equal of King Robert, who was very pious, I admit it, but who wasted his time singing to the lute whilst the Normans ran wild. King Robert let his friends go hang, and actually he retained the mantle. Mimi sent her complete wardrobe to *père* Cadedis, an incomparable action in that Mimi is a woman, young, pretty, coquettish and poor; and take special note, that this dress is necessary to her so that she can go as usual to her shop, to earn her daily bread. Not only then does she deprive herself of the piece of cake which she was going to feast on, but she voluntarily puts herself into the positon of not being able to dine. Moreover, notice that *père* Cadedis is far from being a beggar, and dragging himself on all fours under the table. King Robert, giving up his fringe, did not make any great sacrifice, because it was cut off before he noticed it. It is not known whether this fringe was cut across or not, and if it was possible to mend it; whilst Mimi, voluntarily, far from expecting that she would have her dress stolen, herself tears this covering from her poor body, more precious, more useful than the tinsel of all the lace-makers in Paris. She goes out draped in a curtain; but rest assured that she would not have gone out in this garb to any other place than the church. She would sooner have an arm cut off than show herself arrayed in a bundle of rags at the Luxembourg or the Tuileries; but she dares to show herself to God, because it is the time for her daily prayer. Believe me, Eugène, there is more courage and real religion in Mimi crossing in her curtain the place St. Michel, rue de Tournon and rue de Petit Lion, where she is known to everybody, than in all the hymns of good King Robert, of which all the world talked, from the fat Bossuet to the thin Anquetil, whereas Mimi will die unknown in her fifth story between a pot of flowers and a half-finished dress."

"All the better for her," said Eugène.

"If I wished," resumed Marcel, "to continue to make comparisons, I could draw you a parallel between Mucius Scævola and Rougette. Do you believe, as far as that goes, that it would be more difficult for a Roman of the time of Tarquin to keep his arm for five minutes over a lighted fire than for a present-day grisette to go without food for twenty-four hours? Neither one nor the other made any plaint, but look into their reasons. Mucius was in the middle of a camp, in the presence of an Etruscan king whom he had tried to assassinate; he failed lamentably, he was in the hands of the soldiery. What was going through his mind? Bravado? So that he should be admired before he was hanged? He burnt his fingers with a brand, but it has not been proved that the brazier was really hot, nor that the finger was incinerated. Upon which, the dignified Porsenna, astounded by this high-flown gesture, pardoned him and sent him home. It is debatable if the said Porsenna, capable of such generosity, cut a good figure, and whether Scævola had reason to suppose that in sacrificing his arm he would save his head. Rougette, on the contrary, endures patiently the most horrible, the most tedious of tortures, that of hunger; no one was taking any notice of her. She is alone in the corner of a garret, she has neither Porsenna to admire her, that is to say the baron, nor the Romans, that is to say the neighbors, nor the Etrucans, that is to say her creditors, nor even the brazier, for her stove was out. But why did she suffer without complaint? First, from vanity, that is certain; but the case of Mucius was the same; from nobility of soul, then, and that constitutes her glory; for if she remained quiet behind her locked door it is precisely in order that her friends should not know she was dying, so that she should be spared the humiliation of pity, so that her friend Pinson, whom she knew to be kind-hearted and thoroughly devoted, should not be obliged, as she had done previously, to give her her dress and her food. Mucius, in Rougette's place, would have pretended to die in silence, but that would have been at the cross-roads or some other public place. His taciturn and sublime vanity would have found a delicate way of hinting for a glass of wine and a crust. It is true Rougette asked the baron, whom I insist on comparing with Porsenna, for a louis, but you must realize that the baron was really indebted to Rougette for many kindnesses. That is clear to the least observant. As you have, moreover, wisely remarked, it was possible that the baron was in the country, and if this were so Rougette was lost. And do not think that you can confound me with the usual platitude with which one refers to all the good deeds of women, that they do not know what they are doing, and that they run towards danger as cats make for the tiles. Rougette knows what death means; she has seen it at first hand on the pont d'Jena, for she has already thrown herself in the water once, and I asked her if she had suffered. She said no, that she had felt nothing, except at the moment when she was hauled out, for the boatmen had dragged her by the legs, and they had, so she said, grazed her head on the side of the boat."

"Enough!" said Eugène, "spare me your gruesome pleasantries. Answer me seriously: do you believe that such horrible instances, often repeated, always menacing, can eventually have any good result? These poor girls, living alone, with nothing behind them, without advice, have they enough native good sense to counterbalance their lack of experience? Is there a familiar spirit in attendance on them, who condemns them always to ill-luck and misfortune, but, in spite of such vagaries can they return to better things? Here is one who prays to God, you say; she goes to church, performs her devotions, lives honestly by her work; her friends appear to hold her in esteem; and you other blackguards, you do not treat her yourselves with your usual thoughtlessness. Here is another who goes from one blunder to another, from prodigality to the pangs of hunger. Indeed, she will always have in mind the cruel lessons she has learned. Do you believe that with wise counsel, regular habits, a little help, one could make such women into reasonable beings? If there are any such, tell me. An opportunity is presented to us; let us make our way to poor Rougette; she is doubtless still suffering a great deal, and her friend watches by her bedside. Do not discourage me, let me take action; I would like to guide them back to the straight path, to speak to them in all sincerity; I do not wish to preach to or reproach them. I want to go to them, take their hands, and say to them . . ."

At this moment the two friends passed in front of the café Tortoni. The silhouettes of the two young women, who were eating ices in front of a window, were thrown up by the bright lights. One of them waved her handkerchief and the other one burst out laughing.

"By jingo," exclaimed Marcel, "if you wish to speak to them, we've only to cross the road, for there they are, God bless me! I recognize Mimi by her dress, and Rougette by her white feather, always to be found where there is something good to eat! It appears that M'sieur le baron has done his part handsomely!"

"Does not such irresponsibility frighten you?" said Eugène.

"Undoubtedly," replied Marcel; "but I beg of you when you speak disparingly of grisettes make an exception of the little Pinson. She recited to us the history of a supper, she pawned her dress for four francs, she made herself a mantle out of a curtain; and who says what he knows, who gives what he has, who does what he can, is not called upon to do more."

6

One of Cleopatra's Nights

THÉOPHILE GAUTIER

NINETEEN hundred years ago from the date of this writing, a magnificiently gilded and painted cangia was descending the Nile as rapidly as fifty long, flat oars, which seemed to crawl over the furrowed water like the legs of a gigantic scarabæus, could impel it.

This cangia was narrow, long, elevated at both ends in the form of a new moon, elegantly proportioned, and admirably built for speed; the figure of a ram's head, surmounted by a golden globe, armed the point of the prow, showing that the vessel belonged to some personage of royal blood.

In the center of the vessel arose a flat-roofed cabin—a sort of *naos,* or tent of honor—colored and gilded, ornamented with palm-leaf mouldings, and lighted by four little square windows.

Two chambers, both decorated with hieroglyphic paintings, occupied the horns of the crescent. One of them, the larger, had a second story of lesser height built upon it, like the *chateaux gaillards* of those fantastic galleys of the sixteenth century drawn by Della-Bella; the other and smaller chamber, which also served as a pilot-house, was surmounted with a triangular pediment.

In lieu of a rudder, two immense oars, adjusted upon stakes decorated with stripes of paint, which served in place of our modern row-locks, extended into the water in rear of the vessel like the webbed feet of a swan; heads crowned with *pshents,* and bearing the allegorical horn upon their chins, were sculptured upon the handles of these huge oars, which were maneuvered by the pilot as he stood upon the deck of the cabin above.

He was a swarthy man, tawny as new bronze, with bluish surface gleams playing over his dark skin; long oblique eyes, hair deeply black and all plaited into little cords, full lips, high cheek-bones, ears standing out from the skull—the Egyptian type in all its purity. A narrow strip of cotton about his loins, together with five or six strings of glass beads and a few amulets, comprised his whole costume.

He appeared to be the only one on board the cangia; for the rowers bending over their oars, and concealed from view by the gunwales, made their presence known only through the symmetrical movements of the oars themselves, which spread open alternately on either side of the vessel, like the ribs of a fan, and fell regularly back into the water after a short pause.

Not a breath of air was stirring; and the great triangular sail of the cangia, tied up and bound to the lowered mast with a silken cord, testified that all hope of the wind rising had been abandoned.

The noonday sun shot his arrows perpendicularly from above; the ashen-hued slime of the river banks reflected the fiery glow; a raw light, glaring and blinding in its intensity, poured down in torrents of flame; the azure of the sky whitened in the heat as a metal whitens in the furnace; an ardent and lurid fog smoked in the horizon. Not a cloud appeared in the sky—a sky mournful and changeless as Eternity.

The water of the Nile, sluggish and wan, seemed to slumber in its course, and slowly extend itself in sheets of molten tin. No breath of air wrinkled its surface, or bowed down upon their stalks the cups of the lotus-flowers, as rigidly motionless as though sculptured; at long intervals the leap of a bechir or fabaka expanding its belly scarcely caused a silvery gleam upon the current; and the oars of the cangia seemed with difficulty to tear their way through the fuliginous film of that curdled water. The banks were desolate, a solemn and mighty sadness weighed upon this land, which was never aught else than a vast tomb, and in which the living appeared to be solely occupied in the work of burying the dead. It was an arid sadness, dry as pumice stone, without melancholy, without reverie, without one pearly gray cloud to follow toward the horizon, one secret spring wherein to lave one's dusty feet; the sadness of a sphinx weary of eternally gazing upon the desert, and unable to detach herself from the granite socle upon which she has sharpened her claws for twenty centuries.

So profound was the silence that it seemed as though the world had become dumb, or that the air had lost all power of conveying sound. The only noises which could be heard at intervals were the whisperings and stifled "chuckling" of the crocodiles, which, enfeebled by the heat, were wallowing among the bullrushes by the river banks; or the sound made by some ibis, which, tired of standing with one leg doubled up against its stomach, and its head sunk between its shoulders, suddenly abandoned its motionless attitude, and, brusquely whipping the blue air with its white wings, flew off to perch upon an obelisk or a palm-tree.

The cangia flew like an arrow over the smooth river-water, leaving behind it a silvery wake which soon disappeared; and only a few foam-bubbles rising to break at the surface of the stream bore testimony to the passage of the vessel, then already out of sight.

The ochre-hued or salmon-colored banks unrolled themselves rapidly, like scrolls of papyrus, between the double azure of water and sky so similar in tint that the slender tongue of earth which separated them seemed like a causeway stretching over an immense lake, and that it would have been difficult to determine whether the Nile reflected the sky, or whether the sky reflected the Nile.

The scene continually changed. At one moment were visible gigantic propylæa, whose sloping walls, painted with large panels of fantastic figures, were mirrored in the river; pylons with broad-bulging capitals; stairways guarded by huge crouching sphinxes, wearing caps with lappets of many folds, and crossing their paws of black basalt below their sharply projecting breasts; palaces, immeasurably vast, projecting against the horizon the severe horizontal lines of their entablatures, where the emblematic globe unfolded its mysterious wings like an eagle's vast-extending pinions; temples with enormous columns thick as towers, on which were limned processions of hieroglyphic figures against a background of brilliant white—all the monstrosities of that Titanic architecture. Again the eye beheld only landscapes of desolate aridity—hills formed of stony fragments from excavations and building works, crumbs of that gigantic debauch of granite which lasted for more than thirty centuries; mountains exfoliated by heat, and mangled and striped with black lines which seemed like the cauterizations of a conflagration; hillocks humped and deformed, squatting like the criocephalus of the tombs, and projecting the outlines of their misshapen attitude against the sky-line; expanses of greenish clay, reddle, flour-white tufa; and from time to time some steep cliff of dry, rose-colored granite, where yawned the black mouths of the stone quarries.

This aridity was wholly unrelieved; no oasis of foliage refreshed the eye; green seemed to be a color unknown to that nature; only some meager palm-tree, like a vegetable crab, appeared from time to time in the horizon; or a thorny fig-tree brandished its tempered leaves like sword blades of bronze; or a carthamus-plant, which had found a little moisture to live upon in the shadow of some fragment of a broken column, relieved the general uniformity with a speck of crimson.

After this rapid glance at the aspect of the landscape, let us return to the cangia with its fifty rowers, and, without announcing ourselves, enter boldly into the *naos* of honor.

The interior was painted white with green arabesques, bands of vermillion, and gilt flowers fantastically shaped; an exceedingly fine rush matting covered the floor; at the further end stood a little bed, supported upon griffin's feet, having a back resembling that of a modern lounge or sofa; a stool with four steps to enable one to climb into bed; and (rather an odd luxury according to our ideas of comfort) a sort of hemicycle of cedar wood, supported upon a single leg, and designed to fit the nape of the neck so as to support the head of the person reclining.

Upon this strange pillow reposed a most charming head, one look of which once caused the loss of half a world; an adorable, a divine head; the head of the most perfect woman that ever lived; the most womanly and most queenly of all women; an admirable type of beauty which the imagination of poets could never invest with any new grace, and which dreamers will find forever in the depth of their dreams—it is not necessary to name Cleopatra.

Beside her stood her favorite slave Charmion, waving a large fan of ibis feathers; and a young girl was moistening with scented water the little reed blinds attached to the windows of the *naos,* so that the air might only enter impregnated with fresh odors.

Near the bed of repose, in a striped vase of alabaster with a slender neck and a peculiarly elegant, tapering shape, vaguely recalling the form of a heron, was placed a bouquet of lotus-flowers, some of a celestial blue, others of a tender rose-color, like the finger-tips of Isis the great goddess.

Either from caprice or policy, Cleopatra did not wear the Greek dress that day. She had just attended a panegyris,* and was returning to her summer palace still clad in the Egyptian costume she had worn at the festival.

Perhaps our fair readers will feel curious to know how Queen Cleopatra was attired on her return from the Mammisi of Hermonthis whereat were worshipped the holy triad of the god Mandou, the goddess Ritho, and their son, Harphra; luckily we are able to satisfy them in this regard.

For headdress Queen Cleopatra wore a kind of very light helmet of beaten gold, fashioned in the form of the body and wings of the sacred

---

* *Panegyris;* pl., *panegyreis,* from the Greek πανήγρις, signifies the meeting of a whole people to worship at a common sanctuary or participate in a national religious festival. The assemblies at the Olympic, Pythian, Nemean, or Isthmian games were in this sense *panegyreis.* See Smith's Dict. Antiq. [Trans.]

partridge. The wings, opening downward like fans, covered the temples, and extending below, almost to the neck, left exposed on either side, through a small aperture, an ear rosier and more delicately curled than the shell whence arose that Venus whom the Egyptians named Athor; the tail of the bird occupied that place where our women wear their chignons; its body, covered with imbricated feathers, and painted in variegated enamel, concealed the upper part of the head; and its neck, gracefully curving forward over the forehead of the wearer, formed together with its little head a kind of horn-shaped ornament, all sparkling with precious stones; a symbolic crest, designed like a tower, completed this odd but elegant headdress. Hair dark as a starless night flowed from beneath this helmet, and streamed in long tresses over the fair shoulders whereof the commencement only, alas! was left exposed by a collarette, or goret, adorned with many rows of serpentine stones, azodrachs, and chrysoberyls; a linen robe diagonally cut—a mist of material, of woven air, *ventus textilis* as Petronius says, undulated in vapory whiteness about a lovely body whose outlines it scarcely shaded with the softest shading. This robe had half-sleeves, tight at the shoulder, but widening toward the elbows like our *manches-à-sabot,* and permitting a glimpse of an adorable arm and a perfect hand, the arm being clasped by six golden bracelets, and the hand adorned with a ring representing the sacred scarabæus. A girdle, whose knotted ends hung down in front, confined this free-floating tunic at the waist; a short cloak adorned with fringing completed the costume; and, if a few barbarous words will not frighten Parisian ears, we might add that the robe was called *schenti,* and the short cloak, *calisiris.*

Finally, we may observe that Queen Cleopatra wore very thin, light sandals, turned up at the toes, and fastened over the instep, like the *souliers-à-la-poulaine* of the mediæval *chatelaines.*

But Queen Cleopatra did not wear that air of satisfaction which becomes a woman conscious of being perfectly beautiful and perfectly well dressed. She tossed and turned in her little bed, and her sudden movements momentarily disarranged the folds of her gauzy *conopeum,* which Charmion as often rearranged with inexhaustible patience, and without ceasing to wave her fan.

"This room is stifling," said Cleopatra; "even if Pthah the God of Fire established his forges in here, he could not make it hotter; the air is like the breath of a furnace!" And she moistened her lips with the tip of her little tongue, and stretched out her hand like a feverish patient seeking an absent cup.

Charmion, ever attentive, at once clapped her hands. A black slave clothed in a short tunic hanging in folds like an Albanian petticoat, and a panther-skin thrown over his shoulders, entered with the suddenness of an apparition; with his left hand balancing a tray laden with cups, and slices of watermelon, and carrying in his right a long vase with a spout like a modern teapot.

The slave filled one of these cups, pouring the liquor into it from a considerable height with marvellous dexterity, and placed it before the queen. Cleopatra merely touched the beverage with her lips, laid the cup down beside her, and turning upon Charmion her beautiful liquid black eyes, lustrous with living light, exclaimed:

"O Charmion, I am weary unto death!"

II

Charmion, at once anticipating a confidence, assumed a look of pained sympathy, and drew nearer to her mistress.

"I am horribly weary!" continued Cleopatra, letting her arms fall like one utterly discouraged. "This Egypt crushes, annihilates me; this sky with its implacable azure is sadder than the deep night of Erebus; never a cloud, never a shadow, and always that red, sanguine sun, which glares down upon you like the eye of a Cyclops. Ah, Charmion, I would give a pearl for one drop of rain! From the inflamed pupil of that sky of bronze no tear has ever yet fallen upon the desolation of this land; it is only a vast covering for a tomb—the dome of a necropolis; a sky dead and dried up like the mummies it hangs over; it weighs upon my shoulders like an over-heavy mantle; it constrains and terrifies me; it seems to me that I could not stand up erect without striking my forehead against it. And, moreover, this land is truly an awful land; all things in it are gloomy, enigmatic, incomprehensible. Imagination has produced in it only monstrous chimeras and monuments immeasurable; this architecture and this art fill me with fear; those colossi, whose stone-entangled limbs compel them to remain eternally sitting with their hands upon their knees, weary me with their stupid immobility; they trouble my eyes and my horizon. When, indeed, shall the giant come who is to take them by the hand and relieve them from their long watch of twenty centuries? For even granite itself must grow weary at last! Of what master, then, do they await the coming, to leave their mountain-seats and rise in token of respect? Of what invisible flock are those huge sphinxes the guardians, crouching like dogs on the watch, that they never close their eyelids, and forever extend their claws in readiness to seize? Why are their stony eyes so obstinately fixed upon eternity and infinity? What weird secret do their firmly locked lips retain within their breasts? On the right hand, on the left, whithersoever one turns, only frightful monsters are visible— dogs with the heads of men; men with the heads of dogs; chimeras begotten of hideous couplings in the shadowy depths of the labyrinths; figures of Anubis, Typhon, Osiris; partridges with great yellow eyes that seem to pierce through you with their inquisitorial gaze, and see beyond and behind you things which one dare not speak of—a family of animals and horrible gods with scaly wings, hooked beaks, trenchant claws, ever ready to seize and devour you should you venture to cross the threshold of the temple, or lift a corner of the veil.

"Upon the walls, upon the columns, on the ceilings, on the floors, upon palaces and temples, in the long passages and the deepest pits of the necropoli, even within the bowels of the earth where light never comes, and where the flames of the torches die for want of air, forever and everywhere are sculptured and painted interminable hieroglyphics, telling in language unintelligible of things which are no longer known, and which belong, doubtless, to the vanished creations of the past—prodigious buried works wherein a whole nation was sacrificed to write the epitaph of one king! Mystery and granite—this is Egypt! Truly a fair land for a young woman, and a young queen.

"Menacing and funereal symbols alone meet the eye—the emblems of the *pedum,* the *tau,* allegorical globes, coiling serpents, and the scales in which souls are weighed—the Unknown, death, nothingness. In the place of any vegetation only *stelæ* limned with weird characters; instead of avenues of trees, avenues of granite obelisks; in lieu of soil, vast pavements of granite for which whole mountains could each furnish but one slab; in place of a sky, ceilings of granite—eternity made palpable, a bitter and everlasting sarcasm upon the frailty and brevity of life—stairways built only for the limbs of Titans, which the human foot cannot ascend save by the aid of ladders; columns that a hundred arms cannot encircle; labyrinths in which one might travel for years without discovering the termination—the vertigo of enormity, the drunkenness of the gigantic, the reckless efforts of that pride which would at any cost engrave its name deeply upon the face of the world.

"And, moreover, Charmion, I tell you a thought haunts me which terrifies me. In other lands of the earth, corpses are burned, and their ashes soon mingle with the soil. Here, it is said that the living have no other occupation than that of preserving the dead. Potent balms save them from destruction; the remains endure after the soul has evaporated. Beneath this people lie twenty peoples; each city stands upon twenty layers of necropoli; each generation which passes away leaves a population of mummies to a shadowy city. Beneath the father you find the grandfather and the great-grandfather in their gilded and painted boxes, even as they were during life; and should you dig down forever, forever you would still find the underlying dead.

"When I think upon those bandage-swathed myriads—those multitudes of parched specters who fill the sepulchral pits, and who have been there for two thousand years face to face in their own silence, which nothing ever breaks, not even the noise which the graveworms make in crawling, and who will be found intact after yet another two thousand years, with their crocodiles, their cats, their ibises, and all things that lived in their lifetime—then terrors seize me, and I feel my flesh creep. What do they mutter to each other? For they still have lips, and every ghost would find its body in the same state as when it quitted it, if they should all take the fancy to return.

"Ah, truly is Egypt a sinister kingdom and little suited to me, the laughter-loving and merry one. Everything in it encloses a mummy; that is the heart and the kernel of all things. After a thousand turns you must always end there; the Pyramids themselves hide sarcophagi. What nothingness and madness is this! Disembowel the sky with gigantic triangles of stone—you cannot thereby lengthen your corpse an inch. How can one rejoice and live in a land like this, where the only perfume you can respire is the acrid odor of the naphtha and bitumen which boil in the caldrons of the embalmers, to where the very flooring of your chamber sounds hollow because the corridors of the hypogeum and the mortuary pits extend even under your alcove? To be the queen of mummies, to have none to converse with but statues in constrained and rigid attitudes—this is, in truth, a cheerful lot. Again, if I only had some heartfelt passion to relieve this melancholy, some interest in life; if I could but love somebody or something; if I were even loved; but I am not.

"This is why I am weary, Charmion. With love, this grim and arid Egypt would seem to me fairer than even Greece with her ivory gods, her temples of snowy marble, her groves of laurel, and fountains of living water. There I should never dream of the weird face of Anubis and the ghastly terrors of the cities underground."

Charmion smiled incredulously. "That ought not, surely, to be a source of much grief to you, O queen; for every glance of your eyes transpierces hearts, like the golden arrows of Eros himself."

"Can a queen," answered Cleopatra, "ever know whether it is her face or her diadem that is loved? The rays of her starry crown dazzle the eyes and the hearts. Were I to descend from the height of my throne, would I even have the celebrity or the popularity of Bacchis or Archian-assa, of the first courtesan from Athens or Miletus? A queen is some-thing so far removed from men, so elevated, so widely separated from them, so impossible for them to reach! What presumption dare flatter itself in such an enterprise? It is not simply a woman, it is an august and sacred being that has no sex, and that is worshipped kneeling without being loved. Who was ever really enamoured of Hera the snowy-armed or Pallas of the sea-green eyes? Who ever sought to kiss the silver feet of Thetis or the rosy fingers of Aurora? What lover of the divine beauties ever took unto himself wings that he might soar to the golden palaces of heaven? Respect and fear chill hearts in our presence, and in order to obtain the love of our equals, one must descend into those necropoli of which I have just been speaking."

Although she offered no further objection to the arguments of her mistress, a vague smile which played about the lips of the handsome Greek slave showed that she had little faith in the inviolability of the royal person.

"Ah," continued Cleopatra, "I wish that something would happen to me, some strange, unexpected adventure. The songs of the poets; the dances of the Syrian slaves; the banquets, rose garlanded, and prolonged into the dawn; the nocturnal races; the Laconian dogs; the tame lions; the humpbacked dwarfs; the brotherhood of the Inimitables; the com-bats of the arena; the new dresses; the byssus robes; the clusters of pearls; the perfumes from Asia; the most exquisite of luxuries; the wildest of splendors—nothing any longer gives me pleasure. Everything has be-come indifferent to me, everything is insupportable to me."

"It is easily to be seen," muttered Charmion to herself, "that the queen has not had a lover nor had anyone killed for a whole month."

Fatigued with so lengthy a tirade, Cleopatra once more took the cup placed beside her, moistened her lips with it, and putting her head be-neath her arm, like a dove putting its head under its wing, composed herself for slumber as best she could. Charmion unfastened her sandals and commenced to gently tickle the soles of her feet with a peacock's feather, and Sleep soon sprinkled his golden dust upon the beautiful eyes of Ptolemy's sister.

While Cleopatra sleeps, let us ascend upon deck and enjoy the glorious sunset view. A broad band of violet color, warmed deeply with ruddy tints toward the west, occupies all the lower portions of the sky; encoun-tering the zone of azure above, the violet shade melts into a clear lilac, and fades off through half-rosy tints into the blue beyond; afar, where the sun, red as a buckler fallen from the furnace of Vulcan, casts his burning reflection, the deeper shades turn to pale citron hues, and glow with turquoise tints. The water, rippling under an oblique beam of light, shines with the dull gleam of the quicksilvered side of a mirror, or like a damascened blade. The sinuosities of the bank, the reeds, and all objects along the shore are brought out in sharp black relief against the bright glow. By the aid of this crepuscular light you may perceive afar off, like a grain of dust floating upon quicksilver, a little brown speck trembling in the network of luminous ripples. Is it a teal diving, a tortoise lazily drifting with the current, a crocodile raising the tip of his scaly snout above the water to breathe the cooler air of evening, the belly of a hippopotamus gleaming amidstream, or perhaps a rock left bare by the falling of the river? For the ancient Opi-Mou, Father of Waters, sadly needs to replenish his dry urn from the solstitial rains of the Mountains of the Moon.

It is none of these. By the atoms of Osiris so deftly resewn together, it is a man, who seems to walk, to skate, upon the water! Now the frail bark which sustains him becomes visible, a very nutshell of a boat, a hollow fish; three strips of bark fitted together (one for the bottom and two for the sides), and strongly fastened at either end by cord well smeared with bitumen. The man stands erect, with one foot on either side of this fragile vessel, which he impels with a single oar that also serves the purpose of a rudder; and although the royal cangia moves rapidly under the efforts of the fifty rowers, the little black bark visibly gains upon it.

Cleopatra desired some strange adventure, something wholly unexpected. This little bark which moves so mysteriously seems to us to be conveying an adventure, or, at least, an adventurer. Perhaps it contains the hero of our story; the thing is not impossible.

At any rate he was a handsome youth of twenty, with hair so black that it seemed to own a tinge of blue, a skin blonde as gold, and a form so perfectly proportioned that he might have been taken for a bronze statue by Lysippus. Although he had been rowing for a very long time he betrayed no sign of fatigue, and not a single drop of sweat bedewed his forehead.

The sun half sank below the horizon, and against his broken disk figured the dark silhouette of a far distant city, which the eye could not have distinguished but for this accidental effect of light. His radiance soon faded altogether away, and the stars, fair night-flowers of heaven, opened their chalices of gold in the azure of the firmament. The royal cangia, closely followed by the little bark, stopped before a huge marble stairway, whereof each step supported one of those sphinxes that Cleopatra so much detested. This was the landing-place of the summer palace.

Cleopatra, leaning upon Charmion, passed swiftly, like a gleaming vision, between a double line of lantern-bearing slaves.

The youth took from the bottom of his little boat a great lion-skin, threw it across his shoulders, drew the tiny shell upon the beach, and wended his way toward the palace.

III

Who is this young man, balancing himself upon a fragment of bark, who dares follow the royal cangia, and is able to contend in a race of speed against fifty strong rowers from the land of Kush, all naked to the waist, and anointed with palm-oil? What secret motive urges him to this swift pursuit? That, indeed, is one of the many things we are obliged to know in our character of the intuition-gifted poet, for whose benefit all men, and even all women (a much more difficult matter), must have in their breasts that little window which Momus of old demanded.

It is not a very easy thing to find out precisely what a young man from the land of Kemi, who followed the barge of Cleopatra, queen and goddess Evergetes, on her return from the Mammisi of Hermonthis two thousand years ago, was then thinking of. But we shall make the effort notwithstanding.

Meïamoun, son of Mandouschopsh, was a youth of strange character; nothing by which ordinary minds are affected made any impression upon him. He seemed to belong to some loftier race, and might well have been regarded as the offspring of some divine adultery. His glance had the steady brilliancy of a falcon's gaze, and a serene majesty sat on his brow as upon a pedestal of marble; a noble pride curled his upper lip, and expanded his nostrils like those of a fiery horse. Although owning a grace of form almost maidenly in its delicacy, and though the bosom of the fair and effeminate god Dionysos was not more softly rounded or smoother than his, yet beneath this soft exterior were hidden sinews of steel and the strength of Hercules—a strange privilege of certain antique natures to unite in themselves the beauty of woman with the strength of man.

As for his complexion, we must acknowledge that it was of a tawny orange color, a hue little in accordance with our white-and-rose ideas of beauty; but which did not prevent him from being a very charming young man, much sought after by all kinds of women—yellow, red, copper-colored, sooty-black, or golden skinned, and even by one fair, white Greek.

Do not suppose from this that Meïamoun's lot was altogether enviable. The ashes of aged Priam, the very snows of Hippolytus, were not more insensible or more frigid; the young white-robed neophyte preparing for the initiation into the mysteries of Isis led no chaster life; the young maiden benumbed by the icy shadow of her mother was not more shyly pure.

Nevertheless, for so coy a youth, the pleasures of Meïamoun were certainly of a singular nature. He would go forth quietly some morning with his little buckler of hippopotamus hide, his *harpe* or curved sword, a triangular bow, and a snake-skin quiver filled with barbed arrows; then he would ride at a gallop far into the desert, upon his slender-limbed, small-headed, wild-maned mare, until he could find some lion-tracks. He especially delighted in taking the little lion-cubs from underneath the belly of their mother. In all things he loved the perilous or the unachievable. He preferred to walk where it seemed impossible for any human being to obtain a foothold, or to swim in a raging torrent, and he had accordingly chosen the neighborhood of the cataracts for his bathing place in the Nile. The Abyss called him!

Such was Meïamoun, son of Mandouschopsh.

For some time his humors had been growing more savage than ever. During whole months he buried himself in the Ocean of Sands, returning only at long intervals. Vainly would his uneasy mother lean from her terrace and gaze anxiously down the long road with tireless eyes. At last, after weary waiting, a little whirling cloud of dust would become visible in the horizon, and finally the cloud would open to allow a full view of Meïamoun, all covered with dust, riding upon a mare gaunt as a wolf, with red and bloodshot eyes, nostrils trembling, and huge scars along her flanks—scars which certainly were not made by spurs.

After having hung up in his room some hyena or lion skin, he would start off again.

And yet no one might have been happier than Meïamoun. He was beloved by Nephthe, daughter of the priest Afomouthis, and the loveliest woman of the Nome Arsinoïtes. Only such a being as Meïamoun could have failed to see that Nephthe had the most charmingly oblique and indescribably voluptuous eyes, a mouth sweetly illuminated by ruddy smiles, little teeth of wondrous whiteness and transparency, arms exquisitely round, and feet more perfect than the jasper feet of the statue of Isis. Assuredly there was not a smaller hand nor longer hair than hers in all Egypt. The charms of Nephthe could have been eclipsed only by those of Cleopatra. But who could dare to dream of loving Cleopatra? Ixion, enamoured of Juno, strained only a cloud to his bosom, and must forever roll the wheel of his punishment in hell.

It was Cleopatra whom Meïamoun loved.

He had at first striven to tame this wild passion; he had wrestled fiercely with it; but love cannot be strangled even as a lion is strangled, and the strong skill of the mightiest athlete avails nothing in such a contest. The arrow had remained in the wound, and he carried it with him everywhere. The radiant and splendid image of Cleopatra, with her golden-pointed diadem and her imperial purple, standing above a nation on their knees, illumined his nightly dreams and his waking thoughts. Like some imprudent man who has dared to look at the sun and forever thereafter beholds an impalpable blot floating before his eyes, so Meïamoun ever beheld Cleopatra. Eagles may gaze undazzled at the sun, but what diamond eye can with impunity fix itself upon a beautiful woman, a beautiful queen?

He commenced at last to spend his life in wandering about the neighborhood of the royal dwelling, that he might at least breathe the same air as Cleopatra, that he might sometimes kiss the almost imperceptible print of her foot upon the sand (a happiness, alas! rare indeed). He attended the sacred festivals and *panegyreis,* striving to obtain one beaming glance of her eyes, to catch in passing one stealthy glimpse of her loveliness in some of its thousand varied aspects. At other moments, filled with sudden shame of this mad life, he gave himself up to the chase with redoubled ardor, and sought by fatigue to tame the ardor of his blood and the impetuosity of his desires.

He had gone to the panegyris of Hermonthis, and, in the vague hope of beholding the queen again for an instant as she disembarked at the summer palace, had followed her cangia in his boat—little heeding the sharp stings of the sun—through a heat intense enough to make the panting sphinxes melt in lava-sweat upon their reddened pedestals.

And then he felt that the supreme moment was nigh, that the decisive instant of his life was at hand, and that he could not die with his secret in his breast.

It is a strange situation truly to find oneself enamored of a queen. It is as though one loved a star; yet she, the star, comes forth nightly to sparkle in her place in heaven. It is a kind of mysterious rendezvous. You may find her again, you may see her; she is not offended at your gaze. Oh, misery! to be poor, unknown, obscure, seated at the very foot of the ladder, and to feel one's heart breaking with love for something glittering, solemn, and magnificent—for a woman whose meanest female attendant would scorn you—to gaze fixedly and fatefully upon one who never sees you, who never will see you; one to whom you are no more than a ripple on the sea of humanity, in nowise differing from the other ripples, and who might a hundred times encounter you without once recognizing you; to have no reason to offer should an opportunity for addressing her present itself in excuse for such mad audacity—neither poetical talent, nor great genius, nor any superhuman qualification—nothing but love; and to be able to offer in exchange for beauty, nobility, power, and all imaginable splendor only one's passion and one's youth—rare offerings, forsooth!

Such were the thoughts which overwhelmed Meïamoun. Lying upon the sand, supporting his chin on his palms, he permitted himself to be lifted and borne away by the inexhaustible current of reverie; he sketched out a thousand projects, each madder than the last. He felt convinced that he was seeking after the unattainable, but he lacked the courage to frankly renounce his undertaking, and a perfidious hope came to whisper some lying promises in his ear.

"Athor, mighty goddess," he murmured in a deep voice, "what evil have I done against thee that I should be made thus miserable? Art thou avenging thyself for my disdain of Nephthe, daughted of the priest Afomouthis? Hast thou afflicted me thus for having rejected the love of Lamia, the Athenian hetaira, or of Flora, the Roman courtesan? Is it my fault that my heart should be sensible only to the matchless beauty of thy rival, Cleopatra? Why hast thou wounded my soul with the envenomed arrow of unattainable love? What sacrifice, what offerings dost thou desire? Must I erect to thee a chapel of the rosy marble of Syene with columns crowned by gilded capitals, a ceiling all of one block, and hieroglyphics deeply sculptured by the best workmen of Memphis and of Thebes? Answer me."

Like all gods or goddesses thus invoked, Athor answered not a word, and Meïamoun resolved upon a desperate expedient.

Cleopatra, on her part, likewise invoked the goddess Athor. She prayed for a new pleasure, for some fresh sensation. As she languidly reclined upon her couch she thought to herself that the number of the senses was sadly limited, that the most exquisite refinements of delight soon yielded to satiety, and that it was really no small task for a queen to find means of occupying her time. To test new poisons upon slaves; to make men fight like tigers, or gladiators with each other; to drink pearls dissolved; to swallow the wealth of a whole province—all these things had become commonplace and insipid.

Charmion was fairly at her wit's end, and knew not what to do for her mistress.

Suddenly a whistling sound was heard, and an arrow buried itself, quivering, in the cedar wainscoting of the wall.

Cleopatra well-nigh fainted with terror. Charmion ran to the window, leaned out, and beheld only a flake of foam on the surface of the river. A scroll of papyrus encircled the wood of the arrow. It bore only these words, written in Phœnician characters, "I love you!"

IV

"I love you," repeated Cleopatra, making the serpent-coiling strip of papyrus writhe between her delicate white fingers. "Those are the words I longed for. What intelligent spirit, what invisible genius has thus so fully comprehended my desire?"

And thoroughly aroused from her languid torpor, she sprang out of bed with the agility of a cat which has scented a mouse, placed her little ivory feet in her embroidered *tatbebs,* threw a byssus tunic over her shoulders, and ran to the window from which Charmion was still gazing.

The night was clear and calm. The risen moon outlined with huge angles of light and shadow the architectural masses of the palace, which stood out in strong relief against a background of bluish transparency; and the waters of the river, wherein her reflection lengthened into a shining column, were frosted with silvery ripples. A gentle breeze, such as might have been mistaken for the respiration of the slumbering sphinxes, quivered among the reeds and shook the azure bells of the lotus flowers; the cables of the vessels moored to the Nile's bank groaned feebly, and the rippling tide moaned upon the shore like a dove lamenting for its mate. A vague perfume of vegetation, sweeter than that of the aromatics burned in the *anschir* of the priests of Anubis, floated into the chamber. It was one of those enchanted nights of the Orient, which are more splendid than our fairest days; for our sun can ill compare with the Oriental moon.

"Do you not see far over there, almost in the middle of the river, the head of a man swimming? See, he crosses that track of light, and passes into the shadow beyond! He is already out of sight!" And, supporting herself upon Charmion's shoulder, she leaned out, with half of her fair body beyond the sill of the window, in the effort to catch another glimpse of the mysterious swimmer; but a grove of Nile acacias, dhoum-palms, and sayals flung its deep shadow upon the river in that direction, and protected the flight of the daring fugitive. If Meïamoun had but had the courtesy to look back, he might have beheld Cleopatra, the sidereal queen, eagerly seeking him through the night gloom—he, the poor obscure Egyptian, the miserable lion-hunter.

"Charmion, Charmion, send hither Phrehipephbour, the chief of the rowers, and have two boats despatched in pursuit of that man!" cried Cleopatra, whose curiosity was excited to the highest pitch.

Phrehipephbour appeared, a man of the race of Nahasi, with large hands and muscular arms, wearing a red cap not unlike a Phrygian helmet in form, and clad only in a pair of narrow drawers diagonally striped with white and blue. His huge torso, entirely nude, black and polished like a globe of jet, shone under the lamplight. He received the commands of the queen and instantly retired to execute them.

Two long, narrow boats, so light that the least inattention to equilibrium would capsize them, were soon cleaving the waters of the Nile with hissing rapidity under the efforts of the twenty vigorous rowers, but the pursuit was all in vain. After searching the river banks in every direction, and carefully exploring every patch of reeds, Phrehipephbour returned to the palace, having only succeeded in putting to flight some solitary heron which had been sleeping on one leg, or in troubling the digestion of some terrified crocodile.

So intense was the vexation of Cleopatra at being thus foiled, that she felt a strong inclination to condemn Phrehipephbour either to the wild beasts or to the hardest labor at the grindstone. Happily, Charmion interceded for the trembling unfortunate, who turned pale with fear, despite his black skin. It was the first time in Cleopatra's life that one of her desires had not been gratified as soon as expressed, and she experienced, in consequence, a kind of uneasy surprise; a first doubt, as it were, of her own omnipotence.

She, Cleopatra, wife and sister of Ptolemy—she who had been proclaimed goddess Evergetes, living queen of the regions Above and Below. Eye of Light, Chosen of the Sun (as may still be read within the cartouches sculptured on the walls of the temples) she to find an obstacle in her path, to have wished aught that failed of accomplishment, to have spoken and not been obeyed! As well be the wife of some wretched Paraschistes, some corpse-cutter, and melt natron in a caldron! It was monstrous, preposterous! and none but the most gentle and clement of queens could have refrained from crucifying that miserable Phrehipephbour.

You wished for some adventure, something strange and unexpected.

Your wish has been gratified. You find that your kingdom is not so dead as you deemed it. It was not the stony arm of a statue which shot that arrow; it was not from a mummy's heart that came those three words which have moved even you—you who smilingly watched your poisoned slaves dashing their heads and beating their feet upon your beautiful mosaic and porphyry pavements in the convulsions of death-agony; you who even applauded the tiger which boldly buried its muzzle in the flank of some vanquished gladiator.

You could obtain all else you might wish for—chariots of silver, starred with emeralds; griffin-quadrigeræ; tunics of purple thrice-dyed; mirrors of molten steel, so clear that you might find the charms of your loveliness faithfully copied in them; robes from the land of Serica, so fine and subtly light that they could be drawn through the ring worn upon your little finger; Orient pearls of wondrous color; cups wrought by Myron or Lysippus; Indian paroquets that speak like poets—all things else you could obtain, even should you ask for the Cestus of Venus or the *pshent* of Isis, but most certainly you cannot this night capture the man who shot the arrow which still quivers in the cedar wood of your couch.

The task of the slaves who must dress you tomorrow will not be a grateful one. They will hardly escape with blows. The bosom of the unskilful waiting-maid will be apt to prove a cushion for the golden pins of the toilette, and the poor hairdresser will run great risk of being suspended by her feet from the ceiling.

"Who could have had the audacity to send me this avowal upon the shaft of an arrow? Could it have been the Nomarch Amoun-Ra who fancies himself handsomer than the Apollo of the Greeks? What think you, Charmion? Or perhaps Cheâpsiro, commander of Hermothybia, who is so boastful of his conquests in the land of Kush? Or is it not more likely to have been young Sextus, that Roman debauchee who paints his face, lisps in speaking, and wears sleeves in the fashion of the Persians?"

"Queen, it was none of those. Though you are indeed the fairest of women, those men only flatter you; they do not love you. The Nomarch Amoun-Ra has chosen himself an idol to which he will be forever faithful, and that is his own person. The warrior Cheâpsiro thinks of nothing save the pleasure of recounting his victories. As for Sextus, he is so seriously occupied with the preparation of a new cosmetic that he cannot dream of anything else. Besides, he had just purchased some Laconian dresses, a number of yellow tunics embroidered with gold, and some Asiatic children which absorb all his time. Not one of those fine lords would risk his head in so daring and dangerous an undertaking; they do not love you well enough for that.

"Yesterday, in your cangia, you said that men dared not fix their daz-zled eyes upon you; that they knew only how to turn pale in your pres-ence, to fall at your feet and supplicate your mercy; and that your sole remaining resource would be to awake some ancient, bitumen-perfumed Pharoah from his gilded coffin. Now here is an ardent and youthful heart that loves you. What will you do with it?"

Cleopatra that night sought slumber in vain. She tossed feverishly upon her couch, and long and vainly invoked Morpheus, the brother of Death. She incessantly repeated that she was the most unhappy of queens, that every one sought to persecute her, and that her life had be-come insupportable; woeful lamentations which had little effect upon Charmion, although she pretended to sympathize with them.

Let us for a while leave Cleopatra to seek fugitive sleep, and direct her suspicions successively upon each noble of the court. Let us return to Meïamoun, and as we are much more sagacious than Phrehipephbour, chief of the rowers, we shall have no difficulty in finding him.

Terrified at his own hardihood, Meïamoun had thrown himself into the Nile, and had succeeded in swimming the current and gaining the little grove of dhoum-palms before Phrehipephbour had even launched the two boats in pursuit of him.

When he had recovered breath, and brushed back his long black locks, all damp with river foam, behind his ears, he began to feel more at ease, more inwardly calm. Cleopatra possessed something which had come from him; some sort of communication was now established between them. Cleopatra was thinking of him, Meïamoun. Perhaps that thought might be one of wrath; but then he had at least been able to awake some feeling within her, whether of fear, anger, or pity. He had forced her to the consciousness of his existence. It was true that he had forgotten to inscribe his name upon the papyrus scroll, but what more of him could the queen have learned from the inscription, *Meïamoun, Son of Mandou-schopsh?* In her eyes the slave and the monarch were equal. A goddess in choosing a peasant for her lover stoops no lower than in choosing a patrician or a king. The Immortals from a height so lofty can behold only love in the man of their choice.

The thought which had weighed upon his breast like the knee of a colossus of brass had at last departed. It had traversed the air; it had even reached the queen herself, the apex of the triangle, the inacessible summit. It had aroused curiosity in that impassive heart; a prodigious advance, truly, toward success.

Meïamoun, indeed, never suspected that he had so thoroughly suc-ceeded in this wise, but he felt more tranquil; for he had sworn unto himself by that mystic Bari who guides the souls of the dead to Amenthi, by the sacred birds Bermou and Ghenghen, by Typhon and by Osiris, and by all things awful in Egyptian mythology, that he should be the accepted lover of Cleopatra, though it were but for a single night, though for only a single hour, though it should cost him his life and even his very soul.

If we must explain how he had fallen so deeply in love with a woman whom he had beheld only from afar off, and to whom he had hardly dared to raise his eyes—even he who was wont to gaze fearlessly into the yellow eyes of the lion—or how the tiny seed of love, chance-fallen upon his heart, had grown there so rapidly and extended its roots so deeply, we can answer only that it is a mystery which we are unable to explain. We have already said of Meïamoun—The Abyss called him.

Once assured that Phrehipephbour had returned with his rowers, he again threw himself into the current and once more swam toward the palace of Cleopatra, whose lamp still shone through the window curtains like a painted star. Never did Leander swim with more courage and vigor toward the tower of Sestos; yet for Meïamoun no Hero was waiting, ready to pour vials of perfume upon his head to dissipate the briny odors of the sea and banish the sharp kisses of the storm.

A strong blow from some keen lance or *harpe* was certainly the worst he had to fear, and in truth he had but little fear of such things.

He swam close under the walls of the palace, which bathed its marble feet in the river's depth, and paused an instant before a submerged archway into which the water rushed downward in eddying whirls. Twice, thrice he plunged into the vortex unsuccessfully. At last, with better luck, he found the opening and disappeared.

This archway was the opening to a vaulted canal which conducted the waters of the Nile into the baths of Cleopatra.

V

CLEOPATRA found no rest until morning, at the hour when wandering dreams reënter the Ivory Gate. Amid the illusions of sleep she beheld all kinds of lovers swimming rivers and scaling walls in order to come to her, and, through the vague souvenirs of the night before, her dreams appeared fairly riddled with arrows bearing declarations of love. Starting nervously from time to time in her troubled slumbers, she struck her little feet unconsciously against the bosom of Charmion, who lay across the foot of the bed to serve her as a a cushion.

When she awoke, a merry sunbeam was playing through the window curtain, whose woof it penetrated with a thousand tiny points of light, and thence came familiarly to the bed, flitting like a golden butterfly over her lovely shoulders, which it lightly touched in passing by with a luminous kiss. Happy sunbeam, which the gods might well have envied.

In a faint voice, like that of a sick child, Cleopatra asked to be lifted out of bed. Two of her women raised her in their arms and gently laid her on a tiger-skin stretched upon the floor, of which the eyes were formed of carbuncles and the claws of gold. Charmion wrapped her in a *calasiris* of linen whiter than milk, confined her hair in a net of woven silver threads, tied to her little feet cork *tatbebs* upon the soles of which were painted, in token of contempt, two grotesque figures, representing two men of the races of Nahasi and Nahmou, bound hand and foot, so that Cleopatra literally deserved the epithet, "Conculcatrix of Nations,"* which the royal cartouche inscriptions bestow upon her.

It was the hour for the bath. Cleopatra went to bathe, accompanied by her women.

The baths of Cleopatra were built in the midst of immense gardens filled with mimosas, aloes, carob-trees, citron-trees, and Persian apple-trees, whose luxuriant freshness afforded a delicious contrast to the arid appearance of the neighboring vegetation. There, too, vast terraces uplifted masses of verdant foliage, and enabled flowers to climb almost to the very sky upon gigantic stairways of rose-colored granite; vases of Pentelic marble bloomed at the end of each step like huge lily-flowers, and the plants they contained seemed only their pistils; chimeras caressed into form by the chisels of the most skilful Greek sculptors, and less stern of aspect than the Egyptian sphinxes, with their grim mien and moody attitudes, softly extended their limbs upon the flower-strewn turf, like shapely white leverettes upon a drawing-room carpet. These were charming feminine figures, with finely chiselled nostrils, smooth brows, small mouths, delicately dimpled arms, breasts fair-rounded and daintily formed; wearing earrings, necklaces, and all the trinkets suggested by adorable caprice; whose bodies terminated in bifurcated fishes' tails, like the women described by Horace, or extended into birds' wings, or rounded into lions' haunches, or blended into volutes of foliage, according to the fancies of the artist or in conformity to the architectural position chosen. A double row of these delightful monsters lined the alley which led from the palace to the bathing halls.

At the end of this alley was a huge fountain-basin, approached by four

---

* *Conculcatrice des peuples.* From the Latin *conculcare,* to trample under foot: therefore, the epithet literally signifies the "Trampler of nations." [Trans.]

porphyry stairways. Through the transparent depths of the diamond-clear water the steps could be seen descending to the bottom of the basin, which was strewn with gold-dust in lieu of sand. Here figures of women terminating in pedestals like Caryatides* spurted from their breasts slender jets of perfumed water, which fell into the basin in silvery dew, pitting the clear watery mirror with wrinkle-creating drops. In addition to this task these Caryatides had likewise that of supporting upon their heads an entablature decorated with Nereids and Tritons in bas-relief, and furnished with rings of bronze to which the silken cords of a velarium might be attached. From the portica was visible an extending expanse of freshly humid, bluish-green verdure and cool shade, a fragment of the Vale of Tempe transported to Egypt. The famous gardens of Semiramis would not have borne comparison with these.

We will not pause to describe the seven or eight other halls of various temperature, with their hot and cold vapors, perfume boxes, cosmetics, oils, pumice stone, gloves of woven horsehair, and all the refinements of the antique balneatory art brought to the highest pitch of voluptuous perfection.

Hither came Cleopatra, leaning with one hand upon the shoulder of Charmion. She had taken at least thirty steps all by herself. Mighty effort, enormous fatigue! A tender tint of rose commenced to suffuse the transparent skin of her cheeks, refreshing their passionate pallor; a blue network of veins relieved the amber blondness of her temples; her marble forehead, low like the antique foreheads, but full and perfect in form, united by one faultless line with a straight nose, finely chiselled as a cameo, with rosy nostrils which the least emotion made palpitate like the nostrils of an amorous tigress; the lips of her small, rounded mouth, slightly separated from the nose, wore a disdainful curve; but an unbridled voluptuousness, an indescribable vital warmth, glowed in the brilliant crimson and humid luster of the under lip. Her eyes were shaded by level eyelids, and eyebrows slightly arched and delicately outlined. We cannot attempt by description to convey an idea of their brilliancy. It was a fire, a languor, a sparkling limpidity which might have made even the dog-headed Anubis giddy. Every glance of her eyes was in itself a poem richer than aught of Homer or Mimnermus. An imperial chin, replete with force and power to command, worthily completed this charming profile.

She stood erect upon the upper step of the basin, in an attitude full of proud grace; her figure slightly thrown back, and one foot in suspense,

---

* The Greeks and Romans usually termed such figures Hermæ or Termini. Caryatides were, strictly, entire figures of women. [Trans.]

like a goddess about to leave her pedestal, whose eyes still linger on heaven. Her robe fell in two superb folds from the peaks of her bosom to her feet in unbroken lines. Had Cleomenes been her contemporary and enjoyed the happiness of beholding her thus, he would have broken his Venus in despair.

Before entering the water she bade Charmion, for a new caprice, to change her silver hair-net; she preferred to be crowned with reeds and lotos flowers, like a water divinity. Charmion obeyed, and her liberated hair fell in black cascades over her shoulders, and shadowed her beautiful cheeks in rich bunches, like ripening grapes.

Then the linen tunic, which had been confined only by one golden clasp, glided down over her marble body, and fell in a white cloud at her feet, like the swan at the feet of Leda. . . .

And Meïamoun, where was he?

Oh cruel lot, that so many insensible objects should enjoy the favors which would ravish a lover with delight! The wind which toys with a wealth of perfumed hair, or kisses beautiful lips with kisses which it is unable to appreciate; the water which envelops an adorably beautiful body in one universal kiss, and is yet, notwithstanding, indifferent to that exquisite pleasure; the mirror which reflects so many charming images; the buskin or *tatbeb* which clasps a divine little foot—oh, what happiness lost!

Cleopatra dipped her pink heel in the water and descended a few steps. The quivering flood made a silver belt about her waist, and silver bracelets about her arms, and rolled in pearls like a broken necklace over her bosom and shoulders; her wealth of hair, lifted by the water, extended behind her like a royal mantle; even in the bath she was a queen. She swam to and fro, dived, and brought up handfuls of gold-dust with which she laughingly pelted some of her women. Again, she clung suspended to the balustrade of the basin, concealing or exposing her treasures of loveliness—now permitting only her lustrous and polished back to be seen, now showing her whole figure, like Venus Anadyomene, and incessantly varying the aspects of her beauty.

Suddenly she uttered a cry as shrill as that of Diana surprised by Actæon. She had seen gleaming through the neighboring foliage a burning eye, yellow and phosphoric as the eye of a crocodile or lion.

It was Meïamoun, who, crouching behind a tuft of leaves, and trembling like a fawn in a field of wheat, was intoxicating himself with the dangerous pleasure of beholding the queen in her bath. Though brave even to temerity, the cry of Cleopatra passed through his heart, coldly piercing as the blade of a sword. A death-like sweat covered his whole body; his arteries hissed through his temples with a sharp sound; the iron hand of anxious fear had seized him by the throat and was strangling him.

The eunuchs rushed forward, lance in hand. Cleopatra pointed out to them the group of trees, where they found Meïamoun crouching in concealment. Defence was out of the question. He attempted none, and suffered himself to be captured. They prepared to kill him with that cruel and stupid impassibility characteristic of eunuchs; but Cleopatra, who, in the interim, had covered herself with her *calasiris,* made signs to them to stop, and bring the prisoner before her.

Meïamoun could only fall upon his knees and stretch forth suppliant hands to her, as to the altars of the gods.

"Are you some assassin bribed by Rome, or for what purpose have you entered these sacred precincts from which all men are excluded?" demanded Cleopatra with an imperious gesture of interrogation.

"May my soul be found light in the balance of Amenti, and may Tmeï, daughter of the Sun and goddess of Truth, punish me if I have ever entertained a thought of evil against you, O queen!" answered Meïamoun, still upon his knees.

Sincerity and loyalty were written upon his countenance in characters so transparent that Cleopatra immediately banished her suspicions, and looked upon the young Egyptian wth a look less stern and wrathful. She saw that he was beautiful.

"Then what motive could have prompted you to enter a place where you could only expect to meet death?"

"I love you!" murmured Meïamoun in a low, but distinct voice; for his courage had returned, as in every desperate situation when the odds against him could be no worse.

"Ah!" cried Cleopatra, bending toward him, and seizing his arm with a sudden brusque movement, "so, then, it was you who shot that arrow with the papyrus scroll! By Oms, the Dog of Hell, you are a very foolhardy wretch! . . . I now recognize you. I long observed you wandering like a complaining Shade about the places where I dwell. . . . You were at the Procession of Isis, at the Panegyris of Hermonthis. You followed the royal cangia. Ah! you must have a queen? . . . You have no mean ambitions. You expect, without doubt, to be well paid in return. . . . Assuredly I am going to love you. . . . Why not?"

"Queen," returned Meïamoun with a look of deep melancholy, "do not rail. I am mad, it is true. I have deserved death; that is also true. Be humane; bid them kill me."

"No; I have taken the whim to be clement today. I will give you your life."

"What would you that I should do with life? I love you!"

"Well, then, you shall be satisfied; you shall die," answered Cleopatra. "You have indulged yourself in wild and extravagant dreams; in fancy your desires have crossed an impassable threshold. You imagined yourself to be Cæsar or Mark Antony. You loved the queen. In some moment of delirium you have been able to believe that, under some condition of things which takes place but once in a thousand years, Cleopatra might some day love you. Well, what you thought impossible is actually about to happen. I will transform your dream into a reality. It pleases me, for once, to secure the accomplishment of a mad hope. I am willing to inundate you with glories and splendors and lightnings. I intend that your good fortune shall be dazzling in its brilliancy. You were at the bottom of the ladder. I am about to lift you to the summit, abruptly, suddenly, without a transition. I take you out of nothingness, I make you the equal of a god, and I plunge you back again into nothingness; that is all. But do not presume to call me cruel or to invoke my pity; do not weaken when the hour comes. I am good to you. I lend myself to your folly. I have the right to order you to be killed at once; but since you tell me that you love me, I will have you killed tomorrow instead. Your life belongs to me for one night. I am generous. I will buy it from you; I could take it from you. But what are you doing on your knees at my feet? Rise, and give me your arm, that we may return to the palace."

VI

OUR world of today is puny indeed beside the antique world. Our banquets are mean, niggardly, compared with the appalling sumptuousness of the Roman patricians and the princes of ancient Asia. Their ordinary repasts would in these days be regarded as frenzied orgies, and a whole modern city could subsist for eight days upon the leavings of one supper given by Lucullus to a few intimate friends. With our miserable habits we find it difficult to conceive of those enormous existences, realizing everything vast, strange, and most monstrously impossible that imagination could devise. Our palaces are mere stables, in which Caligula would not quarter his horse. The retinue of our wealthiest constitutional king is as nothing compared with that of a petty satrap or a Roman proconsul. The radiant suns which once shone upon the earth are forever extinguished in the nothingness of uniformity. Above the dark swarm of men no longer tower those Titanic colossi who bestrode the world in three paces, like the steeds of Homer; no more towers of Lylacq; no giant Babel scaling the sky with its infinity of spirals; no temples immeasurable, builded with the fragments of quarried mountains; no kingly terraces for which successive ages and generations could each erect but one step, and from whence some dreamfully reclining prince might gaze on the face of the world as upon a map unfolded; no more of those extravagantly vast cities of cyclopæan edifices, inextricably piled upon one another, with their mighty circumvallations, their circuses roaring night and day, their reservoirs filled with ocean brine and peopled with whales and leviathans, their colossal stairways, their superimposition of terraces, their tower-summits bathed in clouds, their giant palaces, their aqueducts, their multitude-vomiting gates, their shadowy necropoli. Alas! henceforth only plaster hives upon chessboard pavements.

One marvels that men did not revolt against such confiscation of all riches and all living forces for the benefit of a few privileged ones, and that such exorbitant fantasies should not have encountered any opposition on their bloody way. It was because those prodigious lives were the realization by day of the dreams which haunted each man by night, the personifications of the common ideal which the nations beheld living symbolized under one of those meteoric names that flame inextinguishably through the night of ages. Today, deprived of such dazzling spectacles of omnipotent will, of the lofty contemplation of some human mind whose least wish makes itself visible in actions unparalleled, in enormities of granite and brass, the world becomes irredeemably and hopelessly dull. Man is no longer represented in the realization of his imperial fancy.

The story which we are writing, and the great name of Cleopatra which appears in it, have prompted us to these reflections, so ill-sounding, doubtless, to modern ears. But the spectacle of the antique world is something so crushingly discouraging, even to those imaginations which deem themselves exhaustless, and those minds which fancy themselves to have conceived the utmost limits of fairy magnificence, that we cannot here forbear recording our regret and lamentation that we were not contemporaries of Sardanapalus; of Teglathphalazar; of Cleopatra, queen of Egypt; or even of Elagabalus, emperor of Rome and priest of the Sun.

It is our task to describe a supreme orgy—a banquet compared with which the splendors of Belshazzar's feast must pale—one of Cleopatra's nights. How can we picture forth in this French tongue, so chaste, so icily prudish, that unbounded transport of passions, that huge and mighty debauch which feared not to mingle the double purple of wine and blood, those furious outbursts of insatiate pleasure, madly leaping toward the Impossible with all the wild ardor of senses as yet untamed by the long fast of Christianity?

The promised night should well have been a splendid one, for all the joys and pleasures possible in a human lifetime were to be concentrated into the space of a few hours. It was necessary that the life of Meïamoun should be converted into a powerful elixir which he could imbibe at a single draught. Cleopatra desired to dazzle her voluntary victim, and plunge him into a whirlpool of dizzy pleasures; to intoxicate and madden him with the wine of orgie, so that death, though freely accepted, might come invisibly and unawares.

Let us transport our readers to the banquet-hall.

Our existing architecture offers few points for comparison with those vast edifices whose very ruins resemble the crumblings of mountains rather than the remains of buildings. It needed all the exaggeration of the antique life to animate and fill those prodigious palaces, whose halls were too lofty and vast to allow of any ceiling save the sky itself—a magnificent ceiling, and well worthy of such mighty architecture.

The banquet-hall was of enormous and Babylonian dimensions; the eye could not penetrate its immeasurable depth. Monstrous columns—short, thick, and solid enough to sustain the pole itself—heavily expanded their broad-swelling shafts upon socles variegated with hieroglyphics, and sustained upon their bulging capitals gigantic arcades of granite rising by successive tiers, like vast stairways reversed. Between each two pillars a colossal sphinx of basalt, crowned with the *pschent,* bent forward her oblique-eyed face and horned chin, and gazed into the hall with a fixed and mysterious look. The columns of the second tier, receding from the first, were more elegantly formed, and crowned in lieu of capitals with four female heads addorsed, wearing caps of many folds and all the intricacies of the Egyptian headdress. Instead of sphinxes, bull-headed idols—impassive spectators of nocturnal frenzy and the furies of orgy—were seated upon thrones of stone, like patient hosts awaiting the opening of the banquet.

A third story, constructed in a yet different style of architecture, with elephants of bronze spouting perfume from their trunks, crowned the edifice; above, the sky yawned like a blue gulf, and the curious stars leaned over the frieze.*

Prodigious stairways of porphyry, so highly polished that they reflected the human body like a mirror, ascended and decended on every hand, and bound together these huge masses of architecture.

We can only make a very rapid sketch here, in order to convey some idea of this awful structure, proportioned out of all human measurements. It would require the pencil of Martin,† the great painter of enormities passed away, and we can present only a weak pen-picture in lieu of the Apocalyptic depth of his gloomy style; but imagination may supply our deficiencies. Less fortunate than the painter and the musician, we can only present objects and ideas separately in slow succession. We have as yet spoken of the banquet-hall only, without referring to the guests, and yet we have but barely indicated its character. Cleopatra and Meïamoun are waiting for us. We see them drawing near. . . .

Meïamoun was clad in a linen tunic constellated with stars, and a purple mantle, and wore a fillet about his locks, like an Oriental king. Cleopatra was apparelled in a robe of pale green, open at either side, and clasped with golden bees. Two bracelets of immense pearls gleamed around her naked arms; upon her head glimmered the golden-pointed diadem. Despite the smile on her lips, a slight cloud of preoccupation shadowed her fair forehead, and from time to time her brows became knitted in a feverish manner. What thoughts could trouble the great queen? As for Meïamoun, his face wore the ardent and luminous look of one in ecstasy or vision; light beamed and radiated from his brow and

---

* Does not this suggest the lines which DeQuincey so much admired?—

> "A wilderness of building, sinking far,
> And self-withdrawn into a wondrous depth
> Far sinking into splendor, without end.
> Fabric it seemed of diamond, and of bold,
> With alabaster domes and silver spires,
> And blazing terrace upon terrace, high
> Uplifted. Here serene pavilions bright,
> In avenues disposed; their towers begirt
> With *battlements that on their restless fronts*
> *Bore stars.*"

† John Martin, the English painter, whose creations were unparalleled in breadth and depth of composition. His pictures seem to have made a powerful impression upon the highly imaginative author of these Romances. There is something in these descriptions of antique architecture that suggests the influence of such pictured fantasies as Martin's "Seventh Plague"; "The Heavenly City"; and perhaps, especially, the famous "Pandemonium," with its infernal splendor, in Martin's illustrations to "Paradise Lost." [Trans.]

temples, surrounding his head with a golden nimbus, like one of the twelve great gods of Olympus.

A deep, heartfelt joy illumined his every feature. He had embraced his restless-winged chimera, and it had not flown from him; he had reached the goal of his life. Though he were to live to the age of Nestor or Priam, though he should behold his veined temples hoary with locks whiter than those of the high priest of Ammon, he could never know another new experience, never feel another new pleasure. His maddest hopes had been so much more than realized that there was nothing in the world left for him to desire.

Cleopatra seated him beside her upon a throne with golden griffins on either side, and clapped her little hands together. Instantly lines of fire, bands of sparkling light outlined all the projections of the architecture— the eyes of the sphinxes flamed with phosphoric lightnings; the bull-headed idols breathed flame; the elephants, in lieu of perfumed water, spouted aloft bright columns of crimson fire, arms of bronze, each bearing a torch, started from the walls, and blazing aigrettes bloomed in the sculptured hearts of the lotos flowers.

Huge blue flames palpitated in tripods of brass; giant candelabras shook their dishevelled light in the midst of ardent vapors; everything sparkled, glittered, beamed. Prismatic irises crossed and shattered each other in the air. The facets of the cups, the angles of the marbles and jaspers, the chiselling of the vases—all caught a sparkle, a gleam, or a flash as of lightning. Radiance streamed in torrents and leaped from step to step like a cascade, over the porphyry stairways. It seemed the reflection of a conflagration on some broad river. Had the Queen of Sheba ascended thither she would have caught up the folds of her robe, and believed herself walking in water, as when she stepped upon the crystal pavements of Solomon. Viewed through that burning haze, the monstrous figures of the colossi, the animals, the hieroglyphics, seemed to become animated and to live with a factitious life; the black marble rams bleated ironically, and clashed their gilded horns; the idols breathed harshly through their panting nostrils.

The orgy was at its height: the dishes of phenicopters' tongues, and the livers of scarus fish; the eels fattened upon human flesh, and cooked in brine; the dishes of peacock's brains; the boars stuffed with living birds; and all the marvels of the antique banquets were heaped upon the three table-surfaces of the gigantic triclinium. The wines of Crete, of Massicus and of Falernus foamed up in cratera wreathed with roses, and filled by Asiatic pages whose beautiful flowing hair served the guests to wipe their hands upon. Musicians playing upon the sistrum, the tympanum, the sambuke, and the harp with one-and-twenty strings filled all the upper galleries, and mingled their harmonies with the tempest of sound that hovered over the feast. Even the deep-voiced thunder could not have made itself heard there.

Meïamoun, whose head was lying on Cleopatra's shoulder, felt as though his reason were leaving him. The banquet-hall whirled around him like a vast architectural nightmare; through the dizzy glare he beheld perspectives and colonnades without end; new zones of porticoes seemed to uprear themselves upon the real fabric, and bury their summits in heights of sky to which Babel never rose. Had he not felt within his hand the soft, cool hand of Cleopatra, he would have believed himself transported into an enchanted world by some witch of Thessaly or Magian of Persia.

Toward the close of the repast hump-backed dwarfs and mummers engaged in grotesque dances and combats; then young Egyptian and Greek maidens, representing the black and white Hours, danced with inimitable grace a voluptuous dance after the Ionian manner.

Cleopatra herself arose from her throne, threw aside her royal mantle, replaced her starry diadem with a garland of flowers, attached golden *crotali** to her alabaster hands, and began to dance before Meïamoun, who was ravished with delight. Her beautiful arms, rounded like the handles of an alabaster vase, shook out bunches of sparkling notes, and her *crotali* prattled with ever-increasing volubility. Poised on the pink tips of her little feet, she approached swiftly to graze the forehead of Meïamoun with a kiss; then she recommenced her wondrous art, and flitted around him, now backward-leaning, with head reversed, eyes half closed, arms lifelessly relaxed, locks uncurled and loose-hanging like a Bacchante of Mount Mænalus; now again, active, animated, laughing, fluttering, more tireless and capricious in her movements than the pilfering bee. Heart-consuming love, sensual pleasure, burning passion, youth inexhaustible and ever-fresh, the promise of bliss to come—she expressed all. . . .

The modest stars had ceased to contemplate the scene; their golden eyes could not endure such a spectacle; the heaven itself was blotted out, and a dome of flaming vapor covered the hall.

Cleopatra seated herself once more by Meïamoun. Night advanced; the last of the black Hours was about to take flight; a faint blue glow entered with bewildered aspect into the tumult of ruddy light as a moon-

* Antique castanets. [Trans.]

beam falls into a furnace; the upper arcades became suffused with pale azure tints—day was breaking.

Meïamoun took the horn vase which an Ethiopian slave of sinister countenance presented to him, and which contained a poison so violent that it would have caused any other vase to burst asunder. Flinging his whole life to his mistress in one last look, he lifted to his lips the fatal cup in which the envenomed liquor boiled up, hissing.

Cleopatra turned pale, and laid her hand on Meïamoun's arm to stay the act. His courage touched her. She was about to say, "Live to love me yet, I desire it! . . ." when the sound of a clarion was heard. Four heralds-at-arms entered the banquet-hall on horseback; they were officers of Mark Antony, and rode but a short distance in advance of their master. Cleopatra silently loosened the arm of Meïamoun. A long ray of sunlight suddenly played upon her forehead, as though trying to replace her absent diadem.

"You see the moment has come; it is daybreak, it is the hour when happy dreams take flight," said Meïamoun. Then he emptied the fatal vessel at a draught, and fell as though struck by lightning. Cleopatra bent her head, and one burning tear—the only one she had ever shed—fell into her cup to mingle with the molten pearl.

"By Hercules, my fair queen! I made all speed in vain. I see I have come too late," cried Mark Antony, entering the banquet-hall, "the supper is over. But what signifies this corpse upon the pavement?"

"Oh, nothing!" returned Cleopatra, with a smile; "only a poison I was testing with the idea of using it upon myself should Augustus take me prisoner. My dear Lord, will you not please to take a seat beside me, and watch those Greek buffoons dance?"

7

A Simple Heart

GUSTAVE FLAUBERT

I

FOR half a century past the good folk of Pont-l'Évêque had envied Mme. Aubain her servant, Félicité. For a wage of a hundred francs a year she cooked and did all the work of the house, sewing, washing, ironing; she knew how to harness a horse, how to fatten up poultry, and how to make butter; moreover, she remained loyal to her mistress, and her mistress was not an amiable person.

Mme. Aubain had married a handsome fellow, without means, who had died at the beginning of the year 1809, leaving her with two very young children and a quantity of debts. She then sold what landed property she owned, with the exception of two farms, named Toucques and Geffosses, the rents of which brought her in at most five thousand francs a year; and she gave up her Saint Melaine house, and moved into another which was less expensive—one which belonged to her ancestors, and which was situated at the back of the market-place.

This house roofed with slate, stood between a narrow alley and a lane which ended down by the riverside. Within there were differences of level that made one stumble. A narrow vestibule separated the kitchen from the sitting-room in which Mme. Aubain, seated near the window in a wicker armchair, spent the entire day. Eight mahogany chairs stood in line against the wainscoting, which was painted white. A pyramid of small wooden and pasteboard boxes was heaped up on an old piano, beneath a barometer. The yellow marble chimney-piece, style Louis XV, was flanked by two shepherdesses in tapestry. The clock in the center represented a temple of Vesta. An atmosphere of mustiness pervaded the room, which was on a lower level than the adjoining garden.

On the first floor you came at once upon Madame's bedroom, very large, a pale flower-design on its wall-paper, and for its chief decoration a portrait of "Monsieur" in dandified costume. It communicated with a smaller room in which were to be seen two children's beds, without mat-tresses. Next came the drawing-room, always kept closed, and filled with furniture covered over with a dust-sheet. Beyond, a corridor led to a study; books and waste papers occupied the shelves of a book-case, the three sides of which embraced, as it were, a wide desk made of black wood. The opposite walls were almost covered with pen-drawings, water-colors, and l'Audran engravings—souvenirs of better times and vanished luxury. On the second floor was Félicité's room, lit by a dor-mer window which looked out over the fields.

Félicité rose at daybreak so as to be able to get to Mass, and worked on till the evening without interruption; then, dinner over, the plates and dishes cleared, and the door closed and bolted, she would smother the burning log in the ashes and drop off to sleep before the hearth, her rosary in her fingers. There was no better hand at a bargain than Félicité —nobody equalled her in determination. As for her trimness, the polish of her saucepans was the despair of other servants. Very economical, she ate her food slowly and gathered together the breadcrumbs on the table with her fingers—her loaf was baked specially for her, weighed twelve pounds, and lasted her twenty days.

At all times and all seasons she wore a cotton handkerchief over her shoulders, pinned at the back, a bonnet hiding her hair, gray stockings, red petticoat, and, over her bodice, an apron like those of hospital nurses.

Her face was thin and her voice sharp. At twenty-five people had taken her for forty. After she had reached fifty, she had ceased to show any signs of increasing age; and, with her silent ways, her erect carriage and deliberate movements, she gave the impression of a woman made of wood, going through her work like an automaton.

II

Yet, like any other, Félicité had had her love story.

Her father, a stonemason, had been killed by a fall from a scaffolding. Then her mother died, her sisters dispersed, and a farmer took her into his service, setting her, while still a tiny child, to look after the cows in the pastures. She shivered with cold in her thin rags, quenched her thirst in pools—lying full length on the ground to drink—was beaten frequently for nothing, and finally was turned away for a theft of thirty sous, which she had not committed. Then she got into another farm, where she tended the poultry-yard, and where she gave so much satisfaction to her employers that the other servants became jealous of her. One evening in August (she was now eighteen) she was taken to the merry-making at Colleville. She was bewildered, stupefied almost, by the din of the fiddlers, by the dazzling lights hung from the trees, the medley of costumes, the wealth of lace and gold crosses, the immense concourse of people. She was holding timidly aloof when a young man, well-to-do in appearance, who had been smoking his pipe with his two elbows resting upon the pole of a cart, came up and asked her to dance. He treated her to some cider and to coffee, and bought her cakes and a silk handkerchief, and, supposing that she guessed what he had in mind, offered to see her home. As they were passing by a field of oats he threw her backwards roughly. She was frightened and began to scream. He took himself off.

Another evening, on the Beaumont road, as she was trying to hurry past a great wagon of hay which was progressing slowly in the same direction as herself, she recognized Theodore as she rubbed against the wheeels.

He addressed her calmly, saying that she must forgive him everything, as it was "the fault of the drink."

She did not know what reply to make, and her impulse was to take flight.

He went on, however, at once to talk about the crops and about the notable folk of the Commune. It seemed that his father had quitted Colleville and had taken the farm at Écots, so that they were now neighbors. "Oh!" said Félicité. He added that he was anxious to settle down. He was in no hurry, though, and could wait till he found a wife to his taste. She drooped her head. Then he asked her whether she had thought of marriage. She replied, smiling, that he ought not to make fun of her. "I'm not doing so, I swear I'm not," he rejoined, and he put his left arm round her waist; thus supported, she walked along. They slackened their pace. There was a gentle breeze, the stars were shining; in front of them the huge wagon oscillated from side to side, the four horses moving slowly, raising a cloud of dust. Presently, of their own accord, they took a turning to the right. He kissed her once again, and she made off into the darkness.

Next week Theodore got her to meet him.

They met in yard corners, behind walls, under isolated trees. She had not the innocence of young ladies of her age—the ways of animals had been an education to her; but commonsense and the instinct of self-respect safeguarded her virtue. Her resistance so stimulated Theodore's desires that to compass them (perhaps, indeed, ingenuously) he asked her to marry him. She was distrustful at first, but he gave her his word.

Soon, however, he communicated a disturbing piece of news. His parents had bought him a substitute the year previously, but now at any moment he was liable to conscription, and the idea of having to serve in the army frightened him. This cowardice, in Félicité's eyes, was evidence of his devotion to her; and she became increasingly devoted to him. She began to meet him at night, and while they were together Theodore tortured her with his fears and his entreaties.

At last he declared one evening that he would go himself to the Prefecture to make definite inquiries, and that he would come back with his news on the following Sunday between eleven o'clock and midnight.

When the time came Félicité hastened to meet him.

In his place she found one of his friends. He told her that she would not see Theodore again. In order to escape the conscription he had married a very rich old woman, Mme. Lehouassais, of Toucques.

A fit of passionate grief ensued. Félicité threw herself down on the ground, uttering cries of misery and appeals to God. She lay there all alone in the field, weeping and moaning until sunrise. Then she returned to the farm and announced her intention of leaving it; and at the end of the month, having received her wages, she tied up all her belongings in a handkerchief and made her way to Pont-l'Évêque. In front of the inn, she accosted a dame wearing widow's weeds, who happened at that very time to be on the look-out for a cook. The young girl clearly did not know much, but she seemed so willing and so easily pleased that Mme. Aubain ended by saying: "Good. I engage you." Half an hour later Félicité was installed in her new situation.

At first she lived there in a state of nervousness caused by the style of the house and the memories of "Monsieur" by which it seemed to be pervaded. Paul and Virginie, aged respectively seven and barely four, seemed to her beings of a finer clay; she would let them ride upon her back; Mme. Aubain mortified her by telling her not to keep kissing them every minute. She was happy, however. Her sorrow melted away in these pleasant surroundings.

Every Thursday certain friends of Mme. Aubain's came to play a game of "Boston." Félicité had to get ready the cards and the foot-warmers. The guests arrived exactly at eight o'clock, and took their departure before the stroke of eleven.

Every Monday morning the curio-dealer who lived down the street spread out his wares on the ground in front. And on that day the whole town was filled with a babel of sounds, horses neighing, sheep bleating, pigs grunting—all these noises mingling with the sharp clattering of the carts in the streets. Towards midday, when the market was at its height, a tall old peasant with a hooked nose, his cap on the back of his head,

would present himself at the hall door—this was Robelin, the tenant
of the Geffosses farm. Shortly afterwards, Liébard, the Toucques farmer,
would appear, short and fat and ruddy, wearing a gray coat and gaiters
with spurs attached to them.

They both had fowls and cheeses to offer to Mme. Aubain. Félicité
was always more than a match for them in guile, and they went off much
impressed by her astuteness.

At irregular intervals, Mme. Aubain received a visit from the Marquis de Gremanville, one of her uncles, a broken-down rake who lived
now at Falaise on the last remnant of his estate. He always made his
appearance at lunch-time, accompanied by a hideous poodle whose paws
left dirty tracks upon all the furniture. Despite his efforts to maintain the
air of a gentleman of noble birth (he would, for instance, lift his hat
every time he uttered the words "my late father"), he had acquired the
habit of filling himself glass after glass and giving forth questionable
stories. Félicité would put him out of the house quite politely. "You
have had enough, Monsieur de Gremanville! You must come again
another time!" she would say, and shut the door on him.

To M. Bourais, a retired lawyer, Félicité would open the door with
pleasure. His white cravat, his bald head, his shirt-frills, his ample
brown frock-coat, his way of curving his arm when he took a pinch of
snuff—in fact, his whole personality produced in her that slight feeling
of excitement which we experience at the sight of men of mark. As he
looked after Madame's property, he would be shut up in Monsieur's
Sanctum with her for hours at a time; he was cautious always not to
commit himself, had a boundless reverence for the magistracy, and was
by way of being something of a Latin scholar.

With a view to imparting a little instruction to the children in an
agreeable fashion, he presented them with a series of geographical prints
which included representations of scenes in different parts of the world
—cannibals with head-dresses of feathers, an ape carrying off a young
lady, Bedouin Arabs in the desert, the harpooning of a whale, etc.

Paul explained these pictures to Félicité. This, in fact, was her sole
literary education. That of the children was undertaken by Guyot, a
poor wretch employed at the Mairie, famous for his beautiful penman-
ship and for the way he sharpened his penknife on his boot.

In fine weather they went off at an early hour to the Geffosses farm.
The farmyard is on a slope, with the house in the middle; in the distance
is the sea, looking like a spot of gray.

Félicité would take some slices of cold meat out of her basket, and
they would all sit down to their *déjeuner* in a room forming part of the

dairy. It was all that was left of a pleasure-house now disappeared. The wall-paper, falling into shreds, shook as the wind blew through the room. Mme. Aubain leaned forward, a victim to sad memories; the children did not dare to speak. "Why don't you go and play?" she would say to them, and they would run off.

Paul climbed up into the loft, caught birds, played ducks and drakes with flat stones upon the pond, or tapped with a stick the rows of big barrels which sounded like so many drums.

Virginie fed the rabbits, or went to pick cornflowers, her legs moving so quickly that you caught glimpses of her little embroidered drawers.

One evening in autumn they were going back by the cornfields. The moon in its first quarter lit up a portion of the sky, and a mist hung like a cloud over the winding course of the Toucques. Oxen, lying in the meadows, gazed tranquilly at the four passers-by. In the third field, some got up and formed round them in a circle.

"Don't be afraid," said Félicité, and making a soothing kind of noise with her mouth she stroked the back of the animal nearest to her, on which it turned right round and went off followed by others. But the little party had scarcely traversed the adjoining meadow when they heard a fierce bellowing. It was a bull, invisible till then by reason of the mist. He advanced towards the two women. Mme. Aubain began to run. "No! no! don't go so fast!" cried Félicité; they hurried none the less and heard loud snorts closer and closer behind them. His hoofs had begun to beat the ground like strokes of a hammer—he was coming down upon them full gallop! Félicité turned round, and snatching up handfuls of earth threw them into the animal's eyes. He lowered his head, shook his horns, and stood trembling with fury, bellowing terribly. Mme. Aubain had by now reached the end of the field with her children, and was making desperate efforts to climb up the high bank. Félicité backed away slowly from the bull, and continued to throw bits of earth into his eyes. She kept calling out to the others, "Be quick! be quick!"

Mme. Aubain got down into the ditch, pushing Virginie and Paul before her, but fell several times while struggling to climb up the other side, which she pluckily achieved.

The bull had forced Félicité back against some palings. Flakes of foam from his mouth splashed her face, and in another second he would have ripped her up. She had just time to slip between two bars, and the huge animal pulled up short, quite astonished.

This event was a subject of conversation at Pont-l'Évêque for many years. Félicité herself, however, took no pride in it, having no notion that she had achieved anything heroic. Virginie monopolized her attention, for, as a result of the shock, the child had contracted a nervous affection, and M. Pourpart, the doctor, had recommended sea-baths for her at Trouville.

Trouville was not a fashionable watering-place in those days. Mme. Aubain made inquiries about it, and consulted Bourais, making preparations as though for a long journey.

Her luggage was sent on ahead, on the eve of her departure, in a cart of Liébard's. Next day he himself brought round two horses, one provided with a lady's saddle covered with velvet, the other with a cloak rolled up to form a seat. Mme. Aubain got up on one of them, behind Liébard, while Félicité mounted the other with Virginie under her charge, and Paul rode a donkey lent by M. Lechaptois on the express understanding that great care was to be taken of it.

The road was so bad that two hours were taken to compass its eight kilometers. The horses sank in the mud down to their pasterns, and had to make violent movements with their haunches to extricate themselves; now they had to struggle with deep ruts, now clamber over obstacles. Now and again Liébard's mare would come to a standstill. He waited patiently until she decided to go ahead again, and he held forth upon the people whose estates bordered the road and indulged in moral reflections upon their history. Thus in the center of Toucques, while passing under windows full of geraniums, he began with a shrug of his shoulders, "There's a Mme. Lehouassais, who instead of taking a young man. . . ." Félicité did not catch the rest of the remark; the horses broke into a trot, the ass into a gallop; they now went down a narrow path single file, a gateway was opened to them, two boys made their appearance, and all dismounted in front of a dung-heap on the very threshold.

Old "Mère" Liébard on seeing her mistress indulged in warm expressions of delight. She served a *déjeuner* consisting of a sirloin, tripe, black pudding, a fricassee of fowl, sparkling cider, a jam tart, and prunes served in brandy—all to a running accompaniment of compliments to Madame herself who seemed "in the best of health," to Mademoiselle who looked "magnificent," to M. Paul "grown so big and strong," and inquiries after their deceased grandparents whom the Liébards had known, having been in the service of the family for several generations. The farm, like its occupiers, bore the appearance of age. The beams across the ceiling were worm-eaten, the walls blackened with smoke, the tiles gray with dust. An oak cupboard was covered with all sorts of utensils, jugs, plates, tin porringers, wolf-traps, sheep clippers; a huge squirt amused the children. In the three adjoining yards there was not a tree but had mushrooms growing at its base, and tufts of mistletoe sprouting among its branches. The wind had blown down some of them. They had sprouted again, and all were weighed down by their quantity of apples. The thatched roofs of the outhouses, looking like brown velvet and of unequal thickness, withstood the most violent gusts of wind, but the carthouse lay in ruins. Mme. Aubain declared she would have it seen to, and gave orders for the horses to be reharnessed.

Another half-hour elapsed before they reached Trouville. The little caravan dismounted to pass the Ecores, a cliff beneath which boats were moored, and three minutes later, at the end of the quay, they made their way into the courtyard of the "Golden Lamb," kept by "Mère" David.

Virginie began from the very first to feel less weak—the result of the change of air and the action of the baths. She went into the water in her chemise, having no bathing dress, and her nurse dressed her in a custom-house shed which was placed at the disposal of the bathers.

In the afternoon they went with the donkey beyond the Roches Noires, Hennequeville way. The path rose, at first, through a countryside undulating like the greensward of a park, then came to an upland in which meadows alternated with ploughed fields. To either side of the road holly-bushes stood up from among the tangle of briars; while here and there a great lifeless tree made a zigzag pattern against the blue sky with its bare branches.

They nearly always had a rest when they reached a certain meadow, whence they could see Deauville to the left, Havre to the right, and the open sea in front of them. The sea flashed in the sunlight, its surface smooth as a mirror, and so calm that you could scarcely hear its murmuring; sparrows twittered out of sight; the immense vault of the heavens was over all. Mme. Aubain, sitting on the ground, busied herself with her sewing; Virginie, beside her, plaited reeds; Félicité weeded out sprigs of lavender; Paul found it dull and was restless to be off.

On other occasions they would cross over the Toucques by boat and go looking for shells. At low tide they would find sea-urchins, anemones and jelly-fish; and the children would run to catch the flakes of foam carried by the breeze. The tranquil waves, breaking upon the sands, unrolled themselves along the entire length of the beach; the beach stretched out as far as you could see, but to landward it ended in the dunes which divided it from the Marais—a wide extent of meadow-land shaped like a hippodrome. When they returned that way they saw Trouville at the foot of the hillside. At each step they took the town seemed to grow bigger and to spread itself out, with all its multiform dwellings, in gay disorder.

On days when the weather was too hot they did not leave their sitting-room. The dazzling radiance outside formed golden bars of light between the shutters of the Venetian blinds. Not a sound was to be heard in the village. Not a soul stirred in the street below. This pervading silence intensified their sense of restfulness. In the distance the hammers of calkers beat upon keels and the smell of tar was wafted upwards on the heavy air.

Their principal amusement was found in the return of ships to port. As soon as the vessels had passed the buoys they began to tack. They came in, topsails down, their foresails swelling like balloons; they glided along through the chopping waves until they were in the middle of the harbor, when the anchor was suddenly dropped. Finally, the vessel came alongside the quay. The sailors threw out their harvest of fish still palpitating and alive; a long line of carts stood in readiness, and a crowd of women wearing cotton bonnets rushed forward to fill their baskets and give their men a welcome.

One day one of these women went up to Félicité, who a few minutes later re-entered the family sitting-room with her face beaming. She had found a sister; and Nastasie Barette, by marriage Leroux, presented herself, carrying a baby at her breast, while at her right hand was another young child, and at her left a small cabin-boy, with his fists doubled on his hips and his sailor's cap cocked over one ear.

At the end of a quarter of an hour Mme. Aubain signified to her that it was time to go.

They were to be met continually outside the kitchen or on their walks. The husband did not show himself.

Félicité grew fond of them. She bought them a blanket, some shirts, and a stove; it was evident that they were taking advantage of her. This weakness exasperated Mme. Aubain, who, moreover, resented the familiar way in which the boy addressed Paul; and as Virginie had begun to cough and the weather was no longer good, she decided on a return to Pont-l'Évêque.

M. Bourais helped her to choose a college for Paul. That of Caen was considered to be the best, and thither he was sent. He went bravely through with his leave-taking, content to go and live in a house where he was to have companions.

Mme. Aubain resigned herself to the parting from her son because it was absolutely necessary. Virginie missed him less and less, Félicité felt the loss of his noisy ways. A new occupation, however, served to distract her thoughts. After Christmas it became one of her duties to take the little girl to have her catechism lesson every day.

III

Having made a genuflexion at the door of the church, Félicité advanced along the lofty nave between two rows of chairs, opened Mme. Aubain's pew, sat down and allowed her gaze to travel all round her.

Boys to the right, girls to the left, occupied the choir stalls; the curé remained standing by the lectern; a stained-glass window in the apse represented the Holy Ghost overshadowing the Blessed Virgin; another showed her on her knees before the Infant Jesus; and behind the tabernacle there was a wood carving of St. Michael demolishing the dragon.

The priest began with an outline of sacred history. Félicité formed pictures in her mind of Paradise, the Deluge, the Tower of Babel, cities in flames, concourses of people being annihilated, idols being shattered, and these bewildering visions filled her with awe of the Almighty and terror of His wrath. The story of the Passion moved her to tears. Why had Jesus been crucified—He who had cherished little children, who had given food to the multitude, who had cured the blind, and who had chosen, out of love and kindness, to be born in the midst of the poor, in a stable? The seed-times, the harvest-times, the pressing of the grapes, these and all other familiar things spoken of in the Gospel belonged to her life; the coming of the Saviour sanctified them; and she began to love lambs more tenderly for love of the Lamb, doves because of the Holy Ghost. She found it difficult to imagine his Person, for he was not only a bird, but also a flame, and at other times a breath. Perhaps it was his light that flew hither and thither at night by the borders of the marshes, his breath that moved the clouds, his voice that lent harmony to the bells? She remained lost in these moods of adoration, taking pleasure also in the freshness of the walls of the church and its atmosphere of peace. As for the dogmas, she understood nothing of them, made no effort to understand them. The curé discoursed, the children repeated what they had learnt; presently she fell asleep, waking suddenly when they all got up to go and their sabots began to clatter on the flag-stones.

It was in this fashion that she learnt her catechism, hearing it repeated out loud, her religious education having been neglected in her youth, and henceforth she imitated all Virginie's practices, fasting like her and going to confession. On the festival of Corpus Christi they erected a small altar together.

Virginie's first communion was a matter for great consideration to her for many days in advance. She busied herself over the necessary shoes, the rosary beads, the prayerbook and gloves. How her hands trembled as she helped Mme. Aubain to dress her!

Throughout the Mass she endured an agony of nervousness. M. Bourais prevented her from seeing one side of the choir, but immediately in front of her the little troop of maidens, adorned with white crowns above their drooping veils, looked to her like a field of snow; and she recognized her little dear one from afar by her peculiarly slender neck and her devout bearing. The bell rang, the heads bent forward; there was a silence. Then the organ pealed out, and the choristers and the whole congregation sang the "Agnus Dei"; after which the boys moved out of their seats in single file, the girls following. Slowly, with hands joined, they progressed towards the brilliantly lit altar, knelt down upon the first step, received the Sacrament one by one, and returned to their places in the same order. When Virginie's turn came Félicité leant forward to watch her, and in imagination, as happens in such cases of true devotion, she felt as though she herself were this child—Virginie's face had become her own, Virginie's dress clothed her, Virginie's heart was beating in her bosom—when the moment came to open the mouth, with eyelids lowered, she all but fainted.

Next day, early in the morning, Félicité presented herself at the Sacristy and asked M. le Curé to give her communion. She received it devoutly but not with the same rapture.

Mme. Aubain was anxious to make an accomplished person of her daughter, and as Guyot could teach her neither English nor music, she determined to send her as a boarder to the Urusline Convent at Honfleur.

Virginie raised no objection. Félicité sighed, and it seemed to her that Mme. Aubain was unfeeling. Afterwards she reflected that perhaps her mistress was well advised. These things were beyond the scope of her own judgment.

At last an old convent van stopped one day in front of the house, and there stepped out of it one of the nuns who was come to fetch "Mademoiselle." Félicité placed Virginie's luggage on the roof of the conveyance, imparted some instructions to the driver, and put in the box under the driver's seat six pots of jam, a dozen pears, and a bouquet of violets.

At the last moment Virginie burst into tears; she embraced her mother, who kissed her on the forehead, bidding her to be brave. The steps were raised and the vehicle started.

Then Mme. Aubain broke down; in the evening all her friends, the Lormeau household, Mme. Lechaptois, "those" Rochefeuille women, M. de Houppeville and Bourais looked in to console her.

The loss of her daughter was a great grief to her at first. But three times a week she had a letter from her, and on the other day she wrote to her, walked about in the garden or read, and in this way succeeded in passing the time.

From force of habit Félicité continued to enter Virginie's bedroom every morning and looked all round it. It saddened her that she no longer had her hair to comb, her boots to lace, herself to tuck up in bed—that she no longer had her pretty little face to gaze upon or her hand to hold out walking. Feeling the want of occupation, she tried her hand at making lace, but her fingers were too clumsy and she broke the threads; she seemed to herself no good at anything, she became unable to sleep—as she put it herself, she was simply worn out.

To distract her mind, she asked permission to have her nephew Victor to visit her.

He arrived on Sunday after Mass, his cheeks glowing, his breast uncovered, odorous of the country which he had crossed. Félicité had a meal ready for him at once. They sat down to it face to face and Félicité, eating as little as possible herself from motives of economy, so stuffed him up that at last he fell asleep. When the bells began to peal for Vespers she woke him, brushed his trousers, tied his bow, and went off to church with him, leaning on his arm with a kind of maternal pride.

His parents made him bring something home always from these visits; it might be a packet of brown sugar or of soap, or some brandy—sometimes it would be money. And he would leave Félicité his clothes to mend—a task she enjoyed especially because it meant that he had to come back to get them again.

In August his father took him off on a cruise along the coast. It was holiday time. The arrival of the children consoled Félicité. But Paul had become capricious, and Virginie had grown too old to be addressed in the accustomed familiar way, and this produced a feeling of awkwardness, raised a barrier between them.

Victor sailed first to Morlaix, then to Dunkirk, then to Brighton; on his return from each trip he brought Félicité a present. On the first occasion it was a box of contrived shells; next time it was a coffee-cup; the time after a great figure of a man made of gingerbread. The boy was improving in appearance, he was growing into quite a fine fellow; a moustache began to make its appearance, and there was a frank look in his eyes. He wore a little leather hat on the back of his head like a pilot. It amused Félicité to listen to him telling his yarns full of sailor's lingo.

On Monday, July 14, 1819 (she never forgot the date), Victor announced to her that he had signed on for a long voyage, and that on the night of the following day he would have to go away on the Honfleur packet-boat to rejoin his ship, and which was shortly to put in at Havre. It was possible that he might be away two years.

The prospect of so long a separation went to Félicité's heart; and, to say good-bye to him again, on the Wednesday evening, after Madame had dined, she put on her goloshes and trudged the twelve miles between Pont-l'Évêque and Honfleur.

On arriving at the Calvary, instead of turning to the left she went to the right, and getting lost among the shipbuilders' yards she had to retrace her steps; some people of whom she asked the way warned her that she must hurry up. She made her way round the harbor, which was full of ships, stumbling against ropes as she hastened along; then the ground sloped down to the water's edge, there was a confusion of lights, and she thought she must have lost her senses, for she saw horses in the sky.

On the edge of the quay other horses were neighing, frightened at the sea. A crane was lifting them up and lowering them into a vessel, on the decks of which people were shoving their way between barrels of cider, hampers full of cheeses, and sacks of grain; hens were to be heard clucking, and the captain swearing, and a cabin-boy was leaning over the cathead, regardless of all this. Félicité who had not recognized him, called out "Victor." He raised his head; she rushed up, but they suddenly drew back the gangway.

The packet-boat, towed at first by a number of women, cheering, moved out of the port. Her timbers creaked, the heavy waves beat against her prow. Her sail had flapped round and nobody on board could now be seen. Soon nothing was visible upon the sea, silvered by the moon, but a black spot, which gradually grew less distinct, then sank and disappeared.

Félicité, passing close by the Calvary, wished to commend to God him whom she held nearest to her heart; and she stood there a long time praying, her face bathed in tears, her eyes turned towards the clouds. The town lay sleeping, the custom-house officials alone were moving about; there was the sound of water flowing unceasingly, like a torrent through the holes in the lock gates. Two o'clock struck.

The convent would not be open until the morning. Mme. Aubain would be annoyed if she were delayed; and, in spite of her desire to see the other child, she went back. The girls at the inn were getting up when she reached Pont-l'Évêque.

For months and months to come that poor boy was to toss about on the waters of the deep. His cruises until then had given her no uneasiness. You might count on coming back safe from Brittany or from England; but America, the Colonies, the East Indies—these places were in dubious regions, at the other end of the world.

Henceforth all Félicité thoughts were for her nephew. On sunny days she imagined him suffering from thirst; when it was stormy she dreaded the lightning for him. When she heard the wind shrieking down the chimney or blowing slates down from the roof, she saw him battered by this very tempest, on the top of a broken mast, drenched in foam. At another time—her imagination helped by those geographical pictures —she thought of him being eaten by savages, or in the grip of apes in a forest, or perishing on some desert shore. And she never spoke of these anxieties.

Mme. Aubain meanwhile experienced anxieties of another kind concerning her daughter. The good Sisters reported that she was an affectionate child, but delicate.

The least excitement upset her. They found it necessary to give up teaching her the piano.

Mme. Aubain expected the letters from the convent to come to her with fixed regularity. One morning when there was no post she became very impatient. She kept walking up and down the room from her armchair to the window. Really it was too extraordinary! Four whole days and no news!

To console her, Félicité remarked: "It is six months, Madame, since I have heard any news."

"News from whom?"

Félicité replied quite gently: "Why—from my nephew!"

"Oh! Your nephew!" And Madame Aubain, shrugging her shoulders, went on walking up and down, as much as to say, "You don't suppose I was thinking of him? He is nothing to me! A cabin-boy, a little ragamuffin like that! The idea! It is my daughter I am talking about! Think a moment!"

Félicité, though hardened to rudeness by this time, took the affront to heart but presently forgot it. It seemed to her natural enough to lose one's head over the little girl. The two children were of equal importance in her eyes—they shared her heart, and their destinies were to be the same.

The chemist told her that Victor's ship had arrived at Havana. He had seen this item of news in a gazette.

On account of the cigars, Félicité imagined Havana to be a country in which people did nothing but smoke, and Victor went about among the Negroes in a cloud of tobacco. Would it be possible, "in case of need," to return from Havana by land? How far was it from Pont-l'Évêque? To find this out, she put the questions to M. Bourais.

He got out his atlas, and entered upon explanations of longitudes and latitudes, and he smiled a very superior smile as he noted the dumbfounded expression on her face. He ended by pointing out to her a small black spot, barely perceptible, somewhere in the irregular outline of an oval section in the map. "Here it is," he said. She leaned over the map, but the network of colored lines merely tried her eyes and told her nothing; and on Bourais asking her to say what it was that puzzled her, she begged him to point out to her the house in which Victor was staying. Bourais lifted up his arms, roaring with laughter—such simplicity delighted him; but Félicité had no notion what had amused him—how should she, inasmuch as she very likely expected to see even her nephew's portrait in the map, within such narrow limits did her intelligence work?

It was fifteen days after this that Liébard entered the kitchen, at market-time as usual, and handed her a letter from her brother-in-law. As neither of them could read it, she had recourse to her mistress.

Mme. Aubain, who was counting the stitches of her knitting work, now put that aside, broke the seal of the letter, trembled, and said in a deep voice, a grave look in her eyes:

"This is to give you news of a calamity . . . Your nephew . . ."

He was dead. That was all the letter told.

Félicité sank into a chair, and, leaning her head on the back of it, closed her eyes, which became suddenly red. Then bending forward, her eyes fixed, her hands drooping idly, she kept saying over and over again: "Poor little fellow! Poor little fellow!"

Liébard, sighing, stood watching her. Mme. Aubain still trembled slightly. She suggested to Félicité that she should go and visit her sister at Trouville.

Félicité signified by a gesture that she felt no need to do so.

There was a silence. Liébard thought it tactful for him to withdraw.

Then Félicité exclaimed, "It means nothing to them." Her head fell forward again; mechanically from time to time she lifted the long knitting-needles upon the work-table.

Some women passed into the yard with a cart from which odds and ends of linen kept falling out. Seeing them through the window, Félicité remembered her washing. Having soaked the things the day before, she had to wring them out today; she got up and left the room.

Her tub and her board were down by the Toucques. She threw a heap of underlinen down on the river bank, rolled up her sleeves and took her bat in hand; the vigorous blows she dealt with it could be heard in the neighboring gardens. The meadows were empty, the wind ruffled the surface of the stream; lower down, tall grasses leant over its sides, looking like the hair of corpses floating in the water. Félicité restrained her feelings and was very brave until the evening; but in her own room she gave way to her sorrow and lay prostrate on the mattress, her face buried in the pillow, her hands clenched against her temples.

A good deal later she learnt particulars as to Victor's death from the captain of the vessel. The boy had been bled to excess at the hospital for yellow fever. Four doctors had him in hand at the same time. He died immediately, and the principal doctor remarked: "Good, one more!"

Victor's parents had always treated him brutally. Félicité preferred to see no more of them; and they for their part made no advance to her, either because they forgot all about her, or because of the callousness that comes from penury.

Virginie meanwhile was losing strength. A weight on her chest, coughing, continued feverishness, and her flushed cheeks pointed to some deep-seated malady. M. Pourpart had recommended a stay in Provence. Mme. Aubain decided upon this, and she would have had her daughter back home again at once were it not for the climate of Pont-l'Évêque.

She made an arrangement with a man who let out carriages on hire, which enabled her to visit the convent every Tuesday. There was in the garden a terrace from which a glimpse could be caught of the Seine. Virginie would walk up and down here over the vine-leaves fallen on the ground, leaning on her mother's arm. Sometimes the sun, breaking through the clouds, forced her to lower her eyes, as she gazed upon the distant sails and along the entire horizon from the Château of Tancarville to the lighthouses at Havre. Afterwards they would have a rest in an arbor. Mme. Aubain had provided herself with a small cask of excellent Malaga; and, laughing at the idea of its possibly making her tipsy, Virginie would drink two thimblefuls, never more.

The girl's strength seemed to be coming back to her. The autumn passed smoothly. Félicité reassured Mme. Aubain. But one evening when she had been for a walk outside the town she found M. Pourpart's carriage outside the door on her return; and he himself was in the hall Mme. Aubain was putting on her hat.

"Give me my foot-warmer, and my purse and gloves," she cried out. "Hurry up about it."

Virginie was suffering from inflammation of the lungs; perhaps it was already a hopeless case.

"Not yet!" said the doctor; and he and Mme. Aubain stepped into the vehicle, beneath the whirling snowflakes. Night was approaching and the weather was very cold.

Félicité rushed off to the church to light a candle. Then she ran after the carriage, which she caught up an hour later and jumped nimbly up behind, holding on to the hangings until suddenly the reflection came to her, "The yard was not closed. Suppose thieves found their way in!" and she got down.

First thing next day she presented herself at the doctor's. He had come back home, but had gone off again into the country. Then she stopped at the inn, thinking perhaps a letter might be brought thither by some stranger. Finally, towards dusk, she took the diligence for Lisieux.

The convent was situated at the bottom of a steep lane. Halfway down it, she heard strange sounds—a death-knell. "It must be for others," she thought; and knocked vigorously at the convent door.

After several minutes she could hear the shuffling of shoes; the door was half opened and a nun appeared.

The good Sister, with a compassionate look, said that Virginie "had just passed away." At the same moment the knell of Saint Leonard was renewed.

Félicité made her way up to the second floor.

From the door she saw Virginie lying outstretched upon the bed, her hands clasped together, her mouth open, her head poised slightly backwards beneath a black cross leaning over her, between the motionless curtains, less white than her face. Mme. Aubain, clinging to the foot of the bed, gave out sobs of agony. The Mother Superior was standing to the right. Three candlesticks upon the chest of drawers made spots of red, and the fog spread a white mist over the windows. Some nuns led Mme. Aubain away.

For two nights Félicité did not leave the dead girl. She repeated the same prayers over and over again, throwing holy water over the sheets, and sitting down to gaze upon her. At the end of the first watch she noticed that the face had taken on a yellowish tint, the lips had become blue, the nose was thinner, the eyes were sinking in. She kissed them several times, and it would not have surprised her beyond measure had Virginie opened them again; for such souls the supernatural is quite simple. She dressed the body, wrapped it in the shroud, and laid it in the coffin, placed a wreath on her, and spread her hair. It was fair and extraordinarily long for her age. Félicité cut off a big lock of it and put half of it into her bosom, resolved never to part with it.

The corpse was taken back to Pont-l'Évêque, according to the wishes of Mme. Aubain, who followed the hearse in a closed carriage.

After the Mass, it took the funeral cortège three-quarters of an hour to reach the cemetery. Paul walked at its head, sobbing. M. Bourais followed, and then the principal inhabitants of the village, the women wearing black cloaks, Félicité among them. Her thoughts went back to her nephew, and not having been able to render him these tokens of regard, she felt her sadness intensified—as if he also was being taken to the grave.

Mme. Aubain's despair was boundless. At first she revolted against God, accusing Him of injustice in robbing her of her child when she had never done any harm, and her conscience was so pure. . . . But no! she ought to have taken Virginie to the South! . . . Perhaps other doctors would have saved her life! She accused herself, wished to follow her child, and cried out distressfully in her dreams. One in particular obsessed her. Her husband, wearing the garb of a sailor, had returned from a long voyage and was saying to her, weeping the while, that he had been commanded to take Virginie away. Then he and she endeavored together to find a hiding-place somewhere.

Once, she re-entered the house from the garden, quite overcome. A moment ago (she could point out the exact spot) father and child appeared to her side by side. They were doing nothing; they were only looking at her.

For several months she remained in her room, listless. Félicité would lecture her gently—she must rouse herself for the sake of her son, and besides—in remembrance of "her."

"Of her?" replied Mme. Aubain, as though coming back to consciousness. "Oh, of course! . . . You do not forget." She had been scrupulously forbidden any allusion to the cemetery.

Félicité went to it every day. At four o'clock precisely she would walk past the houses, go up the hill, open the gate, and make her way to Virginie's grave. There was a little column of rose-colored marble, with a tablet at its base, and a chain all around enclosing a miniature garden-plot. The borders were almost hidden by flowers. Félicité watered them and renewed the sand, going down on her knees to better dress the ground. Mme. Aubain, when she was able to visit the grave, derived some relief and a kind of consolation from it.

After this years passed by, all very much alike, and without other incidents than the return of the great festivals—Easter, the Assumption,

All Saints. Domestic events constituted dates to serve as landmarks in years to come. Thus, in 1825, two glaziers whitewashed the hall; in 1827, a portion of the roof, falling down into the courtyard, nearly killed a man. In the summer of 1828 it fell to Madame to offer the Blessed Bread; Bourais, about this time, absented himself mysteriously; and gradually old acquaintances passed out of sight; Guyot, Liébard, Mme. Lechaptois, Robelin, l'oncle Gremanville, paralyzed now for a considerable time past.

One night the mail-cart driver announced in Pont-l'Évêque the revolution of July. A new Sub-Prefect was nominated some days later; the Baron de Larsonnière, who had been previously a consul in America, and who brought with him, in addition to his wife, his sister-in-law and her three daughters, almost grown up. They were all to be seen on their lawn, wearing loosely made blouses; they were the owners of a Negro and a parrot. Mme. Aubain received a visit from them and duly returned it. Félicité used always to run to her mistress to let her know whenever she saw any of them approaching, no matter how far off they might be. But the only thing that could now arouse her were the letters from her son.

He could not follow any profession, spending all his time in drinking-houses. She paid his debts, but he contracted new ones; and Mme. Aubain's sighs, as she sat knitting by the window, reached the ears of Félicité, turning her spinning wheel in the kitchen.

They used to walk together under the fruit wall; they talked always of Virginie, speculating as to whether such and such a thing would have pleased her, what she would have said on this occasion or on that.

All her little belongings were gathered together in a cupboard in the double-bedded room. Mme. Aubain abstained as much as possible from inspecting them. One summer's day she resigned herself to doing so, and moths flew out of the cupboard.

Her dresses lay folded under a shelf on which were three dolls, some hoops, a set of doll's-house furniture, and the basin she used. Mme. Aubain and Félicité also took out the petticoats, stockings, and handkerchiefs and spread them out upon the two beds before folding them up again. The sun shining on these poor little treasures revealed spots and stains and the creases made by the movements of the body that had worn them. Outside, the atmosphere was warm and blue mist; a thrush was warbling; the world seemed steeped in peace. Presently they came upon a small plush hat, with deep pile, chestnut-colored; but it was all moth-eaten. Félicité took possession of it for herself. The eyes of the two women met and filled with tears. Then the mistress opened wide her arms and the servant threw herself into them; and they held each other fast, finding vent for their common grief in the kiss that annulled all difference of rank.

It was the first time in their lives that they had embraced, for Mme. Aubain was not demonstrative by nature. Félicité felt grateful to her as for some actual benefit, and henceforth tended her with as much devotion as a dumb animal, and with a religious veneration.

The benevolence of her heart developed. When she heard in the street the drums of a regiment marching past, she would take up her position in front of the door with a jug of cider and invite the soldiers to drink. She helped to nurse those on the sick list. She took the Poles under her special protection, and one of them declared he wanted her to marry him. But she had a tiff with him; for returning one morning from the Angelus, she found him in her kitchen, in which he had settled down comfortably to the consumption of a salad.

After the Poles came Père Colmiche, an old man who was reputed to have been guilty of enormities in '93. He lived down by the riverside in what was left of a disused pigsty. The street urchins spied at him through chinks in the wall, and chucked stones which fell down on the squalid bed upon which he lay, shaken continually by a cough, his hair worn long, his eyelids inflamed, and on one of his arms a tumor bigger than his head. She provided him with linen and made efforts to cleanse his hovel; she wanted, indeed, to establish him in the bakehouse, if only it could be managed without disturbance or annoyance to Madame. When the cancerous growth burst, she doctored the sore every day, sometimes bringing him some cake which she would place in the sun in a box lined with straw. The poor old man, dribbling and trembling, thanked her in his faint voice, and, fearing always lest he should lose her, stretched out his arms as he watched her retreating figure. He died, and she had a Mass said for the repose of his soul.

It was on that day that a piece of great good fortune befell her. Just as dinner was served, the Negro belonging to Mme. Larsonnière made his appearance, carrying the parrot in its cage, with its perch, chain and padlock. A note from the Baronne informed Mme. Aubain that, her husband having been promoted to a Prefecture, they were going away that evening, and begged her to accept the bird as a souvenir and a mark of her regard.

It had long excited Félicité's imagination, for it came from America, and the word recalled Victor—so much so that she had sometimes questioned the Negro on the subject. Once she had gone so far as to say, "How pleased Madame would be if she had it!"

The Negro had repeated the remark to his mistress, who, being unable to take it away with her, was glad to dispose of it in this manner.

IV

Its name was Loulou. Its body was green, the tips of its wings pink, its forehead blue, its throat golden.

But it had a tiresome habit of biting its perch, and it tore out its feathers, splashed about the water in its drinking-trough, and made such a mess that Mme. Aubain found it a nuisance and handed it over altogether to Félicité.

She set about educating it; soon it learnt to say *"Charmant garçon"* ... *"Serviteur, monsieur"* ... *"Je vous salue, Marie."* It was placed by the door, and people used to be surprised that it would not answer to the name of Jacquot, for all parrots are called Jaçquot. It used to be likened sometimes to a turkey, sometimes even to a log of wood. These remarks stabbed Félicité to the heart. Certainly it was very perverse of Loulou to stop talking the moment anyone looked at it.

Yet it liked to have company, for on Sunday when "those" Rochefeuille women, M. de Houppeville, and certain new members of Madame's social circle—the apothecary Onfroy, M. Varin and Captain Mathieu—were playing cards, it would beat against the window-panes with its wings and conduct itself so violently that it was impossible to hear oneself speak.

No doubt old Bourais' countenance struck the bird as very droll. The moment it saw him it always began to laugh—to laugh with all the vigor at its command. Its clattering voice resounded through the courtyard; an echo repeated it, and the neighbors coming to their windows laughed too. M. Bourais, to avoid being seen by the parrot, used to slink along the wall, covering his face with his hat, and, getting down to the river, would enter the house from the gardens; and the looks he would direct toward the bird were lacking in affection.

Loulou had been given a slap by the butcher's boy one morning, having taken the liberty of inserting its head into his basket; and ever since it had tried to pinch him through his shirt-sleeves. Fabu threatened to wring its neck for it, though in reality he was not cruel, despite his tattooed arms and heavy whiskers. Indeed, he had a liking for the parrot, and even insisted in his jovial way on teaching it how to curse. Félicité, horrified, removed it to the kitchen. It was now relieved of its chain and allowed to wander about the house.

When coming downstairs it would first lean its beak upon each step, then raise its right claw, its left following. Félicité used to be afraid that these gymnastic exercises would make it dizzy. It became ill and could no more talk nor eat. There was a thickness under the tongue, such as poultry sometimes suffer from. She cured it by removing this growth with her finger-nail. M. Paul was one day so imprudent as to puff the smoke of his cigar into the bird's nostrils. On another occasion Mme. Lormeau worried it with the end of her umbrella and it snatched at the ferrule. Finally, it got lost.

She had put it out on the grass to give it some fresh air and had gone away for a minute. When she returned there was no parrot to be seen! At first she looked about for it in the bushes, by the river-side, and on the roofs, paying no attention to her mistress, who was crying out to her, "Mind what you are doing. Have you taken leave of your senses?" Then she explored all the gardens of Pont-l'Évêque, and she inquired of every-one she met, "Do you happen by any chance to have seen my parrot?" To those who did not know the parrot she gave a description of its appearance. Suddenly she though she descried something green flying behind the windmills at the bottom of the hill, but when she got near there was no sign of it. A pedlar maintained that he had come across it shortly before at Saint Melaine, in Mère Simon's shop. She ran thither. They knew nothing about it there. At last she returned home quite worn out, her shoes in rags, despair in her heart; and sitting on the bench side by side with Madame, she had begun a recital of all her adventures, when suddenly a light weight fell upon her shoulder—it was Loulou! What in the world had it been up to? Perhaps it had gone for a turn in the neighborhood!

It took her a long time to recover from the effects of her over-exertion —in fact, she never really recovered.

As the result of a cold, she had an attack of quinsy, followed soon after by an affection of the ears. Three years later she was deaf and had got into the way of talking very loud, even in church. Although her sins might have been made known in every corner of the diocese without shame to her or evil effect upon the world at large, the curé deemed it well to hear her confession henceforth only in the sacristy.

She suffered from buzzing in her ears. Often her mistress would cry out, "Mon Dieu! how stupid you are!" and she would answer merely, "Yes, Madame," and go looking about for something close at hand.

The narrow field of her ideas became still further limited, and the pealing of bells and the lowing of cattle no longer existed for her. Living creatures of every description moved and acted with the noiselessness of phantoms. The only sound that penetrated to her ears was the voice of the parrot.

As though to amuse her, it would mimic the tic-tac of the turnspit, the sharp cry of the vendor of fish, the sound of the carpenter's saw from across the road, and when the bell rang, Mme. Aubain's voice calling out "Félicité, the door! the door!"

They would walk together, the bird going through incessantly with its three stock phrases, and Félicité replying in words which were no less inconsequent, yet in which her heart poured itself out. In her isolation Loulou was almost a son to her, or a lover. He walked up and down her fingers, nibbled at her lips, hung on to her kerchief; and when she leaned forward, shaking her head in the way nurses do, the great wings of her cap and the wings of the bird flapped in unison.

When the clouds gathered and the thunder rolled, Loulou would give forth cries, remembering perhaps the inundations of its native forests. The streaming down of the rain made it wild with excitement; it would dash about violently, flying up to the ceiling, knocking everything about, and, escaping out of the window, would dabble about in the garden; but it would soon make its way in again to the fireplace, and, hopping about to dry its feathers, would display now its tail, now its beak.

One morning in the terrible winter of 1837, when Félicité had put the bird in front of the fire on account of the cold, she found it dead in the center of its cage, its head down, its claws grasping the iron bars. Doubtless it had died of a cold, but Félicité attributed its death to poisoning by eating parsley, and despite the lack of any kind of proof her suspicions fell upon Fabu.

She wept so much that her mistress said to her, "Well, well! Have it stuffed!"

She asked the advice of the chemist, who had always been friendly to the parrot.

He wrote to Havre. A certain Fellacher volunteered to undertake the job. As parcels sometimes went astray when sent by diligence, Félicité preferred to take it into Honfleur herself.

Leafless apple trees lined both sides of the road. The water in the ditches was frozen. Dogs barked on the edges of farmyards. Félicité, her hands hidden under her cloak, trudged along briskly in the middle of the road, wearing her little black sabots, and carrying her basket.

She crossed the forest, passed by the Haut-Chêne, and reached Saint-

Gatien. Behind her, in a cloud of dust, gathering momentum as it came, a mail-cart at full gallop rushed down the incline like a waterspout. Catching sight of the woman, who turned neither to the right nor left, the driver jumped up from his seat and the postilion began to shout out warning, but the four horses clattered along ever faster. The two leaders grazed her; with a sudden jerk of the reins he contrived to swerve to one side of the road, but, furiously, he raised his arm and, as he passed, lashed Félicité with his great whip around her stomach and neck so violently that she fell on her back.

Her first action when she regained consciousness was to open the basket. Loulou was all right, thank goodness! She felt a burning pain on her right cheek; putting her hands to it, she found them red. The blood was running.

She sat down on a heap of stones and stopped the bleeding of her face with a handkerchief; then she ate a crust of bread which she had the forethought to put in her basket, and took consolation for her own wound in contemplating the bird.

When she had got to the summit of Ecquemanville, she saw the lights of Honfleur sparkling in the night like stars; beyond, the sea spread out indistinctly. Then a feeling of weakness overcame her, and her childhood's misery, the disillusionment of her first love, her nephew's departure, Virginie's death, came back all at once like a flood-tide, rising to her throat and suffocating her.

She spoke to the captain of the vessel herself, and, without saying what it was she was consigning to his care, she gave him his instructions.

Fellacher kept the parrot a long time. He kept promising it for the following week; at the end of six months he announced its dispatch in a box, and then for a period there was no further news. It looked as though Loulou would never return to her. "They have stolen him from me," she thought.

But at last it arrived—and looking a magnificent sight, perched on the branch of a tree which was fixed onto a mahogany pedestal. One claw was in the air, the head was cocked on one side. Loulou was biting a nut to which the bird-stuffer, carried away by his love for the grandiose, had given a gilt coating!

Félicité put it away safely in her own room.

This spot, to which she admitted very few visitors, had the aspect at once of a chapel and a bazaar; it contained so many religious objects as well as other miscellaneous treasures.

A large cupboard was so placed as to make it difficult to open the door. Opposite the window which overlooked the garden there was a round one from which you could see the courtyard; on a table standing near the folding-bed stood a jug of water, two combs and a piece of blue soap on a notched plate. On the walls were hung rosaries, medals, several statues of the Blessed Virgin, and a holy water font made of cocoa-nut wood; on the chest of drawers, covered with a cloth like an altar, stood the box made of shells that Victor had given her, together with a water-ing-pot, a toy balloon, some copy-books, the series of geographical charts, and a pair of boots; Virginie's little plush hat was tied by its ribbons to the nail from which hung the looking-glass. Félicité carried this form of respect so far as even to keep an old frock-coat of Monsieur's. She took to this room of hers, in fact, all the old belongings for which Mme. Aubain had no use. This accounted for a case of artificial flowers on one side of the chest of drawers, and a portrait of Comte d'Artois at the side of the window.

By means of a small bracket Loulou was set up on a portion of the chimney which projected into the room. Every morning, on waking, she caught sight of it in the clear light of dawn, and without pain, full of peace, she recalled days that had gone and insignificant events in all their slightest details.

Cut off from all communication with everybody, she continued to live on like a somnambulist, in a kind of trance. The Corpus Christi proces-sions revived her. She applied to her neighbors for the loan of torches and colored mats in order to decorate the altar that was being erected in the street.

In church she would sit gazing at the Holy Ghost, and discovered in him some resemblance to the parrot. This resemblance came out in a more marked degree in an Épinal picture representing the Baptism of our Lord. With the purple wings and emerald body, this really repre-sented a portrait of Loulou.

She bought this picture, and hung it up in the place by the window where she had previously put the Comte d'Artois, so that she could see the parrot and it together in the same glance. They became associated together in her mind, the parrot becoming sanctified by this connection with the Holy Ghost, who thus became more real in her eyes and easier to understand. God the Father, to announce Himself, could not have chosen a dove, for these birds have no voice, but rather one of Loulou's ancestors; and Félicité prayed before the sacred picture, but would turn slightly from time to time in the direction of the bird.

She wanted to enroll herself in the confraternity of the "Demoiselles de la Vierge," but Mme. Aubain dissuaded her from doing so.

Presently an important event took place—Paul's marriage.

After having been first a clerk in a notary's office, and then in business, in the Customs and Revenue services, and after making an effort to get into the Rivers and Forests Department, at last in his thirty-sixth year he had discovered, as though by a heavenly inspiration, his natural calling, his *métier:* that of a registrar. He displayed such remarkable qualifications for this position that an inspector had offered him his daughter in marriage, promising at the same time to use his influence in his favor.

Paul, now sobered, brought her to visit his mother. She sniffed at the ways of Pont-l'Évêque, played the princess, and hurt Félicité's feelings. Mme. Aubain felt relieved when she took her departure.

The following week news came of the death of M. Bourais, in Lower Brittany, in an inn. A rumor that he had committed suicide was confirmed, and doubts were raised as to his honesty. Mme. Aubain examined her books and was not long in learning the litany of his misdeeds: misappropriations, fictitious sales of timber, forged receipts, etc. To add to this, he was the father of an illegitimate child, and had had "illicit relations with a creature from Dozule."

These iniquities afflicted her very much. In the month of March, 1853, she began to feel a pain in her chest; her tongue became clouded, and the application of leeches afforded her no relief. On the ninth evening she died, aged seventy-two precisely.

She had been believed to be less old on account of her brown hair, plaits of which framed her pallid face, marked by small-pox. Few friends regretted her, for her proud manners had kept people at a distance.

Félicité, however, mourned her in a way that masters are seldom mourned. It seemed to upset all her calculations that Madame should die before she did; it seemed out of keeping with the order of things, unallowable and uncanny.

Ten days later (it took ten days to hurry up from Besançon) Paul and his wife appeared upon the scene. The latter turned out every drawer in the house, chose some furniture and sold the rest. The pair then returned home.

Mme. Aubain's arm-chair, her round table, her foot-warmer, the eight sitting-room chairs, disappeared. The wall space once occupied by the pictures was now a series of yellow squares. The children's beds with their mattresses had also been carried off, and the cupboard in which Virginie's belongings had been cherished was now empty. Félicité went upstairs, beside herself with misery.

Next day there was a notice posted up on the front door; the apothecary shouted in her ear that the house was for sale.

She tottered and had to sit down. What chiefly troubled her was the idea of having to give up her room—it suited poor Loulou so well. Gazing with anguish at the bird, she prayed fervently to the Holy Ghost. She contracted the idolatrous habit of kneeling in front of the parrot to say her prayers. Sometimes the sun coming through the window struck its glass eye, making it emit a great luminous ray, which threw her into an ecstasy.

She had an income of three hundred and eighty francs a year, bequeathed her by her mistress. The garden provided her with vegetables; as for clothes, she had enough to last her until the end of her days, while she saved lighting by going to bed at dusk.

She rarely went out, not liking to pass the second-hand shop in which some of the old furniture of the house was now displayed for sale. She had dragged one leg since her shock; and as she was losing her strength, Mère Simon, whose grocery business had come to grief, came now every morning to cut wood and draw water for her.

Her eyes became weak. She gave up opening the window-shutters. Many years passed. And the house remained unlet and unsold.

For fear lest they should get rid of her, Félicité refrained from asking for repairs. The laths of the roof began to rot; for an entire winter the bolster on her bed was damp. After the following Easter she spat blood.

Then Mère Simon had recourse to a doctor. Félicité wanted to know what was the matter with her. But, too deaf to hear, she could only catch one word—"Pneumonia." It was familiar to her, and she said softly, "Ah! like Madame!" finding it natural to follow her mistress.

The time for the temporary altars now approached. The first of them was erected always at the foot of the hill, the second in front of the post-office, the third about halfway down the street. There was some contention as to the exact position of this one, and the parishioners had at last decided to place it in Mme. Aubain's courtyard.

Félicité's sufferings increased, and she worried over her inability to do anything for the altar. If only she could have put something on it! Then the parrot occurred to her. The neighbors objected; it was not suitable, they maintained. But the curé granted her his permission, and this made her so happy that she begged him to accept Loulou, her only valuable, when she should die.

From Tuesday until Saturday, the eve of Corpus Christi, she coughed more and more frequently. In the evening her face shrivelled up, her lips clove to her gums, and she began to vomit; next day at early dawn, feeling very low in herself, she sent for the priest.

Three good women stood round her while she received Extreme Unction. Then she declared that she wanted to speak to Fabu.

He arrived in his Sunday clothes, ill at ease in the dismal atmosphere.

"Forgive me," she said to him, trying to hold out her arms; "I believed it was you who killed him!"

What in the world was she talking about? The idea of suspecting a man like him of murder! Fabu grew indignant, and began to get excited. "She is off her head! Anybody can see that!"

From time to time Félicité talked with shadows. The neighbors left her, Mère Simon took her *déjeuner*.

A little later she took Loulou and held him out toward Félicité. "Come! Bid him good-bye!"

Though it was not a corpse, the worms had begun to eat it; one of its wings was broken, and the stuffing had begun to escape from its stomach. But, quite blind now, she kissed it on the forehead and pressed it against her cheek. Then Mère Simon took it away again to place it upon the altar.

V

The scent of flowers came from the meadows; there was a buzzing of flies; the sunshine made the surface of the river sparkle, and warmed the slates upon the roof. Mère Simon had returned to the room, and was slumbering peacefully.

The striking of a bell woke her. People were coming away from Vespers. Félicité's delirium left her, and, her thoughts intent on the procession, she saw it as though she were making part of it.

All the children from the schools, together with the choristers and the firemen, walked along the pavements, whilst in the middle of the road came first the Suisse with his halberd, the beadle with a great cross, the schoolmaster looking after his boys, the Sister watching anxiously the little girls under her charge; three of the smallest of these, with curly hair like angels, threw rose petals into the air as they advanced; the deacon, his arms outstretched, beat time for the music; and two incense-bearers bowed at every step in front of the Blessed Sacrament, carried by M. le Curé wearing his beautiful chasuble, beneath a canopy of red velvet, held up by four churchwardens. A mass of people followed, between the white cloths covering the walls of the houses. They arrived at the foot of the hill.

A cold sweat moistened Félicité's temples. Mère Simon wiped them with a piece of linen, saying to herself that some day her own time would come.

The murmur of the crowd grew in volume, for a moment waxed very loud, then faded away.

A fusillade shook the windows. It was the postilions firing a salute in front of the monstrance. Félicité, rolling her eyes, inquired in as low a tone as she could: "Is he all right?" She was worrying about the parrot.

Her death agony commenced. A rattle, more and more violent, shook her sides. Bubbles of foam rose to the corners of her mouth, and her whole body was in a tremble.

Now, the blare of the wind instruments made itself heard, the clear voices of the children, the deep voices of men. There were intervals of silence, and the trampling of feet, muffled by the flowers strewn along the ground, sounded like the pattering of sheep upon the grass.

The priests appeared in the courtyard. Mère Simon climbed on a chair so that she might look out of the circular window, and thus got a view of the altar.

Green garlands hung over the altar, which was decorated with a frill of English lace. In the center there was a small casket containing relics, two orange trees at either end, and all along it silver candlesticks and porcelain vases, from which rose sunflowers, lilies, peonies, foxgloves, and tufts of hydrangea. This mass of brilliant coloring sloped downwards, extending from above the altar down to the carpet which had been spread over the ground. A variety of rare objects caught the eye. A vermilion sugar-basin had a wreath of violets; pendants of Alençon stone shone on tufts of moss; two Chinese screens depicted landscapes. Loulou, hidden beneath roses, displayed only his blue forehead, which looked like a slab of lapis-lazuli.

The churchwardens, the choristers and the children stood in a line along the three sides of the courtyard. The priest ascended slowly the steps of the altar and put down his great, shining, golden sun upon the lace-work cloth. All knelt down. There was a deep silence, and the incense-burners, swinging to and fro, grated upon their chains.

A cloud of blue smoke rose to Félicité's bedroom. She distended her nostrils, breathing it in with a mystical sensuousness; then closed her eyes. Her lips smiled. The movements of her heart became gradually more faint, more gentle, as a fountain runs out, as an echo fades away; and when she gave up her last breath, she believed she saw in the opening heavens a tremendous parrot hovering above her head.

8

Herodias

GUSTAVE FLAUBERT

THE citadel of Machærus stood on the eastern shore of the Dead sea, on a cone-shaped basaltic peak. Four deep valleys surrounded it, two on the sides, one in front, the fourth behind. Houses clustered about its base, within the enclosure formed by a wall which rose and fell with the undulations of the ground; and by a zigzag road, hewn in the rock, the town was connected with the fortress, whose walls were one hundred and twenty cubits high, with many angles, battlements on the edge, and here and there towers, forming the ornamentation, as it were, of that crown of stone, suspended over the abyss.

Within there was a palace, adorned with porticoes and sheltered by a terrace, about which ran a balustrade of sycamore-wood, with tall poles arranged to hold a tent.

One morning, before dawn, the Tetrarch Herod Antipas leaned on the balustrade and looked forth.

Immediately beneath him the mountains were beginning to show their peaks, while their dense masses, to the lowest depths of the ravines, were still in shadow. The hovering mist was rent asunder, and the outlines of the Dead Sea appeared. The dawn, breaking behind Machærus, diffused a reddish light. Soon it illuminated the sands on the shore, the hills, the desert, and, farther away, all the mountains of Judea, with their jagged gray slopes. En-Gedi, in the center, formed a black bar; Hebron, in the background, was rounded like a dome; Eshtaol was covered with pomegranates, Sorek with vineyards, Carmel with fields of sesame; and the Tower of Antonia, with its monstrous cube, dominated Jerusalem. The Tetrarch turned his eyes to the right, to gaze upon the palm-trees of Jericho; and he thought of the other cities of his Galilee: Capernaum, Endor, Nazareth, Tiberias, whither perhaps he would never go again.

Meanwhile the Jordan flowed through the barren plain. All white, it was as dazzling as a field of snow. Now the lake seemed to be of lapis lazuli; and at its southern point, in the direction of Yemen, Antipas saw what he dreaded to see. Brown tents were scattered here and there; men with lances went to and fro among the horses; and dying fires gleamed like sparks, level with the ground.

They were the troops of the King of the Arabs, whose daughter he had cast aside to take Herodias, wife to one of his brothers, who lived in Italy with no pretension to power.

Antipas was awaiting succor from the Romans; and as Vitellius, Governor of Syria, did not appear, he was consumed with impatience.

Doubtless Agrippa had ruined him in the mind of the Emperor? Philip, his third brother, sovereign of Batanea, was secretly arming. The Jews would have no more of his idolatrous customs, nor all the rest of his domineering sway; so that he was hesitating between two plans: to beguile the Arabs, or to enter into an alliance with the Parthians; and, on the pretext of celebrating his birthday, he had bidden to a great banquet, for that very day, the leaders of his troops, the stewards of his estates, and the chief men of Galilee. With a keen glance he scanned all the roads. They were empty. Eagles flew over his head; the soldiers were sleeping against the walls, along the ramparts; nothing stirred within the castle.

Of a sudden a voice in the distance, as if escaping from the bowels of the earth, made the Tetrarch turn pale. He leaned forward to listen; it had ceased. It began again, and he clapped his hands and called:

"Mannæus! Mannæus!"

A man appeared, naked to the waist, like the masseurs at baths. He was very tall, aged, fleshless, and wore at his hip a cutlass in a copper sheath. His hair, brushed back and held in place by a comb, exaggerated the height of his brow. His eyes were dull with drowsiness, but his teeth gleamed and his toes rested lightly on the flagstones, his whole body having the suppleness of a monkey and his face the impassiveness of a mummy.

"Where is he?" asked the Tetrarch.

Mannæus replied, pointing with his thumb to something behind them: "There! still there!"

"I thought that I heard him!"

And Antipas, having drawn a long breath of relief, inquired concerning Iaokanann, the same man whom the Latins called St. John the Baptist. Had those two men been seen again who had been admitted as a favor to his dungeon some months before; and had the purpose with which they had come been learned since?

Mannæus replied:

"They exchanged some words with him in secret, like thieves at a cross-roads in the night. Then they went away towards Upper Galilee, announcing that they were the bearers of great tidings."

Antipas hung his head, then exclaimed in a tone of alarm:

"Keep him! keep him! And let no one enter! Lock the door fast! Cover the hole! None must even suspect that he lives!"

Before receiving these orders Mannæus had carried them out; for Iaokanann was a Jew; and, like all Samaritans, he abhorred the Jews.

Their temple of Gerizim, intended by Moses to be the center of Israel, had ceased to exist since the time of King Hyrcanus; and that of Jerusalem drove them to frenzy as an outrage and a lasting injustice. Mannæus had made his way into it in order to sully the altar with dead men's bones. His confederates, less swift of foot than he, had been beheaded.

He saw it in the gap between two hills. Its white marble walls and the golden lines of its roof shone resplendent in the sun. It was like a luminous mountain—something superhuman, crushing all else by its magnificence and its pride.

Then he extended his arms towards Zion; and, standing erect, with head thrown back and fists clenched, he hurled a malediction at it, believing that words had real power.

Antipas listened and did not seem shocked.

The Samaritan continued:

"At times he becomes excited, he longs to fly, he hopes for a rescue. At other times he has the tranquil aspect of a sick beast; or else I see him walking to and fro in the darkness, saying: 'What matters it? That He may grow great, I must needs shrink!"

Antipas and Mannæus glanced at each other. But the Tetrarch was weary of reflection.

All those mountains about him, like terraces of huge petrified waves, the black ravines on the sides of the cliffs, the immensity of the blue vault, the brilliant glamor of the day, the depth of the abysses, disturbed him; and a wave of desolation swept over him at the spectacle of the desert, which, in the upheavals of its surface, formed amphitheaters and ruined palaces. The hot wind brought, with the odor of sulphur, an exhalation, as it were, from the accursed cities, buried lower than the banks beneath the heavy waters of the lake. These tokens of an immortal wrath brought dismay to his mind; and he stood, with both elbows on the balustrade, staring eyes, and his hands pressed against his temples. Some one touched him. He turned. Herodias stood before him.

A light purple robe covered her to the sandals. Having come forth hurriedly from her chamber, she wore neither necklace nor earrings; a tress of her black hair fell over one arm, and its end was lost to sight between her breasts. Her two open nostrils throbbed; a joyous expression of triumph lighted up her face; and in a loud voice, shaking the Tetrarch's arm, she said:

"Cæsar loves us! Agrippa is in prison!"

"Who told you so?"

"I know it."

She added:

"It is for having aspired to Caius's* empire!"

While living on their alms, he had schemed to obtain the title of king, which they, like him, coveted. But in the future no more fear! "Tiberius's dungeons are hard to open, and sometimes life is not secure therein!"

Antipas understood her; and, although she was Agrippa's sister, her atrocious purpose seemed to him justified. Such murders were a consequence of the state of affairs, a fatality attached to royal families. In Herod's they had become too numerous to count.

Then she set forth her plan: clients bought, letters discovered, spies at every door; and how she had succeeded in seducing Eutyches the denouncer. "Nothing deterred me! Have I not done even more for you? I have abandoned my daughter!"

After her divorce she had left the child in Rome, hoping to have others by the Tetrarch. She never mentioned her. He wondered why that outburst of affection.

The tent had been spread, and huge cushions were speedily brought to them. Herodias sank upon them and wept, turning her head to him. Then she passed her hand over her eyes, said that she proposed to think no more about it, that she was happy; and she recalled to his mind their chats yonder in the atrium, their meetings at the baths, their strolls along the Via Sacra, and the evenings at the great villas, amid the plashing of fountains, beneath arches of flowers, by the Roman Campagna. She gazed at him as of yore, rubbing against his breast, with cajoling gestures. He pushed her away. The love that she tried to kindle was so far away now! And all his misfortunes had flowed from it, for war had raged well-nigh twelve years. It had aged the Tetrarch. His shoulders were bent; in his sad-colored toga with a violet border, his white hair blended with his beard, and the sun, shining through the veil, bathed

* The Emperor Caligula. [Trans.]

with light his troubled brow. Herodias's too was wrinkled; and, seated face to face, they eyed each other fiercely.

The roads over the mountain began to be peopled. Herdsmen drove their cattle, children dragged donkeys along, grooms led horses. Those who descended the heights above Machærus disappeared behind the castle; others ascended the ravine opposite, and, having reached the town, discharged their burdens in the courtyards. They were the Tetrarch's purveyors, and servants preceding his guests.

But, at the foot of the terrace, on the left, an Essene appeared, in a white robe, barefooted, with a stoical air. Mannæus, on the right, rushed forward, brandishing his cutlass.

"Kill him!" cried Herodias.

"Hold!" said the Tetrarch.

He stood still; the other did likewise.

Then they withdrew, each by a different stairway, walking backward, keeping their eyes fixed on each other.

"I know him!" said Herodias; "his name is Phanuel, and he seeks speech with Iaokanann, since you are blind enough to spare his life!"

Antipas suggested that he might some day be of use. His attacks upon Jerusalem would win to their side the rest of the Jews.

"No!" she said; "they accept all masters and are not capable of forming a fatherland!" As for him who stirred the people with hopes never lost since the days of Nehemiah, the best policy was to suppress him.

There was no need of haste in the Tetrarch's opinion. Iaokanann dangerous! Folly! He feigned to laugh at the idea.

"Hold your peace!" And she repeated the tale of her humiliation one day when she was going towards Gilead to gather balsam. People were putting on their clothes on the bank of a stream. On a low hill near by a man was speaking. He had a camel's skin about his loins, and his head resembled a lion's. "As soon as he saw me he spit out at me all the maledictions of the prophets. His eyes shot fire; his voice roared; he raised his arms as if to tear the thunder from on high. Impossible to fly! the wheels of my chariot were buried in sand to the axles; and I drove away slowly, sheltering myself beneath my cloak, my blood congealed by those insults, which fell like a shower of rain."

Iaokanann made life impossible to her. When he was taken and bound with cords, the soldiers were ordered to stab him if he resisted; he was as gentle as a lamb. They had put serpents in his dungeon; they were dead.

The futility of these tricks drove Herodias mad. Besides, what was the cause of his war against her? What interest guided him? His harangues, delivered to crowds, were circulated, spread abroad; she heard them everywhere, they filled the air. Against legions she would have been stout of heart. But that power, more harmful than the sword, and intangible, was stupefying, and she paced the terrace, livid with wrath, lacking words to express the passion that suffocated her.

She reflected, too, that the Tetrarch, yielding to public opinion, would perhaps deem it best to cast her off. In that case all would be lost! From childhood she had cherished the dream of mighty empire. It was to attain it that, deserting her first husband, she had allied herself to this one, who, she thought, had deceived her.

"I obtained a powerful support when I entered your family!"

"It is equal to yours!" rejoined the Tetrarch, simply.

Herodias felt the blood of the priests and kings who were her ancestors boiling in her veins.

"But your grandfather swept the temple of Ascalon! The others were shepherds, bandits, heads of caravans, a wandering horde, subject to Judah from the time of King David! All my ancestors vanquished yours! The first of the Maccabees drove you forth from Hebron; Hyrcanus forced you to be circumcised!" And, giving vent to the patrician's scorn for the plebeian, Jacob's hatred of Edom,* she reproached him for his indifference to insults, for his mildness towards the Phœnecians, who betrayed him, his cowardly subservience to the people, who detested him. "You are like them, admit it! And you sigh for the Arab girl who danced around the stones! Take her! Go, live with her, in her canvas house! feed on her bread cooked in the ashes; drink the curdled milk of her sheep! Kiss her blue cheeks! And forget me!"

The Tetrarch was no longer listening. He was gazing at the roof of a house, on which there was a young girl, and an old woman holding a parasol with a reed handle as long as a fisher's line. In the center of the rug stood a great travelling-basket, open. Girdles, veils, jewels overflowed from it in a confused mass. Now and again the girl stooped towards those objects and shook them in the air. She was dressed like the Roman women, in a wrinkled tunic, with a peplum adorned with emerald tassels; and blue bands confined her hair, which was doubtless too heavy, for from time to time she put her hand to it. The shadow of the parasol hovered above her, half hiding her. Twice or thrice Antipas caught a glimpse of her shapely neck, the corner of an ear, or of a tiny mouth. But he saw her whole figure, from the hips to the neck, as she bent forward and drew herself up again with supple grace. He watched

* Esau. [Trans.]

for the repetition of that movement, and his breath came faster; flames kindled in his eyes. Herodias observed him.

He asked: "Who is she?"

She answered that she had no knowledge, and left him, suddenly appeased.

The Tetrarch was awaited under the porticoes by the Galileans, the master of the writings, the chief of the pasturage, the director of the salt-wells, and a Jew of Babylon, in command of his horsemen. All hailed him with loud acclamations. Then he vanished towards the inner chambers.

Phanuel appeared at the angle of a passage.

"Ah, again? You came to see Iaokanann doubtless?"

"And you! I have to tell you something of moment."

And, following Antipas, he entered, at his heels, a dark apartment.

The light entered through a barred opening that extended along the wall under the cornice. The walls were painted a dark pomegranate color, almost black. At the end stood an ebony bed, with cords of oxhide. A golden buckler, above, gleamed like a sun.

Antipas walked the whole length of the room, and lay down on the bed.

Phanuel was standing. He raised his arm, and said in the attitude of one inspired:

"The Most High sends one of his sons to earth now and again. Iaokanann is such an one. If you oppress him you will be punished."

"It is he who persecutes me!" cried Antipas. "He demanded of me an impossible act. Since then he has rent me. And I was not harsh at the beginning! He has even sent forth from Machærus men who overturn my provinces. A curse upon his life! Since he attacks me, I defend myself!"

"His fits of anger are too violent," replied Phanuel. "No matter! He must be set free."

"One does not set free raging beasts!" said the Tetrarch.

"Have no fear," the Essene replied. "He will go hence to the Arabs, the Gauls, the Scythians. His work is destined to reach to the ends of the earth!"

Antipas seemed lost in a vision.

"His power is mighty! Against my will, I love him."

"Then let him be free!"

The Tetrarch shook his head. He feared Herodias, Mannæus, and the unknown.

Phanuel strove to persuade him, alleging as a guaranty of his plans the submission of the Essenes to the King. People respected those poor men, unconquerable by torture, always clad in flax, and able to read the future in the stars.

Antipas recalled the words he had let fall a moment before.

"What is this thing which you said was of moment?"

A Negro appeared. His body was white with dust. He gasped for breath and could only say:

"Vitellius!"

"What! Has he arrived?"

"I saw him. Within three hours he will be here!"

The portières at the doors of the corridors were separated as by the wind. A busy hum filled the castle, a tumult of people running to and fro, of furniture being dragged about, of silver plate falling to the floor; and from the towers trumpets sounded, to call the scattered slaves.

II

The ramparts were thronged with people when Vitellius entered the courtyard. He was leaning on his interpreter's arm, followed by a great red litter adorned with plumes and mirrors; he wore the toga, the laticlave, the buskins of a consul, and his person was surrounded by lictors.

They leaned against the door their twelve fasces—staves bound together by a strap, with an axe in the center. Thereupon one and all trembled before the majesty of the Roman people.

The litter borne by eight men, stopped. Then stepped forth a youth with a fat paunch, a blotched face, and pearls along his fingers. He was offered a glass of wine and spices. He drank it and demanded a second.

The Tetrarch had fallen at the Proconsul's feet, grieved, he said, that he had not been sooner informed of the favor of his presence. Otherwise he would have ordered that whatever the Vitellii might require should await them along the roads. They were descended from the goddess Vitellia. A road leading from Janiculum to the sea still bore their name. Quæstorships and consulships were innumerable in the family; and as for Lucius, now his guest, they owed thanks to him as the conqueror of the Cliti and as the father of the young Aulus,* who seemed to be returning to his own domain, since the Orient was the fatherland of the gods.

These hyperbolical compliments were delivered in Latin. Vitellius accepted them impassively.

* Afterwards the Emperor Vitellius. [Trans.]

He replied that the great Herod sufficed to make a nation glorious. The Athenians had entrusted to him the management of the Olympic games. He had built temples in honor of Augustus, had been patient, ingenious, awe-inspiring, and always loyal to the Cæsars.

Between the pillars, with their brazen capitals, Herodias was seen, advancing with the air of an empress, amid women and eunuchs carrying burning perfumes on silver-gilt salvers.

The Proconsul took three steps to meet her; and, having saluted him with an inclination of the head:

"What joy!" she cried; "henceforth, Agrippa, the enemy of Tiberius, is powerless to do harm!"

He knew nothing of the event; it seemed to him perilous; and as Antipas swore that he would do everything for the Emperor, Vitellius added: "Even to the injury of others?"

He had taken hostages from the King of the Parthians, and the Emperor had forgotten it; for Antipas, being present at the conference, to give himself importance, had instantly despatched the news. Hence a deep-rooted hatred, and delay in sending succor.

The Tetrarch stammered, but Aulus said, laughing:

"Fear not; I will protect you!"

The Proconsul pretended not to have heard. The father's fortune depended on the son's debasement; and that flower from the mire of Capræ procured him advantages so considerable that he encompassed it with attentions, distrusting it all the while because it was poisonous.

A tumult arose beneath the gate. A file of white mules was led in, ridden by persons in priestly costume. They were Sadducees and Pharisees, led to Machærus by the same object of ambition, the first wishing to obtain the honorable post of sacrificer, the others to retain it. Their faces were dark, especially those of the Pharisees, foes of Rome and of the Tetrarch. The skirts of their tunics embarrassed them in the press; and their tiaras rested insecurely on their brows, above bands of parchment, whereon words were written.

At almost the same time some soldiers of the vanguard arrived. They had placed their shields in bags, to protect them from the dust; and behind them was Marcellus, lieutenant to the Proconsul, with publicans carrying tablets of wood under their armpits.

Antipas named the principal persons of his suite: Tolmai, Kanthera, Sebon, Ammonius, of Alexandria, who bought asphalt for him, Naaman, captain of his velites, and Jacim the Babylonian.

Vitellius had observed Mannæus.

"Who is that man?"

The Tetrarch, with a gesture, gave him to understand that he was the executioner.

Then he presented the Sadducees.

Jonathas, a small man of free manners, speaking Greek, begged the master to honor them by a visit to Jerusalem. He would probably go thither.

Eleazar, with hooked nose and long beard, demanded for the Pharisees the cloak of the high priest, detained in the Tower of Antonia by the civil authorities.

Then the Galileans denounced Pontius Pilate. Taking advantage of the act of a madman who was seeking David's vessel of gold in a cave near Samaria, he had killed some of the inhabitants. And they all spoke at once, Mannæus with more violence than the others. Vitellius declared that the criminals should be punished.

Loud exclamations arose in front of a portico where the soldiers had hung their shields. The coverings being removed, there was seen on the bosses the image of Cæsar. That, to the Jews, was idolatry. Antipas harangued them, while Vitellius, from an elevated seat on the colonnade, looked on in amazement at their wrath. Tiberius had done well to banish four hundred of them to Sardinia. But at home they were strong; and he ordered the bucklers to be removed.

Thereupon they surrounded the Proconsul, imploring reparation for injustice, privileges, alms. Clothes were torn, they trampled upon one another; and, to make room, slaves struck right and left with staves. Those nearest the gateway went down to the road; others ascended it; the tide flowed back; two currents met in that mass of men, which swayed back and forth, hemmed in by the encircling walls.

Vitellius asked why there were so many people. Antipas told him the reason: his birthday festival; and he pointed out several of his people, who leaned over the battlements, lowering enormous baskets of meat, fruit, vegetables, antelopes and storks, large sky-blue fish, grapes, melons, pomegranates arranged in pyramids. Aulus could not restrain himself. He rushed towards the kitchen, impelled by that gluttony which was destined to surprise the universe.

Passing a cave, he saw stew-pans like cuirasses. Vitellius came to look at them, and demanded that the underground rooms of the fortress should be opened for him.

They were hewn in the rock, with high vaulted roofs, and pillars at intervals. The first contained old armor, but the second was filled to overflowing with pikes, all their points protruding from a bouquet of plumes. The third seemed to be hung with mats of reeds, the slender arrows were arranged so straightly side by side. Scimitar-blades covered the walls of the fourth. In the center of the fifth, rows of helmets, with their crests, formed as it were a battalion of red serpents. In the sixth naught could be seen save quivers; in the seventh, naught but military boots; in the eighth, naught but armlets; in those following, pitchforks, grappling-irons, ladders, ropes, and even poles for catapults, even bells for the breastplates of dromedaries! And as the mountain grew larger at its base, and was hollowed out within like a beehive, beneath these rooms there were others more numerous and deeper.

Vitellius, Phineas his interpreter, and Sisenna, the leader of the publicans, walked through them by the light of torches borne by three eunuchs.

In the shadow they distinguished hideous objects invented by the barbarians: head-crushers studded with nails, javelins that poisoned the wounds they made, pincers resembling a crocodile's jaws; in a word, the Tetrarch had in store in Machærus munitions of war for forty thousand men.

He had gathered them in anticipation of an alliance of his enemies. But the Proconsul might believe, or say, that it was to fight against the Romans, and the Tetrarch sought explanations.

They were not his; many were used for protection against brigands; moreover, they were needed against the Arabs; or else, they had all belonged to his father. And, instead of walking behind the Proconsul, he went before, at a rapid pace. Then he stood against the wall, which he covered with his toga, holding his elbows away from his sides; but the top of a door appeared above his head. Vitellius noticed it and wished to know what was on the other side.

The Babylonian alone could open it.

"Call the Babylonian!"

They awaited his coming.

His father had come from the shores of the Euphrates, to offer his services to Herod the Great, with four hundred horsemen, to defend the eastern frontier. After the partition of the kingdom, Jacim had remained in Philip's service, and now served Antipas.

He appeared, with a bow over his shoulder, a whip in his hand. Cords of many colors were tide tightly about his crooked legs. His huge arms emerged from a sleeveless tunic, and a fur cap cast its shadow over his face, which bore a beard curled in rings.

At first he seemed not to understand the interpreter. But Vitellius cast a glance at Antipas, who instantly repeated his command. Thereupon Jacim placed both his hands against the door. It glided into the wall.

A breath of hot air came forth from the darkness. A winding path sloped downward; they followed it and reached the entrance to a grotto, of greater extent than the other underground apartments.

At the rear there was an arched opening over the precipice, which defended the citadel on that side. The blossoms of a honeysuckle that clung to the wall hung downward in the bright light of day. Along the ground trickled a murmuring thread of water.

There were white horses there, a hundred perhaps, eating barley from a board on a level with their mouths. All had their manes painted blue, their hoofs in bags of esparto, and the hair between the ears curled over the frontal bone, like a wig. With their very long tails they lazily lashed their legs. The Proconsul was struck dumb with admiration.

They were marvellous creatures, supple as serpents, light as birds. They would keep pace with their riders' arrows, overturn men and bite them in the abdomen, traverse the mountainous country with ease, leap ravines, and continue their wild gallop over the level ground through a whole day. A word would stop them. As soon as Jacim entered, they went to him, like sheep when the shepherd appears, and, stretching out their necks, gazed at him restlessly with their childlike eyes. From habit, he uttered a hoarse cry from the bottom of his throat, which aroused their spirits; and they reared, hungry for space, begging leave to run.

Antipas, fearing that Vitellius might take them, had imprisoned them in that place, specially designed for animals in case of seige.

"It is a bad stable," said the Proconsul, "and you run the risk of losing them! Count them, Sisenna!"

The publican took a tablet from his girdle, counted the horses and wrote the number.

The agents of the fiscal companies bribed the provincial governors, in order to pillage the provinces. This one smelt everywhere, with his pole-cat's jaw and his blinking eyes.

At last they went up again to the courtyard.

Bronze shields, set in the pavement here and there, covered the cisterns. He noticed one larger than the rest, which had not their sonority beneath the feet. He struck them all in turn, then shouted, stamping:

"I have it! I have it! Herod's treasure is here!"

The search for his treasure was a mania among the Romans.

It did not exist, the Tetrach swore.

But what was there beneath?

"Nothing! A man, a prisoner."

"Show him to me!" said Vitellius.

The Tetrarch did not obey; the Jews would have learned his secret. His disinclination to raise the shield angered Vitellius.

"Break it in!" he shouted to the lictors.

Mannæus had divined what was happening. Seeing an axe, he thought that they were going to behead Iaokanann—and he stopped the lictor at the first blow on the bronze circle, inserted a sort of hook between it and the pavement, then, straightening his long, thin arms, slowly raised it; it opened, and all marvelled at the old man's strength. Beneath the wood-lined cover was a trapdoor of the same dimensions. At a blow of the fist it folded in two panels; then they saw a hole, a great ditch, surrounded by a staircase without a rail; and they who leaned over the brink saw at the bottom something indistinct and horrifying.

A human being lay on the ground, covered with long hair that mingled with the beast's hair that clothed his back. He rose; his brow touched a horizontal grating; and from time to time he disappeared in the depths of his den.

The sun gleamed on the points of the tiaras and on the sword-hilts, and heated the flagstones beyond measure; and doves, flying from the eaves, fluttered above the courtyard. It was the hour when Mannæus usually threw grain to them. He crouched before the Tetrarch, who stood beside Vitellius. The Galileans, the priests, the soldiers, formed a circle behind them; all held their peace, in agonizing suspense as to what was about to happen.

First there was a profound sigh, uttered in a cavernous voice.

Herodias heard it at the other end of the palace. Overcome by a sort of fascination, she passed through the crowd; and with one hand on Mannæus's shoulder, and body bent forward, she listened.

The voice arose.

"Woe to you, Pharisees and Sadducees, generation of vipers, inflated skins, tinkling cymbals!"

They recognized Iaokanann. His name passed from mouth to mouth. Others hastened to the spot.

"Woe unto you, O people! woe to the traitors of Judah, to the drunkards of Ephraim, to those who dwell in the fat valleys and who are overcome with wine!

"Let them fade away like the water that flows, like the snail that melts as it crawls, like the fœtus of a woman who does not see the sun.

"Thou must take refuge, O Moab, among the cypresses like the sparrows, in caverns like the jerboa. The gates of the fortresses shall be rent assunder more easily than nut shells, walls shall crumble, cities shall burn; and the scourge of the Eternal shall not rest. He shall turn your limbs about in your blood as wool is turned in the dyer's vat. He shall tear you like a new harrow; He shall scatter morsels of your flesh upon the mountains!"

Of what conqueror was he speaking? Was it of Vitellius? The Romans alone could effect such an extermination. Complaints arose:

"Enough! enough! let him finish!"

He continued, in a louder voice:

"Beside their mothers' dead bodies, little children shall drag themselves through the dust. You shall go at night to seek bread among the ruins, at the risk of sword thrusts. The jackals shall fight for your bones on the public squares, where the old men used to talk at evening. Your virgins, swallowing their tears, shall play the lute at the stranger's feasts, and your bravest sons shall bend their backs, crushed by too heavy burdens!"

The people remembered their days of exile, all the calamities of their history. These were the words of the prophets of old. Iaokanann sent them forth, like mighty blows, one after another.

But the voice became sweet, melodious, musical. It proclaimed enfranchisement, splendid portents in the sky, the newly born, with an arm in the dragon's cavern, gold instead of clay, the desert blooming like a rose. "That which is now worthy sixty talents will not cost an obol. Fountains of milk shall gush from the rocks; you shall sleep in the winepresses, with full bellies! When wilt Thou come, whose coming I await? In anticipation, all the peoples kneel, and Thy sway shall be eternal, O Son of David!"

The Tetrarch threw himself back, the existence of a Son of David affronting him like a threat.

Iaokanann anathematized him for his assumption of royalty; "There is no king save the Eternal!" and for his gardens, his statues, his ivory furniture—like the impious Ahab!

Antipas broke the cord of the seal that hung upon his breast, and threw it into the hole, bidding him hold his peace.

The voice replied:

"I will cry aloud like the bear, like a wild ass, like a woman in labor!

"The punishment has already befallen thee in thy incest. God afflicts thee with the sterility of the mule."

And laughter arose, like the plashing of the waves.

Vitellius persisted in remaining. The interpreter, in an unmoved voice, repeated in the Roman tongue all the invectives that Iaokanann roared in his own. The Tetrarch and Herodias were forced to listen to them twice. He panted, while she, open-mouthed, watched the bottom of the hole.

The ghastly man threw back his head, and, grasping the bars, pressed against them his face, which had the aspect of a tangled underbrush, and in which two coals of fire beamed.

"Ah! it is thou, Jezebel!

"Thou dost take his heart captive with the creaking of thy shoes. Thou didst neigh like a mare. Thou didst set thy bed on the mountains, to accomplish thy sacrifices!

"The Lord shall tear away thine earrings, thy purple robes, thy veils of fine linen, the circlets from thine arms, the rings from thy feet; and the little golden crescents that tremble on thy brow, thy silver mirrors, thy fans of ostrich feathers, the mother-of-pearl pattens that increase thy stature, the pride of thy diamonds, the perfumes of thy hair, the painting of thy nails—all the artifices of sensuality; and the stones shall be too few to stone the adulteress!"

She glanced about her for protection. The Pharisees hypocritically lowered their eyes. The Sadducees turned their faces away, fearing to offend the Proconsul. Antipas seemed at the point of death.

The voice grew louder, took on new intonations, rolled hither and thither with a crashing as of thunder, and, repeated by the mountain echoes, struck Machærus with bolt after bolt.

"Stretch thyself in the dust, daughter of Babylon! Grind flour! Remove thy girdle, unloose thy shoes, truss up thy skirts, cross the rivers! Thy shame shall be laid bare, thine approbrium shall be seen! Thy sobs shall break thy teeth! The Eternal abhors the stench of thy crimes! Accursed! Accursed! Die like a dog!"

The trap-door closed, the cover was lowered to its place. Mannæus wished to strangle Iaokanann.

Herodias vanished. The Pharisees were scandalized. Antipas, in their midst, defended himself.

"Doubtless," said Eleazar, "one may marry his brother's wife; but Herodias was not widowed, and, moreover, she had a child, wherein lay the abomination."

"Not so! not so!" objected Jonathas the Sadducee. "The Law condemns such marriages, without proscribing them absolutely."

"It matters not! They are most unjust to me!" said Antipas; "for Absalom lay with his father's wives, Judah with his daughter-in-law, Ammon with his sister, Lot with his daughters."

Aulus, who had been sleeping, reappeared at that moment. When he was informed of the affair, he took sides with the Tetrarch. He should not be disturbed by such foolish ideas; and he laughed aloud at the reprobation of the priests and the frenzy of Iaokanann.

Herodias, on the steps, turned towards him.

"You are wrong, my master! He bids the people refuse to pay the tax."

"Is that true?" instantly asked the publican.

The answers were generally in the affirmative. The Tetrarch confirmed them.

Vitellius thought the prisoner might fly; and, as Antipas's conduct seemed to him equivocal, he posted sentinels at the gates, along the walls, and in the courtyard.

Then he went to his apartment. The deputations of priests attended him.

Each set forth his grievances, without broaching the question of the office of sacrificer.

One and all importuned him. He dismissed them.

Jonathas left him when he saw on the battlements Antipas talking with a man with long hair and in a white robe—an Essene; and he regretted having upheld him.

One thought afforded the Tetrarch consolation. Iaokanann was no longer at his disposal, the Romans had taken charge of him. What a relief! Phanuel was walking on the path around the battlements. He called him and said, pointing to the soldiers:

"They are stronger than I! I cannot set him free; it is not my fault!"

The courtyard was empty. The slaves were at rest. Against the reddening sky, flame-colored on the horizon, the smallest perpendicular objects were outlined in black. Antipas distinguished the salt-wells at the far end of the Dead Sea, and he no longer saw the tents of the Arabs. Doubtless they had gone. The moon rose; a feeling of peace descended upon his heart.

Phanuel, overwhelmed, stood with his chin upon his breast. At last he made known what he had to say.

Since the beginning of the month he had studied the sky before dawn, the constellation Perseus being at the zenith. Agalah was hardly visible, Algol shone less brightly, Mira-Cœti had disappeared, whence he augured the death of a man of mark, that very night, in Machærus.

Who? Vitellius was too well guarded. Iaokanann would not be executed. "Then it is I!" thought the Tetrarch.

Perhaps the Arabs would return. The Proconsul might discover his relations with the Parthians! Hired assassins from Jerusalem escorted the priests; they had daggers under their garments, and the Tetrarch did not doubt Phanuel's learning.

He conceived the idea of having recourse to Herodias. He hated her, however. But she would give him courage, and all the bonds were not broken of the spell she had formerly cast upon him.

When he entered her chamber, cinnamon was smouldering in a bowl of porphyry; and powders, unguents, fabrics like clouds, embroideries lighter than feathers, were scattered about.

He did not mention Phanuel's prediction, or his dread of the Jews and Arabs; she would have accused him of cowardice. He spoke of the Romans only. Vitellius had confided to him none of his military projects. He supposed him to be a friend of Caius, with whom Agrippa consorted, and he would be sent into exile, or perhaps he would be murdered.

Herodias, with indulgent contempt, tried to encourage him. At last she took from a small casket a curious medallion adorned with Tiberius's profile. That was enough to make the lictors turn pale and to base accusations upon.

Antipas, touched with gratitude, asked her how she had obtained it.

"It was given me," she replied.

Beneath a portière opposite, a bare arm protruded, a lovely, youthful arm, that might have been carved in ivory by Polycletus. Somewhat awkwardly, and yet with grace, it felt about in the air, trying to grasp a tunic left upon a stool near the wall.

An old woman silently passed it to her, pulling aside the curtain.

The Tetrarch remembered the face, but could not place it.

"Is that slave yours?"

"What matters it to you?" replied Herodias.

III

The guests filled the banquet-hall.

It had three naves, like a basilica, separated by pillars of algum wood, with bronze capitals covered with carvings. Two galleries with openwork ballustrades overhung it; and a third, in gold filagree, jutted out at one end, opposite an immense arch.

Candelabra burning on long tables extending the whole length of the hall formed bushes of fire, between cups of painted clay and copper platters, cubes of snow and heaps of grapes; but those red gleams one after another were lost in space because of the height of the ceiling, and points of light twinkled, like the stars at night, through the branches. Through the opening of the vast arch, one could see torches on the terraces of the houses; for Antipas feasted his friends, his subjects, and all who had presented themselves.

Slaves, as active as dogs, and with their feet encased in sandals of felt, went to and fro, carrying salvers.

The proconsular table stood upon a platform built of sycamore boards, beneath the gilded tribune. Tapestries from Babylon enclosed it in a sort of pavilion.

Three ivory couches, one opposite the door and one on either side, held Vitellius, his son, and Antipas; the Proconsul being next the door, at the left, Aulus at the right, the Tetrarch in the center.

He wore a heavy black cloak, whose texture was invisible beneath layers of dyestuffs; he had paint on his cheek-bones, his beard trimmed like a fan, and azure powder on his hair, surmounted by a diadem of precious stones. Vitellius retained his purple baldric, which he wore diagonally over a linen tunic. Aulus had the sleeves of his robe of violet silk, shot with silver, tied at his back. The long spiral curls of his hair formed terraces, and a necklace of sapphires sparkled on his breast, which was as plump and white as a woman's. Beside him, on a mat, with legs crossed, sat a very beautiful boy, who smiled incessantly. He had seen him in the kitchen, could not live without him, and having difficulty in remembering his Chaldean name, called him simply the "Asiatic." From time to time he stretched himself out on the triclinium. Then his bare feet overlooked the assemblage.

On one side there were the priests and officers of Antipas, people from Jerusalem, the chief men of the Greek cities; and, under the Proconsul, Marcellus with the publicans, friends of the Tetrarch, the notables of Cana, Ptolemais, and Jericho; then, mingled pell-mell, mountaineers from Libanus and Herod's old soldiers (twelve Thracians, a Gaul, two Germans), gazelle-hunters, Idumean shepherds, the Sultan of Palmyra, seamen of Eziongeber. Each person had before him a cake of soft dough, on which to wipe his fingers; and their arms, stretching out like vultures' necks, seized olives, pistachioes and almonds. All the faces beamed with joy beneath crowns of flowers.

The Pharisees had spurned them as Roman wantonness. They shuddered when they were sprinkled with galburnum and incense, a compound reserved for the use of the Temple.

Aulus rubbed his armpits with it; and Antipas promised him a whole cargo, with three bales of that genuine balsam which caused Cleopatra to covet Palestine.

A captain of his garrison at Tiberius, recently arrived, took his place behind him, to tell him of extraordinary events. But his attention was divided between the Proconsul and what was being said at the neighboring tables.

The talk was of Iaokanann and men of his type; Simon of Gittoy purged sin with fire. A certain Jesus——

• "The worst of all!" cried Eleazer. "An infamous juggler!"

Behind the Tetrarch a man arose, as pale as the hem of his chlamys. He descended from the platform and addressed the Pharisees:

"False! Jesus does miracles!"

Antipas would fain see one.

"You should have brought Him hither! Tell us."

Then he told that he, Jacob, having a daughter who was sick, had betaken himself to Capernaum, to implore the Master to heal her. The master had replied: "Return to thy home, she is healed!" And he had found her in the doorway, having left her bed when the hand of the dial marked three o'clock, the very moment when he had accosted Jesus.

Of course, argued the Pharisees, there are devices, powerful herbs! Sometimes, even there, at Machærus, one found the *baaras*, which made men invulnerable; but to cure without seeing or touching was an impossibility, unless Jesus employed demons.

And the friends of Antipas, the chief men of Galilee, repeated, shaking ther heads:

"Demons, clearly."

Jacob, standing between their table and that of the priests, held his peace, with a haughty yet gentle bearing.

They called upon him to speak: "Explain His power."

He bent his shoulders, and in an undertone, slowly, as if afraid of himself:

"Know you not that He is the Messiah?"

All the priests glanced at one another, and Vitellius inquired the meaning of the word. His interpreter waited a full minute before replying.

They called by that name a liberator who should bring to them the enjoyment of all their goods and power over all peoples. Some indeed maintained that two should be expected. The first would be vanquished by Gog and Magog, demons of the North; but the other would exterminate the Prince of Evil; and for ages they had expected His coming every minute.

The priests having taken counsel together, Eleazer spoke for them.

First, the Messiah would be a Son of David, not of a carpenter. He would confirm the Law; this Nazarene assailed it; and—a yet stronger argument—he was to be preceded by the coming of Elias.

Jacob retorted:

"But Elias has come!"

"Elias! Elias!" echoed the multitude, even to the farthest end of the hall.

All, in imagination, saw an old man beneath a flock of ravens, the lightning shining upon an altar, idolatrous pontiffs cast into raging torrents; and the women in the tribunes thought of the widow of Zarephath.

Jacob wearied himself repeating that he knew him! He had seen him! And so had the people!

"His name?"

Whereupon he shouted with all his strength:

"Iaokanann!"

Antipas fell backward as if stricken full in the chest. The Sadducees leaped upon Jacob. Eleazer harangued, seeking to obtain an audience.

When silence was restored, he folded his cloak about him and propounded questions, like a judge.

"Since the prophet is dead——"

Murmurs interrupted him. It was believed that Elias had disappeared only.

He angrily rebuked the multitude, and asked, continuing his inquiry:

"Think you that he has come to life again?"

"Why not?" said Jacob.

The Sadducees shrugged their shoulders; Jonathas, half closing his little eyes, forced himself to laugh, like a clown. Nothing could be more absurd than the claim of the body to life everlasting; and he declaimed for the Proconsul's benefit, this line from a contemporary poet:

Nec crescit, nec post mortem durare videtur.

But Aulus was leaning over the edge of the triclinium, his forehead bathed in sweat, green of face, his hands on his stomach.

The Sadducees feigned deep emotion—on the morrow the office of sacrificer was restored to them; Antipas made parade of despair; Vitellius remained impassive. None the less his suffering was intense; with his son he would lose his fortune.

Aulus had not finished vomiting when he wished to eat again.

'Give me some marble-dust, schist from Naxos, sea-water, no matter what! Suppose I should take a bath?"

He crunched snow; then, after hesitating between a Commagene stew and pink blackbirds, he decided upon gourds with honey. The

Asiatic stared at him, that faculty of absorbing food denoting a prodigious being of a superior race.

Bulls' kidneys were served, also dormice, nightingales, and minced-meat on vine leaves; and the priests disputed concerning the resurrection. Ammonius, pupil of Philo the Platonist, deemed them stupid, and said as much to Greeks who laughed at the oracles. Marcellus and Jacob had come together. The first described to the second the bliss he had felt during his baptism by Mithra, and Jacob urged him to follow Jesus. Wines made from the palm and the tamarisk, wines of Safed and of Byblos, flowed from amphoræ into crateres, from crateres into drinking-cups, from drinking-cups down thirsty throats; there was much talk, and hearts overflowed. Jacim, although a Jew, did not conceal his adoration of the planets. A merchant of Aphaka stupefied the nomads by detailing the wonders of the Temple of Hierapolis: and they asked how much the pilgrimage would cost. Others clung to their native religion. A German, almost blind, sang a hymn in praise of that promontory of Scandinavia where the gods appeared with halos about their faces; and men from Sichem refused to eat turtle-doves, from respect for the dove Azima.

Many talked, standing in the center of the hall, and the vapor of their breaths, with the smoke of the candles, made a fog in the air. Phanuel passed along the wall. He had been studying the firmament anew, but he did not approach the Tetrarch, dreading the drops of oil, which, to the Essenes, were a great pollution.

Blows rang out against the gate of the castle.

It was known now that Iaokanann was held a prisoner there. Men with torches ascended the path; a black mass swarmed in the ravine; and they roared from time to time:

"Iaokanann! Iaokanann!"

"He disturbs everything!" said Jonathas.

"We shall have no money left if he continues!" added the Pharisees.

And recriminations arose:

"Protect us!"

"Let us make an end of him!"

"You abandon the religion!"

"Impious as the Herods!"

"Less so than you!" retorted Antipas. "It was my father who built your temple!"

Thereupon the Pharisees, the sons of the proscribed, the partisans of the Mattathiases, accused the Tetrarch of the crimes of his family.

They had pointed skulls, bristling beards, weak and evil hands, or flat noses, great round eyes, and the expression of a bulldog. A dozen or more, scribes and servants of the priests, fed upon the refuse of holocausts, rushed as far as the foot of the platform, and with knives threatened Antipas, who harangued them, while the Sadducees listlessly defended him. He spied Mannæus and motioned him to go, Vitellius signifying by his expression that these things did not concern him.

The Pharisees, remaining on their triclinia, worked themselves into a demoniacal frenzy. They broke the dishes before them. They had been served with the favorite stew of Mæcenas—wild ass—unclean meat.

Aulus mocked at them on the subject of the ass's head, which they held in honor, it was said, and indulged in other sarcasms concerning their antipathy for pork. Doubtless it was because that vulgar beast had killed their Bacchus; and they were too fond of wine, since a golden vine had been discovered in the Temple.

The priests did not understand his words. Phineas, by birth a Galilæan, refused to translate them. Thereupon Aulus's wrath knew no bounds, the more as the Asiatic, seized with fright, had disappeared; and the repast failed to please him, the dishes being commonplace, not sufficiently disguised! He became calmer when he saw tails of Syrian sheep, which are bundles of fat.

The character of the Jews seemed hideous to Vitellius. Their god might well be Moloch, whose altars he had noticed along the road; and the sacrifices of children recurred to his mind, with the story of the man whom they were mysteriously fattening. His Latin heart rose in disgust at their intolerance, their iconoclastic frenzy, their brutish stagnation. The Proconsul wished to go, Aulus refused.

His robe fallen to his hips, he lay behind a heap of food, too replete to take more, but persisting in not leaving it.

The excitement of the people increased. They abandoned themselves to schemes of independence. They recalled the glory of Israel. All the conquerors had been punished: Antigonus, Crassus, Varus.

"Villains!" exclaimed the Proconsul; for he understood Syriac; his interpreter simply gave him time to compose his replies.

Antipas quickly drew the medallion of the Emperor, and, watching him tremblingly, held it with the image towards him.

Suddenly the panels of the golden tribune opened, and in the brilliant blaze of candles, between her slaves and festoons of anemone, Herodias appeared—on her head an Assyrian mitre held in place on her brow by a chin-piece; her hair fell in spiral curls over a scarlet peplum, slit along the sleeves. With two stone monsters, like those that guard the treasure of the Atrides, standing against the door, she resembled Cybele flanked by her lions; and from the balustrade above Antipas, she cried, patera in hand:

"Long life to Cæsar!"

This homage was echoed by Vitellius, Antipas, and the priests.

But there came to them from the lower end of the hall a hum of surprise and admiration. A young girl had entered.

Beneath a bluish veil that concealed her breast and her head could be seen her arched eyebrows, the sards at her ears, the whiteness of her skin. A square of variegated silk covered her shoulders and was secured about her hips by a golden girdle. Her black drawers were embroidered with mandrakes, and she tapped the floor indolently with tiny slippers of humming-birds' feathers.

When she reached the platform, she removed her veil. It was Herodias, as she was in her youth. Then she began to dance.

Her feet passed, one before the other, to the music of a flute and a pair of crotala. Her rounded arms seemed to beckon some one, who always fled. She pursued him, lighter than a butterfly, like an inquisitive Psyche, like a wandering soul, and seemed on the point of flying away.

The funereal notes of the gingras succeeded the crotala. Prostration had followed hope. Her attitudes signified sighs, and her whole person a languor so intense that one knew not whether she was weeping for a god or dying for joy in his embrace. Her eyes half closed, she writhed and swayed with billowy undulations of the stomach; her bosoms quivered, her face remained impassive, and her feet did not stop.

Vitellius compared her to Mnester the pantomimist. Aulus was vomiting again. The Tetrarch lost himself in a dream and thought no more of Herodias. He fancied that he saw her near the Sadducees. Then the vision faded away.

It was not a vision. She had sent messengers, far from Machærus, to Salome her daughter, whom the Tetrarch loved; and it was an excellent scheme. She was sure of him now!

Then it was the frenzy of love that demanded to be satisfied. She danced like the priestess of the Indies, like the Nubian girls of the Cataracts, like the Bacchantes of Lydia. She threw herself in all directions, like a flower beaten by the storm. The jewels in her ears leaped about, the silk on her back shone with a changing gleam; from her arms, from her feet, from her garments invisible sparks flashed and set men aflame. A harp sang; the multitude replied with loud applause. By stretching her legs apart, without bending her knees, she stooped so low that her chin touched the floor; and the nomads, accustomed to abstinance, the Roman soldiers, experts in debauchery, the miserly publicans, the old priests soured by disputes, all, distending their nostrils, quivered with desire.

Then she danced about Antipas's table, in a frenzy of excitement, like a witch's rhombus; and in a voice broken by sobs of lust he said: "Come! come!" She danced on; the dulcimers rang out as if they would burst; the crowd roared. But the Tetrarch shouted louder than them all: "Come! come! thou shalt have Capernaum! the plain of Tiberias! my citadels! half of my kingdom!"

She threw herself on her hands, heels in the air, and thus circled the platform like a huge scarab, then stopped abruptly.

Her neck and her vertebræ were at right angles. The colored skirts that enveloped her legs, falling over her shoulders like a rainbow, framed her face a cubit from the floor. Her lips were painted, her eyebrows intensely black, her eyes almost terrible, and drops of sweat on her forehead resembled steam on white marble.

She did not speak. They gazed at each other.

There was a snapping of fingers in the tribune. She went thither, reappeared, and, lisping a little, uttered these words with an infantine air:

"I want you to give me, on a charger, the head——" She had forgotten the name, but she continued with a smile: "The head of Iaokanann!"

The Tetrarch sank back, overwhelmed.

He was bound by his word, and the people were waiting. But the death that had been predicted to him, should it befall another, might avert his own. If Iaokanann were really Elias, he could escape it; if he were not, the murder would be of no importance.

Mannæus was at his side and understood his purpose.

Vitellius recalled him to give him the countersign of the sentinels guarding the moat.

It was a relief. In a moment all would be over.

But Mannæus was hardly prompt in the execution of his function.

He reappeared, but greatly perturbed.

For forty years he had filled the post of executioner. He it was who had drowned Aristobulus, strangled Alexander, burned Mattathias alive, beheaded Zosimus, Pappus, Josephus and Antipates, and he dared not kill Iaokanann! His teeth chattered, his whole body trembled.

He had seen in front of the hole the Great Angel of the Samaritans, all covered with eyes, and brandishing an enormous sword, red and jagged like a flame. Two soldiers brought forward as witnesses could confirm him.

They had seen nothing save a Jewish captain, who had rushed upon them and who had ceased to live.

The frantic rage of Herodias burst forth in a torrent of vulgar and murderous abuse. She broke her nails on the gilded grating of the tribune, and the two carved lions seemed to bite at her shoulders and to roar with her.

Antipas imitated her, so did the priests, the soldiers, the Pharisees, all demanding vengeance; and others indignant that their pleasure was delayed.

Mannæus went forth, hiding his face.

The guests found the time of waiting even longer than before. They were bored.

Suddenly the sound of footsteps echoed in the corridors. The suspense became intolerable.

The head entered; and Mannæus held it by the hair, at arm's length, proud of the applause.

When he laid it on a charger, he offered it to Salome. She ran lightly up to the tribune; some moments later the head was brought back by the same old woman whom the Tetrarch had noticed that morning on the roof of a house, and later in Herodias's chamber.

He recoiled to avoid looking at it. Vitellius cast an indifferent glance upon it.

Mannæus went down from the platform and exhibited it to the Roman captains, then to all those who were eating in that part of the hall.

They examined it.

The sharp blade of the instrument, cutting downward, had touched the jaw. The corners of the mouth were drawn convulsively. Blood, already clotted, studded the beard. The closed eyelids were of a leaden hue, like shells; and the candelabra all about shone upon it.

It reached the priest's table. A Pharisee turned it over curiously, and Mannæus, having turned it back again, placed it in front of Aulus, who was awakened by it. Through their partly open lids the dead eyes and the lifeless eyes seemed to speak to each other.

Then Mannæus presented it to Antipas. Tears flowed down the Tetrarch's cheeks.

The torches were extinguished. The guests took their leave, and Antipas alone remained in the hall, his hands pressed against his temples, still gazing at the severed head; while Phanuel, standing in the center of the great nave, muttered prayers with outstretched arms.

At the moment when the sun rose, two men, previously despatched by Iaokanann, returned with the long-awaited answer.

They confided it to Phanuel, who was enraptured by it.

Then he showed them the sorrowful object on the charger, amidst the remnants of the feast. One of the men said to him:

"Be comforted! He has gone down among the dead to announce the Christ's coming!"

The Essene understood now the words: "That He may grow great, I must needs shrink."

And all three, having taken the head of Iaokanann, went forth in the direction of Galilee.

As it was very heavy, they carried it each in turn.

9

The Torture of Hope

VILLIERS DE L'ISLE-ADAM

MANY years ago, as evening was closing in, the venerable Pedro Arbuez d'Espila, sixth prior of the Dominicans of Segovia, and third Grand Inquisitor of Spain, followed by a *fra redemptor,* and preceded by two familiars of the Holy Office, the latter carrying lanterns, made their way to a subterranean dungeon. The bolt of a massive door creaked, and they entered a mephitic *in pace,* where the dim light revealed between rings fastened to the wall a blood-stained rack, a brazier, and a jug. On a pile of straw, loaded with fetters and his neck encircled by an iron carcan, sat a haggard man, of uncertain age, clothed in rags.

This prisoner was no other than Rabbi Aser Abarbanel, a Jew of Aragon, who—accused of usury and pitiless scorn for the poor—had been daily subjected to torture for more than a year. Yet "his blindness was as dense as his hide," and he had refused to abjure his faith.

Proud of a filiation dating back thousands of years, proud of his ancestors—for all Jews worthy of the name are vain of their blood—he descended Talmudically from Othoniel and consequently from Ipsiboa, the wife of the last judge of Israel, a circumstance which had sustained his courage amid incessant torture. With tears in his eyes at the thought of this resolute soul rejecting salvation, the venerable Pedro Arbuez d'Espila, approaching the shuddering rabbi, addressed him as follows:

"My son, rejoice: your trials here below are about to end. If in the presence of such obstinacy I was forced to permit, with deep regret, the use of great severity, my task of fraternal correction has its limits. You are the fig tree which, having failed so many times to bear fruit, at last withered, but God alone can judge your soul. Perhaps Infinite Mercy will shine upon you at the last moment! We must hope so. There are examples. So sleep in peace tonight. Tomorrow you will be included in

the *auto da fé:* that is, you will be exposed to the *quémadero,* the symbolical flames of the Everlasting Fire: it burns, as you know, only at a
distance, my son; and Death is at least two hours (often three) in coming, on account of the wet, iced bandages with which we protect the
heads and hearts of the condemned. There will be forty-three of you.
Placed in the last row, you will have time to invoke God and offer to
Him this baptism of fire, which is of the Holy Spirit. Hope in the Light,
and rest."

With these words, having signed to his companions to unchain the
prisoner, the prior tenderly embraced him. Then came the turn of the
fra redemptor, who, in a low tone, entreated the Jew's forgiveness for
what he had made him suffer for the purpose of redeeming him; then
the two familiars silently kissed him. This ceremony over, the captive
was left, solitary and bewildered, in the darkness.

Rabbi Aser Abarbanel, with parched lips and visage worn by suffering, at first gazed at the closed door with vacant eyes. Closed? The word
unconsciously roused a vague fancy in his mind, the fancy that he had
seen for an instant the light of the lanterns through a chink between the
door and the wall. A morbid idea of hope, due to the weakness of his
brain, stirred his whole being. He dragged himself toward the strange
appearance. Then, very gently and cautiously, slipping one finger into
the crevice, he drew the door toward him. Marvelous! By an extraordinary accident the familiar who closed it had turned the huge key an
instant before it struck the stone casing, so that the rusty bolt not having
entered the hole, the door again rolled on its hinges.

The rabbi ventured to glance outside. By the aid of a sort of luminous
dusk he distinguished at first a semicircle of walls indented by winding
stairs; and opposite to him, at the top of five or six stone steps, a sort of
black portal, opening into an immense corridor, whose first arches only
were visible from below.

Stretching himself flat he crept to the threshold. Yes, it was really a
corridor, but endless in length. A wan light illumined it: lamps suspended from the vaulted ceiling lightened at intervals the dull hue of
the atmosphere—the distance was veiled in shadow. Not a single door
appeared in the whole extent! Only on one side, the left, heavily grated
loopholes, sunk in the walls, admitted a light which must be that of evening, for crimson bars at intervals rested on the flags of the pavement.
What a terrible silence! Yet, yonder, at the far end of that passage there
might be a doorway of escape! The Jew's vacillating hope was tenacious,
for it was *the last.*

Without hesitating, he ventured on the flags, keeping close under the loopholes, trying to make himself part of the blackness of the long walls. He advanced slowly, dragging himself along on his breast, forcing back the cry of pain when some raw wound sent a keen pang through his whole body.

Suddenly the sound of a sandaled foot approaching reached his ears. He trembled violently, fear stifled him, his sight grew dim. Well, it was over, no doubt. He pressed himself into a niche and, half lifeless with terror, waited.

It was a familiar hurrying along. He passed swiftly by, holding in his clenched hand an intrument of torture—a frightful figure—and vanished. The suspense which the rabbi had endured seemed to have suspended the functions of life, and he lay nearly an hour unable to move. Fearing an increase of tortures if he were captured, he thought of returning to his dungeon. But the old hope whispered in his soul that divine *perhaps,* which comforts us in our sorest trials. A miracle had happened. He could doubt no longer. He began to crawl toward the chance of escape. Exhausted by suffering and hunger, trembling with pain, he pressed onward. The sepulchral corridor seemed to lengthen mysteriously, while he, still advancing, gazed into the gloom where there *must* be some avenue of escape.

Oh! oh! He again heard footsteps, but this time they were slower, more heavy. The white and black forms of two inquisitors appeared, emerging from the obscurity beyond. They were conversing in low tones, and seemed to be discussing some important subject, for they were gesticulating vehemently.

At this spectacle Rabbi Aser Abarbanel closed his eyes; his heart beat so violently that it almost suffocated him; his rags were damp with the cold sweat of agony; he lay motionless by the wall, his mouth wide open, under the rays of a lamp, praying to the God of David.

Just opposite to him the two inquisitors paused under the light of the lamp—doubtless owing to some accident due to the course of their argument. One, while listening to his companion, gazed at the rabbi! And, beneath that look—whose absence of expression the hapless man did not at first notice—he fancied he again felt the burning pincers scorch his flesh, he was to be once more a living wound. Fainting, breathless, with fluttering eyelids, he shivered at the touch of the monk's floating robe. But—strange yet natural fact—the inquisitor's gaze was evidently that of a man deeply absorbed in his intended reply, engrossed by what he was hearing; his eyes were fixed—and seemed to look at the Jew *without seeing him*.

In fact, after the lapse of a few minutes, the two gloomy figures slowly pursued their way, still conversing in low tones, toward the place whence the prisoner had come. HE HAD NOT BEEN SEEN! Amid the horrible confusion of the rabbi's thoughts, the idea darted through his brain: "Can I be already dead that they did not see me?" A hideous impression roused him from his lethargy: in looking at the wall against which his face was pressed, he imagined he beheld two fierce eyes watching him! He flung his head back in a sudden frenzy of fright, his hair fairly bristling! Yet, no! No. His hand groped over the stones: it was the *reflection* of the inquisitor's eyes, still retained in his own, which had been reflected from two spots on the wall.

Forward! He must hasten toward that goal which he fancied (absurdly, no doubt) to be deliverance, toward the darkness from which he was now barely thirty paces distant. He pressed forward faster on his knees, his hands, at full length, dragging himself painfully along, and soon entered the dark portion of this terrible corridor.

Suddenly the poor wretch felt a gust of cold air on the hands resting upon the flags; it came from under the little door to which the two walls led.

Oh, Heaven, if that door should open outward. Every nerve in the miserable fugitive's body thrilled with hope. He examined it from top to bottom, though scarcely able to distinguish its outlines in the surrounding darkness. He passed his hand over it: no bolt, no lock! A latch! He started up, the latch yielded to the pressure of his thumb: the door silently swung open before him.

"Halleluia!" murmured the rabbi in a transport of gratitude as, standing on the threshold, he beheld the scene before him.

The door had opened into the gardens, above which arched a starlit sky, into spring, liberty, life! It revealed the neighboring fields, stretching toward the sierras, whose sinuous blue lines were relieved against the horizon. Yonder lay freedom! Oh, to escape! He would journey all night through the lemon groves, whose fragrance reached him. Once in the mountains and he was safe! He inhaled the delicious air; the breeze revived him, his lungs expanded! He felt in his swelling heart the *Veni foràs* of Lazarus! And to thank once more the God who had bestowed this mercy upon him, he extended his arms, raising his eyes toward Heaven. It was an ecstasy of joy!

Then he fancied he saw the shadow of his arms approach him—fancied that he felt these shadowy arms inclose, embrace him—and that he was pressed tenderly to someone's breast. A tall figure actually did stand directly before him. He lowered his eyes—and remained motionless, gasping for breath, dazed, with fixed eyes, fairly driveling with terror.

Horror! He was in the clasp of the Grand Inquisitor himself, the venerable Pedro Arbuez d'Espila, who gazed at him with tearful eyes, like a good shepherd who had found his stray lamb.

The dark-robed priest pressed the hapless Jew to his heart with so fervent an outburst of love, that the edge of the monochal haircloth rubbed the Dominican's breast. And while Aser Abarbanel with protruding eyes gasped in agony in the ascetic's embrace, vaguely comprehending that *all the phases of this fatal evening were only a prearranged torture, that of* Hope, the Grand Inquisitor, with an accent of touching reproach and a look of consternation, murmured in his ear, his breath parched and burning from long fasting:

"What, my son! On the eve, perchance, of salvation—you wished to leave us?"

10

The Elixir of Father Gaucher

ALPHONSE DAUDET

"DRINK this, neighbor, and tell me what you think of it."

And drop by drop, with the painstaking care of a lapidary counting pearls, the curé of Gravenson poured out for me two fingers of a golden-green, warm, sparkling, exquisite liqueur. My stomach was as if bathed in sunlight.

"This is Father Gaucher's elixir, the joy and health of our Provence," said the worthy man, with a triumphant air; "it is made at the convent of Prémontrés, two leagues from your mill. Isn't it better than all the chartreuses on earth? And if you knew how interesting the story of this elixir is! Listen."

Thereupon, as artlessly as possible, without the slightest tinge of irony, in that parsonage dining-room, so placid and calm, with its *Road to the Cross* in tiny pictures, and its pretty light curtains ironed like surplices, the abbé began a somewhat skeptical and irreverant anecdote, after the fashion of a tale of Erasmus or d'Assoucy.

"Twenty years ago, the Prémontrés, or the White Fathers, as we Provençals call them, had fallen into utter destitution. If you had seen their convent in those days, it would have made your heart ache.

"The high wall, the Pacôme Tower, were falling in pieces. All around the grass-grown cloisters, the pillars were cracked, the stone saints crumbling in their recesses. Not a stained-glass window whole, not a door that would close. In the courtyards, in the chapels, the wind from the Rhône blew as it blows in Camargue, extinguishing the candles, breaking the leaden sashes of the windows, spilling the water from the holy-water vessels. But the saddest of all was the convent belfry, silent as an empty dove-cote; and the fathers, in default of money to buy a bell, were obliged to ring for matins with clappers of almond-wood!

"Poor White Fathers! I can see them now, in the procession on Corpus Christi, pacing sadly along in their patched hoods, pale and thin, fed on pumpkins and watermelons; and behind them monseigneur the abbé, marching with downcast head, ashamed to exhibit in the sunlight his tarnished crook and his worm-eaten mitre of white wool. The ladies of the fraternity wept with compassion in the ranks, and the stout banner-bearers whispered sneeringly to one another as they pointed to the poor monks:

" 'The starlings grow thin when they fly in flocks.'

"The fact is, the unfortunate White Fathers had reached the point where they asked themselves if they would not do better to fly out into the world and to seek pasturage each for himself.

"Now, one day when this grave question was being discussed in the chapter, the prior was informed that Brother Gaucher desired to be heard in the council. I must say for your information that this Brother Gaucher was the drover of the convent; that is to say, he passed his days waddling from arch to arch through the cloister, driving before him two consumptive cows, which tried to find grass between the cracks of the flagstones. Supported until he was twelve years old by an old mad-woman of the Baux country, called Aunt Bégon, then taken in by the monks, the wretched drover had never been able to learn anything except to drive his beasts and to repeat his paternoster; and even that he said in Provençal, for his brain was thick and his mind as dull as a leaden dagger. A fervent Christian, however, although somewhat visionary, comfortable in his haircloth shirt, and inflicting discipline upon himself, with sturdy convicion, and such arms!

"When they saw him come into the chapter-hall, simple and stupid of aspect, saluting the assemblage with a leg thrown back, prior, canons, steward, and everybody began to laugh. That was always the effect produced by that good-natured face with its grizzly, goatlike beard and its slightly erratic eyes, whenever it appeared anywhere; so that Brother Gaucher was not disturbed thereby.

" 'Reverend fathers,' he said in a wheedling voice, playing with his chaplet of olive-stones, 'it is quite true that empty casks make the best music. Just imagine that, by dint of cudgeling my poor brain, which was already so hollow, I believe that I have thought out a way to help us out of our poverty.

" 'This is how. You know Aunt Bégon, that worthy woman who took care of me when I was small—God rest her soul, the old hag! she used to sing some very vile songs after drinking. I must tell you then, reverend fathers, that Aunt Bégon, in her lifetime, knew as much about the mountain herbs as an old Corsican blackbird, and more. In fact, towards the end of her life, she compounded an incomparable elixir by mixing five or six kinds of simples that we picked together in the mountains. That was a good many years ago; but I believe that with the aid of St. Augustine and the permission of our worshipful abbé, I might, by careful search, discover the composition of that mysterious elixir. Then we should only have to bottle it and sell it at a rather high price, to enable the community to get rich as nicely as you please, like our brothers of La Trappe and La Grande——'

"He was not allowed to finish. The prior sprang to his feet and fell upon his neck. The canons seized his hands. The steward, even more deeply moved than all the rest, kissed respectfully the ragged edge of his cowl. Then they all returned to their chairs to deliberate; and the chapter decided on the spot that the cows should be entrusted to Brother Thrasybule, so that Brother Gaucher might devote himself exclusively to the compounding of his elixir.

"How did the excellent monk succeed in discovering Aunt Bégon's recipe? At the price of what efforts, or what vigils? History does not say. But this much is sure, that after six months, the elixir of the White Fathers was very popular. Throughout the Comtat, in all the Arles country, there was not a farmhouse, not a granary, which had not in the depths of its buttery, amid the bottles of mulled wine and the jars of olives *à la picholine,* a little jug of brown earthenware, sealed with the arms of Provence, and with a monk in a trance on a silver label. Thanks to the popularity of its elixir, the convent of the Prémontrés grew rich very rapidly. The Pacôme Tower was rebuilt. The prior had a new mitre, the church some pretty stained windows; and in the fine openwork of the belfry, a whole legion of bells, large and small, burst forth one fine Easter morning, jingling and chiming with all their might.

"As for Brother Gaucher, that unfortunate lay brother, whose rustic manners amused the chapter so much, was never spoken of in the convent. Henceforth they only knew the Reverend Father Gaucher, a man of brains and of great learning, who lived completely apart from the trivial and multifarious occupations of the cloister, and was shut up all day in his distillery, while thirty monks hunted the mountain for him, seeking fragrant herbs. That distillery which no one, not even the prior, had the right to enter, was an old abandoned chapel, at the end of the

canons' garden. The simplicity of the worthy fathers had transformed it
into something mysterious and redoubtable; and if by chance some audacious and inquisitive young monk happened to get as far as the rosework
of the doorway, he retreated very quickly, terrified by the aspect of Father
Gaucher, with his sorcerer's beard, leaning over his furnaces, scales in
hand; and all about him retorts of red sandstone, huge alembics, serpentine glasses, a whole strange outfit, flaming as if bewitched, in the red
gleam of the stained-glass.

"At nightfall, when the last Angelus rang, the door of that abode of
mystery would open softly, and the father would betake himself to the
church for the evening service. You should have seen the welcome that
he received when he passed through the monastery! The brethren drew
up in two lines for him to pass. They said to one another:

" 'Hush! he knows the secret!'

"The steward followed him and spoke to him with downcast eyes.
Amid all this adulation, the father walked along, mopping his forehead,
his broad-brimmed, three-cornered hat placed on the back of his head
like a halo, glancing with an air of condescension at the great courtyards
full of orange-trees, the blue roofs surmounted by new weathervanes;
and, in the cloister, glaringly white between the gracefully carved pillars,
the monks, newly dressed, marching two by two with placid faces.

" 'They owe all this to me!' the father would say to himself; and every
time that thought caused his bosom to swell with pride.

"The poor man was well punished for it, as you will see.

"Imagine that one evening, during the service, he arrived in the church
in a state of extraordinary excitement: red-faced, breathless, his hood
awry, and so perturbed that when he took his holy-water he wet his
sleeves to the elbow. They thought at first that his excitement was due
to being late; but when they saw him make profound reverences to the
organ and the galleries instead of saluting the main altar, when they saw
him rush through the church like a gust of wind, wander about the
choir for five minutes looking for his stall, and, when once seated, bow
to the right and left with a beatific smile, a murmur of amazement ran
through the three naves. From breviary to breviary the monks whispered:

"What can be the matter with our Father Gaucher? What can be the
matter with our Father Gaucher?"

"Twice the prior, in his annoyance, struck his crook on the flagstones
to enjoin silence. In the choir the psalms continued; but the responses
lacked vigor.

"Suddenly, in the very middle of the *Ave verum,* lo and behold Father

Gaucher fell backward in his stall and chanted in a voice of thunder:

    " 'In Paris there is a White Father—
    Patatin, patatan, tarabin, taraban.' "

"General consernation. Everybody rose.

" 'Carry him away! he is possessed!' they cried.

"The canons crossed themselves. Monseigneur's crook waved frantically. But Father Gaucher neither saw nor heard anything; and two sturdy monks were obliged to drag him away through the small door of the choir, struggling like one bewitched and continuing his *patatans* and his *tarabans* louder than ever.

"The next morning, at daybreak, the poor wretch was on his knees in the prior's oratory, confessing his sin with a flood of tears.

" 'It was the elixir, monseigneur, it was the elixir that took me by surprise, he said, beating his breast. And seeing him so heartbroken, so penitent, the good prior was deeply moved himself.

" 'Come, come, Father Gaucher, calm yourself; all this will dry up like the dew in the sunshine. After all, the scandal was not so great as you think. To be sure there was a song which was a little—however, we must hope that the novices did not hear it. Now, tell me just how the thing happened to you. It was while you were trying the elixir, was it not? Your hand was a little too heavy. Yes, yes, I understand. It was like Brother Schwartz, the inventor of powder; you were the victim of your invention. And tell me, my dear friend, is it really necessary that you should try this terrible elixir upon yourself?'

" 'Unluckily, yes, monseigneur. The test-tube, to be sure, gives me the strength and degree of heat of the alcohol; but for the finishing touch, the velvety smoothness, I can trust nothing but my tongue.'

" 'Ah! very good. But listen to what I ask. When you taste the elixir thus as a duty, does it taste good to you? Do you enjoy it?'

" 'Alas! yes, monseigneur,' said the unhappy father, turning as red as a beet; 'for two evenings now I have found such a bouquet, such an aroma in it! It is certainly the devil who has played me this vile trick. So I have determined only to use the test-tube henceforth. If the liqueur is not as fine, if it is not as smooth as before, so much the worse!'

" 'Do nothing of the sort,' interrupted the prior, earnestly. 'We must not take the risk of displeasing our customers. All that you have to do now that you are warned is to be on your guard. Tell me, how much do you need to drink, for your test? Fifteen or twenty drops, is it not? Let us say twenty drops. The devil will be very smart if he can catch you with twenty drops. Moreover, to avert all chance of accident, I excuse you from coming to church henceworth. You will repeat the evening service in the distillery. And now, go in peace, my father, and, above all things, count your drops carefully.'

"Alas! the poor father counted his drops to no purpose; the demon had him in his clutch, and he did not let him go.

"The distillery heard some strange services!

"In the daytime everything went well. The father was tranquil enough; he prepared his retorts, his alembics, carefully assorted his herbs —all Provençal herbs, fine and gray, and burned with perfume and sunlight. But at night, when the simples were steeped and the elixir was cooling in great basins of red copper, the poor man's martyrdom began.

" 'Seventeen, eighteen, nineteen, twenty.'

"The drops fell from the tube into the silver goblet. Those twenty, the father swallowed at one draught, almost without enjoyment. It was only the twenty-first that aroused his longing. Oh! that twenty-first drop! To avoid temptation, he would go and kneel at the end of the laboratory and bury himself in his paternosters. But from the still warm liqueur there ascended a wreath of smoke heavily laden with aromatic odors, which came prowling about him, and drew him back towards the basins, whether he would or no. The liqueur was a beautiful golden-green. Leaning over it, with distended nostrils, the father stirred it gently with his tube, and it seemed to him that he saw, in the sparkling little spangles on the surface of the emerald lake, Aunt Bégon's eyes laughing and snapping as they looked at him.

" 'Nonsense! Just one more drop!'

"And from drop to drop the poor wretch ended by filling his goblet to the brim. Then, at the end of his strength, he would sink down in an easy-chair; and his body relaxed, his eyes half closed, he would enjoy his sin by little sips, murmuring to himself with ecstatic remorse:

" 'Ah! I am damning myself! I am damning myself!'

"The most terrible part of it was, that in the depth of diabolical elixir, he remembered, by some witchery or other, all Aunt Bégon's naughty songs: 'There were three little gossips, who talked of giving a feast'; or, 'Master André's shepherdess goes to the woods alone'; and always the famous one of the White Fathers: 'Patatin, patatan!'

"Imagine his confusion the next day when his old neighbors said to him with a sly expression:

" 'Ha! ha! Father Gaucher, you had grasshoppers in your head when you went to bed last night.'

"Then there were tears, despair, fasting, haircloth, and penance. But nothing could prevail against the demon of the elixir; and every evening, at the same hour, the possession began anew.

"Meanwhile, orders rained upon the abbey like a blessing from Heaven. They came from Nîmes, from Aix, from Avignon, from Marseille. From day to day the convent assumed the aspect of a factory. There were packing brothers, labelling brothers, brothers to attend to the correspondence, draymen brothers; the service of God lost a few strokes of the bell now and then, to be sure, but the poor people of the neighborhood lost nothing, I assure you.

"But one fine Sunday morning, while the steward was reading to the chapter his annual inventory, and the good canons were listening with sparkling eyes and smiling lips, behold Father Gaucher rushed into the midst of the conference, exclaiming:

" 'It is all over! I can't stand it any longer! give me back my cows.'

" 'What is the matter, pray, Father Gaucher?' asked the prior, who had a shrewd idea what the matter might be.

" 'The matter, monseigneur? The matter is that I am laying up for myself an eternity of hell-fire and blows with the pitchfork. The matter is that I am drinking, drinking like a miserable wretch.'

" 'But I told you to count your drops.'

" 'Count my drops! Oh, yes! I should have to count them by goblets now. Yes, my fathers, I have reached that point. Three flasks an evening. You must see that that cannot last. So let whomsoever you choose make the elixir. May God's fire consume me if I touch it again!'

"The chapter laughed no longer.

" 'But you are ruining us, unhappy man!' cried the steward, waving his ledger.

" 'Do you prefer that I should damn myself forever?'

"Thereupon the prior rose.

" 'My fathers,' he said, putting forth his beautiful white hand, upon which the pastoral ring glistened, 'there is a way to arrange everything. It is at night, is it not, my dear son, that the demon tempts you?'

" 'Yes, monsieur prior, regularly every evening. So now, when night comes, a cold sweat takes me, saving your presence, like Capitou's donkey when he saw the saddle coming.

" ' 'Tis well! be comforted. Henceforth, every evening, at the service, we will repeat in your favor the prayer of St. Augustine, to which plenary indulgence is attached. With that, whatever happens, you are safe. It affords absolution during sin.'

" 'Oh well! in that case, thanks, monsieur prior!'

"And, without asking anything more, Father Gaucher returned to his laboratory, as light-hearted as a lark.

"And in truth, from that day forward, every evening at the end of the complines, the officiating father never failed to say:

" 'Let us pray for our poor Father Gaucher, who is sacrificing his soul in the interest of the community. *Oremus, Dominie——*'

"And while the prayer ran quivering over those white hoods, prostate in the shadow of the nave, as a light breeze rushes over the snow, yonder at the other end of the convent, behind the flaming stained-glass of the distillery, Father Gaucher could be heard singing at the top of his lungs:

> " '*In Paris there is a White Father,*
> *Patatin, patatan, tarabin, taraban;*
> *In Paris there is a White Father*
> *Who dances with the nuns,*
> *Trin, trin, trin, in a garden,*
> *Who dances with the ——*' "

Here the good curé stopped, in dismay.

"Merciful Heaven!" he exclaimed, "suppose my parishioners should hear me!"

11

The Last Lesson

ALPHONSE DAUDET

THAT morning it was quite late before I started for school, and I was terribly afraid I should be scolded, for Monsieur Hamel had told us that he would question us upon participles, and I did not know the first thing about them. For a moment I thought of escaping from school and roving through the fields.

The day was so warm, so clear! The blackbirds were whistling on the outskirts of the woods. In Rippert Meadow, behind the sawmill, the Prussians were drilling. All these things were far more attractive to me than the rule for the use of participles. But I mustered up strength to resist temptation, and hurried on to school.

As I reached the town hall, I saw a group of people; they loitered before the little grating, reading the placards posted upon it. For two years every bit of bad news had been announced to us from that grating. There we read what battles had been lost, what requisitions made; there we learned what orders had issued from headquarters. And though I did not pause with the rest, I wondered to myself, "What can be the matter now?"

As I ran across the square, Wachter, the blacksmith, who, in company with his apprentice, was absorbed in reading the notice, exclaimed—

"Not so fast, child! You will reach your school soon enough!"

I believed he was making game of me, and I was quite out of breath when I entered Monsieur Hamel's small domain.

Now, at the beginning of the session there was usually such an uproar that it could be heard as far as the street. Desks were opened and shut, lessons recited at the top of our voices, all shouting together, each of us stopping his ears that he might hear better. Then the master's big ruler would descend upon his desk, and he would say—

"Silence!"

I counted upon making my entrance in the midst of the usual babel and reaching my seat unobserved, but upon this particular morning all was hushed. Sabbath stillness reigned. Through the open window I could see that my comrades had already taken their seats; I could see Monsieur Hamel himself, passing back and forth, his formidable iron ruler under his arm.

I must open that door. I must enter in the midst of that deep silence. I need not tell you that I grew red in the face, and terror seized me.

But, strangely enough, as Monsieur Hamel scrutinized me, there was no anger in his gaze. He said very gently—

"Take your seat quickly, my little Franz. We were going to begin without you."

I climbed over the bench, and seated myself. But when I had recovered a little from my fright, I noticed that our master had donned his beautiful green frock-coat, his finest frilled shirt, and his embroidered black silk calotte, which he wore only on inspection days, or upon those occasions when prizes were distributed. Moreover, an extraordinary solemnity had taken possession of my classmates. But the greatest surprise of all came when my eye fell upon the benches at the farther end of the room. Usually they were empty, but upon this morning the villagers were seated there, solemn as ourselves. There sat old Hauser, with his three-cornered hat, there sat the venerable mayor, the aged carrier, and other personages of importance. All of our visitors seemed sad, and Hauser had brought with him an old primer, chewed at the edges. It lay wide open upon his knees, his big spectacles reposing upon the page.

While I was wondering at all these things, Monsieur Hamel had taken his seat, and in the same grave and gentle tone in which he had greeted me, he said to us—

"My children, this is the last day I shall teach you. The order has come from Berlin that henceforth in the schools of Alsace and Lorraine all instruction shall be given in the German tongue only. Your new master will arrive tomorrow. Today you hear the last lesson you will receive in French, and I beg you will be most attentive."

My "last" French lesson! And I scarcely knew how to write! Now I should never learn. My education must be cut short. How I grudged at that moment every minute I had lost, every lesson I had missed for the sake of hunting birds' nests or making slides upon the Saar! And those books which a moment before were so dry and dull, so heavy to carry, my grammar, my Bible-history, seemed now to wear the faces of old friends, whom I could not bear to bid farewell. It was with them as with Monsieur Hamel, the thought that he was about to leave, that I should see him no more, made me forget all the blows of his ruler, and the many punishments I had received.

Poor man! It was in honor of that last session that he was arrayed in his finest Sunday garb, and now I began to understand why the villagers had gathered at the back of the class-room. Their presence at such a moment seemed to express a regret that they had not visited that school-room oftener; it was their way of telling our master they thanked him for his forty years of faithful service, and desired to pay their respects to the land whose empire was departing.

I was busied with these reflections when I heard my name called. It was now my turn to recite. Ah! what would I not have given then had I been able to repeat from beginning to end that famous rule for the use of participles loudly, distinctly, and without a single mistake; but I became entangled in the first few words, and remained standing at my seat, swinging from side to side, my heart swelling. I dared not raise my head. Monsieur Hamel was addressing me.

"I shall not chide thee, my little Franz; thy punishment will be great enough. So it is! We say to ourselves each day, 'Bah! I have time enough. I will learn tomorrow.' And now see what results. Ah, it has ever been the greatest misfortune of our Alsace that she was willing to put off learning till tomorrow! And now these foreigners can say to us, and justly, 'What! you profess to be Frenchmen, and can neither speak nor write your own language?' And in all this, my poor Franz, you are not the chief culprit. Each of us has something to reproach himself with.

"Your parents have not shown enough anxiety about having you educated. They preferred to see you spinning, or tilling the soil, since that brought them in a few more sous. And have I nothing with which to reproach myself? Did I not often send you to water my garden when you should have been at your tasks? And if I wished to go trout-fishing, was my conscience in the least disturbed when I gave you a holiday?"

One topic leading to another, Monsieur Hamel began to speak of the French language, saying it was the strongest, clearest, most beautiful language in the world, which we must keep as our heritage, never allowing it to be forgotten, telling us that when a nation has become enslaved, she holds the key which shall unlock her prison as long as she preserves her native tongue.[1]

Then he took a grammar, and read our lesson to us, and I was amazed to see how well I understood. Everything he said seemed so very simple, so easy! I had never, I believe, listened to any one as I listened to him at

[1] "S'il tient sa langue il tient la clé qui de ses chaînes le délivre."—F. MISTRAL.

that moment, and never before had he shown so much patience in his explanations. It really seemed as if the poor man, anxious to impart everything he knew before he took leave of us, desired to strike a single blow that might drive all his knowledge into our heads at once.

The lesson was followed by writing. For this occasion Monsieur Hamel had prepared some copies that were entirely new, and upon these were written in a beautiful round hand, *"France, Alsace! France, Alsace!"*

These words were as inspiring as the sight of the tiny flags attached to the rod of our desks. It was good to see how each one applied himself, and how silent it was! Not a sound save the scratching of pens as they touched our papers. Once, indeed, some cockchafers entered the room, but no one paid the least attention to them, not even the tiniest pupil; for the youngest were absorbed in tracing their straight strokes as earnestly and conscientiously as if these too were written in French! On the roof of the schoolhouse the pigeons were cooing softly, and I thought to myself as I listened, "And must they also be compelled to sing in German?"

From time to time, looking up from my page, I saw Monsieur Hamel, motionless in his chair, his eyes riveted upon each object about him, as if he desired to fix in his mind, and forever, every detail of his little school. Remember that for forty years he had been constantly at his post, in that very school-room, facing the same playground. Little had changed. The desks and benches were polished and worn, through long use; the walnut-trees in the playground had grown taller; and the hop-vine he himself had planted curled its tendrils about the windows, running even to the roof. What anguish must have filled the poor man's heart, as he thought of leaving all these things, and heard his sister moving to and fro in the room overhead, busied in fastening their trunks! For on the morrow they were to leave the country, never to return. Nevertheless his courage did not falter; not a single lesson was omitted. After writing came history, and then the little ones sang their *"Ba, Be, Bi, Bo, Bu,"* together. Old Hauser, at the back of the room, had put on his spectacles, and, holding his primer in both hands, was spelling out the letters with the little ones. He too was absorbed in his task; his voice trembled with emotion, and it was so comical to hear him that we all wanted to laugh and to cry at the same moment. Ah! never shall I forget that last lesson!

Suddenly the church clock struck twelve, and then the Angelus was heard.

At the same moment, a trumpet-blast under our window announced that the Prussians were returning from drill. Monsieur Hamel rose in his chair. He was very pale, but never before had he seemed to me so tall as at that moment.

"My friends—" he said, "my friends—I—I—"

But something choked him. He could not finish his sentence.

Then he took a piece of chalk, and grasping it with all his strength, wrote in his largest hand:

"Vive La France!"

He remained standing at the blackboard, his head resting against the wall. He did not speak again, but a motion of his hand said to us—

"That is all. You are dismissed."

12

The Attack on the Mill

EMILE ZOLA

IT WAS high holiday at Father Merlier's mill on that pleasant summer afternoon. Three tables had been brought out into the garden and placed end to end in the shadow of the great elm, and now they were awaiting the arrival of the guests. It was known throughout the length and breadth of the land that that day was to witness the betrothal of old Merlier's daughter, Françoise, to Dominique, a young man who was said to be not over-fond of work, but whom never a woman for three leagues of the country around could look at without sparkling eyes, such a well-favored young fellow was he.

That mill of Father Merlier's was truly a very pleasant spot. It was situated right in the heart of Rocreuse, at the place where the main road makes a sharp bend. The village has but a single street, bordered on either side by a row of low, whitened cottages, but just there where the road curves there are broad stretches of meadow-land, and huge trees, which follow the course of the Morelle, cover the low grounds of the valley with a most delicious shade. All Lorraine has no more charming bit of nature to show. To right and left dense forests, great monarchs of the wood, centuries old, rise from the gentle slopes and fill the horizon with a sea of verdure, while away towards the south extends the plain, of wondrous fertility and checkered almost to infinity with its small enclosures, divided off from one another by their live hedges. But what makes the crowning glory of Rocreuse is the coolness of this verdurous nook, even in the hottest days of July and August. The Morelle comes down from the woods of Gagny, and it would seem as if it gathered to itself on the way all the delicious freshness of the foliage beneath which it glides for many a league; it brings down with it the murmuring sounds, the glacial, solemn shadows of the forest. And that is not the only source of coolness; there are running waters of all kinds singing among the copses; one cannot take a step without coming on a gushing spring, and as he makes his way along the narrow paths he seems to be treading above subterranean lakes that seek the air and sunshine through the moss above and profit by every smallest crevice, at the roots of trees or among the chinks and crannies of the rocks, to burst forth in fountains of crystalline clearness. So numerous and so loud are the whispering voices of these streams that they silence the song of the bullfinches. It is as if one were in an enchanted park, with cascades falling on every side.

The meadows below are never athirst. The shadows beneath the gigantic chestnut trees are of inky blackness, and along the edges of the fields long rows of poplars stand like walls of rustling foliage. There is a double avenue of huge plane trees ascending across the fields towards the ancient castle of Gagny, now gone to rack and ruin. In this region, where drought is never known, vegetation of all kinds is wonderfully rank; it is like a flower garden down there in the low ground between those two wooded hills, a natural garden, where the lawns are broad meadows and the giant trees represent colossal beds. When the noonday sun pours down his scorching rays the shadows lie blue upon the ground, the glowing vegetation slumbers in the heat, while every now and then a breath of icy coldness passes under the foliage.

Such was the spot where Father Merlier's mill enlivened with its cheerful clack nature run riot. The building itself, constructed of wood and plaster, looked as if it might be coeval with our planet. Its foundations were in part washed by the Morelle, which here expands into a clear pool. A dam, a few feet in height, afforded sufficient head of water to drive the old wheel, which creaked and groaned as it revolved with the asthmatic wheezing of a faithful servant who has grown old in her place. Whenever Father Merlier was advised to change it, he would shake his head and say that like as not a young wheel would be lazier and not so well acquainted with its duties, and then would set to work and patch up the old one with anything that came to hand, old hogshead-staves, bits of rusty iron, zinc or lead. The old wheel only seemed the gayer for it, with its old profile, all plumed and feathered with tufts of moss and grass, and when the water poured over it in a silvery tide its gaunt black skeleton was decked out with a gorgeous display of pearls and diamonds.

That portion of the mill which was bathed by the Morelle had something of the look of a barbaric arch that had been dropped down there by chance. A good half of the structure was built on piles; the water came in under the floor, and there were deep holes, famous throughout the whole country for the eels and the huge crawfish that were to be caught there. Below the fall the pool was as clear as a mirror, and when it was not clouded by foam from the wheel one could see troops of great fish swimming about in it with the slow, majestic movements of a squadron. There was a broken stairway leading down to the stream, near a stake to which a boat was fastened, and over the wheel was a gallery of wood. Such windows as there were were arranged without any attempt at order. The whole was a quaint conglomeration of nooks and corners, bits of wall, additions made here and there as after-thoughts, beams and roofs, that gave the mill the aspect of an old, dismantled citadel; but ivy and all sorts of creeping plants had grown luxuriantly and kindly covered up such crevices as were too unsightly, casting a mantle of green over the old dwelling. Young ladies who passed that way used to stop and sketch Father Merlier's mill in their albums.

The side of the house that faced the road was less irregular. A gateway in stone afforded access to the principal courtyard, on the right and left hand of which were sheds and stables. Beside a well stood an immense elm that threw its shade over half the court. At the further end, opposite the gate, stood the house, surmounted by a dovecote, the four windows of its first floor in a symmetrical line. The only vanity that Father Merlier ever allowed himself was to paint this façade every ten years. It had just been freshly whitened at the time of our story, and dazzled the eyes of all the village when the sun lighted it up in the middle of the day.

For twenty years had Father Merlier been mayor of Rocreuse. He was held in great consideration on account of his fortune; he was supposed to be worth something like eighty thousand francs, the result of patient saving. When he married Madeleine Guillard, who brought him the mill as her dowry, his entire capital lay in his two strong arms, but Madeleine had never repented of her choice, so manfully had he conducted their joint affairs. Now his wife was dead, and he was left a widower with his daughter Françoise. Doubtless he might have set himself down to take his rest and suffered the old mill-wheel to sleep among its moss, but he would have found idleness too irksome and the house would have seemed dead to him. He kept on working still for the pleasure of it. In those days Father Merlier was a tall old man, with a long, silent face, on which a laugh was never seen, but beneath which there lay, none the less, a large fund of good-humor. He had been elected mayor on account of his money, and also for the impressive air that he knew how to assume when it devolved on him to marry a couple.

Françoise Merlier had just completed her eighteenth year. She was small, and for that reason was not accounted one of the beauties of the country. Until she reached the age of fifteen she had been even homely;

the good folks of Rocreuse could not see how it was that the daughter of Father and Mother Merlier, such a hale, vigorous couple, had such a hard time of it in getting her growth. When she was fifteen, however, though still remaining delicate, a change came over her and she took on the prettiest little face imaginable. She had black hair, black eyes, and was red as a rose withal; her mouth was always smiling, there were delicious dimples in her cheeks, and a crown of sunshine seemed to be ever resting on her fair, candid forehead. Although small, as girls went in that region, she was far from being thin; she might not have been able to raise a sack of wheat to her shoulder, but she became quite plump as she grew older, and gave promise of becoming eventually as well-rounded and appetizing as a partridge. Her father's habits of taciturnity had made her reflective while yet a young girl; if she always had a smile on her lips it was in order to give pleasure to others. Her natural disposition was serious.

As was no more than to be expected, she had every young man in the countryside at her heels as a suitor, more even for her money than for her attractiveness, and she had made a choice at last, a choice that had been the talk and scandal of the entire neighborhood.

On the other side of the Morelle lived a strapping young fellow who went by the name of Dominique Penquer. He was not to the manor born; ten years previously he had come to Rocreuse from Belgium to receive the inheritance of an uncle who had owned a small property on the very borders of the forest of Gagny, just facing the mill and distant from it only a few musket-shots. His object in coming was to sell the property, so he said, and return to his own home again; but he must have found the land to his liking, for he made no move to go away. He was seen cultivating his bit of a field and gathering the few vegetables that afforded him an existence. He fished, he hunted; more than once he was near coming in contact with the law through the intervention of the keepers. This independent way of living, of which the peasants could not very clearly see the resources, had in the end given him a bad name. He was vaguely looked upon as nothing better than a poacher. At all events he was lazy, for he was frequently found sleeping in the grass at hours when he should have been at work. Then, too, the hut in which he lived, in the shade of the last trees of the forest, did not seem like the abode of an honest young man; the old women would not have been surprised at any time to hear that he was on friendly terms with the wolves in the ruins of Gagny. Still, the young girls would now and then venture to stand up for him, for he was altogether a splendid specimen of manhood, was this individual of doubtful antecedents, tall and straight as a young poplar, with a milk-white skin and ruddy hair and moustaches that seemed to be of gold when the sun shone on them. Now one fine morning it came to pass that Françoise told Father Merlier that she loved Dominique, and that never, never would she consent to marry any other young man.

It may be imagined what a knockdown blow it was that Father Merlier received that day! As was his wont, he said never a word; his countenance wore its usual reflective look, only the fun that used to bubble up from within no longer shone in his eyes. Françoise, too, was very serious, and for a week father and daughter scarcely spoke to each other. What troubled Father Merlier was to know how that rascal of a poacher had succeeded in bewitching his daughter. Dominique had never shown himself at the mill. The miller played the spy a little, and was rewarded by catching sight of the gallant, on the other side of the Morelle, lying among the grass and pretending to be asleep. Françoise could see him from her chamber window. The thing was clear enough; they had been making sheep's eyes at each other over the old mill-wheel, and so had fallen in love.

A week slipped by; Françoise became more and more serious. Father Merlier still continued to say nothing. Then, one evening, of his own accord, he brought Dominique to the house, without a word. Françoise was just setting the table. She made no demonstration of surprise; all she did was to add another plate, but her laugh had come back to her, and the little dimples appeared again upon her cheeks. Father Merlier had gone that morning to look for Dominique at his hut on the edge of the forest, and there the two men had had a conference, with closed doors and windows, that lasted three hours. No one ever knew what they said to each other; the only thing certain is that when Father Merlier left the hut he already treated Dominique as a son. Doubtless the old man had discovered that he whom he had gone to visit was a worthy young fellow, even though he did lie in the grass to gain the love of young girls.

All Rocreuse was up in arms. The women gathered at their doors and could not find words strong enough to characterize Father Merlier's folly in thus receiving a ne'er-do-well into his family. He let them talk. Perhaps he thought of his own marriage. Neither had he possessed a penny to his name at the time he married Madeleine and her mill, and yet that had not prevented him from being a good husband to her. Moreover, Dominique put an end to their tittle-tattle by setting to work in such strenuous fashion that all the countryside was amazed. It so happened just then that the boy of the mill drew an unlucky number and had to go for a soldier, and Dominique would not hear of their engaging another. He lifted sacks, drove the cart, wrestled with the old wheel when it took an obstinate fit and refused to turn, and all so pluckily and cheerfully that people came from far and near merely for the pleasure of seeing him. Father Merlier laughed his silent laugh. He was highly elated that he had read the youngster aright. There is nothing like love to hearten up young men.

In the midst of all that laborious toil Françoise and Dominique fairly worshipped each other. They had not much to say, but their tender smiles conveyed a world of meaning. Father Merlier had not said a word thus far on the subject of their marriage, and they had both respected his silence, waiting until the old man should see fit to give expression to his will. At last, one day toward the middle of July, he had had three tables laid in the courtyard, in the shade of the big elm, and had invited his friends of Rocreuse to come that afternoon and drink a glass of wine with him. When the courtyard was filled with people, and everyone there had a full glass in his hand, Father Merlier raised his own high above his head and said:

"I have the pleasure of announcing to you that Françoise and this lad will be married in a month from now, on St. Louis' fête-day."

Then there was a universal touching of glasses, attended by a tremendous uproar; everyone was laughing. But Father Merlier, raising his voice above the din, again spoke:

"Dominique, kiss your wife that is to be. It is no more than customary."

And they kissed, very red in the face, both of them, while the company laughed louder still. It was a regular fête; they emptied a small cask. Then, when only the intimate friends of the house remained, conversation went on in a calmer strain. Night had fallen, a starlit night, and very clear. Dominique and Françoise sat on a bench, side by side, and said nothing. An old peasant spoke of the war that the Emperor had declared against Prussia. All the lads of the village were already gone off to the army. Troops had passed through the place only the night before. There were going to be hard knocks.

"Bah!" said Father Merlier, with the selfishness of a man who is quite happy, "Dominque is a foreigner; he won't have to go—and if the Prussians come this way, he will be here to defend his wife."

The idea of the Prussians coming there seemed to the company an exceedingly good joke. The army would give them one good conscientious thrashing, and the affair would be quickly ended.

"I have seen them before, I have seen them before," the old peasant repeated, in a low voice.

There was silence for a little, then they all touched glasses once again.

Françoise and Dominique had heard nothing; they had managed to clasp hands behind the bench in such a way as not to be seen by the others, and this condition of affairs seemed so beatific to them that they sat there mute, their gaze lost in the darkness of the night.

What a magnificent, balmy night! The village lay slumbering on either side of the white road as peacefully as a little child. The deep silence was undisturbed save by the occasional crow of a cock in some distant barnyard acting on a mistaken impression that dawn was at hand. Perfumed breaths of air, like long-drawn sighs, came down from the great woods that lay around and above, sweeping softly over the roofs, as if caressing them. The meadows, with their black intensity of shadow, took on a dim, mysterious majesty of their own, while all the springs, all the brooks and water courses that gurgled in the darkness, might have been taken for the cool, rhythmical breathing of the sleeping country. Every now and then the old dozing mill-wheel seemed to be dreaming like a watch-dog that barks uneasily in his slumber; it creaked, it talked to itself, rocked by the fall of the Morelle, whose current gave forth the deep, sustained music of an organ pipe. Never was there a more charming or happier nook, never did a deeper peace come down to cover it.

II

One month later, to a day, on the eve of the fête of St. Louis, Rocreuse was in a state of alarm and dismay. The Prussians had beaten the Emperor, and were advancing on the village by forced marches. For a week past people passing along the road had brought tidings of the enemy: "They are at Lormières, they are at Nouvelles"; and by dint of hearing so many stories of the rapidity of their advance, Rocreuse woke up every morning in the full expectation of seeing them swarming down out of Gagny wood. They did not come, however, and that only served to make the affright the greater. They would certainly fall upon the village in the night-time, and put every soul to the sword.

There had been an alarm the night before, a little before daybreak. The inhabitants had been aroused by a great noise of men tramping upon the road. The women were already throwing themselves upon their knees and making the sign of the cross, when someone, to whom it happily occurred to peep through a half-opened window, caught sight of red trousers. It was a French detachment. The captain had forthwith asked for the mayor, and, after a long conversation with Father Merlier, had remained at the mill.

The sun shone bright and clear that morning, giving promise of a warm day. There was a golden light floating over the woodland, while in the low grounds white mists were rising from the meadows. The pretty village, so neat and trim, awoke in the cool dawning, and the country, with its streams and its fountains, was as gracious as a freshly plucked bouquet. But the beauty of the day brought gladness to the face of no one; the villagers had watched the captain, and seen him circle round and round the old mill, examine the adjacent houses, then pass to the other bank of the Morelle, and from thence scan the country with a field-glass; Father Merlier, who accompanied him, appeared to be giving explanations. After that the captain had posted some of his men behind walls, behind trees, or in hollows. The main body of the detachment had encamped in the courtyard of the mill. So there was going to be a fight, then? And when Father Merlier returned they questioned him. He spoke no word, but slowly and sorrowfully nodded his head. Yes, there was going to be a fight.

Françoise and Dominique were there in the courtyard, watching him. He finally took his pipe from his lips, and gave utterance to these few words:

"Ah! my poor children, I shall not be able to marry you today!"

Dominique, with lips tight set and an angry frown upon his forehead, raised himself on tiptoe from time to time and stood with eyes bent on Gagny wood, as if he would have been glad to see the Prussians appear and end the suspense they were in. Françoise, whose face was grave and very pale, was constantly passing back and forth, supplying the needs of the soldiers. They were preparing their soup in a corner of the courtyard, joking and chaffing one another while awaiting their meal.

The captain appeared to be highly pleased. He had visited the chambers and the great hall of the mill that looked out on the stream. Now, seated beside the well, he was conversing with Father Merlier.

"You have a regular fortress here," he was saying. "We shall have no trouble in holding it until evening. The bandits are late; they ought to be here by this time."

The miller looked very grave. He saw his beloved mill going up in flame and smoke, but uttered no word of remonstrance or complaint, considering that it would be useless. He only opened his mouth to say:

"You ought to take steps to hide the boat; there is a hole behind the wheel fitted to hold it. Perhaps you may find it of use to you."

The captain gave an order to one of his men. This captain was a tall, fine-looking man of about forty, with an agreeable expression of countenance. The sight of Dominique and Françoise seemed to afford him much pleasure; he watched them as if he had forgotten all about the approaching conflict. He followed Françoise with his eyes as she moved about the courtyard, and his manner showed clearly enough that he thought her charming. Then, turning to Dominique:

"You are not with the army, I see, my boy?" he abruptly asked.

"I am a foreigner," the young man replied.

The captain did not seem particularly pleased with the answer; he winked his eyes and smiled. Françoise was doubtless a more agreeable companion than a musket would have been. Dominique, noticing his smile, made haste to add:

"I am a foreigner, but I can lodge a rifle bullet in an apple at five hundred yards. See, there's my rifle behind you."

"You may find use for it," the captain dryly answered.

Françoise had drawn near; she was trembling a little, and Dominique, regardless of the bystanders, took and held firmly clasped in his own the two hands that she held forth to him, as if committing herself to his protection. The captain smiled again, but said nothing more. He remained seated, his sword between his legs, his eyes fixed on space, apparently lost in dreamy reverie.

It was ten o'clock. The heat was already oppressive. A deep silence prevailed. The soldiers had sat down in the shade of the sheds in the courtyard and begun to eat their soup. Not a sound came from the village, where the inhabitants had all barricaded their houses, doors and windows. A dog, abandoned by his master, howled mournfully upon the the road. From the woods and the near-by meadows, that lay fainting in the heat, came a long-drawn, whispering, soughing sound, produced by the union of what wandering breaths of air there were. A cuckoo called. Then the silence became deeper still.

And all at once, upon that lazy, sleepy air, a shot rang out. The captain rose quickly to his feet, the soldiers left their half-empty plates. In a few seconds all were at their posts; the mill was occupied from top to bottom. And yet the captain, who had gone out through the gate, saw nothing; to right and left the road stretched away, desolate and blindingly white in the fierce sunshine. A second report was heard, and still nothing to be seen, not even so much as a shadow; but just as he was turning to re-enter he chanced to look over toward Gagny and there beheld a little puff of smoke floating away on the tranquil air like thistledown. The deep peace of the forest was apparently unbroken.

"The rascals have occupied the wood," the officer murmured. "They know we are here."

Then the firing went on, and became more and more continuous between the French soldiers posted about the mill and the Prussians concealed among the trees. The bullets whistled over the Morelle without doing any mischief on either side. The firing was irregular; every bush seemed to have its marksman, and nothing was to be seen save those bluish smoke wreaths that hung for a moment on the wind before they vanished. It lasted thus for nearly two hours. The officer hummed a tune with a careless air. Françoise and Dominique, who had remained in the courtyard, raised themselves to look out over a low wall. They were more particularly interested in a little soldier who had his post on the bank of the Morelle, behind the hull of an old boat; he would lie face downward on the ground, watch his chance, deliver his fire, then slip back into a ditch a few steps in his rear to reload, and his movements were so comical, he displayed such cunning and activity, that it was difficult for anyone watching him to refrain from smiling. He must have caught sight of a Prussian, for he rose quickly and brought his piece to the shoulder, but before he could discharge it he uttered a loud cry, whirled completely around in his tracks and fell backward into the ditch, where for an instant his legs moved convulsively, just as the claws of a fowl do when it is beheaded. The little soldier had received a bullet directly through his heart. It was the first casualty of the day. Françoise instinctively seized Dominique's hand, and held it tight in a convulsive grasp.

"Come away from there," said the captain. "The bullets reach us here."

As if to confirm his words a slight, sharp sound was heard up in the old elm, and the end of a branch came to the ground, turning over and over as it fell, but the two young people never stirred, riveted to the spot as they were by the interest of the spectacle. On the edge of the wood a Prussian had suddenly emerged from behind a tree, as an actor comes upon the stage from the wings, beating the air with his arms and falling over upon his back. And beyond that there was no movement; the two dead men appeared to be sleeping in the bright sunshine; there was not a soul to be seen in the fields on which the heat lay heavy. Even the sharp rattle of the musketry had ceased. Only the Morelle kept on whispering to itself with its low, musical murmur.

Father Merlier looked at the captain with an astonished air, as if to inquire whether that were the end of it.

"Here comes their attack," the officer murmured. "Look out for yourself! Don't stand there!"

The words were scarcely out of his mouth when a terrible discharge of musketry ensued. The great elm was riddled, its leaves came eddying down as thick as snowflakes. Fortunately the Prussians had aimed too

high. Dominique dragged, almost carried, Françoise from the spot, while
Father Merlier followed them, shouting:

"Get into the small cellar, the walls are thicker there."

But they paid no attention to him; they made their way to the main
hall, where ten or a dozen soldiers were silently waiting, watching events
outside through the chinks of the closed shutters. The captain was left
alone in the courtyard, where he sheltered himself behind the low wall,
while the furious fire was maintained uninterruptedly. The soldiers
whom he had posted outside only yielded their ground inch by inch;
they came crawling in, however, one after another, as the enemy dis-
lodged them from their positions. Their instructions were to gain all the
time they could, taking care not to show themselves, in order that the
Prussians might remain in ignorance of the force they had opposed to
them. Another hour passed, and as a sergeant came in, reporting that
there were now only two or three men left outside, the officer took his
watch from his pocket, murmuring:

"Half-past two. Come, we must hold out for four hours yet."

He caused the great gate of the courtyard to be tightly secured, and
everything was made ready for an energetic defense. The Prussians were
on the other side of the Morelle, consequently there was no reason to fear
an assault at the moment. There was a bridge indeed, a mile and a
quarter away, but they were probably unaware of its existence, and it
was hardly to be supposed that they would attempt to cross the stream
by fording. The officer, therefore, simply caused the road to be watched;
the attack, when it came, was to be looked for from the direction of the
fields.

The firing had ceased again. The mill appeared to lie there in the sunlight, void of all life. Not a shutter was open, not a sound came from
within. Gradually, however, the Prussians began to show themselves at
the edge of the Gagny wood. Heads were protruded here and there; they
seemed to be mustering up their courage. Several of the soldiers within
the mill brought up their pieces to an aim, but the captain shouted:

"No, no; not yet; wait. Let them come nearer."

They displayed a great deal of prudence in their advance, looking at
the mill with a distrustful air; they seemed hardly to know what to make
of the old structure, so lifeless and gloomy, with its curtain of ivy. Still
they kept on advancing. When there were fifty of them or so in the open,
directly opposite, the officer uttered one word:

"Now!"

A crashing, tearing discharge burst from the position, succeeded by an
irregular, dropping fire. Françoise, trembling violently, involuntarily

raised her hands to her ears. Dominique, from his position behind the soldiers, peered out upon the field, and when the smoke drifted away a little, counted three Prussians extended on their backs in the middle of the meadow. The others had sought shelter among the willows and the poplars. And then commenced the siege.

For more than an hour the mill was riddled with bullets; they beat and rattled on its old walls like hail. The noise they made was plainly audible as they struck the stonework, were flattened, and fell back into the water; they buried themselves in the woodwork with a dull thud. Occasionally a creaking sound would announce that the wheel had been hit. Within the building the soldiers husbanded their ammunition, firing only when they could see something to aim at. The captain kept consulting his watch every few minutes, and as a ball split one of the shutters in halves and then lodged in the ceiling:

"Four o'clock," he murmured. "We shall never be able to hold the position."

The old mill, in truth, was gradually going to pieces beneath that terrific fire. A shutter that had been perforated again and again, until it looked like a piece of lace, fell off its hinges into the water, and had to be replaced by a mattress. Every moment, almost, Father Merlier exposed himself to the fire in order to take account of the damage sustained by his poor wheel, every wound of which was like a bullet in his own heart. Its period of usefulness was ended this time for certain; he would never be able to patch it up again. Dominique had besought Françoise to retire to a place of safety, but she was determined to remain with him; she had taken a seat behind a great oaken clothes-press, which afforded her protection. A ball struck the press, however, the sides of which gave out a dull hollow sound, whereupon Dominique stationed himself in front of Françoise. He had as yet taken no part in the firing, although he had his rifle in his hand; the soldiers occupied the whole breadth of the windows, so that he could not get near them. At every discharge the floor trembled.

"Look out! look out!" the captain suddenly shouted.

He had just descried a dark mass emerging from the wood. As soon as they gained the open they set up a telling platoon fire. It struck the mill like a tornado. Another shutter parted company, and the bullets came whistling in through the yawning aperture. Two soldiers rolled upon the floor; one lay where he fell and never moved a limb; his comrades pushed him up against the wall because he was in their way. The other writhed and twisted, beseeching someone to end his agony, but no one had ears for the poor wretch; the bullets were still pouring in, and everyone was looking out for himself and searching for a loophole whence he might answer the enemy's fire. A third soldier was wounded; that one said not a word, but with staring, haggard eyes sank down beneath a table. Françoise, horror-stricken by the dreadful spectacle of the dead and dying men, mechanically pushed away her chair and seated herself on the floor, against the wall; it seemed to her that she would be smaller there and less exposed. In the meantime men had gone and secured all the mattresses in the house; the opening of the window was partially closed again. The hall was filled with débris of every description, broken weapons, dislocated furniture.

"Five o'clock," said the captain. "Stand fast, boys. They are going to make an attempt to pass the stream."

Just then Françoise gave a shriek. A bullet had struck the floor, and, rebounding, grazed her forehead on the ricochet. A few drops of blood appeared. Dominique looked at her, then went to the window and fired his first shot, and from that time kept on firing uninterruptedly. He kept on loading and discharging his piece mechanically, paying no attention to what was passing at his side, only pausing from time to time to cast a look at Françoise. He did not fire hurriedly or at random, moreover, but took deliberate aim. As the captain had predicted, the Prussians were skirting the belt of poplars and attempting the passage of the Morelle, but each time that one of them showed himself he fell with one of Dominique's bullets in his brain. The captain, who was watching the performance, was amazed; he complimented the young man, telling him that he would like to have many more marksmen of his skill. Dominique did not hear a word he said. A ball struck him in the shoulder, another raised a contusion on his arm. And still he kept on firing.

There were two more deaths. The mattresses were torn to shreds and no longer availed to stop the windows. The last volley that was poured in seemed as if it would carry away the mill bodily, so fierce it was. The position was no longer tenable. Still, the officer kept repeating: "Stand fast. Another half-hour yet."

He was counting the minutes, one by one, now. He had promised his commanders that he would hold the enemy there until nightfall, and he would not budge a hair's-breadth before the moment that he had fixed on for his withdrawal. He maintained his pleasant air of good humor, smiling at Françoise by way of reassuring her. He had picked up the musket of one of the dead soldiers and was firing away with the rest.

There were but four soldiers left in the room. The Prussians were showing themselves *en masse* on the other side of the Morelle, and it was evident that they might now pass the stream at any moment. A few moments more elapsed; the captain was as determined as ever, and would not give the order to retreat, when a sergeant came running into the room, saying:

"They are on the road; they are going to take us in the rear."

The Prussians must have discovered the bridge. The captain drew out his watch again.

"Five minutes more," he said. "They won't be here within five minutes."

Then exactly at six o'clock he at last withdrew his men through a little postern that opened on a narrow lane, whence they threw themselves into the ditch, and in that way reached the forest of Sauval. The captain took leave of Father Merlier with much politeness, apologizing profusely for the trouble he had caused. He even added:

"Try to keep them occupied for a while. We shall return."

While this was occurring, Dominique had remained alone in the hall. He was still firing away, hearing nothing, conscious of nothing; his sole thought was to defend Françoise. The soldiers were all gone, and he had not the remotest idea of the fact; he aimed and brought down his man at every shot. All at once there was a great tumult. The Prussians had entered the courtyard from the rear. He fired his last shot, and they fell upon him with his weapon still smoking in his hand.

It required four men to hold him; the rest of them swarmed about him, vociferating like madmen in their horrible dialect. Françoise rushed forward to intercede with her prayers. They were on the point of killing him on the spot, but an officer came in and made them turn the prisoner over to him. After exchanging a few words in German with his men he turned to Dominique and said to him, in very good French:

"You will be shot in two hours from now"

III

It was the standing regulation, laid down by the German staff, that every Frenchman, not belonging to the regular army, taken with arms in his hands should be shot. Even the *compagnies franches* were not recognized as belligerents. It was the intention of the Germans, in making such terrible examples of the peasants who attempted to defend their firesides, to prevent a rising *en masse,* which they greatly dreaded.

The officer, a tall, square man of about fifty years old, subjected Dominique to a brief examination. Although he spoke French fluently, he was unmistakably Prussian in the stiffness of his manner.

"You are a native of this country?"

"No, I am a Belgian."

"Why did you take up arms? These are matters with which you have no concern."

Dominique made no reply. At this moment the officer caught sight of Françoise where she stood listening, very pale; her slight wound had marked her white forehead with a streak of red. He looked from one to the other of the young people and appeared to understand the situation. He merely added:

"You do not deny having fired on my men?"

"I fired as long as I was able to do so," Dominique quietly replied.

The admission was scarcely necessary, for he was black with powder, wet with sweat, and the blood from the wound in his shoulder had trickled down and stained his clothing.

"Very well," the officer repeated. "You will be shot two hours hence."

Françoise uttered no cry. She clasped her hands and raised them above her head in a gesture of mute despair. Her action was not lost upon the officer. Two soldiers had led Dominique away to an adjacent room, where their orders were to guard him and not lose sight of him. The girl had sunk upon a chair; her strength had failed her, her legs refused to support her; she was denied the relief of tears, it seemed as if her emotion was strangling her. The officer continued to examine her attentively, and finally addressed her:

"Is that young man your brother?" he inquired.

She shook her head in negation. He was as rigid and unbending as ever, without the suspicion of a smile on his face. Then, after an interval of silence, he spoke again:

"Has he been living in the neighborhood long?"

She answered yes, by another motion of the head.

"Then he must be well acquainted with the woods about here?"

This time she made a verbal answer. "Yes, sir," she said, looking at him with some astonishment.

He said nothing more, but turned on his heel, requesting that the mayor of the village should be brought before him. But Françoise had risen from her chair, a faint tinge of color on her cheeks, believing that she had caught the significance of his questions, and with renewed hope she ran off to look for her father.

As soon as the firing had ceased Father Merlier had hurriedly descended by the wooden gallery to have a look at his wheel. He adored his daughter and had a strong feeling of affection for Dominique, his son-in-law who was to be; but his wheel also occupied a large space in his heart. Now that the two little ones, as he called them, had come safe and sound out of the fray, he thought of his other love, which must have suffered sorely, poor thing, and bending over the great wooden skeleton he was scrutinizing its wounds with a heartbroken air. Five of the buckets were reduced to splinters, the central framework was honeycombed. He was thrusting his fingers into the cavities that the bullets had made to see how deep they were and reflecting how he was ever to repair all that damage. When Françoise found him he was already plugging up the crevices with moss and such débris as he could lay hands on.

"They are asking for you, father," said she.

And at last she wept as she told him what she had just heard. Father Merlier shook his head. It was not customary to shoot people like that. He would have to look into the matter. And he re-entered the mill with his usual placid, silent air. When the officer made his demand for supplies for his men, he answered that the people of Rocreuse were not accustomed to be ridden roughshod, and that nothing would be obtained from them through violence; he was willing to assume all the responsibility, but only on condition that he was allowed to act independently. The officer at first appeared to take umbrage at this easy way of viewing matters, but finally gave way before the old man's brief and distinct representations. As the latter was leaving the room the other recalled him to ask:

"Those woods there, opposite, what do you call them?"

"The woods of Sauval."

"And how far do they extend?"

The miller looked him straight in the face. "I do not know," he replied.

And he withdrew. An hour later the subvention in money and provisions that the officer had demanded was in the courtyard of the mill. Night was coming on; Françoise followed every movement of the soldiers with an anxious eye. She never once left the vicinity of the room in which Dominique was imprisoned. About seven o'clock she had a harrowing emotion; she saw the officer enter the prisoner's apartment, and for a quarter of an hour heard their voices raised in violent discussion. The officer came to the door for a moment and gave an order in German which she did not understand, but when twelve men came and formed in the courtyard with shouldered muskets, she was seized with a fit of trembling and felt as if she should die. It was all over, then; the execution was about to take place. The twelve men remained there ten minutes; Dominique's voice kept rising higher and higher in a tone of vehement denial. Finally the officer came out, closing the door behind him with a vicious bang and saying:

"Very well; think it over. I give you until tomorrow morning."

And he ordered the twelve men to break ranks by a motion of his hand. Françoise was stupefied. Father Merlier, who had continued to puff away at his pipe while watching the platoon with a simple, curious air, came and took her by the arm with fatherly gentleness. He led her to her chamber.

"Don't fret," he said to her; "try to get some sleep. Tomorrow it will be light and we shall see more clearly."

He locked the door behind him as he left the room. It was a fixed principle with him that women are good for nothing, and that they spoil everything whenever they meddle in important matters. Françoise did not lie down, however; she remained a long time seated on her bed, listening to the various noises in the house. The German soldiers quartered in the courtyard were singing and laughing; they must have kept up their eating and drinking until eleven o'clock, for the riot never ceased for an instant. Heavy footsteps resounded from time to time through the mill itself, doubtless the tramp of the guards as they were relieved. What had most interest for her was the sounds that she could catch in the room that lay directly under her own; several times she threw herself prone upon the floor and applied her ear to the boards. That room was the one in which they had locked up Dominique. He must have been pacing the apartment, for she could hear for a long time his regular, cadenced tread passing from the wall to the window and back again; then there was a deep silence; doubtless he had seated himself. The other sounds ceased too; everything was still. When it seemed to her that the house was sunk in slumber she raised her window as noiselessly as possible and leaned out.

Without, the night was serene and balmy. The slender crescent of the moon, which was just setting behind Sauval wood, cast a dim radiance over the landscape. The lengthening shadows of the great trees stretched far athwart the fields in bands of blackness, while in such spots as were unobscured the grass appeared of a tender green, soft as velvet. But Françoise did not stop to consider the mysterious charm of night. She was scrutinizing the country and looking to see where the Germans had posted their sentinels. She could clearly distinguish their dark forms outlined along the course of the Morelle. There was only one stationed opposite the mill, on the far bank of the stream, by a willow whose branches dipped in the water. Françoise had an excellent view of him; he was a tall young man, standing quite motionless with his face upturned towards the sky, with the meditative air of a shepherd.

When she had completed her careful inspection of localities she returned and took her former seat upon the bed. She remained there an hour, absorbed in deep thought. Then she listened again; there was not a breath to be heard in the house. She went again to the window and took another look outside, but one of the moon's horns was still hanging above the edge of the forest, and this circumstance doubtless appeared to her unpropitious, for she resumed her waiting. At last the moment seemed to have arrived; the night was now quite dark; she could no longer discern the sentinel opposite her, the landscape lay before her, black as a sea of ink. She listened intently for a moment, then formed her resolve. Close beside her window was an iron ladder made of bars set in the wall, which ascended from the mill-wheel to the granary at the top of the building, and had formerly served the miller as a means of inspecting certain portions of the gearing, but a change having been made in the machinery the ladder had long since become lost to sight beneath the thick ivy that covered all that side of the mill.

Françoise bravely climbed over the balustrade of the little balcony in front of her window, grasped one of the iron bars and found herself suspended in space. She commenced the descent; her skirts were a great hindrance to her. Suddenly a stone became loosened from the wall and fell into the Morelle with a loud splash. She stopped, benumbed with fear, but reflection quickly told her that the waterfall, with its continuous roar, was sufficient to deaden any noise that she could make, and then she descended more boldly, putting aside the ivy with her foot, testing each round of her ladder. When she was on a level with the room that had been converted into a prison for her lover she stopped. An unforeseen difficulty came near depriving her of all her courage: the window of the room beneath was not situated directly under the window of her bedroom; there was a wide space between it and the ladder, and when she extended her hand it only encountered the naked wall.

Would she have to go back the way she came and leave her project unaccomplished? Her arms were growing very tired; the murmuring of the Morelle, far down below, was beginning to make her dizzy. Then she broke off bits of plaster from the wall and threw them against Dominique's window. He did not hear; perhaps he was asleep. Again she crumbled fragments from the wall, until the skin was peeled from her fingers. Her strength was exhausted; she felt that she was about to fall back into the stream when at last Dominique softly raised his sash.

"It is I," she murmured. "Take me quick; I am about to fall." Leaning from the window he grasped her and drew her into the room, where she had a paroxysm of weeping, stifling her sobs in order that she might not be heard. Then, by a supreme effort of the will she overcame her emotion.

"Are you guarded?" she asked in a low voice.

Dominique, not yet recovered from his stupefaction at seeing her there, made answer by simply pointing toward his door. There was a sound of snoring audible on the outside; it was evident that the sentinel had been overpowered by sleep and had thrown himself upon the floor close against the door in such a way that it could not be opened without arousing him.

"You must fly," she continued earnestly. "I came here to bid you fly and say farewell."

But he seemed not to hear her. He kept repeating:

"What, is it you, is it you? Oh, what a fright you gave me! You might have killed yourself." He took her hands, he kissed them again and again. "How I love you, Françoise! You are as courageous as you are good. The only thing I feared was that I might die without seeing you again; but you are here, and now they may shoot me when they will. Let me but have a quarter of an hour with you and I am ready."

He had gradually drawn her to him; her head was resting on his shoulder. The peril that was so near at hand brought them closer to each other, and they forgot everything in that long embrace.

"Ah, Françoise!" Dominique went on in low, caressing tones, "today is the fête of St. Louis, our wedding day, that we have been waiting for so long. Nothing has been able to keep us apart, for we are both here, faithful to our appointment, are we not? It is now our wedding morning."

"Yes, yes," she repeated after him, "our wedding morning."

They shuddered as they exchanged a kiss. But suddenly she tore herself from his arms; the terrible reality arose before her eyes.

"You must fly, you must fly," she murmured breathlessly. "There is not a moment to lose." And as he stretched out his arms in the darkness to draw her to him again, she went on in tender, beseeching tones: "Oh! listen to me, I entreat you. If you die, I shall die. In an hour it will be daylight. Go, go at once; I command you to go."

Then she rapidly explained her plan to him. The iron ladder extend-

ing downward to the wheel; once he had got so far he could climb down
by means of the buckets and get into the boat, which was hidden in a
recess. Then it would be an easy matter for him to reach the other bank
of the stream and make his escape.

"But are there no sentinels?" said he.

"Only one, directly opposite here, at the foot of the first willow."

"And if he sees me, if he gives the alarm?"

Françoise shuddered. She placed in his hand a knife that she had
brought down with her. They were silent.

"And your father—and you?" Dominique continued. "But no, it is
not to be thought of; I must not fly. When I am no longer here those
soldiers are capable of murdering you. You do not know them. They
offered to spare my life if I would guide them into Sauval forest. When
they discover that I have escaped, their fury will be such that they will
be ready for every atrocity."

The girl did not stop to argue the question. To all the considerations
that he adduced to her one simple answer was: "Fly. For the love of me,
fly. If you love me, Dominique, do not linger here a single moment
longer."

She promised that she would return to her bedroom; no one should
know that she had helped him. She concluded by folding him in her
arms and smothering him with kisses, in an extravagant outburst of
passion. He was vanquished. He only put one more question to her:

"Will you swear to me that your father knows what you are doing,
and that he counsels my flight?"

"It was my father who sent me to you," Françoise unhesitatingly replied.

She told a falsehood. At that moment she had but one great, over-
mastering longing, to know that he was in safety, to escape from the
horrible thought that the morning's sun was to be the signal for his
death. When he should be far away, then calamity and evil might burst
upon her head; whatever fate might be in store for her would seem en-
durable, so that only his life might be spared. Before and above all other
considerations, the selfishness of her love demanded that he should be
saved.

"It is well," said Dominique; "I will do as you desire."

No further word was spoken. Dominique went to the window to raise
it again. But suddenly there was a noise that chilled them with affright.
The door was shaken violently; they thought that someone was about to
open it; it was evidently a party going the rounds who had heard their
voices. They stood by the window, closely locked in each other's arms,

awaiting the event with anguish unspeakable. Again there came the rattling at the door, but it did not open. Each of them drew a deep sigh of relief; they saw how it was. The soldier lying across the threshold had turned over in his sleep. Silence was restored indeed, and presently the snoring began again.

Dominique insisted that Françoise should return to her room first of all. He took her in his arms, he bade her a silent farewell, then helped her to grasp the ladder, and himself climbed out on it in turn. He refused to descend a single step, however, until he knew that she was in her chamber. When she was safe in her room she let fall, in a voice scarce louder than a whisper, the words:

"*Au revoir.* I love you!"

She kneeled at the window, resting her elbows on the sill, straining her eyes to follow Dominique. The night was still very dark. She looked for the sentinel, but could see nothing of him; the willow alone was dimly visible, a pale spot upon the surrounding blackness. For a moment she heard the rustling of the ivy as Dominique descended, then the wheel creaked, and there was a faint splash which told that the young man had found the boat. This was confirmed when, a minute later, she descried the shadowy outline of the skiff on the gray bosom of the Morelle. Then a horrible feeling of dread seemed to clutch her by the throat. Every moment she thought she heard the sentry give the alarm; every faintest sound among the dusky shadows seemed to her overwrought imagination to be the hurrying tread of soldiers, the clash of steel, the click of musket-locks. The seconds slipped by, however, the landscape still preserved its solemn peace. Dominique must have landed safely on the other bank. Françoise no longer had eyes for anything. The silence was oppressive. And she heard the sound of trampling feet, a hoarse cry, the dull thud of a heavy body falling. This was followed by another silence, even deeper than that which had gone before. Then, as if conscious that Death had passed that way, she became very cold in presence of the impenetrable night.

IV

At early daybreak the repose of the mill was disturbed by the clamor of angry voices. Father Merlier had gone and unlocked Françoise's door. She descended to the courtyard, pale and very calm, but when there, could not repress a shudder upon being brought face to face with the body of a Prussian soldier that lay on the ground beside the well, stretched out upon a cloak.

Around the corpse soldiers were shouting and gesticulating angrily. Several of them shook their fists threateningly in the direction of the village. The officer had just sent a summons to Father Merlier to appear before him in his capacity as mayor of the commune.

"Here is one of our men," he said, in a voice that was almost unintelligible from anger, "who was found murdered on the bank of the stream. The murderer must be found, so that we may make a salutary example of him, and I shall expect you to cooperate with us in finding him."

"Whatever you desire," the miller replied, with his customary impassiveness. "Only it will be no easy matter."

The officer stooped down and drew aside the skirt of the cloak which concealed the dead man's face, disclosing as he did so a frightful wound. The sentinel had been struck in the throat and the weapon had not been withdrawn from the wound. It was a common kitchen-knife, with a black handle.

"Look at that knife," the officer said to Father Merlier. "Perhaps it will assist us in our investigation."

The old man had started violently, but recovered himself at once; not a muscle of his face moved as he replied:

"Everyone about here has knives like that. Like enough your man was tired of fighting and did the business himself. Such things have happened before now."

"Be silent!" the officer shouted in a fury. "I don't know what it is that keeps me from setting fire to the four corners of your village."

His anger fortunately kept him from noticing the great change that had come over Françoise's countenance. Her feelings had compelled her to sit down upon the stone bench beside the well. Do what she would she could not remove her eyes from the body that lay stretched upon the ground, almost at her feet. He had been a tall, handsome young man in life, very like Dominique in appearance, with blue eyes and yellow hair. The resemblance went to her heart. She thought that perhaps the dead man had left behind him in his German home some sweetheart who would weep for his loss. And she recognized her knife in the dead man's throat. She had killed him.

The officer, meantime, was talking of visiting Rocreuse with some terrible punishment, when two or three soldiers came running in. The guard had just that moment ascertained the fact of Dominique's escape. The agitation caused by the tidings was extreme. The officer went to inspect the locality, looked out through the still open window, saw at

once how the event had happened, and returned in a state of exaspera-
tion.

Father Merlier appeared greatly vexed by Dominique's flight. "The
idiot!" he murmured; "he has upset everything."

Françoise heard him, and was in an agony of suffering. Her father,
moreover, had no suspicion of her complicity. He shook his head, saying
to her in an undertone:

"We are in a nice box now!"

"It was that scoundrel! It was that scoundrel!" cried the officer. "He
has got away to the woods; but he must be found, or the village shall
stand the consequences." And addressing himself to the miller: "Come,
you must know where he is hiding?"

Father Merlier laughed in his silent way, and pointed to the wide
stretch of wooded hills.

"How can you expect to find a man in that wilderness?" he asked.

"Oh! there are plenty of hiding places that you are acquainted with.
I am going to give you ten men; you shall act as guide to them."

"I am perfectly willing. But it will take a week to beat up all the woods
of the neighborhood."

The old man's serenity enraged the officer; he saw, indeed, what a
ridiculous proceeding such a hunt would be. It was at that moment that
he caught sight of Françoise where she sat, pale and trembling, on her
bench. His attention was aroused by the girl's anxious attitude. He was
silent for a moment, glancing suspiciously from father to daughter and
back again.

"Is not that man," he at last coarsely asked the old man, "your
daughter's lover?"

Father Merlier's face became ashy pale, and he appeared for a moment
as if about to throw himself on the officer and throttle him. He straight-
ened himself up and made no reply. Françoise had hid her face in her
hands.

"Yes, that is how it is," the Prussian continued; "you or your daughter
have helped him to escape. You are his accomplices. For the last time,
will you surrender him?"

The miller did not answer. He had turned away and was looking at
the distant landscape with an air of indifference, just as if the officer were
talking to some other person. That put the finishing touch on the latter's
wrath.

"Very well, then!" he declared, "you shall be shot in his stead."

And again he ordered out the firing party. Father Merlier was as imperturbable as ever. He scarcely did so much as shrug his shoulders; the whole drama appeared to him to be in very doubtful taste. He probably believed that they would not take a man's life in that unceremonious manner. When the platoon was on the ground he gravely said:

"So, then, you are in earnest? Very well, I am willing it should be so. If you feel you must have a victim, it may as well be I as another."

But Françoice arose, greatly troubled, stammering: "Have mercy, sir: do not harm my father. Kill me instead of him. It was I who helped Dominique to escape; I am the only guilty one."

"Hold your tongue, my girl," Father Merlier exclaimed. "Why do you tell such a falsehood? She passed the night locked in her room, sir: I assure you that she does not speak the truth."

"I *am* speaking the truth," the girl eagerly replied. "I got down by the window; I incited Dominique to fly. It is the truth, the whole truth."

The old man's face was very white. He could read in her eyes that she was not lying, and her story terrified him. Ah, those children! those children! how they spoiled everything, with their hearts and their feelings! Then he said angrily:

"She is crazy; do not listen to her. It is a lot of trash she is telling you. Come, let us get through with this business."

She persisted in her protestations; she kneeled, she raised her clasped hands in supplication. The officer stood tranquilly by and watched the harrowing scene.

"Mon Dieu!" he said at last, "I take your father because the other has escaped me. Bring me back the other man, and your father shall have his liberty."

She looked at him for a moment with eyes dilated by the horror which his proposal inspired in her.

"It is dreadful?" she murmured. "Where can I look for Dominique now? He is gone; I know nothing beyond that."

"Well, make your choice between them; him or your father."

"Oh, my God! how can I choose? Even if I knew where to find Dominique I could not choose. You are breaking my heart. I would rather die at once. Yes, it would be more quickly ended thus. Kill me, I beseech you, kill me——"

The officer finally became weary of this scene of despair and tears. He cried:

"Enough of this! I wish to treat you kindly; I will give you two hours. If your lover is not here within two hours, your father shall pay the penalty that he has incurred."

And he ordered Father Merlier away to the room that had served as a prison for Dominique. The old man asked for tobacco, and began to smoke. There was no trace of emotion to be described on his impassive face. Only when he was alone he wept two big tears that coursed slowly down his cheeks. His poor, dear child, what a fearful trial she was enduring!

Françoise remained in the courtyard. Prussian soldiers passed back and forth, laughing. Some of them addressed her with coarse pleasantries which she did not understand. Her gaze was bent upon the door through which her father had disappeared, and with a slow movement she raised her hand to her forehead, as if to keep it from bursting. The officer turned sharply on his heel, and said to her:

"You have two hours. Try to make good use of them."

She had two hours. The words kept buzzing, buzzing in her ears. Then she went forth mechanically from the courtyard; she walked straight ahead with no definite end. Where was she to go? What was she to do? She did not even endeavor to arrive at any decision, for she felt how utterly useless were her efforts. And yet she would have liked to see Dominique; they could have come to some understanding together, perhaps they might have hit on some plan to extricate them from their difficulties. And so, amid the confusion of her whirling thoughts, she took her way downwards to the bank of the Morelle, which she crossed below the dam by means of some stepping-stones which were there. Proceeding onwards, still involuntarily, she came to the first willow, at the corner of the meadow, and stooping down, beheld a sight that made her grow deathly pale—a pool of blood. It was the spot. And she followed the track that Dominique had left in the tall grass; it was evident that he had run, for the footsteps that crossed the meadow in a diagonal line were separated from one another by wide intervals. Then, beyond that point, she lost the trace, but thought she had discovered it again in an adjoining field. It led her onwards to the border of the forest, where the trail came abruptly to an end.

Though conscious of the futility of the proceeding, Françoise penetrated into the wood. It was a comfort for her to be alone. She sat down for a moment, then, reflecting that time was passing, rose again to her feet. How long was it since she left the mill? Five minutes, or a half-hour? She had lost all idea of time. Perhaps Dominique had sought concealment in a clearing that she knew of, where they had gone together one afternoon and eaten hazel nuts. She directed her steps towards the clearing; she searched it thoroughly. A blackbird flew out, whistling his sweet and melancholy note; that was all. Then she thought that he might have taken refuge in a hollow among the rocks where he went sometimes with his gun, but the spot was untenanted. What use was there in looking for him? She would never find him, and little by little the desire to discover the hiding-place became a passionate longing. She proceeded at a more rapid pace. The idea suddenly took possession of her that he had climbed into a tree, and thenceforth she went along with eyes raised aloft and called him by name every fifteen or twenty steps, so that he might know she was near him. The cuckoos answered her; a breath of air that rustled the leaves made her think that he was there and was coming down to her. Once she even imagined that she saw him; she stopped with a sense of suffocation, with a desire to run away. What was she to say to him? Had she come there to take him back with her and have him shot? Oh! no, she would not mention those things; she would not tell him that he must fly, that he must not remain in the neighborhood. Then she thought of her father awaiting her return, and the reflection caused her most bitter anguish. She sank upon the turf, weeping hot tears, crying aloud.

"My God! My God! Why am I here?"

It was a mad thing for her to have come. And as if seized with sudden panic, she ran hither and thither. She sought to make her way out of the forest. Three times she lost her way, and had begun to think she was never to see the mill again, when she came out into a meadow, directly opposite Rocreuse. As soon as she caught sight of the village she stopped. Was she going to return alone?

She was standing there when she heard a voice calling her by name, softly:

"Françoise! Françoise!"

And she beheld Dominique raising his head above the edge of a ditch. Just God! She had found him.

Could it be, then, that Heaven willed his death? She suppressed a cry that rose to her lips, and slipped into the ditch beside him.

"You were looking for me?" he asked.

"Yes," she replied bewilderedly, scarcely knowing what she was saying.

"Ah! what has happened?"

She stammered, with eyes downcast: "Why, nothing; I was anxious, I wanted to see you."

Thereupon, his fears alleviated, he went on to tell her how it was that he had remained in the vicinity. He was alarmed for them. Those rascally Prussians were not above wreaking their vengeance on women and old men. All had ended well, however, and he added, laughing:

"The wedding will be put off for a week, that's all."

He became serious, however, upon noticing that her dejection did not pass away.

"But what is the matter? You are concealing something from me."

"No, I give you my word I am not. I am tired; I ran all the way here."

He kissed her, saying it was imprudent for them both to talk there any longer, and was about to climb out of the ditch in order to return to the forest. She stopped him; she was trembling violently.

"Listen, Dominique; perhaps it will be as well for you to stay here, after all. There is no one looking for you; you have nothing to fear."

"Françoise, you are concealing something from me," he said again.

Again she protested that she was concealing nothing. She only liked to know that he was near her. And there were other reasons still that she gave in stammering accents. Her manner was so strange that no consideration could now have induced him to go away. He believed, moreover, that the French would return presently. Troops had been seen over towards Sauval.

"Ah! let them make haste; let them come as quickly as possible," she murmured fervently.

At that moment the clock of the church at Rocreuse struck eleven; the strokes reached them, clear and distinct. She arose in terror; it was two hours since she had left the mill.

"Listen," she said, with feverish rapidity, "should we need you, I will go up to my room and wave my handkerchief from the window."

And she started off homeward at a run, while Dominique, greatly disturbed in mind, stretched himself at length beside the ditch to watch the mill. Just as she was about to enter the village Françoise encountered an old beggar man, Father Bontemps, who knew everyone and everything in that part of the country. He saluted her; he had just seen the miller, he said, surrounded by a crowd of Prussians; then, making numerous signs of the cross and mumbling some inarticulate words, he went his way.

"The two hours are up," the officer said when Françoise made her appearance.

Father Merlier was there, seated on the bench beside the well. He was smoking still. The young girl again proffered her supplication, kneeling before the officer and weeping. Her wish was to gain time. The hope that she might yet behold the return of the French had been gaining strength in her bosom, and amid her tears and sobs she thought she could distinguish in the distance the cadenced tramp of an advancing army. Oh! if they would but come and deliver them all from their fearful trouble!

"Hear me, sir: grant us an hour, just one little hour. Surely you will not refuse to grant us an hour!"

But the officer was inflexible. He even ordered two men to lay hold of her and take her away, in order that they might proceed undisturbed with the execution of the old man. Then a dreadful conflict took place in Françoise's heart. She could not allow her father to be murdered in that manner; no, no, she would die in company with Dominique rather; and she was just darting away in the direction of her room in order to signal to her *fiancé,* when Dominique himself entered the courtyard.

The officer and his soldiers gave a great shout of triumph, but he, as if there had been no soul there but Françoise, walked straight up to her: he was perfectly calm, and his face wore a slight expression of sternness.

"You did wrong," he said. "Why did you not bring me back with you? Had it not been for Father Bontemps I should have known nothing of all this. Well, I am here, at all events."

V

It was three o'clock. The heavens were piled high with great black clouds, the tail-end of a storm that had been raging somewhere in the vicinity. Beneath the coppery sky and ragged scud the valley of Rocreuse, so bright and smiling in the sunlight, became a grim chasm, full of sinister shadows. The Prussian officer had done nothing with Dominique beyond placing him in confinement, giving no indication of his ultimate purpose in regard to him. Françoise, since noon, had been suffering unendurable agony; notwithstanding her father's entreaties, she would not leave the courtyard. She was waiting for the French troops to appear, but the hours slipped by, night was approaching, and she suffered all the more since it appeared as if the time thus gained would have no effect on the final result.

About three o'clock, however, the Prussians began to make their preparations for departure. The officer had gone to Dominique's room and remained closeted with him for some minutes, as he had done the day before. Françoise knew that the young man's life was hanging in the balance; she clasped her hands and put up fervent prayers. Beside her sat Father Merlier, rigid and silent, declining, like the true peasant he was, to attempt any interference with accomplished facts.

"Oh! my God! my God!" Françoise exclaimed, "they are going to kill him!"

The miller drew her to him, and took her on his lap as if she had been a little child. At this juncture the officer came from the room, followed by two men conducting Dominique between them.

"Never, never!" the latter exclaimed. "I am ready to die."

"You had better think the matter over," the officer replied. "I shall have no trouble in finding someone else to render us the service which you refuse. I am generous with you; I offer you your life. It is simply a matter of guiding us across the forest to Montredon; there must be paths."

Dominique made no answer.

"Then you persist in your obstinacy?"

"Shoot me, and let's have done with it," he replied.

Françoise, in the distance, entreated her lover with clasped hands; she was forgetful of all considerations save one—she would have had him commit a treason. But Father Merlier seized her hands, that the Prussians might not see the wild gestures of a woman whose mind was disordered by her distress.

"He is right," he murmured, "it is best for him to die."

The firing party was in readiness. The officer still had hopes of bringing Dominique over, and was waiting to see him exhibit some signs of weakness. Deep silence prevailed. Heavy peals of thunder were heard in the distance, the fields and woods lay lifeless beneath the sweltering heat. And it was in the midst of this oppressive silence that suddenly the cry arose: "The French! The French!"

It was a fact; they were coming. The line of red trousers could be seen advancing along the Sauval road, at the edge of the forest. In the mill the confusion was extreme; the Prussian soldiers ran to and fro, giving vent to guttural cries. Not a shot had been fired as yet.

"The French! The French!" cried Françoise, clapping her hands for joy. She was like a woman possessed. She had escaped from her father's embrace and was laughing boisterously, her arms raised high in the air. They had come at last, then, and had come in time, since Dominique was still there, alive!

A crash of musketry that rang in her ears like a thunderclap caused her to suddenly turn her head. The officer had muttered, "We will finish this business first," and with his own hands pushing Dominique up against the wall of a shed, had given the command to the squad to fire. When Françoise turned, Dominique was lying on the ground, pierced by a dozen bullets.

She did not shed a tear; she stood there like one suddenly rendered senseless. Her eyes were fixed and staring, and she went and seated herself beneath the shed, a few steps from the lifeless body. She looked at it wistfully; now and then she would make a movement with her hands in an aimless, childish way. The Prussians had seized Father Merlier as a hostage.

It was a pretty fight. The officer, perceiving that he could not retreat without being cut to pieces, rapidly made the best disposition possible of his men; it was as well to sell their lives dearly. The Prussians were now the defenders of the mill, and the French were the attacking party. The musketry fire began with unparalleled fury; for half an hour there was no lull in the storm. Then a deep report was heard, and a ball carried away a main branch of the old elm. The French had artillery; a battery, in position just beyond the ditch where Dominique had concealed himself, commanded the main street of Rocreuse. The conflict could not last long after that.

Ah! the poor old mill! The cannon balls raked it from wall to wall. Half the roof was carried away; two of the walls fell in. But it was on the side towards the Morelle that the damage was most lamentable. The ivy, torn from the tottering walls, hung in tatters, débris of every description floated away upon the bosom of the stream, and through a great breach Françoise's chamber was visible, with its little bed, the snow-white curtains of which were carefully drawn. Two balls struck the old wheel in quick succession, and it gave one parting groan; the buckets were carried away down stream, the frame was crushed into a shapeless mass. It was the soul of the stout old mill parting from the body.

Then the French came forward to carry the place by storm. There was a mad hand-to-hand conflict with the bayonet. Under the dull sky the pretty valley became a huge slaughter-pen; the broad meadows looked on in horror, with their great isolated trees and their rows of poplars, dotting them with shade, while to right and left the forest was like the walls of a tilting ground enclosing the combatants, and in Nature's universal panic the gentle murmur of the springs and watercourses sounded like sobs and wails.

Françoise had not stirred from the shed where she remained hanging over Dominique's body. Father Merlier had met his death from a stray bullet. Then the French captain, the Prussians being exterminated and the mill on fire, entered the courtyard at the head of his men. It was the first success that he had gained since the breaking out of the war, so, all inflamed with enthusiasm, drawing himself up to the full height of his lofty stature, he laughed pleasantly, as a handsome cavalier like him might laugh. Then, perceiving poor idiotic Françoise where she crouched between the corpses of her father and her betrothed, among the smoking ruins of the mill, he saluted her gallantly with his sword, and shouted:
"Victory! Victory!"

13

The Procurator of Judaea

ANATOLE FRANCE

L. ÆLIUS LAMIA, born in Italy of illustrious parents, had not yet discarded the *toga prætexta* when he set out for the schools of Athens to study philosophy. Subsequently he took up his residence at Rome, and in his house on the Esquiline, amid a circle of youthful wastrels, abandoned himself to licentious courses. But being accused of engaging in criminal relations with Lepida, the wife of Sulpicius Quirinus, a man of consular rank, and being found guilty, he was exiled by Tiberius Cæsar. At that time he was just entering his twenty-fourth year. During the eighteen years that his exile lasted he traversed Syria, Palestine, Cappadocia, and Armenia, and made prolonged visits to Antioch, Cæsarea, and Jerusalem. When, after the death of Tiberius, Caius was raised to the purple, Lamia obtained permission to return to Rome. He even regained a portion of his possessions. Adversity had taught him wisdom.

He avoided all intercourse with the wives and daughters of Roman citizens, made no efforts towards obtaining office, held aloof from public honors, and lived a secluded life in his house on the Esquiline. Occupying himself with the task of recording all the remarkable things he had seen during his distant travels, he turned, as he said, the vicissitudes of his years of expiation into a diversion for his hours of rest. In the midst of these calm employments, alternating with assiduous study of the works of Epicurus, he recognized with a mixture of surprise and vexation that age was stealing upon him. In his sixty-second year, being afflicted with an illness which proved in no slight degree troublesome, he decided to have recourse to the waters at Baiæ. The coast at that point, once frequented by the halcyon, was at this date the resort of the wealthy Roman, greedy of pleasure. For a week Lamia lived alone, without a friend in the brilliant crowd. Then one day, after dinner, an inclination to which he yielded urged him to ascend the incline, which, covered with vines that resembled bacchantes, looked out upon the waves.

Having reached the summit he seated himself by the side of a path beneath a terebinth, and let his glances wander over the lovely landscape. To his left, livid and bare, the Phlegræan plain stretched out towards the ruins of Cumæ. On his right, Cape Misenum plunged its abrupt spur beneath the Tyrrhenian sea. Beneath his feet luxurious Baiæ, following the graceful outline of the coast, displayed its gardens, its villas thronged with statues, its porticoes, its marble terraces along the shores of the blue ocean where the dolphins sported. Before him, on the other side of the bay, on the Campanian coast, gilded by the already sinking sun, gleamed the temples which far away rose above the laurels of Posilippo, whilst on the extreme horizon Vesuvius looked forth smiling.

Lamia drew from a fold of his toga a scroll containing the *Treatise upon Nature,* extended himself upon the ground, and began to read. But the warning cries of a slave necessitated his rising to allow of the passage of a litter which was being carried along the narrow pathway through the vineyards. The litter being uncurtained permitted Lamia to see stretched upon the cushions as it was borne nearer to him the figure of an elderly man of immense bulk, who, supporting his head on his hand, gazed out with a gloomy and disdainful expression. His nose, which was aquiline, and his chin, which was prominent, seemed desirous of meeting across his lips, and his jaws were powerful.

From the first moment Lamia was convinced that the face was familiar to him. He hesitated a moment before the name came to him. Then suddenly hastening towards the litter with a display of surprise and delight—

"Pontius Pilate!" he cried. "The gods be praised who have permitted me to see you once again!"

The old man gave a signal to the slaves to stop, and cast a keen glance upon the stranger who had addressed him.

"Pontius, my dear host," resumed the latter, "have twenty years so far whitened my hair and hollowed my cheeks that you no longer recognize your friend Ælius Lamia?"

At this name Pontius Pilate dismounted from the litter as actively as the weight of his years and the heaviness of his gait permitted him, and embraced Ælius Lamia again and again.

"Gods! what a treat it is to me to see you once more! But, alas! you call up memories of those long-vanished days when I was Procurator of

Judæa in the province of Syria. Why, it must be thirty years ago that I first met you. It was at Cæsarea, whither you came to drag out your weary term of exile. I was fortunate enough to alleviate it a little, and out of friendship, Lamia, you followed me to that depressing place Jerusalem, where the Jews filled me with bitterness and disgust. You remained for more than ten years my guest and my companion, and in converse about Rome and things Roman we both of us managed to find consolation— you for your misfortunes, and I for my burdens of State."

Lamia embraced him afresh.

"You forget two things, Pontius; you are overlooking the facts that you used your influence on my behalf with Herod Antipas, and that your purse was freely open to me."

"Let us not talk of that," replied Pontius, "since after your return to Rome you sent me by one of your freedmen a sum of money which repaid me with usury."

"Pontius, I could never consider myself out of your debt by the mere payment of money. But tell me, have the gods fulfilled your desires? Are you in the enjoyment of all the happiness you deserve? Tell me about your family, your fortunes, your health."

"I have withdrawn to Sicily, where I possess estates, and where I cultivate wheat for the market. My eldest daughter, my best-beloved Pontia, who has been left a widow, lives with me, and directs my household. The gods be praised, I have preserved my mental vigor; my memory is not in the least degree enfeebled. But old age always brings in its train a long procession of griefs and infirmities. I am cruelly tormented with gout. And at this very moment you find me on my way to the Phlegræan plain in search of a remedy for my sufferings. From that burning soil, whence at night flames burst forth, proceed acrid exhalations of sulphur, which, so they say, ease the pains and restore suppleness to the stiffened joints. At least, the physicians assure me that it is so."

"May you find it so in your case, Pontius. But, despite the gout and its burning torments, you scarcely look as old as myself, although in reality you must be my senior by ten years. Unmistakably you have retained a greater degree of vigor than I ever possessed, and I am overjoyed to find you looking so hale. Why, dear friend, did you retire from the public service before the customary age? Why, on resigning your governorship in Judæa, did you withdraw to a voluntary exile on your Sicilian estates? Give me an account of your doings from the moment that I ceased to be a witness of them. You were preparing to suppress a Samaritan rising when I set out for Cappadocia, where I hoped to draw some profit from the breeding of horses and mules. I have not seen you since then. How did that expedition succeed? Pray tell me. Everything interests me that concerns you in any way."

Pontius Pilate sadly shook his head.

"My natural disposition," he said, "as well as a sense of duty, impelled me to fulfill my public responsibilities, not merely with diligence, but even with ardor. But I was pursued by unrelenting hatred. Intrigues and calumnies cut short my career in its prime, and the fruit it should have looked to bear has withered away. You ask me about the Samaritan insurrection. Let us sit down on this hillock. I shall be able to give you an answer in few words. Those occurrences are as vividly present to me as if they had happened yesterday.

"A man of the people, of persuasive speech—there are many such to be met with in Syria—induced the Samaritans to gather together in arms on Mount Gerizim (which in that country is looked upon as a holy place) under the promise that he would disclose to their sight the sacred vessels which in the ancient days of Evander and our father, Æneas, had been hidden away by an eponymous hero, or rather a tribal deity, named Moses. Upon this assurance the Samaritans rose in rebellion; but having been warned in time to forestall them, I dispatched detachments of infantry to occupy the mountain, and stationed cavalry to keep the approaches to it under observation.

"These measures of prudence were urgent. The rebels were already laying siege to the town of Tyrathaba, situated at the foot of Mount Gerizim. I easily dispersed them, and stifled the as yet scarcely organized revolt. Then, in order to give a forcible example with as few victims as possible, I handed over to execution the leaders of the rebellion. But you are aware, Lamia, in what strait dependence I was kept by the proconsul Vitellius, who governed Syria not in, but against the interests of Rome, and looked upon the provinces of the Empire as territories which could be farmed out to tetrarchs. The head-men among the Samaritans, in their resentment against me, came and fell at his feet lamenting. To listen to them, nothing had been further from their thoughts than to disobey Cæsar. It was I who had provoked the rising, and it was purely in order to withstand my violence that they had gathered together round Tyrathaba. Vitellius listened to their complaints, and handing over the affairs of Judæa to his friend Marcellus, commanded me to go and justify my proceedings before the Emperor himself. With a heart overflowing with grief and resentment I took ship. Just as I approached the shores of Italy, Tiberius, worn out with age and the cares of empire, died suddenly on the self-same Cape Misenum, whose peak we see from this very spot magnified in the mists of evening. I demanded justice of Caius, his successor, whose perception was naturally acute, and who was acquainted with Syrian affairs. But marvel with me, Lamia, at the maliciousness of fortune, resolved on my discomfiture. Caius then had in his suite at Rome the Jew Agrippa, his companion, the friend of his childhood, whom he cherished as his own eyes. Now Agrippa favored Vitellius, inasmuch as Vitellius was the enemy of Antipas, whom Agrippa pursued with his hatred. The Emperor adopted the prejudices of his beloved Asiatic and refused even to listen to me. There was nothing for me to do but bow beneath the stroke of unmerited misfortune. With tears for my meat and gall for my portion, I withdrew to my estates in Sicily, where I should have died of grief if my sweet Pontia had not come to console her father. I have cultivated wheat, and succeeded in producing the fullest ears in the whole province. But now my life is ended; the future will judge between Vitellius and me."

"Pontius," replied Lamia, "I am persuaded that you acted towards the Samaritans according to the rectitude of your character, and solely in the interests of Rome. But were you not perchance on that occasion a trifle too much influenced by that impetuous courage which has always swayed you? You will remember that in Judæa it often happened that I who, younger than you, should naturally have been more impetuous than you, was obliged to urge you to clemency and suavity."

"Suavity towards the Jews!" cried Pontius Pilate. "Although you have lived amongst them, it seems clear that you ill understand those enemies of the human race. Haughty and at the same time base, combining an invincible obstinacy with a despicably mean spirit, they weary alike your love and your hatred. My character, Lamia, was formed upon the maxims of the divine Augustus. When I was appointed Procurator of Judæa, the world was already penetrated with the majestic ideal of the *Pax Romana*. No longer, as in the days of our internecine strife, were we witnesses to the sack of a province for the aggrandisement of a proconsul. I knew where my duty lay. I was careful that my actions should be governed by prudence and moderation. The gods are my witnesses that I was resolved upon mildness, and upon mildness only. Yet what did my benevolent intentions avail me? You were at my side, Lamia, when, at the outset of my career as ruler, the first rebellion came to a head. Is there any need for me to recall the details to you? The garrison had been transferred from Cæsarea to take up its winter quarters at Jerusalem. Upon the ensigns of the legionaries appeared the presentment of Cæsar. The inhabitants of Jerusalem, who did not recognize the indwelling divinity of the Emperor, were scandalized at this, as though, when obedience is compulsory, it were not less abject to obey a god than a man. The priests of their nation appeared before my tribunal imploring me with supercilious humility to have the ensigns removed from within the holy city. Out of reverence for the divine nature of Cæsar and the majesty of the empire, I refused to comply. Then the rabble made common cause with the priests, and all around the pretorium portentous cries of supplication arose. I ordered the soldiers to stack their spears in front of the tower of Antonia, and to proceed, armed only with sticks like lictors, to disperse the insolent crowd. But, heedless of blows, the Jews continued their entreaties, and the more obstinate amongst them threw themselves on the ground and, exposing their breasts to the rods, deliberately courted death. You were a witness of my humiliation on that occasion, Lamia. By the order of Vitellius I was forced to send the insignia back to Cæsarea. That disgrace I had certainly not merited. Before the immortal gods I swear that never once during my term of office did I flout justice and the laws. But I am grown old. My enemies and detractors are dead. I shall die unavenged. Who will now retrieve my character?"

He moaned and lapsed into silence. Lamia replied—

"That man is prudent who neither hopes nor fears anything from the uncertain events of the future. Does it matter in the least what estimate men may form of us hereafter? We ourselves are after all our own witnesses, and our own judges. You must rely, Pontius Pilate, on the testimony you yourself bear to your own rectitude. Be content with your own personal respect and that of your friends. For the rest, we know that mildness by itself will not suffice for the work of government. There is but little room in the actions of public men for that indulgence of human frailty which the philosophers recommend."

"We'll say no more at present," said Pontius. "The sulphureous fumes which rise from the Phlegræan plain are more powerful when the ground which exhales them is still warm beneath the sun's rays. I must hasten on. Adieu! But now that I have rediscovered a friend, I should wish to take advantage of my good fortune. Do me the favor, Ælius Lamia, to give me your company at supper at my house tomorrow. My house stands on the seashore, at the extreme end of the town in the direction of Misenum. You will easily recognize it by the porch, which bears a painting representing Orpheus surrounded by tigers and lions, whom he is charming with the strains from his lyre.

"Till tomorrow, Lamia," he repeated, as he climbed once more into his litter. "Tomorrow we will talk about Judæa."

The following day at the supper hour Lamia presented himself at the house of Pontius Pilate. Two couches only were in readiness for occupants. Creditably but simply equipped, the table held a silver service in which were set out beccaficos in honey, thrushes, oysters from the Lucrine lake, and lampreys from Sicily. As they proceeded with their repast, Pontius and Lamia interchanged inquiries with one another about their ailments, the symptoms of which they described at considerable length, mutually emulous of communicating the various remedies which had been recommended to them. Then, congratulating themselves on being thrown together once more at Baiæ, they vied with one another in praise of the beauty of that enchanting coast and the mildness of the climate they enjoyed. Lamia was enthusiastic about the charms of the courtesans who frequented the seashore laden with golden ornaments and trailing draperies of barbaric broidery. But the aged Procurator deplored the ostentation with which by means of trumpery jewels and filmy garments foreigners and even enemies of the empire beguiled the Romans of their gold. After a time they turned to the subject of the great engineering feats that had been accomplished in the country; the prodigious bridge constructed by Caius between Puteoli and Baiæ, and the canals which Augustus excavated to convey the waters of the ocean to Lake Avernus and the Lucrine lake.

"I also," said Pontius, with a sigh, "I also wished to set afoot public works of great utility. When, for my sins, I was appointed Governor of Judæa, I conceived the idea of furnishing Jerusalem with an abundant supply of pure water by means of an aqueduct. The elevation of the levels, the proportionate capacity of the various parts, the gradient for the brazen reservoirs to which the distribution pipes were to be fixed— I had gone into every detail, and decided everything for myself with the assistance of mechanical experts. I had drawn up regulations for the superintendents so as to prevent individuals from making unauthorized depredations. The architects and the workmen had their instructions. I gave orders for the commencement of operations. But far from viewing with satisfaction the construction of that conduit, which was intended to carry to their town upon its massive arches not only water but health, the inhabitants of Jerusalem gave vent to lamentable outcries. They gathered tumultuously together, exclaiming against the sacrilege and impiousness, and, hurling themselves upon the workmen, scattered the very foundation stones. Can you picture to yourself, Lamia, a filthier set of barbarians? Nevertheless, Vitellius decided in their favor, and I received orders to put a stop to the work."

"It is a knotty point," said Lamia, "how far one is justified in devising things for the commonweal against the will of the populace."

Pontius Pilate continued as though he had not heard this interruption.

"Refuse an aqueduct! What madness! But whatever is of Roman origin is distasteful to the Jews. In their eyes we are an unclean race, and our very presence appears a profanation to them. You will remember that they would never venture to enter the pretorium for fear of defiling themselves, and that I was consequently obliged to discharge my magisterial functions in an open-air tribunal on that marble pavement your feet so often trod.

"They fear us and they despise us. Yet is not Rome the mother and warden of all those peoples who nestle smiling upon her venerable bosom? With her eagles in the van, peace and liberty have been carried to the very confines of the universe. Those whom we have subdued we look on as our friends, and we leave those conquered races, nay, we secure to them the permanence of their customs and their laws. Did Syria, aforetime rent asunder by its rabble of petty kings, ever even begin to taste of peace and prosperity until it submitted to the armies of Pompey? And when Rome might have reaped a golden harvest as the price of her goodwill, did she lay hands on the hoards that swell the treasuries of barbaric temples? Did she despoil the shrine of Cybele at Pessinus, or the Morimene and Cilician sanctuaries of Jupiter, or the temple of the Jewish god at Jerusalem? Antioch, Palmyra, and Apamea, secure despite their wealth, and no longer in dread of the wandering Arab of the desert, have erected temples to the genius of Rome and the divine Cæsar. The Jews alone hate and withstand us. They withhold their tribute till it is wrested from them, and obstinately rebel against military service."

"The Jews," replied Lamia, "are profoundly attached to their ancient customs. They suspected you, unreasonably, I admit, of a desire to abolish their laws and change their usages. Do not resent it, Pontius, if I say that you did not always act in such a way as to disperse their unfortunate illusion. It gratified you, despite your habitual self-restraint, to play upon their fears, and, more than once have I seen you betray in their presence the contempt with which their beliefs and religious ceremonies inspired you. You irritated them particularly by giving instructions for the sacerdotal garments and ornaments of their high priest to be kept in ward by your legionaries in the Antonine tower. One must admit that though they have never risen like us to an appreciation of things divine the Jews celebrate rites which their very antiquity renders venerable."

Pontius Pilate shrugged his shoulders.

"They have very little exact knowledge of the nature of the gods," he said. "They worship Jupiter, yet they abstain from naming him or erecting a statue of him. They do not even adore him under the semblance of a rude stone, as certain of the Asiatic peoples are wont to do. They know nothing of Apollo, of Neptune, of Mars, nor of Pluto, nor of any goddess. At the same time, I am convinced that in days gone by they worshipped Venus. For even to this day their women bring doves to the altar as victims; and you know as well as I that the dealers who trade beneath the arcades of their temple supply those birds in couples for sacrifice. I have even been told that on one occasion some madman proceeded to overturn the stalls bearing these offerings, and their owners with them. The priests raised an outcry about it, and looked on it as a case of sacrilege. I am of opinion that their custom of sacrificing turtledoves was instituted in honor of Venus. Why are you laughing, Lamia?"

"I was laughing," said Lamia, "at an amusing idea which, I hardly know how, just occurred to me. I was thinking that perchance some day the Jupiter of the Jews might come to Rome and vent his fury upon you. Why should he not? Asia and Africa have already enriched us with a considerable number of gods. We have seen temples in honor of Isis and the dog-faced Anubis erected in Rome. In the public squares, and even on the race-courses, you may run across the Bona Dea of the Syrians mounted on an ass. And did you never hear how, in the reign of Tiberius, a young patrician passed himself off as the horned Jupiter of the Egyptians, Jupiter Ammon, and in this disguise procured the favors of an illustrious lady who was too virtuous to deny anything to a god? Beware, Pontius, lest the invisible Jupiter of the Jews disembark some day on the quay at Ostia!"

At the idea of a god coming out of Judæa, a fleeting smile played over the severe countenance of the Procurator. Then he replied gravely—

"How would the Jews manage to impose their sacred law on outside peoples when they are in a perpetual state of tumult amongst themselves as to the interpretation of that law? You have seen them yourself, Lamia, in the public squares, split up into twenty rival parties, with staves in their hands, abusing each other and clutching one another by the beard. You have seen them on the steps of the temple, tearing their filthy garments as a symbol of lamentation, with some wretched creature in a frenzy of prophetic exaltation in their midst. They have never realized that it is possible to discuss peacefully and with an even mind those matters concerning the divine which yet are hidden from the profane and wrapped in uncertainty. For the nature of the immortal gods remains hidden from us, and we cannot arrive at a knowledge of it. Though I am of opinion, none the less, that it is a prudent thing to believe in the providence of the gods. But the Jews are devoid of philosophy, and cannot tolerate any diversity of opinions. On the contrary, they judge worthy of the extreme penalty all those who on divine subjects profess opinions opposed to their law. And as, since the genius of Rome has towered over them, capital sentences pronounced by their own tribunals can only be carried out with the sanction of the proconsul or the procurator, they harry the Roman magistrate at any hour to procure his signature to their baleful decrees, they besiege the pretorium with their cries of 'Death!' A hundred times, at least, have I known them, mustered, rich and poor together, all united under their priests, make a furious onslaught on my ivory chair, seizing me by the skirts of my robe, by the thongs of my sandals, and all to demand of me—nay, to exact from me— the death sentence on some unfortunate whose guilt I failed to perceive, and as to whom I could only pronounce that he was as mad as his accusers. A hundred times, do I say! Not a hundred, but every day and all day. Yet it was my duty to execute their law as if it were ours, since I was appointed by Rome not for the destruction, but for the upholding of their customs, and over them I had the power of the rod and the axe. At the outset of my term of office I endeavored to persuade them to hear reason; I attempted to snatch their miserable victims from death. But this show of mildness only irritated them the more; they demanded their prey, fighting around me like a horde of vultures with wing and beak. Their priests reported to Cæsar that I was violating their law, and their appeals, supported by Vitellius, drew down upon me a severe reprimand. How many times did I long, as the Greeks used to say, to dispatch accusers and accused in one convoy to the crows!

"Do not imagine, Lamia, that I nourish the rancor of the discomfited, the wrath of the superannuated, against a people which in my person has prevailed against both Rome and tranquillity. But I foresee the extremity to which sooner or later they will reduce us. Since we cannot govern them, we shall be driven to destroy them. Never doubt it. Always in a state of insubordination, brewing rebellion in their inflammatory minds, they will one day burst forth upon us with a fury beside which the wrath of the Numidians and the mutterings of the Parthians are mere child's play. They are secretly nourishing preposterous hopes, and madly premeditating our ruin. How can it be otherwise, when, on the strength of an oracle, they are living in expectation of the coming of a prince of their own blood whose kingdom shall extend over the whole earth? There are no half measures with such a people. They must be exterminated. Jerusalem must be laid waste to the very foundation. Perchance, old as I am, it may be granted me to behold the day when her walls shall fall and the flames shall envelop her houses, when her inhabitants shall pass under the edge of the sword, when salt shall be strown on the place where once the temple stood. And in that day I shall at length be justified."

Lamia exerted himself to lead the conversation back to a less acrimonious note.

"Pontius," he said, "it is not difficult for me to understand both your longstanding resentment and your sinister forebodings. Truly, what you have experienced of the character of the Jews is nothing to their advantage. But I lived in Jerusalem as an interested onlooker, and mingled freely with the people, and I succeeded in detecting certain obscure virtues in these rude folk which were altogether hidden from you. I have met Jews who were all mildness, whose simple manners and faithfulness of heart recalled to me what our poets have related concerning the Spartan lawgiver. And you yourself, Pontius, have seen perish beneath the cudgels of your legionaries simple-minded men who have died for a cause they believed to be just without revealing their names. Such men do not deserve our contempt. I am saying this because it is desirable in all things to preserve moderation and an even mind. But I own that I never experienced any lively sympathy for the Jews. The Jewesses, on the contrary, I found extremely pleasing. I was young then, and the Syrian women stirred all my senses to response. Their ruddy lips, their liquid eyes that shone in the shade, their sleepy gaze pierced me to the very marrow. Painted and stained, smelling of nard and myrrh, steeped in odors, their physical attractions are both rare and delightful."

Pontius listened impatiently to these praises.

"I was not the kind of man to fall into the snares of the Jewish women," he said; "and since you have opened the subject yourself, Lamia, I was never able to approve of your laxity. If I did not express with sufficient emphasis formerly how culpable I held you for having intrigued at Rome with the wife of a man of consular rank, it was because you were then enduring heavy penance for your misdoings. Marriage from the patrician point of view is a sacred tie; it is one of the institutions which are the support of Rome. As to foreign women and slaves, such relations as one may enter into with them would be of little account were it not that they habituate the body to a humiliating effeminacy. Let me tell you that you have been too liberal in your offerings to the Venus of the Market-place; and what, above all, I blame in you is that you have not married in compliance with the law and given children to the Republic, as every good citizen is bound to do."

But the man who had suffered exile under Tiberius was no longer listening to the venerable magistrate. Having tossed off his cup of Falernian, he was smiling at some image visible to his eye alone.

After a moment's silence he resumed in a very deep voice, which rose in pitch little by little:

"With what languorous grace they dance, those Syrian women! I knew a Jewess at Jerusalem who used to dance in a poky little room, on a threadbare carpet, by the light of one smoky little lamp, waving her arms as she clanged her cymbals. Her loins arched, her head thrown back, and, as it were, dragged down by the weight of her heavy red hair, her eyes swimming with voluptuousness, eager, languishing, compliant, she would have made Cleopatra herself grow pale with envy. I was in love with her barbaric dances, her voice—a little raucous and yet so sweet—her atmosphere of incense, the semi-somnolescent state in which she seemed to live. I followed her everywhere. I mixed with the vile rabble of soldiers, conjurers, and extortioners with which she was surrounded. One day, however, she disappeared, and I saw her no more. Long did I seek her in disreputable alleys and taverns. It was more difficult to learn to do without her than to lose the taste for Greek wine. Some months after I lost sight of her, I learned by chance that she had attached herself to a small company of men and women who were followers of a young Galilean thaumaturgist. His name was Jesus; he came from Nazareth, and he was crucified for some crime, I don't quite know what. Pontius, do you remember anything about the man?"

Pontius Pilate contracted his brows, and his hand rose to his forehead in the attitude of one who probes the deeps of memory. Then after a silence of some seconds:

"Jesus?" he murmured, "Jesus—of Nazareth? I cannot call him to mind."

14

Crainquebille

ANATOLE FRANCE

I

IN EVERY sentence pronounced by a judge in the name of the sovereign people, dwells the whole majesty of justice. The august character of that justice was brought home to Jérôme Crainquebille, costermonger, when, accused of having insulted a policeman, he appeared in the police court. Having taken his place in the dock, he beheld in the imposing somber hall magistrates, clerks, lawyers in their robes, the usher wearing his chains, *gendarmes,* and, behind a rail, the bare heads of the silent spectators. He, himself, occupied a raised seat, as if some sinister honor were conferred on the accused by his appearance before the magistrate. At the end of the hall, between two assessors, sat President Bourriche. The palm-leaves of an officer of the Academy decorated his breast. Over the tribune were a bust representing the Republic and a crucifix, as if to indicate that all laws divine and human were suspended over Crainquebille's head. Such symbols naturally inspired him with terror. Not being gifted with a philosophic mind, he did not inquire the meaning of the bust and the crucifix; he did not ask how far Jesus and the symbolical bust harmonized in the Law Courts. Nevertheless, here was matter for reflection; for, after all, pontifical teaching and canon law are in many points opposed to the constitution of the Republic and to the civil code. So far as we know the Decretals have not been abolished. Today, as formerly, the Church of Christ teaches that only those powers are lawful to which it has given its sanction. Now the French Republic claims to be independent of pontifical power. Crainquebille might reasonably say:

'Gentlemen and magistrates, insomuch as President Loubet has not been anointed, the Christ, whose image is suspended over your heads, repudiates you through the voice of councils and of Popes. Either he is here to remind you of the rights of the Church, which invalidate yours, or His presence has no rational signification.'

Whereupon President Bourriche might reply:

'Prisoner Crainquebille, the kings of France have always quarrelled with the Pope. Guillaume de Nogaret was excommunicated, but for so trifling a reason he did not resign his office. The Christ of the tribune is not the Christ of Gregory VII or of Boniface VIII. He is, if you will, the Christ of the Gospels, who knew not one word of canon law, and had never heard of the holy Decretals.'

Then Crainquebille might not without reason have answered:

'The Christ of the Gospels was an agitator. Moreover, he was the victim of a sentence, which for nineteen hundred years all Christian peoples have regarded as a grave judicial error. I defy you, Monsieur le Président, to condemn me in His name to so much as forty-eight hours' imprisonment.'

But Crainquebille did not indulge in any considerations either historical, political or social. He was wrapped in amazement. All the ceremonial, with which he was surrounded, impressed him with a very lofty idea of justice. Filled with reverence, overcome with terror, he was ready to submit to his judges in the matter of his guilt. In his own conscience he was convinced of his innocence; but he felt how insignificant is the conscience of a costermonger in the face of the panoply of the law, and the ministers of public prosecution. Already his lawyer had half persuaded him that he was not innocent.

A summary and hasty examination had brought out the charges under which he labored.

II. Crainquebille's Misadventure

Up and down the town went Jérôme Crainquebille, costermonger, pushing his barrow before him and crying: 'Cabbages! Turnips! Carrots!' When he had leeks he cried: 'Asparagus!' For leeks are the asparagus of the poor. Now it happened that on October 20, at noon, as he was going down the Rue Montmartre, there came out of her shop the shoemaker's wife, Madame Bayard. She went up to Crainquebille's barrow and scornfully taking up a bundle of leeks, she said:

'I don't think much of your leeks. What do you want a bundle?'

'Sevenpence halfpenny, mum, and the best in the market!'

'Sevenpence halfpenny for three wretched leeks?'

And disdainfully she cast the leeks back into the barrow.

Then it was that Constable 64 came and said to Crainquebille: 'Move on.'

Moving on was what Crainquebille had been doing from morning till evening for fifty years. Such an order seemed right to him, and perfectly in accordance with the nature of things. Quite prepared to obey, he urged his customer to take what she wanted.

'You must give me time to choose,' she retorted sharply.

Then she felt all the bundles of leeks over again. Finally, she selected the one she thought the best, and held it clasped to her bosom as saints in church pictures hold the palm of victory.

'I will give you sevenpence. That's quite enough; and I'll have to fetch it from the shop, for I haven't anything on me.'

Still embracing the leeks, she went back into the shop, whither she had been preceded by a customer carrying a child.

Just at this moment Constable 64 said to Crainquebille for the second time:

'Move on.'

'I'm waiting for my money,' replied Crainquebille.

'And I'm not telling you to wait for your money; I'm telling you to move on,' retorted the constable grimly.

Meanwhile, the shoemaker's wife in her shop was fitting blue slippers on to a child of eighteen months, whose mother was in a hurry. And the green heads of the leeks were lying on the counter.

For the half-century that he had been pushing his barrow through the streets, Crainquebille had been learning respect for authority. But now his position was a peculiar one: he was torn asunder between what was his due and what was his duty. His was not a judicial mind. He failed to understand that the possession of an individual's right in no way exonerated him from the performance of a social duty. He attached too great importance to his claim to receive sevenpence, and too little to the duty of pushing his barrow and moving on, forever moving on. He stood still.

For the third time Constable 64 quietly and calmly ordered him to move on. Unlike Inspector Montauciel, whose habit it is to threaten constantly but never to take proceedings, Constable 64 is slow to threaten and quick to act. Such is his character. Though somewhat sly he is an excellent servant and a loyal soldier. He is as brave as a lion and as gentle as a child. He knows naught save his official instructions.

'Don't you understand when I tell you to move on?'

To Crainquebille's mind his reason for standing still was too weighty for him not to consider it sufficient. Wherefore, artlessly and simply, he explained it:

'Good Lord! Don't I tell you that I am waiting for my money?'

Constable 64 merely replied:

'Do you want me to summons you? If you do, you have only to say so.'

At these words Crainquebille slowly shrugged his shoulders, looked sadly at the constable, and then raised his eyes to heaven, as if he would say:

'I call God to witness! Am I a law-breaker? Am I one to make light of the by-laws and ordinances which regulate my ambulatory calling? At five o'clock in the morning I was at the market. Since seven, pushing my barrow and wearing my hands to the bone, I have been crying: "Cabbages! Turnips! Carrots!" I am turned sixty. I am worn out. And you ask me whether I have raised the black flag of rebellion. You are mocking me and your joking is cruel!'

Either because he failed to notice the expression on Crainquebille's face, or because he considered it no excuse for disobedience, the constable inquired curtly and roughly whether he had been understood.

Now, just at that moment the block of traffic in the Rue Montmartre was at its worst. Carriages, drays, carts, omnibuses, trucks, jammed one against the other, seemed indissolubly welded together. From their quivering immobility proceeded shouts and oaths. Cabmen and butchers' boys grandiloquent and drawling insulted one another from a distance, and omnibus conductors, regarding Crainquebille as the cause of the block, called him 'a dirty leek.'

Meanwhile, on the pavement the curious were crowding round to listen to the dispute. Then the constable, finding himself the center of attention, began to think it time to display his authority.

'Very well,' he said, taking a stumpy pencil and a greasy notebook from his pocket.

Crainquebille persisted in his idea, obedient to a force within. Besides, it was now impossible for him either to move or to draw back. The wheel of his barrow was unfortunately caught in that of a milkman's cart.

Tearing his hair beneath his cap he cried:

'But don't I tell you I'm waiting for my money! Here's a fix! *Misère de misère! Bon sang de bon sang!*'

By these words, expressive rather of despair than of rebellion, Constable 64 considered he had been insulted. And, because to his mind all insults must necessarily take the consecrated, regular, traditional, litur-

gical, ritual form so to speak of *Mort aux vaches,** thus the offender's
words were heard and understood by the constable.

'Ah! You said: *Mort aux vaches!* Very good. Come along.'

Stupefied with amazement and distress, Crainquebille opened his
great rheumy eyes and gazed at Constable 64. With a broken voice proceeding now from the top of his head and now from the heels of his
boots, he cried, with his arms folded over his blue blouse:

'I said "*Mort aux vaches?*" I? . . . Oh!'

The tradesmen and errand boys hailed the arrest with laughter. It
gratified the taste of all crowds for violent and ignoble spectacles. But
there was one serious person who was pushing his way through the
throng; he was a sad-looking old man, dressed in black, wearing a high
hat; he went up to the constable and said to him in a low voice very
gently and firmly:

'You are mistaken. This man did not insult you.'

'Mind your own business,' replied the policeman, but without threatening, for he was speaking to a man who was well dressed.

The old man insisted calmly and tenaciously. And the policeman ordered him to make his declaration to the Police Commissioner.

Meanwhile Crainquebille was explaining:

'Then I did say "*Mort aux vaches!*" Oh! . . .'

As he was thus giving vent to his astonishment, Madame Bayard, the
shoemaker's wife, came to him with sevenpence in her hand. But Constable 64 already had him by the collar; so Madame Bayard, thinking
that no debt could be due to a man who was being taken to the police-
station, put her sevenpence into her apron pocket.

Then, suddenly beholding his barrow confiscated, his liberty lost, a
gulf opening beneath him and the sky overcast, Crainquebille murmured:

'It can't be helped!'

Before the Commissioner, the old gentleman declared that he had
been hindered on his way by the block in the traffic, and so had witnessed
the incident. He maintained that the policeman had not been insulted,
and that he was laboring under a delusion. He gave his name and profession: Dr. David Matthieu, chief physician at the Ambroise-Paré Hospital, officer of the Legion of Honor. At another time such evidence
would have been sufficient for the Commissioner. But just then men of
science were regarded with suspicion in France.

Crainquebille continued under arrest. He passed the night in the

* It is impossible to translate this expression. As explained later, it means 'down
with spies,' the word spies being used to indicate the police.

lock-up. In the morning he was taken to the Police Court in the prison van.

He did not find prison either sad or humiliating. It seemed to him necessary. What struck him as he entered was the cleanliness of the walls and of the brick floor.

'Well, for a clean place, yes, it is a clean place. You might eat off the floor.'

'When he was left alone, he wanted to draw out his stool; but he perceived that it was fastened to the wall. He expressed his surprise aloud:

'That's a queer idea! Now there's a thing I should never have thought of, I'm sure.'

Having sat down, he twiddled his thumbs and remained wrapped in amazement. The silence and the solitude overwhelmed him. The time seemed long. Anxiously he thought of his barrow, which had been confiscated with its load of cabbages, carrots, celery, dandelion, and corn-salad. And he wondered, asking himself with alarm: 'What have they done with my barrow?'

On the third day he received a visit from his lawyer, Maître Lemerle, one of the youngest members of the Paris Bar, President of a section of La Ligue de la Patrie Française.

Crainquebille endeavored to tell him his story; but it was not easy, for he was not accustomed to conversation. With a little help he might perhaps have succeeded. But his lawyer shook his head doubtfully at everything he said; and, turning over his papers, muttered:

'Hm! Hm! I don't find anything about all this in my brief.'

Then, in a bored tone, twirling his fair moustache he said:

'In your own interest it would be advisable, perhaps, for you to confess. Your persistence in absolute denial seems to me extremely unwise.'

And from that moment Crainquebille would have made confession if he had known what to confess.

III. Crainquebille before the Magistrates

President Bourriche devoted six whole minutes to the examination of Crainquebille. The examination would have been more enlightening if the accused had replied to the questions asked him. But Crainquebille was unaccustomed to discussion; and in such a company his lips were sealed by reverence and fear. So he was silent: and the President answered his own question; his replies were staggering. He concluded: 'Finally, you admit having said, *"Mort aux vaches!"*'

'I said, *"Mort aux vaches!"* because the policeman said, *"Mort aux vaches!"* so then I said, *"Mort aux vaches!"* '

He meant that, being overwhelmed by the most unexpected of accusations, he had in his amazement merely repeated the curious words falsely attributed to him, and which he had certainly never pronounced. He had said, *'Mort aux vaches!'* as he might have said, "I capable of insulting any one! how could you believe it?'

President Bourriche put a different interpretation on the incident.

'Do you maintain,' he said, 'that the policeman was, himself, the first to utter the exclamation?'

Crainquebille gave up trying to explain. It was too difficult.

'You do not persist in your statement. You are quite right,' said the President.

And he had the witness called.

Constable 64, by name Bastien Matra, swore he spoke the truth and nothing but the truth. Then he gave evidence in the following terms:

'I was on my beat on October 20, at noon, when I noticed in the Rue Montmartre a person who appeared to be a hawker, unduly blocking the traffic with his barrow opposite No. 328. Three times I intimated to him the order to move on, but he refused to comply. And when I gave him warning that I was about to charge him, he retorted by crying: *"Mort aux vaches!"* Which I took as an insult.'

This evidence, delivered in a firm and moderate manner, the magistrates received with obvious approbation. The witnesses for the defense were Madame Bayard, shoemaker's wife, and Dr. David Matthieu, chief physician to the Hospital Ambroise-Paré, officer of the Legion of Honor. Madame Bayard had seen nothing and heard nothing. Dr. Matthieu was in the crowd which had gathered round the policeman, who was ordering the costermonger to move on. His evidence led to a new episode in the trial.

'I witnessed the incident,' he said. 'I observed that the constable had made a mistake; he had not been insulted. I went up to him and called his attention to the fact. The officer insisted on arresting the costermonger, and told me to follow him to the Commissioner of Police. This I did. Before the Commissioner, I repeated my declaration.'

'You may sit down,' said the President. 'Usher, recall witness Matra.'

'Matra, when you proceeded to arrest the accused, did not Dr. Matthieu point out to you that you were mistaken?'

'That is to say, Monsieur le Président, that he insulted me.'

'What did he say?'

'He said, *"Mort aux vaches!"'*

Uproarious laughter arose from the audience.

'You may withdraw,' said the President hurriedly.

And he warned the public that if such unseemly demonstrations occurred again he would clear the court. Meanwhile, Counsel for the defense was haughtily fluttering the sleeves of his gown, and for the moment it was thought that Crainquebille would be acquitted.

Order having been restored, Maître Lemerle rose. He opened his pleading with a eulogy of policemen: 'those unassuming servants of society who, in return for a trifling salary, endure fatigue and brave incessant danger with daily heroism. They were soldiers once, and soldiers they remain; soldiers, that word expresses everything. . . .'

From this consideration Maître Lemerle went on to descant eloquently on the military virtues. He was one of those, he said, who would not allow a finger to be laid on the army, on that national army, to which he was so proud to belong.

The President bowed. Maître Lemerle happened to be lieutenant in the Reserves. He was also nationalist candidate for Les Vieilles Haudriettes. He continued:

'No, indeed, I do not esteem lightly the invaluable services, unassumingly rendered, which the valiant people of Paris receive daily from the guardians of the peace. And had I beheld in Crainquebille, gentlemen, one who had insulted an ex-soldier, I should never have consented to represent him before you. My client is accused of having said: *"Mort aux vaches!"* The meaning of such an expression is clear. If you consult *Le Dictionnaire de la Langue Verte* (slang) you will find: *"Vachard,* a sluggard, an idler, one who stretches himself out lazily like a cow instead of working. *Vache,* one who sells himself to the police; spy." *Mort aux vaches!* is an expression employed by certain people. But the question resolves itself into this: how did Crainquebille say it? And, further, did he say it at all? Permit me to doubt it, gentlemen.

'I do not suspect Constable Matra of any evil intention. But, as we have said, his calling is arduous. He is sometimes harassed, fatigued, overdone. In such conditions he may have suffered from an aural hallucination. And, when he comes and tells you, gentlemen, that Dr. David Matthieu, officer of the Legion of Honor, chief physician at the Ambroise-Paré Hospital, a gentleman and a prince of science, cried: *"Mort aux vaches!"* then we are forced to believe that Matra is obsessed, and if the term be not too strong, suffering from the mania of persecution.

'And even if Crainquebille did cry: *"Mort aux vaches!"* it remains to be proved whether such words on his lips can be regarded as an offense.

Crainquebille is the natural child of a costermonger, depraved by years of drinking and other evil courses. Crainquebille was born alcoholic. You behold him brutalized by sixty years of poverty. Gentlemen you must conclude that he is irresponsible.'

Maître Lemerle sat down. Then President Bourriche muttered a sentence condemning Jérôme Crainquebille to pay fifty francs fine and to go to prison for a fortnight. The magistrates convicted him on the strength of the evidence given by Constable Matra.

As he was being taken down the long dark passage of the Palais, Crainquebille felt an intense desire for sympathy. He turned to the municipal guard who was his escort and called him three times:

"Cipal! . . . 'cipal! . . . Eh! 'cipal!' And he sighed:

'If any one had told me only a fortnight ago that this would happen!'

Then he reflected:

'They speak too quickly, these gentlemen. They speak well, but they speak too quickly. You can't make them understand you. . . . 'Cipal, don't you think they speak too quickly?'

But the soldier marched straight on without replying or turning his head.

Crainquebille asked him:

'Why don't you answer me?'

The soldier was silent. And Crainquebille said bitterly:

'You would speak to a dog. Why not to me? Do you never open your mouth? Is it because your breath is foul?'

IV. An Apology for President Bourriche

After the sentence had been pronounced, several members of the audience and two or three lawyers left the hall. The clerk was already calling another case. Those who went out did not reflect on the Crainquebille affair, which had not greatly interested them; and they thought no more about it. Monsieur Jean Lermite, an etcher, who happened to be at the Palais, was the only one who meditated on what he had just seen and heard. Putting his arm on the shoulder of Maître Joseph Aubarrée, he said:

'President Bourriche must be congratulated on having kept his mind free from idle curiosity, and from the intellectual pride which is determined to know everything. If he had weighed one against the other the contradictory evidence of Constable Matra and Dr. David Matthieu, the magistrate would have adopted a course leading to nothing but doubt and uncertainty. The method of examining facts in a critical spirit would be fatal to the administration of justice. If the judge were so imprudent as to follow that method, his sentences would depend on his personal sagacity, of which he has generally no very great store, and on human infirmity which is universal. Where can he find a criterion? It cannot be denied that the historical method is absolutely incapable of providing him with the certainty he needs. In this connection you may recall a story told of Sir Walter Raleigh.

' "One day, when Raleigh, a prisoner in the Tower of London, was working, as was his wont, at the second part of his *History of the World,* there was a scuffle under his window. He went and looked at the brawlers; and when he returned to his work, he thought he had observed them very carefully. But on the morrow, having related the incident to one of his friends who had witnessed the affair and had even taken part in it, he was contradicted by his friend on every point. Reflecting, therefore, that if he were mistaken as to events which passed beneath his very eyes, how much greater must be the difficulty of ascertaining the truth concerning events far distant, he threw the manuscript of his history into the fire."

'If the judges had the same scruples as Sir Walter Raleigh, they would throw all their notes into the fire. But they have no right to do so. They would thus be flouting justice; they would be committing a crime. We may despair of knowing, we must not despair of judging. Those who demand that sentences pronounced in Law Courts should be founded upon a methodical examination of facts, are dangerous sophists, and perfidious enemies of justice both civil and military. President Bourriche has too judicial a mind to permit his sentences to depend on reason and knowledge, the conclusions of which are eternally open to question. He founds them on dogma and moulds them by tradition, so that the authority of his sentences is equal to that of the Church's commandments. His sentences are indeed canonical. I mean that he derives them from a certain number of sacred canons. See, for example, how he classifies evidence, not according to the uncertain and deceptive qualities of appearance and of human veracity, but according to intrinsic, permanent, and manifest qualities. He weighs them in the scale, using weapons of war for weights. Can anything be at once simpler and wiser? Irrefutable for him is the evidence of a guardian of the peace, once his humanity be abstracted, and he conceived as a registered number, and according to the categories of an ideal police. Not that Matra (Bastien), born at Cinto-Monte in Corsica, appears to him incapable of error. He never thought that Bastien Matra was gifted with any great faculty of observation, nor that he applied any secret and vigorous method to the examination of facts. In truth it is not Bastien Matra he is considering, but Constable 64. A man is fallible, he thinks. Peter and Paul may be mistaken. Descartes and Gassendi, Leibniz and Newton, Bichat and Claude Bernard were capable of error. We may all err at any moment. The causes of error are innumerable. The perceptions of our senses and the judgment of our minds are sources of illusion and causes of uncertainty. We dare not rely on the evidence of a single man: *Testis unus, testis nullus*. But we may have faith in a number. Bastien Matra, of Cinto-Monte, is fallible. But Constable 64, when abstraction has been made of his humanity, cannot err. He is an entity. An entity has nothing in common with a man, it is free from all that confuses, corrupts and deceives men. It is pure, unchangeable and unalloyed. Wherefore the magistrates did not hesitate to reject the evidence of the mere man, Dr. David Matthieu, and to admit that of Constable 64, who is the pure idea, an emanation from divinity come down to the judgment bar.

'By following such a line of argument, President Bourriche attains to a kind of infallibility, the only kind to which a magistrate may aspire. When the man who bears witness is armed with a sword, it is the sword's evidence that must be listened to, not the man's. The man is contemptible and may be wrong. The sword is not contemptible and is always right. President Bourriche has seen deeply into the spirit of laws. Society rests on force; force must be respected as the august foundation of society. Justice is the administration of force. President Bourriche knows that Constable 64 is an integral part of the Government. The Government is immanent in each one of its officers. To slight the authority of Constable 64 is to weaken the State. To eat the leaves of an artichoke is to eat the artichoke, as Bossuet puts it in his sublime language. (*Politique tirée de l'Écriture sainte, passim*.)

'All the swords of the State are turned in the same direction. To oppose one to the other is to overthrow the Republic. For that reason, Crainquebille, the accused, is justly condemned to a fortnight in prison and a fine of fifty francs, on the evidence of Constable 64. I seem to hear President Bourriche, himself, explaining the high and noble considerations which inspired his sentence. I seem to hear him saying:

' "I judged this person according to the evidence of Constable 64, because Constable 64 is the emanation of public force. And if you wish to prove my wisdom, imagine the consequences had I adopted the opposite course. You will see at once that it would have been absurd. For if my judgments were in opposition to force, they would never be executed. Notice, gentlemen, that judges are only obeyed when force is on their side. A judge without policemen would be but an idle dreamer. I should be doing myself an injury if I admitted a policeman to be in the wrong. Moreover, the very spirit of laws is in opposition to my doing so. To disarm the strong and to arm the weak would be to subvert that social order which it is my duty to preserve. Justice is the sanction of established injustice. Was justice ever seen to oppose conquerors and usurpers? When an unlawful power arises, justice has only to recognize it and it becomes lawful. Form is everything; and between crime and innocence there is but the thickness of a piece of stamped paper. It was for you, Crainquebille, to be the strongest. If, after having cried: '*Mort aux vaches!*' you had declared yourself emperor, dictator, President of the Republic, or even town councillor, I assure you you would not have been sentenced to pass a fortnight in prison, and to pay a fine of fifty francs. I should have acquitted you. You may be sure of that."

'Such would have doubtless been the words of President Bourriche; for he has a judicial mind, and he knows what a magistrate owes to society. With order and regularity he defends social principles. Justice is social. Only wrong-headed persons would make justice out to be human and reasonable. Justice is administered upon fixed rules, not in obedience to physical emotions and flashes of intelligence. Above all things do not ask justice to be just, it has no need to be just since it is justice, and I might even say that the idea of just justice can have only arisen in the brains of an anarchist. True, President Magnaud pronounces just sentences; but if they are reversed, that is still justice.

'The true judge weighs his evidence with weights that are weapons. So it was in the Crainquebille affair, and in other more famous cases.'

Thus said Monsieur Jean Lermite as he paced up and down the Salle des Pas-Perdus.

Scratching the tip of his nose, Maître Joseph Aubarrée, who knows the Palais well, replied:

'If you want to hear what I think, I don't believe that President Bourriche rose to so lofty a metaphysical plane. In my opinion, when he received as true the evidence of Constable 64, he merely acted according to precedent. Imitation lies at the root of most human actions. A respectable person is one who conforms to custom. People are called good when they do as others do.'

V. Crainquebille submits to the Laws of the Republic

Having been taken back to his prison, Crainquebille sat down on his chained stool, filled with astonishment and admiration. He, himself, was not quite sure whether the magistrates were mistaken. The tribunal had concealed its essential weakness beneath the majesty of form. He could not believe that he was in the right, as against magistrates whose reasons he had not understood: it was impossible for him to conceive that anything could go wrong in so elaborate a ceremony. For, unaccustomed to attending Mass or frequenting the Élysée, he had never in his life witnessed anything so grand as a police court trial. He was perfectly aware that he had never cried: *'Mort aux vaches!'* That for having said it he should have been sentenced to a fortnight's imprisonment seemed to him an august mystery, one of those articles of faith to which believers adhere without understanding them, an obscure, striking, adorable and terrible revelation.

This poor old man believed himself guilty of having mystically offended Constable 64, just as the little boy learning his first Catechism believes himself guilty of Eve's sin. His sentence had taught him that he had cried: *'Mort aux vaches!'* He must, therefore have cried: *'Mort aux vaches!'* in some mysterious manner, unknown to himself. He was transported into a supernatural world. His trial was his apocalypse.

If he had no very clear idea of the offense, his idea of the penalty was still less clear. His sentence appeared to him a solemn and superior ritual, something dazzling and incomprehensible, which is not to be discussed, and for which one is neither to be praised no pitied. If at that moment he had seen President Bourriche, with white wings and a halo round his forehead, coming down through a hole in the ceiling, he would not have been surprised at this new manifestation of judicial glory. He would have said: 'This is my trial continuing!'

On the next day his lawyer visited him:

'Well, my good fellow, things aren't so bad after all! Don't be discouraged. A fortnight is soon over. We have not much to complain of.'

'As for that, I must say the gentlemen were very kind, very polite: not a single rude word. I shouldn't have believed it. And the *'cipal* was wearing white gloves. Did you notice?'

'Everything considered, we did well to confess.'

'Perhaps.'

'Crainquebille, I have a piece of good news for you. A charitable person, whose interest I have elicited on your behalf, gave me fifty francs for you. The sum will be used to pay your fine.'

'When will you give me the money?'

'It will be paid into the clerk's office. You need not trouble about it.'

'It does not matter. All the same I am very grateful to this person.' And

Crainquebille murmured meditatively: 'It's something out of the common that's happening to me.'

'Don't exaggerate, Crainquebille. Your case is by no means rare, far from it.'

'You couldn't tell me where they've put my barrow?'

VI. Crainquebille in the Light of Public Opinion

After his discharge from prison, Crainquebille trundled his barrow along the Rue Montmarte, crying: 'Cabbages! Turnips! Carrots!' He was neither ashamed nor proud of his adventure. The memory of it was not painful. He classed it in his mind with dreams, travels, and plays. But, above all things, he was glad to be walking in the mud, along the paved streets, and to see overhead the rainy sky as dirty as the gutter, the dear sky of the town. At every corner he stopped to have a drink; then, gay and unconstrained, spitting in his hands in order to moisten his horny palms, he would seize the shafts and push on his barrow. Meanwhile a flight of sparrows, as poor and as early as he, seeking their livelihood in the road, flew off at the sound of his familiar cry: 'Cabbages! Turnips! Carrots!' An old housewife, who had come up, said to him as she felt his celery:

'What's happened to you, Père Crainquebille? We haven't seen you for three weeks. Have you been ill? You look rather pale.'

'I'll tell you, M'ame Mailloche, I've been doing the gentleman.'

Nothing in his life changed, except that he went oftener to the pub, because he had an idea it was a holiday and that he had made the acquaintance of charitable folk. He returned to his garret rather gay. Stretched on his mattress he drew over him the sacks borrowed from the chestnut-seller at the corner which served him as blankets and he pondered: 'Well, prison is not so bad; one has everything one wants there. But all the same one is better at home.'

His contentment did not last long. He soon perceived that his customers looked at him askance.

'Fine celery, M'ame Cointreau!'

'I don't want anything.'

'What! nothing! do you live on air then?'

And M'ame Cointreau without deigning to reply returned to the large bakery of which she was the mistress. The shopkeepers and caretakers, who had once flocked round his barrow all green and blooming, now turned away from him. Having reached the shoemaker's, at the sign of l'Ange Gardien, the place where his adventures with justice had begun, he called:

'M'ame Bayard, M'ame Bayard, you owe me sevenpence halfpenny from last time.'

But M'ame Bayard, who was sitting at her counter, did not deign to turn her head.

The whole of the Rue Montmartre was aware that Père Crainquebille had been in prison, and the whole of the Rue Montmartre gave up his acquaintance. The rumor of his conviction had reached the Faubourg and the noisy corner of the Rue Richer. There, about noon, he perceived Madame Laure, a kind and faithful customer, leaning over the barrow of another costermonger, young Martin. She was feeling a large cabbage. Her hair shone in the sunlight like masses of golden threads loosely twisted. And young Martin, a nobody, a good-for-nothing, was protesting with his hand on his heart that there were no finer vegetables than his. At this sight Crainquebille's heart was rent. He pushed his barrow up to young Martin's, and in a plaintive broken voice said to Madame Laure: 'It's not fair of you to forsake me.'

As Madame Laure herself admitted, she was no duchess. It was not in society that she had acquired her ideas of the prison van and the police-station. But can one not be honest in every station in life? Every one has his self-respect; and one does not like to deal with a man who has just come out of prison. So the only notice she took of Crainquebille was to give him a look of disgust. And the old costermonger resenting the affront shouted:

'Dirty wench, go along with you.'

Madame Laure let fall her cabbage and cried:

'Eh! Be off with you, you bad penny. You come out of prison and then insult folk!'

If Crainquebille had had any self-control he would never have reproached Madame Laure with her calling. He knew only too well that one is not master of one's fate, that one cannot always choose one's occupation, and that good people may be found everywhere. He was accustomed discreetly to ignore her customers' business with her; and he despised no one. But he was beside himself. Three times he called Madame Laure drunkard, wench, harridan. A group of idlers gathered round Madame Laure and Crainquebille. They exchanged a few more insults as serious as the first; and they would soon have exhausted their vocabulary, if a policeman had not suddenly appeared, and at once, by his silence and immobility, rendered them as silent and as motionless as himself. They separated. But this scene put the finishing touch to the discrediting of Crainquebille in the eyes of the Faubourg Montmartre and the Rue Richer.

VII. Results

The old man went along mumbling:

'For certain she's a hussy, and none more of a hussy than she.'

But at the bottom of his heart that was not the reproach he brought against her. He did not scorn her for being what she was. Rather he esteemed her for it, knowing her to be frugal and orderly. Once they had liked to talk together. She used to tell him of her parents who lived in the country. And they had both resolved to have a little garden and keep poultry. She was a good customer. And then to see her buying cabbages from young Martin, a dirty, good-for-nothing wretch; it cut him to the heart; and when she pretended to despise him, that put his back up, and then . . . !

But she alas! was not the only one who shunned him as if he had the plague. Every one avoided him. Just like Madame Laure, Madame Cointreau the baker, Madame Bayard of l'Ange Gardien scorned and repulsed him. Why! the whole of society refused to have anything to do with him.

So because one had been put away for a fortnight one was not good enough even to sell leeks! Was it just? Was it reasonable to make a decent chap die of starvation because he had got into difficulties with a copper? If he was not to be allowed to sell vegetables then it was all over with him. Like a badly doctored wine he turned sour. After having had words with Madame Laure, he now had them with every one. For a mere nothing he would tell his customers what he thought of them and in no ambiguous terms, I assure you. If they felt his wares too long he would call them to their faces chatterer, soft head. Likewise at the wine-shop he bawled at his comrades. His friend, the chestnut-seller, no longer recognized him; old Père Crainquebille, he said, had turned into a regular porcupine. It cannot be denied: he was becoming rude, disagreeable, evil-mouthed, loquacious. The truth of the matter was that he was discovering the imperfections of society; but he had not the facilities of a Professor of Moral and Political Science for the expression of his ideas concerning the vices of the system and the reforms necessary; and his thoughts evolved devoid of order and moderation.

Misfortune was rendering him unjust. He was taking his revenge on those who did not wish him ill and sometimes on those who were weaker than he. One day he boxed Alphonse, the wine-seller's little boy, on the ear, because he had asked him what it was like to be sent away. Crainquebille struck him and said:

'Dirty brat! it's your father who ought to be sent away instead of growing rich by selling poison.'

A deed and a speech which did him no honor; for, as the chestnut-seller justly remarked, one ought not to strike a child, neither should one reproach him with a father whom he had not chosen.

Crainquebille began to drink. The less money he earned the more brandy he drank. Formerly frugal and sober, he himself marvelled at the change.

'I never used to be a waster,' he said. 'I suppose one doesn't improve as one grows old.'

Sometimes he severely blamed himself for his misconduct and his laziness:

'Crainquebille, old chap, you ain't good for anything but liftin' your glass."

Sometimes he deceived himself and made out that he needed the drink.

'I must have it now and then; I must have a drop to strengthen me and cheer me up. It seems as if I had a fire in my inside; and there's nothing like the drink for quenching it.'

It often happened that he missed the auction in the morning and so had to provide himself with damaged fruit and vegetables on credit. One day, feeling tired and discouraged, he left his barrow in its shed, and spent the livelong day hanging round the stall of Madame Rose, the tripe-seller, or lounging in and out of the wine-shops near the market. In the evening, sitting on a basket, he mediated and became conscious of his deterioration. He recalled the strength of his early years: the achievements of former days, the arduous labors and the glad evenings: those days quickly passing, all alike and fully occupied; the pacing in the darkness up and down the market pavement, waiting for the early auction; the vegetables carried in armfuls and artistically arranged in the barrow; the piping hot black coffee of Mère Théodore swallowed standing, and at one gulp; the shafts grasped vigorously; and then the loud cry, piercing as cock crow, rending the morning air as he passed through the crowded streets. All that innocent, rough life of the human pack-horse came before him. For half a century on his travelling stall, he had borne to townsfolk worn with care and vigil the fresh harvest of kitchen gardens. Shaking his head he sighed: "No! I'm not what I was.

I'm done for. The pitcher goes so often to the well that at last it comes home broken. And then I've never been the same since my affair with the magistrates. No, I'm not the man I was.'

In short he was demoralized. And when a man reaches that condition he might as well be on the ground and unable to rise. All the passers-by tread him under foot.

VIII. The Final Result

Poverty came, black poverty. The old costermonger who used to come back from the Faubourg Montmartre with a bag full of five-franc pieces, had not a single coin now. Winter came. Driven out of his garret, he slept under the carts in a shed. It had been raining for days; the gutters were overflowing, and the shed was flooded.

Crouching in his barrow, over the pestilent water, in the company of spiders, rats and half-starved cats, he was meditating in the gloom. Having eaten nothing all day and no longer having the chestnut-seller's sacks for a covering, he recalled the fortnight when the Government had provided him with food and clothing. He envied the prisoner's fate. They suffer neither cold not hunger, and an idea occurred to him:

'Since I know the trick why don't I use it?'

He rose and went out into the street. It was a little past eleven. The night was dark and chill. A drizzling mist was falling, colder and more penetrating than rain. The few passers-by crept along under cover of the houses.

Crainquebille went past the Church of Saint-Eustache and turned into the Rue Montmartre. It was deserted. A guardian of the peace stood on the pavement, by the apse of the church. He was under a gas-lamp, and all around fell a fine rain looking reddish in the gaslight. It fell on to the policeman's hood. He looked chilled to the bone; but, either because he preferred to be in the light or because he was tired of walking he stayed under the lamp, and perhaps it seemed to him a friend, a companion. In the loneliness of the night the flickering flame was his only entertainment. In his immobility he appeared hardly human. The reflection of his boots on the wet pavement, which looked like a lake, prolonged him downwards and gave him from a distance the air of some amphibious monster half out of water. Observed more closely he had at once a monkish and a military appearance. The coarse features of his countenance, magnified under the shadow of his hood, were sad and placid. He wore a thick moustache, short and gray. He was an old copper, a man of some two-score years. Crainquebille went up to him softly, and in a weak hesitating voice, said: '*Mort aux vaches!*'

Then he awaited the result of those sacred words. But nothing came of them. The constable remained motionless and silent, with his arms folded under his short cloak. His eyes were wide open; they glistened in the darkness and regarded Crainquebille with sadness, vigilance, and scorn.

Crainquebille, astonished, but still resolute, muttered:

'*Mort aux vaches!* I tell you.'

There was a long silence in the chill darkness and the falling of the fine penetrating rain. At last the constable spoke:

'Such things are not said. . . . For sure and for certain they are not said. At your age you ought to know better. Pass on.'

'Why don't you arrest me?' asked Crainquebille.

The constable shook his head beneath his dripping hood:

'If we were to take up all the addlepates who say what they oughtn't to, we should have our work cut out! . . . And what would be the use of it?'

Overcome by such magnanimous disdain, Crainquebille remained for some time stolid and silent, with his feet in the gutter. Before going, he tried to explain:

'I didn't mean to say: *Mort aux vaches!* to you. It was not for you more than for another. It was only an idea.'

The constable replied sternly but kindly:

'Whether an idea or anything else, it ought not to be said, because when a man does his duty and endures much, he ought not to be insulted with idle words. . . . I tell you again to pass on.'

Crainquebille, with head bent and arms hanging limp, plunged into the rain and the darkness.

15

The Diamond Necklace

GUY DE MAUPASSANT

S HE was one of those pretty, charming young ladies, born, as if through an error of destiny, into a family of clerks. She had no dowry, no hopes, no means of becoming known, appreciated, loved, and married by a man either rich or distinguished; and she allowed herself to marry a petty clerk in the office of the Board of Education.

She was simple, not being able to adorn herself; but she was unhappy, as one out of her class; for women belong to no caste, no race; their grace, their beauty, and their charm serving them in the place of birth and family. Their inborn finesse, their instinctive elegance, their suppleness of wit are their only aristocracy, making some daughters of the people the equal of great ladies.

She suffered incessantly, feeling herself born for all delicacies and luxuries. She suffered from the poverty of her apartment, the shabby walls, the worn chairs, and the faded stuffs. All these things, which another woman of her station would not have noticed, tortured and angered her. The sight of the little Breton, who made this humble home, awoke in her sad regrets and desperate dreams. She thought of quiet antechambers, with their Oriental hangings, lighted by high, bronze torches, and of the two great footmen in short trousers who sleep in the large armchairs, made sleepy by the heavy air from the heating apparatus. She thought of large drawing-rooms, hung in old silks, of graceful pieces of furniture carrying bric-à-brac of inestimable value, and of the little perfumed coquettish apartments, made for five o'clock chats with most intimate friends, men known and sought after, whose attention all women envied and desired.

When she seated herself for dinner, before the round table where the tablecloth had been used three days, opposite her husband who uncovered the tureen with a delighted air, saying: "Oh! the good potpie! I know nothing better than that—" she would think of the elegant dinners, of the shining silver, of the tapestries peopling the walls with ancient personages and rare birds in the midst of fairy forests; she thought of the exquisite food served on marvelous dishes, of the whispered gallantries, listened to with the smile of the sphinx, while eating the rose-colored flesh of the trout or a chicken's wing.

She had neither frocks nor jewels, nothing. And she loved only those things. She felt that she was made for them. She had such a desire to please, to be sought after, to be clever and courted.

She had a rich friend, a schoolmate at the convent, whom she did not like to visit, she suffered so much when she returned. And she wept for whole days from chagrin, from regret, from despair, and disappointment.

One evening her husband returned elated, bearing in his hand a large envelope.

"Here," said he, "here is something for you."

She quickly tore open the wrapper and drew out a printed card on which were inscribed these words:

"The Minister of Public Instruction and Madame George Ramponneau ask the honor of Mr. and Mrs. Loisel's company Monday evening, Janunary 18, at the Minister's residence."

Instead of being delighted as her husband had hoped, she threw the invitation spitefully upon the table, murmuring:

"What do you suppose I want with that?"

"But, my dearie, I thought it would make you happy. You never go out, and this is an occasion, and a fine one! I had a great deal of trouble to get it. Everybody wishes one, and it is very select; not many are given to employees. You will see the whole official world there."

She looked at him with an irritated eye and declared impatiently:

"What do you suppose I have to wear to such a thing as that?"

He had not thought of that; he stammered:

"Why, the dress you wear when we go to the theater. It seems very pretty to me—"

He was silent, stupefied, in dismay, at the sight of his wife weeping. Two great tears fell slowly from the corners of his eyes toward the corners of his mouth; he stammered:

"What is the matter? What is the matter?"

By a violent effort, she had controlled her vexation and responded in a calm voice, wiping her moist cheeks:

"Nothing. Only I have no dress and consequently I cannot go to this affair. Give your card to some colleague whose wife is better fitted out than I."

He was grieved, but answered:

"Let us see, Matilda. How much would a suitable costume cost, something that would serve for other occasions, something very simple?"

She reflected for some seconds, making estimates and thinking of a sum that she could ask for without bringing with it an immediate refusal and a frightened exclamation from the economical clerk.

Finally she said, in a hesitating voice:

"I cannot tell exactly, but it seems to me that four hundred francs ought to cover it."

He turned a little pale, for he had saved just this sum to buy a gun that he might be able to join some hunting parties the next summer, on the plains at Nanterre, with some friends who went to shoot larks up there on Sunday. Nevertheless, he answered:

"Very well. I will give you four hundred francs. But try to have a pretty dress."

The day of the ball approached and Mme. Loisel seemed sad, disturbed, anxious. Nevertheless, her dress was nearly ready. Her husband said to her one evening:

"What is the matter with you? You have acted strangely for two or three days."

And she responded: "I am vexed not to have a jewel, not one stone, nothing to adorn myself with. I shall have such a poverty-laden look. I would prefer not to go to this party."

He replied: "You can wear some natural flowers. At this season they look very *chic*. For ten francs you can have two or three magnificent roses."

She was not convinced. "No," she replied, "there is nothing more humiliating than to have a shabby air in the midst of rich women."

Then her husband cried out: "How stupid we are! Go and find your friend Mrs. Forestier and ask her to lend you her jewels. You are well enough acquainted with her to do this."

She uttered a cry of joy: "It is true!" she said. "I had not thought of that."

The next day she took herself to her friend's house and related her story of distress. Mrs. Forestier went to her closet with the glass doors, took out a large jewel-case, brought it, opened it, and said: "Choose, my dear."

She saw at first some bracelets, then a collar of pearls, then a Venetian cross of gold and jewels and of admirable workmanship. She tried the jewels before the glass, hesitated, but could neither decide to take them nor leave them. Then she asked:

"Have you nothing more?"

"Why, yes. Look for yourself. I do not know what will please you."

Suddenly she discovered, in a black satin box, a superb necklace of diamonds, and her heart beat fast with an immoderate desire. Her hands trembled as she took them up. She placed them about her throat against her dress, and remained in ecstasy before them. Then she asked, in a hesitating voice, full of anxiety:

"Could you lend me this? Only this?"

"Why, yes, certainly."

She fell upon the neck of her friend, embraced her with passion, then went away with her treasure.

The day of the ball arrived. Mme. Loisel was a great success. She was the prettiest of all, elegant, gracious, smiling, and full of joy. All the men noticed her, asked her name, and wanted to be presented. All the members of the Cabinet wished to waltz with her. The Minister of Education paid her some attention.

She danced with enthusiasm, with passion, intoxicated with pleasure, thinking of nothing, in the triumph of her beauty, in the glory of her success, in a kind of cloud of happiness that came of all this homage, and all this admiration, of all these awakened desires, and this victory so complete and sweet to the heart of woman.

She went home toward four o'clock in the morning. Her husband had been half asleep in one of the little salons since midnight, with three other gentlemen whose wives were enjoying themselves very much.

He threw around her shoulders the wraps they had carried for the coming home, modest garments of everyday wear, whose poverty clashed with the elegance of the ball costume. She felt this and wished to hurry away in order not to be noticed by the other women who were wrapping themselves in rich furs.

Loisel retained her. "Wait," said he. "You will catch cold out there. I am going to call a cab."

But she would not listen and descended the steps rapidly. When they were in the street, they found no carriage; and they began to seek one, hailing the coachmen whom they saw at a distance.

They walked along toward the Seine, hopeless and shivering. Finally they found on the dock one of those old nocturnal *coupés* that one sees in Paris after nightfall, as if they were ashamed of their misery by day.

It took them as far as their door in Martyr street, and they went wearily up to their apartment. It was all over for her. And on his part, he remembered that he would have to be at the office by ten o'clock.

She removed the wraps from her shoulders before the glass, for a final view of herself in her glory. Suddenly she uttered a cry. Her necklace was not around her neck.

Her husband, already half undressed, asked: "What is the matter?"

She turned toward him excitedly:

"I have—I have—I no longer have Mrs. Forestier's necklace."

He arose in dismay. "What! How is that? It is not possible."

And they looked in the folds of the dress, in the folds of the mantle, in the pockets, everywhere. They could not find it.

He asked: "You are sure you still had it when we left the house?"

"Yes, I felt it in the vestibule as we came out."

"But if you had lost it in the street, we should have heard it fall. It must be in the cab."

"Yes. It is probable. Did you take the number?"

"No. And you did not notice what it was?"

"No."

They looked at each other utterly cast down. Finally, Loisel dressed himself again.

"I am going," said he, "over the track where we went on foot, to see if I can find it."

And he went. She remained in her evening gown, not having the force to go to bed, stretched upon a chair, without ambition or thoughts.

Toward seven o'clock her husband returned. He had found nothing.

He went to the police and to the cab offices, and put an advertisement in the newspapers, offering a reward; he did everything that afforded them a suspicion of hope.

She waited all day in a state of bewilderment before this frightful disaster. Loisel returned at evening with his face harrowed and pale; he had discovered nothing.

"It will be necessary," said he, "to write to your friend that you have broken the clasp of the necklace and that you will have it repaired. That will give us time to turn around."

She wrote as he dictated.

At the end of a week, they had lost all hope. And Loisel, older by five years, declared:

"We must take measures to replace this jewel."

The next day they took the box which had inclosed it to the jeweler whose name was on the inside. He consulted his books:

"It is not I, Madame," said he, "who sold this necklace; I only furnished the casket."

Then they went from jeweler to jeweler seeking a necklace like the other one, consulting their memories, and ill, both of them, with chagrin and anxiety.

In a shop on the Palais-Royal, they found a chaplet of diamonds which seemed to them exactly like the one they had lost. It was valued at forty thousand francs. They could get it for thirty-six thousand.

They begged the jeweler not to sell it for three days. And they made an arrangement by which they might return it for thirty-four thousand francs if they found the other one before the end of February.

Loisel possessed eighteen thousand francs which his father had left him. He borrowed the rest.

He borrowed it, asking for a thousand francs of one, five hundred of another, five louis of this one, and three louis of that one. He gave notes, made ruinous promises, took money of usurers and the whole race of lenders. He compromised his whole existence, in fact, risked his signature, without even knowing whether he could make it good or not, and, harassed by anxiety for the future, by the black misery which surrounded him, and by the prospect of all physical privations and moral torture, he went to get the new necklace, depositing on the merchant's counter thirty-six thousand francs.

When Mrs. Loisel took back the jewels to Mrs. Forestier, the latter said to her in a frigid tone:

"You should have returned them to me sooner, for I might have needed them."

She did not open the jewel-box as her friend feared she would. If she should perceive the substitution, what would she think? What should she say? Would she take her for a robber?

Mrs. Loisel now knew the horrible life of necessity. She did her part, however, completely, heroically. It was necessary to pay this frightful debt. She would pay it. They sent away the maid; they changed their lodgings; they rented some rooms under a mansard roof.

She learned the heavy cares of a household, the odious work of a kitchen. She washed the dishes, using her rosy nails upon the greasy pots and the bottoms of the stewpans. She washed the soiled linen, the chemises and dishcloths, which she hung on the line to dry; she took down the refuse to the street each morning and brought up the water, stopping at each landing to breathe. And, clothed like a woman of the people, she went to the grocer's, the butcher's, and the fruiterer's, with her basket on her arm, shopping, haggling, defending to the last sou her miserable money.

Every month it was necessary to renew some notes, thus obtaining time, and to pay others.

The husband worked evenings, putting the books of some merchants in order, and nights he often did copying at five sous a page.

And this life lasted for ten years.

At the end of ten years, they had restored all, all, with interest to the usurer, and accumulated interest besides.

Mrs. Loisel seemed old now. She had become a strong hard woman, the crude woman of the poor household. Her hair badly dressed, her skirts awry, her hands red, she spoke in a loud tone, and washed the floors in large pails of water. But sometimes, when her husband was at the office, she would seat herself before the window and think of that evening party of former times, of that ball where she was so beautiful and so flattered.

How would it have been if she had not lost that necklace? Who knows? Who knows? How singular is life, and how full of changes! How small a thing will ruin or save one!

One Sunday, as she was taking a walk in the Champs-Elysées to rid herself of the cares of the week, she suddenly perceived a woman walking with a child. It was Mrs. Forestier, still young, still pretty, still attractive. Mrs. Loisel was affected. Should she speak to her? Yes, certainly. And now that she had paid, she would tell her all. Why not?

She approached her. "Good morning, Jeanne."

Her friend did not recognize her and was astonished to be so familiarly addressed by this common personage. She stammered:

"But, Madame—I do not know—You must be mistaken—"

"No, I am Matilda Loisel."

Her friend uttered a cry of astonishment: "Oh! my poor Matilda! How you have changed—"

"Yes, I have had some hard days since I saw you; and some miserable ones—and all because of you—"

"Because of me? How is that?"

"You recall the diamond necklace that you loaned me to wear to the Commissioner's ball?"

"Yes, very well."

"Well, I lost it."

"How is that, since you returned it to me?"

"I returned another to you exactly like it. And it has taken us ten years to pay for it. You can understand that it was not easy for us who have nothing. But it is finished and I am decently content."

Madame Forestier stopped short. She said:

"You say that you bought a diamond necklace to replace mine?"

"Yes. You did not perceive it then? They were just alike."

And she smiled with a proud and simple joy. Madame Forestier was touched and took both her hands as she replied:

"Oh! my poor Matilda! Mine were false. They were not worth over five hundred francs!"

16

Madame Tellier's Excursion

GUY DE MAUPASSANT

MEN went there every evening at about eleven o'clock, just as they went to the café. Six or eight of them used to meet there; always the same set, not fast men, but respectable tradesmen, and young men in government or some other employ; and they used to drink their Chartreuse, and tease the girls, or else they would talk seriously with Madame, whom everybody respected, and then would go home at twelve o'clock! The younger men would sometimes stay the night.

It was a small, comfortable house, at the corner of a street behind Saint Etienne's church. From the windows one could see the docks, full of ships which were being unloaded, and on the hill the old, gray chapel, dedicated to the Virgin.

Madame, who came of a respectable family of peasant proprietors in the department of the Eure, had taken up her profession, just as she would have become a milliner or dressmaker. The prejudice against prostitution, which is so violent and deeply rooted in large towns, does not exist in the country places in Normandy. The peasant simply says: "It is a paying business," and sends his daughter to keep a harem of fast girls, just as he would send her to keep a girls' school.

She had inherited the house from an old uncle, to whom it had belonged. Monsieur and Madame, who had formerly been innkeepers near Yvetot, had immediately sold their house, as they thought that the business at Fécamp was more profitable. They arrived one fine morning to assume the direction of the enterprise, which was declining on account of the absence of a head. They were good people enough in their way, and soon made themselves liked by their staff and their neighbors.

Monsieur died of apoplexy two years later, for as his new profession kept him in idleness and without exercise, he had grown excessively stout, and his health had suffered. Since Madame had been a widow, all the frequenters of the establishment had wanted her; but people said that personally she was quite virtuous, and even the girls in the house could not discover anything against her. She was tall, stout, and affable, and her complexion, which had become pale in the dimness of her house, the shutters of which were scarcely ever opened, shone as if it had been varnished. She had a fringe of curly, false hair, which gave her a juvenile look, which in turn contrasted strongly with her matronly figure. She was always smiling and cheerful, and was fond of a joke, but there was a shade of reserve about her which her new occupation had not quite made her lose. Coarse words always shocked her, and when any young fellow who had been badly brought up called her establishment by its right name, she was angry and disgusted.

In a word, she had a refined mind, and although she treated her women as friends, yet she very frequently used to say that she and they were not made of the same stuff.

Sometimes during the week she would hire a carriage and take some of her girls into the country, where they used to enjoy themselves on the grass by the side of the little river. They behaved like a lot of girls let out from a school, and used to run races, and play childish games. They would have a cold dinner on the grass, and drink cider, and go home at night with a delicious feeling of fatigue, and in the carriage kiss Madame as a kind mother who was full of goodness and complaisance.

The house had two entrances. At the corner there was a sort of low café, which sailors and the lower orders frequented at night, and she had two girls whose special duty it was to attend to that part of the business. With the assistance of the waiter, whose name was Frederic, and who was a short, light-haired, beardless fellow, as strong as a horse, they set the half bottles of wine and the jugs of beer on the shaky marble tables and then, sitting astride on the customers' knees, would urge them to drink.

The three other girls (there were only five in all), formed a kind of aristocracy, and were reserved for the company on the first floor, unless they were wanted downstairs, and there was nobody on the first floor. The salon of Jupiter, where the tradesmen used to meet, was papered in blue, and embellished with a large drawing representing Leda stretched out under the swan. That room was reached by a winding staircase, which ended at a narrow door opening on to the street, and above it, all night long a little lamp burned, behind wire bars, such as one still sees in some towns, at the foot of the shrine of some saint.

The house, which was old and damp, rather smelled of mildew. At times there was an odor of eau de Cologne in the passages, or a half open door downstairs allowed the noise of the common men sitting and drinking downstairs to reach the first floor, much to the disgust of the gentlemen who were there. Madame, who was quite familiar with those of her customers with whom she was on friendly terms, did not leave the salon. She took much interest in what was going on in the town, and they regularly told her all the news. Her serious conversation was a change from the ceaseless chatter of the three women; it was a rest from the doubtful jokes of those stout individuals who every evening indulged in the commonplace amusement of drinking a glass of liquor in company with girls of easy virtue.

The names of the girls on the first floor were Fernande, Raphaelle, and Rosa "the Jade." As the staff was limited, Madame had endeavored that each member of it should be a pattern, an epitome of each feminine type so that every customer might find as nearly as possible, the realization of his ideal. Fernande represented the handsome blonde; she was very tall, rather fat, and lazy; a country girl, who could not get rid of her freckles, and whose short, light, almost colorless, tow-like hair, which was like combed-out flax, barely covered her head.

Raphaelle, who came from Marseilles, played the indispensable part of the handsome Jewess. She was thin, with high cheek-bones covered with rouge, and her black hair, which was always covered with pomatum, curled on to her forehead. Her eyes would have been handsome, if the right one had not had a speck in it. Her Roman nose came down over a square jaw, where two false upper teeth contrasted strangely with the bad color of the rest.

Rosa the Jade was a little roll of fat, nearly all stomach, with very short legs. From morning till night she sang songs, which were alternately indecent or sentimental, in a harsh voice, told silly, interminable tales, and only stopped talking in order to eat, or left off eating in order to talk. She was never still, was as active as a squirrel, in spite of her fat and her short legs; and her laugh, which was a torrent of shrill cries, resounded here and there, ceaselessly, in a bedroom, in the loft, in the café, everywhere, and always about nothing.

The two women on the ground floor were Louise, who was nicknamed "la Cocotte," and Flora, whom they called "Balançière,"* because she limped a little. The former always dressed as Liberty, with a tri-colored sash, and the other as a Spanish woman, with a string of copper coins, which jingled at every step she took, in her carroty hair. Both looked like

* Swing, or seesaw.

cooks dressed up for the carnival, and were like all other women of the lower orders, neither uglier nor better looking than they usually are. In fact they looked just like servants at an inn, and were generally called "the Two Pumps."

A jealous peace, very rarely disturbed, reigned among these five women, thanks to Madame's conciliatory wisdom and to her constant good humor; and the establishment, which was the only one of the kind in the little town, was very much frequented. Madame had succeeded in giving it such a respectable appearance; she was so amiable and obliging to everybody, her good heart was so well known, that she was treated with a certain amount of consideration. The regular customers spent money on her, and were delighted when she was especially friendly toward them. When they met during the day, they would say: "This evening, you know where," just as men say: "At the café, after dinner." In a word, Madame Tellier's house was somewhere to go to, and her customers very rarely missed their daily meetings there.

One evening, toward the end of May, the first arrival, Monsieur Poulin, who was a timber merchant, and had been mayor, found the door shut. The little lantern behind the grating was not alight; there was not a sound in the house; everything seemed dead. He knocked, gently at first, and then more loudly, but nobody answered the door. Then he went slowly up the street, and when he got to the market place, he met Monsieur Duvert, the gun-maker, who was going to the same pace, so they went back together, but did not meet with any better success. But suddenly they heard a loud noise close to them, and on going round the corner of the house, they saw a number of English and French sailors, who were hammering at the closed shutters of the café with their fists.

The two tradesmen immediately made their escape, for fear of being compromised, but a low *Pst* stopped them; it was Monsieur Tournevau, the fish-curer, who had recognized them, and was trying to attract their attention. They told him what had happened, and he was all the more vexed at it, as he, a married man, and father of a family, only went there on Saturdays—*securitatis causa,* as he said, alluding to a measure of sanitary policy, which his friend Doctor Borde had advised him to observe. That was his regular evening, and now he would be deprived of it for the whole week.

The three men went as far as the quay together, and on the way they met young Monsieur Philippe, the banker's son, who frequented the place regularly, and Monsieur Pinipesse, the collector. They all returned to the Rue aux Juifs together, to make a last attempt. But the exasperated sailors were besieging the house, throwing stones at the shutters, and shouting, and the five first-floor customers went away as quickly as possible, and walked aimlessly about the streets.

Presently they met Monsieur Dupuis, the insurance agent, and then Monsieur Vassi, the Judge of the Tribunal of Commerce, and they all took a long walk, going to the pier first of all. There they sat down in a row on the granite parapet, and watched the rising tide, and when the promenaders had sat there for some time, Monsieur Tournevau said: "This is not very amusing!"

"Decidedly not," Monsieur Pinipesse replied, and they started off to walk again.

After going through the street on the top of the hill, they returned over the wooden bridge which crosses the Retenue, passed close to the railway, and came out again on to the market place, when suddenly a quarrel arose between Monsieur Pinipesse and Monsieur Tournevau, about an edible fungus which one of them declared he had found in the neighborhood.

As they were out of temper already from annoyance, they would very probably have come to blows, if the others had not interfered. Monsieur Pinipesse went off furious, and soon another altercation arose between the ex-mayor, Monsieur Poulin, and Monsieur Dupuis, the insurance agent, on the subject of the tax-collector's salary, and the profits which he might make. Insulting remarks were freely passing between them, when a torrent of formidable cries were heard, and the group of sailors, who were tired of waiting so long outside a closed house, came into the square. They were walking arm-in-arm, two and two, and formed a long procession, and were shouting furiously. The landsmen went and hid themselves under a gateway, and the yelling crew disappeared in the direction af the abbey. For a long time they still heard the noise, which diminished like a storm in the distance, and then silence was restored. Monsieur Poulin and Monsieur Dupuis, who were enraged with each other, went in different directions, without wishing each other good-bye.

The other four set off again, and instinctively went in the direction of Madame Tellier's establishment, which was still closed, silent, impenetrable. A quiet, but obstinate, drunken man was knocking at the door of the café; then he stopped and called Frederic, the waiter, in a low voice, but finding that he got no answer, he sat down on the doorstep, and awaited the course of events.

The others were just going to retire, when the noisy band of sailors reappeared at the end of the street. The French sailors were shouting the "Marseillaise," and the Englishmen, "Rule Britannia." There was a general lurching against the wall, and then the drunken brutes went on their way toward the quay, where a fight broke out between the two nations, in the course of which an Englishman had his arm broken, and a Frenchman his nose split.

The drunken man, who had stopped outside the door, was crying by this time, as drunken men and children cry when they are vexed, and the others went away. By degrees, calm was restored in the noisy town; here and there, at moments, the distant sound of voices could be heard, only to die away in the distance.

One man was still wandering about, Monsieur Tournevau, the fish-curer, who was vexed at having to wait until the next Saturday. He hoped for something to turn up, he did not know what; but he was exasperated at the police for thus allowing an establishment of such public utility, which they had under their control, to be thus closed.

He went back to it, examined the walls, and tried to find out the reason. On the shutter he saw a notice stuck up, so he struck a wax vesta, and read the following, in a large, uneven hand: "Closed on account of the Confirmation."

Then he went away, as he saw it was useless to remain, and left the drunken man lying on the pavement fast asleep, outside the inhospitable door.

The next day, all the regular customers, one after the other, found some reason for going through the Rue aux Juifs with a bundle of papers under their arm, to keep them in countenance, and with a furtive glance they all read that mysterious notice:

"Closed on Account of the Confirmation."

II

Madame had a brother, who was a carpenter in their native place, Virville, in the department of Eure. When Madame had still kept the inn at Yvetot, she had stood godmother to that brother's daughter, who had received the name of Constance, Constance Rivet; she herself being a Rivet on her father's side. The carpenter, who knew that his sister was in a good position, did not lose sight of her, although they did not meet often, as they were both kept at home by their occupations, and lived a long way from each other. But when the girl was twelve years old, and about to be confirmed, he seized the opportunity to write to his sister, and ask her to come and be present at the ceremony. Their old parents were dead, and as Madame could not well refuse, she accepted the invitation. Her brother, whose name was Joseph, hoped that by dint of showing his sister attentions, she might be induced to make her will in the girl's favor, as she had no children of her own.

His sister's occupation did not trouble his scruples in the least, and, besides, nobody knew anything about it at Virville. When they spoke of her, they only said: "Madame Tellier is living at Fécamp," which might mean that she was living on her own private income. It was quite twenty leagues from Fécamp to Virville, and for a peasant, twenty leagues on land are more than is crossing the ocean to an educated person. The people at Virville had never been further than Rouen, and nothing attracted the people from Fécamp to a village of five hundred houses, in the middle of a plain, and situated in another department. At any rate, nothing was known about her business.

But the Confirmation was coming on, and Madame was in great embarrassment. She had no under-mistress, and did not at all care to leave her house, even for a day. She feared the rivalries between the girls upstairs and those downstairs would certainly break out; that Frederic would get drunk, for when he was in that state, he would knock anybody down for a mere word. At last, however, she made up her mind to take them all with her, with the exception of the man, to whom she gave a holiday, until the next day but one.

When she asked her brother, he made no objection, but undertook to put them all up for a night. So on Saturday morning the eight o'clock express carried off Madame and her companions in a second-class carriage. As far as Beuzeille they were alone, and chattered like magpies, but at that station a couple got in. The man, an aged peasant dressed in a blue blouse with a folding collar, wide sleeves tight at the wrist, and ornamented with white embroidery, wore an old high hat with long nap. He held an enormous green umbrella in one hand, and a large basket in the other, from which the heads of three frightened ducks protruded. The woman, who sat stiffly in her rustic finery, had a face like a fowl, and with a nose that was as pointed as a bill. She sat down opposite her husband and did not stir, as she was startled at finding herself in such smart company.

There was certainly an array of striking colors in the carriage. Madame was dressed in blue silk from head to foot, and had over her dress a dazzling red shawl of imitation French cashmere. Fernande was panting in a Scottish plaid dress, whose bodice, which her companions had laced as tight as they could, had forced up her falling bosom into a double dome, that was continually heaving up and down, and which seemed liquid beneath the material. Raphaelle, with a bonnet covered with feathers, so that it looked like a nest full of birds, had on a lilac dress with gold spots on it; there was something Oriental about it that suited her Jewish face. Rosa the Jade had on a pink petticoat with large flounces, and looked like a very fat child, an obese dwarf; while the Two Pumps looked as if they had cut their dresses out of old, flowered curtains, dating from the Restoration.

Perceiving that they were no longer alone in the compartment, the ladies put on staid looks, and began to talk of subjects which might give the others a high opinion of them. But at Bolbec a gentleman with light whiskers, with a gold chain, and wearing two or three rings, got in, and put several parcels wrapped in oil cloth into the net over his head. He looked inclined for a joke, and a good-natured fellow.

"Are you ladies changing your quarters?" he asked. The question embarrassed them all considerably. Madame, however, quickly recovered her composure, and said sharply, to avenge the honor of her corps:

"I think you might try and be polite!"

He excused himself, and said: "I beg your pardon, I ought to have said your nunnery."

As Madame could not think of a retort, or perhaps as she thought herself justified sufficiently, she gave him a dignified bow, and pinched in her lips.

Then the gentleman, who was sitting between Rosa the Jade and the old peasant, began to wink knowingly at the ducks, whose heads were sticking out of the basket. When he felt that he had fixed the attention of his public, he began to tickle them under their bills, and spoke funnily to them, to make the company smile.

"We have left our little pond, qu-ack! qu-ack! to make the acquaintance of the little spit, qu-ack! qu-ack!"

The unfortunate creatures turned their necks away to avoid his caresses, and made desperate efforts to get out of their wicker prison, and then, suddenly, all at once, uttered the most lamentable quacks of distress. The women exploded with laughter. They leaned forward and pushed each other, so as to see better; they were very much interested in the ducks, and the gentleman redoubled his airs, his wit, and his teasing.

Rosa joined in, and leaning over her neighbor's legs, she kissed the three animals on the head. Immediately all the girls wanted to kiss them in turn, and the gentleman took them on to his knees, made them jump up and down and pinched them. The two peasants, who were even in greater consternation than their poultry, rolled their eyes as if they were possessed, without venturing to move, and their old wrinkled faces had not a smile nor a movement.

Then the gentleman, who was a commercial traveler, offered the ladies braces by way of a joke, and taking up one of his packages, he opened it. It was a trick, for the parcel contained garters. There were blue silk, pink silk, red silk, violet silk, mauve silk garters, and the buckles were made of two gilt metal Cupids, embracing each other. The girls uttered exclamations of delight, and looked at them with that gravity which is natural to a woman when she is hankering after a bargain. They consulted one another by their looks or in a whisper, and replied in the same manner, and Madame was longingly handling a pair of orange garters that were broader and more imposing than the rest; really fit for the mistress of such an establishment.

The gentleman waited, for he was nourishing an idea.

"Come, my kittens," he said, "you must try them on."

There was a torrent of exclamations, and they squeezed their petticoats between their legs, as if they thought he was going to ravish them, but he quietly waited his time, and said: "Well, if you will not, I shall pack them up again."

And he added cunningly: "I offer any pair they like, to those who will try them on."

But they would not, and sat up very straight, and looked dignified.

But the Two Pumps looked so distressed that he renewed the offer to them. Flora especially hesitated, and he pressed her:

"Come, my dear, a little courage! Just look at that lilac pair; it will suit your dress admirably."

That decided her, and pulling up her dress she showed a thick leg fit for a milk-maid, in a badly-fitting, coarse stocking. The commercial traveler stooped down and fastened the garter below the knee first of all and then above it; and he tickled the girl gently, which made her scream and jump. When he had done, he gave her the lilac pair, and asked: "Who next?"

"I! I!" they all shouted at once, and he began on Rosa the Jade, who uncovered a shapeless, round thing without any ankle, a regular "sausage of a leg," as Raphaelle used to say.

The commercial traveler complimented Fernande, and grew quite enthusiatic over her powerful columns.

The thin tibias of the handsome Jewess met with less flattery, and Louise Cocotte, by way of a joke, put her petticoats over the man's head, so that Madame was obliged to interfere to check such unseemly behavior.

Lastly, Madame herself put out her leg, a handsome, muscular, Norman leg, and in his surprise and pleasure the commercial traveler gallantly took off his hat to salute that master calf, like a true French cavalier.

The two peasants, who were speechless from surprise, looked askance, out of the corners of their eyes. They looked so exactly like fowls, that the man with the light whiskers, when he sat up, said "Co—co—ri—co," under their very noses, and that gave rise to another storm of amusement.

The old people got out at Motteville, with their basket, their ducks, and their umbrella, and they heard the woman say to her husband, as they went away:

"They are sluts, who are off to that cursed place, Paris."

The funny commercial traveler himself got out at Rouen, after behaving so coarsely that Madame was obliged sharply to put him into his right place. She added, as a moral: "This will teach us not to talk to the first comer."

At Oissel they changed trains, and at a little station further on Monsieur Joseph Rivet was waiting for them with a large cart and a number of chairs in it, which was drawn by a white horse.

The carpenter politely kissed all the ladies, and then helped them into his conveyance.

Three of them sat on three chairs at the back, Raphaelle, Madame, and her brother on the three chairs in front, and Rosa, who had no seat, settled herself as comfortably as she could on tall Fernande's knees, and then they set off.

But the horse's jerky trot shook the cart so terribly, that the chairs began to dance, throwing the travelers into the air, to the right and to the left, as if they had been dancing puppets. This made them make horrible grimaces and screams, which, however, were cut short by another jolt of the cart.

They clung to the sides of the vehicle, their bonnets fell on to their backs, their noses on their shoulders, and the white horse trotted on, stretching out his head and holding out his tail quite straight, a little hairless rat's tail, with which he whisked his buttocks from time to time.

Joseph Rivet, with one leg on the shafts and the other bent under him, held the reins with elbows high and kept uttering a kind of chuckling sound, which made the horse prick up its ears and go faster.

The green country extended on either side of the road, and here and there the colza in flower presented a waving expanse of yellow, from which there arose a strong, wholesome, sweet and penetrating smell, which the wind carried to some distance.

The cornflowers showed their little blue heads among the rye, and the women wanted to pick them, but Monsieur Rivet refused to stop.

Then sometimes a whole field appeared to be covered with blood, so thickly were the poppies growing, and the cart, which looked as if it were filled with flowers of more brilliant hue, drove on through the fields colored with wild flowers, to disappear behind the trees of a farm, then to reappear and go on again through the yellow or green standing crops studded with red or blue.

One o'clock struck as they drove up to the carpenter's door. They were tired out, and very hungry, as they had eaten nothing since they left home. Madame Rivet ran out, and made them alight, one after another, kissing them as soon as they were on the ground. She seemed as if she would never tire of kissing her sister-in-law, whom she apparently wanted to monopolize. They had lunch in the workshop, which had been cleared out for the next day's dinner.

A capital omelette, followed by boiled chitterlings, and washed down by good, sharp cider, made them all feel comfortable.

Rivet had taken a glass so that he might hob-nob with them, and his wife cooked, waited on them, brought in the dishes, took them out, and asked all of them in a whisper whether they had everything they wanted. A number of boards standing against the walls, and heaps of shavings that had been swept into the corners, gave out the smell of planed wood, of carpentering, that resinous odor which penetrates the lungs.

They wanted to see the little girl, but she had gone to church, and would not be back until evening, so they all went out for a stroll in the country.

It was a small village, through which the high road passed. Ten or a dozen houses on either side of the single street had for tenants the butcher, the grocer, the carpenter, the innkeeper, the shoemaker, and the baker, and others.

The church was at the end of the street. It was surrounded by a small churchyard, and four enormous lime-trees, which stood just outside the porch, shaded it completely. It was built of flint, in no particular style, and had a slated steeple. When you got past it, you were in the open country again, which was broken here and there by clumps of trees which hid some homestead.

Rivet had given his arm to his sister, out of politeness, although he was in his working clothes, and was walking with her majestically. His wife, who was overwhelmed by Raphaelle's gold-striped dress, was walking between her and Fernande, and rotund Rosa was trotting behind with Louise Cocotte and Flora, the see-saw, who was limping along, quite tired out.

The inhabitants came to their doors, the children left off playing, and a window curtain would be raised, so as to show a muslin cap, while an old woman with a crutch, who was almost blind, crossed herself as if it were a religious procession. They all looked for a long time after those handsome ladies from the town, who had come so far to be present at the confirmation of Joseph Rivet's little girl, and the carpenter rose very much in the public estimation.

As they passed the church, they heard some children singing; little shrill voices were singing a hymn, but Madame would not let them go in, for fear of disturbing the little cherubs.

After a walk, during which Joseph Rivet enumerated the principal landed proprietors, spoke about the yield of the land, and the productiveness of the cows and sheep, he took his flock of women home and installed them in his house, and as it was very small, he had put them into the rooms, two and two.

Just for once, Rivet would sleep in the workshop on the shavings; his wife was going to share her bed with her sister-in-law, and Fernande and Raphaelle were to sleep together in the next room. Louise and Flora were put into the kitchen, where they had a mattress on the floor, and Rosa had a little dark cupboard at the top of the stairs to herself, close to the loft, where the candidate for confirmation was to sleep.

When the girl came in, she was overwhelmed with kisses; all the women wished to caress her, with that need of tender expansion, that habit of professional wheedling, which had made them kiss the ducks in the railway carriage.

They took her on to their laps, stroked her soft, light hair, and pressed her in their arms with vehement and spontaneous outbursts of affection, and the child, who was very good-natured and docile, bore it all patiently.

As the day had been a fatiguing one for everybody, they all went to bed soon after dinner. The whole village was wrapped in that perfect stillness of the country, which is almost like a religious silence, and the girls, who were accustomed to the noisy evenings of their establishment, felt rather impressed by the perfect repose of the sleeping village. They shivered, not with cold, but with those little shivers of solitude which come over uneasy and troubled hearts.

As soon as they were in bed, two and two together, they clasped each other in their arms, as if to protect themselves against this feeling of the calm and profound slumber of the earth. But Rosa the Jade, who was alone in her little dark cupboard, felt a vague and painful emotion come over her.

She was tossing about in bed, unable to get to sleep, when she heard the faint sobs of a crying child close to her head, through the partition. She was frightened, and called out, and was answered by a weak voice, broken by sobs. It was the little girl who, being used to sleeping in her mother's room, was frightened in her small attic.

Rosa was delighted, got up softly so as not to awaken anyone, and went and fetched the child. She took her into her warm bed, kissed her and pressed her to her bosom, caressed her, lavished exaggerated manifestations of tenderness on her, and at last grew calmer herself and went to sleep. And till morning, the candidate for confirmation slept with her head on Rosa's naked bosom.

At five o'clock, the little church bell ringing the "Angelus" woke these women up, who as a rule slept the whole morning long.

The peasants were up already, and the women went busily from house to house, carefully bringing short, starched, muslin dresses in bandboxes, or very long wax tapers, with a bow of silk fringed with gold in the middle, and with dents in the wax for the fingers.

The sun was already high in the blue sky, which still had a rosy tint toward the horizon, like a faint trace of dawn, remaining. Families of fowls were walking about the henhouses, and here and there a black cock, with a glistening breast, raised his head, crowned by his red comb, flapped his wings, and uttered his shrill crow, which the other cocks repeated.

Vehicles of all sorts came from neighboring parishes, and discharged tall, Norman women, in dark dresses, with neck-handkerchiefs crossed over the bosom, and fastened with silver brooches, a hundred years old.

The men had put on blouses over their new frock coats, or over their old dress coats of green cloth, the tails of which hung down below their blouses. When the horses were in the stable, there was a double line of rustic conveyances along the road; carts, carbriolets, tilburies, char-à-bancs, traps of every shape and age, resting on their shafts, or pointing them in the air.

The carpenter's house was as busy as a beehive. The ladies, in dressing jackets and petticoats, with their long, thin, light hair, which looked as if it were faded and worn by dyeing, were busy dressing the child, who was standing motionless on a table, while Madame Tellier was directing the movements of her battalion. They washed her, did her hair, dressed her, and with the help of a number of pins, they arranged the folds of her dress, and took in the waist, which was too large.

Then, when she was ready, she was told to sit down and not to move, and the women hurried off to get ready themselves.

The church bell began to ring again, and its tinkle was lost in the air, like a feeble voice which is soon drowned in space. The candidates came out of the houses, and went toward the parochial building which contained the school and the mansion house. This stood quite at one end of the village, while the church was situated at the other.

The parents, in their very best clothes, followed their children with awkward looks, and with the clumsy movements of bodies that are always bent at work.

The little girls disappeared in a cloud of muslin, which looked like whipped cream, while the lads, who looked like embryo waiters in a café, and whose head shone with pomatum, walked with their legs apart, so as not to get any dust or dirt on to their black trousers.

It was something for the family to be proud of; a large number of relatives from distant parts surrounded the child, and, consequently, the carpenter's triumph was complete.

Madame Tellier's regiment, with its mistress at its head, followed Constance; her father gave his arm to his sister, her mother walked by the side of Raphaelle. Fernande with Rosa, and the Two Pumps together. Thus they walked majestically through the village, like a general's staff in full uniform, while the effect on the village was startling.

At the school, the girls arranged themselves under the Sister of Mercy, and the boys under the schoolmaster, and they started off, singing a hymn as they went. The boys led the way, in two files, between the two rows of vehicles, from which the horses had been taken out, and the girls followed in the same order. As all the people in the village had given the town ladies the precedence out of politeness, they came immediately behind the girls, and lengthened the double line of the procession still more, three on the right and three on the left, while their dresses were as striking as a bouquet of fireworks.

When they went into the church, the congregation grew quite excited. They pressed against each other, they turned round, they jostled one another in order to see. Some of the devout ones almost spoke aloud, so astonished were they at the sight of these ladies, whose dresses were trimmed more elaborately than the priest's chasuble.

The Mayor offered them his pew, the first one on the right, close to the choir, and Madame Tellier sat there with her sister-in-law; Fernande and Raphaelle, Rosa the Jade, and the Two Pumps occupied the second seat, in company with the carpenter.

The choir was full of kneeling children, the girls on one side, and the boys on the other, and the long wax tapers which they held, looked like lances, pointing in all directions. Three men were standing in front of the lecturn, singing as loud as they could.

They prolonged the syllables of the sonorous Latin indefinitely, holding on to the Amens with interminable *a—a's,* which the serpent of the organ kept up in the monotonous, long-drawn-out notes, emitted by the deep-throated pipes.

A child's shrill voice took up the reply, and from time to time a priest sitting in a stall and wearing a biretta, got up, muttered something, and sat down again. The three singers continued, with their eyes fixed on the big book of plain-song lying open before them on the outstretched wings of an eagle, mounted on a pivot.

Then silence ensued. The service went on, and toward the end of it, Rosa, with her head in both her hands, suddenly thought of her mother, and her village church on a similar occasion. She almost fancied that that day had returned, when she was so small, and almost hidden in her white dress, and she began to cry.

First of all she wept silently, the tears dropped slowly from her eyes, but her emotion increased with her recollections, and she began to sob. She took out her pocket-handkerchief, wiped her eyes, and held it to her mouth, so as not to scream, but it was useless.

A sort of rattle escaped her throat, and she was answered by two other profound, heart-breaking sobs; for her two neighbors, Louise and Flora, who were kneeling near her, overcome by similar recollections, were sobbing by her side. There was a flood of tears, and as weeping is contagious, Madame soon found that her eyes were wet, and on turning to her sister-in-law, she saw that all the occupants of the pew were crying.

Soon, throughout the church, here and there, a wife, a mother, a sister, seized by the strange sympathy of poignant emotion, and agitated by the grief of those handsome ladies on their knees, who were shaken by their sobs, was moistening her cambric pocket-handkerchief, and pressing her beating heart with her left hand.

Just as the sparks from an engine will set fire to dry grass, so the tears of Rosa and of her companions infected the whole congregation in a moment. Men, women, old men, and lads in new blouses were soon sobbing; something superhuman seemed to be hovering over their heads—a spirit, the powerful breath of an invisible and all-powerful being.

Suddenly a species of madness seemed to pervade the church, the noise of a crowd in a state of frenzy, a tempest of sobs and of stifled cries. It passed over the people like gusts of wind which bow the trees in a forest, and the priest, overcome by emotion, stammered out incoherent prayers, those inarticulate prayers of the soul, when it soars toward heaven.

The people behind him gradually grew calmer. The cantors, in all the dignity of their white surplices, went on in somewhat uncertain voices, and the organ itself seemed hoarse, as if the instrument had been weeping. The priest, however, raised his hand, as a sign for them to be still, and went to the chancel steps. All were silent, immediately.

After a few remarks on what had just taken place, which he attributed to a miracle, he continued, turning to the seats where the carpenter's guests were sitting:

"I especially thank you, my dear sisters, who have come from such a distance, and whose presence among us, whose evident faith and ardent piety have set such a salutary example to all. You have edified my parish; your emotion has warmed all hearts; without you, this day would not, perhaps, have had this really divine character. It is sufficient, at times, that there should be one chosen to keep in the flock, to make the whole flock blessed."

His voice failed him again, from emotion, and he said no more, but concluded the service.

They all left the church as quickly as possible; the children themselves were restless, tired with such a prolonged tension of the mind. Besides, the elders were hungry, and one after another left the churchyard, to see about dinner.

There was a crowd outside, a noisy crowd, a babel of loud voices, in which the shrill Norman accent was discernible. The villagers formed two ranks, and when the children appeared, each family seized their own.

The whole houseful of women caught hold of Constance, surrounded her and kissed her, and Rosa was especially demonstrative. At last she took hold of one hand, while Madame Tellier held the other, and Raphaelle and Fernande held up her long muslin petticoat, so that it might not drag in the dust. Louise and Flora brought up the rear with Madame Rivet, and the child, who was very silent and thoughtful, set off home, in the midst of this guard of honor.

The dinner was served in the workshop, on long boards supported by trestles, and through the open door they could see all the enjoyment that was going on. Everywhere people were feasting; through every window could be seen tables surrounded by people in their Sunday clothes. There was merriment in every house—men sitting in their shirt sleeves, drinking cider, glass after glass.

In the carpenter's house the gaiety took on somewhat of an air of reserve, the consequence of the emotion of the girls in the morning. Rivet was the only one who was in good cue, and he was drinking to excess. Madame Tellier was looking at the clock every moment, for, in order not to lose two days following, they ought to take the 3.55 train, which would bring them to Fécamp by dark.

The carpenter tried very hard to distract her attention, so as to keep his guests until the next day. But he did not succeed, for she never joked when there was business to be done, and as soon as they had had their coffee she ordered her girls to make haste and get ready. Then, turning to her brother, she said:

"You must have the horse put in immediately," and she herself went to complete her preparations.

When she came down again, her sister-in-law was waiting to speak to her about the child, and a long conversation took place, in which, however, nothing was settled. The carpenter's wife finessed, and pretended to be very much moved, and Madame Tellier, who was holding the girl on her knees, would not pledge herself to anything definite, but merely gave vague promises: she would not forget her, there was plenty of time, and then, they were sure to meet again.

But the conveyance did not come to the door, and the women did not come downstairs. Upstairs, they even heard loud laughter, falls, little screams, and much clapping of hands, and so, while the carpenter's wife went to the stable to see whether the cart was ready, Madame went upstairs.

Rivet, who was very drunk and half undressed, was vainly trying to kiss Rosa, who was choking with laughter. The Two Pumps were holding him by the arms and trying to calm him, as they were shocked at such a scene after that morning's ceremony; but Raphaelle and Fernande were urging him on, writhing and holding their sides with laughter, and they uttered shrill cries at every useless attempt that the drunken fellow made.

The man was furious, his face was red, his dress disordered, and he was trying to shake off the two women who were clinging to him, while he was pulling Rosa's bodice, with all his might, and ejaculating: "Won't you, you slut?"

But Madame, who was very indignant, went up to her brother, seized him by the shoulders, and threw him out of the room with such violence that he fell against a wall in the passage, and a minute afterward, they heard him pumping water on to his head in the yard. When he came back with the cart, he was already quite calmed down.

They seated themselves in the same way as they had done the day before, and the little white horse started off with his quick, dancing trot. Under the hot sun, their fun, which had been checked during dinner, broke out again. The girls now were amused at the jolts which the wagon gave, pushed their neighbors' chairs, and burst out laughing every moment, for they were in the vein for it, after Rivet's vain attempt.

There was a haze over the country, the roads were glaring, and dazzled their eyes. The wheels raised up two trails of dust, which followed the cart for a long time along the highroad, and presently Fernande, who was fond of music, asked Rosa to sing something. She boldly struck up the "Gros Curé de Meudon," but Madame made her stop immediately, as she thought it a song which was very unsuitable for such a day, and added:

"Sing us something of Béranger's."

After a moment's hesitation, Rosa began Béranger's song, "The Grandmother," in her worn-out voice, and all the girls, and even Madame herself, joined in the chorus:

> "How I regret
>   My dimpled arms,
> My well-made legs,
>   And my vanished charms."

"That is first-rate," Rivet declared, carried away by the rhythm. They shouted the refrain to every verse, while Rivet beat time on the shafts with his foot, and on the horse's back with the reins. The animal, himself, carried away by the rhythm, broke into a wild gallop, and threw all the women in a heap, one on the top of the other, in the bottom of the conveyance.

They got up, laughing as if they were crazy, and the song went on, shouted at the top of their voices, beneath the burning sky and among the ripening grain, to the rapid gallop of the little horse, who set off every time the refrain was sung, and galloped a hundred yards, to their great delight. Occasionally a stone breaker by the roadside sat up, and looked at the wild and shouting female load, through his wire spectacles.

When they got out at the station, the carpenter said:

"I am sorry you are going; we might have had some fun together."

But Madame replied very sensibly: "Everything has its right time, and we cannot always be enjoying ourselves."

And then he had a sudden inspiration: "Look here, I will come and see you at Fécamp next month." And he gave a knowing look, with his bright and roguish eyes.

"Come," Madame said, "you must be sensible; you may come if you like, but you are not to be up to any of your tricks."

He did not reply, and as they heard the whistle of the train he immediately began to kiss them all. When it came to Rosa's turn, he tried to get to her mouth, which she, however, smiling with her lips closed, turned away from him each time by a rapid movement of her head to one side. He held her in his arms, but he could not attain his object, as his large whip, which he was holding in his hand and waving behind the girl's back in desperation, interfered with his efforts.

"Passengers for Rouen, take your seats, please!" a guard cried, and they got in. There was a slight whistle followed by a loud one from the engine, which noisily puffed out its first jet of steam, while the wheels began to turn a little, with visible effort. Rivet left the station and went to the gate by the side of the line to get another look at Rosa, and as the carriage full of human merchandise passed him, he began to crack his whip and to jump, singing at the top of his voice:

"How I regret
    My dimpled arms,
My well-made legs,
    And my vanished charms!"

And then he watched a white pocket-handkerchief, which somebody was waving, as it disappeared in the distance.

III

They slept the peaceful sleep of quiet consciences, until they got to Rouen. When they returned to the house, refreshed and rested, Madame could not help saying:

"It was all very well, but I was already longing to get home."

They hurried over their supper, and then, when they had put on their usual light evening costumes, waited for their usual customers. The little colored lamp outside the door told the passers-by that the flock had returned to the fold, and in a moment the news spread, nobody knew how, or by whom.

Monsieur Philippe, the banker's son, even carried his audacity so far as to send a special messenger to Monsieur Tournevau, who was in the bosom of his family.

Every Sunday the fish-curer used to have several cousins to dinner, and they were having coffee, when a man came in with a letter in his hand. Monsieur Tournevau was much excited; he opened the envelope and grew pale; it only contained these words in pencil:

"The cargo of fish has been found; the ship has come into port; good business for you. Come immediately."

He felt in his pockets, gave the messenger two-pence, and suddenly blushing to his ears, he said: "I must go out." He handed his wife the laconic and mysterious note, rang the bell, and when the servant came in, he asked her to bring him his hat and overcoat immediately. As soon as he was in the street, he began to run, and the way seemed to him to be twice as long as usual, in consequence of his impatience.

Madame Tellier's establishment had put on quite a holiday look. On the ground floor, a number of sailors were making a deafening noise, and Louise and Flora drank with one and the other, so as to merit their name of the Two Pumps more than ever. They were being called for everywhere at once; already they were not quite sober enough for their business, and the night bid fair to be a very jolly one.

The upstairs room was full by nine o'clock. Monsieur Vassi, the Judge of the Tribunal of Commerce, Madame's usual Platonic wooer, was talking to her in a corner, in a low voice, and they were both smiling, as if they were about to come to an understanding.

Monsieur Poulin, the ex-mayor, was holding Rosa on his knees; and she, with her nose close to his, was running her hands through the old gentleman's white whiskers.

Tall Fernande, who was lying on the sofa, had both her feet on Monsieur Pinipesse the tax-collector's stomach, and her back on young Monsieur Philippe's waistcoat; her right arm was round his neck, and she held a cigarette in her left.

Raphaelle appeared to be discussing matters with Monsieur Dupuis, the insurance agent, and she finished by saying: "Yes, my dear, I will."

Just then, the door opened suddenly, and Monsieur Tournevau came in. He was greeted with enthusiastic cries of: "Long live Tournevau!" and Raphaelle, who was twirling round, went and threw herself into his arms. He seized her in a vigorous embrace, and without saying a word, lifting her up as if she had been a feather, he carried her through the room.

Rosa was chatting to the ex-mayor, kissing him every moment, and pulling both his whiskers at the same time in order to keep his head straight.

Fernande and Madame remained with the four men, and Monsieur Philippe exclaimed: "I will pay for some champagne; get three bottles, Madame Tellier." And Fernande gave him a hug, and whispered to him: "Play us a waltz, will you?" So he rose and sat down at the old piano in the corner, and managed to get a hoarse waltz out of the entrails of the instrument.

The tall girl put her arms round the tax-collector, Madame asked Monsieur Vassi to take her in his arms, and the two couples turned round, kissing as they danced. Monsieur Vassi, who had formerly danced in good society, waltzed with such elegance that Madame was quite captivated.

Frederic brought the champagne; the first cork popped, and Monsieur Philippe played the introduction to a quadrille, through which the four dancers walked in society fashion, decorously, with propriety of deportment, with bows, and curtsies, and then they began to drink.

Monsieur Philippe next struck up a lively polka, and Monsieur Tournevau started off with the handsome Jewess, whom he held up in the air, without letting her feet touch the ground. Monsieur Pinipesse and Monsieur Vassi had started off with renewed vigor and from time to time one or other couple would stop to toss off a long glass of sparkling wine. The dance was threatening to become never-ending, when Rosa opened the door.

"I want to dance," she exclaimed. And she caught hold of Monsieur Dupuis, who was sitting idle on the couch, and the dance began again.

But the bottles were empty. "I will pay for one," Monsieur Tournevau said.

"So will I," Monsieur Vassi declared.

"And I will do the same," Monsieur Dupuis remarked.

They all began to clap their hands, and it soon became a regular ball. From time to time, Louise and Flora ran upstairs quickly, had a few turns while their customers downstairs grew impatient, and then they returned regretfully to the café. At midnight they were still dancing.

Madame shut her eyes to what was going on, and she had long private talks in corners with Monsieur Vassi, as if to settle the last details of something that had already been agreed upon.

At last, at one o'clock, the two married men, Monsieur Tournevau and Monsieur Pinipesse, declared that they were going home, and wanted to pay. Nothing was charged for except the champagne, and that only cost six francs a bottle, instead of ten, which was the usual price, and when they expressed their surprise at such generosity, Madame, who was beaming, said to them:

"We don't have a holiday every day."

17

Vain Beauty

GUY DE MAUPASSANT

A VERY elegant victoria, with two beautiful black horses, was drawn up in front of the mansion. It was a day in the latter end of June, about half past five in the afternoon, and the sun shone warm and bright into the large courtyard.

The Countess de Mascaret came down just as her husband, who was coming home, appeared in the carriage entrance. He stopped for a few moments to look at his wife and grew rather pale.

She was very beautiful, graceful, and distinguished looking, with her long oval face, her complexion like gilt ivory, her large gray eyes, and her black hair; and she got into her carriage without looking at him, without even seeming to have noticed him, with such a particularly high-bred air, that the furious jealousy by which he had been devoured for so long again gnawed at his heart. He went up to her and said: "You are going for a drive?"

She merely replied disdainfully: "You see I am!"

"In the Bois de Boulogne?"

"Most probably."

"May I come with you?"

"The carriage belongs to you."

Without being surprised at the tone of voice in which she answered him, he got in and sat down by his wife's side, and said: "Bois de Boulogne." The footman jumped up by the coachman's side, and the horses as usual pawed the ground and shook their heads until they were in the street. Husband and wife sat side by side, without speaking. He was thinking how to begin a conversation, but she maintained such an obstinately hard look, that he did not venture to make the attempt. At last, however, he cunningly, accidentally as it were, touched the Countess's gloved hand with his own, but she drew her arm away, with a

movement which was so expressive of disgust, that he remained thoughtful, in spite of his usual authoritative and despotic character. "Gabrielle!"
said he at last.

"What do you want?"

"I think you are looking adorable."

She did not reply, but remained lying back in the carriage, looking like
an irritated queen. By that time they were driving up the Champs-
Elysées, toward the Arc de Triomphe. That immense monument, at the
end of the long avenue, raised its colossal arch against the red sky, and
the sun seemed to be sinking on to it, showering fiery dust on it from
the sky.

The streams of carriages, with the sun reflecting from the bright,
plated harness and the shining lamps, were like a double current flowing,
one toward the town and one toward the wood, and the Count de
Mascaret continued: "My dear Gabrielle!"

Then, unable to bear it any longer, she replied in an exasperated voice:
"Oh! do leave me in peace, pray; I am not even at liberty to have my
carriage to myself, now." He, however, pretended not to hear her, and
continued: "You have never looked so pretty as you do today."

Her patience was decidedly at an end, and she replied with irrepres-
sible anger: "You are wrong to notice it, for I swear to you that I will
never have anything to do with you in that way again." He was stupefied
and agitated, and his violent nature gaining the upper hand, he exclaimed: "What do you mean by that?" in such a manner as revealed
rather the brutal master than the amorous man. But she replied in a low
voice, so that the servants might not hear, amid the deafening noise of
the wheels:

"Ah! What do I mean by that? What do I mean by that? Now I recognize you again! Do you want me to tell everything?"

"Yes."

"Everything that has been on my heart, since I have been the victim
of your terrible selfishness?"

He had grown red with surprise and anger, and he growled between
his closed teeth: "Yes, tell me everything."

He was a tall, broad-shouldered man, with a big, red beard, a handsome man, a nobleman, a man of the world, who passed as a perfect husband and an excellent father, and now for the first time since they had
started she turned toward him, and looked him full in the face: "Ah!
You will hear some disagreeable things, but you must know that I am
prepared for everything, that I fear nothing, and you less than anyone,
today."

He also was looking into her eyes, and already was shaking with passion; then he said in a low voice: "You are mad."

"No, but I will no longer be the victim of the hateful penalty of maternity, which you have inflicted on me for eleven years! I wish to live like a woman of the world, as I have the right to do, as all women have the right to do."

He suddenly grew pale again, and stammered: "I do not understand you."

"Oh! yes; you understand me well enough. It is now three months since I had my last child, and as I am still very beautiful, and as, in spite of all your efforts you cannot spoil my figure, as you just now perceived, when you saw me on the outside flight of steps, you think it is time that I should become *enceinte* again."

"But you are talking nonsense!"

"No, I am not; I am thirty, and I have had seven children, and we have been married eleven years, and you hope that this will go on for ten years longer, after which you will leave off being jealous."

He seized her arm and squeezed it, saying: "I will not allow you to talk to me like that for long."

"And I shall talk to you till the end, until I have finished all I have to say to you, and if you try to prevent me, I shall raise my voice so that the two servants, who are on the box, may hear. I only allowed you to come with me for that object, for I have these witnesses, who will oblige you to listen to me, and to contain yourself; so now, pay attention to what I say. I have always felt an antipathy for you, and I have always let you see it, for I have never lied, Monsieur. You married me in spite of myself; you forced my parents, who were in embarrassed circumstances, to give me to you, because you were rich, and they obliged me to marry you, in spite of my tears.

"So you bought me, and as soon as I was in your power, as soon as I had become your companion, ready to attach myself to you, to forget your coercive and threatening proceedings, in order that I might only remember that I ought to be a devoted wife and to love you as much as it might be possible for me to love you, you became jealous—you—as no man has ever been before, with the base, ignoble jealousy of a spy, which was as degrading for you at it was for me. I had not been married eight months, when you suspected me of every perfidiousness, and you even told me so. What a disgrace! And as you could not prevent me from being beautiful, and from pleasing people, from being called in drawing-rooms, and also in the newspapers, one of the most beautiful women in Paris, you tried everything you could think of to keep admirers from me, and you hit upon the abominable idea of making me spend my life in a constant state of motherhood, until the time when I should disgust every man. Oh! do not deny it! I did not understand it for some time, but then I guessed it. You even boasted about it to your sister, who told me of it, for she is fond of me and was disgusted at your boorish coarseness.

"Ah! Remember our struggles, doors smashed in, and locks forced! For eleven years you have condemned me to the existence of a brood mare. Then as soon as I was pregnant, you grew disgusted with me, and I saw nothing of you for months, and I was sent into the country, to the family mansion, among fields and meadows, to bring forth my child. And when I reappeared, fresh, pretty, and indestructible, still seductive and constantly surrounded by admirers, hoping that at last I should live a little like a young rich woman who belongs to society, you were seized by jealousy again, and you recommenced to persecute me with that infamous and hateful desire from which you are suffering at this moment, by my side. And it is not the desire of possessing me—for I should never have refused myself to you—but it is the wish to make me unsightly.

"Besides this, that abominable and mysterious circumstance took place, which I was a long time in penetrating (but I grew acute by dint of watching your thoughts and actions). You attached yourself to your children with all the security which they gave you while I bore them in my womb. You felt affection for them, with all you aversion for me, and in spite of your ignoble fears, which were momentarily allayed by your pleasure in seeing me a mother.

"Oh! how often have I noticed that joy in you! I have seen it in your eyes and guessed it. You loved your children as victories, and not because they were of your own blood. They were victories over me, over my youth, over my beauty, over my charms, over the compliments which were paid me, and over those who whispered round me, without paying them to me. And you are proud of them, you make a parade of them, you take them out for drives in your coach in the Bois de Boulogne, and you give them donkey rides at Montmorency. You take them to theatrical matinées so that you may be seen in the midst of them, and that people may say: 'What a kind father!' and that repeated."

He had seized her wrist with savage brutality, and squeezed it so violently that she was quiet, though she nearly cried out with the pain. Then he said to her in a whisper:

"I love my children, do you hear? What you have just told me is disgraceful in a mother. But you belong to me; I am master—your master. I can exact from you what I like and when I like—and I have the law on my side."

He was trying to crush her fingers in the strong grip of his large, muscular hand, and she, livid with pain, tried in vain to free them from that vise which was crushing them; the agony made her pant, and the tears came into her eyes. "You see that I am the master, and the stronger," he said. And when he somewhat loosened his grip, she asked him: "Do you think that I am a religious woman?"

He was surprised and stammered: "Yes."

"Do you think that I could lie, if I swore to the truth of anything to you, before an altar on which Christ's body is?"

"No."

"Will you go with me to some church?"

"What for?"

"You shall see. Will you?"

"If you absolutely wish it, yes."

She raised her voice and said: "Philip!" And the coachman, bending down a little, without taking his eyes from his horses, seemed to turn his ear alone toward his mistress, who said: "Drive to St. Philip-du-Roule's." And the victoria, which had reached the entrance of the Bois de Boulogne, returned to Paris.

Husband and wife did not exchange a word during the drive. When the carriage stopped before the church, Madame de Mascaret jumped out, and entered it, followed by the Count, a few yards behind her. She went, without stopping, as far as the choir-screen, and falling on her knees at a chair, she buried her face in her hands. She prayed for a long time, and he, standing behind her, could see that she was crying. She wept noiselessly, like women do weep when they are in great and poignant grief. There was a kind of undulation in her body, which ended in a little sob, hidden and stifled by her fingers.

But Count de Mascaret thought that the situation was long drawn out, and he touched her on the shoulder. That contact recalled her to herself, as if she had been burned, and getting up, she looked straight into his eyes.

"This is what I have to say to you. I am afraid of nothing, whatever you may do to me. You may kill me if you like. One of your children is not yours, and one only; that I swear to you before God, who hears me here. That is the only revenge which was possible for me, in return for all your abominable male tyrannies, in return for the penal servitude of childbearing to which you have condemned me. Who was my lover? That you will never know! You may suspect everyone, but you will never find out. I gave myself up to him, without love and without pleasure, only for the sake of betraying you, and he made me a mother. Which

is his child? That also you will never know. I have seven; try and find
out! I intended to tell you this later, for one cannot completely avenge
oneself on a man by deceiving him, unless he knows it. You have driven
me to confess it today; now I have finished."

She hurried through the church, toward the open door, expecting to
hear behind her the quick steps of her husband whom she had defied,
and to be knocked to the ground by a blow of his fist, but she heard
nothing, and reached her carriage. She jumped into it at a bound, overwhelmed with anguish, and breathless with fear; she called out to the
coachman, "Home!" and the horses set off at a quick trot.

II

The Countess de Mascaret was waiting in her room for dinner time,
like a criminal sentenced to death awaits the hour of his execution. What
was he going to do? Had he come home? Despotic, passionate, ready for
any violence as he was, what was he mediating, what had he made up
his mind to do? There was no sound in the house, and every moment
she looked at the clock. Her maid had come and dressed her for the
evening, and had then left the room again. Eight o'clock struck; almost
at the same moment there were two knocks at the door, and the butler
came in and told her that dinner was ready.

"Has the Count come in?"

"Yes, Madame la Comtesse; he is in the dining-room."

For a moment she felt inclined to arm herself with a small revolver,
which she had bought some weeks before, foreseeing the tragedy which
was being rehearsed in her heart. But she remembered that all the children would be there, and she took nothing except a smelling-bottle. He
rose somewhat ceremoniously from his chair. They exchanged a slight
bow, and sat down. The three boys, with their tutor, Abbé Martin, were
on her right, and the three girls, with Miss Smith, their English gov-
erness, were on her left. The youngest child, who was only three months
old, remained upstairs with his nurse.

The Abbé said grace, as was usual when there was no company, for
the children did not come down to dinner when there were guests present; then they began dinner. The Countess, suffering from emotion
which she had not at all calculated upon, remained with her eyes cast
down, while the Count scrutinized, now the three boys, and now the
three girls with uncertain, unhappy looks, which traveled from one to
the other. Suddenly, pushing his wineglass from him, it broke, and the
wine was spilt on the tablecloth, and at the slight noise caused by this

little accident, the Countess started up from her chair, and for the first time they looked at each other. Then, almost every moment, in spite of themselves, in spite of the irritation of their nerves caused by every glance, they did not cease to exchange looks, rapid as pistol shots.

The Abbé, who felt that there was some cause for embarrassment which he could not divine, tried to get up a conversation, and started various subjects, but his useless efforts gave rise to no ideas and did not bring out a word. The Countess, with feminine tact and obeying the instincts of a woman of the world, tried to answer him two or three times, but in vain. She could not find words, in the perplexity of her mind, and her own voice almost frightened her in the silence of the large room, where nothing else was heard except the slight sound of plates and knives and forks.

Suddenly, her husband said to her, bending forward: "Here, amid your children, will you swear to me that what you told me just now is true?"

The hatred which was fermenting in her veins suddenly roused her, and replying to that question with the same firmness with which she had replied to his looks, she raised both her hands, the right pointing toward the boys and the left toward the girls, and said in a firm, resolute voice, and without any hesitation: "On the heads of my children, I swear that I have told you the truth."

He got up, and throwing his table napkin on to the table with an exasperated movement, turned round and flung his chair against the wall. Then he went out without another word, while she, uttering a deep sigh, as if after a first victory, went on in a calm voice: "You must not pay any attention to what your father has just said, my darlings; he was very much upset a short time ago, but he will be all right again, in a few days."

Then she talked with the Abbé and with Miss Smith, and had tender, pretty words for all her children; those sweet spoiling mother's ways which unlock little hearts.

When dinner was over, she went into the drawing room with all her little following. She made the elder ones chatter, and when their bedtime came she kissed them for a long time, and then went alone into her room.

She waited, for she had no doubt that he would come, and she made up her mind then, as her children were not with her, to defend her human flesh, as she defended her life as a woman of the world; and in the pocket of her dress she put the little loaded revolver which she had bought a few weeks before. The hours went by, the hours struck, and every sound was hushed in the house. Only the cabs continued to rumble through the streets, but their noise was only heard vaguely through the shuttered and curtained windows.

She waited, energetic and nervous, without any fear of him now, ready for anything, and almost triumphant, for she had found means of torturing him continually, during every moment of his life.

But the first gleams of dawn came in through the fringe at the bottom of her curtains, without his having come into her room, and then she awoke to the fact, much to her surprise that he was not coming. Having locked and bolted her door, for greater security, she went to bed at last, and remained there, with her eyes open, thinking, and barely understanding it all, without being able to guess what he was going to do.

When her maid brought her tea, she at the same time gave her a letter from her husband. He told her that he was going to undertake a longish journey, and in a postscript he added that his lawyer would provide her with such money as she might require for her expenses.

III

It was at the opera, between two of the acts in "Robert the Devil." In the stalls, the men were standing up, with their hats on, their waistcoats cut very low so as to show a large amount of white shirt front, in which the gold and precious stones of their studs glistened. They were looking at the boxes crowded with ladies in low dresses, covered with diamonds and pearls, women who seemed to expand like flowers in that illuminated hot-house, where the beauty of their faces and the whiteness of their shoulders seemed to bloom for inspection, in the midst of the music and of human voices.

Two friends, with their backs to the orchestra, were scanning those parterres of elegance, that exhibition of real or false charms, of jewels, of luxury, and of pretension which showed itself off all round the Grand Theater. One of them, Roger de Salnis, said to his companion, Bernard Grandin: "Just look how beautiful Countess de Mascaret still is."

Then the elder, in turn, looked through his opera glasses at a tall lady in a box opposite, who appeared to be still very young, and whose striking beauty seemed to appeal to men's eyes in every corner of the house. Her pale complexion, of an ivory tint, gave her the appearance of a statue, while a small, diamond coronet glistened on her black hair like a cluster of stars.

When he had looked at her for some time, Bernard Grandin replied with a jocular accent of sincere conviction: "You may well call her beautiful!"

"How old do you think she is?'"

"Wait a moment. I can tell you exactly, for I have known her since she was a child, and I saw her make her *début* into society when she was quite a girl. She is—she is—thirty—thirty-six."

"Impossible!"

"I am sure of it."

"She looks twenty-five."

"She has had seven children."

"It is incredible."

"And what is more, they are all seven alive, as she is a very good mother. I go to the house, which is a very quiet and pleasant one, occasionally, and she presents the phenomenon of the family in the midst of the world."

"How very strange! And have there never been any reports about her?"

"Never."

"But what about her husband? He is peculiar, is he not?"

"Yes and no. Very likely there has been a little drama between them, one of those little domestic dramas which one suspects, which one never finds out exactly, but which one guesses pretty nearly."

"What is it?"

"I do not know anything about it. Mascaret leads a very fast life now, after having been a model husband. As long as he remained a good spouse, he had a shocking temper and was crabbed and easily took offense, but since he has been leading his present, rackety life, he has become quite indifferent; but one would guess that he has some trouble, a worm gnawing somewhere, for he has aged very much."

Thereupon the two friends talked philosophically for some minutes about the secret, unknowable troubles, which differences of character or perhaps physical antipathies, which were not perceived at first, give rise to in families. Then Roger de Salnis, who was still looking at Madame de Mascaret through his opera-glasses, said:

"It is almost incredible that that woman has had seven children."

"Yes, in eleven years; after which, when she was thirty, she put a stop to her period of production in order to enter into the brilliant period of entertaining, which does not seem near coming to an end."

"Poor women!"

"Why do you pity them?"

"Why? Ah! my dear fellow, just consider! Eleven years of maternity, for such a woman! What a hell! All her youth, all her beauty, every hope of success, every poetical ideal of a bright life, sacrificed to that abominable law of reproduction which turns the normal woman into a mere machine for maternity."

"What would you have? It is only Nature!"

"Yes, but I say that Nature is our enemy, that we must always fight against Nature, for she is continually bringing us back to an animal state. You may be sure that God has not put anything on this earth that is clean, pretty, elegant, or accessory to our ideal, but the human brain has done it. It is we who have introduced a little grace, beauty, unknown charm, and mystery into creation by singing about it, interpreting it, by admiring it as poets, idealizing it as artists, and by explaining it as learned men who make mistakes, but who find ingenious reasons, some grace and beauty, some unknown charm and mystery in the various phenomena of nature.

"God only created coarse beings, full of the germs of disease, and who, after a few years of bestial enjoyment, grow old and infirm, with all the ugliness and all the want of power of human decrepitude. He only seems to have made them in order that they may reproduce their species in a repulsive manner, and then die like ephemeral insects. I said, *reproduce their species in a repulsive manner,* and I adhere to that expression. What is there as a matter of fact, more ignoble and more repugnant than that ridiculous act of the reproduction of living beings, against which all delicate minds always have revolted, and always will revolt? Since all the organs which have been invented by this economical and malicious Creator serve two purposes, why did he not choose those that were unsullied, in order to intrust them with that sacred mission, which is the noblest and the most exalted of all human functions? The mouth which nourishes the body by means of material food, also diffuses abroad speech and thought. Our flesh revives itself by means of itself, and at the same time, ideas are communicated by it. The sense of smell, which gives the vital air to the lungs, imparts all the perfumes of the world to the brain: the smell of flowers, of woods, of trees, of the sea. The ear, which enables us to communicate with our fellowmen, has also allowed us to invent music, to create dreams, happiness, the infinite, and even physical pleasure, by means of sounds!

"But one might say that the Creator wished to prohibit men from ever ennobling and idealizing his commerce with women. Nevertheless, man has found love, which is not a bad reply to that sly Deity, and he has ornamented it so much with literary poetry, that woman often forgets the contact she is obliged to submit to. Those among us who are power-less to deceive themselves have invented vice and refined debauchery, which is another way of laughing at God, and of paying homage, im-modest homage, to beauty.

"But the normal man makes children; just a beast that is coupled with another by law.

"Look at that woman! Is it not abominable to think that such a jewel, such a pearl, born to be beautiful, admired, fêted, and adored, has spent eleven years of her life in providing heirs for the Count de Mascaret?"

Bernard Grandin replied with a laugh: "There is a great deal of truth in all that, but very few people would understand you."

Salnis got more and more animated. "Do you know how I picture God myself?" he said. "As an enormous, creative organ unknown to us, who scatters millions of worlds into space, just as one single fish would deposit its spawn in the sea. He creates, because it is His function as God to do so, but He does not know what He is doing, and is stupidly prolific in His work, and is ignorant of the combinations of all kinds which are produced by His scattered germs. Human thought is a lucky little local, passing accident, which was totally unforeseen, and is condemned to disappear with this earth, and to recommence perhaps here or elsewhere, the same or different, with fresh combinations of eternally new begin-nings. We owe it to this slight accident which has happened to His in-tellect, that we are very uncomfortable in this world which was not made for us, which had not been prepared to receive us, to lodge and feed us, or to satisfy reflecting beings, and we owe it to Him also that we have to struggle without ceasing against what are still called the designs of Providence, when we are really refined and civilized beings."

Grandin, who was listening to him attentively, as he had long known the surprising outbursts of his fancy, asked him: "Then you believe that human thought is the spontaneous product of blind, divine parturition?"

"Naturally. A fortuitous function of the nerve-centers of our brain, like some unforeseen chemical action which is due to new mixtures, and which also resembles a product of electricity, caused by friction or the unexpected proximity of some substance, and which, lastly, resembles the phenomena caused by the infinite and fruitful fermentations of living matter.

"But, my dear fellow, the truth of this must be evident to anyone who looks about him. If human thought, ordained by an omniscient Creator, had been intended to be what it has become, altogether different from mechanical thoughts and resignation, so exacting, inquiring, agitated, tormented, would the world which was created to receive the beings which we now are have been this unpleasant little dwelling place for poor fools, this salad plot, this rocky, wooded, and spherical kitchen garden where your improvident Providence has destined us to live naked, in caves or under trees, nourished on the flesh of slaughtered animals, our brethren, or on raw vegetables nourished by the sun and the rain.

"But it is sufficient to reflect for a moment, in order to understand that this world was not made for such creatures as we are. Thought, which is developed by a miracle in the nerves of the cells in our brain, powerless, ignorant, and confused as it is, and as it will always remain, makes all of us who are intellectual beings eternal and wretched exiles on earth.

"Look at this earth, as God has given it to those who inhabit it. Is it not visibly and solely made, planted and covered with forests, for the sake of animals? What is there for us? Nothing. And for them? Everything. They have nothing to do but to eat, or go hunting and eat each other, according to their instincts, for God never foresaw gentleness and peaceable manners. He only foresaw the death of creatures which were bent on destroying and devouring each other. Are not the quail, the pigeon, and the partridge the natural prey of the hawk? the sheep, the stag, and the ox that of the great flesh-eating animals, rather than meat that has been fattened to be served up to us with truffles, which have been unearthed by pigs, for our special benefit?

"As to ourselves, the more civilized, intellectual, and refined we are, the more we ought to conquer and subdue that animal instinct, which represents the will of God in us. And so, in order to mitigate our lot as brutes, we have discovered and made everything, beginning with houses, then exquisite food, sauces, sweetmeats, pastry, drink, stuffs, clothes, ornaments, beds, mattresses, carriages, railways, and innumerable machines, besides arts and sciences, writing and poetry. Every ideal comes from us as well as the amenities of life, in order to make our existence as simple reproducers, for which divine Providence solely intended us, less monotonous and less hard.

"Look at this theater. Is there not here a human world created by us, unforeseen and unknown by Eternal destinies, comprehensible by our minds alone, a sensual and intellectual distraction, which has been invented solely by and for that discontented and restless little animal that we are.

"Look at that woman, Madame de Mascaret. God intended her to live in a cave naked, or wrapped up in the skins of wild animals, but is she not better as she is? But, speaking of her, does anyone know why and how her brute of a husband, having such a companion by his side, and especially after having been boorish enough to make her a mother seven times, has suddenly left her, to run after bad women?"

Grandin replied: "Oh! my dear fellow, this is probably the only reason. He found that always living with her was becoming too expensive in the end, and from reasons of domestic economy, he has arrived at the same principles which you lay down as a philosopher."

Just then the curtain rose for the third act, and they turned round, took off their hats, and sat down.

IV

The Count and Countess Mascaret were sitting side by side in the carriage which was taking them home from the opera, without speaking. But suddenly the husband said to his wife: "Gabrielle!"

"What do you want?"

"Don't you think that this has lasted long enough?"

"What?"

"The horrible punishment to which you have condemned me for the last six years."

"What do you want? I cannot help it."

"Then tell me which of them it is?"

"Never."

"Think that I can no longer see my children or feel them round me, without having my heart burdened with this doubt. Tell me which of them it is, and I swear that I will forgive you, and treat it like the others."

"I have not the right to."

"You do not see that I can no longer endure this life, this thought which is wearing me out, or this question which I am constantly asking myself, this question which tortures me each time I look at them. It is driving me mad.'"

"Then you have suffered a great deal?" she said.

"Terribly. Should I, without that, have accepted the horror of living by your side, and the still greater horror of feeling and knowing that there is one among them whom I cannot recognize, and who prevents me from loving the others?"

She repeated: "Then you have really suffered very much?" And he replied in a constrained and sorrowful voice:

"Yes, for do I not tell you every day that it is intolerable torture to me? Should I have remained in that house, near you and them, if I did not love them? Oh! You have behaved abominably toward me. All the affection of my heart I have bestowed upon my children, and that you know. I am for them a father of the olden time, as I was for you a husband of one of the families of old, for by instinct I have remained a natural man, a man of former days. Yes, I will confess it, you have made me terribly jealous, because you are a woman of another race, of another soul, with other requirements. Oh! I shall never forget the things that you told me, but from that day, I troubled myself no more about you. I did not kill you, because then I should have had no means on earth of ever discovering which of our—of your children is not mine. I have waited, but I have suffered more than you would believe, for I can no longer venture to love them, except, perhaps, the two eldest; I no longer venture to look at them, to call them to me, to kiss them; I cannot take them on to my knee without asking myself: 'Can it be this one? I have been correct in my behavior toward you for six years, and even kind and complaisant; tell me the truth, and I swear that I will do nothing unkind."

He thought, in spite of the darkness of the carriage, that he could perceive that she was moved, and feeling certain that she was going to speak at last, he said: "I beg you, I beseech you to tell me."

"I have been more guilty than you think perhaps," she replied; "but I could no longer endure that life of continual pregnancy, and I had only one means of driving you from my bed. I lied before God, and I lied, with my hand raised to my children's heads, for I have never wronged you."

He seized her arm in the darkness, and squeezing it as he had done on that terrible day of their drive in the Bois de Boulogne, he stammered: "Is that true?"

"It is true."

But he in terrible grief said with a groan: "I shall have fresh doubts that will never end! When did you lie, the last time or now? How am I to believe you at present? How can one believe a woman after that? I shall never again know what I am to think. I would rather you had said to me: 'It is Jacques, or, it is Jeanne.' "

The carriage drove them into the courtyard of their mansion, and when it had drawn up in front of the steps, the Count got down first as usual, and offered his wife his arm, to help her up. And then, as soon as they had reached the first floor he said: "May I speak to you for a few moments longer?"

And she replied: "I am quite willing."

They went into a small drawing-room, while a footman in some surprise, lit the wax candles. As soon as he had left the room and they were alone, he continued: "How am I to know the truth? I have begged you a thousand times to speak, but you have remained dumb, impenetrable, inflexible, inexorable, and now today, you tell me that you have been lying. For six years you have actually allowed me to believe such a thing! No, you are lying now, I do not know why, but out of pity for me, perhaps?"

She replied in a sincere and convincing manner: "If I had not done so, I should have had four more children in the last six years!"

And he exclaimed: "Can a mother speak like that?"

"Oh!" she replied, "I do not at all feel that I am the mother of children who have never been born, it is enough for me to be the mother of those that I have, and to love them with all my heart. I am—we are—women who belong to the civilized world, Monsieur, and we are no longer, and we refuse to be, mere females who restock the earth."

She got up, but he seized her hands. "Only one word, Gabrielle. Tell me the truth!"

"I have just told you. I have never dishonored you."

He looked her full in the face, and how beautiful she was, with her gray eyes, like the cold sky. In her dark hairdress, on that opaque night of black hair, there shone the diamond coronet, like a cluster of stars. Then he suddenly felt, felt by a kind of intuition, that this grand creature was not merely a being destined to perpetuate his race, but the strange and mysterious product of all the complicated desires which have been accumulating in us for centuries but which have been turned aside from their primitive and divine object, and which have wandered after a mystic, imperfectly seen, and intangible beauty. There are some women like that, women who blossom only for our dreams, adorned with every poetical attribute of civilization, with that ideal luxury, coquetry, and æsthetic charm which should surround the living statue who brightens our life.

Her husband remained standing before her, stupefied at the tardy and obscure discovery, confusedly hitting on the cause of his former jealousy, and understanding it all very imperfectly. At last he said: "I believe you, for I feel at this moment that you are not lying, and formerly, I really thought that you were."

She put out her hand to him: "We are friends then?"

He took her hand and kissed it, and replied: "We are friends. Thank you, Gabrielle."

Then he went out, still looking at her, and surprised that she was still so beautiful, and feeling a strange emotion arising in him, which was, perhaps, more formidable than antique and simple love.

18

The Sacrifice

GEORGES DUHAMEL

WE had had all the windows opened. From their beds, the wounded could see, through the dancing waves of heat, the heights of Berru and Nogent l'Abbesse, the towers of the Cathedral, still crouching like a dying lion in the middle of the plain of Reims, and the chalky lines of the trenches intersecting the landscape.

A kind of torpor seemed to hang over the battle-field. Sometimes, a perpendicular column of smoke rose up, in the motionless distance, and the detonation reached us a little while afterwards, as if astray, and ashamed of outraging the radiant silence.

It was one of the fine days of the summer of 1915, one of those days when the supreme indifference of Nature makes one feel the burden of war more cruelly, when the beauty of the sky seems to proclaim its remoteness from the anguish of the human heart.

We had finished our morning round when an ambulance drew up at the entrance.

"Doctor on duty!"

I went down the steps. The chauffeur explained:

"There are three slightly wounded men. I am going to take on further, and then there are some severely wounded . . ."

He opened the back of his car. On one side three soldiers were seated, dozing. On the other, there were stretchers, and I saw the feet of the men lying upon them. Then, from the depths of the vehicle came a low, grave, uncertain voice which said:

"I am one of the severely wounded, Monsieur."

He was a lad rather than a man. He had a little soft down on his chin, a well-cut aquiline nose, dark eyes to which extreme weakness gave an appearance of exaggerated size, and the gray pallor of those who have lost much blood.

"Oh! how tired I am!" he said.

He held on to the stretcher with both hands as he was carried up the steps. He raised his head a little, gave a glance full of astonishment, distress, and lassitude at the green trees, the smiling hills, the glowing horizon, and then he found himself inside the house.

Here begins the story of Gaston Léglise. It is a modest story and a very sad story; but indeed, are there any stories now in the world that are not sad?

I will tell it day by day, as we lived it, as it is graven in my memory, and as it is graven in your memory and in your flesh, my friend Léglise.

Léglise only had a whiff of chloroform, and he fell at once into a sleep closely akin to death.

"Let us make haste," said the head doctor. "We shall have the poor boy dying on the table."

Then he shook his head, adding:

"Both knees! Both knees! What a future!"

The burden of experience is a sorrowful one. It is always sorrowful to have sufficient memory to discern the future.

Small splinters from a grenade make very little wounds in a man's legs; but great disorders may enter by way of those little wounds, and the knee is such a complicated, delicate marvel!

Corporal Léglise is in bed now. He breathes with difficulty, and catches his breath now and again like a person who has been sobbing. He looks about him languidly, and hardly seems to have made up his mind to live. He contemplates the bottle of serum, the tubes, the needles, all the apparatus set in motion to revive his fluttering heart, and he seems bowed down by grief. He wants something to drink, but he must not have anything yet; he wants to sleep, but we have to deny sleep to those who need it most; he wants to die perhaps, and we will not let him.

He sees again the listening post where he spent the night, in advance of all his comrades. He sees again the narrow doorway bordered by sandbags through which he came out at dawn to breathe the cold air and look at the sky from the bottom of the communication-trench. All was quiet, and the early summer morning was sweet even in the depths of the trench. But some one was watching and listening for the faint sound of his footsteps. An invisible hand hurled a bomb. He rushed back to the door; but his pack was on his back, and he was caught in the aperture like a rat in a trap. The air was rent by the detonation, and his legs were rent, like the pure air, like the summer morning, like the lovely silence.

The days pass, and once more, the coursing blood begins to make the vessels of the neck throb, to tinge the lips, and give depth and brilliance to the eye.

Death, which had overrun the whole body like an invader, retired, yielding ground by degrees; but it has halted now, and makes a stand at the legs; these it will not relinquish; it demands something by way of spoil; it will not be balked of its prey entirely.

We fight for the portion Death has chosen. The wounded Corporal looks on at our labors and our efforts, like a poor man who has placed his cause in the hands of a knight, and who can only be a spectator of the combat, can only pray and wait.

We shall have to give the monster a share; one of the legs must go. Now another struggle begins with the man himself. Several times a day I go and sit by his bed. All our attempts at conversation break down one by one. We always end in the same silence and anxiety. Today Léglise said to me:

"Oh! I know quite well what you're thinking about!"

As I made no answer, he intreated:

"Perhaps we could wait a little longer? Perhaps tomorrow I may be better . . ."

Then suddenly, in great confusion:

"Forgive me. I do trust you all. I know what you do is necessary. But perhaps it will not be too late in two or three days. . . ."

Two or three days! We will see tomorrow.

The nights are terribly hot; I suffer for his sake.

I come to see him in the evening for the last time, and encourage him to sleep. But his eyes are wide open in the night and I feel that they are anxiously fixed on mine.

Fever makes his voice tremble.

"How can I sleep with all the things I am thinking about?"

Then he adds faintly:

"Must you? Must you?"

The darkness gives me courage, and I nod my head: "Yes!"

As I finish his dressings, I speak from the depths of my heart:

"Léglise, we will put you to sleep tomorrow. We will make an examination without letting you suffer, and we will do what is necessary."

"I know quite well that you will take it off."

"We shall do what we must do."

I divine that the corners of his mouth are drawn down a little, and that his lips are quivering. He thinks aloud:

"If only the other leg was all right!"

I have been thinking of that too, but I pretend not to have heard. Sufficient unto the day is the evil thereof.

I spend part of the afternoon sewing pieces of waterproof stuff together. He asks me:

"What are you doing?"

"I am making you a mask, to give you ether."

"Thank you; I can't bear the smell of chloroform."

I answer "Yes, that's why." The real reason is that we are not sure he could bear the brutal chloroform, in his present state.

Léglise's leg was taken off at the thigh this morning. He was still unconscious when we carried him into the dark room to examine his other leg under the X-rays.

He was already beginning to moan and to open his eyes, and the radiographer was not hurrying. I did all I could to hasten the business, and to get him back into his bed. Thus he regained consciousness in bright sunshine.

What would he, who once again was so close to the dark kingdom, have thought if he had awakened in a gloom peopled by shadows, full of whisperings, sparks and flashes of light?

As soon as he could speak, he said to me:

"You have cut off my leg?"

I made a sign. His eyes filled, and as his head was low, the great tears trickled on to the pillow.

Today he is calmer. The first dressings were very painful. He looked at the raw, bloody, oozing stump, trembling, and said:

"It looks pretty horrible!"

We took so many precautions that now he is refreshed for a few hours.

"They say you are to have the Military Medal," the head doctor told him.

Léglise confided to me later, with some hesitation:

"I don't suppose they would really give me the medal!"

"And why not?"

"I was punished; one of my men had some buttons off his overcoat."

Oh, my friend, scrupulous lad, could I love my countrymen if they could remember those wretched buttons for an instant?

"My men!" he said gravely. I look at his narrow chest, his thin face, his boyish forehead with the serious furrow on it of one who accepts all responsibilities, and I do not know how to show him my respect and affection.

Léglise's fears were baseless. General G—— arrived just now. I met him on the terrace. His face pleased me. It was refined and intelligent.

"I have come to see Corporal Léglise," he said.

I took him into the ward, full of wounded men, and he at once went towards Léglise unhesitatingly, as if he knew him perfectly.

"How are you?" he asked, taking the young man's hand.

"*Mon Général,* they've cut off my leg . . ."

"Yes, yes, I know, my poor fellow. And I have brought you the Military Medal."

He pinned it on to Léglise's shirt, and kissed my friend on both cheeks, simply and affectionately.

Then he talked to him again for a few minutes.

I was greatly pleased. Really, this General is one of the right sort.

The medal has been wrapped in a bit of muslin, so that the flies may not soil it, and hung on the wall over the bed. It seems to be watching over the wounded man, to be looking on at what is happening. Unfortunately, what it sees is sad enough. The right leg, the only leg, is giving us trouble now. The knee is diseased, it is in a very bad state, and all we have done to save it seems to have been in vain. Then a sore has appeared on the back, and then another sore. Every morning, we pass from one misery to another, telling the beads of suffering in due order.

So a man does not die of pain, or Léglise would certainly be dead. I see him still, opening his eyes desperately and checking the scream that rises to his lips. Oh! I thought indeed that he was going to die. But his agony demands full endurance; it does not even stupefy those it assails.

I call on every one for help.

"Genest, Barrassin, Prévôt, come, all of you."

Yes, let ten of us do our best if necessary, to support Léglise, to hold him, to soothe him. A minute of his endurance is equal to ten years of such effort as ours.

Alas! were there a hundred of us he would still have to bear the heaviest burden alone.

All humanity at this hour is bearing a very cruel burden. Every minute aggravates its sufferings, and will no one, no one come to its aid?

We made an examination of the wounded man, together with our chief, who muttered almost inaudibly between his teeth:

"He must be prepared for another sacrifice."

Yes, the sacrifice is not yet entirely consummated.

But Léglise understood. He no longer weeps. He has the weary and somewhat bewildered look of the man who is rowing against the storm.

I steal a look at him, and he says at once in a clear, calm, resolute voice:
"I would much rather die."

I go into the garden. It is a brilliant morning, but I can see nothing, I want to see nothing. I repeat as I walk to and fro:

"He would much rather die."

And I ask despairingly whether he is not right perhaps.

All the poplars rustle softly. With one voice, the voice of Summer itself, they say: "No! No! He is not right!"

A little beetle crosses the path before me. I step on it unintentionally, but it flies away in desperate haste. It too has answered in its own way: "No, really, your friend is not right."

"Tell him he is wrong," sing the swarm of insects that buzz about the lime-tree.

And even a loud roar from the guns that travels across the landscape seems to say gruffly: "He is wrong! He is wrong!"

During the evening the chief came back to see Léglise, who said to him with the same mournful gravity:

"No, I won't, Monsieur, I would rather die."

We go down into the garden, and the chief says a strange thing to me:

"Try to convince him. I begin at last to feel ashamed of demanding such a sacrifice from him."

And I too . . . am I not ashamed?

I consult the warm, star-decked night; I am quite sure now that he is wrong, but I don't know how to tell him so. What can I offer him in exchange for the thing I am about to ask him? Where shall I find the words that induce a man to live? Oh you, all things around me, tell me, repeat to me that it is sweet to live, even with a body so grievously mutilated.

This morning I extracted a little projectile from one of his wounds. He secretly concluded that this would perhaps make the great operation unnecessary, and it hurt me to see his joy. I could not leave him this satisfaction.

The struggle began again; this time it was desperate. For we have no time to lose. Every hour of delay exhausts our man further. A few days more, and there will be no choice open to him: only death, after a long ordeal. . . ."

He repeats:

"I am not afraid, but I would rather die."

Then I talk to him as if I were the advocate of Life. Who gave me this right? Who gave me eloquence? The things I said were just the right

things, and they came so readily that now and then I was afraid of holding out so sure a promise of a life I am not certain I can preserve, of guar-
anteeing a future that is not in man's hands.

Gradually, I feel his resistance weakening. There is something in Léglise which involuntarily sides with me and pleads with me. There are
moments when he does not know what to say, and formulates trivial
objections, just because there are others so much weightier.

"I live with my mother," he says. "I am twenty years old. What work
is there for a cripple? Ought I to live to suffer poverty and misery?"

"Léglise, all France owes you too much, she would blush not to pay
her debt."

And I promise again, in the name of our country, sure that she will
never fall short of what I undertake for her. The whole French nation is
behind me at this moment, silently ratifying my promise.

We are at the edge of the terrace; evening has come. I hold his burning
wrist in which the feeble pulse beats with exhausted fury. The night is
so beautiful, so beautiful! Rockets rise above the hills, and fall slowly
bathing the horizon in silvery rays. The lightning of the guns flashes
furtively, like a winking eye. In spite of all this, in spite of war, the night
is like waters dark and divine. Léglise breathes it in to his wasted breast
in long draughts, and says:

"Oh, I don't know, I don't know! . . . Wait another day, please,
please. . . ."

We waited three whole days, and then Léglise gave in.

"Well, do what you must. Do what you like."

On the morning of the operation, he asked to be carried down to the
ward by the steps into the park. I went with him, and I saw him looking
at all things round him, as if taking them to witness.

If only, only it is not too late!

Again he was laid on the table. Again we cut through flesh and bones.
The second leg was amputated at the thigh.

I took him in my arms to lay him on his bed, and he was so light, so
light. . . .

This time when he woke he asked no question. But I saw his hands
groping to feel where his body ended.

A few days have passed since the operation. We have done all it was
humanly possible to do, and Léglise comes back to life with a kind of
bewilderment.

"I thought I should have died," he said to me this morning, while I
was encouraging him to eat.

He added:

"When I went down to the operation-ward, I looked well at everything, and I thought it was for the last time."

"Look, dear boy. Everything is just the same, just as beautiful as ever."

"Oh!" he says, going back to his memories, "I had made up my mind to die."

To make up one's mind to die is to take a certain resolution, in the hope of becoming quieter, calmer, and less unhappy. The man who makes up his mind to die severs a good many ties, and indeed actually dies to some extent.

With secret anxiety, I say gently, as if I were asking a question:

"It is always good to eat, to drink, to breathe, to see the light. . . .

He does not answer. He is dreaming. I spoke too soon. I go away, still anxious.

We have some bad moments yet, but the fever gradually abates. I have an impression that Léglise bears his pain more resolutely, like one who has given all he had to give, and fears nothing further.

When I have finished the dressing, I turned him over on his side, to ease his sore back. He smiled for the first time this morning, saying:

"I have already gained something by getting rid of my legs. I can lie on my side now."

But he cannot balance himself well; he is afraid of falling.

Think of him, and you will be afraid with him and for him.

Sometimes he goes to sleep in broad daylight and dozes for a few minutes. He has shrunk to the size of a child. I lay a piece of gauze over his face, as one does to a child, to keep the flies off. I bring him a little bottle of Eau de Cologne and a fan, they help him to bear the final assaults of the fever.

He begins to smoke again. We smoke together on the terrace, where I have had his bed brought. I show him the garden and say: "In a few days, I will carry you down into the garden."

He is anxious about his neighbors, asks their names, and inquires about their wounds. For each one he has a compassionate word that comes from the depths of his being. He says to me:

"I hear that little Camus is dead. Poor Camus!"

His eyes fill with tears. I was almost glad to see them. He had not cried for so long. He adds:

"Excuse me, I used to see Camus sometimes. It's so sad."

He becomes extraordinarily sensitive. He is touched by all he sees around him, by the sufferings of others, by their individual misfortunes. He vibrates like an elect soul, exalted by a great crisis.

When he speaks of his own case, it is always to make light of his misfortune:

"Dumont got it in the belly. Ah, it's lucky for me that none of my organs are touched; I can't complain."

I watch him with admiration, but I am waiting for something more, something more. . . .

His chief crony is Legrand.

Legrand is a stonemason with a face like a young girl. He has lost a big piece of his skull. He has also lost the use of language, and we teach him words, as to a baby. He is beginning to get up now, and he hovers round Léglise's bed to perform little services for him. He tries to master his rebellious tongue, but failing in the attempt, he smiles, and expresses himself with a limpid glance, full of intelligence.

Léglise pities him too:

"It must be wretched not to be able to speak."

Today we laughed, yes, indeed, we laughed heartily. Léglise, the orderlies and I.

We were talking of his future pension while the dressings were being prepared, and someone said to him:

"You will live like a little man of means."

Léglise looked at his body and answered:

"Oh, yes, a little man, a very little man."

The dressing went off very well. To make our task easier, Léglise suggested that he should hold on to the head of the bed with both hands and throw himself back on his shoulders, holding his stumps up in the air. It was a terrible, an unimaginable sight; but he began to laugh, and the spectacle became comic. We all laughed. But the dressing was easy and was quickly finished.

The stumps are healing healthily. In the afternoon, he sits up in bed. He begins to read and to smoke, chatting to his companions.

I explain to him how he will be able to walk with artificial legs. He jokes again:

"I was rather short before; but now I can be just the height I choose."

I bring him some cigarettes that had been sent me for him, some sweets and dainties. He makes a sign that he wants to whisper to me, and says very softly:

"I have far too many things. But Legrand is very badly off; his home is in the invaded district, and he has nothing, they can't send him anything."

I understand. I come back presently with a packet in which there are tobacco, some good cigarettes, and also a little note. . . .

"Here is something for Legrand. You must give it to him. I'm off."

In the afternoon I find Léglise troubled and perplexed.

"I can't give all this to Legrand myself, he would be offended."

So then we have to devise a discreet method of presentation.

It takes some minutes. He invents romantic possibilities. He becomes flushed, animated, interested.

"Think," I say, "find a way. Give it to him yourself, from some one or other."

But Léglise is too much afraid of wounding Legrand's susceptibilities. He ruminates on the matter till evening.

The little parcel is at the head of Legrand's bed. Léglise calls my attention to it with his chin, and whispers:

"I found someone to give it to him. He doesn't know who sent it. He has made all sorts of guesses; it is very amusing!"

Oh, Léglise, can it be that there is still something amusing, and that it is to be kind? Isn't this alone enough to make it worth while to live?

So now we have a great secret between us. All the morning, as I come and go in the ward, he looks at me meaningly, and smiles to himself. Legrand gravely offers me a cigarette; Léglise finds it hard not to burst out laughing. But he keeps his counsel.

The orderlies have put him on a neighboring bed while they make his. He stays there very quietly, his bandaged stumps in view, and sings a little song, like a child's cradle-song. Then, all of a sudden, he begins to cry, sobbing aloud.

I put my arm round him and ask anxiously:

"Why? What is the matter?"

Then he answers in a broken voice:

"I am crying with joy and thankfulness."

Oh! I did not expect so much. But I am very happy, much comforted. I kiss him, he kisses me, and I think I cried a little too.

I have wrapped him in a flannel dressing-gown, and I carry him in my arms. I go down the steps to the park very carefully, like a mother carrying her new-born babe for the first time, and I call out: "An arm-chair! An arm-chair."

He clings to my neck as I walk, and says in some confusion:

"I shall tire you."

No indeed! I am too well pleased. I would not let any one take my place. The arm-chair has been set under the trees, near a grove. I deposit

Léglise among the cushions. They bring him a *képi*. He breathes the scent of green things, of the newly mown lawns, of the warm gravel. He looks at the façade of the mansion, and says:

"I had not even seen the place where I very nearly died."

All the wounded who are walking about come and visit him; they almost seem to be paying him homage. He talks to them with a cordial authority. Is he not the chief among them, in virtue of his sufferings and his sacrifice?

Someone in the ward was talking this morning of love and marriage, and a home.

I glanced at Léglise now and then; he seemed to be dreaming and he murmured:

"Oh, for me, now . . ."

Then I told him something I knew: I know young girls who have sworn to marry only a mutilated man. Well, we must believe in the vows of these young girls. France is a country richer in warmth of heart than in any other virtue. It is a blessed duty to give happiness to those who have sacrificed so much. And a thousand hearts, the generous hearts of women, applaud me at this moment.

Léglise listens, shaking his head. He does not venture to say "No."

Léglise has not only the Military Medal, but also the War Cross. The notice has just come. He reads it with blushes.

"I shall never dare to show this," he says; "it is a good deal exaggerated."

He hands me the paper, which states, in substance, that Corporal Léglise behaved with great gallantry under a hail of bombs, and that his left leg has been amputated.

"I didn't behave with great gallantry," he says; "I was at my post, that's all. As to the bombs, I only got one."

I reject this point of view summarily.

"Wasn't it a gallant act to go to that advanced post, so near the enemy, all alone, at the head of all the Frenchmen? Weren't they all behind you, to the very end of the country, right away to the Pyrenees? Did they not all rely on your coolness, your keen sight, your vigilance? You were only hit by one bomb, but I think you might have had several, and still be with us. And besides, the notice, far from being exaggerated, is really insufficient; it says you have lost a leg, whereas you have lost two! It seems to me that this fully compensates for anything excessive with regard to the bombs."

"That's true!" agrees Léglise, laughing. "But I don't want to be made out a hero."

"My good lad, people won't ask what you think before they appreciate and honor you. It will be quite enough to look at your body."

Then we had to part, for the war goes on, and every day there are fresh wounded.

Léglise left us nearly cured. He left with some comrades, and he was not the least lively of the group.

"I was the most severely wounded man in the train," he wrote to me, not without a certain pride.

Since then, Léglise has written to me often. His letters breathe a contented calm. I receive them among the vicissitudes of the campaign; on the highways, in wards where other wounded men are moaning, in fields scoured by the gallop of the cannonade.

And always something beside me murmurs, mutely:

"You see, you see, he was wrong when he said he would rather die."

I am convinced of it, and this is why I have told your story. You will forgive me, won't you, Léglise, my friend?

19

The Escape

JOSEPH KESSEL

IT WAS raining. The police-van slowly picked its way up and down the grades of the slippery road that followed the curves of the hills. Gerbier was alone in the interior of the car with a gendarme. Another gendarme was driving. The one who was guarding Gerbier had peasant cheeks and a rather strong body odor.

As the car turned into a side road, the gendarme observed,

"We're making a little detour, but I suppose you're not in any hurry."

"No, I'm really not," said Gerbier with a brief smile.

The police-van stopped before an isolated farm. Through the grilled opening Gerbier could see only a bit of sky and field. He heard the driver leave his seat.

"It's not going to take long," said the gendarme. "My partner is going to get a few provisions. Have to do the best you can in these wretched times."

"That's perfectly natural," said Gerbier.

The gendarme took in his prisoner and shook his head. This man was well dressed and he had a straightforward way of speaking, a pleasant face. What wretched times. . . . He wasn't the first one he was embarrassed to see wearing handcuffs.

"You won't be too badly off in that camp!" said the gendarme. "I'm not talking about the food, of course. Before the war the dogs wouldn't have touched it. But aside from that it's the best concentration camp in France, I've been told. It's the German camp."

"I don't quite follow you," said Gerbier.

"During the phony war I guess we were expecting to take a lot of prisoners," the gendarme explained. "A big center was set up for them in this part of the country. Naturally not a single one came. But today it comes in handy."

"A real stroke of luck, you might say," Gerbier suggested.

"You said it, Monsieur, you said it!" the gendarme exclaimed.

The driver climbed back in his seat. The police-van started off again. The rain continued to pour down on the Limousin countryside.

II

Gerbier, his hands free, but standing, was waiting for the camp commander to address him. The camp commander was reading Gerbier's dossier. From time to time he would dig the thumb of his left hand into the hollow of his cheek and slowly withdraw it. The fat, soft and unhealthy flesh would keep the white imprint for a few seconds and swell again with difficulty like an old rubber ball that has lost its elasticity. This movement marked the tempo of the commander's reflections.

"The same old story," he thought to himself. "We no longer know whom we get, nor how to treat them."

He sighed as he remembered the pre-war, when he was a prison warden. All you had to worry about then was getting your percentage of profit on the food. The rest presented no difficulties. The prisoners of their own accord fell into known categories and for each category there was a corresponding rule of conduct. Now, on the contrary, you could get as big a cut as you wanted on the camp rations (no one concerned himself about it), but it was a headache to sort the people. Those who came without trial, without sentence, remained locked up indefinitely. Others, with a terrible record, would get out very quickly and regain influence in the department, the regional prefecture, in fact even in Vichy.

The commander did not look at Gerbier. He had given up trying to form an opinion from faces and clothes. He was trying to read between the lines of the police notes which the gendarmes had handed him at the same time that they had delivered the prisoner.

"An independent character, a quick mind; a distant and ironic attitude," the commander read. And he translated, "Break him." Then, "Distinguished bridge and highway engineer," and with his thumb in his cheek the commander would say to himself, "Spare him."

"Suspected of De Gaullist activities." "Break him, break him." But immediately after, "Freed for lack of evidence." "Influence, influence," the commander would say to himself, "spare him."

The commander's thumb sank deeper into the adipose flesh. It seemed to Gerbier that the cheek would never come back to its normal level.

However, the edema disappeared little by little. Then the commander declared with a certain solemnity,

"I'm going to put you in a building that was intended for German officers."

"I appreciate the honor," said Gerbier.

For the first time the commander looked up, with the vague and heavy gaze of a man who eats too much, at the face of his new prisoner.

The latter was smiling, or rather half smiling—his lips were thin and contracted.

"Spare him, yes," the camp commander thought to himself, "but keep an eye on him."

III

The storekeeper gave Gerbier some wooden shoes and a fatigue suit of red homespun.

"This was intended," he began, "for the . . ."

"German prisoners—I know," said Gerbier.

He took off his clothes and slipped on the fatigue suit. Then on the doorstep of the shop he let his eyes roam across the camp. It was a level, grassy plateau around which undulations of uninhabited terrain rose and fell. A drizzle still fell from the low sky. Evening was coming on. The barbed-wire networks and the patrol road that separated them were already harshly lighted by projectors. But the buildings of different sizes scattered over the plateau remained dark. Gerbier headed for one of the smallest of these.

IV

The cabin sheltered five red fatigue suits.

The colonel, the pharmacist and the traveling salesman, sitting with their legs crossed near the door, were playing dominoes with pieces of cardboard on the back of a mess-tin. The other two prisoners were in the back of the cabin, talking in low voices.

Armel was stretched out on his straw bed, wrapped in the single blanket issued to internees. Legrain had spread his own over it, but this did not prevent Armel from shivering. He had lost a good deal more blood in the course of the afternoon. His blond hair was matted with the sweat of fever. His fleshless face wore an expression of rather qualified, but unalterable gentleness.

"I assure you, Roger, I assure you that if only you had faith you wouldn't be unhappy because you would no longer be in a state of revolt," Armel murmured.

"But I want to be, I want to," said Legrain.

He clenched his thin fists and a kind of wheeze issued from his collapsed chest. He resumed angrily.

"You came here, you were twenty, and I was seventeen. We were healthy, we hadn't done anybody any harm, all we asked was to be let alone. Look at us today. And everything that's going on all around! I just can't understand that this exists and that there can be a God."

Armel had shut his eyes. His features seemed to have been worn away by an inner torment and by the growing darkness.

"It's only with God that everything becomes comprehensible," he answered.

Armel and Legrain were among the first internees of the camp. And Legrain had no other friend in the world. He would have done anything to bring rest to that bloodless and angelic face. It inspired him with a tenderness, a pity that were the only bonds that linked him to mankind. But there was in him an even stronger, an inflexible feeling—which prevented him from falling in with Armel's murmured plea.

"I can't believe in God," he said. "It's too convenient for those sons of bitches, to pay up in the next world. I want to see justice on this earth. I want . . ."

The stir in the doorway caused Legrain to break off. A new red fatigue suit had just come in.

"My name is Philippe Gerbier," said the new arrival.

Colonel Jarret du Plessis, Aubert the pharmacist and Octave Bonnafous, the traveling salesman, introduced themselves each in turn.

"I don't know, Monsieur, what brings you here," said the colonel.

"Neither do I," said Gerbier, half smiling.

"But I want to know right away why I was interned," the coloned continued. "I made the statement, in a café, that Admiral Darlan was a scoundrel. Yes."

The colonel made a rather emphatic pause, and continued emphatically,

"Today I add that Marshal Petain is another scoundrel who lets soldiers be bullied by sailors. Yes!"

"At least, colonel, you're suffering for an idea!" the traveling salesman exclaimed. "But I was simply going about my business, crossing a square where there was a De Gaullist demonstration . . ."

"And I," broke in Aubert, the pharmacist, "with me it's even worse." He turned abruptly to Gerbier.

"Do you know what a Malher shell is?" he asked.

"No," said Gerbier.

"That general ignorance is what killed me," Aubert went on. "The Malher shell, Monsieur, is a container in the shape of a pointed cylinder for producing chemical reactions under pressure. I am an expert chemist, Monsieur. I couldn't help having a Malher shell, after all. I was reported for illegal possession of a shell. I have never been able to obtain a hearing from the authorities."

"There is no longer any authority, there are only scoundrels. Yes!" said the colonel. "They've cut off my pension. . . ."

Gerbier realized that he would hear these stories a hundred times. With extreme politeness, he asked which was the place he was to occupy in the cabin. The colonel, who did duty as barracks-officer, pointed to a free straw bed in back. In bringing his valise over to it Gerbier approached his other companions. He held out his hand to Legrain, who gave his name and said,

"Communist."

"Aleady?" asked Gerbier.

Legrain turned a deep red.

"I was too young to have my party card, that's true," he hurriedly explained, "but it's all the same thing. I was arrested with my father and other militants. They were sent to some other place. It seems that life was too easy for them here. I asked to go with them, but the bastards wouldn't let me."

"How long ago was that?" Gerbier then asked.

"Right after the armistice."

"That makes almost a year," said Gerbier.

"I'm the oldest in the camp," said Roger Legrain.

"The longest," Gerbier corrected, smiling.

"Next to me it's Armel," Legrain went on, ". . . the young school-teacher who's lying down."

"Is he asleep?" Gerbier asked.

"No, he's very sick," Legrain murmured. "A rotten dysentery."

"What about the infirmary?" asked Gerbier.

"No room," said Legrain.

At their feet a soft, listless voice spoke,

"Any place is good enough to die in."

"Why are you here?" Gerbier asked, leaning over Armel.

"I gave notice that I would never be able to teach children hatred of the Jews and the English," said the schoolteacher, without having the strength to open his eyes.

Gerbier got up again. He showed no emotion. Only his lips had turned a slightly darker color.

Gerbier put his valise at the head of the straw bed assigned to him. The cabin was completely devoid of furniture and accessories, except for the inevitable soil-tub in the middle.

"There was everything that was needed for the German officers, who never came," said the colonel. "But the warden and the guards helped themselves, and the rest went to the black market."

"Do you play dominoes?" the pharmacist asked Gerbier.

"No, sorry," the latter answered.

"We can teach you," the traveling salesman suggested.

"Thanks, but I really haven't any aptitude for it," said Gerbier.

"Then you will excuse us?" exclaimed the colonel. "There is just time for a game before it gets dark."

Night fell. Roll was called. The doors were shut. There was no light in the cabin. Legrain's breathing was wheezy and oppressed. In his corner the little schoolteacher moaned softly. Gerbier reflected. "The camp commander isn't so dumb. He stuffs me away between three imbeciles and two lost children."

V

The following day when Roger Legrain stepped out of the cabin it was raining. In spite of this and in spite of the chill in the April morning air on a plateau exposed to all the winds Gerbier, naked in his clogs and wearing a towel tied around his middle, was doing setting-up exercises. His body was flat-colored, of a dry and hard consistence. His muscles were not visible, but their even, compact play gave the feeling of a block not easily dented. Legrain considered these movements with melancholy. Merely breathing deeply made his lungs whistle like a hollow bladder.

"Already out walking!" Gerbier shouted between exercises.

"I'm going to the camp power-plant," said Legrain. "I work there."

Gerbier completed a body bend and went over to Legrain.

"A good job?" he asked.

A bright flush came into Legrain's hollow cheeks. This tendency to blush occasionally was the only trace of his extreme youth. For the rest, privations, confinement and above all the constant wear and tear of a weighty, obsessing inner revolt had matured his face and his behavior frightfully.

"I don't even get a crust of bread for my work," said Legrain. "But it's a job I like and I don't want to lose the knack. That's all there is to it."

Gerbier's nose was very slender at the bridge. Because of this his eyes seemed very close together. When Gerbier looked at someone attentively, as he was looking at Legrain at this moment, his eternal half-smile became set in a severe fold and it was as though his eyes dissolved in a single black fire. As Gerbier remained silent, Legrain pivoted on his clogs. Gerbier said softly.

"Good-by, comrade."

Legrain whirled round and faced him as suddenly as though he had been burned.

"You are . . . you are . . . a communist," he stammered.

"No, I'm not a communist," said Gerbier.

He allowed a second to pass and added with a smile,

"But that doesn't prevent me from having comrades."

Gerbier tightened his towel round his waist and resumed his exercises. Legrain's red fatigue clothes were slowly blotted out on the rain-swept plateau.

VI

In the afternoon, the sky having cleared a little, Gerbier made the round of the camp. It took him several hours. The plateau was immense and was occupied entirely by the prisoners' city. One could see that it had grown haphazardly and piecemeal, as Vichy's orders progressively drained the ever-growing population of captives to this elevated stretch of bare ground. In the center rose the original nucleus that had been built for the German prisoners. Its buildings were decent and substantial. The penitentiary administration offices were set up in the best of these. All around, shacks built of wooden boards, corrugated iron, tarpaper, spread as far as the eye could see. It looked like the slums that hedge great cities. More and more, and still more room had been needed.

Room for foreigners. For traffickers. For Freemasons. For Kabyles. For those who were opposed to the Legion. For Jews. For refractory peasants. For vagrants. For former convicts. For political suspects. For those whose intents were suspect. For those who embarrassed the government. For those whose influence over the people was feared. For those who had been accused without proof. For those who had served their sentence but whom the authorities did not want to set free. For those whom the judges refused to sentence, to try, and who were being punished for their innocence. . . .

Here were hundreds of men taken from their families, from their work, from their town, from their truth, and corralled in camps on the mere decision of an official or a ministry for an indefinite period of time, like wreckage thrown up on a muddy beach beyond the reach of the tides.

To keep these men whose legions augmented day by day, other men had been needed, who also grew more and more numerous. They had been recruited by chance, in haste, among the lowest elements of the un-employed, the incompetent, the alcoholics, the degenerates. Their only uniform, worn with their wretched clothes, was a beret and an armband. They were very badly paid. These outcasts suddenly found themselves with power. They displayed more ferocity than professional brutes. They made money out of everything: out of the famine rations which they managed to cut by half, the tobacco, the soap, the basic toilet articles which they resold at monstrous prices. Corruption was the only thing that had any effect on these guards.

During his walk Gerbier thus was able to win over two purveyors. He also exchanged a few words with some prisoners lying in front of their shacks. He had the feeling of approaching a kind of mold, of reddish mushrooms in human forms. These undernourished people, flapping and shivering in their fatigue suits, at loose ends, unshaved, unwashed, had vacant, roaming eyes, limp mouths that had lost their elasticity. Gerbier reflected that this laxness was quite natural. Real rebels, when they were caught, were usually kept in deep, voiceless prisons, or handed over to the Gestapo. There were no doubt, even in this camp, a few resolute men who did not give way to the rotting process. But it would take time to discover them in the midst of this immense flock broken by adversity. Gerbier remembered Roger Legrain, his exhausted but in-flexible features, his courageous emaciated shoulders. Yet it was he who had spent the greatest number of months in this humus-bin. Gerbier made for the power station which was located among the central group of buildings, known in the camp as the German quarter.

As he neared it Gerbier ran into a file of skeleton-like Kabyles pushing wheelbarrows loaded with garbage-cans. They moved very slowly. Their wrists seemed to be on the point of breaking. Their heads were too heavy for their bony necks. One of them stumbled and his wheelbarrow tipped, upsetting the garbage-can. Peelings, sordid remnants scattered on the ground. Before Gerbier knew what was happening he saw a kind of mute, frantic pack throw itself on the offals. Then he saw another pack come running. The guards began to strike about with their fists, their feet, bludgeons, black-jacks. At first they struck out of duty, to bring back order. But before long they began to enjoy it, to be carried away as by a kind of intoxication. They would aim at the man's fragile and vulnerable areas—in the middle, in the small of the back, the liver, the sexual parts. They relinquished their victim only when he had become inanimate.

Gerbier suddenly heard Legrain's muffled, wheezing voice.

"It drives me mad," the young man said. "It drives me mad to think that we went and got those wretches in Africa and took them from their homes. They were told about France, beautiful France, and about the Marshal, the grand old man. They were promised ten francs a day. At the yards they only got half of that. They asked why. Then they were sent here. They croak like flies. And when they haven't had time to croak, this is what happens. . . . ."

Out of breath, Legrain began to cough a long, hollow cough.

"All debts will be paid," said Gerbier.

At this moment his half-smile assumed an extreme sharpness. Most people experienced a feeling of uneasiness when this expression passed over Gerbier's features. But it inspired Legrain with great confidence.

VII

Toward mid-May fine weather set in for good. The late spring burst all at once in full splendor. Thousands of tiny flowers sprang up in the field of grass. The prisoners began to take sunbaths. The sharp hip-bones, the prominent ribs, the limp skins, the arms reduced to the form of the bones, rested among the fresh flowers. Gerbier who passed the plateau all day long would ceaselessly run into this hospital humanity stunned by spring. No one could have told whether his feeling for them was one of disgust or pity or indifference. He himself did not know. But when, at the noon-hour, he discovered Legrain exposing himself like the rest he hurried over to him.

"Don't do that, cover yourself right away," he said. As Legrain did not obey, Gerbier threw a fatigue jacket over the young man's pitiful torso.

"I hear you breathing and coughing in your sleep," said Gerbier. "You've surely got something wrong with your lungs. The sun is very dangerous for you."

Gerbier had never shown a greater interest in Legrain than in the pharmacist or his other cabin-mates.

"You don't look like a doctor," said Legrain with astonishment.

"And I'm not," said Gerbier, "but I once directed the construction of a power line in Savoy. There were some establishments there for tuberculars. I used to talk with the doctors."

Legrain's eyes had lighted up.

"You're an electrician!" he exclaimed.

"Like yourself," said Gerbier jovially.

"Oh no! I can see that you're a *Monsieur* in the game," said Legrain. "But we might talk shop just the same."

Legrain was afraid he was being indescreet and added,

"From time to time."

"Right away, if you like," said Gerbier.

He lay down beside Legrain and while chewing grass-blades and flower-stems listened to the young man talk about the generating set, the voltage, the light and power mains.

"Would you like me to take you there?" Legrain asked at last.

Gerbier was shown a station that was rather primitive, but run with knowledge and taste. Gerbier likewise saw Legrain's assistant. He was an old Austrian engineer of Jewish origin. He must have fled from Vienna to Prague and from Prague to France. He was very timid. He tried to make himself as small as possible. After so many adversities and fears he seemed satisfied with his fate.

VIII

The estimate Gerbier had formed of this man enabled him to understand the full significance of a scene that took place some time after this.

A Gestapo car stopped before the entrance to the concentration camp. The gates were swung open. A few guards with berets and armbands jumped up on the running-boards and the gray auto drove slowly in the direction of the German quarter. When it got close to the electrical plant an S.S. officer stepped out and signaled to the guards to follow him inside the building. It was sun-bathing time. Many of the prisoners gathered round the car. The uniformed driver was smoking a cigar and was blowing the smoke through the nostrils of his broad, turned-up nose. He did not look at the hedge of bony, half-naked and silent men. In the midst of this silence there was a cry—then another, and again another. Now they were strung together into a single lamentation, which was close to an animal wail. The half-naked men gave a start of panic. But the fascination of horror was stronger in them than fear. They waited. The guards appeared, dragging a white-haired man from the building. The old engineer was struggling, still shrieking. Suddenly he caught sight of the hedge of men, half-naked, silent and pale. He began to utter broken words. Only a few phrases were distinguishable: "French soil . . . French government . . . free zone. . . ."

Gerbier, who at first had kept at a distance from the spectators, did not notice that he was drawing close to them, that he was edging his way through the last row, edging his way through the next, that he was reaching the first, that he was still advancing. A trembling, warm hand alighted on his wrist. Gerbier's body all at once relaxed and his eyes lost their expression of morbid fixity.

"Thank you," he said to Legrain.

Gerbier took a deep breath. After which, with a kind of avid detestation, he watched the guards throw the old engineer into the car and the driver continue to blow rings of smoke through his wide nostrils.

"Thank you," Gerbier said again.

He smiled to Legrain with that half-smile in which the eyes had no share.

The same evening, in the cabin, Legrain wanted to speak of the incident but Gerbier avoided all conversation. So it was the following days. Besides, Armel the schoolteacher was going from bad to worse and Legrain no longer had any thoughts but for his friend.

IX

The young schoolteacher died one night. His delirium had been no worse than usual. Some Kabyles carried his body away early in the morning. Legrain went to his work. The day flowed by and he behaved no differently than the day before. When he came back to the cabin the colonel, the pharmacist and the traveling salesman stopped their domino game and wanted to console him.

"I'm not sad," said Legrain. "Armel is better off as he is."

Gerbier said nothing to Legrain. He handed him the package of cigarettes he had bought from a guard in the afternoon. Legrain smoked three in succession, in spite of the cough that was exhausting him. Night came. Roll was called. The doors were closed. The colonel, the traveling salesman, the pharmacist went to sleep one after the other. Legrain appeared calm. Gerbier in turn fell asleep.

He was awakened by a familiar sound. Legrain was coughing. Yet Gerbier could not go back to sleep. He listened more attentively. And he understood. Legrain was forcing himself to cough to choke his sobs. Gerbier fumbled for Legrain's hand and said to him in a very low voice,

"I'm here, old man."

For several seconds there was no other sound from the place where Legrain's straw bed was. "He's fighting for his dignity," thought Gerbier. He had guessed rightly. But Legrain was only a child, just the same. Gerbier suddenly felt a body without weight and a pair of small bony shoulders contract against him. He heard a thin, barely audible wail.

"Now I'm all alone in the world. . . . Armel has left me. He's perhaps with his God. He believed in Him so much. But I can't see him there. . . . I don't believe in Him, Monsieur Gerbier . . . I beg your pardon . . . but I can't go on any more. I haven't got anybody in the world. Talk to me once in a while, Monsieur Gerbier, will you?"

Then Gerbier said in Legrain's ear,

"We never let a comrade down in the resistance movement."

Legrain had become silent.

"The resistance. Do you hear?" Gerbier said again in a voice that was secret and heavy as the night. "Go to sleep with that word in your mind. In these days it's the finest word in the whole French language. You've had no chance to learn it. It came into existence while you were being destroyed here. Go to sleep. I'll promise to teach it to you."

X

Gerbier was accompanying Legrain to his work. They walked slowly, and Gerbier was speaking.

"You understand, they came in their tanks, with their blank eyes. They thought that the treads of tanks are made to trace the new law of peoples. As they had manufactured many tanks, they had the assurance of having been born to write this law. They have a horror of liberty, of thought. Their true war aim is the death of thinking man, of free man. They want to exterminate everyone who has not blank eyes. They have found in France people who had the same tastes and those have gone into their service. And those have put you to rot here, you who had not even begun to live. They have caused the death of young Armel. You saw them hand over the poor fellow who believed in the right of asylum. At the same time they published the claim that the conqueror was magnanimous. A foul Old Man tried to suborn the country. 'Be good, be cowardly,' he preached. 'Forget that you have been proud, joyous and free. Obey and smile to the victor. He will let you rub along unmolested.' The people who surrounded the Old Man calculated that France was credulous and that she was gentle, that she was the country of moderation and of the happy medium. 'France is so civilized, so weakened,' they thought, 'that she no longer knows the meaning of underground warfare and of secret death. She will accept, she will go to sleep. And in her sleep we shall put her eyes out.' And they thought, furthermore, 'We are not afraid of extremists. They have no connections. They have no weapons. And we have all the German divisions to defend us.' While they were rejoicing in this way, the resistance was being born."

Roger Legrain walked on without daring to turn his head toward Gerbier. It was as though he were afraid of intervening in the accomplishment of a miracle. This man, so distant, so sparing of words, suddenly burst into words of fire. . . . And the universe which suddenly became an altogether different universe . . . Legrain saw the grass and the shacks of the camp and the red fatigue suits and the starved figures of the Kabyles dragging themselves about at their forced labor. But all this was changing its form and its function. The life of the camp no longer stopped at the barbed-wire fences. It extended over the whole country. It was becoming illuminated, assuming a meaning. The Kabyles and Armel and himself were entering into a great human order. Legrain felt himself becoming liberated little by little from the sense of revolt that had filled him until now—from that blind, desperate, chained, confused, obtuse feeling, that was without issue and that struggled within him, tearing and ravaging all his substance. He felt himself approaching a great mystery. And he was too ignorant and too puny to contemplate the companion who was lifting the veils of this mystery for him.

"How it came about I don't know," said Gerbier. "I think no one will ever know. But one day a peasant cut a rural telephone wire. An old woman put her cane athwart the legs of a German soldier. Tracts circulated. A butcher threw into the cold storage room a captain who was requisitioning meat with too much arrogance. A bourgeois gives a wrong address to the victors who are trying to find their way. Railroad workers, curates, poachers, bankers help escaped prisoners to get through by the hundreds. Farmers shelter British soldiers. A prostitute refuses to go to bed with the conquerors. French officers, soldiers, masons, painters conceal weapons. You know nothing of all this. You were here. But for one who felt this awakening, this first stirring, it was the most inspiring thing in the world. It was the sap of liberty that was beginning to rise in the French earth. Then the Germans and their servants and the Old Man decided to eradicate the rank growth. But the more of it they tore up the better it grew. They have filled the prisons, they have multiplied the camps. They have become frantic. They have locked up the colonel, the traveling salesman, the pharmacist. And they have acquired even more enemies. They have resorted to the firing squad. Now blood was what the plant most needed to grow and to spread. Blood has flowed. Blood is flowing. Rivers of it will flow. And the plant will become a forest."

Gerbier and Legrain made the round of the power station. Gerbier continued.

"He who joins the resistance aims at the Germans. But at the same time he strikes Vichy and its Old Man, and the Old Man's henchmen and the director of our camp, and the guards you see at work every day. The resistance is composed of all Frenchmen who don't want the eyes of France to turn dead and blank."

Legrain and Gerbier were sitting in the grass. The wind from the slopes was turning cool. Evening was approaching; Gerbier spoke to the young man about the newspapers of the resistance movement.

"And the people who make them dare to write what they think?" asked Legrain, his cheeks blazing.

"They can dare anything, they have no other law, no other master than their idea," said Gerbier. "This idea is stronger in them than life. The men who publish these sheets are unknown, but some day monuments will be erected to their work. The fellow who finds the paper risks death. Those who compose the pages risk death. Those who write the articles risk death. And those who transport the newspapers risk death. Nothing can stop them. Nothing can choke the cry that rises from the mimeograph machines hidden in dingy chambers, from the presses buried away in the depths of cellars. Don't think these sheets have anything like the appearance of those that are sold in broad daylight. They are miserable little squares of paper. Clumsy sheets that somehow get printed or typed. The characters are blurred, the headings thin. The ink often smudges. The people turn them out as they can. One week in one town and one week in another. They take what lies to hand. But the paper appears. The articles follow subterranean channels. Someone collects them, someone secretly arranges them. Furtive groups set them up. The police, the agents, the spies, the informers agitate, search, nose about. The newspaper starts out on the roads of France. It isn't big, it doesn't look impressive. It swells worn, cracking, disjointed suitcases. But every line is like a ray of gold. A ray of free thought."

"My father was a typographer . . . so I can realize . . ." said Legrain. "There can't be many of these papers."

"There are flocks of them," said Gerbier. "Each important movement of the resistance has its own, and turns out tens of thousands of copies. And then there are those of the isolated groups. And those of the provinces. And the doctors have theirs, and the musicians, and the students, and the teachers, and the university professors, and the painters, and the writers, and the engineers."

"What about the communists?" asked Legrain in a low voice.

"Why naturally, they have *L'Humanité*. As before."

"*L'Huma* . . ." said Legrain, "*L'Huma* . . ."

His hollow eyes were full of ecstasy. He wanted to say more, but a series of coughing fits prevented him.

XI

It was noon. The prisoners had swallowed the mess-tin of dirty water which served as a meal and lay motionless in the sun. Legrain was with Gerbier, in the shadow of the cabin.

"They know how to die in the resistance movement," Gerbier was saying. "The daughter of an industrialist was to be executed by the Gestapo because she refused to reveal anything about the organization to which she belonged. Her father was granted permission to see her. He begged her to talk. She insulted him and *ordered* the German officer who witnessed the interview to take her father away. . . . A militant of the Christian Syndicates became friendly with the Germans, either out of weakness or interest. His wife put him out of the house. And his very young son volunteered with an action group. He did sabotage, killed some sentinels. When he was caught he wrote to his mother, 'Everything has been washed away. I die as a good Frenchman and a good Christian.' I saw the letter. . . .

"A famous professor was arrested, thrown into a Gestapo cell in Fresnes. They tortured him to make him reveal names. He resisted. . . . He resisted. . . . But at last he reached his limit of endurance. He became afraid of himself. He tore up his shirt and hanged himself. . . . After a violent demonstration, in the course of which German blood flowed in Paris, a dozen men were condemned to die. They were to be shot the following day at dawn. They knew it. And one of them, who was a worker, began to tell funny stories. During the whole night he made his comrades laugh. It was the German chaplain of the prison who told the worker's family about it."

Legrain averted his eyes and asked hesitantly,

"Tell me . . . Monsieur Gerbier . . . weren't there any communists among those demonstrators?"

"They all were," answered Gerbier. "And it was a communist, Gabriel

Peri, who before he died spoke the finest words, perhaps, that have come out of the resistance movement: 'I am glad,' he wrote. 'We are building tomorrows that will sing.' "

Gerbier placed his hand on Legrain's narrow wrist and said to him gently,

"I should like you to understand me once and for all. There are no longer suspicions, hatreds or barriers of any sort between communists and others. Today we are French. We are all in the same fight. And it is the communists against whom the enemy is most rabid. We know it. And we know that they are as brave as the bravest and better organized. They help us and we help them. They like us and we like them. Everything has become very simple."

"Talk, Monsieur Gerbier, talk some more," Legrain murmured.

XII

It was especially at night that Gerbier had time to talk.

Their little cabin, closed tight, gave back the heat accumulated during the day. The straw beds burned the men's backs. And the darkness was suffocating. The companions in captivity turned and turned again in their sleep. But nothing mattered to Legrain, not even the accelerated whistling of his lungs which sometimes, without his noticing it, forced him to press his chest between his two hands. And Gerbier told about how radio stations hidden in towns or in hamlets made it possible to speak every day with friends in the free world. He told about the work of the secret operatives, their tricks, their patience, their risks and the marvelous music which the ciphered messages make. He showed the immense network of listening posts and observers that enveloped the enemy, counted its regiments, broke through its defenses, found access to its documents. And Gerbier also said that in every season, at every hour, liaison agents were traveling back and forth, riding, walking, crawling their way all over France. And he depicted this underground France, this France of buried arms depots, of command posts going from refuge to refuge, of unknown leaders, of men and women who ceaselessly changed their name, their appearance, their address and their face.

"These people," Gerbier would say, "could have kept quiet. Nothing forced them into action. Wisdom, good sense told them to eat and sleep in the shadow of the German bayonets and to watch their business flourish, their women smile, their children grow. Material goods and the goods of narrow tenderness were thereby assured them. They even had the benediction of the Old Man of Vichy to appease and lull their conscience. Really, nothing forced them to fight, nothing but their free soil.

"Do you know," he said, "what the life of the outlaw, of the man of the underground is like? He no longer has any identity, or else he has so many that he has forgotten his own. He has no ration card. He can no longer even half allay his hunger. He sleeps in a loft, or in the house of a prostitute, or on the floor-tiles of a shop or in a deserted barn, or on a station bench. He can no longer see his family, who are being watched by the police. If his wife—which often happens—is also in the resistance movement, his children grow at random. The threat of being caught doubles his shadow. Every day comrades vanish, are tortured and shot. He goes from one precarious shelter to another, without hearth or home, hunted, obscure, a phantom of himself."

And Gerbier continued,

"But he is never alone. He feels around him the faith and the tenderness of a whole enslaved people. He finds accomplices, he finds friends in the fields and in the factory. In the suburbs and in the chateaux, among gendarmes, railroad workers, smugglers, merchants and priests. Among old notaries and young girls. The poorest one shares his meager ration of bread with him, who has not even the right to go into a baker's shop because he is fighting for all the harvests of France."

So spoke Gerbier. And Legrain on his burning pallet, in the choking darkness, was discovering a wholly new and enchanted country peopled with combatants without number, and without weapons, a fatherland of sacred friends, more beautiful than any fatherland ever was on earth. The resistance movement was this fatherland.

XIII

One morning on going to his work Legrain suddenly asked,

"Monsieur Gerbier, are you a leader in the resistance movement?"

Gerbier considered Legrain's burning and ravaged young face with an almost cruel attention. He saw in it a limitless loyalty and devotion.

"I was on the general staff of a movement," he said. "No one here knows it. I was coming from Paris. I was arrested in Toulouse—some informer, I think. But no proof. They didn't even dare to try me. So they sent me here."

"For how long?" asked Legrain.

Gerbier shrugged his shoulders and smiled.

"For as long as they please, of course," he said. "You know that better than anyone."

Legrain stopped and stared at the ground. Then he said in a choked voice, but with great firmness,

"Monsieur Gerbier, you've got to get away from here." He paused, then raised his head and added, "They need you out there."

As Gerbier did not answer, Legrain continued, "I have an idea . . . I've had it a long time . . . I'll tell you about it tonight."

They took leave of each other. Gerbier bought some cigarettes from the guard who acted as his purveyor. He made the round of the plateau. He wore his usual smile. He was reaching the objective he had been working toward through the stories and the images with which he had patiently intoxicated Legrain.

XIV

"I'll tell you what my idea is," whispered Legrain when he had made sure the colonel, the traveling salesman and the pharmacist were fast asleep.

Legrain collected his thoughts and chose his words. Then he spoke.

"What stands in the way of escape? There are two things: the barbed wires and the patrols. As for the barbed wires, the ground isn't the same level everywhere, and there are places where a slender man like yourself, Monsieur Gerbier, can squeeze under, though he might rip his clothes a little."

"I know all those places," said Gerbier.

"So much for the barbed wires," said Legrain. "That leaves the patrols. How many minutes do you need to run as far as the patrol road, pass it and be absorbed in the landscape?"

"Twelve. . . . Fifteen at the most," said Gerbier.

"Well, I can manage to make the guards blind for longer than that," said Legrain.

"I think so," said Gerbier placidly. "It's not difficult for a skillful electrician to fix it in advance so the current will break down."

"You thought of it," Legrain murmured. "And you never said a word."

"I like to command or to accept. I don't know how to ask a favor," said Gerbier. "I was waiting for it to come from you."

Gerbier leaned on one shoulder as if to try to make out his companion's face in the dark. And he said,

"I have often wondered why, when you had this means at your disposal, you never took advantage of it."

Legrain had a coughing fit before he answered.

"In the beginning I discussed the matter with Armel. He wasn't for it. He was too easily resigned, perhaps. But in a sense what he said was true. With our fatigue suits and no papers, without ration cards, we wouldn't have gone very far. Then Armel got sick. I couldn't leave him. And things weren't going so well any more with me either. For you it's quite different. With your friends of the resistance . . ."

"I've already established a contact through the guard who sells me cigarettes," said Gerbier. Without transition, he added, "In a week—two at the most—we can leave."

There was a silence. And Legrain's heart pounded so hard against his emaciated ribs that Gerbier could hear its beating. With a faltering voice the young man asked,

"You said *we,* didn't you, Monsieur Gerbier?"

"Why, of course," said Gerbier. "What did you suppose?"

"I thought at certain moments that you would take me with you. But I didn't dare to be sure," said Legrain.

"So you were willing," Gerbier asked, speaking slowly, emphasizing every syllable, "to make the preparations for my escape and stay here yourself?"

"That's how I had worked it out for myself," said Legrain.

"And you would have done it?"

"They need you, Monsieur Gerbier, in the resistance movement."

For some minutes Gerbier had felt a violent craving for a smoke. Yet he waited before lighting a cigarette. He hated to show the least emotion on his features.

XV

As he was beginning his game of dominoes Colonel Jarret du Plessis made this remark to his companions,

"The little communist looks all perked up. I hear him humming every morning as he goes to work."

"It's the spring," the traveling salesman assured.

"It's rather that you get used to everything," sighed the pharmacist. "He, like everybody else, poor kid."

The three men had no hostility toward Legrain. On the contrary his age, his misfortune, his physical condition touched them, for they were naturally good-hearted. They had offered to take turns in watching over Armel. But Legrain, who was jealous of his friend, had declined their services. When they received packages containing a little food from outside they always wanted to give Legrain a share. But knowing that he would have no opportunity to reciprocate these kindnesses Legrain had stubbornly refused. Little by little, because of this uncompromising behavior, the domino-players had come to forget the young man's existence. His change of attitude brought their attention back to him. One evening when the pharmacist was passing around some chocolate tablets which he had found in a package from his family Legrain held out his hand.

"Hurrah!" exclaimed Colonel Jarret du Plessis. "The little communist is getting broken in."

The colonel turned toward Gerbier and said,

"It's your influence, Monsieur, and I congratulate you."

"I rather think it's the chocolate," said Gerbier.

A few hours later, when they were the only ones still awake, Gerbier said to Legrain,

"You've picked a rather bad time to draw comments on your sweet tooth."

"It's because I thought . . . I thought I'd be able to send him something in return soon," the young man murmured.

"The same thought may have occurred to them. It's never a good idea to assume other people are more stupid than you are," said Gerbier.

They fell into silence. After a few moments Legrain asked humbly,

"Are you angry with me, Monsieur Gerbier?"

"No, of course not. That's the end of it," said Gerbier.

"Then you won't mind telling me what's going to happen after the current breaks down?" begged Legrain.

"I already went into the details of that yesterday and the day before," said Gerbier.

"If you don't tell me again," said Legrain, "I just can't bring myself to believe it, and I can't sleep. . . . Then there will really be a car?"

"A gasogene,"* said Gerbier. "And I think Guillaume will be at the wheel."

"The former sergeant of the Foreign Legion? The hard-boiled guy? The one they also call the Bison?" Legrain whispered.

"There will be civilian clothes in the car," Gerbier went on. "We'll be driven to a presbytery. After that we'll see."

"And friends in the resistance movement will give us false papers?" asked Legrain.

---

* A car in use since the war equipped with a wood-burning device that produces a gasoline substitute.

"And ration cards for food."

"And you'll let me meet some communists, Monsieur Gerbier? And I'll work with them in the underground?"

"I promise you."

"But we'll keep on seeing each other, you and I, Monsieur Gerbier?"

"If you're a liaison agent."

"That's what I want to be," said Legrain.

And during the nights that followed, Legrain would ask each time,

"Tell me about Guillaume, the Bison, Monsieur Gerbier, and about anything you like."

XVI

A day came when Gerbier, on opening a package of cigarettes that he had just bought, found inside it a folded sheet of onionskin paper. He went to the latrines, read the message attentively and burned it. Then he made the round of the barbed-wire fences, as he habitually did. Late in the afternoon he said to Legrain,

"Everything is arranged. We're leaving Saturday."

"In four days," Legrain stammered.

The blood completely left his pinched cheeks, then came back with a rush, and once more drained them. He leaned against Gerbier.

"Excuse me . . ." he said. "My head is turning. I'm so glad."

Legrain let himself drop gently to the ground. Gerbier realized that the last week had taxed the young man terribly. His face had shrunk and his eyes had grown larger. His nose was thin as a fish bone. His Adam's apple was much more prominent.

"You must calm yourself and control your feelings," said Gerbier severely, "and before Saturday you've got to get some strength back. Don't forget, we've got five kilometers to walk. You're going to take my soup at noon, do you hear?"

"I'll do it, Monsieur Gerbier."

"And you don't sleep enough. Tomorrow you're going to go and ask for some sleeping pills at the infirmary."

"I will, Monsieur Gerbier."

Legrain left the cabin earlier than usual and Gerbier accompanied him as far as the doorstep.

"Only three more nights here, and it's the Bison's car," said Legrain.

He started off at a run. Gerbier watched him and thought to himself, "He's young, he'll hold out."

At the noon-day meal Gerbier gave Legrain his mess-tin. But the young man shook his head.

"I know we agreed on that, but I can't. It turns my stomach," he said.

"Then take my bread," said Gerbier, "you can eat it while you work."

Legrain stuffed the blackish slice into his fatigue jacket. His movement was limp, lifeless, his face was vacant.

"You look down in the mouth," Gerbier observed.

Legrain did not answer and walked off in the direction of the power station. That evening he did not ask Gerbier to talk to him about the Bison and the other wonders.

"Did you take your sleeping pill?" asked Gerbier.

"I took it. I'll fall asleep in no time, I guess," said Legrain.

On Thursday his behavior was even stranger. He did not eat any lunch, and in the cabin, while waiting for nightfall, he watched the game of dominoes instead of talking with Gerbier. He seemed to fall asleep all at once.

On Friday Legrain had an absurd argument with the pharmacist and accused him of being a dirty bourgeois. Gerbier said nothing at the moment, but in the darkness and the silence he roughly seized Legrain's arm as the latter seemed already asleep and asked,

"What's wrong?"

"Why . . . nothing, Monsieur Gerbier," said Legrain.

"I beg you to answer," said Gerbier. "Don't you trust me any more? Your nerves played out? I give you my word that for my part everything is going to be ready."

"I know, Monsieur Gerbier."

"What about your end of it?"

"I'll do a clean job, I give you my word."

"Then—what's wrong?"

"I don't know, Monsieur Gerbier, really . . . . Headache. Heart's in a knot. . . ."

Gerbier's eyes narrowed, as they did in daylight when he wanted to penetrate to the secret of a face. But they were impotent in the darkness.

"You must have taken too many pills," said Gerbier at last.

"That's surely it, Monsieur Gerbier," said Legrain.

"You'll feel better tomorrow," Gerbier said in turn, "when you see the car with the Bison."

"The Bison," Legrain repeated.

But he did not go on.

Gerbier often remembered subsequently the unconscious and frightful cruelty of this dialogue in the night.

XVII

Saturday morning, in the course of his usual walk, Gerbier passed by the power station where Legrain had been working alone since the removal of the old Austrian engineer. Gerbier saw with satisfaction that Legrain was calm.

"Everything is ready," said the young man.

Gerbier examined Legrain's work. The clocklike mechanism which was to create the short circuit had been conceived with consummate intelligence and skill. The current would be broken at the hour required.

"And don't worry," Legrain reassured him, "those dumbbells on the night shift will take forty minutes to repair it."

"Nobody could have done better than you've done. We're as good as out," said Gerbier.

"Thanks, Monsieur Gerbier," the young man murmured.

His eyes were very bright.

XVIII

The colonel, the pharmacist and the traveling salesman were finishing their game of dominoes by the last glimmer of daylight. The twilight was gathering its gray smoke over the plateau. But a belt of hard, fixed light imprisoned the twilight within the camp. The patrol road between the network of metallic brambles was violently illuminated. Behind this belt and by contrast it was already night. In front of their cabin, Gerbier and Legrain were looking in silence at the glistening barbed wires. From time to time Gerbier would reach to the bottom of his pocket to feel the tool Legrain had brought back to spring the locks. A guard in a beret cried,

"Roll-call!"

Legrain and Gerbier went inside. The guard counted the occupants of the hut and shut the doors. Darkness once more. Each one fumbled his way to his straw bed. For some time the colonel, the traveling salesman and the pharmacist exchanged remarks that became increasingly desultory. Gerbier and Legrain were silent. Their mates dozed off with their habitual sighs and groans. Gerbier and Legrain were silent.

Gerbier was pleased with Legrain's silence. He had feared that Legrain would be too excited for this wait. The mechanism Legrain had rigged up was to go off at midnight. They still had about an hour. Gerbier smoked several cigarettes, then went to the door and forced the lock without making any noise. He pushed the door. He saw the brutal light that encircled the plateau. Gerbier came back to the straw bed and notified Legrain.

"Be ready, Roger, it won't be long now."

Then once more Gerbier heard the movements of Legrain's heart.

"Monsieur Gerbier," the young man murmured with difficulty, "I've got to tell you something."

He got his breath again with an effort.

"I'm not going," he said.

In spite of all his self-control Gerbier was on the point of raising his voice in an imprudent way. But he got the better of himself and spoke in the usual pitch of these conversations in the dark.

"You're afraid?" he asked very softly.

"Oh, Monsieur Gerbier," Legrain moaned.

And Gerbier felt sure that Legrain was inaccessible to fear. As sure as if he could have seen his face.

"You think you're too tired to make it?" said Gerbier. "I'll carry you if necessary."

"I would have made it. I would have made it, even much farther," said Legrain.

And Gerbier felt that he was telling the truth.

"I'll explain to you, Monsieur Gerbier, only don't talk to me," said Legrain. "I've got to make it fast, and it isn't easy to do."

Legrain's lungs wheezed. He coughed, and went on,

"When I went to get the pills to sleep as you told me, I saw the doctor. He's a nice fellow, the doctor. He's an old man who understands. He had us put here, Armel and me, because at least it doesn't rain through the roof and the floor stays dry. He couldn't do anything more. What I mean is you can talk to him. He didn't think I looked well. He examined me. I didn't understand everything he told me. But enough anyway to gather that one of my lungs is gone and the other is in bad shape. He seemed pretty upset about seeing me shut up here with no hope of getting out. Then I asked him what would happen if I was free. He told me that with two years in a sanitarium I could be well again. Otherwise I wouldn't be good for anything. I came away from his office stunned. You saw me. . . . I was thinking all the time about what you had told me of the life in the underground. It took me until this morning to realize that I couldn't go."

Gerbier considered himself pretty hardened. And he was. He believed he never acted without due reflection. And this was true. He had inflamed Legrain with his stories only in order to have an accomplice he could trust. Yet it was without reflection, without calculation and seized by an unfamiliar contraction that he said,

"I'm not going to leave you. I have ways of getting money, and I'll find others. You'll be safe and cared for. You'll have all the time you need to get back into shape."

"That's not why I was leaving, Monsieur Gerbier," said the calm voice of the invisible young man. "I wanted to be a liaison agent. I don't want to take ration cards from the comrades for my poor little health. I don't want to hinder the resistance. You've shown me too well what it's like."

Gerbier felt himself physically unable to answer. And Legrain continued,

"But just the same I'm very glad to know about the resistance movement. I won't be so unhappy any more. I understand life and I love it. I'm like Armel, now. I have faith."

He became a little animated, and said in a fiercer tone,

"But it's not in the next world that I look for justice, Monsieur Gerbier. Tell our friends here and on the other side of the water, tell them to hurry. I should like to have time to see the end of the men with blank eyes."

He stopped talking, and the silence that followed was one whose duration neither of them measured. Without knowing it they both had their eyes fixed on the slit in the doorway through which they could see the glare of the lights on the patrol road.

They got up at the same time because that luminous thread suddenly snapped. The darkness of freedom had joined the imprisoned darkness. Gerbier and Legrain were at the door.

Against all prudence, against all good sense, Gerbier spoke again,

"They'll discover the sabotage, they'll see that I've escaped. They'll make the connection. They'll think of you."

"What more can they do to us?" murmured Legrain.

Gerbier still did not leave.

"On the contrary, I'll be useful to you," said the young man. "They'll come and get me to make the repair. I'll go out so fast that they won't see your empty straw bed and I'll keep them running around another half hour. You'll be far away with the Bison."

Gerbier crossed the doorstep.

"Think it over for the last time," he almost pleaded.

"I was never the kind to be a burden to anyone," answered Legrain. "I'm not going to begin with the resistance movement."

Gerbier slipped between the door and the jamb without turning round and headed straight for the opening in the barbed wire. He had studied it a hundred times and he had counted a hundred times the number of steps he would have to take to reach the spot.

Legrain carefully closed the door, went back to his straw bed, dug his teeth into the ticking that covered it and lay very still.

20

Prisoner of the Sand

ANTOINE DE SAINT EXUPÉRY

WE HAD been flying for three hours. A brightness that seemed to me a glare spurted on the starboard side. I stared. A streamer of light which I had hitherto not noticed was fluttering from a lamp at the tip of the wing. It was an intermittent glow, now brilliant, now dim. It told me that I had flown into a cloud, and it was on the cloud that the lamp was reflected.

I was nearing the landmarks upon which I had counted; a clear sky would have helped a lot. The wing shone bright under the halo. The light steadied itself, became fixed, and then began to radiate in the form of a bouquet of pink blossoms. Great eddies of air were swinging me to and fro. I was navigating somewhere in the belly of a cumulus whose thickness I could not guess. I rose to seventy-five hundred feet and was still in it. Down again to three thousand, and the bouquet of flowers was still with me, motionless and growing brighter.

Well, there it was and there was nothing to do about it. I would think of something else, and wait to get clear of it. Just the same, I did not like this sinister glitter of a one-eyed grog-shop.

"Let me think," I said to myself. "I am bouncing round a bit, but there's nothing abnormal about that. I've been bumped all the way, despite a clear sky and plenty of ceiling. The wind has not died down, and I must be doing better than the 190 m.p.h. I counted on." This was about as far as I could get. Oh, well, when I got through the cloud-bank I would try to take my bearings.

Out of it we flew. The bouquet suddenly vanished, letting me know I was in the clear again. I stared ahead and saw, if one can speak of "seeing" space, a narrow valley of sky and the wall of the next cumulus. Already the bouquet was coming to life again. I was free of that viscous mess from time to time but only for a few seconds each time. After three

and a half hours of flying it began to get on my nerves. If I had made
the time I imagined, we were certainly approaching the Nile. With a
little luck I might be able to spot the river through the rifts, but they
were getting rare. I dared not come down, for if I was actually slower
than I thought, I was still over high-lying country.

Thus far I was entirely without anxiety; my only fear was that I might
presently be wasting time. I decided that I would take things easy until I
had flown four and a quarter hours: after that, even in a dead calm
(which was highly unlikely) I should have crossed the Nile. When I
reached the fringes of the cloud-bank the bouquet winked on and off
more and more swiftly and then suddenly went out. Decidedly, I did
not like these dot-and-dash messages from the demons of the night.

A green star appeared ahead of me, flashing like a lighthouse. Was it
a lighthouse? or really a star? I took no pleasure from this supernatural gleam, this star the Magi might have seen, this dangerous decoy.

Prévot, meanwhile, had waked up and turned his electric torch on
the engine dials. I waved him off, him and his torch. We had just sailed
into the clear between two clouds and I was busy staring below. Prévot
went back to sleep. The gap in the clouds was no help; there was nothing
below.

Four hours and five minutes in the air. Prévot awoke and sat down
beside me.

"I'll bet we're near Cairo," he said.

"We must be."

"What's that? A star? or is it a lighthouse?"

I had throttled the engine down a little. This, probably, was what had
awakened Prévot. He is sensitive to all the variations of sound in flight.

I began a slow descent, intending to slip under the mass of clouds.
Meanwhile I had had a look at my map. One thing was sure—the land
below me lay at sea level, and there was no risk of conking against a
hill. Down I went, flying due north so that the lights of the cities would
strike square into my windows. I must have overflown them, and should
therefore see them on my left.

Now I was flying below the cumulus. But alongside was another cloud
hanging lower down on the left. I swerved so as not to be caught in its
net, and headed north-northeast. This second cloud-bank certainly went
down a long way, for it blocked my view of the horizon. I dared not
give up any more altitude. My altimeter registered 1200 feet, but I had
no notion of the atmospheric pressure here. Prévot leaned towards me
and I shouted to him, "I'm going out to sea. I'd rather come down on it
than risk a crash here."

As a matter of fact, there was nothing to prove that we had not drifted over the sea already. Below that cloud-bank visibility was exactly nil. I hugged my window, trying to read below me, to discover flares, signs of life. I was a man raking dead ashes, trying in vain to retrieve the flame of life in a hearth.

"A lighthouse!"

Both of us spied it at the same moment, that winking decoy! What madness! Where was that phantom light, that invention of the night? For at the very second when Prévot and I leaned forward to pick it out of the air where it had glittered nine hundred feet below our wings, suddenly, at that very instant . . .

"Oh!"

I am quite sure that this was all I said. I am quite sure that all I felt was a terrific crash that rocked our world to its foundations. We had crashed against the earth at a hundred and seventy miles an hour. I am quite sure that in the split second that followed, all I expected was the great flash of ruddy light of the explosion in which Prévot and I were to be blown up together. Neither he nor I had felt the least emotion of any kind. All I could observe in myself was an extraordinary tense feeling of expectancy, the expectancy of that resplendent star in which we were to vanish within the second.

But there was no ruddy star. Instead there was a sort of earthquake that splintered our cabin, ripped away the windows, blew sheets of metal hurtling through space a hundred yards away, and filled our very entrails with its roar. The ship quivered like a knife-blade thrown from a distance into a block of oak, and its anger mashed us as if we were so much pulp.

One second, two seconds passed, and the plane still quivered while I waited with a grotesque impatience for the forces within it to burst it like a bomb. But the subterranean quakings went on without a climax of eruption while I marveled uncomprehendingly at its invisible travail. I was baffled by the quaking, the anger, the interminable postponement. Five seconds passed; six seconds. And suddenly we were seized by a spinning motion, a shock that jerked our cigarettes out of the window, pulverized the starboard wing—and then nothing, nothing but a frozen immobility. I shouted to Prévot:

"Jump!"

And in that instant he cried out:

"Fire!"

We dove together through the wrecked window and found ourselves standing side by side, sixty feet from the plane. I said:

"Are you hurt?"

He answered:

"Not a bit."

But he was rubbing his knee.

"Better run your hands over yourself," I said; "move about a bit. Sure no bones are broken?"

He answered:

"I'm all right. It's that emergency pump."

Emergency pump! I was sure he was going to keel over any minute and split open from head to navel there before my eyes. But he kept repeating with a glassy stare:

"That pump, that emergency pump."

He's out of his head, I thought. He'll start dancing in a minute.

Finally he stopped staring at the plane—which had not gone up in flames—and stared at me instead. And he said again:

"I'm all right. It's that emergency pump. It got me in the knee."

Why we were not blown up, I do not know. I switched on my electric torch and went back over the furrow in the ground traced by the plane. Two hundred and fifty yards from where we stopped the ship had begun to shed the twisted iron and sheet-metal that spattered the sand the length of her traces. We were to see, when day came, that we had run almost tangentially into a gentle slope at the top of a barren plateau. At the point of impact there was a hole in the sand that looked as if it had been made by a plough. Maintaining an even keel, the plane had run its course with the fury and the tail-lashings of a reptile gliding on its belly at the rate of a hundred and seventy miles an hour. We owed our lives to the fact that this desert was surfaced with round black pebbles which had rolled over and over like ballbearings beneath us. They must have rained upward to the heavens as we shot through them.

Prévot disconnected the batteries for fear of fire by short-circuit. I leaned against the motor and turned the situation over in my mind. I had been flying high for four hours and a quarter, possibly with a thirty-mile following wind. I had been jolted a good deal. If the wind had changed since the weather people forecast it, I was unable to say into what quarter it had veered. All I could make out was that we had crashed in an empty square two hundred and fifty miles on each side.

Prévot came up and sat down beside me.

"I can't believe that we're alive," he said.

I said nothing. Even that thought could not cheer me. A germ of an idea was at work in my mind and was already bothering me. Telling

Prévot to switch on his torch as a landmark, I walked straight out, scrutinizing the ground in the light of my own torch as I went.

I went forward slowly, swung round in a wide arc, and changed direction a number of times. I kept my eyes fixed on the ground like a man hunting a lost ring.

Only a little while before I had been straining just as hard to see a gleam of light from the air. Through the darkness I went, bowed over the traveling disk of white light. "Just as I thought," I said to myself, and I went slowly back to the plane. I sat down beside the cabin and ruminated. I had been looking for a reason to hope and had failed to find it. I had been looking for a sign of life, and no sign of life had appeared.

"Prévot, I couldn't find a single blade of grass."

Prévot said nothing, and I was not sure he had understood. Well, we could talk about it again when the curtain arose at dawn. Meanwhile I was dead tired and all I could think was, "Two hundred and fifty miles more or less in the desert."

Suddenly I jumped to my feet. "Water!" I said.

Gas tanks and oil tanks were smashed in. So was our supply of drinking-water. The sand had drunk everything. We found a pint of coffee in a batteerd thermos flask and half a pint of white wine in another. We filtered both, and poured them into one flask. There were some grapes, too, and a single orange. Meanwhile I was computing: "All this will last us five hours of tramping in the sun."

We crawled into the cabin and waited for dawn. I stretched out, and as I settled down to sleep I took stock of our situation. We didn't know where we were; we had less than a quart of liquid between us; if we were not too far off the Benghazi-Cairo lane we should be found in a week, and that would be too late. Yet it was the best we could hope for. If, on the other hand, we had drifted off our course, we shouldn't be found in six months. One thing was sure—we could not count on being picked up by a plane; the men who came out for us would have two thousand miles to cover.

"You know, it's a shame," Prévot said suddenly.

"What's a shame?"

"That we didn't crash properly and have it over with."

It seemed pretty early to be throwing in one's hand. Prévot and I pulled ourselves together. There was still a chance, slender as it was, that we might be saved miraculously by a plane. On the other hand, we couldn't stay here and perhaps miss a near-by oasis. We would walk all

day and come back to the plane before dark. And before going off we
would write our plan in huge letters in the sand.

With this I curled up and settled down to sleep. I was happy to go to
sleep. My weariness wrapped me round like a multiple presence. I was
not alone in the desert: my drowsiness was peopled with voices and
memories and whispered confidences. I was not yet thirsty; I felt strong;
and I surrendered myself to sleep as to an aimless journey. Reality lost
ground before the advance of dreams.

Ah, but things were different when I awoke!

In times past I have loved the Sahara. I have spent nights alone in
the path of marauding tribes and have waked up with untroubled mind
in the golden emptiness of the desert where the wind like a sea had
raised sandwaves upon its surface. Asleep under the wing of my plane
I have looked forward with confidence to being rescued next day. But
this was not the Sahara!

Prévot and I walked along the slopes of rolling mounds. The ground
was sand covered over with a single layer of shining black pebbles. They
gleamed like metal scales and all the domes about us shone like coats of
mail. We had dropped down into a mineral world and were hemmed
in by iron hills.

When we reached the top of the first crest we saw in the distance
another just like it, black and gleaming. As we walked we scraped the
ground with our boots, marking a trail over which to return to the
plane. We went forward with the sun in our eyes. It was not logical to
go due east like this, for everything—the weather reports, the duration
of the flight—had made it plain that we had crossed the Nile. But I
had started tentatively towards the west and had felt a vague foreboding
I could not explain to myself. So I had put off the west till tomorrow,
In the same way, provisionally, I had given up going north, though that
led to the sea.

Three days later, when scourged by thirst into abandoning the plane
and walking straight on until we dropped in our tracks, it was still eastward that we tramped. More precisely, we walked east-northeast. And
this too was in defiance of all reason and even of all hope. Yet after we
had been rescued we discovered that if we had gone in any other direction we should have been lost.

Northward, we should never have had the endurance to reach the sea.
And absurd as it may appear, it seems to me now, since I had no other
motive, that I must have chosen the east simply because it was by going

eastward that Guillaumet had been saved in the Andes, after I had hunted for him everywhere. In a confused way the east had become for me the direction of life.

We walked on for five hours and then the landscape changed. A river of sand seemed to be running through a valley, and we followed this river-bed, taking long strides in order to cover as much ground as possible and get back to the plane before night fell, if our march was in vain. Suddenly I stopped.

"Prévot!"

"What's up?"

"Our tracks!"

How long was it since we had forgotten to leave a wake behind us? We had to find it or die.

We went back, bearing to the right. When we had gone back far enough we would make a right angle to the left and eventually intersect our tracks where we had still remembered to mark them.

This we did and were off again. The heat rose and with it came the mirages. But these were still the commonplace kind—sheets of water that materialized and then vanished as we neared them. We decided to cross the valley of sand and climb the highest dome in order to look round the horizon. This was after six hours of march in which, striding along, we must have covered twenty miles.

When we had struggled up to the top of the black hump we sat down and looked at each other. At our feet lay our valley of sand, opening into a desert of sand whose dazzling brightness seared our eyes. As far as the eye could see lay empty space. But in that space the play of light created mirages which, this time, were of a disturbing kind, fortresses and minarets, angular geometric hulks. I could see also a black mass that pretended to be vegetation, overhung by the last of those clouds that dissolve during the day only to return at night. This mass of vegetation was the shadow of a cumulus.

It was no good going on. The experiment was a failure. We would have to go back to our plane, to that red and white beacon which, perhaps, would be picked out by a flyer. I was not staking great hopes on a rescue party, but it did seem to me our last chance of salvation. In any case, we had to get back to our few drops of liquid, for our throats were parched. We were imprisoned in this iron circle, captives of the curt dictatorship of thirst.

And yet, how hard it was to turn back when there was a chance that we might be on the road to life! Beyond the mirages the horizon was perhaps rich in veritable treasures, in meadows and runnels of sweet water. I knew I was doing the right thing by returning to the plane, and yet as I swung round and started back I was filled with portents of disaster.

We were resting on the ground beside the plane. Nearly forty miles of wandering this day. The last drop of liquid had been drained. No sign of life had appeared to the east. No plane had soared overhead. How long should we be able to hold out? Already our thirst was terrible.

We had built up a great pyre out of bits of the splintered wing. Our gasoline was ready, and we had flung on the heap sheets of metal whose magnesium coating would burn with a hard white flame. We were waiting now for night to come down before we lighted our conflagration. But where were there men to see it?

Night fell and the flames rose. Prayerfully we watched our mute and radiant fanion mount resplendent into the night. As I looked I said to myself that this message was not only a cry for help, it was fraught also with a great deal of love. We were begging for water, but we were also begging the communion of human society. Only man can create fire: let another flame light up the night; let man answer man!

I was haunted by a vision of my wife's eyes under the halo of her hat. Of her face I could see only the eyes, questioning me, looking at me yearningly. I am answering, answering with all my strength! What flame could leap higher than this that darts up into the night from my heart?

What I could do, I have done. What we could do, we have done. Nearly forty miles, almost without a drop to drink. Now there was no water left. Was it our fault that we could wait no longer? Suppose we had sat quietly by the plane, taking suck at the mouths of our water-bottles? But from the moment I breathed in the moist bottom of the tin cup, a clock had started up in me. From the second when I had sucked up the last drop, I had begun to slip downhill. Could I help it if time like a river was carrying me away? Prévot was weeping. I tapped him on the shoulder and said, to console him:

"If we're done for we're done for, and that's all there is to it."

He said:

"Do you think it's me I'm bawling about?"

I might have known it. It was evident enough. Nothing is unbearable. Tomorrow, and the day after, I should learn that nothing was really unbearable. I had never really believed in torture. Reading Poe as a kid,

I had already said as much to myself. Once, jammed in the cabin of a plane, I thought I was going to drown; and I had not suffered much. Several times it had seemed to me that the final smash-up was coming, and I don't remember that I thought of it as a cosmic event. And I didn't believe this was going to be agonizing either. There will be time tomorrow to find out stranger things about it. Meanwhile, God knows that despite the bonfire I had decidedly given up hope that our cries would be heard by the world.

"Do you think it's me . . ." There you have what is truly unbearable! Every time I saw those yearning eyes it was as if a flame were searing me. They were like a scream for help, like the flares of a sinking ship. I felt that I should not sit idly by: I should jump up and run—anywhere! straight ahead of me!

What a strange reversal of rôles! But I have always thought it would be like this. Still, I needed Prévot beside me to be quite sure of it. Prévot was a level-headed fellow. He loved life. And yet Prévot no more than I was wringing his hands at the sight of death the way we are told men do. But there did exist something that he could not bear any more than I could. I was perfectly ready to fall asleep, whether for a night or for eternity. If I did fall asleep, I could not even know whether it was for the one or for the other. And the peace of sleep! But that cry that would be sent up at home, that great wail of desolation—that was what I could not bear. I could not stand idly by and look on at that disaster. Each second of silence drove the knife deeper into someone I loved. At the thought, a blind rage surged up in me. Why do these chains bind me and prevent me from rescuing those who are drowning? Why does our conflagration not carry our cry to the ends of the world? Hear me, you out here! Patience. We are coming to save you.

The magnesium had been licked off and the metal was glowing red. There was left only a heap of embers round which we crouched to warm ourselves. Our flaming call had spent itself. Had it set anything in the world in motion? I knew well enough that it hadn't. Here was a prayer that had of necessity gone unheard.

That was that.

I ought to get some sleep.

At daybreak I took a rag and mopped up a little dew on the wings. The mixture of water and paint and oil yielded a spoonful of nauseating liquid which we sipped because it would at least moisten our lips. After this banquet Prévot said:

"Thank God we've got a gun."

Instantly I became furious and turned on him with an aggressiveness which I regretted directly I felt it. There was nothing I should have loathed more at that moment than a gush of sentimentality. I am so made that I have to believe that everything is simple. Birth is simple. Growing up is simple. And dying of thirst is simple. I watched Prévot out of the corner of my eye, ready to wound his feelings, if that was necessary to shut him up.

But Prévot had spoken without emotion. He had been discussing a matter of hygiene, and might have said in the same tone, "We ought to wash our hands." That being so, we were agreed. Indeed already yesterday, my eye falling by chance on the leather holster, the same thought had crossed my mind, and with me too it had been a reasonable reflex, not an emotional one. Pathos resides in social man, not in the individual; what was pathetic was our powerlessness to reassure those for whom we were responsible, not what we might do with the gun.

There was still no sign that we were being sought; or rather they were doubtless hunting for us elsewhere, probably in Arabia. We were to hear no sound of plane until the day after we had abandoned our own. And if ships did pass overhead, what could that mean to us? What could they see in us except two black dots among the thousand shadowy dots in the desert? Absurd to think of being distinguishable from them. None of the reflections that might be attributed to me on the score of this torture would be true. I should not feel in the least tortured. The aerial rescue party would seem to me, each time I sighted one, to be moving through a universe that was not mine. When searchers have to cover two thousand miles of territory, it takes them a good two weeks to spot a plane in the desert from the sky.

They were probably looking for us all along the line from Tripoli to Persia. And still, with all this, I clung to the slim chance that they might pick us out. Was that not our only chance of being saved? I changed my tactics, determining to go reconnoitering by myself. Prévot would get another bonfire together and kindle it in the event that visitors showed up. But we were to have no callers that day.

So off I went without knowing whether or not I should have the stamina to come back. I remembered what I knew about this Libyan desert. When, in the Sahara, humidity is still at forty per cent of saturation, it is only eighteen here in Libya. Life here evaporates like a vapor. Bedouins, explorers, and colonial officers all tell us that a man may go nineteen hours without water. Thereafter his eyes fill with light, and that marks the beginning of the end. The progress made by thirst is swift and terrible. But this northeast wind, this abnormal wind that had blown us out off our course and had marooned us on this plateau, was now prolonging our lives. What was the length of the reprieve it would grant us before our eyes began to fill with light? I went forward with the feeling of a man canoeing in mid-ocean.

I will admit that at daybreak this landscape seemed to me less infernal, and that I began my walk with my hands in my pockets, like a tramp on a highroad. The evening before we had set snares at the mouths of certain mysterious burrows in the ground, and the poacher in me was on the alert. I went first to have a look at our traps. They were empty.

Well, this meant that I should not be drinking blood today; and indeed I hadn't expected to. But though I was not disappointed, my curiosity was aroused. What was there in the desert for these animals to live on? These were certainly the holes of fennecs, a long-eared carnivorous sand-box the size of a rabbit. I spotted the tracks made by one of them, and gave way to the impulse to follow them. They led to a narrow stream of sand where each footprint was plainly outlined and where I marveled at the pretty palm formed by the three toes spread fanwise on the sand.

I could imagine my little friend trotting blithely along at dawn and licking the dew off the rocks. Here the tracks were wider apart: my fennec had broken into a run. And now I see that a companion has joined him and they have trotted on side by side. These signs of a morning stroll gave me a strange thrill. They were signs of life, and I loved them for that. I almost forgot that I was thirsty.

Finally I came to the pasture-ground of my foxes. Here, every hundred yards or so, I saw sticking up out of the sand a small dry shrub, its twigs heavy with little golden snails. The fennec came here at dawn to do his marketing. And here I was able to observe another of nature's mysteries.

My fennec did not stop at all the shrubs. There were some weighed down with snails which he disdained. Obviously he avoided them with some wariness. Others he stopped at but did not strip of all they bore. He must have picked out two or three shells and then gone on to another restaurant. What was he up to? Was he nurseryman to the snails, encouraging their reproduction by refraining from exhausting the stock on a given shrub, or a given twig? Or was he amusing himself by delaying repletion, putting off satiety in order to enhance the pleasure he took from his morning stroll?

The tracks led me back to the hole in which he lived. Doubtless my fennec crouched below, listening to me and startled by the crunching of my footsteps. I said to him:

"Fox, my little fox, I'm done for; but somehow that doesn't prevent me from taking an interest in your mood."

And there I stayed a bit, ruminating and telling myself that a man was able to adapt himself to anything. The notion that he is to die in thirty years has probably never spoiled any man's fun. Thirty years . . . or thirty days: it's all a matter of perspective.

Only, you have to be able to put certain visions out of your mind.

I went on, finally, and the time came when, along with my weariness, something in me began to change. If those were not mirages, I was inventing them.

"Hi! Hi! there!"

I shouted and waved my arms, but the man I had seen waving at me turned out to be a black rock. Everything in the desert had grown animate. I stopped to waken a sleeping Bedouin and he turned into the trunk of a black tree. A tree-trunk? Here in the desert? I was amazed and bent over to lift a broken bough. It was solid marble.

Straightening up I looked round and saw more black marble. An antediluvian forest littered the ground with its broken tree-tops. How many thousand years ago, under what hurricane of the time of Genesis, had this cathedral of wood crumbled in this spot? Countless centuries had rolled these fragments of giant pillars at my feet, polished them like steel, petrified and vitrified them and indued them with the color of jet.

I could distinguish the knots in their branches, the twistings of their once living boughs, could count the rings of life in them. This forest had rustled with birds and been filled with music that now was struck by doom and frozen into salt. And all this was hostile to me. Blacker than the chain-mail of the hummocks, these solemn derelicts rejected me. What had I, a living man, to do with this incorruptible stone? Perishable as I was, I whose body was to crumble into dust, what place had I in this eternity?

Since yesterday I had walked nearly fifty miles. This dizziness that I felt came doubtless from my thirst. Or from the sun. It glittered on these hulks until they shone as if smeared with oil. It blazed down on this universal carapace. Sand and fox had no life here. This world was a gigantic anvil upon which the sun beat down. I strode across this anvil and at my temples I could feel the hammer-strokes of the sun.

"Hi! Hi, there!" I called out.

"There is nothing there," I told myself. "Take it easy. You are delirious."

I had to talk to myself aloud, had to bring myself to reason. It was hard for me to reject what I was seeing, hard not to run towards that caravan plodding on the horizon. There! Do you see it?

"Fool! You know very well that you are inventing it."

"You mean that nothing in the world is real?"

Nothing in the world is real if that cross which I see ten miles off on the top of a hill is not real. Or is it a lighthouse? No, the sea does not lie in that direction. Then it must be a cross.

I had spent the night studying my map—but uselessly, since I did not know my position. Still, I had scrutinized all the signs that marked the marvelous presence of man. And somewhere on the map I had seen a little circle surmounted by just such a cross. I had glanced down at the legend to get an explanation of the symbol and had read: "Religious institution."

Close to the cross there had been a black dot. Again I had run my finger down the legend and had read: "Permanent well." My heart had jumped and I had repeated the legend aloud: "Permanent well, permanent well." What were all of Ali Baba's treasures compared with a permanent well? A little farther on were two white circles. "Temporary wells," the legend said. Not quite so exciting. And round about them was nothing . . . unless it was the blankness of despair.

But this must be my "religious institution"! The monks must certainly have planted a great cross on the hill expressly for men in our plight! All I had to do was to walk across to them. I should be taken in by those Dominicans. . . .

"But there are only Coptic monasteries in Libya!" I told myself.

. . . by those learned Dominicans. They have a great cool kitchen with red tiles, and out in the courtyard a marvelous rusted pump. Beneath the rusted pump; beneath the rusted pump . . . you've guessed it! . . . beneath the rusted pump is dug the permanent well! Ah, what rejoicing when I ring at their gate, when I get my hands on the rope of the great bell.

"Madman! You are describing a house in Provence; and what's more, the house has no bell!"

. . . on the rope of the great bell. The porter will raise his arms to Heaven and cry out, "You are the messenger of the Lord!" and he will call aloud to all the monks. They will pour out of the monastery. They will welcome me with a great feast, as if I were the Prodigal Son. They will lead me to the kitchen and will say to me, "One moment, my son, one moment. We'll just be off to the permanent well." And I shall be trembling with happiness.

No, no! I will *not* weep just because there happens to be no cross on the hill.

The treasures of the west turned out to be mere illusion. I have veered due north. At least the north is filled with the sound of the sea.

Over the hilltop. Look there, at the horizon! The most beautiful city in the world!

"You know perfectly well that is a mirage."

Of course I know it is a mirage! Am I the sort of man who can be fooled? But what if I *want* to go after that mirage? Suppose I enjoy indulging my hope? Suppose it suits me to love that crenelated town all beflagged with sunlight? What if I choose to walk straight ahead on light feet—for you must know that I have dropped my weariness behind me, I am happy now. . . . Prévot and his gun! Don't make me laugh! I prefer my drunkenness. I am drunk. I am dying of thirst.

It took the twilight to sober me. Suddenly I stopped, appalled to think how far I was from our base. In the twilight the mirage was dying. The horizon had stripped itself of its pomp, its palaces, its priestly vestments. It was the old desert horizon again.

"A fine day's work you've done! Night will overtake you. You won't be able to go on before daybreak, and by that time your tracks will have been blown away and you'll be properly nowhere."

In that case I may as well walk straight on. Why turn back? Why should I bring my ship round when I may find the sea straight ahead of me?

"When did you catch a glimpse of the sea? What makes you think you could walk that far? Meanwhile there's Prévot watching for you beside the *Simoon*. He may have been picked up by a caravan, for all you know."

Very good. I'll go back. But first I want to call out for help.

"Hi! Hi!"

By God! You can't tell me this planet is not inhabited. Where are its men?

"Hi! Hi!"

I was hoarse. My voice was gone. I knew it was ridiculous to croak like this, but—one more try:

"Hi! Hi!"

And I turned back.

I had been walking two hours when I saw the flames of the bonfire that Prévot, frightened by my long absence, had sent up. They mattered very little to me now.

Another hour of trudging. Five hundred yards away. A hundred yards. Fifty yards.

Good Lord!"

Amazement stopped me in my tracks. Joy surged up and filled my heart with its violence. In the firelight stood Prévot, talking to two Arabs who were leaning against the motor. He had not noticed me, for he was too full of his own joy. If only I had sat still and waited with him! I should have been saved already. Exultantly I called out:

"Hi! Hi!"

The two Bedouins gave a start and stared at me. Prévot left them standing and came forward to meet me. I opened my arms to him. He caught me by the elbow. Did he think I was keeling over? I said:

"At last, eh?"

"What do you mean?"

"The Arabs!"

"What Arabs?"

"Those Arabs there, with you."

Prévot looked at me queerly, and when he spoke I felt as if he was very reluctantly confiding a great secret to me:

"There are no Arabs here."

This time I know I am going to cry.

A man can go nineteen hours without water, and what have we drunk since last night? A few drops of dew at dawn. But the northeast wind is still blowing, still slowing up the process of our evaporation. To it, also, we owe the continued accumulation of high clouds. If only they would drift straight overhead and break into rain! But it never rains in the desert.

"Look here, Prévot. Let's rip up one of the parachutes and spread the sections out on the ground, weighed down with stones. If the wind stays in the same quarter till morning, they'll catch the dew and we can wring them out into one of the tanks."

We spread six triangular sections of parachute under the stars, and Prévot unhooked a fuel tank. This was as much as we could do for ourselves till dawn. But, miracle of miracles! Prévot had come upon an orange while working over the tank. We share it, and though it was little enough to men who could have used a few gallons of sweet water, still I was overcome with relief.

Stretched out beside the fire I looked at the glowing fruit and said to myself that men did not know what an orange was. "Here we are, condemned to death," I said to myself, "and still the certainty of dying cannot compare with the pleasure I am feeling. The joy I take from this half of an orange which I am holding in my hand is one of the greatest joys I have ever known."

I lay flat on my back, sucking my orange and counting the shooting stars. Here I was, for one minute infinitely happy. "Nobody can know anything of the world in which the individual moves and has his being," I reflected. "There is no guessing it. Only the man locked up in it can know what it is."

For the first time I understood the cigarette and glass of rum that are handed to the criminal about to be executed. I used to think that for a man to accept these wretched gifts at the foot of the gallows was beneath human dignity. Now I was learning that he took pleasure from them. People thought him courageous when he smiled as he smoked or drank. I knew now that he smiled because the taste gave him pleasure. People could not see that his perspective had changed, and that for him the last hour of his life was a life in itself.

We collected an enormous quantity of water—perhaps as much as two quarts. Never again would we be thirsty! We were saved; we had a liquid to drink!

I dipped my tin cup into the tank and brought up a beautifully yellow-green liquid the first mouthful of which nauseated me so that despite my thirst I had to catch my breath before swallowing it. I would have swallowed mud, I swear; but this taste of poisonous metal cut keener than thirst.

I glanced at Prévot and saw him going round and round with his eyes fixed to the ground as if looking for something. Suddenly he leaned forward and began to vomit without interrupting his spinning. Half a minute later it was my turn. I was seized by such convulsions that I went down on my knees and dug my fingers into the sand while I puked. Neither of us spoke, and for a quarter of an hour we remained thus shaken, bringing up nothing but a little bile.

After a time it passed and all I felt was a vague, distant nausea. But our last hope had fled. Whether our bad luck was due to a sizing on the parachute or to the magnesium lining of the tank, I never found out. Certain it was that we needed either another set of cloths or another receptacle.

Well, it was broad daylight and time we were on our way. This time we should strike out as fast as we could, leave this cursed plateau, and tramp till we dropped in our tracks. That was what Guillaumet had done in the Andes. I had been thinking of him all the day before and had determined to follow his example. I should do violence to the pilot's unwritten law, which is to stick by the ship; but I was sure no one would be along to look for us here.

Once again we discovered that it was not we who were shipwrecked, not we but those who were waiting for news of us, those who were alarmed by our silence, were already torn with grief by some atrocious and fantastic report. We could not but strive towards them. Guillaumet had done it, had scrambled towards his lost ones. To do so is a universal impulse.

"If I were alone in the world," Prévot said, "I'd lie down right here. Damned if I wouldn't."

East-northeast we tramped. If we had in fact crossed the Nile, each step was leading us deeper and deeper into the desert.

I don't remember anything about that day. I remember only my haste. I was hurrying desperately towards something—towards some finality. I remember also that I walked with my eyes to the ground, for the mirages were more than I could bear. From time to time we would correct our course by the compass, and now and again we would lie down to catch our breath. I remember having flung away my waterproof, which I had held on to as covering for the night. That is as much as I recall about the day. Of what happened when the chill of evening came, I remember more. But during the day I had simply turned to sand and was a being without mind.

When the sun set we decided to make camp. Oh, I knew as well as anybody that we should push on, that this one waterless night would finish us off. But we had brought along the bits of parachute, and if the poison was not in the sizing, we might get a sip of water next morning. Once again we spread our trap for the dew under the stars.

But the sky in the north was cloudless. The wind no longer had the same taste on the lip. It had moved into another quarter. Something was rustling against us, but this time it seemed to be the desert itself. The wild beast was stalking us, had us in its power. I could feel its breath in my face, could feel it lick my face and hands. Suppose I walked on: at the best I could do five or six miles more. Remember that in three days I had covered one hundred miles, practically without water.

And then, just as we stopped, Prévot said:

"I swear to you I see a lake!"

"You're crazy."

"Have you ever heard of a mirage after sunset?" he challenged.

I didn't seem able to answer him. I had long ago given up believing my own eyes. Perhaps it was not a mirage; but in that case it was a hallucination. How could Prévot go on believing? But he was stubborn about it.

"It's only twenty minutes off. I'll go have a look."

His mulishness got on my nerves.

"Go ahead!" I shouted. "Take your little constitutional. Nothing better for a man. But let me tell you, if your lake exists it is salt. And whether it's salt or not, it's a devil of away off. And besides, there is no damned lake!"

Prévot was already on his way, his eyes glassy. I knew the strength of these irresistible obsessions. I was thinking: "There are somnambulists who walk straight into locomotives." And I knew that Prévot would not come back. He would be seized by the vertigo of empty space and would be unable to turn back. And then he would keel over. He somewhere, and I somewhere else. Not that it was important.

Thinking thus, it struck me that this mood of resignation was doing me no good. Once when I was half drowned I had let myself go like this. Lying now flat on my face on the stony ground, I took this occasion to write a letter for posthumous delivery. It gave me a chance, also, to take stock of myself again. I tried to bring up a little saliva: how long was it since I had spit? No saliva. If I kept my mouth closed, a kind of glue sealed my lips together. It dried on the outside of the lips and formed a hard crust. However, I found I was still able to swallow, and I bethought me that I was still not seeing a blinding light in my eyes. Once I was treated to that radiant spectacle I might know that the end was a couple of hours away.

Night fell. The moon had swollen since I last saw it. Prévot was still not back. I stretched out on my back and turned these few data over in my mind. A familiar impression came over me, and I tried to seize it. I was . . . I was . . . I was at sea. I was on a ship going to South America and was stretched out, exactly like this, on the boat deck. The tip of the mast was swaying to and fro, very slowly, among the stars. That mast was missing tonight, but again I was at sea, bound for a port I was to make without raising a finger. Slave-traders had flung me on this ship.

I thought of Prévot who was still not back. Not once had I heard him complain. That was a good thing. To hear him whine would have been unbearable. Prévot was a man.

What was that! Five hundred yards ahead of me I could see the light of his lamp. He had lost his way. I had no lamp with which to signal back. I stood up and shouted, but he could not hear me.

A second lamp, and then a third! God in Heaven! It was a search party and it was me that they were hunting!

"Hi! Hi!" I shouted.

But they had not heard me. The three lamps were still signaling me.

"Tonight I am sane," I said to myself. "I am relaxed. I am not out of my head. Those are certainly three lamps and they are about five hundred yards off." I stared at them and shouted again, and again I gathered that they could not hear me.

Then, for the first and only time, I was really seized with panic. I could still run, I thought. "Wait! Wait!" I screamed. They seemed to be turning away from me, going off, hunting me elsewhere! And I stood tottering, tottering on the brink of life when there were arms out there ready to catch me! I shouted and screamed again and again.

They had heard me! An answering shout had come. I was strangling, suffocating, but I ran on, shouting as I ran, until I saw Prévot and keeled over.

When I could speak again I said: "Whew! When I saw all those lights . . ."

"What lights?"

God in Heaven, it was true! He was alone!

This time I was beyond despair. I was filled with a sort of dumb fury.

"What about your lake?" I rasped.

"As fast as I moved towards it, it moved back. I walked after it for about half an hour. Then it seemed still too far away, so I came back. But I am positive, now, that it is a lake."

"You're crazy. Absolutely crazy. Why did you do it? Tell me. Why?"

What had he done? Why had he done it? I was ready to weep with indignation, yet I scarcely knew why I was so indignant. Prévot mumbled his excuse:

"I felt I had to find some water. You . . . your lips were awfully pale."

Well! My anger died within me. I passed my hand over my forehead as if I were waking out of sleep. I was suddenly sad. I said:

"There was no mistake about it. I saw them as clearly as I see you now. Three lights there were. I tell you, Prévot, I saw them!"

Prévot made no comment.

"Well," he said finally, "I guess we're in a bad way."

In this air devoid of moisture the soil is swift to give off its temperature. It was already very cold. I stood up and stamped about. But soon a violent fit of trembling came over me. My dehydrated blood was moving sluggishly and I was pierced by a freezing chill which was not merely the chill of night. My teeth were chattering and my whole body had begun to twitch. My hand shook so that I could not hold an electric torch. I who had never been sensitive to cold was about to die of cold. What a strange effect thirst can have!

Somewhere, tired of carrying it in the sun, I had left my waterproof drop. Now the wind was growing bitter and I was learning that in the desert there is no place of refuge. The desert is as smooth as marble. By day it throws no shadow; by night it hands you over naked to the wind. Not a tree, not a hedge, not a rock behind which I could seek shelter. The wind was charging me like a troop of cavalry across open country. I turned and twisted to escape it: I lay down, stood up, lay down again, and still I was exposed to its freezing lash. I had no strength to run from the assassin and under the sabre-stroke I tumbled to my knees, my head between my hands.

A little later I pieced these bits together and remembered that I had struggled to my feet and had started to walk on, shivering as I went. I had started forward wondering where I was and then I had heard Prévot. His shouting had jolted me into consciousness.

I went back towards him, still trembling from head to foot—quivering with the attack of hiccups that was convulsing my whole body. To myself I said: "It isn't the cold. It's something else. It's the end." The simple fact was that I hadn't enough water in me. I had tramped too far yesterday and the day before when I was off by myself, and I was dehydrated.

The thought of dying of the cold hurt me. I preferred the phantoms of my mind, the cross, the trees, the lamps. At least they would have killed me by enchantment. But to be whipped to death like a slave! ...

Confound it! Down on my knees again! We had with us a little store of medicines—a hundred grammes of ninety per cent alcohol, the same of pure ether, and a small bottle of iodine. I tried to swallow a little of the ether: it was like swallowing a knife. Then I tried the alcohol: it contracted my gullet. I dug a pit in the sand, lay down in it, and flung handfuls of sand over me until all but my face was buried in it.

Prévot was able to collect a few twigs, and he lit a fire which soon burnt itself out. He wouldn't bury himself in the sand, but preferred to stamp round and round in a circle. That was foolish.

My throat stayed shut, and though I knew that was a bad sign, I felt better. I felt calm. I felt a peace that was beyond all hope. Once more, despite myself, I was journeying, trussed up on the deck of my slave-ship under the stars. It seemed to me that I was perhaps not in such a bad pass after all.

So long as I lay absolutely motionless, I no longer felt the cold. This allowed me to forget my body buried in the sand. I said to myself that I would not budge an inch, and would therefore never suffer again. As a matter of fact, we really suffer very little. Back of all these torments there is the orchestration of fatigue or of delirium, and we live on in a kind of picture-book, a slightly cruel fairy-tale.

A little while ago the wind had been after me with whip and spur, and I was running in circles like a frightened fox. After that came a time when I couldn't breathe. A great knee was crushing in my chest. A knee. I was writhing in vain to free myself from the weight of the angel who had overthrown me. There had not been a moment when I was alone in this desert. But now I have ceased to believe in my surroundings; I have withdrawn into myself, have shut my eyes, have not so much as batted an eyelid. I have the feeling that this torrent of visions is sweeping me away to a tranquil dream: so rivers cease their turbulence in the embrace of the sea.

Farewell, eyes that I loved! Do not blame me if the human body cannot go three days without water. I should never have believed that man was so truly the prisoner of the springs and freshets. I had no notion that our self-sufficiency was so circumscribed. We take it for granted that a man is able to stride straight out into the world. We believe that man is free. We never see the cord that binds him to wells and fountains, that umbilical cord by which he is tied to the womb of the world. Let man take but one step too many ... and the cord snaps.

Apart from your suffering, I have no regrets. All in all, it has been a good life. If I got free of this I should start right in again. A man cannot live a decent life in cities, and I need to feel myself live. I am not thinking of aviation. The airplane is a means, not an end. One doesn't risk one's life for a plane any more than a farmer ploughs for the sake of the plough. But the airplane is a means of getting away from towns and their bookkeeping and coming to grips with reality.

Flying is a man's job and its worries are a man's worries. A pilot's business is with the wind, with the stars, with night, with sand, with the sea. He strives to outwit the forces of nature. He stares in expectancy for the coming of dawn the way a gardener awaits the coming of spring. He looks forward to port as to a promised land, and truth for him is what lives in the stars.

I have nothing to complain of. For three days I have tramped the desert, have known the pangs of thirst, have followed false scents in the sand, have pinned my faith on the dew. I have struggled to rejoin my kind, whose very existence on earth I had forgotten. These are the cares of men alive in every fibre, and I cannot help thinking them more important than the fretful choosing of a night-club in which to spend the evening. Compare the one life with the other, and all things considered this is luxury! I have no regrets. I have gambled and lost. It was all in the day's work. At least I have had the unforgettable taste of the sea on my lips.

I am not talking about living dangerously. Such words are meaningless to me. The toreador does not stir me to enthusiasm. It is not danger I love. I know what I love. It is life.

The sky seemed to me faintly bright. I drew up one arm through the sand. There was a bit of the torn parachute within reach, and I ran my hand over it. It was bone dry. Let's see. Dew falls at dawn. Here was dawn risen and no moisture on the cloth. My mind was befuddled and I heard myself say: "There is a dry heart here, a dry heart that canno! know the relief of tears."

I scrambled to my feet. "We're off, Prévot," I said. "Our throats are still open. Get along, man!"

The wind that shrivels up a man in nineteen hours was now blowing out of the west. My gullet was not yet shut, but it was hard and painful and I could feel that there was a rasp in it. Soon that cough would begin that I had been told about and was now expecting. My tongue was becoming a nuisance. But most serious of all, I was beginning to see shining spots before my eyes. When those spots changed into flames, I should simply lie down.

The first morning hours were cool and we took advantage of them to get on at a good pace. We knew that once the sun was high there would be no more walking for us. We no longer had the right to sweat. Certainly not to stop and catch our breath. This coolness was merely the coolness of low humidity. The prevailing wind was coming from the desert, and under its soft and treacherous caress the blood was being dried out of us.

Our first day's nourishment had been a few grapes. In the next three days each of us ate half an orange and a bit of cake. If we had had anything left now, we couldn't have eaten it because we had no saliva with which to masticate it. But I had stopped being hungry. Thirsty I was, yes, and it seemed to me that I was suffering less from thirst itself than from the effects of thirst. Bullet hard. Tongue like plaster-of-Paris. A rasping in the throat. A horrible taste in the mouth.

All these sensations were new to me, and though I believed water could rid me of them, nothing in my memory associated them with water. Thirst had become more and more a disease and less and less a craving. I began to realize that the thought of water and fruit was now less agonizing than it had been. I was forgetting the radiance of the orange, just as I was forgetting the eyes under the hat-brim. Perhaps I was forgetting everything.

We had sat down after all, but it could not be for long. Nevertheless, it was impossible to go five hundred yards without our legs giving way. To stretch out on the sand would be marvelous—but it could not be.

The landscape had begun to change. Rocky places grew rarer and the sand was now firm beneath our feet. A mile ahead stood dunes and on those dunes we could see a scrubby vegetation. At least this sand was preferable to the steely surface over which we had been trudging. This was the golden desert. This might have been the Sahara. It was in a sense my country.

Two hundred yards had now become our limit, but we had determined to carry on until we reached the vegetation. Better than that we could not hope to do. A week later, when we went back over our traces in a car to have a look at the *Simoon,* I measured this last lap and found that it was just short of fifty miles. All told we had done one hundred and twenty-four miles.

The previous day I had tramped without hope. Today the word "hope" had grown meaningless. Today we were tramping simply because we were tramping. Probably oxen work for the same reason. Yesterday I had dreamed of a paradise of orange-trees. Today I would not give a button for paradise; I did not believe oranges existed. When I thought about myself I found in me nothing but a heart squeezed dry. I was tottering but emotionless. I felt no distress whatever, and in a way I regretted it: misery would have seemed to me as sweet as water. I might then have felt sorry for myself and commiserated with myself as with a friend. But I had not a friend left on earth.

Later, when we were rescued, seeing our burnt-out eyes men thought we must have called aloud and wept and suffered. But cries of despair, misery, sobbing grief are a kind of wealth, and we possessed no wealth. When a young girl is disappointed in love she weeps and knows sorrow. Sorrow is one of the vibrations that prove the fact of living. I felt no sorrow. I was the desert. I could no longer bring up a little saliva; neither could I any longer summon those moving visions towards which I should have loved to stretch forth arms. The sun had dried up the springs of tears in me.

And yet, what was that? A ripple of hope went through me like a faint breeze over a lake. What was this sign that had awakened my instinct before knocking on the door of my consciousness? Nothing had changed, and yet everything was changed. This sheet of sand, these low hummocks and sparse tufts of verdure that had been a landscape, were now become a stage setting. Thus far the stage was empty, but the scene was set. I looked at Prévot. The same astonishing thing had happened to him as to me, but he was as far from guessing its significance as I was.

I swear to you that something is about to happen. I swear that life has sprung in this desert. I swear that this emptiness, this stillness, has suddenly become more stirring than a tumult on a public square.

"Prévot! Footprints! We are saved!"

We had wandered from the trail of the human species; we had cast ourselves forth from the tribe; we had found ourselves alone on earth and forgotten by the universal migration; and here, imprinted in the sand, were the divine and naked feet of man!

"Look, Prévot, here two men stood together and then separated."

"Here a camel knelt."

"Here . . ."

But it was not true that we were already saved. It was not enough to squat down and wait. Before long we should be past saving. Once the cough has begun, the progress made by thirst is swift.

Still, I believed in that caravan swaying somewhere in the desert, heavy with its cargo of treasure.

We went on. Suddenly I heard a cock crow. I remembered what Guillaumet had told me: "Towards the end I heard cocks crowing in the Andes. And I heard the railway train." The instant the cock crowed I thought of Guillaumet and I said to myself: "First it was my eyes that played tricks on me. I suppose this is another of the effects of thirst. Probably my ears have merely held out longer than my eyes." But Prévot grabbed my arm:

"Did you hear that?"

"What?"

"The cock."

"Why . . . why, yes, I did."

To myself I said: "Fool! Get it through your head! This means life!"

I had one last hallucination—three dogs chasing one another. Prévot looked, but could not see them. However, both of us waved our arms at a Bedouin. Both of us shouted with all the breath in our bodies, and laughed for happiness.

But our voices could not carry thirty yards. The Bedouin on his slow-moving camel had come into view from behind a dune and now he was moving slowly out of sight. The man was probably the only Arab in this desert, sent by a demon to materialize and vanish before the eyes of us who could not run.

We saw in profile on the dune another Arab. We shouted, but our shouts were whispers. We waved our arms and it seemed to us that they must fill the sky with monstrous signals. Still the Bedouin stared with averted face away from us.

At last, slowly, slowly he began a right angle turn in our direction. At the very second when he came face to face with us, I thought, the curtain would come down. At the very second when his eyes met ours, thirst would vanish and by this man would death and the mirages be wiped out. Let this man but make a quarter-turn left and the world is changed. Let him but bring his torso round, but sweep the scene with a glance, and like a god he can create life.

The miracle had come to pass. He was walking towards us over the sand like a god over the waves.

The Arab looked at us without a word. He placed his hands upon our shoulders and we obeyed him: we stretched out upon the sand. Race, language, religion were forgotten. There was only this humble nomad with the hands of an archangel on our shoulders.

Face to the sand, we waited. And when the water came, we drank like calves with our faces in the basin, and with a greediness which alarmed the Bedouin so that from time to time he pulled us back. But as soon as his hand fell away from us we plunged our faces anew into the water.

Water, thou hast no taste, no color, no odor; canst not be defined, art relished while ever mysterious. Not necessary to life, but rather life itself, thou fillest us with a gratification that exceeds the delight of the senses. By thy might, there return into us treasures that we had abandoned. By thy grace, there are released in us all the dried-up runnels of our heart. Of the riches that exist in the world, thou art the rarest and also the most delicate—thou so pure within the bowels of the earth! A man may die of thirst lying beside a magnesium spring. He may die within reach of a salt lake. He may die though he hold in his hand a jug of dew, if it be inhabited by evil salts. For thou, water, art a proud divinity, allowing no alternation, no foreignness in thy being. And the joy that thou spreadest is an infinitely simple joy.

You, Bedouin of Libya who saved our lives, though you will dwell for ever in my memory yet I shall never be able to recapture your features. You are Humanity and your face comes into my mind simply as man incarnate. You, our beloved fellowman, did not know who we might be, and yet you recognized us without fail. And I, in my turn, shall recognize you in the faces of all mankind. You came towards me in an aureole of charity and magnanimity bearing the gift of water. All my friends and all my enemies marched towards me in your person. It did not seem to me that you were rescuing me: rather did it seen that you were forgiving me. And I felt I had no enemy left in all the world.

This is the end of my story. Lifted on to a camel, we went on for three hours. Then, broken with weariness, we asked to be set down at a camp while the cameleers went on ahead for help. Towards six in the evening a car manned by armed Bedouins came to fetch us. A half-hour later we were set down at the house of a Swiss engineer named Raccaud who was operating a soda factory beside saline deposits in the desert. He was unforgettably kind to us. By midnight we were in Cairo.

I awoke between white sheets. Through the curtains came the rays of a sun that was no longer an enemy. I spread butter and honey on my bread. I smiled. I recaptured the savor of my childhood and all its marvels. And I read and re-read the telegram from those dearest to me in all the world whose three words had shattered me:

"So terribly happy!"

21

Tank Trap

ANDRÉ MALRAUX

A ROAD forever the same edged by trees forever the same, and the rocks of Flanders forever as hard beneath the treads of the tanks. The monotony of the columns advancing across the plain. Our last stretch of monotony. From now on we shall know exaltation or fear; we are moving up to the front lines. Our attention smolders beneath the state of stupor, the heat, the din of the motors and the hammering of the treads that seem to pound our heads as they do the road. I know how we look when we emerge from our tanks after a long march, our faces flabby and our eyes blinking as though we had been stunned—faces of comedians beneath our lansquenets' helmets.

To infinity, the Flemish night. Behind us, nine months of barracks and billetings; the time it takes to make a man.

Nine months ago, in a hotel in Quercy, some young voices were discussing the only thing people talked about then. A smell of gasoline, of dust and sun-scorched flowers came in through the window, and I heard someone say, "To me the war isn't just a war. It's another war. And I begin to realize I'm getting old."

The servant girls could not tear themselves from the radio. They were old women. One morning I passed two of them on the stairs. They were running with little steps up to their room, and tears streamed down their worn faces. This is how I learned that the German army had entered Poland.

In the afternoon, in Beaulieu-de-Corrèze, I saw the mobilization posters. The church of Beaulieu has one of the finest Romanesque tympana in the world, the only one in which, behind the arms of the Christ held out to the world, the sculptor has represented those of the cross as a menacing shadow. A tropical shower streamed down on the village. Before the church there is a statue of the Virgin; as they had done every year for five hundred years, to celebrate the grape harvest, the vineyard growers had hung one of the loveliest clusters on the hand of the Infant. The rain ceased. On the deserted square the posters which had become unglued began to curl down; before the eternal language of the old sculptor, the drops of water on the cluster would slip from grape to grape and fall with a tiny splash into a puddle, one after another, in the silence.

Our tanks roll toward the German lines. There are four of us in ours. There is nothing to do but to follow this night road and get closer to the war. The life of each of my companions becomes a destiny: it is perhaps tonight that they are going to die. A destiny forever unintelligible. Like my own.

I saw them leave by the thousands, at the beginning of September, the anonymous ones, who are like my three comrades. Five million men went off to the barracks without a word; that is already a thing of the past, a past which in memory is only a great silence.

On the Place de Moulins the loudspeaker was announcing the first battles. Evening was falling. Two or three thousand draftees listened, awkward in their new uniforms because they were new, or in their old ones because they were dirty. Not one of them said a word. On all the roads the men were joining the colors, the bitter-faced women were leading requisitioned horses to the depots. There was a somber firmness in all this, the resoluteness of the peasant before a flood. They were going out to meet the calamity.

In almost the same way my three companions are riding tonight toward the German tanks and guns, along the dreary road.

They believe themselves to be very different from one another. They are only around thirty, but of the four of us I am the one who seems the youngest. The soldiers who at the beginning of 1914 appeared to me to be grandfathers were perhaps of the same age as these. Now I know what a *poilu* is: a fighter who is too old to be called a soldier.

They are half-peasants, half-workers, and jacks-of-all-trades first and foremost.

Bonneau, the mechanic, ought to be in the engine compartment. I am sure he is in the communication alley. In all these tanks that follow one behind the other down the dark road there is not one mechanic who has not left the engine compartment where regulations require him to be. As Bonneau cannot talk to any of us, no doubt he talks to himself, his endless monologue crushed by the hammering of the treads.

When he first came to the squadron in the custody of the gendarmes, in a leather jacket, unshaved, he looked so brawny that the captain called for the roll of corporals and was delighted to find among them a professional boxer. The latter promptly received delivery of Bonneau, not without working himself into a fine funk. I have rarely seen real courage among devotees of boxing.

There was no boxing match, however. Merely, to begin with, a certain uneasiness. Bonneau arrived rigged out like a pimp, accustomed to inspiring contempt or fear, and all the more anxious to inspire fear as he more often met contempt. But common soldiers are not much given to contempt, and when Bonneau, sticking out his jaw, would ask, "What're you lookin' at me that way for?" he would be answered by a casual "Me? I'm not even lookin' at you . . ."

He claimed to have killed a man in a brawl, which undoubtedly was untrue, for he would have been detailed to the disciplinary battalions. But the office was not long in letting it be known in the barracks-rooms that he had three convictions for assault on his record. The common people are much less impressed than the middle class by the romance of murder. In their eyes the murderer is only a particular species, like the wolf. The only question was whether Bonneau actually belonged to the species, whether what he told was true or "all a cock-and-bull story." Slaves have a strong instinct for lying.

The only one who believed in this romance was himself. He was full of stories of prison and pimps. To avoid shaving and keep his mug looking like a killer's he announced that he was growing a goatee; and he had the accent of the outer slums of Paris, and the rebel songs of Montéhus were always on his lips while he was on fatigue, to which he was perpetually condemned. The child of misfortune. . . . When the whole squadron, jammed in a stairway, was waiting for shoes to be distributed, he would suddenly burst out singing "Le Légionnaire," and then a monologue would begin. "Ah, I had the swellest little woman, I can tell you! I sure was crazy about her! They got her, those cops did. . . ." We could guess that behind this lay some story of a hospital in which "they" referred both to the doctors and to all who abide by the law; and his suspicious barracks-room mates, though they would nudge one another like schoolboys listening to a smart-aleck, would prudently work out complicated schemes to prevent him from ever being on barracks-room duty. And they became initiated to a folklore of music-hall denizens of which all of them, to be sure, were not wholly ignorant: the victim of society whom drunkenness or sexual vice has made an outcast; the troublemaker of the disciplinary battalions; the outlaw who fights alone against the whole police in some assassin's hideout; the notorious Bonnot (whose name he surely did not forget he almost bore) who fires on the Prefect through the crook of his arm; but above all the heroic and sentimental pimp, wicked but above-board, faithful to his friends and a murderer for love, who escapes from the penitentiary and ends his dark career among the crocodiles of the Maroni River. For Bonneau's hell, whether the damned who inhabit it are epic figures or wretches, has only one circle, and it is a circle of victims.

When he brought in a wounded finch and announced his intention of raising it, the fear grew. For my companions the murderer is first of all a madman.

Each barracks-room had methods of camouflage that were the more ingenious as the lights-out regulation was the more rigorous. The non-commissioned officers would remove the light bulbs, but other bulbs would emerge from under the bolsters when the time came. One evening two plugs got out of order. Bonneau announced that "he had worked in electricity," went down and secretly struggled with the switchboards of the entire building, with the result that the following evening not a single plug would work in his room or in four of the others. In the dark someone growled: "How the hell do they get that way? Of all the damn fool things! Here I'm an electrician, but I wouldn't dare to go tinkering around without being told. And then this guy comes along!" By the way the door of the first barracks-room slammed every-one understood it was he who was coming in; suddenly all was quiet. Then began a muffled altercation, and one voice became very clear, calm and hard, a voice which was not that of the boxer-corporal:

"Look here, Bonneau, we're getting damn well fed up with you. Tough guys don't go over big with me. If they try to monkey with my light bulb, there's going to be trouble. And if you don't like it, here's my face." A face appeared, fully illuminated in the small circle of light projected by a flashlight. "So if you're looking for it tomorrow it won't be hard for you to find it!"

It was the first time I heard Pradé.

Whereupon Bonneau began to explain in the dark that "It wasn't his fault, the current—the fuses . . ." I was waiting for all of them to accuse him of being yellow. The general impression was that "He wasn't exactly pulling in his horns, that he was on the level, and didn't want to start a row when he knew he was in the wrong. . . ." So he wasn't so crazy, after all. The squadron was getting ready to adopt him, but the barracks-room remained without light.

A tank driver, who before this had been driving a bus, began to sing "Le P'tit Quinquin." There were quite a few soldiers from Flanders, but it was not the memories it brought up that gave so much force to his song; it was the slowness. He sang it as a dirge. And, in thus catching the true rhythm of the old-time laments, he also caught their nasal quality, as though here in the dark a miserable voice would have been all that was needed to give its full meaning to a song of misery. And the soldiers kept asking for stanza after stanza, as they would ask for glass after glass at the canteen, determined to get drunk with sadness in this war that was like a prison.

The singer, tired of this inglorious music, intoned the great aria from *La Tosca*. With catastrophic results. An embarrassed silence followed the last howls; the bus-driver growled angrily, "All right, if you gentlemen don't enjoy it!" and went back to bed, and the awkward feeling of a destroyed communion was added to the melancholy of the first song. Bonneau was forgotten. Everyone sank into his private bitterness. Who was the first to pull out his wife's picture from his pocketbook to look at it in the clandestine glow of a flashlight? Five minutes later, in little groups, the pictures were being passed around, four or five peaked caps around a muffled light, a voice bursting out angrily when occasionally a snapshot would drop from between clumsy fingers into the hay. No one, for that matter, gave a damn about the others' wives, and looked at them only in order to be able to show their own. And yet, in this confidential light, they appeared like secrets, the dresses suddenly suggesting the husbands' lives better than their own pictures in civilian clothes would have done. Pradé's wife is a housekeeper, hard and wooden, with her hair firmly parted down the middle; Bonneau was the only one to possess four photographs, one more whorish than the other. And little Léonard with the beet-red nose—our radio-operator tonight—reticent and having to be coaxed, finally pulled out a post card of a very beautiful girl in a glamorous feather-costume. A few lines were written at the bottom. And the buddies, their heads glued together under the nose fantastically lighted from below, deciphered by bringing the flashlight up close, "To my dear little darling Louis" and the signature of one of the glories of the music halls.

Léonard used to be a fireman at the Casino de Paris. Each day, with the same admiration, he would watch the star come backstage, all blushing from the applause. He claims he never spoke to her. His face is appealing in spite of his extraordinary snout; gentle spaniel's eyes, and the kind of expression, sometimes so poignant, that knows nothing of pride. Was the dancer touched by this unwearying admiration, or did she yield to a whim? One evening when she had received a great ovation, "So you could still hear the applause all the way up the stairs," she led him into her dressing room and went to bed with him. "And then, the thing that got me was. . . . Anyway when we were in bed, well, she looked at my uniform on the chair, and then says to me as if she was going to jump out, 'Look here, you're not on the police force, I hope?' 'Of course not, can't you see it's a fireman's!' 'Because if you were . . .' Can you beat it, she'd been seeing me every night, and she didn't know what a fireman's uniform looked like! Of course I was younger then . . ."

Everyone has his dream—of Marlene Dietrich, or Mistinguett, or the Duchess of Windsor. But it remains a dream. And they do not regard this buddy on whom the gods have smiled—the dumbbell of the barracks-room—as merely lucky, but in a dim way as one predestined. His curly little head and red nose are there to prove to them the mysterious role of love, and what fascinates them, without their knowing it, beneath the star's caprice, is the love potion of Iseult.

"And what happened after that?" they asked in chorus, and their fingers tingled as they once more held the photograph.

"The days that followed she didn't even give me a look; so I got the idea. . . ." He answered without resentment, even without resignation; to him this was as it should be.

Their hereditary experience has not made them casual about good fortune.

Naturally, after Léonard's photo the greatest success was Bonneau's harem. He was definitely being adopted by the squadron. And little by little—seeing him stoop during the marches to pick up a paring-knife, put it in his cartridge-belt with a new sermon—"Got to be careful; I'm suspicious of these tools," invariably ending with "It might be of some use"—they caught on to the fact that this terror of the music halls was at heart a junk collector. Anyone knows what a junk collector is. Then time brought out a new facet of this anarchist's personality. He was a respecter of priests. "My old lady didn't teach me much," he would say, "but she taught me to respect those fellows. Why'd the State take away everything they had? I say it's robbery. It's the Rothschilds, the bankers, guys like that who done it; they always take from the poor!" He would sport the Ruhr occupation medal, and worshipped Captain de Mortemart "under whom I served in the hussars at Strasbourg, who was nothing like these fat-heads around here, and knew how to command, always ready to take off his stripes and say to a fellow: Come on outside if you're a man!" Quite prepared, if he got to be corporal, to think of himself as a model soldier—hard-headed and soft-hearted, though in no mood to give up the songs of Montéhus. Member of a company union, and respectful of respectability.

"Come, Bonneau," the lieutenant would say, "you're not as bad as you'd like to make out!"

"Me, Lieutenant? Why, I'm not bad! It's the others who've made me bad." And his thick lips would protrude, his black eyebrows lift, and it was as if the mask of ferocity that was torn off suddenly revealed his incurably childish soul.

More brutal than bad, indeed. He bore Pradé no grudge for his speech. We are tank mates, and often go to the canteen together. The minute Bonneau begins to rave, Pradé slowly shrugs his shoulders, looks at him and says nothing. Bonneau splutters, conscious of being in the presence of a man of a different race—the kind that never dreams.

Thus one day we were sitting with a liter of red wine before us, after listening to a lecture to which we had been sent, in columns of fours, to learn about the necessity of dismembering Germany. I was curious to know what the soldiers thought of this noble speech, for which the dinner hour had been put off.

"Would do better to let us eat on time!" said Bonneau. And Léonard: "Me, I like to listen to educated people . . ." And others around us: "I couldn't understand it all; he talks like a book. The hell with it, what we want to do is go home!" Still another: "Fine words to make us do things that are ignoble . . .!" "What things?" A vague gesture. All were thinking, deep down, that no one would ask them their opinion about dismembering Germany; and that when the powerful wanted to convince them of anything they had reason to be on their guard. Pradé, tight-lipped like the Asiatics whom he resembles by his flat face and his slant eyes, again had said nothing.

We started back toward the barracks-room. We had gone a good hundred meters when he made up his mind and, not looking at me at first, said with his heavy Eastern accent and his very slow delivery, "It's about what you were asking the boys: what they think of the youngster's speech. Pradé thinks that if they're talking to soldiers it's one thing, and if they're talking to French citizens it's another. As a soldier I'm ready to listen to anything. I won't understand any more than I understand! But if they talk to me as a citizen, that's something else. That's something else!" Whatever he says, he always seems to be talking angrily to some invisible liar. "In that case I don't like to be forced to think. And I don't like to be told a lot of bosh. I know something about those Fritzes. When they hit our town in 1915, everybody was in the cellars. They banged on the doors with their riflebutts. I was just a kid, and they sent me up to let them in. I was shaking like this. . . . Some of them boxed our ears, and others gave us bread. It's like everywhere else!" He repeats, with his toothless jaw stuck out, still indignant at the imaginary liar, "It's like everywhere else!" and he adds in the same tone, "Only *they* don't talk about citizens!"

It often seems to me that these soldiers with whom I am living are of another age. France is still full of faces whose Gothic character is made manifest by the uniform. As civilians' faces they seemed merely those of peasants. It is full, too, of ancient souls, and in listening to Pradé I seemed to hear the old Republican dignity speaking, a voice barely changed in the course of a century. He took a liking for me, and confided to me that a brother of his, who was a hothead, had returned from the brigades of Spain. "And when a fellow gets back from there, you can take Pradé's word for it, there's no use trying to look for a job!"

One day he came over to talk to me and, in the same slow voice, in a tone that seems to accentuate everything with the fist, and make of each sentence the peremptory summary of a meditation, said, "The captain's orderly is leaving. Of all the things you can do in the army the job of orderly is still one of the least silly." I waited. When he comes and talks to me in this way, starting with a general affirmation, it is to ask me for help or advice. He went on, "There's nothing worse than an officer." "Then why put yourself in his clutches, especially in a servant's job?" "A servant (and once more he bares his tooth-stumps bitterly), who isn't a servant around here? I say if you're an orderly you have to deal more with the wife than with the old son of a bitch. A fellow who's serious and does his work: I say, who does his work (and that gesture he so often makes, which means: I'm serving you, but leave me alone; I'm a slave, but I don't want to know you), a fellow like that can have peace. With an officer, and all those who're between them and us, you can never have peace. A woman is nothing but a woman; but anyway she doesn't wear stripes!"

I did not dare to use the word dignity, and resorted to circumlocutions. But he used it immediately, "If a man has dignity he has it wherever he goes; otherwise I say he hasn't got it anywhere!" And as I tried to explain to him that the military relationship is at least impersonal, he bared his worn teeth in a bitter smile; and I felt that he was right, that he could live for ten years side by side with a man he doesn't like and see him die as though the man had never existed.

None of my comrades has taught me more about the people of his country. At heart, the Frenchman is a solitary animal, obsessed with defending himself against everything that is not his own little cell. His definitive attitude toward the world is one of suspicion. "When I got the pension for my accident," Pradé said, "they would have loved to find out how much I was getting. They could have, through the postman. But I asked not to have the money sent to my house. . . ." And, in the tone of one who has surmounted all obstacles to carry out a great design, slowly striking his fist upon a table that wasn't there, he said, "I had it sent to another address!"

His son is the only absolute in that humiliating, dismal and harrowing thing called Life. When he asks me if I think the war will be a long one, it isn't because he wants to know how long he will be in the army. "Sonny's eleven, that's a little more than I was in the last war. That's what prevented me getting an education. They managed to send me to Sunday school, all right, but they didn't manage to send me to school. . . . The kid's smart. I'd get him a scholarship. I don't like to ask, but I'd get a scholarship. What's goin' to happen to all those scholarships, with this war? For him to go on studying I'd have to work, and all I'm working at is playing the idiot with a gun. And afterwards, suppose he loses two years, there's nothing can be done about it; it'll be too late. He would have been the first one in the family to get an education! A kid at that age's got to have some kind of guidance. I could do it myself, at a pinch. Not when he got past his certificate, but I could now, except for the spelling. I used to be good at arithmetic. I can guide him. The wife, what can she do? She's one of a large family . . ." And, in that tone of summary judgment that he always resorts to, melancholy this time, instead of being vehement, "She's not very bright, my wife . . ."

What does he think about the war? I don't believe he knows himself. Not that he is incapable of reflection, like Léonard or Bonneau; but the things our propaganda tells him don't count for him. He is like someone who has seen three of his children die of tuberculosis and to whom someone should come and talk about original sin when his fourth child came down with it. "This summer I had a little time. I gathered some wood. I sawed my wood. In pieces big as this, very even. In my shed I've piled, I don't know, a thousand, fifteen hundred kilos!" and as always slowly summarizing, "Now, it's the Fritzes who'll burn my wood. . . ."

It is he who is driving. Since on our tanks, though they are quite new, the phone system does not work between the tank commander and the driver, I am joined to him by two pieces of string, attached to his arms, that I hold in my hand.

In spite of the shattering din of the treads, we suddenly seem to have returned to silence. The tanks have just left the road. Like the boat pushed clear of the sand, like the plane lifting from the ground, we enter into our element. Our muscles, contracted by the vibration of the armor plate, by the endless hammering of the treads on the road, relax, become attuned to the peace of the moonlit night. . . .

For a minute we roll on thus, liberated, among squat orchards blooming in the night and trailing banks of mist. With the smell of castor oil in my nostrils, I nervously hold my strings, ready to stop the tank for firing; the pitching is too great even in these apparently even fields to fire while in motion; our shells would pass above the orchards. Since we have left the road and the few forms barely visible may become targets, we are more aware of our rocking motion, like that of angular galleys. The clouds mask the moon. We enter the wheat fields.

This is the moment when the war begins.

The feeling of marching on the enemy has no name, and yet it is as specific, as strong as sexual desire or anguish. The universe is an indifferent menace. We steer by the compass and can make out only what is outlined against the sky: telegraph posts, roofs, treetops; the orchards, barely more distinct than the mist, have disappeared, the darkness seems to be massed on the level of the fields that rock us or furiously shake us. If a tread breaks, we are dead or prisoners. I know with what intensity Pradé's slant eyes are watching his instrument board. I feel the string in my hands each second, as though a jerk were about to give me warning. And we are not yet in contact. The war awaits us a little farther on, perhaps behind the rolling hills bristling here and there with concrete telegraph poles that are phosphorescent in the moonlight which has just reappeared.

The great blurred lines of the darkling plain, the banks of mist that emerge again in all their whiteness, rise and fall with the tossing of the tank. Against the jerking, against the frenzied vibrations the moment we find ourselves again on hard ground between wheat fields, our whole bodies are contracted as in an automobile at the moment of an accident. I clutch the turret no less with the muscles of my back than with my hands. Were the furious vibrations to crack one of the feedpipes, the tank, with one tread paralyzed, would await the shells while turning round upon itself like an epileptic cat. But the treads continue to hammer the fields and the rocks, and through the observation slits of my turret, beyond what I can make out of short-stalked wheat, mist, orchards, I watch the rise and fall against the night sky of the horizon as yet unstreaked by the flame of any gun.

The German positions are before us. In front, our tanks can be effectively hit only by telescopic sight and direct fire. We have confidence in our armor plate. The enemy is not German; it is the breaking of a tread, the mine and the trap.

The most obsessing is the trap. We don't speak of the mine any more than about death; one gets blown up or one doesn't; it's not a subject of conversation. But the trap is. We have listened to stories of the last war—and in training school we have seen the modern pits, their bottoms slanted to prevent the tank from raising its bow, their four anti-tank guns set off by the fall. Léonard, Bonneau, Pradé—there is not one of us who has not imagined himself in the cross-fire of the four anti-tank guns, at the moment when they are about to fire on him. And the world of the anti-tank traps is vast, from this sure death to the hastily camouflaged excavation in which the fall sets off a signal for a heavy gun trained on it somewhere in the distance, to the pit on which no gun is leveled. Of the old communion between man and the earth, nothing remains. These wheat fields in which we pitch in the dark are no longer wheat fields, but camouflages. There is no longer an earth of harvests, only an earth of traps, an earth of mines; and I have the feeling that the tank bounds of its own accord toward some self-dug ambush, that the future species are tonight beginning their own combat, beyond the human adventure. . . .

On a low hill a series of very rapid mauve flames finally appear: the German heavy artillery. Was their brief flare invisible in the bright moonlight, or has the firing just begun? It spreads quickly from our right to our left, as far as our swaying turrets enable us to see, as though an immense match were scratching the whole horizon. But near us there is not an explosion. Our motors cover every sound; we are undoubtedly out of the wheat (I cannot see twenty meters away), for the furious forge of the treads begins to hammer us again. For a second I bring the tank to a stop.

From the silence that sweeps over me rises the cannonade whose reverberations are carried away by the wind. And to my ears, in which the din of our own tank still dimly rumbles, the same wind, beneath the explosions of a few shells behind us and the hurried pounding of the treads of our companions, brings a deep forest sound, the shudder of great curtains of poplar trees: the advance of the French tanks whose invisible columns extend into the depth of the night. . . .

The firing ceases. Behind us, then in front, a few very scattered shells still explode and, after their garnet-red flashing has subsided, a silence of expectation rises again, a silence teaming with the passage of our tanks.

We start off again, force our speed in order to rejoin our invisible group. The hammering of the treads has resumed and we are once more deafened, Pradé and I again glued to the armor plate and the controls, our aching eyes on the watch for a new bursting of rocks and earth above a red explosion which we will not hear. The wind drives toward the German lines a rout of enormous clouds and pools of stars.

Nothing is slower than a march to battle. To our left in the May mist, the other two tanks of our group advance; beyond, the other groups; still beyond and behind, all the sections plow forward beneath the moon. I am sure that Léonard and Bonneau, blind against the plates, know it as well as Pradé, glued to his periscope, as I to my observation slits. I feel even in my body, just as I do the slapping of the treads on the clayey ground, the parallel drive of our tanks through the night. Other tanks, on the other side, are advancing toward us in the same bright night. Men equally tense, equally listless, but who for seven years have been formed for war. To my left our dim bows rise and fall against the less opaque background of the wheat. Behind them advance the shock regiments in the light tanks; and, further off, the deep masses of the French infantry. The peasants whom I saw marching in silence to join the army on all the roads of France, at the beginning of September, are converging toward the sinister crawling of our squad across the Flemish plain. Ah, may victory remain with those who have made war without loving it!

Does this exaltation that sweeps over me come from the communion of an obligation met at the cost of blood, does it come from that which is always obscure and solemn in human sacrifice? How I want none of these men to die! In the young wheat our furrows glisten in the moonlight. . . .

Suddenly all the nearby forms disappear, except the treetops; nothing remains of the ground; darkness envelops the tanks that accompany us. No doubt a cloud masks the moon, which is too high in the sky now for me to see it through the observation slits. And again we think of the mine toward which this movement of well-oiled gears is taking us through the springy wheat, and the comradely shadows that surround us vanish. Cut off from all that is not Pradé, Bonneau, Léonard, Berger: a crew—alone.

Léonard's hand passes between my hip and the turret, places a piece of paper beside the compass. I turn on a light and my eyes, blinded by the sudden glare, finally are able to decipher, letter by letter, in a whirl of red suns, "Tank B–21 encountered trap."

Pradé has turned out the light. Through the rifts in the clouds, the moonlight passes in a succession of shafts across the sky. Now our tanks emerge a little behind us; we had outdistanced them. Then, one hundred meters ahead, a shell bursts, exactly as in a motion picture, even to the vibration of our armor plate. The smoke, which for a second seemed red, is beaten down by the wind, a strange lusterless black beneath the moon. . . .

Other explosions. Very few of them. It is not even a barrage. Our whole squad advances more rapidly, without as yet putting on full speed. What can be the purpose of this scattered shelling?

My glance returns to my vaguely luminous compass which quivers, deviates, returns, seems to want to escape the direction, and, with the jerks of the steering lever returns again, like our vainly and wearilessly contested lives around their destiny. From time to time I have to tug at one of the strings, rectify Pradé's direction. The tank tends to go off its course on the ground which has become uneven and very hard. Suddenly we feel ourselves slipping in a panicky way on springy ground, and . . .

Underneath me someone yells. Is it Bonneau? It is not true that one sees one's life pass before one at the moment of death. I try to get my balance in the slanting turret, but Léonard is clutching my legs with both arms, shouting, "Pradé! Pradé!" I hear him through my thighs, and his yells are thin, sharp as bird cries in the cataclysmic silence which has settled since Pradé, feeling the fall, jammed on the brakes.

The tank trap.

I yell, too. The starting up again of the motor covers my whole voice. Pradé has started going forward.

"Back! Back!"

I pull with all my might on the right string; it is broken.

The shells which were falling only spasmodically were those that were blowing up the located traps. The ground vibrates with the noise of the free tanks which, all around our death, are passing by. . . .

Pradé had merely been giving himself momentum, and now goes into reverse. How many seconds before the shell? All of us keep our heads sunk between our shoulders as hard as we are able, and Bonneau is still yelling. The tank, precariously tipped forward, its tail in the air like a Japanese fish, plunges its rear end at an angle into the wall of the pit, vibrating, as an ax quivers in a treetrunk. It slips, falls back. Is it blood or sweat that flows along my nose? We have fallen lopsided. Bonneau, who is still screaming, tries to open the side door, succeeds but closes it again. It must now open almost underneath the tank. One tread goes round in empty space; Pradé lurches the tank forward on the other, and it drops back into an upright position, as though it were crashing into a second trap. My helmet bangs into the turret, and it seems to me that my head swells and swells, although the expectation of the shell keeps burying it between my shoulders like a screw. If the bottom of the trap is soft, we are stuck, and the shell can take its time. No, the tank advances, backs, again goes forward. The bottoms of modern traps wedge the tanks, and the anti-tank guns would already have fired. Which leaves the located traps. The rear wall is unassailable; if the front wall is vertical or slanting we can perhaps get out. . . . If we are in a funnel we will never get out. I strain my eyes till they ache, in order to see; drops glide toward my temples; my orbits are cold with sweat. The invisible wall is surely close by. Bonneau, crazed, keeps opening and shutting his door with all his might, and the armor plate, in spite of the din of the motor in this hole, resounds like a bell. Why doesn't the shell come? Léonard has let go my legs and is violently kicking them. How have I understood that he wants to open the door of my turret? The shell will burst in the trap. One can't get out of a trap; running out of a tank is even more foolish that to remain paralyzed within, between a madman who tries to break your legs and another, crazed with fear of leaving and fear of remaining, who with precipitous blows of armor plate beats the sinister tom-tom of delirium. My calmness is not that of a calm man; I am beyond the crisis. I leave the turret, bend down to go over to Pradé, who suddenly turns on the lights. The shell will not come; they are killing only out in the night.

Léonard, during the movement that I made to bend down and get into the communication alley, has slipped into the turret in my place. He finally opens the door, stops, with his mouth open; he does not jump out, but suddenly crouches and turns around toward me without saying anything; his toper's nose is extraordinarily red in the raw light; terror leaves his head motionless, but he shrugs his shoulders against the black background of the door opening upon the trap. The treads do not catch. We are in a funnel. On hands and knees I crawl down toward Pradé. I take hold of Bonneau, who still keeps shaking the side door while screaming at the top of his lungs, and send him rolling. "Shut up!" I yell. "Me? I'm not saying anything . . ." answers his normal voice which I recognize in spite of the roar of the motor. He gets up, his helmet striking the ceiling of the alley full force, falls back on his knees. His movie-gangster's mug, in the face of death, has assumed an expression of frightful innocence. He looks at me with the rolling eyes, the quivering of the whole face of children who know they are in for a good spanking. "I'm not saying anything . . ." he repeats (at the same time, like myself, like all of us, he listens, expecting the shell). Flinging the door open again, he fixes his eyes on mine, and, with his hands open, his helmet dented by the bump, like a felt hat, shaking with the jolts of the treads, he screams, screams without averting his eyes from me.

I get alongside of Pradé, am able to straighten up a little. We are at the extreme front of the tank whose bow is lifting, and little by little my suspended body rises as though the illuminated tank in the trap were offering it to death as a sacrifice. Are we going to fall back again? At last I am firmly braced. All my strength goes into burying my head between my shoulders. The treads are still slipping; my oily, blood-covered hands scrape the air in the manner of burrowing animals, as though I myself were the tank. . . .

The treads catch!

Can it be a camouflaged ditch? In a trap the treads would not catch. Will we get out before the shell comes? My three companions have become lifelong friends. Like an explosion, a door is still banging! It may be that the German artillerymen have failed to see the signal of the tank's fall because of a relief, because the look-out man is snoozing, because. . . . All this is idiotic! But even more idiotic to hope that there are tank traps without guns leveled on them! The treads are still catching.

Pradé cuts off the ignition.

"What the hell are you doing?"

In spite of my craze to get out, I feel the silence rising around us like an armor. As long as we do not hear a whistling sound, for four seconds we are alive. Will that door stop banging? I listen with the same frenzy as I have been looking until now, and I hear beneath the gong of the door only the rumbling of our waves of tanks, magnified by the trap and by the plate, passing and fading away. . . . My helmet glued to Pradé's, I yell "Up!" into the hole of his ear-flap, my voice filling the tank in the strange silence that has returned. Pradé, his legs in the air, bracing himself in his seat in the motionless and up-ended tank, turns toward me. Like the face of Bonneau, his face of an old man, in spite of the helmet, has become innocent; his slits of eyes and his three teeth sketch an indulgent death-smile.

"This time I guess sonny's out of luck. . . . Now the tracks are slipping again. . . ." He speaks almost in a whisper. I try to hear beneath the words the first imperceptible whistling of a shell. "If we keep on we'll belly the damn thing. . . ."

The whistling . . . We no longer have necks. Pradé's legs have left the pedals with a froglike movement, protecting his belly. The shell bursts thirty meters behind us.

The light has gone out. Shriveled into knots, we wait for the next shell—no longer for the explosion or the whistling, but for the distant starting signal of the shot—the very voice of death. And now Pradé's Chinese face looms imperceptibly out of the dark, becomes distinct with the leaden solemnity of faces of the dead; a mysterious light, blurred and very faint, fills the tank. And with it a terror that shatters my madman's calm: death is giving us warning. Pradé's motionless face, extraordinarily absent, drained of all life to make room for fear, emerges more and more from the shadows. I do not turn around, I no longer peer ahead, I no longer have to listen. I know that the shell is coming. Death is already in the tank. Pradé turns his head toward me, sees me and throws back his hunted neck, freed even from the shell by this supernatural terror, his head crashing with full force against the armor. And, as if the bell-stroke of the helmet that rings out in the silence had swept away the frightful presence and hurled us back to the expectation of the shell as to serenity, I finally see the periscope mirror. The up-ended tank looks up at the sky where the moon has just emerged, and what is thus lighting up our faces drained of life is the mirror that reflects the moonlit sky, immense and again full of stars. . . .

The door begins to bang. A hand has fastened itself to my back, shakes it. I would like to push it away, but I am hanging on with both hands. "We can get out, boys! We can get out!" bellows Léonard's childish voice. It is he who is tugging at my back. He climbs down into the vertical alley as into a well. "We're in a kind of pit! It's at least twenty meters, thirty meters across! Caved in in places!" Pradé immediately puts the tank into reverse. Léonard and I roll over, thrown on our bellies. The tank is once more horizontal. I get up again, jump out through the side door that Léonard has left open, go rolling once more while the tank backs and stops to my left, the lighted shaft of the doorway in the center of its thick mass. Pradé has been able to turn on the ignition again.

I get back on my feet with the smell of clay all around me; up there, on the earth's surface, our armored division, with a frailer sound than the one we heard from within the tank-armor, is still passing. . . . The shells seem to start very slowly, and then to rush when they are upon us. When the whistling begins it always seems to concern us, to be directed toward our trap. Not always are guns trained on the camouflaged pits. But there is no cave-in, Léonard is mad, we have fallen into an inverted funnel. No, it is an optical illusion. The trap's camouflage has been broken through in the center by the tank; everything that is not exactly underneath this great hole full of stars is pitch-black and seems to converge toward it. I advance cautiously, holding out my hands in front of me; at a little distance the wall we have been attacking slants . . . Not to be killed before we can get out! I don't dare to turn on my flashlight. As a matter of fact, I have left it in the tank. "We can try . . ." says Pradé close beside me in the dark.

He too clings to the wall. Outside of our armor we feel naked. From the clay wall, a smell of mushrooms oozes, full of childhood memories; the one who is waiting here for the next shell is not only a man of forty, but also a child in Jean-Bart, lying outstretched in the leaf-mold . . . Pradé scratches a match; it only lights up a radius of two meters. Another whistling rushes toward us, its shrill note descending the scale as it gains momentum. With our shoulders digging into the clay, fascinated by the hole of sky which the flashing red illumination is about to replace, we wait once more. One does not get used to dying. The match is extraordinarily motionless, and its flame flickers. How vulnerable and soft a human body is! We are flattened against the wall of our pauper's grave: Berger, Léonard, Bonneau, Pradé—a single cross. Our bit of sky disappears, the match goes out, some clods come tumbling down on our helmets and our shoulders.

Undoubtedly the Germans have not had time to locate exactly the pits they have camouflaged, and are pounding them at random. The shells are coming closer together.

The waves of tanks are still passing up above, but in the opposite direction. Have they just set up a refuelling depot around here, or are they in retreat? Will we get out only to fall upon the German armored columns?

Bonneau's flashlight appears. He is no longer screaming. All four of us advance, still clinging to the clay. I have become calm again, but there is a corner of my heart which nothing distracts, which nothing will distract from the shell. The camouflage extends everywhere well beyond the hole made by the tank in its fall; here the caved-in wall rises in an almost gentle slope. We climb it till we run into the tree trunks that cover the pit.

Never will we reach the hole. It is as if we were in one of those prison cells that let in light only through an inaccessible trapdoor; prisoners do not escape through the ceiling. We must try to separate the two nearest trunks. Crouching under them, whispering, "One, two, three . . ." we try to budge them with our shoulders, petrified into Peruvian mummies by each explosion, but recovering immediately. Since we are able to act, fear has become action. If we are powerless against the tree trunks, perhaps the tank will smash the whole thing apart. It is behind us, silent, blacker than the trap; from its half-open door comes a shaft of light in which a night insect flutters. . . .

We rush over to it without shielding ourselves, jump back into it as into a fortress. The din of the motors again fills the trap. Pradé maneuvers to bring us in front of the cave-in. Loose ground is piled around it. The waves, up above, continue to flow back toward the French lines. . . . We are beginning to get bogged. Pradé brings down the emergency block; the tank lifts, gropes. The treads catch hold like hands. The tank lifts again, gets stuck, slips again. The ceiling of trunks jams us. If it does not give way, our efforts will sink us in deeper and deeper; before two minutes the tank will be bellied and the treads will be turning in the air.

The emergency block can now be of some use.

"Let's go and get some rocks!"

Pradé does not answer.

With the motor at full speed, the quivering mass of steel noses into the earth, the whole shell of armor plate stiffens; with the furious comeback of a dying bull, the tank tosses me like a rock against the wall in a resounding crash of trunks that rain down on the plates; in the rear someone shouts, a helmet clangs, and now we are gliding forward like a boat. Back on my feet, I punch aside Pradé's head, glued to the periscope, and turn out the lights. In the mirror, to infinity, the open plain.

We advance at full speed amid the explosions, thinking only of the traps that lie ahead, each one doubled up at his post. Another tank must not fall in after us. When we are already far away, it occurs to me, stupidly, that I should have gone around the trap and posted our tank in front of it, or waited for our fuel convoys to have warning sent to the command (but we have orders to advance) or light a fire (but with what?). And we were not supposed to remain there; we have to advance. To stop is to escape the traps. But nothing at this moment, neither the risk which the comrades behind us are running, nor the one we ourselves are running, counts in the face of the order received; we advance. It is not courage; it is a reflex. And yet the night which is no longer the sepulchre of the trap, the living night appears to me as a prodigious gift, as an immense germination. . . .

When we reach the village, the Germans have evacuated it. Everything is in wild confusion. My three tank-mates and I walk with a strange swaying movement which I begin to recognize—the movement of the last stage of fatigue, when soldiers no longer even drag their feet, walk with their heads forward, their jaws hanging, and can no longer see straight. Our tank poorly camouflaged (like the others), we sink into the hay in a grange. In the beam of my flashlight, which I turn on for a second, I see Pradé stretched out with his arms around a pile of hay that he clutches as though he were clutching life itself.

"We got out of it this time," I said.

No doubt he is thinking that "his kid has had a lucky break."

"It'll begin all over again. . . ." he answers with his eternal smile of rancor. He lets go the hay and shuts his eyes.

Perhaps we will come to life again tomorrow.

The morning is as pure as though there were no war. Day has already dawned. Pradé awakened me as he got up; he has always been the first of us to get up. "When I'm dead I'll have plenty of time to lie down!" I go out in search of a water pump. It seems to me that the cold water awakens me not only from the night's sleep, but also from the trap. A few meters away, Pradé looks in front of him, smiles bitterly with his three teeth and shakes his head.

"I say that if anyone had tried to tell me I would look at chickens and not consider it natural, I'd've thought he was crazy!"

There is nothing in this morning which I too do not look at with a stranger's eyes. I say to myself, "I'm on the earth," as in days gone by I have said, "I'm in Persia." The chickens that have not yet been stolen wander about, seemingly oblivious to the war, though their little round eyes follow us with a sly prudence. They form white specks in the distant fields; close by a few of them peck for food in front of a barn where soldiers are sleeping. They are the ones Pradé was looking at; I too watch their mechanical pecking, the sharp jab of the head released by a spring, but their warmth seems to invade my hands as though I were holding them tight, the warmth of fresh eggs—the warmth of life; the animals are alive on this strange earth. We walk in the peasantless dawn. Barbary ducks, magpies. . . . This morning the picturesque or complex forms of life are the ones which most suggest its mystery: a mosquito that circles around me seems to me to be the most perturbing sign of the cosmos. And before the sudden and supple shying away of a cat I discover myself to be dumbfounded that that twiching fur actually exists. . . . All the cats, for that matter, run away. Whereas the dogs hold their ground, as perhaps they did when our tanks arrived. And something within me is full of wonder (my constant feeling since I am up is surprise) that, on this admirably regulated earth, dogs always behave like dogs, and cats like cats. Some gray pigeons fly up ahead of me, leaving a tomcat beneath them clutching the extremity of his futile leap; they describe a silent arc in the water-blue sky, break it, and becoming suddenly all white, continue in another direction. I am quite prepared to see them return, and chase after the cat who will fly away. The time when animals could talk, the ambiguous poetry of the oldest tales, these are things one brings back from the other side of life. . . .

Like one who sees China or India for the first time, I seem to hear, beneath this picturesque profusion, a vast murmur of centuries that reach almost as far back as the darkness of last night. These granges brimming over with corn and hay, these granges with beams hidden by husks, full of harrows, yokes, shafts, wooden carriages, these granges where all is corn, wood, hay or leather (the rest has been requisitioned), all surrounded by the extinguished fires of refugees and soldiers, are the granges of Gothic times; our tanks at the end of the street are being filled with water, monsters kneeling before the Biblical wells. . . . Oh life, so old!

And so obstinate! In each farmyard, wood has been gathered for the winter. Our soldiers who are waking us use it to light their first fires. Neat vegetable patches everywhere. . . . There is nothing here that does not bear man's imprint. In each farmyard the clothespins on the lines dance in the wind like swallows. The clothes are not yet quite dry: slender stockings, dress gloves, farmers' and workers' blues; and, in the midst of this exodus, in the midst of this disaster, napkins bear initials. . . .

We and those on the other side are no longer good for anything but our mechanical contraptions, our courage and our cowardice. But the old race of men whom we have chased away and which has left here only its implements, its linen and its initialed napkins, seems to me to have come, through thousands of years, out of the darkness encountered last night—slowly, avariciously loaded with all the paraphernalia which it has just abandoned before us: the wheelbarrows and the harrows, the Biblical carts, the kennels and the rabbit hutches, the empty furnaces. . . .

Yet the harvests that are ripening, the trees, the solemn drift of the Flemish clouds make of all this jetsam and even of the long human course which has abandoned it here an ephemeral hazard. Humanity is an accident and futile man roams upon the geological solitude with his abandoned initials, with his conscience, with his pity. The most unwonted presence. Before me are two sprinkling pots with those mushroom spouts that I loved when I was a child; and it seems to me suddenly that man has come out of the depths of time merely in order to invent a sprinkling pot. Beyond the quiet or furtive passage of the stray fowl, a Russian rabbit with a too heavy behind tries to dash like a real wild rabbit; the millstones glisten in the morning; a little dazed, I gaze for a long time at a preposterous flower, born of humanity as the mutilated flowers that surround it are born of the earth. A broom—there are brooms on the earth! We cross a football field, its wooden goalposts solitary in the middle of the trampled grass—and I remember that men play . . .

On a bench, two very old peasants are seated; the man's coat is still dirty with cobwebs from his cellar. Pradé goes over to him, smiling, his three teeth showing.

"Well, Grandfather, sunning yourself?"

By his accent the old man thinks he has recognized another peasant; he looks at him with absentminded friendliness, as though he were at the same time looking beyond him. The woman's hair hangs in a poor little gray plait, very tight. It is she who answers.

"What could we do? You, you're young; we're old; when you're old you're not good for anything any more. . . ."

She says this with a smile—in harmony with the universe, like a stone.

We walk. The farms abound with forage where hens run for shelter; neither the Germans nor we have had time to roast them. The geese and the ducks cackle at the soldiers who begin to appear. The abandoned cattle look at us, motionless, and suddenly run away. Above the farm, in a curtain of tall poplars, the wind shudders with a sound of disappearing tanks. . . .

My legs remember Bonneau's arms clutching them; in my head, far away, his cries beneath the hammering of the tank, still vibrate like flies. Shall I always remember that childish expression which I had never seen on Pradé's face before, and Bonneau's dumbfounded look when he broke off a shriek to say to me; "Me? I'm not saying anything." I know now how humanity becomes haggard. But those phantoms are before the granges, before the sun that quivers on the tips of the young branches, only to give them more sparkle.

Once more I remember a passage from Pascal: "Let us imagine a number of men in chains, all condemned to die, and some of them slaughtered every day in the sight of the rest, who see their own fate in that of their companions. . . . This is a picture of the condition of men." Never have I felt to this point how much such a meditation can cause men to clasp their share of happiness to their bosoms. Perhaps anguish is always the stronger; perhaps joy is poisoned at its source, the joy that was given to the only animal that knows it is not eternal. But this morning I am aware only of birth. I still carry within me the bursting upon us of the earthly night as we emerged from the trap, that germination in the darkness deepened with drifting clouds and constellations; and even as I saw the full and rumbling night loom up from the trap, so now out of the night rises the miraculous revelation of day.

The world could have been simple, like the sky or the sea. And looking at the frenzied multiplicity of its forms, these forms which before me are only those of an abandoned, doomed village; looking at these granges of Paradise and these clothespins and these wells, these scattered wild rosebushes, this voracious grass which perhaps in a year will have overrun everything here, these animals, these trees, these houses, I feel myself before an inexplicable gift—an apparition. All this might not have been—might not have been thus. How unique everything is, how attuned to the earth! There exist other worlds, that of the crystallizations of the sea-depths. . . . With its trees as ramified as veins, the universe is whole, dazzling and mysterious as a young body. The door of the farmhouse I am passing has been left open by the fleeing farmers; I catch a glimpse of a half-pillaged room. Ah! the Magi did not bring gifts to the Child, they only told him that on that night when he arrived the doors of the humble were opened to life, which is revealed to me this morning for the first time—strong as night and strong as death.

I know now the meaning of the ancient myths of men snatched from the kingdom of the dead. Hardly do I remember the terror; what I bear within me is the discovery of a simple and holy secret. I have seen the earth with divine eyes. I find myself back upon it as if it had suddenly been given to me; I discover it although I bear it within me; thus, perhaps, God looked upon the first man. . . .

If a shell comes I shall again fling myself to the ground; I shall duck my head under the fire of bullets; if I fall into another trap, I shall experience the same convulsive dementia and the same madman's calm.

But this morning I am not afraid of death.

22

The Wall

JEAN-PAUL SARTRE

THEY pushed us into a large white room and my eyes began to blink because the light hurt them. Then I saw a table and four fellows seated at the table, civilians, looking at some papers. The other prisoners were herded together at one end and we were obliged to cross the entire room to join them. There were several I knew, and others who must have been foreigners. The two in front of me were blond with round heads. They looked alike. I imagine they were French. The smaller one kept pulling at his trousers, out of nervousness.

This lasted about three hours. I was dog-tired and my head was empty. But the room was well-heated, which struck me as rather agreeable; we had not stopped shivering for twenty-four hours. The guards led the prisoners in one after the other in front of the table. Then the four fellows asked them their names and what they did. Most of the time that was all—or perhaps from time to time they would ask such questions as: "Did you help sabotage the munitions?" or, "Where were you on the morning of the ninth and what were you doing?" They didn't even listen to the replies, or at least they didn't seem to. They just remained silent for a moment and looked straight ahead, then they began to write. They asked Tom if it was true he had served in the International Brigade. Tom couldn't say he hadn't because of the papers they had found in his jacket. They didn't ask Juan anything, but after he told them his name, they wrote for a long while.

"It's my brother José who's the anarchist," Juan said. "You know perfectly well he's not here now. I don't belong to any party. I never did take part in politics." They didn't answer.

Then Juan said, "I didn't do anything. And I'm not going to pay for what the others did."

His lips were trembling. A guard told him to stop talking and led him away. It was my turn.

"Your name is Pablo Ibbieta?"

I said yes.

The fellow looked at his papers and said, "Where is Ramon Gris?"

"I don't know."

"You hid him in your house from the sixth to the nineteenth."

"I did not."

They continued to write for a moment and the guards led me away. In the hall, Tom and Juan were waiting between two guards. We started walking. Tom asked one of the guards, "What's the idea?" "How do you mean?" the guard asked. "Was that just the preliminary questioning, or was that the trial?" "That was the trial," the guard said. "So now what? What are they going to do with us?" The guard answered drily, "The verdict will be told you in your cell."

In reality, our cell was one of the cellars of the hospital. It was terribly cold there because it was very drafty. We had been shivering all night long and it had hardly been any better during the day. I had spent the preceding five days in a cellar in the archbishop's palace, a sort of dungeon that must have dated back to the Middle Ages. There were lots of prisoners and not much room, so they housed them just anywhere. But I was not homesick for my dungeon. I hadn't been cold there, but I had been alone, and that gets to be irritating. In the cellar I had company. Juan didn't say a word; he was afraid, and besides, he was too young to have anything to say. But Tom was a good talker and knew Spanish well.

In the cellar there were a bench and four straw mattresses. When they led us back we sat down and waited in silence. After a while Tom said, "Our goose is cooked."

"I think so too," I said. "But I don't believe they'll do anything to the kid."

Tom said, "They haven't got anything on him. He's the brother of a fellow who's fighting, and that's all."

I looked at Juan. He didn't seem to have heard.

Tom continued, "You know what they do in Saragossa? They lay the guys across the road and then they drive over them with trucks. It was a Moroccan deserter who told us that. They say it's just to save ammunition."

I said, "Well, it doesn't save gasoline."

I was irritated with Tom; he shouldn't have said that.

He went on, "There are officers walking up and down the roads with their hands in their pockets, smoking, and they see that it's done right. Do you think they'd put 'em out of their misery? Like hell they do. They just let 'em holler. Sometimes as long as an hour. The Moroccan said the first time he almost puked."

"I don't believe they do that here," I said, "unless they really are short of ammunition."

The daylight came in through four air vents and a round opening that had been cut in the ceiling, to the left, and which opened directly onto the sky. It was through this hole, which was ordinarily closed by means of a trapdoor, that they unloaded coal into the cellar. Directly under the hole, there was a big pile of coal dust; it had been intended for heating the hospital, but at the beginning of the war they had evacuated the patients and the coal had stayed there unused; it even got rained on from time to time, when they forgot to close the trapdoor.

Tom started to shiver. "God damn it," he said, "I'm shivering. There, it is starting again."

He rose and began to do gymnastic exercises. At each movement, his shirt opened and showed his white, hairy chest. He lay down on his back, lifted his legs in the air and began to do the scissors movement. I watched his big buttocks tremble. Tom was tough, but he had too much fat on him. I kept thinking that soon bullets and bayonet points would sink into that mass of tender flesh as though it were a pat of butter.

I wasn't exactly cold, but I couldn't feel my shoulders or my arms. From time to time, I had the impression that something was missing and I began to look around for my jacket. Then I would suddenly remember they hadn't given me a jacket. It was rather awkward. They had taken our clothes to give them to their own soldiers and had left us only our shirts and these cotton trousers the hospital patients wore in mid-summer. After a moment, Tom got up and sat down beside me, breathless.

"Did you get warmed up?"

"Damn it, no. But I'm all out of breath."

Around eight o'clock in the evening, a Major came in with two Falangists.

"What are the names of those three over there?" he asked the guard.

"Steinbock, Ibbieta and Mirbal," said the guard.

The Major put on his glasses and examined his list.

"Steinbock—Steinbock . . . Here it is. You are condemned to death. You'll be shot tomorrow morning."

He looked at his list again.

"The other two, also," he said.

"That's not possible," said Juan. "Not me."

The Major looked at him with surprise. "What's your name?"

"Juan Mirbal."

"Well, your name is here," said the Major, "and you're condemned to death."

"I didn't do anything," said Juan.

The Major shrugged his shoulders and turned toward Tom and me.

"You are both Basque?"

"No, nobody's Basque."

He appeared exasperated.

"I was told there were three Basques. I'm not going to waste my time running after them. I suppose you don't want a priest?"

We didn't even answer.

Then he said, "A Belgian doctor will be around in a little while. He has permission to stay with you all night."

He gave a military salute and left.

"What did I tell you?" Tom said. "We're in for something swell."

"Yes," I said. "It's a damned shame for the kid."

I said that to be fair, but I really didn't like the kid. His face was too refined and it was disfigured by fear and suffering, which had twisted all his features. Three days ago, he was just a kid with a kind of affected manner some people like. But now he looked like an aging fairy, and I thought to myself he would never be young again, even if they let him go. It wouldn't have been a bad thing to show him a little pity, but pity makes me sick, and besides, I couldn't stand him. He hadn't said anything more, but he had turned gray. His face and hands were gray. He sat down again and stared, round-eyed, at the ground. Tom was good-hearted and tried to take him by the arm, but the kid drew himself away violently and made an ugly face. "Leave him alone," I said quietly. "Can't you see he's going to start to bawl?" Tom obeyed regretfully. He would have liked to console the kid; that would have kept him occupied and he wouldn't have been tempted to think about himself. But it got on my nerves. I had never thought about death, for the reason that the question had never come up. But now it had come up, and there was nothing else to do but think about it.

Tom started talking. "Say, did you ever bump anybody off?" he asked me. I didn't answer. He started to explain to me that he had bumped off six fellows since August. He hadn't yet realized what we were in for, and I saw clearly he didn't *want* to realize it. I myself hadn't quite taken it in. I wondered if it hurt very much. I thought about the bullets; I imagined their fiery hail going through my body. All that was beside the real question; but I was calm, we had all night in which to realize it. After a while

Tom stopped talking and I looked at him out of the corner of my eye. I saw that he, too, had turned gray and that he looked pretty miserable. I said to myself, "It's starting." It was almost dark, a dull light filtered through the air vents across the coal pile and made a big spot under the sky. Through the hole in the ceiling I could already see a star. The night was going to be clear and cold.

The door opened and two guards entered. They were followed by a blond man in a tan uniform. He greeted us.

"I'm the doctor," he said. "I've been authorized to give you any assistance you may require in these painful circumstances."

He had an agreeable, cultivated voice.

I said to him, "What are you going to do here?"

"Whatever you want me to do. I shall do everything in my power to lighten these few hours."

"Why did you come to us? There are lots of others: the hospital's full of them."

"I was sent here," he answered vaguely. "You'd probably like to smoke, wouldn't you?" he added suddenly. "I've got some cigarettes and even some cigars."

He passed around some English cigarettes and some *puros,* but we refused them. I looked him straight in the eye and he appeared uncomfortable.

"You didn't come here out of compassion," I said to him. "In fact, I know who you are. I saw you with some fascists in the barracks yard the day I was arrested."

I was about to continue, when all at once something happened to me which surprised me: the presence of this doctor had suddenly ceased to interest me. Usually, when I've got hold of a man I don't let go. But somehow the desire to speak had left me. I shrugged my shoulders and turned away. A little later, I looked up and saw he was watching me with an air of curiosity. The guards had sat down on one of the mattresses. Pedro, the tall thin one, was twiddling his thumbs, while the other one shook his head occasionally to keep from falling asleep.

"Do you want some light?" Pedro suddenly asked the doctor. The other fellow nodded, "Yes." I think he was not over-intelligent, but doubtless he was not malicious. As I looked at his big, cold, blue eyes, it seemed to me the worst thing about him was his lack of imagination. Pedro went out and came back with an oil lamp which he set on the corner of the bench. It gave a poor light, but it was better than nothing; the night before we had been left in the dark. For a long while I stared at the circle of light the lamp threw on the ceiling. I was fascinated. Then, suddenly, I came to, the light circle paled, and I felt as if I were being crushed under an enormous weight. It wasn't the thought of death, and it wasn't fear; it was something anonymous. My cheeks were burning hot and my head ached.

I roused myself and looked at my two companions. Tom had his head in his hands and only the fat, white nape of his neck was visible. Juan was by far the worst off; his mouth was wide open and his nostrils were trembling. The doctor came over to him and touched him on the shoulder, as though to comfort him; but his eyes remained cold. Then I saw the Belgian slide his hand furtively down Juan's arm to his wrist. Indifferent, Juan let himself be handled. Then, as though absent-mindedly, the Belgian laid three fingers over his wrist; at the same time, he drew away somewhat and managed to turn his back to me. But I leaned over backward and saw him take out his watch and look at it a moment before relinquishing the boy's wrist. After a moment, he let the inert hand fall and went and leaned against the wall. Then, as if he had suddenly remembered something very important that had to be noted down immediately, he took a notebook from his pocket and wrote a few lines in it. "The son-of-a-bitch," I thought angrily. "He better not come and feel my pulse; I'll give him a punch in his dirty jaw."

He didn't come near me, but I felt he was looking at me. I raised my head and looked back at him. In an impersonal voice, he said, "Don't you think it's frightfully cold here?"

He looked purple with cold.

"I'm not cold," I answered him.

He kept looking at me with a hard expression. Suddenly I understood, and I lifted my hands to my face. I was covered with sweat. Here, in this cellar, in mid-winter, right in a draft, I was sweating. I ran my fingers through my hair, which was stiff with sweat; at the same time, I realized my shirt was damp and sticking to my skin. I had been streaming with perspiration for an hour, at least, and had felt nothing. But this fact hadn't escaped that Belgian swine. He had seen the drops rolling down my face and had said to himself that it showed an almost pathological terror; and he himself had felt normal and proud of it because he was cold. I wanted to get up and go punch his face in, but I had hardly started to make a move before my shame and anger had disappeared. I dropped back onto the bench with indifference.

I was content to rub my neck with my handkerchief because now I felt the sweat dripping from my hair onto the nape of my neck and that was disagreeable. I soon gave up rubbing myself, however, for it didn't do any good; my handkerchief was already wringing wet and I was still sweating. My buttocks, too, were sweating, and my damp trousers stuck to the bench.

Suddenly, Juan said, "You're a doctor, aren't you?"

"Yes," said the Belgian.

"Do people suffer—very long?"

"Oh! When . . .? No, no," said the Belgian, in a paternal voice, "it's quickly over."

His manner was as reassuring as if he had been answering a paying patient.

"But I . . . Somebody told me—they often have to fire two volleys."

"Sometimes," said the Belgian, raising his head, "it just happens that the first volley doesn't hit any of the vital organs."

"So then they have to reload their guns and aim all over again?" Juan thought for a moment, then added hoarsely, "But that takes time!"

He was terribly afraid of suffering. He couldn't think about anything else, but that went with his age. As for me, I hardly thought about it any more and it certainly was not fear of suffering that made me perspire.

I rose and walked toward the pile of coal dust. Tom gave a start and looked at me with a look of hate. I irritated him because my shoes squeaked. I wondered if my face was as putty-colored as his. Then I noticed that he, too, was sweating. The sky was magnificent; no light at all came into our dark corner and I had only to lift my head to see the Big Bear. But it didn't look the way it had looked before. Two days ago, from my cell in the archbishop's palace, I could see a big patch of sky and each time of day brought back a different memory. In the morning, when the sky was a deep blue, and light, I thought of beaches along the Atlantic; at noon, I could see the sun, and I remembered a bar in Seville where I used to drink manzanilla and eat anchovies and olives; in the afternoon, I was in the shade, and I thought of the deep shadow which covers half of the arena while the other half gleams in the sunlight: it really gave me a pang to see the whole earth reflected in the sky like that. Now, however, no matter how much I looked up in the air, the sky no longer recalled anything. I liked it better that way. I came back and sat down next to Tom. There was a long silence.

Then Tom began to talk in a low voice. He had to keep talking, otherwise he lost his way in his own thoughts. I believe he was talking to me, but he didn't look at me. No doubt he was afraid to look at me, because I was gray and sweating. We were both alike and worse than mirrors for each other. He looked at the Belgian, the only one who was alive.

"Say, do you understand? I don't."

Then I, too, began to talk in a low voice. I was watching the Belgian.

"Understand what? What's the matter?"

"Something's going to happen to us that I don't understand."

There was a strange odor about Tom. It seemed to me that I was more sensitive to odors than ordinarily. With a sneer, I said, "You'll understand, later."

"That's not so sure," he said stubbornly. "I'm willing to be courageous, but at least I ought to know ... Listen, they're going to take us out into the courtyard. All right. The fellows will be standing in line in front of us. How many of them will there be?"

"Oh, I don't know. Five, or eight. Not more."

"That's enough. Let's say there'll be eight of them. Somebody will shout 'Shoulder arms!' and I'll see all eight rifles aimed at me. I'm sure I'm going to feel like going through the wall. I'll push against the wall as hard as I can with my back, and the wall won't give in. The way it is in a nightmare. . . . I can imagine all that. Ah, if you only knew how well I can imagine it!"

"Skip it!" I said. "I can imagine it too."

"It must hurt like the devil. You know they aim at your eyes and mouth so as to disfigure you," he added maliciously. "I can feel the wounds already. For the last hour I've been having pains in my head and neck. Not real pains—it's worse still. They're the pains I'll feel tomorrow morning. And after that, then what?"

I understood perfectly well what he meant, but I didn't want to seem to understand. As for the pains, I, too, felt them all through my body, like a lot of little gashes. I couldn't get used to them, but I was like him, I didn't think they were very important.

"After that," I said roughly, "you'll be eating daisies."

He started talking to himself, not taking his eyes off the Belgian, who didn't seem to be listening to him. I knew what he had come for, and that what we were thinking didn't interest him. He had come to look at our bodies, our bodies which were dying alive.

"It's like in a nightmare," said Tom. "You want to think of something, you keep having the impression you've got it, that you're going to understand, and then it slips away from you, it eludes you and it's gone again. I say to myself, afterwards, there won't be anything. But I don't really understand what that means. There are moments when I almost do— and then it's gone again. I start to think of the pains, the bullets, the noise of the shooting. I am a materialist, I swear it; and I'm not going crazy, either. But there's something wrong. I see my own corpse. That's not hard, but it's *I* who see it, with *my* eyes. I'll have to get to the point where I think—where I think I won't see anything more. I won't hear anything more, and the world will go on for the others. We're not made to think that way, Pablo. Believe me, I've already stayed awake all night waiting for something. But this is not the same thing. This will grab us from behind, Pablo, and we won't be ready for it."

"Shut up," I said. "Do you want me to call a father confessor?"

He didn't answer. I had already noticed that he had a tendency to prophesy and call me "Pablo" in a kind of pale voice. I didn't like that very much, but it seems all the Irish are like that. I had a vague impression that he smelled of urine. Actually, I didn't like Tom very much, and I didn't see why, just because we were going to die together, I should like him any better. There are certain fellows with whom it would be different—with Ramon Gris, for instance. But between Tom and Juan, I felt alone. In fact, I liked it better that way. With Ramon I might have grown soft. But I felt terribly hard at that moment, and I wanted to stay hard.

Tom kept on muttering, in a kind of absent-minded way. He was certainly talking to keep from thinking. Naturally, I agreed with him, and I could have said everything he was saying. It's not *natural* to die. And since I was going to die, nothing seemed natural any more: neither the coal pile, nor the bench, nor Pedro's dirty old face. Only it was disagreeable for me to think the same things Tom thought. And I knew perfectly well that all night long, within five minutes of each other, we would keep on thinking things at the same time, sweating or shivering at the same time. I looked at him sideways and, for the first time, he seemed strange to me. He had death written on his face. My pride was wounded. For twenty-four hours I had lived side by side with Tom, I had listened to him, I had talked to him, and I knew we had nothing in common. And now we were as alike as twin brothers, simply because we were going to die together. Tom took my hand without looking at me.

"Pablo, I wonder . . . I wonder if it's true that we just cease to exist."

I drew my hand away.

"Look between your feet, you dirty dog."

There was a puddle between his feet and water was dripping from his trousers.

"What's the matter?" he said, frightened.

"You're wetting your pants," I said to him.

"It's not true," he said furiously. "I can't be . . . I don't feel anything."

The Belgian had come closer to him. With an air of false concern, he asked, "Aren't you feeling well?"

Tom didn't answer. The Belgian looked at the puddle without comment.

"I don't know what that is," Tom said savagely, "but I'm not afraid.
I swear to you, I'm not afraid."

The Belgian made no answer. Tom rose and went to the corner. He
came back, buttoning his fly, and sat down, without a word. The Belgian
was taking notes.

We were watching the doctor. Juan was watching him too. All three
of us were watching him because he was alive. He had the gestures of a
living person, the interests of a living person; he was shivering in this
cellar the way living people shiver; he had an obedient, well-fed body.
We, on the other hand, didn't feel our bodies any more—not the same
way, in any case. I felt like touching my trousers, but I didn't dare to. I
looked at the Belgian, well-planted on his two legs, master of his muscles
—and able to plan for tomorrow. We were like three shadows deprived
of blood; we were watching him and sucking his life like vampires.

Finally he came over to Juan. Was he going to lay his hand on the
nape of Juan's neck for some professional reason, or had he obeyed a
charitable impulse? If he had acted out of charity, it was the one and
only time during the whole night. He fondled Juan's head and the nape
of his neck. The kid let him do it, without taking his eyes off him. Then,
suddenly, he took hold of the doctor's hand and looked at it in a funny
way. He held the Belgian's hand between his own two hands and there
was nothing pleasing about them, those two gray paws squeezing that
fat red hand. I sensed what was going to happen and Tom must have
sensed it, too. But all the Belgian saw was emotion, and he smiled pater-
nally. After a moment, the kid lifted the big red paw to his mouth and
started to bite it. The Belgian drew back quickly and stumbled toward
the wall. For a second, he looked at us with horror. He must have suddenly understood that we were not men like himself. I began to laugh,
and one of the guards started up. The other had fallen asleep with his
eyes wide open, showing only the whites.

I felt tired and over-excited at the same time. I didn't want to think
any more about what was going to happen at dawn—about death. It
didn't make sense, and I never got beyond just words, or emptiness. But
whenever I tried to think about something else I saw the barrels of rifles
aimed at me. I must have lived through my execution twenty times in
succession; one time I thought it was the real thing; I must have dozed
off for a moment. They were dragging me toward the wall and I was
resisting; I was imploring their pardon. I woke with a start and looked
at the Belgian. I was afraid I had cried out in my sleep. But he was
smoothing his mustache; he hadn't noticed anything. If I had wanted to,
I believe I could have slept for a while. I had been awake for the last

forty-eight hours, and I was worn out. But I didn't want to lose two hours of life. They would have had to come and wake me at dawn. I would have followed them, drunk with sleep, and I would have gone off without so much as "Gosh!" I didn't want it that way, I didn't want to die like an animal. I wanted to understand. Besides, I was afraid of having nightmares. I got up and began to walk up and down and, so as to think about something else, I began to think about my past life. Memories crowded in on me, helter-skelter. Some were good and some were bad—at least that was how I had thought of them *before*. There were faces and happenings. I saw the face of a little *novilero* who had gotten himself horned during the *Feria,* in Valencia. I saw the face of one of my uncles, of Ramon Gris. I remembered all kinds of things that had happened: how I had been on strike for three months in 1926, and had almost died of hunger. I recalled a night I had spent on a bench in Granada; I hadn't eaten for three days, I was nearly wild, I didn't want to give up the sponge. I had to smile. With what eagerness I had run after happiness, and women, and liberty! And to what end? I had wanted to liberate Spain, I admired Py Margall, I had belonged to the anarchist movement, I had spoken at public meetings. I took everything as seriously as if I had been immortal.

At that time I had the impression that I had my whole life before me, and I thought to myself, "It's all a god-damned lie." Now it wasn't worth anything because it was finished. I wondered how I had ever been able to go out and have a good time with girls. I wouldn't have lifted my little finger if I had ever imagined that I would die like this. I saw my life before me, finished, closed, like a bag, and yet what was inside was not finished. For a moment I tried to appraise it. I would have liked to say to myself, "It's been a good life." But it couldn't be appraised, it was only an outline. I had spent my time writing checks on eternity, and had understood nothing. Now, I didn't miss anything. There were a lot of things I might have missed: the taste of manzanilla, for instance, or the swims I used to take in summer in a little creek near Cadiz. But death had taken the charm out of everything.

Suddenly the Belgian had a wonderful idea.

"My friends," he said to us, "if you want me to—and providing the military authorities give their consent—I could undertake to deliver a word or some token from you to your loved ones . . . ."

Tom growled, "I haven't got anybody."

I didn't answer. Tom waited for a moment, then he looked at me with curiosity. "Aren't you going to send any message to Concha?"

"No."

I hated that sort of sentimental conspiracy. Of course, it was my fault, since I had mentioned Concha the night before, and I should have kept my mouth shut. I had been with her for a year. Even as late as last night, I would have cut my arm off with a hatchet just to see her again for five minutes. That was why I had mentioned her. I couldn't help it. Now I didn't care any more about seeing her. I hadn't anything more to say to her. I didn't even want to hold her in my arms. I loathed my body because it had turned gray and was sweating—and I wasn't even sure that I didn't loathe hers too. Concha would cry when she heard about my death; for months she would have no more interest in life. But still it was I who was going to die. I thought of her beautiful, loving eyes. When she looked at me something went from her to me. But I thought to myself that it was all over; if she looked at me *now* her gaze would not leave her eyes, it would not reach out to me. I was alone.

Tom too, was alone, but not the same way. He was seated astride his chair and had begun to look at the bench with a sort of smile, with surprise, even. He reached out his hand and touched the wood cautiously, as though he were afraid of breaking something, then he drew his hand back hurriedly, and shivered. I wouldn't have amused myself touching that bench, if I had been Tom, that was just some more Irish play-acting. But somehow it seemed to me too that the different objects had something funny about them. They seemed to have grown paler, less massive than before. I had only to look at the bench, the lamp or the pile of coal dust to feel I was going to die. Naturally, I couldn't think clearly about my death, but I saw it everywhere, even on the different objects, the way they had withdrawn and kept their distance, tactfully, like people talking at the bedside of a dying person. It was *his own death* Tom had just touched on the bench.

In the state I was in, if they had come and told me I could go home quietly, that my life would be saved, it would have left me cold. A few hours, or a few years of waiting are all the same, when you've lost the illusion of being eternal. Nothing mattered to me any more. In a way, I was calm. But it was a horrible kind of calm—because of my body. My body—I saw with its eyes and I heard with its ears, but it was no longer I. It sweat and trembled independently, and I didn't recognize it any longer. I was obliged to touch it and look at it to know what was happening to it, just as if it had been someone else's body. At times I still felt it, I felt a slipping, a sort of headlong plunging, as in a falling airplane, or else I heard my heart beating. But this didn't give me confidence. In fact, everything that came from my body had something damned dubious about it. Most of the time it was silent, it stayed put and I didn't feel anything other than a sort of heaviness, a loathsome presence against me. I had the impression of being bound to an enormous vermin.

The Belgian took out his watch and looked at it.

"It's half-past three," he said.

The son-of-a-bitch! He must have done it on purpose. Tom jumped up. We hadn't yet realized the time was passing. The night surrounded us like a formless, dark mass; I didn't even remember it had started.

Juan started to shout. Wringing his hands, he implored, "I don't want to die! I don't want to die!"

He ran the whole length of the cellar with his arms in the air, then he dropped down onto one of the mattresses, sobbing. Tom looked at him with dismal eyes and didn't even try to console him any more. The fact was, it was no use; the kid made more noise than we did, but he was less affected, really. He was like a sick person who defends himself against his malady with a high fever. When there's not even any fever left, it's much more serious.

He was crying. I could tell he felt sorry for himself; he was thinking about death. For one second, one single second, I too felt like crying, crying out of pity for myself. But just the contrary happened. I took one look at the kid, saw his thin, sobbing shoulders, and I felt I was inhuman. I couldn't feel pity either for these others or for myself. I said to myself, "I want to die decently."

Tom had gotten up and was standing just under the round opening looking out for the first signs of daylight. I was determined, I wanted to die decently, and I only thought about that. But underneath, ever since the doctor had told us the time, I felt time slipping, flowing by, one drop at a time.

It was still dark when I heard Tom's voice.

"Do you hear them?"

"Yes."

People were walking in the courtyard.

"What the hell are they doing? After all, they can't shoot in the dark."

After a moment, we didn't heard anything more. I said to Tom, "There's the daylight."

Pedro got up yawning, and came and blew out the lamp. He turned to the man beside him. "It's hellish cold."

The cellar had grown gray. We could hear shots at a distance.

"It's about to start," I said to Tom. "That must be in the back courtyard."

Tom asked the doctor to give him a cigarette. I didn't want any; I didn't want either cigarettes or alcohol. From that moment on, the shooting didn't stop.

"Can you take it in?" Tom said.

He started to add something, then he stopped and began to watch the door. The door opened and a lieutenant came in with four soldiers. Tom dropped his cigarette.

"Steinbock?"

Tom didn't answer. Pedro pointed him out.

"Juan Mirbal?"

"He's the one on the mattress."

"Stand up," said the Lieutenant.

Juan didn't move. Two soldiers took hold of him by the armpits and stood him up on his feet. But as soon as they let go of him he fell down. The soldiers hesitated a moment.

"He's not the first one to get sick," said the Lieutenant. You'll have to carry him, the two of you. We'll arrange things when we get there." He turned to Tom. "All right, come along."

Tom left between two soldiers. Two other soldiers followed, carrying the kid by his arms and legs. He was not unconscious; his eyes were wide open and tears were rolling down his cheeks. When I started to go out, the Lieutenant stopped me.

"Are you Ibbieta?"

"Yes."

"You wait here. They'll come and get you later on."

They left. The Belgian and the two jailers left too, and I was alone. I didn't understand what had happened to me, but I would have liked it better if they had ended it all right away. I heard the volleys at almost regular intervals; at each one, I shuddered. I felt like howling and tearing my hair. But instead, I gritted my teeth and pushed my hands deep into my pockets, because I wanted to stay decent.

An hour later, they came to fetch me and took me up to the first floor in a little room which smelt of cigar smoke and was so hot it seemed to me suffocating. Here there were two officers sitting in comfortable chairs, smoking, with papers spread out on their knees.

"Your name is Ibbieta?"

"Yes."

"Where is Ramon Gris?"

"I don't know."

The man who questioned me was small and stocky. He had hard eyes behind his glasses.

"Come nearer," he said to me.

I went nearer. He rose and took me by the arms, looking at me in a way calculated to make me go through the floor. At the same time he pinched my arms with all his might. He didn't mean to hurt me; it was quite a game; he wanted to dominate me. He also seemed to think it was necessary to blow his fetid breath right into my face. We stood like that for a moment, only I felt more like laughing than anything else. It takes a lot more than that to intimidate a man who's about to die: it didn't work. He pushed me away violently and sat down again.

"It's your life or his," he said. "You'll be allowed to go free if you tell us where he is."

After all, these two bedizened fellows with their riding crops and boots were just men who were going to die one day. A little later than I, perhaps, but not a great deal. And there they were, looking for names among their papers, running after other men in order to put them in prison or do away with them entirely. They had their opinions on the future of Spain and on other subjects. Their petty activities seemed to me to be offensive and ludicrous. I could no longer put myself in their place. I had the impression they were crazy.

The little fat fellow kept looking at me, tapping his boots with his riding crop. All his gestures were calculated to make him appear like a spirited, ferocious animal.

"Well? Do you understand?"

"I don't know where Gris is," I said. "I thought he was in Madrid."

The other officer lifted his pale hand indolently. This indolence was also calculated. I saw through all their little tricks, and I was dumbfounded that men should still exist who took pleasure in that kind of thing.

"You have fifteen minutes to think it over," he said slowly. "Take him to the linen-room, and bring him back here in fifteen minutes. If he continues to refuse, he'll be executed at once."

They knew what they were doing. I had spent the night waiting. After that, they had made me wait another hour in the cellar, while they shot Tom and Juan, and now they locked me in the linen-room. They must have arranged the whole thing the night before. They figured that sooner or later people's nerves wear out and they hoped to get me that way.

They made a big mistake. In the linen-room I sat down on a ladder because I felt very weak, and I began to think things over. Not their proposition, however. Naturally I knew where Gris was. He was hiding in his cousins' house, about two miles outside of the city. I knew, too, that I would not reveal his hiding place, unless they tortured me (but they didn't seem to be considering that). All that was definitely settled and didn't interest me in the least. Only I would have liked to understand the reasons for my own conduct. I would rather die than betray Gris. Why? I no longer liked Ramon Gris. My friendship for him had died shortly before dawn along with my love for Concha, along with my own desire to live. Of course I still admired him—he was hard. But it was not for that reason that I was willing to die in his place; his life was no more valuable than mine. No life was of any value. A man was going to be stood up against a wall and fired at till he dropped dead. It didn't make any difference whether it was I or Gris or somebody else. I knew perfectly well he was more useful to the Spanish cause than I was, but I didn't give a God damn about Spain or anarchy, either; nothing had any importance now. And yet, there I was. I could save my skin by betraying Gris and I refused to do it. It seemed more ludicrous to me than anything else; it was stubbornness.

I thought to myself, "Am I hard-headed!" And I was seized with a strange sort of cheerfulness.

They came to fetch me and took me back to the two officers. A rat darted out under our feet and that amused me. I turned to one of the falangists and said to him, "Did you see that rat?"

He made no reply. He was gloomy, and took himself very seriously. As for me, I felt like laughing, but I restrained myself because I was afraid that if I started, I wouldn't be able to stop. The falangist wore mustaches. I kept after him, "You ought to cut off those mustaches, you fool."

I was amused by the fact that he let hair grow all over his face while he was still alive. He gave me a kind of half-hearted kick, and I shut up.

"Well," said the fat officer, "have you thought things over?"

I looked at them with curiosity, like insects of a very rare species.

"I know where he is," I said. "He's hiding in the cemetery. Either in one of the vaults, or in the gravediggers' shack."

I said that just to make fools of them. I wanted to see them get up and fasten their belts and bustle about giving orders.

They jumped to their feet.

"Fine. Moles, go ask Lieutenant Lopez for fifteen men. And as for you," the little fat fellow said to me, "if you've told the truth, I don't go back on my word. But you'll pay for this, if you're pulling our leg."

They left noisily and I waited in peace, still guarded by the falangists. From time to time I smiled at the thought of the face they were going to make. I felt dull and malicious. I could see them lifting up the gravestones, or opening the doors of the vaults one by one. I saw the whole situation as though I were another person: the prisoner determined to play the hero, the solemn falangists with their mustaches and the men in uniform running around among the graves. It was irresistibly funny.

After half an hour, the little fat fellow came back alone. I thought he had come to give the order to execute me. The others must have stayed in the cemetery.

The officer looked at me. He didn't look at all foolish.

"Take him out in the big courtyard with the others," he said. "When military operations are over, a regular tribunal will decide his case."

I thought I must have misunderstood.

"So they're not—they're not going to shoot me?" I asked.

"Not now, in any case. Afterwards, that doesn't concern me."

I still didn't understand.

"But why?" I said to him.

He shrugged his shoulders wthout replying, and the soldiers lead me away. In the big courtyard there were a hundred or so prisoners, women, children and a few old men. I started to walk around the grass plot in the middle. I felt absolutely idiotic. At noon we were fed in the dining hall. Two or three fellows spoke to me. I must have known them, but I didn't answer. I didn't even know where I was.

Toward evening, about ten new prisoners were pushed into the courtyard. I recognized Garcia, the baker.

He said to me, "Lucky dog! I didn't expect to find you alive."

"They condemned me to death," I said, "and then they changed their minds. I don't know why."

"I was arrested at two o'clock," Garcia said.

"What for?"

Garcia took no part in politics.

"I don't know," he said. "They arrest everybody who doesn"t think the way they do."

He lowered his voice.

"They got Gris."

I began to tremble.

"When?"

"This morning. He acted like a damned fool. He left his cousins' house Tuesday because of a disagreement. There were any number of fellows who would have hidden him, but he didn't want to be indebted to anybody any more. He said, 'I would have hidden at Ibbieta's, but since they've got him, I'll go hide in the cemetery.' "

"In the cemetery?"

"Yes. It was the god-damnedest thing. Naturally they passed by there this morning; that had to happen. They found him in the gravediggers' shack. They opened fire at him and they finished him off."

"In the cemetery!"

Everything went around in circles, and when I came to I was sitting on the ground. I laughed so hard the tears came to my eyes.

23

The Professor and the Mussels

EDITH THOMAS

MY DEAR," said Mme. Ponce-
let, as she opened the door of the study, "my dear, you must excuse me
for disturbing you."

The old professor looked up and laid his pen on the round felt wiper.
Beyond the *Aeneid,* he perceived the face of his wife as through a haze.
Then the haze disappeared. The old man made an enormous leap
through time and saw his wife wrapped in a canton-flannel dressing
gown with an old black broadcloth coat pulled up around her ears; and
he saw his wife's gentle, faded face reflecting, like a mirror, the secret
smile she had had already at twenty-five, when he married her, because
little by little this smile had become indispensable to his life, and had
remained so ever since.

"What is it, my dear?" he asked.

"You'll have to go see if our number has been posted at the tripe shop,"
she said. "And then, on your way back, you might, perhaps, stop at the
fish shop."

"I'd better stop at the fish shop first," said M. Poncelet.

"Whatever you think best, my dear." And she went back to the
kitchen. He put on his fur-lined coat with the worn collar and pulled
his beret down on his head. He wouldn't have to hold it even if it should
be windy. Also, it was more convenient for standing in line. And after
giving a look of mixed melancholy and regret, with perhaps a bit of
irony, at his desk, he went to the kitchen and took down the oilcloth
shopping bag with the handle that had been mended with string.

"You're not going to wash the kitchen in this cold weather," he
said.

"Well, we can't live in it dirty like this all winter. Besides, today
there's a certain let-up."

The only fire they had was in his study because it was essential for him to try to continue his great work on *The Origins of the Aeneid*—his great life work—because it was essential for him to continue. In spite of everything. But they had put a divan in the study and it was there that they slept, worked, ate and cooked their meals on a little stove.

She began to stir the contents of one of the pots.

"Oh, I must be making a noise," she said. "Forgive me, my dear."

"You know, my dear, you never disturb me," he replied. "The fact of living like this all the time has brought us closer than ever to each other."

No, it was not the last days he had dreamed of either for her, or for himself. No, it was not the last days.

Despite the fact that she was advanced in years and that sometimes she had heart attacks which frightened him, he could not get her a servant, nor even an occasional cleaning woman. The Germans paid much higher wages than a retired professor could pay. Nor could he take her to Cannes or Nice, during the dark months, as he had always promised her he would do "when he retired." For this they would have to cross the line of demarcation which cut France in two; and life on the other side was even more expensive than in Paris, on account of all the rich people who had gone there for the duration of the war. And besides, in Paris you felt you were resisting. You were resisting. And, as he walked toward the fish shop, in the face of a sharp wind that seemed to cut his face in two—where was that let-up Annette had noticed?— the old gentleman began to think that maybe he, too, had performed an act of resistance, that he, too, represented a tiny but necessary link in the firm chain of history.

There was a long line of people already waiting on the sidewalk, a long line composed of women all muffled up with head-scarfs tied under their chins. They were pressing against the closed gate of the fish shop like ants against the corpse of an earthworm. And what are we except ants hunting for food, ants whose nest has been demolished by the kick of a boot? This was not a very original comparison. M. Poncelet was aware of this. But with this wind and cold, try and find another one. In fact, having become obliged to return constantly to these preoccupations of heat and food, were we really still superior to animals? Man begins later on. He thought for a moment of his great work on the *Aeneid* which, for him, was the aim and justification of his life, and he gave a shrug.

All around him he saw faces grown blue with cold. He knew some of them, from having met them every day, waiting anxiously before the shop doors. He knew that the husband of that young woman standing there was a prisoner, that she was waiting for him to return. But the days, the months and the years were passing in an atmosphere of waiting and apprehension, in an atmosphere of mire. He knew that old peasant woman, with her lips drawn like pursestrings, had come from way up in the Pyrenees to "stand in line" for her daughter who worked in a factory. "When you have two children to feed, sir, and a husband who doesn't even earn enough for himself."

All kinds of rumors were going the rounds, rumors which were constantly being repeated by word of mouth and magnified. Thus the professor saw the beginnings of the heroic accomplishment of an entire people as it became organized and spread throughout the country. This phenomenon of the oral tradition made him think of Homer or the *Chanson de Roland,* and he smiled despite the cold.

The fish shop gate was now open and he was moving up at the rate of one step every five minutes. Life was a curious thing.

From time to time, the sound of boots could be heard on the sidewalk. A soldier in a field-gray uniform passed by. As he disappeared, a woman said, "The swine, and goodness aren't there a lot of them! They're like lice. When will the day come when we shan't have to see them any more?"

This met with general approval from the others.

At that time the German newspapers written in French were talking about collaboration between France and Germany. But the people were not taken in by it. They had understood right away—much more quickly and certainly than the bourgeois class, M. Poncelet recognized this fact— that this collaboration was another name for an imposture intended to cover up the enslavement of an entire continent; the most absolute subjection that had been witnessed for many centuries. It will only be possible to consider real collaboration later, when man himself will have been rediscovered, M. Poncelet thought to himself, as the sound of boots grew less and less audible. And it will not be the ruling classes who will establish that collaboration, but the peoples themselves, when they will have grown weary with suffering.

There he was again imagining himself in front of his pupils astride the big calm Percheron of history, for them to admire. He smiled, poking fun at himself, then advanced one step.

By now he could see inside the store where there were several large baskets of mussels.

"There'll be enough for everybody," said a woman beside him.

"If the 'priorities' don't show up," said the old peasant woman bitterly, opening for a moment her tightly closed lips. If the "priorities" don't show up. How do you expect a mother to ever have three children, if they let the other two die of hunger before the arrival of the third?

What always surprised the professor was the common sense of these women, and their courage. Few complaints. A sort of unconscious stoicism. In reality, human beings were worth much more than he had realized when he stayed at home with his nose in his books. What would all these people have done under other circumstances more favorable to their development? Nothing was known about this. So far, nothing.

He advanced a step. The baskets of mussels were being rapidly emptied.

"There won't be enough for everybody," the woman next to him remarked.

What an enormous adventure man is, he mused, despite the fact that the wind was roaring through the street and made his nose and ears smart; that it was absurd to wait hours for a pound of mussels which, before, he had never liked, and that *The Origins of the Aeneid* had not advanced one line during all this time.

"There's no use waiting any longer," said the woman beside him; "there won't be any left for us."

And, in fact, the last basket was almost empty. Nevertheless, M. Poncelet stayed a little longer; out of intellectual scrupulousness, out of a desire for proofs and verifications. When the last mussel had disappeared into a wicker basket, the professor left.

Now he would have to go by the tripe shop. It didn't take long; his number was not posted. Getting food was a sort of lottery in which nobody ever won. So he walked slowly home, his old shopping bag hanging empty over his arm.

"Well, my dear, did you get anything?"

"No," he replied, a bit contritely.

After all, he should have left home a little earlier, he should have stopped working on the *Aeneid* of his own accord, and not waited for his wife to ask him to do so.

"But you are half-frozen," she said, taking his hand. "I'm going to make you some herb tea to warm you up."

He sat down at his desk. He heard his wife stirring about the stove. He sensed her presence.

"Take a piece of sugar," she said.

He was aware that she denied herself for him. He looked at her secret smile, the tenderness of which he knew so well.

Yes, life was a marvelous adventure.

Biographical Notes

Biographical Notes ⋆

MOST FAMOUS of French novelists, Honoré de Balzac was born in Tours, May 16, 1799, and died in Paris, August 18, 1850. Yielding to family opposition to writing as a career, Balzac studied law for three years, but at the same time produced a dozen novels which were published under various pseudonyms. For a time he earned a living as publisher, editor and typefounder, but these efforts proved to be financial failures and he abandoned them to devote himself entirely to literature. In the years between 1829 and his death his output was prodigious. The series of novels which appeared under the generic title of *La Comédie Humaine* is a vast panorama of French society from peasant to banker, from rogue to saint, in which the unifying theme is the influence of environment on the personality and behavior of the individual. His death followed close on the heels of his marriage to a wealthy Polish widow, Madame Hanska.

IN HIS lifetime, Prosper Mérimée, who was born in Paris, September 28, 1803, was equally celebrated as scholar, archaeologist, novelist, historian and Senator. It was Mérimée who first made translations from Pushkin, Turgenev and Gogol available to the French. But for the general public it is only his reputation as a novelist that has survived, and that principally from the chance that his novelette, *Carmen,* was selected by Bizet for the theme of an opera. He died on September 23, 1870.

ARMANDINE LUCILE AURORE DUPIN DUDEVANT, better known by her pen name of George Sand, was an ardent feminist and radical, famous (or infamous to the respectable) during her lifetime as a trouser-wearing, cigar-smoking flouter of the conventions. In spite of a convent education, her early marriage to Baron Dudevant was not a success and she ran away to Paris in search of independence and a literary career. Today she is remembered less for her innumerable novels than for her affairs with Chopin and Alfred de Musset and her friendships with Flaubert, Liszt, Balzac and Delacroix. George Sand was born in Paris, July 5, 1804, and died June 8, 1876.

BORN IN PARIS, November 11, 1810, Alfred de Musset published his first verse at the age of twenty and within a few years had won a reputation as one of the leading poets of France. In 1833 he came under the spell of George Sand and traveled with her to Italy. He returned to France alone and heartbroken, after a quarrel with his mistress, and proceeded to pour out his romantic anguish in a series of exquisite short stories, plays and poems. He died in May, 1857.

THÉOPHILE GAUTIER was born at Tarbes, August 31, 1811. After a brief fling at painting he plunged headlong into the romantic movement then sweeping French literature. Experimental and restless in temperament, an admirable critic of art, drama and literature, an avid traveler, Gautier tried every literary form, but is best known in this country for his novel, *Mademoiselle de Maupin* and for his short stories. He died in 1872.

GUSTAVE FLAUBERT was a student of law before he turned to writing. His first and greatest novel, *Madame Bovary,* was published in 1857 in *La Revue de Paris* and immediately involved the author in legal prosecution on the grounds of immorality. He was ultimately acquitted. With this novel Flaubert established himself as the master of the school of naturalism. A meticulous stylist, he spent agonized hours in his search for the "exact word." He had a profound influence on the writers of his period, particularly Guy de Maupassant, an ardent disciple. Flaubert was born in Rouen, December 12, 1821, and died on May 8, 1880.

VILLIERS DE L'ISLE-ADAM was a romantic aristocrat who is chiefly remembered today for his drama, *Axël,* one of the high points of the symbolist movement in French literature. His collection of short stories, *Contes Cruels,* from which "The Torture of Hope" was taken, is considered a French classic. Hating respectability, Villiers lived a wildly romantic life and left behind a fabulous legend. One of his most celebrated exploits was to drag a lobster through the streets of Paris by a blue ribbon. When asked for an explanation, he replied, "Lobsters neither bark nor bite and they know the secrets of the sea!" He was born in Britanny in 1838 and died in Paris, August 19, 1889.

AFTER a depressing childhood in Nîmes, where he was born on May 13, 1840, Alphonse Daudet fled to Paris. Poems, plays, novels and stories written with a certain Dickensesque combination of humor, pathos and sentiment, brought him fame and fortune. His best-known character is that endearing and delightful braggart, *Tartarin of Tarascon* and his best-known novel, *Sapho*. He died in 1897.

EMILE ZOLA, the son of an Italian engineer, was born in Paris, April 2, 1840, and died in 1902. He was the leading exponent of the documentary novel, assiduous in research, relentless in his piling up of photographic detail. The twenty novels which comprise the Rougon-Macquart series were a sociological history of unsparing and insistent realism. With superb courage Zola risked reputation and safety by the publication of his famous pamphlet, *J'Accuse,* in which he denounced the military authorities who had convicted Captain Alfred Dreyfus of treason.

ANATOLE FRANCE was born Jacques Anatole Thibault, April 16, 1844, the son of a Paris bookseller. His first writing efforts were publishers' blurbs, a weekly newspaper column and some collections of poems. In 1883 he met Mme. Arman de Caillavet, a clever and charming woman who helped to guide his hesitant steps into the world of literature. His vehicle was the satirical and philosophic novel; his peculiar gift a skeptical, polished and wickedly worldly wit. Thanks to this gift and to his ambitious mistress, he dominated the French literary scene for many years, but his influence had markedly declined before his death in 1924.

IN ALL nations and in all languages Guy de Maupassant is acknowledged the master of the short story. In a single decade he wrote, in the abundance of his creative fervor, about 300 short stories, almost all of which convey the vigor of his genius. Born in Normandy, August 5, 1850, he participated in the Franco-Prussian War as he reached maturity. Immediately afterward he came under the guidance of Gustave Flaubert and served a seven-year apprenticeship. His first story was *Boule de suif*. From then on until he died in 1893, a victim of insanity, his writing virtually dominated the field of the short story.

GEORGES DUHAMEL is a physician who alternated between his medical practice and his literary work until World War I. Born in Paris, June 30, 1884, the early life of this poet, novelist and playwright was one of poverty and hardship. During the war he devoted himself exclusively to the care of the wounded, and his two books, *Civilization* and *New Book of Martyrs* (from which "The Sacrifice" is taken), are eloquent testimony to his aversion to the horrors of war. Besides writing a series of important novels, Duhamel has, in recent years, published a number of essays dedicated to the promotion of co-operation among the peoples of the world.

WHEN JOSEPH KESSEL was born in the Argentine in 1898 his Russian parents hardly could forsee that he would become a Frenchman who would serve his country loyally and with distinction through two wars and an invasion. At the time of his enlistment in the French Air Force in World War I, he was the youngest Doctor of Letters at the Sorbonne. Before he was thirty he had written four novels and received France's highest award for fiction—the Grand Prix du Roman of the French Academy. Kessel traveled the world over as a war correspondent until the fall of France in 1940, when he joined the French underground and for three years served the cause of democracy against the German invaders. In 1943 he had to flee for his life to London, where he is now living.

ANTOINE DE SAINT EXUPÉRY, who was born in Lyon, June 29, 1900, made his first flight at the age of eleven, when he was taken up in an old-fashioned monoplane. He became a full-fledged pilot at twenty-one and published his first book at twenty-six. His two prize-winning books, *Night Flight* and *Wind, Sand and Stars* were written while he was a pilot in the French airmail service. Saint Exupéry flew over South America, Africa and Indo-China and cracked up in the Libyan desert and again in Guatemala. During the war he served as a reconnaissance officer until the fall of France. After his demobilization he lived in the United States until the American landings in North Africa, when he was able to resume his place in his old flying squadron. In the summer of 1944 he disappeared over the Mediterranean while returning from a reconnaissance flight over the South of France pursued by German planes. Nothing has since been heard from him.

WHEN asked how he could write while taking an active part in the war, André Malraux replied, "It gets dark at night." Thus simply he affirmed his ardent belief that the ivory tower is no place for writers in the present-day world. In China, Spain and, most recently, in his own country, France, the forty-four-year-old author of *Man's Fate, Man's Hope* and *Days of Wrath* has fought passionately in the cause of democracy. This daring and heroic writer led a band of maquis in their fight to liberate Alsace and Lorraine during the very time he was at work on a novel and a biography of D. H. Lawrence. The life of action has inspired him, given him a subject, a passion in expressing it, an imaginative intensity unmatched by any novelist of his generation.

THE WAR has forced many French writers into unforeseen activities. After twelve years as a teacher of philosophy and after having written two esoteric works of philosophy, forty-year-old Jean-Paul Sartre was ca... in the maelstrom of war and was made a prisoner of the Germans. From the moment he managed his escape until the Nazis were expelled he became a leader of the militant resistance movement and its foremost writer. He founded the clandestine journal, *Les Lettres Francaises,* and wrote for *Figaro* and *Combat.* Even while engaged in his dangerous underground work, he found the energy and will to complete a series of psychological essays and two plays which ran simultaneously, successfully and quite openly in Paris during the Occupation.

THE NAME of Edith Thomas is more English than French, yet she is a Parisienne who had made a firm place for herself in French liberal and intellectual circles before the war. With the arrival of the Germans, she became an active organizer of the underground movement and wrote stirring short stories under a variety of pseudonyms, to the bafflement and chagrin of the enemy. "The Professor and the Mussels," a subtle but effective weapon in the unremitting war of ideas against the Nazi intruder, appeared clandestinely in a little paper-bound Midnight Editions volume called *Contes d'Auxois.*

u
of